BOOKS BY

REYNOLDS PRICE

"Reynolds Price has really astonishing gifts of observation and style. . . . I predict for him a long and distinguished life in American letters."

—Harper Lee

"Reynolds Price is the most sensitive prose stylist of his generation."

—Allen Tate

A Long and Happy Life

"An appealing tale of a young girl who does not quite know how to land her laggard suitor. . . . The honesty and art of Price's telling should make 'should she or shouldn't she' seem a new and agonizing problem—as it usually is in life and seldom is in novels. . . . Touching and true."

—*Time*

"A moment of truth that is art."

—Charles Poore, *The New York Times*

"A very funny and a very sorrowful book . . . brilliantly honest. The writing is beautiful."

—Richard Sullivan, *Chicago Tribune*

"A love story, and one of the simplest and most poignant I have ever read. His insight is phenomenal. . . . An achievement that most mature novelists might envy."

—Granville Hicks, *Saturday Review*

"A prize. . . . It is a lesson in love and irony, wonderfully funny and masterfully true . . . blended with great art."

—Diana Poteat Hobby, *The Houston Post*

"This is fiction that is also an experience, as real as rain. Even the minor characters come alive and walk off the pages into your mind."

—Lon Tinkle, *Dallas News*

"A stunningly perceptive, crisply humorous novel . . . subtly fabricating a world of startling and compelling beauty."

—Time

"A *Generous Man* is so beautifully written, so right in characterization, that we are enthralled with Price's strange gallery from beginning to end. Everything he tells us we believe—furthermore, whatever is to be felt, seen, heard, or smelled we pick up with the senses. Seldom has the youth-to-manhood theme been treated with such power and such satisfying indiscretion."

—ROY NEWQUIST, *New York Post*

"The dialogue is a joy . . . and there are many descriptive and narrative passages that fill the reader with admiration for the acuteness of Price's eye and the precision of his language."

—GRANVILLE HICKS, *Saturday Review*

"Yes, we are back with the Mustians in backwoods North Carolina, and you will meet again the delightful Rosacoke, her older brother Milo, her second brother Rato, and the rest of that word-happy household. If you can remember the ingrown togetherness of the earlier book, you will feel instantly at home in the new one."

—JOHN BARKHAM, *Saturday Review Syndicate*

"It bubbles with ribald wit . . . Reynolds Price has the style, the attitude, the sense of wonder of an artist. And he is generous with his gifts."

—WILLIAM McPHERSON, *Life*

"A *Generous Man* celebrates youth, remembered through a glass brightly. It dances without faltering among the pitfalls that confront a writer dealing with such a dangerous subject."

—CONRAD KNICKERBOCKER, *The New York Times*

"Everything in Price's story seems to happen under a bright golden spotlight so that the world he portrays casts a shadow larger than life itself around it. . . . Everything aims toward one ultimate moment when understanding and truth will break over reader and character alike."

—*Newsweek*

GOOD HEARTS

"Voice is Reynolds Price's most precious commodity, and Rosacoke can say more in one or two jaw-drop sentences than most folks do all week."

—*The Boston Globe*

"Superb storytelling by an enduring craftsman. The tone and rhythms of Reynolds Price's language are masterful. . . . In every sense of the word, the novel abounds with pleasure."

—*The New York Times Book Review*

"The stamp of Reynolds Price is unmistakable. . . . There is much pleasure to be taken in the characters' honesty, humor, and stubborn integrity—qualities they share with their creator."

—*Newsday*

"Reynolds Price has a rare intelligence, a generous imagination, a master's way with words, and unflagging energy."

—*The San Francisco Chronicle*

"*A Long and Happy Life* began the story and the characters Reynolds Price has now fashioned into this sequel. Reading both books intensified my pleasure and extended my admiration. They are marvelous books, rich in a fluid and lyrical grasp of language, wise and compelling in their vision. . . . It is Price's creation of the men and women he places in the southern landscape that gives his books their haunting beauty and power."

—*Chicago Tribune*

REYNOLDS PRICE

A SINGULAR FAMILY

ROSACOKE AND HER KIN

SCRIBNER PAPERBACK FICTION
PUBLISHED BY SIMON & SCHUSTER

SCRIBNER PAPERBACK FICTION
Simon & Schuster Inc.
Rockefeller Center
1230 Avenue of the Americas
New York, NY 10020

SCRIBNER PAPERBACK FICTION and design are trademarks of Jossey-Bass, Inc.,
used under license by Simon & Schuster, the publisher of this work.

Manufactured in the United States of America

1   3   5   7   9   10   8   6   4   2

Library of Congress Cataloging-in-Publication Data
Price, Reynolds, 1933–
[Selections. 1999]
A singular family : Rosacoke and her kin / Reynolds Price.
p.   cm.
1. Mustian, Rosacoke (Fictitious character)—Fiction. 2. Women—North Carolina—
Family relationships—Fiction. 3. Family—North Carolina—Fiction. 4. Domestic
fiction, American. I. Title.
PS3566.R54A6   1999
813'.54—dc21   99-17175
CIP

ISBN 0-684-85188-1

These works were previously published separately.
A *Long and Happy Life, A Chain of Love, A Generous Man,* and the preface
were published in a collection entitled *Mustian* in 1983.

CONTENTS

PREFACE:
A PLACE TO STAND

A "young novelist" is a contradiction in terms. The subject and essence of a novel is inevitably time, its motions and effects on the shapes and actions of human creatures and the scenes they inhabit. Any hope of comprehending, ordering, and exhibiting such clandestine and gradual effects is dependent upon intense and deeply registered personal witness. Premature skills in music, graphic art, oral expression, mathematics, even lyric poetry are not rare. But a child prodigy of the novel is almost unthinkable, even now when prose-narrative techniques are commonplace items in grade-school curricula. Raymond Radiguet's *The Devil in the Flesh*, produced at the age of seventeen, stands almost alone (and isn't it significant that Radiguet was dead at twenty?). A glance through the lists of serious novelists is likely to show first novels emerging late in the third decade of life, towards age thirty. Even the most uncanny of fictional debuts waits till age twenty-nine — Emily Brontë's in *Wuthering Heights*, a first and only novel, cyclonic in intensity.

Intensity is never the problem. Most five-year-olds are already the managers of bank vaults of memory, indelibly etched. The generally overwhelming dilemma for a young aspirant to the novel is perspective, distance, literal length-of-deposit in the vault. Those images of crucial stasis and gesture that any child hoards as his debit and capital seem to demand long submersion in the lower reaches of the mind—the zones in which transformation can occur; the alchemies beyond any conscious control that may in five, ten, or forty years accomplish an altered deliverable object, larger and more useful than the initial private matter. Anyone younger than, say, twenty-five is unlikely therefore to have had sufficient time for the unconscious marinade of the first experiences of adult life, the passions and desolations of adolescence. Hence the classic subject matter of the apprentice short story—childhood and youth. And external pressure is generally required to extract even those, the pressure of class assignment or other undeniable request.

In the spring of 1955, I was twenty-two years old, a senior at Duke University, enrolled in William Blackburn's English 104 (Narrative Writing). For nine years I had been writing sporadically but with some persistence—first, plays and film scripts (in the never-realized hope of directing my friends in productions), a few short stories and sketches, numerous high-minded school-newspaper editorials, a steady issue of poems in direct proportion to the hormonal drench and ensuing bafflement of the decade. Only the poems, and a partially autobiographical story called "Michael Egerton," bore any obvious relation to my visible experience; and that relation had made them the most difficult experiments I'd tackled—most of the plays and prose narratives had been in the nature of fantasy and therefore as easy as warmwater floating. In my first three years of college, I'd continued to think of myself as a writer; but though "Michael Egerton" and a few poems of love and solitude surfaced, I'd gladly accepted the pressure of course-work as an excuse for not writing. Only the idle summers at my parents' quiet and congenial house—a room of my own, no insistence that I take a moneymaking job—forced me to confront the fact that I had no presently accessible subject for narrative prose. I recall a good many vacant hours, prone in my locked room, gasping at the ceiling like a ravenous carp. Time, I'd suspected—and all my reading assured me—would furnish the food at its own wise rate. Till the day of delivery then, I had worked at my courses with a fervor that was two parts natural bent and two parts dread of the hot wind blowing our way in those days—the Korean War draft and its aftermath, Khrushchev and Berlin. Most of my male contemporaries were enrolled in the various officers-training corps to insure four uninterrupted years of college. On the advice of the state director of Selective Service, I had tight-roped on a shaky line of grades, gambling on an armistice.

Three weeks after my twenty-first birthday, my father had died of lung cancer. Less than a month before, he had seemed his normal strong self—a fifty-four-year-old traveling salesman in improving financial condition after twenty-odd years of serious straits, a desperate lover of family, a cured alcoholic, a ceaseless hypochondriac, a brilliant natural mime and verbal wit. From the day of the confirmed diagnosis, he requested, quietly but firmly, as much of my presence as I could give. We had not been a casual father-and-son. With all his laughter, his compulsion to win love through performance, he was late-Victorian in his sense of self and dignity. Neither my younger brother nor I romped on his large immaculate body. He played few child's games with us; we were treated from birth like confirmed, if fragile, adults. But from the age of five, I'd been conscious that my own birth—a first child and a dangerous labor—had been the occasion of his soon-successful undertaking to abandon alcohol. And our always unstated awareness of that mutually sacrificial bond proved stronger than either of us had suspected.

In the final two weeks of his life, I was with him more or less steadily; and in the ghastly aftermath of the removal of his lung, I spent all the nights on a chair in his hospital room, his main companion through the rush of mutilations and reductions that killed him. On the night before his death, however, I accepted my mother's persuasion and went home to bathe and sleep. When Father discovered my absence, he raged and lashed in his oxygen tent till they phoned me at dawn and urged my return in the hope of calming him. Once I was back and he'd seen me, he sank without a word into deep sleep. The day was Sunday and numerous witnesses passed in and out, his sisters, various relations of my mother, doctors, nurses, short visits from my mother (who continued to respect his implicit demand to have mainly me now, telling herself he was sparing her the gasping sight). Whenever I'd leave his side for a moment, I'd find a small clutch of kin at the door, quietly searching me for omens. And always beyond them, across the hall, the open door of another patient's room.

I no longer recall who the patient was—male or female, young or old—but in traditional rural fashion, other members of the family had set up a rudimentary yet thriving brand of housekeeping in the rented room. Their patient left them sufficient relaxed time in which to stare nakedly at my father's door, presumably on the chance of catching a view unusual enough to redeem their wait. I remember three young men who looked like brothers, all with long necks and thick country-skin. There seemed to be no women in attendance, not in my recollection. I was partly repelled by their eavesdropping but secretly helped by their obvious sense that I was the main visible actor in a veiled but plainly serious drama.

Just after dark I was back in Father's room with my friend Patricia Cowden. The nurse had gone to get his next sedative. I sat by the bed and held his left wrist; he'd never stirred since morning. A thin thready pulse was the sign of life. Suddenly, beneath my fingers, it stopped. The body enacted a long convulsion. A half-hour later as we left the room for the final time, our country watchers were undauntedly in place, upright in their open door, unblinking as we passed.

Three weeks into official adulthood then, I had seen, at the closest possible range, a death I'd feared since infancy. His mortality had been both a frightening and a comic mutual concern. One of my earliest clear memories is of the night when he powdered his hair, came into my room, and sang "When I Grow Too Old To Dream" (I'd recently deduced that gray hair meant age; I was three and he was thirty-six, just at the end of his drinking and well before he developed its substitute, hypochondria—the dread and hope of death). In the dazed months that followed—a return to college work, a summer of study at Harvard, new expectations at home—I did not suspect that a gear had engaged and was waiting to turn.

But almost exactly a year after the death, two things conspired. First, as I've mentioned, was the necessity to produce a final short story for William Blackburn's class (in the fall semester I had only revised "Michael Egerton," a story conceived three years before). Second was the sort of apparent accident that eventually seems a peculiar gift of writers. I had gone to Duke Hospital to visit an ailing friend; and as I walked through the usual stunned population of hospital corridors, I encountered the nameless trio of men who'd stared so fixedly at my father's door. They were coming towards me, no visible purpose; and as I passed, they showed no recognition. Were they there a year later, in another town, with the same sick kinsman? Did they have any real home or merely haunt hospitals, doomed to watch pain? Were they actual men? Were they messengers to me? Unconsciously I chose the last question and answered Yes. I would let them signal my move into sustained work; they would be both fuel and steering column. In a matter of days, I was planning their story.

Yet it never was theirs. By a process I can no longer reconstruct, I began to generate a fictional center—a girl who had not been part of their family. The name of a fellow student, Rosa Coke Boyle (whom I think I never met, though I knew her sister), was additional fuel. But the moment of ignition was another chance meeting. A friend, Fernando Almeida, and I had gone to Howard Johnson's for a late Sunday lunch. A young couple entered and sat at the counter. He left no impression; she is still intact in every line—a tall girl, maybe nineteen or twenty, with the strong bones and skull that would carry her beauty undimmed to the grave; long ash-blond hair, a straw church-hat, a white good-dress, and pale blue eyes that alternated looks of grave self-sufficiency and half-smiling bottomless imagined need: all aimed at the boy.

She would be Rosacoke, I knew at once—Rosacoke a few years younger in life. The fact that I chose instinctively to show her first in adolescence was, I understood later, the central clue to her origin and meaning (for me at least, at that time in my life). She was the fictional equivalent of any one of a dozen girls who had treated me kindly eleven years before when we moved to my parents' home, a small county-seat in eastern North Carolina. My counterparts in the town itself quickly rejected me—childish violence, real as any. But my rural schoolmates, bused in from distant tobacco farms, accepted me warmly; and for a long three years, age eleven to fourteen, I resorted gladly for validation to the daughters and sons of subsistence farmers. They were ebullient and trusting, if prematurely long-sighted; and they were calmly primed for early adulthood—marriage, children—and lives of hard work at the sufferance of nature, the cruelest employer.

My choice of them—a female delegate from them, imagined though credible—as a lens for examining a parent's death was an act of gratitude for old friendship. More important for the resulting fiction, it was an unconscious annexation of a sufficiently distant perspective yet one still capable of radiant energy—the heat of admiration for a generous heart. Narrative has always refused to function for me unless I prime it with at least one partly admirable protagonist.

The first draft of a story grew quickly through the conflicting chores of winter and spring—I was also writing a senior history thesis on John Milton's politics—and when it was submitted in May to the composition class as "A Chain of Love," I sensed for the first time from my colleagues' responses that eerie pleasure of having been the medium through which an independent life has chosen to emerge. Though her story was not published for nearly three years, and though I continued to tinker at minor details, Rosacoke had stood up, live from her first paragraph—in my mind at least and those of a few friends who dealt with her at once like a palpable creature, warm to the touch.

Four months after I'd released her in the final sentence of the story, I left home for three years of graduate study in England. That was another turn pressed on me by the accident of winning a particular scholarship. Since I'd long planned to live by teaching English literature, I'd have gone to graduate school in any case; but the luck of a long stretch of work abroad was a further, and crucially timed, gift of perspective. I was awarded not only money but four thousand miles of distance from recent experience, the leisurely pace of advanced study in England (virtually all one's time dangerously at one's own disposal), a larger circle of literarily-inclined contemporaries than any young American of the time could have found in the States, and (I soon knew) a low-grade but durable case of homesickness.

Despite the startling, if eccentric, warmth of my welcome in an Oxford that more nearly resembled Max Beerbohm's and Evelyn Waugh's than the crowded welfare-outpost of today, I found myself thinking and feeling steadily about — and maybe longing for — not my home in Raleigh with my mother and brother (however much I missed them) but a largely imaginary childhood home built from my present needs and raised on a foundation of the credible people and landscape of Warren County, North Carolina. The facts that the actual place and its inhabitants were greatly, if subtly, different from any I'd read of (their nearest relations appeared to exist in Tolstoy, Turgenev, and Chekhov) and that no one had yet memorialized them in fiction were further strong components of both the longing and the pressure to capture, fix, and transmit.

In my first two unbroken years abroad, I therefore stole perilous amounts of time from my studies and wrote stories called "The Warrior Princess Ozimba" and "The Anniversary," both redolent of the distant air of eastern Carolina. I also continued to tinker with "A Chain of Love." The sustained exploration and creation of that real and fantastic world of memory became so large a concern of my life that, by January 1957, I found myself seated in freezing digs in the home of a working-class couple, unknowingly on the edge of another accident of the sort that had so far proved propitious. One of my father's sisters had given me a subscription to our county newspaper, *The Warren Record*; and I was reading through a stack of issues delayed in mid-Atlantic by the Christmas rush — the usual murmur of village politics, love-brawls and knifings, social notes of monumental placidity, and (a seasonal feature) children's letters to Santa Claus. When I'd scanned a few of the want-lists — burp-guns, dolls, sweets — my mind suddenly produced a picture. I developed it backward in a matter of seconds. A young woman dressed in a makeshift costume was seated with a live baby in her arms; she was Mary in a small-church Christmas pageant, the kind I'd acted in as a boy; she was Rosacoke Mustian; she was pregnant though unwed; the father was Wesley Beavers, a boy evoked but never shown in "A Chain of Love."

I went to my worktable and wrote down the impulse in skeletal notes. Propped against the wall before me was a color postcard I'd acquired after seeing the original in Holland the previous summer — Vermeer's pregnant girl in blue at a window, absorbed in a one-page letter in her hands, a large map suspended on the plaster behind her.

Surely it had silently inserted itself into whatever crowd of motives had brought me my own instant picture, so slowly evolved.

In the next few days other images flew to the central figure and my notes continued. But by then, caution had knocked. I was midway through the second year of a two-year scholarship. Fiction writing, travel, and my first tempestuous acquaintance with requited romantic love had left me little time to work on the substantial thesis required for my degree. My director, Helen Gardner, was rumbling ominously. A pair of certainties faced me—in the new Rosacoke idea, I had the components of at least a novella; but unless I meant to return home in disgrace, I could not begin to write it now. The thesis took precedence. A smaller but real impediment was my sense that, given an inveterately chameleonic nature, I should wait till my immersion in British voices and rhythms had ended in a homecoming.

For twenty-one months then I turned to, first, a study of Milton and Greek tragedy (steady days in the Bodleian); and then an extension of my scholarship when it became apparent that I wasn't going to finish in two years and that, in any case, I wanted to stay a little longer in a place so conducive to fermentation; and finally to an instructor's job at my undergraduate alma mater and a return there to life in a trailer in the woods by a pond. Through the diversions and travel, I added almost daily to my notes for another Rosacoke story—long and short meditations on plot, character, psychology, language, theme, narrative strategy, the lessons of my concurrent reading (Tolstoy and Hardy were especially instructive), my own doubts and insufficiencies, and the relations of it all to my own luxuriant toils of early love and work.

By October 1958 I'd settled into my trailer, my first autumn back at home was in gorgeous cry at the windows, my mother and brother were in stronger shape twenty-five miles away, my first scouting trips to Warren County were just behind me; and I sat at a new worktable to write what I was already calling *A Long and Happy Life* (the title, though a common phrase, had volunteered some months before when I first saw the film *Bridge on the River Kwai* and heard William Holden wish it for a young soldier doomed to swift destruction). Still propped before me was Vermeer's girl in blue; and beside her stood the forthright mysterious Botticelli portrait of a young man from the

National Gallery, London—he had served as the image of Wesley in my plans.

I was teaching a full schedule at Duke, two courses of freshman composition and one in major British writers. I managed to arrange my university duties on a three-day cycle, thereby freeing three days for writing (I took Sundays off). And slowly, with many balks and falls, I entered the long peculiar tunnel of novel-writing. Strangely, through the entire process, I continued to believe I was writing a longish short story or at most a novella; in fact, even when I'd finished, I submitted it to publishers as the final piece in a volume of short stories and was only with difficulty persuaded to publish it alone as the novel it plainly was. But my life quickly took on the tone and shape of a novelist's life—long days of silent solitary work (relieved importantly, in my case, by easy access to a pond; woods with deer, foxes, swarms of birds; and fields under broomstraw), work that soon exerts an imperious sway over one's other activities: job, friendships, loves, family duties. One lives so steadily, waking and sleeping, in an imagined world that the tangible world of houses, meetings, comrades begins both to fade and to swell in urgency. Throughout the writing, I found that an almost actual door stood ready to burst open between life and work. For long unnerving stretches, daily actions seemed manipulated to the point of puppetry by the needs and discoveries of fictional people. Other times, the intensest strands of private emotion would pour into the work with the vibrance and rhythmic inevitability of strong music. And always through the door came the pure inventions that gave the real joy.

It lasted a little more than two years. In December 1960 I completed the final revision of the scene that embodied my initial image—Rosacoke, pregnant, as the Virgin in a pageant in Delight Church at Christmas. It had taken four years, mostly happy, of my life to bring me and her back to the starting point; and the happiness was largely a product of the time spent in her and her family's growing presence, the malleable shapes of their gestures and choices. (I notice only now that I transformed the three anonymous watchers of my father into the three young men of the stories—Wesley, Milo, Rato.) As I released them into the typescript that was ultimately to become the book that delivered them to readers in thirteen languages, I remember a newly clear glimpse of adulthood. I, and my ROTC friends, had escaped armed combat. The Korean War had ended before we were tapped; Berlin, though ticking, had never exploded. We'd been left alive and unappalled to pursue past and future. There had been no public socially-certified rite of passage for our middle-class generation. When I'd finished, I suspected I'd been through a private rite and had someway described it—death and survival, freedom and love—by setting it loose to roam as it would, far from my own dreads and bafflements. If not an old soldier, then a parent of sorts and marked with the normal parental badges.

It was published fifteen months later. By then I was back at Oxford for a year. I'd abandoned the thought of a doctoral degree but had saved enough money in the three years of teaching to allow myself a stretch of time in the hope of new work. A few weeks after completing *A Long and Happy Life*, I'd conceived the idea of a story that would complete a volume of stories (now that the novel had been corralled out of my five earlier stories). It would be, I noted in March 1961,

> ... 'about' my father and me: I could write about a man who six years after his marriage was childless and an alcoholic, whose wife became pregnant. Her labor was long and painful, and the man promised God that if the child were born alive and unharmed, he would not drink again. The child was born, unharmed; but the mother died—he had forgot to ask for *her* life. My story would be about the relation of father and son.

That summer, in my old freshman rooms in Merton College, I tried to begin it—total recalcitrance. It wouldn't come. With considerable anxiety (I'd touted my trip to friends and employers as one of guaranteed productivity), I set the notes aside, not knowing that they'd season at their own rate and produce *The Surface of Earth* more than ten years later. I turned to translations of Hölderlin and Rimbaud, to one more polishing of "A Chain of Love," and then (on a commission from Stephen Spender for the hundredth number of *Encounter*) to a story called "Uncle Grant"—a Warren County story but this time a memoir. Those, and my friends, saw me through the frigid months till March when A *Long and Happy Life* appeared complete in a single issue of *Harper's* and simultaneously from Atheneum in America and Chatto and Windus in Britain. Its generally handsome reception consumed the remaining months abroad, and only when I returned to America in the summer was I able to begin a story called "The Names and Faces of Heroes" to flesh the older stories to a volume. The story dealt again—fictionally, at a distance—with my father's death. And for years to come, it closed that account.

Another was opening. I had come home again to the trailer to find my mother in Raleigh, fifty-seven years old, going rapidly blind for no reason doctors could at first discover. The next year saw her finally diagnosed with twin aneurysms deep in her skull—drastic surgery followed by a partial slow recovery of vision, all under the sentence of imminent stroke. As I returned to teaching, the external world served up the Cuban missile crisis; then the murder in Dallas of John Kennedy. Running beneath, a constant thirst, was a private relation in which I released more havoc than I'd thought could flow from what had first seemed the wish to protect. Through the months I had gone on with notes for a father-son novel, but by August 1963 even those had stopped.

So it was in a state resembling crucial need of peaceful employment that, in bed one night in January 1964, I thought of a story that promised to be comic. A few days later with no pause for plans or notes, I began to write it under the working title A *Mad Dog and a Boa Constrictor*. By the time it was finished in October 1965, my mother had died of the hemorrhage that had hung fire above her. The apparently comic story had become a muted near-tragic romance—a long fiction but not a realistic novel—and its final title was A *Generous Man*. It had explored in a thoroughly different, almost hallucinatory way the lives of Rosacoke's brother Milo and Rosacoke herself some years earlier than "A Chain of Love." That it had also explored my own simultaneous concerns, private and public, was inevitable (I've discussed its development elsewhere*).

---

*"News for the Mineshaft" in Reynolds Price, *Things Themselves* (Atheneum, 1972), p. 70.

With its publication in March 1966, I had come to the end of eleven years' involvement in the imagined life of a single family. There were to be at least two more engagements with them—a commissioned but still-unproduced screenplay of *A Long and Happy Life* and a stage play called *Early Dark* that examines the relations of Rosacoke and Wesley from a distinctly altered perspective—and of course they'd never kept exclusive hold on my attention, even in their long run. But when I'd revealed Milo's final choice at the end of *A Generous Man*, I had (it now appears) no further need of reliance on his family's history. Strangers occasionally inquire the whereabouts and present fortune of a particular Mustian; and in 1970 I thought briefly of taking them up again, almost in middle age. But no story came; they were silent by then as disused oracles. Other actions and lives stood to fill other needs.

Yet from here, twenty-seven years after the invention of the family, maybe I can be allowed to look back with some degree of puzzled gratitude at the odd arrangements of fate, luck, and will that led a young writer—long on ardor but short on distance—to adopt a fictional family and their satellites (in most ways different from my own kin and friends) as the means of watching, subduing, and transmitting large tracts of his own experience. When they receded as available tools for further work, it was probably because of the peculiarly complete set of jobs they'd so patiently and variously done for me. That "A Chain of Love" and the two novels have been continuously in print since their first appearances—and that they are now read by generations of students young enough to be the grandchildren of Wesley and Rosacoke—suggests, in this present Dark Age of American reading, that their ability to do serious duty was not an offer to me alone. If they say nothing else, they attempt to say now, as they always did, the fixed unalterable injunction of narrative, to me and all readers— *The world exists. It is not yourself. Plunge in it for healing, blessed exhaustion, and the risk of warmth.*

When I wrote those pages in November 1982, I couldn't foresee that, eighteen months later, my life would collide with the reality of an initially unremovable spinal malignancy. After an unsuccessful first surgery and weeks of radiation, I rapidly lost the power to stand and walk; and my work stalled in melancholy. Five months of idleness ensued, with the confirmation of paraplegia, before I was able to write again. Then in rapid order, I completed a delayed novel *Kate Vaiden*, numerous poems, and a trilogy of plays *New Music*. As life continued and I contemplated ideas for more long fiction, I lingered in the shallows of a number of projects before being struck by the old notion of returning to the Mustian family and observing their present lives. I knew at once that I wanted to set them in the present of the mid-1980s; and the one situation that presented itself as firmly as the Christmas scene had presented itself three decades earlier was the fact of Wesley's recent disappearance from his job and his marriage, a vanishing that took him miles from home and detained him at length.

In *A Whole New Life* I've written in detail about that time in my life; so I won't speculate here as to why, in a dark passage, I recalled these fictional companions of my youth. In any case, they responded to the summons and diverted me when diversion was needed. It's no mystery, though, why I knew at once that I'd find Wesley and Rosa (as she was now called) on the verge of a gulf in their middle age, a gravely dangerous domestic gulf which they'd come to feel they must bridge, at whatever cost, if life were to last. The final sentence of that third Mustian novel, which is called *Good Hearts* in forthright tribute, would seem to preclude my watching them further; but I've long since abandoned prophecy in regard to one family anyhow.

R.P., August 1998

A GENEROUS MAN

Come degnasti d'accedere al monte?
non sapei tu che qui è l'uom felice?
DANTE, *Purgatorio*, XXX

ONE

"Milo. Son?" Emma Mustian spoke from the foot of the steps for the third time that morning, still not raising her voice, trusting her natural power to wake him. But it had not and did not. It was Saturday, no school and Milo was dreaming, and because he so rarely dreamed—waking or sleeping—he clung to it now, her his dream, like money smuggled into his head, chest, hips and abandoned there, sudden and perilous. So Emma gave up and went to the kitchen and told Rosacoke to wake her brother and see him dressed.

Rosacoke said, "How am I going to feed Baby Sister and cook a big breakfast for Papa and Milo and wake up Milo all at once?"

Emma said, "I'll cook—I've cooked thirty years—and if Baby Sister can't feed herself at three years old, she will have to starve."

Rosacoke sighed but quickly went and was glad to go, not having seen Milo since the previous supper. The door to his room was shut—which was new, so new Rosa did not think of knocking but entered, and there was Milo asleep, stretched on top of sheets creased as storm water, naked hair to heel.

The sound of her entry, her happy gasping, finished his dream, opened his eyes. He looked, said "Morning," then clamped down again.

Rosacoke said, "Morning? It's nearly noon." (It was seven-fifteen.) "Mama says get up, she needs you now." She went to the foot of his walnut bed and waited there.

Milo said "What for?"

"To take us to Warrenton."

"Papa can take you."

"No Papa can't."

"Why?" Milo said.

"Papa's too old," she said. "You have got to go and stick with Rato and explain about Phillip."

"What's wrong with Phillip?"

"If you ever came home when people were awake, you'd know a lot more about all of us. Phillip hasn't moved out of his house since Thursday. Rato has washed him and wormed him good, but he still acts sick so we're taking him in to Dr. Fuller, and you've got to supervise while Mama shops."

"I hadn't got to do nothing but die."

"And you may have to do that shortly," she said, "lying there naked in early October. Where do you think you are?—Africa?"

"I was near enough to Africa late last night." He buried his dark head entirely in pillows (skin dark from sun, hair gold as crowns).

"I knew it when I saw you walking off that porch. I read it on your back as clear as light—Going To The Fair. Well, if the Warren County Fair is your idea of Africa, I pity the natives."

"I'm just talking about that snake."

"What snake?" she said.

Emma called up to her, "Is he wake yet, Rosa?"

Rosa ran to the railing. "Wake and buck-naked. Slept buck-naked on October eighth."

"Naked? You come straight down here then. You're too old for that."

"I'm not but eleven and he's lying on his stomach."

Emma didn't answer. She said, "Get him dressed" and went back to Baby Sister's oatmeal.

Rosa went back to Milo, fully awake now but playing at sleep. She crept to his feet and tickled the soles so rindy they lasted from summer to summer, not softening. He did not flinch, did not seem to breathe. "Ever try to tickle an elephant?" she said and laid a flat hand hot and sudden on his butt.

That stood him upright among the sheets, rocking with the springs. He lifted his arms and floated them out as though he were soaring—he was only balancing—and looked through the window to the bright morning sky, the road hid by trees. (The leaves would last another six weeks.) Then he said as if to the trees but to Rosa, to tantalize, "If these damned leaves would ever die, I could see through the branches to that ferris wheel."

"If you can see five miles with naked eyes, you got a better night's sleep than I did," she said.

Then he took two sinking steps through the mattress, one long loud step to the floor, then a series of jabs at his underpants. When they were on—they were actually Rato's—he said, "I didn't sleep three good hours."

"Why not?"

"Because I found a friend at the fair."

"Anybody I know?"

"You been to Clearwater, Florida lately?"

"No," she said.

"Then you don't," he said.

"A girl?"

"A *woman*."

"Milo," she said, neither smiling nor frowning.

So he turned in his shirttails, faced her fully, folded his right arm across his waist, his left on his back and gave her the crisp bow boys learn in school.

> "Milo's my name,
> Afton's my hame,
> Heaven's my destination."

Rosa smiled but said, "What heaven? Dog Heaven—you at fifteen sitting up till day with a carnival woman."

"A woman and a five-hundred-dollar boa constrictor. And we weren't sitting."

"What were you doing then?"

He was into his wrinkled trousers, his shoes, so he flung himself upend onto his hands. Pennies rang from his pockets and rolled towards her, and he said from there, "We were taking that snake for a walk through the woods." He stood again, smiling with his eyes flared white. "And we're exercising him again tonight, just her and me."

Rosa laughed and touched him once on the belly, low as she dared, instant and ended as though this were Tag or he were a stove. "Come on and eat or *I'll* snake you. Phillip needs help or Rato will die."

"Let Phillip die. He can blaze my way to Dog Heaven in advance."

"Milo!" She ran.

And he ran behind her, chin held high in the wind Rosa made, arm thrust up as if lifting a desperate flag through war—"On to save Rato, spare him pain, return him to his rightful place in his home!"

Rato waited by the kitchen door—or blocked their charge with Phillip in his arms in an Army blanket, only his neck and head uncovered, the terrier half, white with one black eye. The wrapped half was mystery. (Rato said "Airedale"—he had never seen one—Milo said "Traveling salesman," but whatever, it was Rato's life, had been his companion day and night, waking and sleeping for nearly three years since Milo had found it on the road one Christmas—abandoned by someone too weak to drown it—and brought it in his pocket for Rato's gift.)

Milo stopped and said, "Phillip, smile. Milo's on duty. You're half-cured already" and entered the kitchen and walked to the table where Papa (their own dead father's father) was eating, having finished his morning duties (which was walking to the end of the cleared back-yard and staring for a while in those directions—over cotton stalks, tobacco stalks, pine woods beyond as if staring might revive, make grow, harvest). Emma had gone to dress Baby Sister so Milo sat on Papa's right, Rosacoke went to the oven for his plate and Rato laid Phillip by the fired wood-stove.

Papa studied Milo, then said to his eyes, "You look like you slept three hours last night."

"I didn't know you slept in your hearing aid."

Papa said, "I don't—wouldn't if I had one—but I heard you. So would everybody else if they weren't doped up." (He meant the children's mother, his daughter-in-law. She took two aspirins at nine every night.)

"Well," Milo said, "since they were all drugged senseless, let's don't tell anything that might just confuse them."

As Rosacoke came to the table with his plate, they could hear their mother two rooms away forcing Baby Sister into something warm so Rosacoke lowered her voice and said "Such as what?" Milo questioned her with dumb open mouth.

She said, "What might confuse the people that didn't hear you come in at four a.m.?"

Papa said "Yeah."

Milo told it above his eating, hoarsely, pretending to whisper to Rosa and his grandfather (Rato hunkered on below beside Phillip, half-listening but not caring). "The main thing would be that I went to the fair."

Papa said "No!"

Milo said, "You know I did—or knew I was planning to."

"Never crossed my mind," Papa said, "never knew you knew plans existed."

"Papa, I got more plans than Douglas MacArthur."

Papa said, "I wish you luck then, General, but I still never dreamed you were planning on the fair." •

"Then how come you locked the truck last night for the first time in history? Because some mule was plotting to straight-wire it and drive to the fair and enter himself in the livestock show?"

"Not exactly"—Papa pointed to the trembling dog—"I didn't want Phillip driving in his condition. No telling what he might do."

"Oh I hadn't thought of that. But I wish you had told me—saved me half an hour poking with a rusty wire in that shut lock."

Papa said, "Excuse me. I meant to tell you. Hope I didn't put you out too much."

"I won't say how much but I will just say that Macey Gupton saved five Mustian lives."

Rosacoke said "How?" She had taken a seat on Milo's right. Now they filled three sides of the long dark table, facing or half-facing Rato and Phillip.

"By coming along in his old truck while I was standing down by the road gazing up here and planning axe murders."

Rosa said, "Calm down and tell us the rest."

Milo said, "I'm calm as that frying pan"—holding out one still hand to prove it—"and was last night till oh eleven o'clock."

"What happened then?"

Papa said, "Don't rush him ahead of his story. If I'm going to listen— with all the better stuff I got to do—I mean to understand. So Macey Gupton passed in his Daddy's truck and stopped and you told him you was killing your people and then flagging down a ride to the fair?"

Milo said, "That's it. Except Macey said he'd killed his people—he had the truck and he ain't sixteen—so to let's just save you all till later and make tracks now."

Rosacoke said, "Milo, what sort of talk is that?"

Milo said, "Lies. But from now on it's true—what I can tell of it any-how." He stopped awhile, chewing, swallowing, then faced Rosacoke and Papa again. "You are looking at me like I went to the moon."

Rosa said "You said Africa."

Milo said, "Hush. It was nothing but the Warren County Fair— from eight o'clock till midnight, that is. We took in the rides and ate a lot of mess that Phillip wouldn't eat—would you, son?" (Phillip slowly looked towards the use of his name)—"and got up with a bunch of girls that are in our grade. They all had tickets in a drawing sponsored by the furniture store so we went indoors for that at nine."

Rosa said, "What were they giving away?"

"A bed about the size of Afton—innerspring mattress and pillows thrown in."

Rosa said "Who got it?"

Milo laughed. "Guess."

Papa said "Puss Ellis."

Rosa said "Papa!"

Milo fell back, struck himself on the forehead. "She *did*. Puss won it!"

"And needed it much as anybody could," Papa said, not smiling.

Rosa said, "Papa, what do you know about her?"

"I know she uses a bed in her work."

Rosa said "Hush."

Milo said "Plug your ears" and Rosacoke did.

Papa said, "Was Puss on hand to claim it?"

"Not only claimed it but stretched out and bounced. You ought to seen people's faces, Papa."

Papa said, "They all ought to been very glad. Giving it to Puss is just the same thing as giving it to the male population. She's slept with them all."

Rosacoke said, "She has not either. Shame on both of you."

Milo said, "Warrenton ain't such a big town, Rosa."

Rosa said, "All right, let's change the subject. What did you do next?"

Milo said, "Same subject. Me and Macey got in the hootchy-kootchy show."

Rosa said, "What happened to the Warrenton girls?"

"We lost them after Puss won her bed. Then after the kootch-show I lost Macey too."

"What happened to him?"

"It happened to his glasses. After they strip down completely, you see, the women come out in the tent where the men are. Me and Macey were sitting about halfway up but on the aisle—Macey was on the aisle, beat me to it, thank God, because this woman (Phyllis the star) came towards us naked as a skinned mole except for a little slave bracelet. The closer she came, the further I moved—I admit it; she was making fools right and left (I got splinters in my tail right now)—but Macey was in a trance. He couldn't take his eyes off of her so after she had ruined some fellow's cigar, she stepped up to Macey and he commenced to shrink and nudge towards me. Too late. She said to him, 'Strip off them glasses, son—you'll melt the frames.' And she reached down and flipped off Macey's glasses and tucked them away."

Rosacoke said, "Where?—if she was naked?"

"She found a place—and told Macey he'd have to come rescue them, her backing up the steps laughing and beckoning him on. He finally went and she stood still while he hunted his glasses and brought them back to me and said, 'What do they look like, Milo?' I told him if they were mine I'd leave them in the sun awhile to purify. Then I said, 'No, Macey, I was joking. They look all right. Just polish them some.' But Macey's night was over. He wouldn't put them on, and he's blind without them. Put them in his pocket and said 'Let's go home.' It was just ten-thirty and *I* could still see so I told him to drive on without me. I'd catch a ride."

Rosa said, "Drive? You said he was blind."

"Shoot, he could drive laying down. Lot of people can."

Papa said, "Not only can but do. What next?"

Milo said "The snake show."

Papa said "What did that cost?"

"Fifteen cents."

Papa said, "If you'd ever take a work-tool in hand and go back yonder in your family's garden you'd be in snakes knee-deep—no charge."

Milo said "Not boa constrictors."

"Yeah, we got them too."

"Twenty feet long? Three feet around? Weighing two hundred-eighty pounds? I grant you I hadn't been in the garden lately—"

Papa said "Never been."

"—But I overlooked meeting anything that size."

Papa said, "Nothing ain't naturally that size. All fair shows is fakes—rubber and mirrors."

Milo said, "Well, this fake last night ate a live white rabbit—feet and fur—right before these eyes." He flipped both thumbs towards his blaring eyes. "And the rabbit didn't act like *he* knew it was faked. That's what she says he lives on—live rabbits, white rats, chickens, dogs. Excuse me, Phillip. I forgot you were here."

Rosa said, "Who is *she* and what was that foolishness about you and her taking that snake to walk?"

"You couldn't keep a secret for God Almighty, could you?"

Emma said "What secret?" She and Baby Sister stood in the door, dressed for Warrenton, ready.

Rosacoke stood and began scraping dishes. "Nothing, Mama. I was just teasing Milo."

"What about?" Emma said.

Papa said, "About a new woman he's got him."

Rosacoke standing and Milo sitting—both gazed at the floor, shrunk into their collars, and Emma said, "What is the meaning of that, Milo?"

From the floor, from under Rato's hand Phillip barked—or tried. What came from his throat was nearer to moaning—grated, weak— and Rato said, "What is the meaning of this to Phillip? You set there talking mess while my dog is suffering and dying maybe."

Milo stood and walked to Phillip, bent above him, scratched in the short hot hair of his throat, lifted one side of his upper lip. Over the long teeth his gums were white.

He gave that feeble moan and Rato said, "See what I mean—his whole voice has changed." He touched Phillip's throat—"Can't eat or drink"— showed Phillip's legs, worked one leg gently—"Can't stand or move."

Milo said, "How long has he been this way?"

Rato said, "He ain't been well since Thursday, but since last night he can't do his will."

Emma said, "Thursday, nothing. He hasn't been right since he brought that bat home two weeks ago. I said at the time to get that thing and burn it up—they swarm with lice—but Rato said to let him play, he was having fun. Fun! Gnawing on gristle and leather wings and dirty fur? Well, fun or not, that bat was the start of Phillip's trouble, whatever it is." Phillip moaned again. "See what I tell you? *He* knows the cause."

Rato said, "He knows he's dying, that's all he knows."

Milo said, "He ain't dying, Rato. He's got rheumatism—or some-thing similar. You couldn't kill him."

Rato partly closed his hand on Phillip's throat. "I could kill him in a minute before your eyes. And maybe I should—to keep him from hearing your mess while he hurts. Just because you ain't never hurt, don't mean other things ain't." The tight noose of his fingers slackened.

Milo touched the short hair Rato had pressed. "A lot of things hurt in silence, don't they, Phillip?"

Rato stood to button the collar of his shirt (an old shirt of Milo's), then he leaned to Phillip, took him again in both his arms and walked through the kitchen door down the hall.

Emma said to Baby Sister, "See where he's going."

Baby Sister ran but Rato had heard. He opened the front door, then turned and said towards the kitchen firmly, "Phillip and me are walking to town."

They heard the door shut, heard Baby Sister pound back with the news—as if it were news, had happened at a distance—but before she could start, Milo said to Papa, "Papa, get ready. We can catch him up. He don't know what he's doing today."

Papa stood in obedience, stumped to the mantel, combed his dry white hair in the mirror propped there, and behind him the others twined in preparation—Rosacoke stacking dishes, rinsing her hands, Emma kneeling to inspect Baby Sister again, Milo stabbing his blue shirt into his trousers. Then at once they were ready—lacking only coats which only Baby Sister and Papa needed, it being that warm—and stood for a moment in silence, hands down.

Papa said to Milo "Who's driving?" and Milo's hand went out for the keys.

But Emma said, "Papa. For Rato's sake, let's get there at least."

Milo accepted that and led them out, down the hall, the three porch steps to the smooth tan stones of the yard. They moved out of step towards the truck, passing singly, successively, suddenly through ragged plates of October sun—no longer bleaching but ripening, curing, the color of gold simply though none of them noticed, had ever noticed—Milo, Baby Sister, Emma, Rosa, Papa.

Baby Sister noticed what was noticed, stopped the line, pointed— "Rato!" It was—farther on his way than they had expected, nearly at the trees that would hide him entirely.

Rosacoke said, "He'll never get there, starting that fast. Phillip must weigh thirty pounds at least."

Milo said, "He'd make it—Phillip ain't yours, Rosa—but we got to help him now if he'll let us. Papa, you drive. Mama, you and Baby Sister sit up front. Me and Rosa will ride in the back. Papa, drive past Rato, then slow down and stop a good ways ahead so he has to pass us. We got to give him time to change his mind."

They looked again and Rato was gone—vanished, blanked by pines—so they moved on urgently, silent, to the truck which Papa managed now as if he were younger—reversing, turning, proceeding quickly, smoothly as the ground allowed, then slowing as Rato showed ahead—his high narrow back, head, shoulders, arms spidered inward on Phillip to warm, shield, hide him. They came to Rato, flanked him silently—Rosacoke waved but he didn't look up—then passed on a little. The dirt of the road was damp and soft so they spared him dust at their stopping, yards ahead. And he and Phillip came on unaltered, refusing to acknowledge by look, gait or course that five people waited in a humming truck to make their amends. When Rato had covered half the gap, Milo stood to his knees and dropped the tail gate. At the clang Phillip looked and continued staring till they were close enough for Milo to use his natural voice.

He said, "Phillip, climb in. It ain't as smooth a trip as you're getting now but it's quicker at least." Then he beckoned once (a wide slow scoop), and Phillip scrambled, near panic for a moment in Rato's grip till his forelegs were free—surely the most he had moved since Thursday—so Rato took the truck in stride as if it were one more rise in the road. A foot on the bumper, a hand in Milo's, a seat up forward against the cab, shelter. Nobody spoke, nobody signaled Papa to start, but when Rato was with them and Milo had slammed the tail gate, he started—poorly now because they were safe, together, lurching—and soon they were on the concrete for town.

They still went dumbly—the children behind, separately lighted, their rounded features flat in the wind as if stones washed and smoothed by its streaming—and in fifteen minutes when they passed the fairground (Papa slowing), it seemed they would not even speak of that. But Milo and Rosacoke looked to the left past the white-washed exhibit hall to shapes on the sky of silver wheel, red octopus, swings, brown tented roof of the merry-go-round, all seeming shrunk and squat so early in the day and in natural light so spent, frail, dangerous that Milo quickly thought, "I'm not wasting no money there tonight" and meant it till the truck took a final curve and the back of the fairgrounds spread before them—worse at first than the front, dented old trailers with muffled portholes, rags of black oil smoke lounging from the roofs, but then by one, in a blue bathrobe, chafing her black hair between a towel was a girl maybe sixteen.

Milo waved. The girl saw at once and waved in return with her hand and then the towel as if to flag the truck, quickly, not smiling, as if she were captive and pled for rescue. Her sudden panic thrust Milo scrambling towards the cab to pound and say "Stop," but at the window, seeing Mama's neck, he halted and facing the girl again, merely pointed towards town and said with his lips "Come on, come on." She smiled and nodded, he sat again, and Rosacoke said, "If she's a woman, I'm the mother of a litter of hungry puppies."

Milo said, "She is my age exactly—just a few months older. I know I'm a man and I know she's not, which makes her a woman."

Rosa said, "Well, if you've arranged to meet her, hide her from Mama or we'll all pay for it till after Christmas."

Milo studied the fading fair not his sister, then said, "I got a Ph.D. in hiding things from Mama."

That silenced Rosacoke and seeming the pit of the morning's play, flushed her eyes, seized her throat. She knew already, was learning daily (and mostly from Milo) what she would always have to ignore to live her life, and she huddled lower on the slats of the truck and told it to herself or still hoping, asked it, "When will I learn a way to protect him?"—her face hid from him.

But he felt her trouble, had not yet ceased to know her entirely, and resenting her hold, her try on his life, he left her under the weight she had drawn on herself for almost the final mile. Not until they were in the heart of town—Papa parking the truck by a sidewalk black and laughing with Negroes—did he move to free her. Then he took two steps on his knees towards her, bent to her bowed ear, began the truth. "Rosa, I'm fooling. She is nothing to me, just a girl named Lois Provo from Florida. Her aunt runs the snake show back at the fair and Lois helps her."

Rosacoke looked up, faced him unsmiling but listening.

And the sight of her face locked the truth within him. "Last night when Macey had left me alone, I wandered in the snake show because it was cheap, and since I was almost the only one there, Mrs. Provo (the aunt) and Lois started talking (standing in the midst of dozens of snakes but they were mostly asleep—it was cool last night). Lois talked that is—Mrs. Provo watched me from the minute she saw me like something hurtful, a hawk in a henhouse—and I talked back and watched while they woke up some snakes and put on their show two or three more times for some colored boys. Then at midnight when I said I'd be going, Mrs. Provo finally spoke to me, said, 'Whoever you are, I need your help.' I said I was Milo and volunteered gladly to prove my good nature. 'What help?' I said. 'The big snake,' she said. 'Help us put him in his box.' So we all three did—their helper was drunk—and then Mrs. Provo gave me one more look and left, left *flat*—lights on, snakes loose. Lois said, 'Aunt Selma keeps a lot inside'—in her heart, I guess, but I didn't ask. So Lois and me shut down for the night and then took a walk together round the fair— mostly closed by then— and I hitched home, walked most of the way. That's all."

It was not. There was, and would be, more. And what he had told was mainly lies, told to shield her from his own growing, as if his life, his sudden needs and powers, were a rising light that could stunt, sear. Meeting his smile, she accepted his shielding, believed his story, suspected no more. But she could not mirror his lasting smile. She knew her day—feared her life—was ruined.

Papa gouged the truck tires into the curb, the engine died, Baby Sister turned and flattened her nose on the glass above them, a Negro girl two yards away said to a boy "*Lead* kindly light!"

Rosacoke stood and said, "Come on, Phillip. It's your turn now." She could smile at him.

Dr. Fuller blocked them in the door of his office, five-foot-four in brown shirt sleeves, straw hat to his ears, round purple face grinning young for his age, stumpy legs set wide in bloused gabardine to brace him on the stream of reek and yelp that washed around him down the steps to the Mustians—all but Emma and the baby who were shop- ping. They waited in the sun till the doctor moved, told them come or go. He came to them or at least to Phillip, spoke to him not the family—"What's wrong, boy?" knowing his sex though his sex was hid—and taking one hand from the package he held (a thick short cylinder, wrapped and tied), touched Phillip's skull with three fingers suddenly frail, roved for a moment on the waves of bone round the eyes as if the dog were a boy as he said and would show fever there. No one answered—the question was to Phillip—and Phillip with- drew from beneath the hand and strained with his neck to smell the package, moaning in pain and discovery as he moved. Dr. Fuller smiled to Rato, then pointed to the package—"He knows what I got"—meaning Rato to ask. Rato did not so the doctor stepped back, looked round to the rest, tapped the end of his package and said, "Guess what I am heading to mail."

Milo said "Something round—a snake?"

"No, a mad dog's head. Belongs to a lady in Macon—or did till he bit her cook and she sawed off his head and brought it to me, and I'm shipping it to Raleigh to see was he mad or was she mistaken."

Rato stepped back, removing Phillip's nose from touch of the package, and Papa said, "I was bit by a mad dog—here on the lip, my son's pet hound. She didn't mean me harm, she didn't know she was mad no more than I did, just thought the world of me and tried to show it so one summer evening I come up the porch steps to eat my supper and bent down a little to scratch her stomach and she jumped to kiss me and snagged my lip. Two weeks later she was crazy as a bat, foaming at the mouth, and I shot her dead on a Wednesday evening. I say it was Wednesday and I know it because I waited till then when my boy was at prayer meeting. Shot her, soaked her with kerosene, set fire to her and buried the ashes in the hour or so Rato was gone." Rato at the curb wore horror like a gauze so Papa said, "Rato my *son*, these children's Daddy, that's dead nearly four years. Well, early that Saturday they brought me in here to Dr. Sledge, and he commenced the treatment on me—fourteen shots in the belly with a needle like a twenty-penny nail. No sir, you children step back"—he made shielding wings of his long thin arms. "We don't want no more treatments to pay for."

Dr. Fuller said, "It ain't half as bad as it used to be. I've had it three times. Gave it to myself. But the health office will do it for nothing, and it's not but seven shots now."

Papa said, "That's seven more than we need. What's wrong with this boy's dog?" He ducked his head to the curb and Rato.

Rato stayed still, not moving closer, but Dr. Fuller asked him, "How's your dog been acting, son?"

Rato said "Sad" and bound Phillip closer inwards to him, offering no more.

Milo stepped up—he had come, been sent for this—"He has been depressed for some time, Doctor, but since last Thursday he won't eat his food, and now this morning he can't seem to walk. Just trembles—don't he, Rato?" Rato swallowed, nodded. "And moans like you heard."

Dr. Fuller said, "Worms. Take him inside and I'll see to him when I've mailed this head. Won't take me long. I'm not insuring it."

He turned right to leave them, and they all entered his door but Milo. Milo meant to wait awhile on the stoop, looking down towards Main Street to see who passed, to see if Lois followed his beckoning hand.

So it was to Milo the doctor spoke after he had gone ten yards, stopped, thought, lifted his straw hat, scratched, turned, walked back halfway—"Who are you, son? I know I know you."

"No sir, you don't. You never seen me. I just let my animals die if they can't find weeds to cure themselves. I'm Milo Mustian from out behind Afton. That in yonder"—he thumbed towards the screen door—"is my Granddaddy Mustian and my sister Rosacoke and Rato my brother. The dog is Rato's."

"What's *his* name?"

"Phillip."

"Phillip. You certainly do have unusual names around Afton."

Milo said, "I never looked at it like that. We use the names they give us, that's all. They called me Milo so that's how I act."

The doctor thought a moment, hitched up his package. "The only other Milo I ever knew was a Baptist preacher—Dr. Milo Candler. Fact he used to ride the circuit out around Afton—oh forty years ago. You named for him?"

"No sir, I'm fifteen. I'm named for Milo the old Greek wrestler."

"He one of the fellows wrestles in Raleigh every Saturday?"

"No sir, he's been dead about three thousand years. He used to wrestle in the Olympic games and always won. The first time he won—to celebrate—he brought in a four-year-old heifer on his shoulders and carried her clean across the stadium and then on the far side slaughtered her, cooked her and ate her by himself in one afternoon. Then when he was old one day walking through the woods, he came to a tree some men had halfway split and left, and Milo thought he would finish the job with just his bare hands. He almost did but he slipped a little and the tree clamped on him, and before he could wrench himself loose, wolves passed and they tore him limb from limb and ate him. He was old then though—I said that, didn't I?"

"Yes, you said that. About my age, don't you estimate?"

Milo said, "I can't tell you that. I don't know your age."

"Seventy-one."

"That's about what he was, just a little younger maybe."

Dr. Fuller jammed on his straw hat again. "I'll be stepping on. Back in a minute though—won't keep you waiting with a name like that."

"No sir, please don't"—the doctor went a little—"and keep a good lookout for wolves as you go. I saw some last night out at the fair. They smell that mad dog, you're done for, Doctor."

"And so would half of Warrenton be. That fair's a disgrace—brute beasts cooped up in nothing but chicken wire, blood in their eye, death in their heart, waiting for the chance to bolt and kill." He pointed ahead to the sun-lit junction where men and girls—mostly black—seethed slowly. "Let them *all* bolt loose—wolves and vipers. This town needs a drenching, a scourging, I tell you. It's Nineveh now, drinking and lying and hating your neighbor."

Milo thought he was joking and threw back towards him, "Doctor, you be the Jonah."

But the doctor didn't hear, didn't answer at least. He had finally wheeled on his own last word and was at the corner, rounding it right-ward when Milo's speech lapped on his back, on the print of the pint bottle riding his hip.

Two people heard—a boy at the corner (white, about four, rushed by his mother into dwarf man's pants, bow tie, feathered felt hat: he frowned, waved; Milo grinned, waved) and Rosacoke. She had listened inside unseen through the screen till she knew the doctor was safely gone. Then still inside she moved into sight, raking one finger loudly on the wire of the door.

Milo threw up his arms, shied back in mock fright. "It's one of them violent beasts tearing out!"

She said, "Calm down, it's your sister Rosa, and you're no more Milo for some old Greek than I am Rosa for the roses that bloom."

Milo dropped his arms, said, "Sure you are—you're my own rose" and leapt to the screen, bent, kissed the wire at the height of her lips, wore a grid of rust on his mouth when he stood.

She smiled and said, "I am *Rosa* for Mama's mother, *Coke* for Daddy's, and you are Milo for—who was it Papa?"

From deep in the waiting room—"My old blind mule that died the day Emma had the scoundrel."

Milo said, "That's part of my namesake—you're right, I forgot."

Rosa said, "You are named for our human ancestors. I can't remember which one but Mama'll tell me."

"Mama don't know. She named me Milo for her own reasons when I was defenseless. Now I'm a man I choose to be Milo for Milo the great, strong and brave."

"Milo the *great*? Nobody ever heard of him around here."

"Shoot, he's well known. Anybody's been in the eighth grade knows him. He's in the myth book you study that year."

"I'll recognize him when I get there then. That's something to live for."

Papa said from inside, "What is *my* name?"

Milo said "Mr. Mustian."

Rosacoke turned to where Papa sat, the doctor's Bible open in his lap. "You are *Jasper*, aren't you?"

"Yeah. But *Jasper* for what?"

Milo said, "For your old dead Daddy."

Papa said, "No, for Aaron's breastplate," and he read to them, each word separate, surrounded by waiting—"'the breastplate of judgment with cunning work . . . and thou shalt set in it settings of stones, even four rows of stones. The first row shall be a sardius, a topaz and a carbuncle—this shall be the first row. And the second row shall be an emerald, a sapphire and a diamond. And the third row a ligure, an agate and an amethyst. And the fourth row a beryl and an onyx and a jasper. They shall be set in gold in their inclosings.'"

Milo said, "The *fourth* row? If I'd have been picking, I'd have picked me one in the first row anyhow—*Topaz* Mustian, how does that strike you? Topaz Mustian up on Aaron's breast."

Rosa said, "Milo, Aaron was a man and Papa was named for his own father."

Papa said, "If Milo can choose his namesake at fifteen, I can sure choose me one at seventy. But maybe you're right—fourth row is pretty poor. Hold on a minute though. Listen to this. I do a lot better in the New Testament." He riffled from Exodus to The Revelation, slowly sought his place, found it, lined it on the air with a stained forefinger— "'And he carried me away in the spirit to a great and high mountain and shewed me that great city, the holy Jerusalem, descending out of heaven from God, having the glory of God, and her light was like unto a stone most precious, even like a jasper stone clear as crystal.'"

Milo said, "That's better. I admit that's better. I'd be named for that verse if I was you."

Papa said, "Well, you ain't and there's better yet—'And the foundations of the wall of the city were garnished with all manner of precious stones. The first foundation was jasper.' The *first*—hear that? My name is the cornerstone of New Jerusalem. That beats most wrestlers I ever heard of."

Milo said, "Heaven's hard to beat I grant you that." But Papa barely heard it. It was said not to him nor to Rosacoke but downwards to the corner, meaning Milo was finished discussing names and had moved on to looking, to hunting Lois Provo's face if she came.

Rosacoke heard that in the tone of his voice, and to spare herself watching his hunt, his face, she turned to Rato seated upright on a bench by the wall. He had not looked at a magazine nor studied the dirty framed dogs hung around him but neither had he shut his eyes to rest. She watched a whole minute to see if he blinked, and in the dull room his open eyes seemed to dry as she watched—what shine they had soaking inward till they matched his face (that sallow, that lightless), till they seemed so dry he could never shut them. "Rato!" she said.

He blinked slowly, turned. The deep lower rims of his eyes held tears.

She had made him show his pain, his fear, his weakness to help the little he valued—the huddle of dog cupped now in his lap—so she said, "*Horatio*. If I was a boy I would want your name, and if I have a son I'll name him for you—you and our Daddy."

His name was Horatio—Rato's name—and though he was second

son, he was the Junior. He nodded to her offer, locked his eyes onto blank space again (a hand on Phillip's butt, not moving), and Papa looked up from The Revelation. "He was my only son and I gladly paid for most of his food—even the little he ate at the end—but Horatio's a name ought to stop with this Rato. It hadn't brought none of us no satisfaction—I don't mean you, boy" (but he did half-mean him)—"I mean the drinking I never understood that killed him, drove him wild when he had a good wife, a house, hot food, three growing children and one in Emma. Maybe it was me—I think about that—a judgment on me. Nobody else deserved what he done—walking straight under the wheels of a truck, leaving it all on me, this old. I must have deserved it. He done it to me."

Milo was not beyond them completely. At the end of a moment when nobody answered, assured, denied, Milo threw in the rescue—"Put down the doctor's Bible, Papa. You'll wear it out."

Papa obeyed, set it gently on a table white with dust.

And Rosacoke slowly fled to Milo, relieved by his joking and seeking his help now to soften the knot that had gathered beneath her breastbone since they passed the fair, the standing girl—collecting its mass like a river snag from the sound of their private names, Rato's dumb pain, the inward sight of her dead father, Papa's blame, Milo's adjacent absence. She opened the whining screen and stood to within her arms' length of Milo, silently, trusting her nearness to turn him, return him to his natural friends.

He did not turn, allowed her to stand unacknowledged behind him, laying upon her only the backward edge of his shadow as he balanced upright on the thin iron rail of the stoop. At first the shadow seemed shelter enough, seemed promise of care, but he thrust his loose hands deep in his pockets, hooked his feet on the bars beneath him and hunched far forward, all his body prowed and set for landfall—sight of the girl he had called and expected.

Then his shadow seemed a stain, a small squat bellows as his arms pumped time. Rosacoke stepped back, cleaned herself of its touch and weight and stared at the broad flat base of his neck, scraped bare by Mama the week before of darker twined hair that had gathered since summer. She would stare and wait till she knew his thoughts.

For most of her life till lately she had done this—known Milo in sudden right leaps up his spine through his brain to the core of his simple needs, leaps he allowed her, had heretofore (even in anger) not blocked. She stood awhile waiting, then straining to hear—only the sounds of cars and Negroes, desperate exhausted barks from the kennel. So she clamped her jaws to start the ringing that would flood her ears, let her only hear her inward thinking. She heard herself. "He is aimed away from me, hunched like that, but his main aim—the aim of all this sorry morning—is to throw me off, shut me out of his life who had been there eleven years till yesterday evening." Suddenly she knew one way to reclaim him, a way to test if he could be reclaimed. Still behind him, separate, she began to sing

> *Oh I went down South for to see my Sal,*
> *Singing Polly-wolly-doodle all day.*
> *My Sal she is a spunky gal,*
> *Singing Polly-wolly-doodle all day.*
> *Fare thee well—*

Milo was meant to answer "Fare thee well"—the only three words he would ever sing and had sung without fail since before he could read, in a fake bass croak. But he failed this time, allowed the burden to drop uncaught.

To save the rhythm Rosa caught it herself, took it on to the first stopping place—

> *. . . Fare thee well,*
> *Fare thee well my fairy-fay—*

then stopped and knew he was set to hurt her.

He was not. What she didn't know (mercifully didn't—the truth being harder than any guess) was this, this simply: he had not thought of her (to care or spurn) since facing the corner, since the night before, since this year had rammed him beyond her, for now beyond his own understanding but not beyond his joy in what he was, was becoming daily.

He flagged up a hand in sudden recognition, called "Lois" once, no louder than he ever called anybody, and beckoned inwards to himself, his chest.

Lois heard (people always heard) but waited where she stopped—having followed him this far, quick pride halted her (and fear and shame).

So he rang the railing as his feet unhooked, leapt the four feet down to the pavement and rolled on forward, head half-down, arms bowed again at his hips, hands hid. She had made him a gift (the first such gift he had ever received), and he was still new enough to feel grateful to her, but only grateful—and ready to ask, asking already in his stride, his grin for the gift again, hoping to read guarantee in her eyes. In the little space around her among the Negroes, he stopped, smiled fully, gave her his deep waist bow. "Morning," he said.

"—Which is what it is," she said, looking to the day, the unmarked sky, her waves of black hair chestnut in the light, the white wandering of her nose, chin, neck seeming dusted and dry—for all her quick walk, her helpless search which was ended now (maybe still helpless). Her hands worked rapid pleats in her yellow dress as if by working she could finally lower her eyes to face him.

But she looked on up (at birds now, southward) till Milo said, "I hope you got more sleep than me. I didn't get home till four a.m."

"I slept some," she said and made herself face him. "I can always sleep. Anybody works like me and my aunt could sleep with murder on their soul, I guess."

Milo lurched a step back, walled his eyes in mock concern. "How many murders you got on your soul?"

That eased her. She puffed a little snort through her nose but not in disgust and shook off the hair that lay on her shoulders. Then she smiled a moment.

"How did you get to town so fast?"

She said, "It wasn't so fast. A mile isn't halfway round the earth. On my two poor feet. Thanks for the ride."

Milo said, "I'm sorry. We couldn't stop, you see. We were rushing my brother's sick dog to the vet."

"What's wrong with him?"

"Nothing but worms. The vet's gone to ship off a mad dog's head. He'll be back directly."

"Good thing you didn't stop for me then. If I get the smell of dogs on my hands, the snakes won't touch me for two or three days."

"I don't guess Phillip—Phillip's the dog—would take to you either. Gentle as a baby but show him a snake, he's the Hound of the Baskervilles. I've seen him fight a dead blacksnake the best part of a hot afternoon, wring it to shreds."

"Tell him not to try himself with no pythons though. He wouldn't need a vet—just an undertaker then."

"Not old Phillip. If he don't want you to catch him, God help you—doesn't matter whether you're snake or human. Phillip's *gone* if he wants to be, days at a time, then comes prancing in thin as a slat, tore to ribbons but healing already. He's a expert doctor—eating weeds and grass."

Lois looked to Dr. Fuller's porch. "Who is that girl you were talking to yonder?"

Milo looked. It was Rosacoke still—or until they had turned on her. Then she vanished inward. "That's just my sister. And we weren't talking. I was waiting for you. She was just waiting."

"Looks like I am too, don't it?"

"What for?"

"You tell me that. You called me in here."

Milo said, "I didn't have nothing big in mind. I just saw you yonder drying your hair, waving at me, and the natural thing was to call you on."

"You waved first."

"I beg your pardon for causing you the trip if you didn't want to see me. I don't have no presents to give you, no big plans—not till tonight. There's nothing to do in town, God knows, and when Dr. Fuller comes I've got to go back in there with him and handle all that. And anyhow I couldn't let my mother see you. It would ruin her day—she thinks I'm a child. So I beg your pardon—I said that before—but there you stood at the back of the fair when we were all worried about Rato's dog, and I said to myself, 'Yonder stands Lois. I'm meeting her tonight,' and then instead of waving and waiting for tonight, I was haling you in. I didn't think it out."

"You ought to," she said.

"—*Milo*," he said.

"Milo. *Milo*, I know it's *Milo*—know it by heart—and I don't mind a morning walk in sun like this, but don't you know I work mornings too? You got your duties, I got mine."

"Such as what?" he said.

"My correspondence school (the Law makes show people study too) and I'm learning palm-reading on my own free time. And forty-odd snakes need a lot of love and care."

"I ought to been a snake then."

Lois laughed, half-whispered "You near about *were*."

Milo blushed scaldingly, the cords of his face locked by rushing blood. Then recalling his age, his powers (but looking at the pavement not her), he said, "Look. I got to go back to my family or they'll be asking a million questions, and I'll be stuck at home tonight. You can go to the fair now and study, can't you? And wait till tonight?" He faced her again.

Lois said, "Sure I *can*. I can tell you to go to Hell too. *Wait till tonight*—what for, I ask you? Forty-five minutes in dirty pine straw with a teen-age farmer that I'll never see after sunup tomorrow? If that's all you're offering, if that's all you're hauling me round town for, you keep it, boy. Keep it on ice for some poor girl that hasn't wandered up the seaboard coast of the U.S.A. since she could remember with four dozen snakes and crooks for friends, no family but an aunt that cannot sit still—wanders and drags me behind her like a load and slides in and out of some speechless grief the way normal people change a suit of clothes."

In fifteen years no one had ever said more to Milo than *Come* or *Go*, *Stop* or *Start*, and to those the answers were *Yes* or *No*. Now faced with pride and hurt and honest need, with all the questions twined and crossed, with new orders rising like *Take* and *Use*, he lacked an answer. He had the age, the abundant power to cause her demands but neither knowledge nor strength to fill or reject them. He said, "Lois, I have begged your pardon two times this morning. That is all the angels in Heaven can do." He touched her brown forearm—"Look."

She looked. Her eyes were dry but coiled, crouched.

He did not even have a sight to show her, except himself. Having gained her look he had meant to urge her gently again to leave him now, to wait for night, but he paused a moment, held (again for the first time in fifteen years) by an upward flood in his throat which he did not know was gratitude, unspoken, unspeakable thanks.

To save him, Dr. Fuller appeared—from town, behind them. He seized Milo by the shoulder and said, "Wrestle me, son. If I lose I'll kill you."

Milo said, "You outweigh me, Doctor. How come you didn't mail your mad dog?" The package was still pressed into his side, looking hotter, more dangerous.

The doctor looked to it as though it had manifested fresh that moment—a wen, a tumor—in the crook of his body. "Damned if I didn't forget it," he said. "But it's just as well. It would just have to sit all Sunday in some hot post office, baking. I'll put it back in the ice box till Monday. Who's your friend here? Is she sick too?"

"No sir. She works out at—" Milo stopped. Catching at once the doctor's sweet liquor breath and recalling his rampage against the fair, he said, "She's a friend of my sister's from out of town."

The doctor studied her. "She sure outgrew your sister, didn't she? Must have good air where she comes from—where is it, girl?"

"Clearwater, Florida. But I travel mostly."

Milo frowned to halt her there.

"Travel is broadening," the doctor said, then walked on beyond them towards his office. Milo saw that the bottle he had carried was gone, surely emptied, but before he could turn to Lois and explain, the doctor stopped and called back to them. "Come on, I tell you. Both of you, now. I'll need all the help I can get with that dog."

Where he stood Milo said, "I thought you said it was nothing but worms."

"Maybe I did but I've had time to think, and recalling his face, I don't like his looks. This time of year and the fair going strong, fouling the air—he could be worse-off than anybody knows. So come on and help me." His face was all one downward frown, he seemed in earnest and however wild with drink and age, to wait at the edge of some necessary leap he must make for Phillip—with or without their company or help.

Milo looked to Lois, said, "Stick with me, Lois. God knows what's coming," and they went together behind the doctor, through slotted light (the heat and cold) towards Phillip suddenly the center of the day, their separate lives.

Surrounded at wait on the doctor's table, Phillip seemed to know that—that he bore their fear on his ribbed skull, the color and weight of walnut shell—and at first he spared them by refusing to meet their eyes, even Rato's (Rato still touched him). He watched the empty door where the doctor would come. The doctor had sent them ahead to this room, saying, "Take that poor dog in and stand clear," vanishing himself into some side closet where they heard a drawer open, the sounds of swallowing, the drawer shut quietly, the whisper "Dear God." They listened to that so intently, pressed it so hard for meaning and promise that no one thought to ask Lois's name nor stare at her eyes.

And for all her unease, she stood as what Milo had said she was—his sister's friend—beside Rosacoke on Milo's right in the circle around the bare wood table, and when Dr. Fuller shuffled in towards Phillip (flanked in the door by diplomas on the walls, proving what his gait and smell denied) and Phillip shuddered under Rato's touch, Lois laid a natural unthinking hand on his nose to stroke, to calm them both—Phillip and her, the two in the room who most needed calming.

But sick as he was, Phillip took the old scent sunk in her pores, beneath her scrubbing and the new smell of Milo—the oil of snakes, their leathery threat, his mortal foes. Whatever sickness he bore was light now. He tensed his throat and began a crooning which stood for a growl, not to Lois herself (he saw she was safe) but to what lurked near her, beneath her, behind her. She—understanding—withdrew her hand but Phillip was sure, and he growled on unbroken as Dr. Fuller neared, then seeing the doctor's weaving shape, lifted his lip over ready teeth.

Two feet away, Dr. Fuller halted, stooped from the knees to Phillip's eye level, took his hot cocked gaze, then reached to a bench, took a leather muzzle and held it to Rato—"Muzzle him, son. He's worse than he was."

Rato refused it, shaking his head.

But Papa said, "Do it. You heard the doctor."

So rubbing Phillip's taut neck with one gentle hand (deepening the pitch of the growl as he rubbed), Rato slipped the muzzle on, buckled it down. And Phillip rose or fought through the blanket till his front legs braced and lifted his head which jerked round the circle of faces, growling to each but louder towards Lois, loudest towards the doctor as he finally came and drew back the blanket and started to probe into Phillip's soft thighs, the pits of his chest, his hard hot throat. Phillip yielded his body but none of his mind—his voice continued to rake out defiance and flipped to his back, he staked his legs in the air above him.

The doctor asked him "What you been eating?"

Nobody spoke. Then Rato said "Mostly cold corn bread."

Dr. Fuller said, "I meant the dog. I know your diet."

Rato said, "I meant him too. He eats corn bread after us at night. The rest of his food he gets in the woods."

"He hunts, you mean?"

Rato nodded. He had already said much more than his quota.

"Hunts for himself? What does he catch?"

Milo said, "He's Hell on snakes. But he don't eat them. Squirrels, foxes, muskrats, owls—we got a backyard full of their bones, clean as whistles. He's a clean dog, Phillip. I'll give him that."

"A bat ain't clean." It had slid out of Papa (helpless to hold it), and everything clenched—everybody's face and Dr. Fuller's hands.

He thrust those stiff hands up over Phillip as in sudden surrender. "Who said *bat* and what did you mean?" He looked first to Lois.

She said, "Not I. I don't know nobody here but him" (touching Milo's arm). "I work at the fair and I work with snakes, but I wouldn't touch a bat—filth, lice, needles for teeth."

"Hold everything," Dr. Fuller said and looked to Milo. "Who are you and whose dog is this, and what is this news about eating bats? You said you were Mustians from Afton, I thought, and now this child comes here from the fair saying she runs a snake show. Who *are* you?"

"I am Milo Mustian like I told you, Doctor, and these are my people—my Granddaddy, sister, my brother Rato. The dog is his. The stranger is a girl named Lois Provo. She works at the fair and come in

here to see me today. I vouch for her though. She's all right. The bat
Papa mentioned was two weeks ago. Phillip caught him on the wing
one evening. I was out back and I saw him do it. The bat divebombed
after some bug, I guess, and Phillip shot up and snatched him
down—and played with his body for a day or so till nobody knew
where it was any more, buried maybe."

"*Buried* nothing—*eaten*, that's what." Papa again.

Dr. Fuller said, "Of course it was eaten. This dog ate it and you
haul him in here, teeth bared to kill me."

Papa said, "Doctor, hold it. *You* hold it now. You said it was worms.
I heard you say it and that was my thought. Now how come all this
noise about teeth? He ain't got worms in his teeth, I know."

"You're right, old brother. Worms are the least of your worries now.
You got you a mad dog all to yourself." Dr. Fuller broke off and strode
to the door, to flee the danger, turn them out, call the police—he had
not thought which.

And they had not thought, only spread back from Phillip one uni-
son step at the sudden news—all but Rato; Rato stayed. Then Papa
drew breath and still in retreat said, "*Mad dog?* Look at him—gentle
as a lamb, lying there still, dry at the mouth. I seen mad dogs—I told
you that. They foam at the mouth and run till they drop."

Dr. Fuller stopped, wheeled where he stood. "They foam and run
unless they have got what your dog has got—*dumb* rabies. There's two
kinds of mad dogs, and this dog is one kind—the dumb kind that just
lies there till he dies, taking you with him if you stand too close. He's
paralyzed—*half*-paralyzed, you heard his voice. Now gradually he'll
turn to stone, that still, that dumb."

Rato rolled Phillip back to his stomach—Phillip was quiet now—
and stroking his neck said, "Nothing dumb about him. Smart as some
people that finished school. I ain't saying who."

Milo said "No don't."

And Dr. Fuller said, "For all I know he's a Philadelphia lawyer, but
he's also mad and deadly as a dart." He took two more long steps to leave.

But Papa said, "Wait. Don't run from us now. Hell, do something
for him." Dr. Fuller stopped again, turned, faced Papa. "Doctor, what
can you do?"

"Kill him, that's what." He retracted a step.

Rato said, "Kill him. You try it. Lay one finger on him and you die. Drunk or sober, I don't care which." Again he ringed Phillip's neck with his hand—a finger, a thumb were enough to do it.

Dr. Fuller walked completely back and with his own thumb strummed Phillip's spine. Phillip turned to see him but stayed silent now to listen with the rest. "Oh drunk, I guess." He took out his watch. "Ten-thirteen a.m. by God and more than half-gone. Me, I mean." He looked over Phillip to Lois's face, offered it to her. She nodded receipt. "It's because of—" he stopped; they waited with him. "There's no excuse. It is ten-fourteen. At noon I will lock up here and leave, the best I can, walking home, *home*"—he pointed through plaster and brick as through glass, paused while they looked. "I will eat some rat cheese and soda crackers and stretch out to rest, and if I am lucky I'll sleep a little and *if*"—still to Lois—"if God hears prayer, my heart will seize and I'll never wake." Lois frowned. "I'll wake. Don't worry. I'll wake about ten p.m. in the dark and lie in that empty house, not a sound except what I tell myself—'Get up, Joel (my name is Joel) and take a-*hold*.' I ask myself, 'Take a-hold of what?'—'Your own sorry life, your sorry self.'—'Take hold for who? Who gives a damn?' I spare myself the answer to that. It's one care I take, but I'll tell *you*—not a breathing soul; oh four or five dogs in the dark down here, fouling their cages, waiting for daylight and me to feed them. Well, daylight will come and so will I and any poor bastard that's lasted the night can eat what I give. If one of them's died the others get extra. That's what I take a-hold for every daybreak—three or four dogs that whatever I do, if I was to rise at *three* a.m., will die anyhow, run over, poisoned, shot by neighbors, and nobody grieves more than twenty-four hours. That is my life. Who would have guessed it, who would have thought a man could live it? And you come in here to break my heart with this poor son"—meaning Phillip and still touching Phillip but all said clear-eyed, unblinking, slowly to Lois because he had started with her, could not face the strain of another judge.

For personal reasons she took the burden, said, "Nobody's aiming to break nothing, Doctor. They are just asking you to do what you can."

Milo brushed her flank beneath the table.

Dr. Fuller said "Right" and walked to a cabinet, took an empty syringe, screwed on a needle, held it to the light, withdrew the plunger to fill it with air, then stepped back to Phillip.

Papa said, "Is that some new discovery, Doctor?"

"It's fresh air," he said. "New as air."

Rato understood—but only Rato—and covered Phillip's heart with the flat of his hand.

Milo said, "Phillip, we're pumping you up."

Papa said, "What'll that do for him, Doctor?"

"Put him to sleep."

"For how long, Doctor?"

"Till Judgment Day. That's the best I can do."

"That's *all* you can do?"

"All any human being could do—the shape he's in. I'm sorry to tell you."

Papa said, "We are sorry to hear it, Doctor," and they were, thus: they sensed where they stood among one another, who was left or right ten inches away, kin or strangers—the doctor farthest, opposite, alone; Phillip on the table; Rato at one end and strung out from him down one side together—Papa, Rosacoke, Lois, Milo. They all watched Phillip or chipped quick glances off Dr. Fuller like stones or hooks. They did not, could not face one another nor speak nor touch—and did not know why. Lois knew—she stood in their midst. She had learned that much in sixteen years. So she took a step back, moved left round the table and stopped beyond at the vacant end, on Milo's left. The space she had held shrank as she went; without conscious movement Rosacoke stood now closer to Milo, and Milo said, "Then there's nothing else to do" (which was not a question). "Do you see that, Rato?" Rato nodded. Milo said "Doctor." The doctor extended his left hand to Phillip, Rato bared Phillip's tufted heart, and the doctor aimed the empty syringe, saying "Shut your eyes."

Papa said, "Hold on, Doctor. Excuse me a minute. What do you charge for this fresh air treatment?"

"The consultation is three dollars even; this thing now will be five dollars more—eight dollars total." He was still poised to act.

Papa said, "Just hold it. Doctor, five dollars is more than I've give to *feed* this dog in all his life. Where am I going to find five to kill him?"

Dr. Fuller said, "I can't help you there. I offer a service that would wear and tear the nerves in a rock. I can't do it free."

"I know that. I won't asking that. What I am thinking is, since Rato's handled him all this week with no trouble yet and since you say he is half-paralyzed and will be completely—well, if we could borrow that little leather mask and take Phillip home, we could handle him there. One of us could. Shoot him, I mean, and Milo could bring you your mask on Monday. He comes in to school on Monday, you see."

None of the family objected to that. It seemed—once mentioned—natural and fitting, and no one had real money to offer. There even rose in them, cool and quick, a sense of reprieve that allowed them to move—scrape feet, scratch arms, face one another. All but Rato whose visible future was silent grief, locked at his end, no longer touching Phillip who had failed, abandoned him.

Even the doctor showed relief though slowly. He continued to feel for Phillip's heart, but he said, "You choose. What I can do is no fun for me, and he might prefer your way after all. Just give me your word—that you'll have this poor son underground by noon today."

Papa said "You got it" and while the doctor dismantled the needle, found in his purse three old dollars to pay for the morning, the news, the duty that lay ahead of him yet, saying, "We thank you, Doctor. Take care of yourself," then "Take up your dog" as he turned to Rato and took the first step to finish the day.

Having their word for Phillip's death, Dr. Fuller let them leave unattended, preceding them only to his dark side closet, entering without a backward look—both saving and depriving them further speech. So they passed single file through the hall, the lobby, then stopped outside in a huddle on the steps in sun again. Papa said, "Now listen. Nobody's telling Emma this news. It would just scare her and start her talking. When we get to the truck, you all shut up and I'll get us home quick as I can." He pointed to Phillip in Rato's arms (seeming smaller now, compressed by his doom)—"Stay way from his mouth but treat him easy. I can't be bringing nobody to Warrenton for fourteen mad dog shots if he strikes. He ain't going to strike. He knows he's licked. All right, let's go."

Lois was gone—three steps before even Milo noticed. He said, "Lois?"—no turn, slowing, goodbye, arrangement to meet—so he said to Papa, "You don't need me. You and Rato do it. I got to catch her." He rattled off three long steps of his own.

Then Papa said, "Hold it. You are needed here and will be, at home. We don't even know that child's last name."

Rosacoke said, "I heard—it's Provo. Milo, stay."

But Papa said "Girl—" and Lois turned. "Are you headed for the fair?"

She nodded. "Yes sir."

"Then we can take you with us in the truck" and he started towards her, Rato following.

Rosacoke hung back knowing she had lost, delaying acceptance, and Milo even said, "Papa, you've ruined it. Wait till Mama sees her."

Papa threw back, "I said to keep shut and leave that to me. I've answered Emma since she caught my son and ruined his life. She's the least of my worries. Now let's go home." He spoke the last four words to Lois, having faced her again as he walked ahead and, thinking, smiled. She seemed to be waiting for him—the girl—seemed gently nudged from behind by sunlight to meet him, greet him. And smile she did but he gave the greeting. "What you reckon is the trouble with him?—the doctor, I mean?"

Lois said, "Oh drinking and living alone and your sick dog—"

"—Old age," Papa said, looking down on her (the crown of her dark hair coppered by sun) as she took stride beside him, accepting his lead, his final answer—"Just pure old age."

There was little cause to sing and now no right, yet once they had climbed on the truck (Emma waiting), heard Papa say "He's bad sick, Emma," heard her say "Who's the black-haired girl?," then the cranking engine to drown Papa's lie—once they were washed again by wind, Milo (of all the family) was singing though silently. He had no gift nor love for music, never sang in church nor school nor for joy, only if he thought he could make a girl laugh or to echo Rosacoke's

"Fare thee well," yet now the spent morning and its opposite parts spun in his mind as music, melody—broadening to bear all he saw and felt, needed or merely wanted for pleasure this Saturday morning his fifteenth October, dawn to the previous night with Lois.

For Lois had caused the song he felt—by giving the gift he had grown to demand (entrance, a hot loud grip on his life), giving it simply because he had asked: not aloud but by leading her tired at midnight around the fair, then through rusty trailers, dusty cars to the dark edge of trees where just as his heart rose in him to ask, she turned and spoke—not "Take me back" nor "Why are we here?" nor "What are you after?" but only "Far enough," looking out of the dark where they stood towards the fair (her home) that was dying rapidly light by light on the rim of the sky. *"Far enough,"* meaning this is the place, the time for us both, which he had agreed to, dropping to his knees, not looking for fear she would change and leave, waiting till she lay to her place beside him, open to the night and presently simply open to him for whatever reason—he wondered that as he huddled above her: why? why me when she barely knows my name or face by day anyhow?—the shelter of pines only ten yards away which she would not use.

She would use it tonight. He would lead her there—into trees— tonight. And to test his will, he looked to where she faced him now in the bed of the truck, seeming darker even by day than night, heavy (among his brother and sister) not so much with memory as promise— of the night ahead, his sudden life he had finally begun in her tight fork and would surely continue (farther from now than he could dream) on handfuls of others of whom Lois Provo was only the first.

But still the first. She knew that and smiled, taking his gaze now through all the wind, confirming his hope, her similar wish. Tonight she would go wherever he led. "Oh will follow wherever I lead," he said—or sang, still silent—and blinded now by his memories and hopes, he tasted in an upward rush from his chest one more feeling he had not yet known. To know it and name it, he rolled back his head to rest on the truck side, accepted the light on his shut eyelids— and found that the taste was gratitude, plain thanks for Lois. So he did not contain his song any longer. Eyes still shut, his mouth burst open on the surge of his joy, the sudden manhood that stood in his groin, that firmed the bones of his face and wrists as the truck bore him on through this clear day among his family, his first known girl, towards his life to come, his life he would make for himself as he wished. What he finally sang—aloud to them all—were the only words and tune he knew.

> Fare thee well,
> > (Fare thee well.)
> Fare thee well,
> > (Fare thee well.)
> Fare thee well, my fairy fay.

He bore the burden in his own bass voice and nearing the end, he half-expected—from years of habit and because she was near—that Rosacoke would join and help him, that now she would feel and share his fullness. But no answer came and when he had lunged on alone to the end, he peered from eyes that still seemed shut at three people crying—or in silent tears not caused by the wind: Lois, Rato and Rosacoke. Really not knowing their separate reasons nor trying to guess, he sat up to speak, said, "The funeral's not till after dinner. *Smile* till then."

Before anyone could strike back at that, the truck stopped beneath them. They looked—all but Rato—and saw they had come to the edge of the fair (the town edge; the woods lay beyond towards home). Lois pressed with her hands to rise and leave, meaning to go without a word—to Milo at least who had not spoken except to sing some children's song—but the truck door opened and Papa leaned out and said, "Where must I leave you?"

She stood now. "Oh here will be fine. I thank you, sir."

"That ain't what I mean. I mean where is your tent?" Papa half-stood himself on the running board and waved towards the fair still dead before them so early in the day—ten forty-five, one or two shaggy men with buckets of water, the distant cry of a wrench on metal (someone tightening the ferris wheel in hopes of its lasting another night).

"I'm not headed there," Lois said. "I'm headed home now."

"But we ain't going as far as Florida."

"I meant that trailer." She clutched her black hair with one hand and pointed over tents and rides towards the trees. "The road runs by it but I can walk."

"No'm," Papa said, "Sit tight. I'll take you *home.*" He slammed his door and rolled them forward but she did not sit. She stumbled towards the cab—towards Papa's side—and kneeling on the scraped ribbed-steel floor there, she stared at the fleeing asphalt road which was surely as steady as anything else—any person or place—in her shifting life.

Everyone watched her openly now—Emma and Baby Sister backwards through the window in blank curiosity (Papa had told them the girl was a nurse that toured with the fair and helped the vet in her mornings off); Rosacoke, opposite, propped by the cab, in understanding hatred; even Rato at the tailgate cupped round Phillip, in hope of finding relief on her person (never having looked to a person for that since he was a child: he was fourteen now)—but nobody spoke, least of all Milo.

Milo watched for signs in her face of what would become of tonight—his plan, her promise, their mutual wish. He could only see half (she turned from him), and though she did not smile, she did not frown, and the recent tears had sunk and dried. How could he, why should he spend his days, his precious life, in straining to know what other people meant—this Lois, his sister, his grieving mother—when they would not speak and ask for their needs?

He would ask his need when the right time came. He looked and the time was almost on him. They were slowing beside the huddle of trailers, and once more Lois was crouching to leave—when Papa turned into the dust and ruts and stopped by instinct at Lois's trailer.

She stood and walked down the truck to Rato. He had gone back to watching Phillip not her, but he roused now, let down the chain for her, drew back his legs so she could pass. She jumped the long step, Rato drew back the tailgate, but she faced him over it—no one but him—and said, "I'm sorry to slow you from getting him home. I have lived with animals all my life—since my parents died. I can guess how he feels if I don't know for sure."

Rato nodded. "You know," he said with that much force.

Lois flagged out a hand to Phillip, then moved along the truck on Milo's side, not towards Milo but towards her duty to the waiting old man who had brought her back and leaned out grinning to take her thanks. How could he know, old as he was, that his kindness had ground her—her expectation, promise, pride—like a slow water wheel every inch of the way (his kindness on the base of his grandson's silence)? She would tell him thank you and leave them for good and, walking, she forced a smile towards his grin.

But Milo laid a hand on the truck side and whispered as she passed, "Ten o'clock, Lois. Like we said—o.k.? I'll be needing to see you and say goodbye."

She stopped and faced him, canceling the smile. "What you'll be needing is a set of feelings and some eyes to notice you are not alone in this world, boy—not after last night—and had better stop grinding on other people that you hardly know, for no better reason than because you *need* to. If anything of yours starts *needing* tonight, you haul it to Phyllis's"—she pointed to the kootch tent—"and if she laughs you out, knot a string around it till your feelings grow to fit it. And as for goodbye, I can say that now—say, Fare thee well. Fare-*thee*-well." She bowed her head, swallowed, looked up smiling—"And you don't learn that in Clearwater, Florida, not at sixteen anyhow." She turned again to Papa, deepened the smile and told him "Thank you."

Papa had not heard—no one had but Milo and Rosacoke and they were both stunned (for separate reasons) into slack-jawed stares. Papa only saw, when she stepped near enough, the face she had instantly prepared for him. "My pleasure," he said. She moved left homeward. He reached in the air as if to touch her (she was ten feet gone)—"I would pay you to show me your show right now—I don't drive at night—if it won't for the dog."

"I'm sorry for him. Be careful now."

"No'm, he's no harm."

"Well—" she said and stroked the air once, moving on again.

"Clearwater, Florida, didn't you say?"

Lois only nodded, continuing to leave (twelve feet gone, nearer to home than to them now, to the trailer at least).

And Papa threw towards her "Wait," then turned back to Emma rigid beyond Baby Sister—"Won't that the last place I heard from Tommy?"

"Tommy who, Mr. Mustian?" Her fears of the girl, her cocked outrages were tripping one another from speech to speech like a sweep of dominoes.

"Tommy Ryden my boy, my favorite cousin that ran off from home when he was fourteen in nineteen-and-thirty. You ought to know that."

"I've heard, yes sir, but I didn't know he was such a favorite of yours. You hadn't said his name since the middle of the war."

"Hell, Emma, he was *killed*. Killed overseas and buried in a hole three years ago. You want me to march around naming my griefs the rest of my life? I got to forget. I got work to do."

"Well, I have forgot. I never saw him to know who he was, and I don't know if he moved to Florida—or Baltimore. I just know, since you mention work, I ought to be home right now and cooking."

Papa did not answer that but turned to Lois who had waited at command. "Did you know anybody down there named Ryden? Tommy Ryden?—a middle-sized boy." He measured up five-foot-six with his hand. "Rusty-headed, did a lot of laughing?"

She thought a moment, "No sir. Three years ago I was already traveling, been traveling since I was three in fact."

"*I* knew him"—some new woman's voice entered from beyond, firm and deep. "What you want to know?" All the Mustians looked for the voice—Lois knew. It came from a short plain woman, maybe fifty, walking as she spoke, coming from the tents towards the trailer and Lois, to stop like a shield between Lois and the truck. (Milo knew her—it was Lois's aunt—but she had not seen him and he would not speak, being already in trouble with his mother that would take weeks to clear.)

Papa said, "Good morning. I am Jasper Mustian," bowing as best he could from the running board. "I rode this girl from town out here, and when she said she was from Clearwater, I recalled Tommy wrote me his last word from there before he was killed—ten years before so it won't a goodbye and I never knew what he done down there."

"He done plenty. He kept busy. I am this child's aunt, Selma Provo, her mother's elder sister and the child's only kin."

Papa stepped to the ground, bowed again, kept his hat in his hand. "When was the last time you saw Tommy, please ma'm?"

"Nineteen thirty-five."

Papa said, "Oh. I thought you had seen him nearer to his death."

"No sir. I heard of that ten years after I saw him last, read it in the paper. Somebody mailed it to me out on the road. You haven't got any of his money left, have you?—his death insurance?"

Papa frowned. "I never had it to start with, lady. What do you mean?"

"I mean he disappeared owing me money—for room and board, various things."

Papa said, "Listen, lady. I was nothing but his cousin, and I ain't seen him in eighteen years—since he left home with maybe a dime in his pocket. I can't go taking on his debts this late. Not with these to feed." With his hand he directed her eyes to his truck, his waiting family.

She looked in a sweep, landing last on Milo's helpless smile. Then she laughed, kept laughing, came forward saying, "Is this your boy, mister? How come you hid him?" She even looked back to mystified paralyzed appalled Lois—"Lois, did you see who's sitting here grinning?"—but did not care nor wait for Lois's "Yes." She came till she stood three feet from the truck—"*Milo*, aren't you?"

"Yes ma'm. From last night. He is my Granddaddy. That's my mother." He pointed to the small back window of the truck, expecting Mama's face, prepared to take it, braced for the blow that would land on his eyes. But she was not there, only half of the powdered back of her neck. She was waiting now for an explanation—later at home—and the force of her wait shook the truck like voltage, had stunned Baby Sister to sit and shut up, heated the metal beneath Milo's hand. He lifted it again—"That's my sister Rosa and this is Rato my only brother."

Mrs. Provo studied them all for a while, then said to Milo, "Let me get this straight, help me get this straight—every one of you are Tommy Ryden's cousins?"

Milo said, "If Papa says so, it may be so and may not be. Papa thinks everybody is kin to him. Some of his people way back were

Hulls so he thinks he is kin to Cordell Hull, just having the name rattling round in the family. He's been waiting for a call to Washington all these years from his cousin Cordell. Hadn't you, Papa?"

Papa smiled but nodded his confidence. "Yes'm there's Rydens that are kin to us. I don't know how close kin though."

Rosa said, "They couldn't be too distant for me."

Mrs. Provo said, "What you got against them?"

Milo said, "Oh she's just talking. There's a Ryden girl in her grade at school that beats her time with the boy she likes."

Mrs. Provo smiled but Rosacoke said, "That's a bluefaced lie. I don't like boys yet. Dora Ryden is nice to me. It's Claiborn her twin that ruins everything. I wouldn't even tell the things he does—to girls mainly, putting things on them. Snakes—slimy!" She shuddered of course.

And eight feet away, Phillip cocked his head at the sound of snakes. He knew the word as his order to charge—like "Sic" or "Rabbit" to other dogs—but Rato gripped him.

Mrs. Provo said, "They are cleaner than any human being *I* know, shed their whole skin if it gets a little dirty—scale by scale and it's no fun either by the look on their faces. Name me a person that'll go that far."

"Not me," Papa said. He had moved up to join them. "Every seven years is enough for me. But I've seen them do it—grab hold to something with their tail and *strip* and leave it lying there like so much trash."

"Even the worn-out surface of their eyes, peeled off clean," Mrs. Provo said. "I got one in yonder, shedding now"—she thumbed behind her; Milo knew she was aiming at the snake tent—"Come on and see it. All of you, get out. No charge till noon!" She turned back for Lois—"Lois, you and Milo get the snakes out. I already started."

Phillip clenched again and Lois was gone, where she had stood seeming violent, smoky as if she had been snatched away or had vanished in anguish like a speechless ghost.

Mrs. Provo said, "She must have gone in to fix up better. She tore off to town so fast this morning, she barely dressed. I didn't know where she was—or what hit her."

"Milo did," Rosacoke said firmly.

"Did what, honey?"

"Hit your niece. When we drove by here two hours ago, she was drying her hair—standing yonder—and Milo waved and she trailed him in to where we was at the veterinarian's with poor old Phillip. Phillip is the dog."

Mrs. Provo said, "What's wrong with Phillip?" walking towards the tailgate and Rato and Phillip. "You ought to have brought him here to me. I can heal most animals just with my hands." She extended her spread fingers into the light, fanned them twice in preparation.

"No'm," Papa said. "Don't touch him now. He's feeling low and his temper is up."

"These are soothing hands," she said and touched him. And at first it seemed she was right in her claim. Phillip loosened beneath her palms, laid a calmer head back on Rato's arm. "What did you say was the trouble he's having?"

Milo snatched the undrawn breaths of his family, open-mouthed around him. "Worms," he said.

She proceeded to stroke, both strong hands in the pit of Phillip's throat (he had raised to admit her).

Papa neared a little, looked, said to Rato, "What have you done with his harness, son?—that leather thing the doctor lent you?" Rato fished behind him and held out the muzzle which he had removed once the truck was rolling, to let Phillip breathe out his last minutes free. Papa glanced to Milo, then said to Rato more gently than ever in fourteen years, "Strap him up, son, like the doctor told you."

Before Rato could decide to obey, Mrs. Provo said, "Muzzling a dog for nothing but worms? What kind of doctor did you take him to?"

Milo said, "A cracked old drunk but he's all we got."

"Well, any fool knows how to worm a dog, and it doesn't take a muzzle and torture to do it. Bring him on over to Jake Hasty's trailer. Jake runs the dog show. He'll worm him for you and no muzzles needed."

Papa said, "No'm, thank you. We got all the treatment he needs at home." He pointed towards what he thought was west.

Mrs. Provo kept rubbing but said to Milo, "I don't think your

Granddaddy trusts me. He thinks I'm after Tommy Ryden's insurance."

"Lady, you are wrong. It ain't I mistrust you. And Tommy didn't have no penny I've seen. His Mama died two years ago—poor as Niggers—so if *she* got a penny she must of buried it."

Milo said, "Old Miss Jack Ryden? Fat as she was, she couldn't of dug a post hole much less buried ten thousand dollars."

"Who said a word about ten thousand dollars?" Mrs. Provo said—but quietly to Phillip.

Milo said, "Nobody. It's just what you get if some of your kin people die in the war. The Bullocks got it when their boy died—and he never left Norfolk, died in port."

They paused as they always did for death—time for one long breath. Then Mrs. Provo looked to Papa. "Excuse me talking so hard about Tommy. I was coming from the tent—from watering the snakes—and Tommy's name struck me like a hand on my teeth. Then I saw Lois facing all you strangers—not seeing Milo grinning over here—and I went cold scared. I didn't know what you might know and tell her, to ruin her life." Her hands on Phillip had stilled when she started, and now they lifted and hung blank before her as part of her asking and offering pardon. "We never told her and I never knew Tommy had living kin till this boy strolled in the tent last night"—Milo gravely accepted her gesture to him—"and my blood froze. It was Tommy *walking*—his face, his voice—like thirteen years had never rolled by so how could I refuse when he took to Lois and she took to him? It was time going backwards like I knew it would, like it always does. Who was I to stop it? But I never knew you were her blood kin too. Well, still, don't tell her. Leave me that much and I'll find a way to ease her the news, later when she can use it."

She had lost them all but in natural courtesy, they tried to hold back the mystery from their faces, the smiles that threatened to replace understanding so they could not look to one another but held their eyes separate, fixed on the lady who was silent now—having opened her life like a vein before them. Her eyes were filled and though her lips parted again and again, her throat was locked.

Papa, being oldest, was now the one to speak. Each silent moment laid the duty harder on him—to comfort or clarify, both if he could. He could not. The mystery craved instant light. "Tell her what, lady?" he said at last.

She had held her open hands suspended this long. They oared once now—"*You* know. Her name, her life, her . . ." They waited as they had not waited before, dreading her tears that were visibly rising to drown the news. She shook her head, blinked, the tears rushed down across a smile broad and sudden as a morning glory—"Let's go see the snakes!" Her healing hands slapped together like cymbals.

And Phillip vaulted the tailgate neatly—from Rato's lap and loose arms to the ground without touching metal, striking all fours a yard from the truck unmuzzled in a small cloud of dust, buckling at the rear knees, then facing Mrs. Provo and rapidly sniffing the air she laid down, the promise of snakes she had trailed from the tent, advancing towards her. The Mustians were frozen in their previous poses, then Milo began a relay of looking—he to Papa, Papa to Rato, Rato to Rosacoke, Rosacoke backward to her mother's neck, all knowing help was needed but helpless, motionless except their eyes.

The first to move was Mrs. Provo. She took a meeting step towards Phillip, leaned to greet him, saying "Looks cured to me," surrendering her fingers to his nose that sucked up, winnowed her scents from palm to elbow. She was squatting now for Phillip's convenience, but she turned to Papa. "See, I told you these hands had healing in them."

Papa broke the family relay of looks by turning to the background, the trailers and tents, in search of help. The only man moving was as old as himself—Jake Hasty the dog man—whom Papa's dimming vision and the twenty yards distance aged and slowed to feebleness. They were on their own. So he spoke to Mrs. Provo in the voice he reserved for corners, blank walls, black-bottomed trouble—"Just hold off your hands if you aim to keep them. Lady."

Mrs. Provo was the one in mystery now. She stood straight with difficulty, backed two steps, then looked to Papa for whatever was needed—a stick, a pistol, relieving laughter—then to Phillip again whose nose had slid to her ankles, her socks, the heels of her shoes, the powdered dust, all in slow motion like a learning child, drunk and lurching but bent on success, a goal in sight and bound to succeed the moment his joints firm and bear him, his nerves obey. "What's his trouble?" she said.

Papa said "He's mad."

"Why mad at me?"

Papa said, "He's mad at the world at large. He's a mad dog, you see. Hold still in your tracks. He used to be gentle. Phillip, lie down, son." He had never said the dog's proper name before, and if Phillip heard it in this strange new voice, it was past too late—he had ceased to fear or love or even care. He was all dog now, with no memories maybe of his life with them. Their last chance was that he recalled his life. Papa said "Rato, catch your dog."

Rato slowly turned from Rosa down to Phillip, free and looking healed as the lady had promised—or visibly healing with each breath he drew, spared of present death. "Phillip?" Rato said.

Phillip looked gradually but accurately to Rato. He partly remembered.

So Rato raised his voice and said, "*Snake*. Snake, boy, snake. Go get it. You are free."

He went of course and everybody stood in respect as he went— those that were seated: Rato, Milo, Rosacoke; Emma and the baby remained sealed off. Mrs. Provo pointed—only pointed to prove she had lived to see this, a mad dog aimed at her livelihood, her twining snakes, the golden python drowsed in the pit. And Phillip pursued the line she pointed, the trail she had laid in the ground as she came, seeming as he went to be wolfing a strip of irresistible food, now in the dust, now floating in air at the level of his head cocked and unappeased. Yet he went so drunk, so slowly at first that each step he took might have been his last—his rear legs delayed, hung swaying backwards, either not receiving or not obeying the fury that sucked his hot eyes on. Mrs. Provo looked to Papa—"Do something, man. You know where he's aiming." By then he had stopped—for good, the Mustians thought; all but Rato. Rato knew he was on the spot where the lady had paused when she came from the snakes and announced her acquaintance with Tommy Ryden, and he circled the spot in what— to the others—seemed a whirlpool safely funneled towards death.

Papa said, "Lady, your snakes are safe. He's dumb mad, you see. He's paralyzed and dying right now."

Phillip stopped in the midst of a whirl facing them, took Papa's words with stiffening ears, used them some private way in his brain, wheeled on himself and plunged on as quickly as in his youth, crooked but silent between the first tents.

"Paralyzed!" Mrs. Provo said. "He's giving a good imitation of lightning—Mr. Jake, stop that dog running yonder." She abandoned the Mustians, yelled to the old man Papa had seen who had a broom now and was sweeping the ground by his trailer steps, then she broke into a run more crippled than even the worst of Phillip's (she suffered rheumatism).

Mr. Jake saw the black O of her mouth, her flinging arms, but before he could cup a hand to his ear, the words had streaked past. Still he saw the Mustians standing in the distant swimming light and Selma Provo in flight from them so he legged out to meet her, broom raised as weapon, arms stretched wide as a safe port for Selma.

But she only saw Phillip—his vanishing trail—and rammed Mr. Jake full-force head-on. They struck dust together, scuffed head and heel, he crying from the cloud, "I'm with you. You're safe;" she crying, "Safe! We're in awful danger. Turn loose, old fool!" He turned loose and lay flat, small on the ground, wounded at heart far worse than in limb, and she strained to rise—camel-wise, humps and knees—but when she set weight on her thick right ankle, it buckled and threw her down useless, frantic. She looked to the Mustians through settling dust, rage and plea plugged dumb in her throat.

Papa looked to Rato, "Boy, you have ruined me—a mad dog streaking towards a wild snake show and now she'll sue me for a broken leg. Emma! Oh Emma!" Emma slowly looked through the dirty glass. "Help that woman. She has broke a leg." Then he limped off tentward, calling, "Come on, children. We got to go face him. He used to be ours. We can't wait here."

But the great snake waited in his canvas pit, roofless this day as he was dazed mild by the rabbit slowly dissolving within him—the meager appalled unworthy offering that had suddenly crouched before him last night from unknown hands. He had roused to accept it in two airless coils only because of blind hunger, starved pride, and it lay within him humbly, invisibly. Yet though it had not faintly swelled his sides, the rabbit was steadily feeding his pride. He dimly knew that in his warming doze and calmly awaited this mysterious healing, return of the strength he had known in his home—the trees, brown water, white sun of Burma: all stripped from him in his treacherous capture (sated, asleep), his black boxed journey that had ended thus in dry canvas walls, despondent giant among knots of pygmies, the target of a thousand daily laughs or shudders from throats he could crush in one coil. But impervious target, unscathed, immortal because of his skin which at least they had left him, the scraped but living roots of his former strength, watered by his blood all night, all morning with the rabbit's bright eyes, tense speed, cold fire. He was healing for a purpose, a deed, a foe. He waited to know it and his skin drew towards him the one shaft of sun that pierced the tent. It flowed warm and thick on his still loose coils and flamed his pattern, the outward show of his inner pride: pale brown scales as the ground on which darker shapes were encrusted—unmatched shapes of night, birth, dream, huddled death, darkest at their centers but edged with gold or—now! as he flickered—with amber, bronze, violet, green. Hide and armor for a warrior king. Such a king wore it now, restored and waiting.

So he felt—and was—as Phillip burst on him, no prologue or warning but silent and firm in every joint as he took the top of the pit in stride, landed a foot from the dreaming head and halted amazed, having seen for the first time a foe so grand, so far beyond hope, fear or former strategy that an instant of worship was compelled upon him. Phillip thrust his front legs flat before him, half-crouched behind and laying his head to the cool wood floor, bore that lidless gaze, sleeping? waking?—for such eyes shone as hard in sleep; in death, he knew—as in dangerous life. Which did he face? He waited to know. His awe was now curiosity, *justice*, and he knelt on, losing this vital moment, dazed by the eyes to his own natural aim—restoration of his ruined pride: he tan-haired, torn-eared, welted, called *mad* and thus doomed and desperate but held, fixed. The black eyes soared in their own amazement two feet above him, borne on the flat head that swayed once back over tightening coils, bared a hundred teeth and—awake!—lunged, locking Phillip's heart in one cold coil and humped for the next as Rato's voice came "Phillip, his throat!"

When Milo and Papa reached home at last it was Sunday morning though full night still, and the house was black except the porch light. Papa choked the engine and striking a match, looked exhausted but proud at his pocket watch. "Two in the morning. We left here at eight o'clock Saturday morning—eighteen hours. I ain't been away from home this many hours since Pauline died, since Prohibition maybe." (Pauline was his wife.) "And two in the morning, Great God Almighty! The last time I read a watch this late—well, I hate to tell you what I was doing. I won't telling time, I'll say that much, and neither was she. What the Hell was her name?—married that cross-eyed fellow in Elberon?"

"Old ugly Mrs. Luck, you talking about?"

"You got her, you got her. Ugly, I grant you. Ugly as sin but she let me in every time I knocked. And I knocked regular. She won't *old* though. Fifty-five years ago, who was old?—just my Mama and Papa. I was younger than you."

"You're holding up better than me now, Papa. I died at midnight. Let's go rest. We got tomorrow to get through, remember."

Papa waited and then said "Yes, I forgot," and they walked to the house as softly as possible, slowing at the steps from now useless habit to let Phillip know it was family, safe, that he could sleep on till light woke him naturally.

Inside the house was as silent as dark, but as they tipped past the dim hall lamp, Milo saw a tablet propped against it. In Rosacoke's round open hand was a note—

Dear Milo and Papa and Rato,

Mama fried a chicken which is in the oven. Where in the world have you all been? We are worried but have finally gone to bed, being sick and tired. Please be quiet as we have company in the downstairs bed- room and in my room. Milo, you and me are sleeping together in your room, hear? Papa, you and Rato sleep as usual. If anything bad has happened, wake me up. I know something bad which I'll tell you in the morning. Sleep good.

Rosacoke

There was bad news enough but Rosa woke herself when Milo laid his hand on the doorknob, before he even turned it. She had been in the depths of a dream about him—a sensible story, clear and possible like most of her dreams: he stood in the fork of a tree high above her (his present age and face), then as she looked up he turned loose his hold, high as he was, and spread his arms to jump. She said, "You will die and ruin us, Milo." He said, not looking, "I am almost a man. I must fall to rise." He jumped and he rose and the last she saw—before she woke—was him rising not falling as he had foretold, above limbs and leaves into steady light, a single figure in clear day alone, no thought of when that day might end.

Though torn awake she did not move at first. She lay in total dark, eyes open, hearing him shut the door, walk towards the bed. She knew she was conscious—she always broke sharply with sleep, no confusion—yet as he slid and hunched out of his clothes (his body lined on the unshaded window), he still seemed to lift, his dark body darker than the visible night, to be past retrieving. Nor did she speak. She had not yet hooked from her mind the question that would drain the mild grief she felt and had felt all day so she concentrated on moving silently to leave him a fair share of bed when he came. And when he came—having stripped to Rato's underwear—and lay on his back to face the ceiling, she said what she suddenly needed to say, what rose unsought, "Well, you came back."

"Barely," he said. "More dead than alive," showing no surprise that she was awake. (He was someone you could not surprise if you tried. Not that he kept up perpetual guard—just that he always expected what happened, accepted it however sudden or wild.)

"We thought you might be completely dead when Papa at least wasn't here by bedtime. I hope you won't taking him and Rato to Phyllis's right after stopping poor Phillip for good."

"No'm, not tonight. I wish I had. I wish I had stopped poor Phillip too. Papa and me and four show men and the sheriff and deputies been looking for Rato and Phillip and Death. Death is the name of an Indian python, twenty feet long, weighing two hundred pounds. We still hadn't found them, not even their tracks. Now let's shut up and get some rest."

Rosa propped on an elbow, "Rest? *Milo*. You mean to say Rato is not in Papa's room?"

"No, and God don't even know where he is tonight—could be the woods behind the fair, could be he's in Death's jaws or belly."

"Milo."

"I'm kidding. No, Rosa, everything's true but that last. The snake ain't hungry. He ate Friday night. Rato is safe for a week or more."

"Milo, you're lying. After you ran Mr. Hasty got up—he was not hurt—and went to the tent and came back directly saying you had caught the dog and no harm was done but that you all would stay there and shoot him right then and he would drive us to town with Mrs. Provo to fix her leg."

"He was the one that was lying, Rosa. Papa told him to." She was speechless again but she stayed propped up so he knew he must start at the first and explain. "Rato outrun us all to the tent—a lot of men joined us before we got there—and when I tore in ten seconds behind him, he was down in the pit on his knees, wrestling Death. Phillip had jumped in first of course and was already locked in one of Death's coils—"

"Just call it a snake. I'll know who you mean." She had lain to her side, turned to face his black profile.

"Phillip was already strangling (you could hear him), but he had his teeth in the snake somewhere—where does a snake's throat begin and end?—and Rato was struggling with both hands and feet to hold off the snake from casting again. Two coils—you're lost, Mrs. Provo says. The four of us were alone there another ten seconds, and I was waiting for some more men to help me. I figured it was no sense the whole Mustian family getting strangled or rabies, but I want you to know in that twenty seconds of grunting and thrashing, Rato tore Phillip loose from Death and took him in his arms—Phillip, I mean—and jumped the far side of that pit and was gone, and so was the snake like lightning behind them. All of that happened with me standing there not moving a muscle but to open my mouth, and when Papa and the extra men arrived, there was nothing to see but a swinging tent flap and my big mouth and four dozen egg-sucking baby snakes, pop-eyed and crazy—I say *baby*; beside Death, I mean. Well, Papa said, 'Where is the mad dog, son?' and I pointed to the flap and said, 'Gone yonder in Rato's arms and a boa constrictor with them.' The man that is Mrs. Provo's help said, 'That ain't no boa constrictor. That's a python. She just calls it a boa since that sounds worse.' Then all of us scuffled around to the flap and looked out for signs. The snake tent is back on the woods side, you see, and unless they were sucked up in a tornado, they had hit those woods thirty seconds before. Some fellow yelled out 'Get your guns, boys'—they have to travel armed—but Papa said, 'Hold it. Don't get no guns. My boy's in them woods—my second grandson—and he ain't a scholar so we got to be extra careful to save him. Take me to a phone and I'll call the sheriff. If we got to have guns, have legal guns.' Just then Mr. Hasty run in and said Mrs. Provo had broke a bone and was suffering. Papa bowed a minute and then said to him, 'Go back please sir, and tell the women we got it in hand but will be delayed, shooting the dog. Have you got a car?' The man said Yes. 'Then you drive them all to the doctor, will you? Emma Mustian is the big woman's name, my daughter-in-law. She's good in a sickness.' The man took orders and Papa called the sheriff, and him and two deputies came right out, and we been scourging those woods every since. Not a trace of nothing— boy, dog or snake—once the pine trees start. Pine straw doesn't show tracks too well, but we all kept looking till around five o'clock when the fair people had to go back and work and the sheriff had to leave to round up the drunks. He left us a deputy—Yancey Breedlove—and him and me and Papa hunted with flashlights till an hour ago. We were God knows how deep back in the briars when Yancey stopped and said, 'Son of a bitch, them bastards live in *trees*,' meaning pythons. Papa said 'Do they, Milo?' and I said they did, having thought of that at sundown. So we gave up and came on out to the truck and come home."

"Just leaving Rato under the stars?"

"Shoot, it's warm tonight. And listen, Rosa, if Rato has got through fourteen years on less than half-rations in the brain department, he can sure last till noon in his own home county."

"Why noon?" she said.

"Because the search party is gathering here in the yard at noon soon as church turns out—all the men we can get, white or black, and the sheriff and deputies and two blood hounds. We are going to spread out and comb every step of the woods from here back in to town and the fair. We figure they are aimed this way."

Rosa sat up finally. "I better go wake Mama up right now."

"You lost your mind? It ain't but two-thirty. You'll worry her to death."

"Well, who's going to cook for all those men between sunup and noon? We ought to start now, killing chickens at least."

"Calm down, Rosa. You are eleven years old. You ain't a woman yet, however you act. You got three or four years so lay back and rest. Your time will come. Mama will make out. She'll know how. It ain't your worry. Rest now or hush up and let me rest."

She said "I'll hush" and fell back beside him. "But who's going to rest, knowing their brother is wandering through briars in the dark of night with a mad dog by him—and running from a snake that is going mad too?"

"Where did you get that?—the snake going mad?"

"You said Phillip bit him. So unless snakes are vaccinated, he's going mad."

Milo waited. "I hadn't thought of that. And he's got a hundred teeth, Mrs. Provo says." His neck strained upward, waited, relaxed. "What is to be will be. Close your eyes." He closed his before he finished speaking.

And Rosa closed hers. She lay flat like him, having fallen that way with her hand on her chest, and thought through a quick hard plea for Rato. As it ended her fingers had warmed on her chest and seemed, despite the gauze of her gown, to touch flesh there—the close firm muscle, tanned hide, brown circles where her breasts would be when her time came. She pressed, even kneaded there (careful not to move the bed beneath her), searching for buried but tangible proof—a core, a seed—that her time would come, that what had happened to most human beings would happen in her—fullness, the burden of fertility of which her body bore no certain promise, cleft though it was and had always been, dryly dusted in every pore with faint gold hair. And she found no surer signs tonight. Her hand stopped, she thought in her mother's voice, "Most things are not meant to be understood;" then in her own, "This surely is one—my terrible future. Oh let my time come;" then in Milo's drowsily, "What is to be will be." But they did not calm her. How could she, why should she wait here behind—three years, four—when she knew the shape her future must have and when people she knew (girls in her grade only six months older), people she loved and had understood were passing her, changing before her eyes: Milo beside her breathing slowly but not with the depth or rhythm of sleep? She rolled to her right side, reached and touched him. Whatever had become of in him in these few months, whatever he would be in time to come—would learn and yield—he was this near now, one hand away, a narrow hand.

He drew a deep breath but did not speak, finding nothing to give her.

So she volunteered what she had meant to avoid. "Don't you want to know who our company is?"

"I guess I know."

"Who do you guess?"

"Mrs. Provo and Lois."

"How did you know?"

"Because their trailer was the only one left when we came through the fairgrounds awhile ago—everything else had broke up and gone, snake show included—and their lights were out and the shades were up so I figured Mrs. Provo was hurt and was here."

"And you didn't ask me?"

"I figured what she broke wouldn't knit before morning."

"She didn't break nothing. She tore some gristle and that's more painful. I'll tell you, hear?" He did not say No. "Well, when you all ran, me and Mama and the baby went to Mrs. Provo. She was still right down in the dust, moaning. Even Mr. Hasty had run off and left her, hot behind you all. Mama didn't know a thing about Phillip— Papa lied to her; she thought he could live—and whenever Mrs.

Provo began about Phillip, Mama would look up from rubbing her ankle and tell her not to worry, he wouldn't harm a flea. Finally when she still couldn't get on her feet and the pain was getting worse, Mama said to me 'Go find that nurse'—Papa had told her that girl was a nurse, that girl you know—"

"Her name is Lois."

"I know her name. And I knew she was no more a nurse at her age than I'm a bride, but I ran to that trailer and when nobody answered, I went in and found her crying already, flung down and sobbing like she had second sight and knew what had happened. She didn't though. I told her and she asked where you were so I had to tell her that—about Phillip running. Then she got up and came out and acted like a nurse. She felt her aunt's leg and said, 'No bones broke but the gristle is loose.' Then she asked Mama was there a doctor in town, and Mama said, 'Several—ours is Dr. Sledge. We can take you to him when the men get back.' So I want you to know we squatted in the sun around that woman for a good quarter hour—she couldn't stand up and how could we tote her? She's no bantam hen—till the old dog man Mr. Hasty come back and passed on that stream of lies from Papa: everything was in hand and you all were held up, shooting Phillip. Well, we had to put our shoulders to it and get Mrs. Provo in Mr. Hasty's car. Dog hair! I thought Phillip shed bad enough, but he sheds outdoors—or used to, didn't he?—and he's just one dog. Mr. Hasty has twelve and they ride with him. Anyhow it got us there—the car, I mean—and Dr. Sledge said what Lois had said: torn gristle and was there anybody that could look after her for a day or so till she could walk? Mrs. Provo said she had a white boy working for her that was sober enough to handle the snake show—everyone of Mama's pores stood up; it was the first she had heard of snakes—but all else she had was her one niece and mighty poor cooking equipment in her trailer. What could Mama say? She had seen enough to know we were mainly responsible so she said 'Come to us' and Mrs. Provo accepted. Mr. Hasty drove us back to the fair. You all were still gone and Mama's groceries were spoiling in the heat so he said why didn't he ride us on home? Lois got their clothes and locked the trailer, and here we've been since two p.m., waiting for you. Gradually Mama learned all the facts the rest of us knew, but they didn't seem to scare her half as much as me—because she was busy every minute, I guess: giving Mrs. Provo aspirins and footbaths and frying two chickens. Lois seemed to worry more than anybody else. She sat with her aunt while we ate supper, and she must have been wringing and twisting a lot because we heard Mrs. Provo say, 'Lois, for God's sake, when I was your age I didn't know nerves existed. Get up from here and breathe some fresh air. Take you a walk out in the yard while it's daylight.' Lois didn't answer but she got up and left—and walked beyond the yard and outstayed daylight. When she still wasn't back by seven o'clock, Mama went to Mrs. Provo to ask where was Lois. Mrs. Provo said 'Emma, shut the door'—she used Mama's first name. Mama went in and shut it, and they must have talked an hour in there while I washed dishes—whispering mostly as not a word came through the door to me. Then Mama came out and *she* had been crying. She told me these curious sleeping arrangements—she and the baby would sleep with Mrs. Provo (Mrs. Provo's been in Mama's room from the start). Then Lois came in all dusty from somewhere. Mama and me were standing in the hall. Mama took one look and cried again. Lois said, 'I've just been walking in the road. I knew where I was,' but the tears ran on and that worried me more than all the waiting and wondering about you. When has anybody seen Mama cry? I asked her the trouble. She just said 'Someday you'll understand.' Understand *what*? I want to know. And *when* will my day come? If people just tell me what's going on, I understand more now than they ever guess. What do you reckon she could mean, Milo?" He did not answer nor even seem to breathe. "You are fifteen. Maybe you understand?" Still deeper silence. "This is your day, Milo. I'm not that blind. Tell me what you know." His only reply, only move was breath. "Then how come you stay up till four a.m. just to walk some girl as common as dirt round a county fair if you don't learn something for your efforts?" She was not expecting an answer but she could not stop. Rosacoke had tripped within her a hot brown stream that till now had run buried. "It's not but two-thirty yet, Milo. It's not your bedtime. How come you don't go ask your girl what the secret is. She's older even than you, you know, and she's yonder in my room through that wall."

She did not point but still the wall seemed to melt between rooms and Lois to be there ten yards away, waiting, awake. Rosacoke tensed where she lay and listened—for any sound, threat or rescue. What came was the pulse of sleep from Milo—half-counterfeit but calming, beckoning—and when she had linked her breath with his and had thought of sinking, she sank and slept.

For how long, how deeply she did not know nor what had seized Milo and shook him, but she woke again cleanly in full possession when he eased back the cover and slid to the floor and stood a long moment against the dark window holding his arms still shuddering, then picked his way through the floor like a minefield (safely, silently), took a whole minute to open the door, left it cracked behind him and started the five steps to where Lois was. Rosacoke widened her eyes to the dark. Before this past day, the previous night, she had understood Milo—him, at least—and now she forced her mind out to him, not to warn or halt or even protect him but to share his life as she shared his mother, dead father, home, bed. She knew the thing he aimed to do—had learned it from older girls at school, boys' drawings, the poems they yelled—and she knew from frequent sight of his body that whatever he wished, he could now perform. What she did not know was why?—what force could hold him awake bone-tired, could seize and rattle his teeth with need and send him half-naked in Rato's drawers through the black crowded house past Papa's open door to one narrow girl on her own iron bed, suspended above Mama's snoring body? And what would he have at the end for his trouble, the dangers he dared?—unless simple calm, the shuddering eased, sleep at last?

He did not know, might well not have cared or tried to prevent her, but Rosacoke was with him, as surely with him now as if she were laid against his back or had entered him ghostly and tapped the currents of his sight and touch. The stalking paused. Here was the door. Body drew tall, fists clenched, toes grasped. Then right hand felt as gently for the knob as for warm bird eggs, twisted the cool cracked china rightward, pressed a half-inch—then the lock took hold and shaking swept again from eyes through shoulders. The lock was a screen-door hook Rosacoke had screwed there herself the previous summer to give her the sense at least of peace for occasional thinking, and here now it threatened to hold off answers she needed far worse than privacy, peace. Probe finger into crack, lift hook free. But there is not space for both skin and bone, and the nearest thin blade is below in the kitchen. O speak! Surely she waits for word? Say "Lois." It was said in Milo's whisper. "Lois, it's me." The rustle of cover, complaint of springs surrounded her waking, her slow understanding, but once formed, her answer hurled sudden and final—"No. Leave me alone. You have lost your mind."

That drove Rosacoke back into herself, instantly, violently. Her actual eyes stayed open but were blind, her hands felt only her own dry chest, ears heard only one rooster crow, then a second, a third—a relay of pride, for daybreak and light were hours away, might never dawn.

She almost wished darkness would last on. She was that exhausted. She strained to stay conscious, to see Milo back, not that she hung large hopes on him still, but she wanted to know he was safe, resting, calmed, that—barefoot, half-naked—he would not take cold. Both of her brothers were valuable to her for all their lack of attention and care. She already knew, thought it four years before when her father was killed—"These are the two persons I will know when everyone else here now is gone. They will outlast my mother and certainly Papa. I must tend to them." And here they were both wandering lost tonight—one maybe miles from here and in danger; one, yards away maybe in worse danger (from inward where deadliest dangers lie).

Yet she slept, suddenly, and did not dream, did not even stir when half an hour later Milo stopped his vigil, came and lay again beside her. He had stood that whole time against Lois's door, looking down towards a window at the end of the hall. Beyond were the tops of trees, invisible. He thought he could stand till light would show through their final leaves and Papa start coughing. He was no longer tired, no longer in hope of any sort of entry but sick with balked want (not need; not yet, whatever he thought) and with shame and bafflement: how could people change like this in a day?—take all you could give one night and leave, promising; then the next night seal you out like a thief, call you crazy through the crack in a door?

Still as he stood from one foot to the next and the last dregs of heat

seeped out of the house, his question rested and finally he was calm —
a different calm from what he had sought. What pulled him now was
his own warm bed, and the moment his head touched pillow he slept
and began to forget. He was the agent, had made the try, taken defeat,
but he would forget in the rush of his growing, his swelling life. It was
his sister, trapped in childhood, who would not forget.

TWO

"Milo." Their mother stood in the open door and spoke towards the bed, firmly, to wake them both with the single name. It was almost eleven and the strong light fell on her worried face and her hands that held the tablet of paper.

Rosa woke first but seeing Mama's forehead, did not dare speak, only rolled to Milo, shook him and said, "Wake up. Mama wants to ask you something."

"*Something!*" Emma said. "I guess I do. I got a list of questions long as my leg" and in proof extended her columnar leg.

Milo said "Shoot" but into his pillow.

Emma said, "Sit up and honor your mother. I have let you sleep past time for church. The least you can do is ease my mind."

He sat up in bed and bowed to his knees. "I'll do what I can but if you're needing ease you better get your aspirins. I'm as full of bad news as a Christmas turkey is of you-know-what—but Papa told you, didn't he?"

"Papa hasn't told me so much as Good Morning. Him and Lois left in the truck about sunup. Didn't wake a soul, didn't eat a mouthful—just took a loaf of lightbread and two hot Pepsis and left me this note." She shook the tablet at him.

His feet hit the floor. "Let me see that."

Emma pressed it to her, "Tell me this first—what is the sheriff doing downstairs now, asking for you, and three men with him milling in the yard, badges shining and hound dogs—they must be—in a rusty wire trailer? What have you done, son? Tell me that first please."

Milo hopped to his clothes, struggled into them, pointed to Rosacoke still in bed—"Rosa knows it all. She can tell you. I'm going," and he tore past her, taking the tablet by force, reading as he went—

Emma,

Me and the girl are leaving early to get a headstart. Milo will tell you on what when he wakes up. But you let him sleep. He needs it bad. Then tell him I said the girl and me will go to the fairgrounds and strike in from there. Him and his men strike in from here and meet us at the old Ryden place at dark.

Emma called after him, "Come back and put your shoes on—it's Sunday," but she knew it was useless, bent for the shoes to take them to him (the laces were knotted) and turning to Rosacoke above the dry shuffle of his feet descending, said "Tell the worst first."

"We got to cook dinner for them" Rosa said and pointed towards the yard. "No, that ain't the worst. Here, sit down, Mama." Emma sat in the warmth where Milo had lain and Rosa began.

But Milo was nearly at the sheriff by then—downstairs, outdoors, across the porch, through the yard (half-asleep, half-buttoned, barefoot). And being barefoot he had come in silence—no one had noticed—so he stopped a little short of the various men, gathered his eyes against broad daylight and searched among the men till he found the sheriff, studied him—or his back which was turned: a big man wide but firm in khaki shirt and pants, stained Panama hat, waddled down on his hams (holster plowing the dirt) by a little wire trailer where the two hounds lay.

He was speaking to the hounds as if they were children, straining to console their obvious grief. "Rest on, boys. Soon as church lets out, you got to go track us a snake and a mad dog." They looked towards his voice but did not even blink.

Then a low dark man (unhitching the trailer) said, "Take more than livestock to scare *my* dogs. They seen and caught worse than any Mustians can offer—rapers, murderers, maniacs, Republicans. You name it, they've tracked it, treed it and *bayed* and been offered as proof in eight courts of law in two different states. Put a man in the Chair last month in Raleigh."

Yancey Breedlove, propped by the big oak, laughed. (He had hunted for Rato the night before.) He said, "Buddy, we gas them in North Carolina."

"But not standing *up*, fool," the hound man said.

"They don't set them down, do they, Sheriff?" Yancey said.

The sheriff faced round onto Milo not Yancey and seemed for a moment not to recognize him or to recognize him as someone else—his narrow mouth bubbled open on a name (not *Milo* certainly), and his eyes frowned in pain. Then he knew the boy, his pain passed on, his mouth smiled broadly, and he half-ran to Milo, saying, "Here's the *man*. This man *here* knows." He shook him by the shoulder—"Tell me all you know."

Milo said, "I know things you'd die to know—die in agony, smiling—but I want to know how come he's yelling *Chair* when all my brother done is chase a sick dog?" He bore the sheriff's heavy stare (Milo could stare-down a statue of God) and pointed to the hound man.

The sheriff said, "Son, *he* ain't running this hunt. I am and I won't named Rooster for nothing. Rooster Pomeroy is running this hunt. That fellow's nothing but a Capps from the river that owns these dogs and runs his mouth, but I give the orders because it's my duty—the duty I can *do*, was elected four times to do like F.D.R. So lean on me. Lean on Rooster, son." He reached for Milo's tangled head to make him lean momentarily.

But Milo coiled back, then surrendered, smiled and looked up for the sun. "Ain't you early, Sheriff? I'd of been up and ready, but I thought you said noon."

Rooster said "I did," then dropped his voice. "I did but I tell you, my wife she—" He stopped. "How old are you, son?"

Milo said "Fifteen."

"You know my wife?—Mrs. Kate Pomeroy?"

"No," Milo said.

So Rooster thought back through thirty-nine years till he was fifteen, then changed his mind and raised his voice—"No, I tell you, I just wasn't sleeping last night so I got up early and drove to the river to get these dogs and come here thinking we could stop by your church (since this thing is serious and they all know you) and ask for helpers. Catch them in a body with women present, they'll volunteer like flies to cream." He fished out his watch. It was quarter past eleven. "It's close by, ain't it? If we go right now we can beat the sermon and make our call." He saw Milo's bare feet, ruined clothes. "I'll go in but you ride with me."

Milo said, "Maybe I better stay here—explain to my mother. She's still in the dark."

Rooster said "So am I." He clamped his eyes shut, groped blind for a moment, looked again (not smiling)—"I need you, son" and started for the car.

Milo followed him.

They had covered more than half the distance in silence—Rooster watching the road as if it were a trap; Milo watching the sky, what birds there were—when Rooster laughed and said, "We're going to find your brother, don't worry. The cause for *worry* is your old Granddaddy. What's he up to with that snake girl?" He looked to Milo who had just seen a quail and did not respond. "We are liable to find him dead of a stroke or burned out clean as a cotton gin, ain't we?—" Still no answer. "How old is he? A heap older than me. Well, I tip him my hat." He tipped his straw hat. "I'm fifty-four, my wife is twenty-seven. I married late, you see, and *I* can't—" He stopped again, again charged tack. "That girl is more your style, isn't she, son? How come you ain't in there guarding your interest, grabbing your share?"

Milo did not turn. He said "I overslept," then leaned to see the sun. "But the day isn't over—not *my* day at least. Hadn't hardly begun. I hadn't lost yet." He smiled but he meant it, believed it entirely.

Rooster grabbed Milo's knee. "The Hell you hadn't. You've told your secrets to the wrong man, son, and you're under arrest—corrupting a minor female child." Then he laughed for a while—Milo not joining in. "No, I *am* sheriff and sheriffs are paid—not much—to keep order (if I kept the order I was *paid* to keep, this county'd be a thicket of gnashing teeth), but this is Sunday and till those dogs start, I'm on private time so I'll set you free"—he lifted his hand—"spare you what you deserve (you'll get it quick enough) but on one condition: that you listen to this. This is something I know and it won't cost you nothing." He looked to Milo who would not face him. "Please look," he said.

So Milo looked. "You guarantee it's free?"

"Free as day," Rooster said.

"Guarantee it's true?"

"Oh it's *true*," Rooster said. "Anybody can lie. I ain't paid to *lie.*"

"Then I'm listening," Milo said—and he was, eyes on Rooster as if Rooster were a place he must occupy.

Rooster said "What's the time?"

"Maybe eleven twenty-five."

"And you think it's morning?"

"For half an hour—sure."

Rooster said "What's your age?"

"I told you—fifteen."

"And you think that's young?"

"Well, I've met one or two older people through the years."

Rooster said it to the road. "It is eleven twenty-five, a clear broad morning that will be noon soon. You are fifteen, a man and the Lord has hung gifts on you like a *hatrack.*"

Milo looked down searching, brushed his chest, his thighs but did not speak.

And Rooster went on—"Use what the good Lord give you *now*, and use it every chance the day provides—Hell, day *and* night—till it's wore to a nub and that'll be before you have hardly got started. Son, I *know.* Thirty-nine years ago when I was fifteen, I could of bored through hickory wood with the auger I had and I *wanted* to, but I listened to my Mama and got religion and let shoals of women go streaming by me in *technicolor*—white, black, gray, tan, red, yellow. I could of had me one of each—Hell, I'm *sheriff*—but no, I waited and did my duty by God and my Mama, and then she died ten years ago, and I got married to a girl seventeen, the jail-keeper's daughter. Too late, too late." He took his hand back to his own fat crotch, cupped the fullness there. "This won't stir a warm rice *pudding*, not now, no more. Remember this, son. It won't cost you nothing but it cost Rooster Pomeroy most of the sweetness life can afford—don't wait, don't wait. Don't think it's morning when it's late afternoon."

The car had slowed to a crawl through that, and Milo had watched Rooster through to the end, but when silence settled he turned to the window, the yellowing trees. "Thank you, Sheriff, but I hadn't been waiting, not since Saturday nohow, around midnight. And I ain't going to wait till dark today so let's get moving. I got to find my brother, a snake and a dog. Then I can pull out my throttle full-steam." Milo pulled an imaginary throttle on the dashboard, pulled with both hands not pausing to his groin and rested them there.

Rooster pulled his own throttle, roared the last quarter-mile and turned rightward into the sandy churchyard, stopped at a distance from the fifteen black cars frosted with dust, baking in the sun, killed the motor and sat still, ear cocked towards the building. A hymn streamed out through open windows—the hymn before collection—so Rooster pointed and said to Milo, "Is that the choir door standing open?"

Milo said "Yes."

"Then I'm going to go and call the preacher out while the singing's still on and ask will he make an announcement for me before the benediction." He looked again at Milo's feet. "You wait. Wait for *me*." Then he struggled to the ground and went three yards, stopped, thought, shook his head and turned back to Milo, face urgently crouched. "And when I get back don't fail to remind me—I *mean* this, son—to tell you one thing I forgot that goes with the rest of my free advice. It's dangerous without it, a loaded gun."

Milo nodded, smiled. "I give you ten minutes."

Rooster said "Thank you" and the flagging congregation launched another stanza (final or not, they would not last another) so Rooster pointed to the gun on his hip, tapped its bright black butt. "A loaded *gun*. How come I forgot?"—meaning it for Milo—and went towards the choir door, turned again on the highest step. "Remind me, hear?" But Milo's head was back, already asleep.

＊   ＊   ＊

Till the full doxology was finished and he had the money, the preacher (Mr. Favro—tall, stooped, yellow) had had to set Rooster in the high black chair behind the pulpit, pistol at his side, hat between his feet, his small hands creeping about for shelter. Then the preacher shut the Bible and said, "My friends. We all see before us a face we know and trust and depend on, a face that we all sleep better because of. He has just come to us with an urgent need. Danger has struck and still roams among us. Our brotherly help is needed, he says, and I have asked him to come before you now (the Lord won't mind) and say a few words in explanation—Sheriff Rob Pomeroy." Some Guptons clapped. Mr. Favro frowned but stepped back and sat.

Rooster clasped the pulpit like the last floating timber in total ship-wreck and began speaking softly, pumping up words with frequent long battings of his round blue eyes. "Reverend, I thank you for those good words. I never thought about my work like that, but now you mention it, if anybody here that has voted for me sleeps better at night knowing I'm on duty—well, God bless their heart, I *am* on duty. Even in my own home and in my bed, I am ready, I am eager, to do whatever I can to serve so sleep tight, friends—Rob Pomeroy's awake. He's awake if he ain't one other thing else, and if you're in need any hour of the night or day, call him—call me, *I'm* him. And I'm ready. For instance, one of your members had some trouble yesterday and called on me with no hesitation, and that's why I'm here—Jasper Mustian, you know him. I got his grandson out in my car—*one* of his grandsons. Wouldn't let him come in. He forgot his shoes. But anyhow all the Mustians rode in to Warrenton yesterday morning, and on the way home as they passed the fairgrounds about eleven-thirty—" He paused, drew his watch out. "Twenty-four hours ago exactly." He turned to Mr. Favro behind him. "It's *your* fault, Doctor. You dragged me in here and now I've took over. Looks like I'm preaching the sermon, don't it? Give me your text."

Rooster had only meant it in fun, but Mr. Favro's face drained potato-white, and his purple lips recited from memory, still seated—"And when Jehu was come to Jezreel, Jezebel heard of it, and she painted her face and tired her head and looked out at a window. And as Jehu entered in at the gate, she said, 'Had Zimri peace, who slew his master?' And he lifted up his face to the window and said, 'Who is on my side? who?' And there looked out to him two or three eunuchs. And he said 'Throw her down.' So they threw her down and some of her blood was sprinkled on the wall and on the horses, and he trod her under foot. And when he was come in, he did eat and drink and said, 'Go, see now this cursed woman and bury her, for she is a king's daughter.' And they went to bury her, but they found no more of her than the skull and the feet and the palms of her hands. Wherefore they came again and told him. And he said, 'This is the word of the Lord which he spake by his servant Elijah and Tishbite, saying, "In the portion of Jezreel shall dogs eat the flesh of Jezebel. And the carcase of Jezebel shall be as dung upon the face of the field in the portion of Jezreel so that they shall not say 'This is Jezebel.'"

Rooster said, "*Uhhh!* You bound to know. Somebody *told* you!" Mr. Favro shook his head in denial. "Then the Lord laid it on you. That's *my* text too—'the skull and the feet and the palms of her hands.' Raving dogs." He faced the congregation. "The Mustians' dog got loose at the fair and run through the snake show and on in the woods. Well, the dog is mad and he's loose right now with the *other* Mustian boy and—I'm sorry to tell you—one of the snakes. Twenty foot long. Can swallow a calf. Break every bone in a grown man's body."

Everyone shrunk about six inches inwards, and for maybe ten seconds nobody looked at anyone else nor moved more than hand to open mouth. Then Arnold Gupton stood to leave while he could—not to help but to run; he had no mind—but Macey his brother wrestled him down. "Arnold, it ain't coming in no *church.*"

Rooster leaned to them across the Bible, "In the words of Jehu from his great book, 'Who is on my side? Oh *who?*' I come here to ask your help today. I got two bloodhounds and two armed deputies setting in the Mustians' yard right now, waiting for reinforcements to hunt. Mr. Jasper has been in the woods since sunup—him and the girl that owns the snake." (Macey fought down a laugh that rose stronger than Arnold.) "I'm calling on every strong man and boy— just so he's fifteen—to join me soon as your preacher is finished. Don't bring no guns. I got four guns and they'll more than kill what might need killing." He bowed to Mr. Favro and motioned him forward, "Preacher, I thank you. It's all yours again."

But Mr. Favro was looking ahead and could see. His face resembled all leaders abandoned—say Moses' face as he came from direct sight of God, the Law in hand, and found his men on their face in the dust, bowed to a gold calf flashing above them.

The men were rising and shuffling towards the aisles. The first to rise had been Buck Russell. His wife had said, "Sit down, Buck. This is Sunday." But his coattail carried her detaining hand with him— "That snake don't know it's Sunday. Come on. I'm riding you home and getting the pistol." He did not turn to hear her say "I'll walk," and though they had tried to whisper their quarrel, the whole church had heard, and the men were pulled silently up and out.

It had not been his purpose to end the service, but Rooster did not try to turn the flow. He had not raised his voice till now and would not—that was the duty of an ordained preacher. He only watched them go and when there were four men left in the church (Mr. Favro, himself, Arnold and Macey Gupton), he said, "Reverend, I never meant to ruin your day, but I know you have heard of the ox in the ditch—Jesus Himself rescued it on Sunday—and anyhow most of your ladies have stayed." He surveyed the remnant—seventeen women, some scared knots of children, Macey and Arnold. He did not know Arnold's mental history, but seeing his size he said to him gently "Ain't you coming?" Arnold shook his head. "You're a big strapping boy. You could handle that snake right by yourself. He'd never swallow *them* shoulders, one sure thing." Arnold's shoulders shook and he pointed to the choir and the women there but did not speak.

Macey said, "Sheriff, his pleasure is music. Louise Rodwell was going to sing a solo. He's living for that."

Rooster smiled to Arnold, "Live on, son," then turned to the choir. "Miss Louise, I don't know which one is you, but excuse me please for taking your crowd. I hope you'll give this boy his song." He bowed again in an arc to all and aimed for the door he had entered by.

Before he was out the piano began. Miss Louise was giving—or starting to give.

Every volunteer had gone home first (for whatever reasons—mainly for guns) so when Milo and Rooster and Macey Gupton (invited by Milo to ride with them) stopped in the Mustian yard again, there were just the two deputies and Mr. Capps, and they were all standing at the porch steps together, drinking cold Pepsis, eating cold biscuits and looking up to where Selma Provo sat at the edge of the steps in a rocking chair, Emma beside her standing with a plate and Milo's shoes.

Selma was dressed though her hair still hung in one long plait, but her face was pale as a ghost in need and seeing Milo rolling towards her through leaf-broken light, she paled even further and whispered to his mother, "You say you never saw him. I don't understand. Not knowing Tommy, how could you make his picture?" She pointed to Milo.

Yards away he accepted her notice and said to her loudly, "You lasted the night. Now maybe you'll live."

Selma's mouth opened towards him but no sound came, and her gray lips wrenched in memory and grief though Milo chalked it up to pain. Then she said, "Your mother has told me the news and helped me out here to see these men."

Rooster tipped his hat, said, "Sheriff Pomeroy, lady. Hope you ain't hurting or worrying no more. Help's on the way. I have just broke up a whole Baptist service, and all the men are coming on here. Your snake's good as dead—and your boy's good as caught." The last was to Emma.

But Selma said, "Dead! You kill that snake and you owe me five hundred dollars cash. What do you think he is?—an eel? He's an Indian python from the jungles of Burma. I've nursed him through more than twelve long years—from a scrawny baby to a strapping beauty—and I won't have him shot by a hot-headed gang just because a mad dog scared him into running and him full of rabbit, drowsy and slow. Excuse me, Emma, but if I hadn't fed him Saturday night, he could save himself, could wrap any one of you in lightning hoops of steel, but full as he is, he's asleep yonder somewhere gentle as a lamb." She made a wide sweep towards the visible woods.

"I'd hate to be a lamb and cross his path." Mr. Capps said that, having nothing to lose—or so he thought.

But Selma pointed towards his trailer in the yard, his valuable hounds. "Laugh all you want but he loves a nice dog. I feed him puppies from city dog-pounds when he gets homesick or is shedding his hide."

Milo said, "Macey here smells like a dog. We can use him as bait and save the bloodhounds." Macey butted him flat and they rolled down the yard twenty feet towards the road till Macey had won and rode Milo's chest, knees in his armpits, both of them laughing to strangulation.

Emma said, "Shame! Shame on both of you. Get up—it's Sunday—and here come the helpers." The boys struggled up, covered with white dust. "I can't smell from here but no dog would get as filthy as you two."

They did not even brush at the dirt with their hands or acknowledge Emma but ran towards the help—two trucks and a car turning into the yard, loaded with faces, not one of them smiling.

Rooster said "Lady" gently to Selma. "Please do me a favor. When my men are all here, just talk to them *calm*. They are doing this free and despite my warning, they have all got guns hid on them somewhere so be nice please, but make a little speech about how you are grateful and how much you trust them with your private property, and then tell us some of that snake's likes and dislikes."

Emma said, "Selma, listen to the sheriff. That's just good sense. You told me last night you had ruined your life through hot-blooded words—"

"—*Acts*," Selma said but nodded agreement, and Emma went in to the kitchen and Rosa, leaving Milo's shoes (Rosa was working on refreshments there, and the baby was with her).

Meanwhile Milo was bringing up his men—Macey and seven that had good sense. They had all but Macey changed to hunting clothes—the oldest dirtiest stuff they owned—so they all matched Macey, and with Milo half-dressed, they resembled a set of old cyclones coming, tan and gray, torn and creased, spent. Rooster said, "General Lee has finally surrendered. Praise God, here come our boys *home!* Welcome home, boys." They heard him but the oldest was in his sixties so they still did not smile as they reached the porch, and to make amends Rooster quickly said, "Thank you, gentlemen. You know me I guess—I am Rooster Pomeroy, the Apple King."

"Apple *what?*" Milo said.

Rooster said, "Apple *King*. That's what Pomeroy means."

"Means in *what?*" Milo said.

"In the language of love—what else? Now you know. But if I don't know everyone of you boys—well, all that means is I ain't arrested you for bootlegging, tom-catting or beating your women, ain't caught you anyhow! I'll have to get all your names in a minute, but this sick lady— she's tore her ankle—is Mrs. Provo from Clearwater, Florida. She runs the snake show that travels with the fair, and the snake we are hunting belongs to her. She raised him from a baby and knows his mind, and she's agreed to tell us all she knows." He gestured to Selma.

Selma said "Nothing."

"*Nothing?*"

"Nothing. I have had that python for thirteen years, and if he knows me from Adam's housecat, *I* don't know it. He lets me touch him and eats the rats and rabbits I give him—when the spirit moves him. One time he fasted from Christmas day till my next birthday, September tenth, nine long months. Laid there and let rats crawl all across him. Then he struck one day, ate a two-pound rat and has eaten regularly ever since—two or three times a week in hot weather."

Macey said "You call today hot?"

Selma tilted her chin to test the day. "Yes sir, I do."

"I figured you did." He slapped the crown of his head and dust flew.

"I'm calling him *him*," she said, "but I don't know that even. The boy that gave him to me way back when, he said you could tell by him having big feet. Pythons got feet out beside their behinds, and the male's feet are bigger—so this boy said—since they hide their nature, their thing, in there. One in each foot, drawn in and covered. That's what he said—the boy he belonged to, that gave him to me. I never have seen it but I call him *him*. And that's all I know—nothing, like I said. I've raised him thirteen years from a baby—three foot long to eighteen foot. I say he's twenty foot when I show him on the road, just to round it off. Maybe he is. You ever try to measure a live python? Anyhow he's been with me all these years, never tried to escape and know me or not, he means something to me. He has been one thing that stayed, and he didn't leave now of his own free will. So when you find him, he'll be asleep. Two or three of you just move on him gentle—he hasn't got ears but he feels you in the ground—and take him by his neck and middle and tail. He won't struggle much. I bet he'll be glad. You won't *know* that though. He won't show feelings. It took me five years of standing in snakes ankle-deep day and night to figure out the terrible thing about them—they haven't got faces, just eyes and a mouth. Dogs, cats, horses, even pigs smile or frown but a snake just stares."

Milo said, "Sounds like your Mama, don't it, Macey?" Then to Mrs. Provo—"Macey's Mama has lost all her teeth and won't crack her mouth, even eats in private." Macey sucked in his lips, crossed eyes to show his mother's predicament, and then another truck pulled into the yard. Milo looked and said, "Hide your money. It's Hawkins Ryden. Who told him?" and a high lean man maybe forty years old started towards them.

"Ryden?" Selma whispered urgently to Milo. "Any kin to Tommy?"

"Who's Tommy?" Milo said.

Selma searched him as disbelievingly as though he had asked, "Who is God? Who am *I*?" Then she gradually found herself and said, "Your Granddaddy's favorite cousin that's dead, your *own* cousin—killed."

Emma stepped out of the door with more biscuits. She had heard that last and catching Selma's eye, gave a deep shaking frown.

Milo said, "I can't tell you that but don't ask Hawkins. He'd charge you for an answer."

Macey nodded. "Listen at him squeak—tightest man in America."

Hawkins came on and Rooster said "Morning, Mr. Ryden."

Hawkins nodded. "Sheriff. I didn't know you knew me."

"I know everybody that's voted for me."

"I never voted."

"Costs too much"—it was Macey whispering, clear as a bell.

"My wife come home from church and said you was wanting some men to help you hunt."

"Need all I can get."

"What are you hunting?"

"A boy, a mad dog and a twenty-foot snake."

"That's what my wife said. I never believed her."

"She's right today. Welcome to the crowd."

"Hold on a minute here. How much you paying?"

"Mr. Ryden, I'm paying out the best thing there is, that will outlast money by a hundred years—a satisfied heart, knowing you have helped a friend."

Hawkins thought a moment. "Who are you speaking of?"

"Mrs. Mustian here and this poor lady that owns the snake."

Hawkins thought again.

Milo said, "Hell-fire, Hawkins. You are blood-kin to us. What else do you want?"

"I don't know," he said, "but I wasn't looking forward to donating time on my day of rest."

"Isn't your name Ryden?" Selma said. "I'm Selma Provo that owns the snake."

"Yes'm, it is."

"Are you any kin to a Tommy Ryden?"

"I was. He's dead."

"I know that," she said. "How well I know."

"Selma—" Emma said.

Selma paddled a silencing hand. "What kin were you when Tommy was breathing?"

Hawkins thought, then worked it out on his fingers. "Tommy's Daddy was my Uncle Gid, my Daddy's brother. His Mama won't a bit of kin to me, but I had her to feed after Tommy left—and she lived till nearly two years ago, back in them woods." He pointed them all to the woods they knew, behind and around. "What do you know about Tommy, lady? None of us saw him after 1930—cleared out of here and never sent his Daddy or Mama a penny. But I knew he wouldn't. I grew up with him. He wouldn't of give a aspirin to a dying woman."

"He give me the snake that's lost today."

Hawkins laughed. "Might of known but I bet it was just part-pay-ment—won't it?—on some big debt. He was famous for paying on things piecemeal even as a boy. Never paid for all of nothing in his life."

Rooster said "Amen" but no one seemed to hear.

Emma said, "He paid for *freedom* with his life. What was that please if not total payment?"

"Shirking," Hawkins said. "Just one more way to shirk his duty and throw his old folks on his relatives to keep. Broke his Mama's heart, I can tell you that. Starved her to death on pure cold grief."

Selma said, "I know what you mean."

Milo said, "*I* don't—old Miss Jack Ryden? Starved to death? I saw her the Sunday before she died. I was squirrel hunting back yonder in the woods, and late in the day I come on her place. Well, I had to do my business and there was her johnny-house standing empty, nobody in sight, so I went in and took a seat, and directly buck-shot was blasting the walls. Talk about business! I never knew you had to buy a ticket. Anyhow once I got hold of myself, I looked through a knothole and saw this woman on the porch of the house, old as a turtle, holding a shotgun and looking like she weighed three hundred pounds stripped—except she looked like she hadn't stripped in years. It was Miss Jack Ryden and don't tell me she was starving. She won't. *I* was thin though and I saw a loose board at the back of the johnny— just a six-inch scantling—but I squeezed through like a ounce of butter, gun and all, and when I got to the edge of the trees and out of her range, I hollered, 'Miss Jack, it's Milo Mustian. I won't doing nothing but borrowing your johnny. Ain't that what it's for?' 'Hell no,' she said. 'The woods is for that.' She flung out her arm at all them pines. 'There's woods enough here to hold all you can do, you and every other thieving scoundrel. That johnny is mine!' So I been using the woods ever since, and don't tell me Miss Jack Ryden starved. She died of meanness."

Selma said, "There's more than one way to starve."

"Amen," Hawkins said. "She was full of fatback and bread till she died and I bought every slice."

Rooster said, "I'm glad she could die on a full stomach. Now Mr. Ryden, are you with me or not? We got to get moving."

Hawkins said, "How long is that snake again, Sheriff?"

"He *was* twenty foot but he'll be a heap longer if we don't get moving. This day is hot and everything's *growing*."

Macey said to Milo, hand cupped for secrecy, "Milo's growing— from the hip outwards, ain't you?"

Milo frowned but seeing his mother had not heard, nodded and grinned and measured off his forward growth with both hands as if it were a fat catfish he had caught.

Hawkins said, "Listen, if I catch that snake, can I have his skin? That's what I'll ask. I'm the best snake hunter in the U.S.A., and I call that a bargain."

Milo said, "If he catches you, can I have yours?"

"Hold it," Selma said and wept. Everyone waited, watching the ground, till she swallowed her grief—its sudden plug at least. "I've said it strongly and I'll said it again—don't kill the snake." She thrust her bandaged ankle at the men's eye level. "If this fool foot would bear my fat, I'd be with you now, be leading the pack and I'd get him whole. But I've been struck down by the hand of God so I'm pleading to you." She paused and stared every man in the eye, separate in turn, then coming last to Milo she rested on him, and said the rest to him. "I can see you thinking, 'She is cracked as deep as the Liberty Bell, raving on a snake like it was human.' And maybe I am. But I've told you he's worth over five hundred dollars, and I've told you the thirteen years I've struggled, bringing him to his full color and power. Still to tell you the truth, he's fully insured, and I've also told you he don't know me—I don't know he does—and I know you are worried with him running free. *I* know he's gentle, has been mostly gentle with me and Lois, but if he took a mind he could do real harm—kill a grown man and I've got a book that says a python swallowed a boy in Sumatra, head and heels. So why am I pleading round a knot like a fist in my foolish throat?" The knot constricted, then eased, gave her breath. "Because like I said, he was *given* to me—by someone more harmful than any live snake, any cobra that spits. Snakes don't strike unless they're cornered or hungry but *that* boy—" She stopped. The boy had been hungry. She saw that now, after so much time. "It was his first cousin"—she pointed to Hawkins—"and some kin of yours"—she pointed to Milo. "And Tommy said to me, 'I'll leave you my snake'—he called it Death even then as a baby—'and if I leave he will be my spirit and carry my messages to you from the grave.' I laughed but took it and have kept it and waited. Not a sound, not a sign."

Emma touched Selma's shoulder. "Take a ham biscuit, Selma.

They were hot awhile ago." Selma took one and ate it like the last shard of food on Judgment Day.

Then the plate passed round to every man, and over his loud chewing Hawkins said, "You got any papers to prove he's yours?"

Selma said "Why do you ask?"

"Because if you ain't and Tommy died owning him, rightly he may be mine not yours. I'm Tommy's nearest living kin and five hundred dollars—if I caught him and sold him—would be partial payment on the food I poured down his hungry Mama when he broke her heart and left her penniless."

The biscuit plate had returned to Emma in the course of that, empty again. Her wish was to sling it into Hawkins' teeth, but looking, she saw it was Rosacoke's, a gift from her drunk dead father (Emma's husband)—thick blue, Captain John Smith bearded, *Jamestown Exposition* 1907. Where had he got it?—the year he was born? She had never thought to ask him, too late, too late. She said, "Hawkins Ryden, this ain't my house and it ain't my land. I come here a bride twenty-one years ago, and I've scoured and scrubbed every inch of it since till my hands are raw." She extended her right hand—it nearly was, flamed with labor. "But it still ain't mine, not a splinter of it. I tell you this though—it'll be my children's when their Granddaddy dies, and in their name I am telling you to leave. Nobody needs your kind around here. Mean people grow on trees, Hawkins Ryden. Start making tracks." He walked three steps and Emma turned to Rooster. "There's one big thing all of you have forgot and that *is* mine—Rato my boy. Carrying on all this time about a snake when a human being is in dreadful trouble every second you waste here fanning your gums. Selma, I know what the snake means to you but you didn't *bear* it. It was just a gift to you. Rato is something I worked on, believe me. And if you say he's a mighty poor job, that he hadn't got the sense of a snake or a dog and sure-God wouldn't bring five hundred dollars nowhere on earth—well, I'll say you're right, but he's *my* job, *my* failure, mine and his sorry dead Daddy's, Sheriff. So please get moving or next election I'll stand in the street like a prophet of God and shame folks into not voting for you."

Rosacoke broke the following silence by coming through the door with a stack of lunches, wax-paper parcels of fresh ham biscuits, and

Baby Sister tagging behind. Rooster's eyes seized her like port in a storm. "Little lady, did you make these?" She smiled and nodded.

But Milo said, "No, Rosacoke's religious. She just blessed the crumbs from last night's supper and lo and behold!"

Rosa gave him the snaking length of her tongue, and Rooster said to Emma, "I need Hawkins Ryden. He's well known for hunting and anyhow I ain't got enough without him."

Emma nodded. Then she said towards Hawkins who was leaving, "Hawkins, I'm sorry. I'm out of my mind. Come back and help them find my boy. All I can pay you is a ham-biscuit dinner, but he is kin to you. Help your people."

Hawkins took another step, stopped in his tracks, his back to Emma. His shoulders hunched. Then he turned and came towards her, eyes down, carefully reusing his previous tracks in the crusty ground, a secret economy. He stopped a little way from the others, and nobody faced him but Emma. She thanked him.

"All right," Rooster said, "let's call the roll. I got to get everybody's name and age. In case that snake should swallow one of us, I got to know who to notify!" He took out an old envelope and a pencil and licking the lead, said, "File by me and I'll write you down. You might get a medal from the governor, who knows?" They came as he wished in Indian file.

"Milo Mustian, going on sixteen."

"Macey Gupton, ditto but smarter."

"Staley Goins, and I'm going strong. Sixty-three last May thirteenth."

"Buck Russell, forty-two."

"Felton Driver, twenty-nine."

"Ballard Stegall, twenty-one."

"Ernest Umphlett, thirty-six."

"Malvin Thrower, a hundred and one." (His voice cracked saying it. He was nineteen.)

"Hawkins Ryden, forty."

Rooster looked up. "That's all but the paid employees then." He began to list them, "Me and Mr. Capps, sixteen plus. Deputy Lonnie Wilson—how old are you, Lonnie?"

"Thirty-five, Sheriff."

"And Yancey Breedlove?" He looked to Yancey—"Pushing fifty, ain't you?"

Yancey said "Twenty-one last Tuesday."

Rooster said, "That's right. You're just *looking* old lately—wore out, Yancey. Ease up, boy." He grinned towards Selma. "Yancey got married two weeks ago. If the snake swallows you, boy—and well he might, you looking so pale—we'll feed him your wife too. She'd die anyhow, grieve her heart out, the Widow Breedlove. See, it hurts me to say it." Rooster drew a dark line at the end of his list and began to count it backwards.

"Speaking of Breedlove," Macey said, "ain't you going to list Mr. Mustian and his girl? They are in the worst sort of danger, I think. Especially that girl." Macey looked to Milo and fought not to smile.

Milo said, "She can handle herself all right, let me tell you. Anyhow I'll be meeting her soon. I'll give her a hand."

Rooster had counted—"Thirteen exactly."

Selma gasped. "One of you drop out or Fate's sure to strike."

Milo said, "Shoot, that's the number of Jesus and *His* men. And all the apostles could handle snakes harmless as fishing worms. That's well known. Macey, you be the Jesus—Macey's beard has started and he walks on water."

Macey raised both hands in grave benediction—"Who is my Judas?" and waited for an answer.

Nobody looked at anybody else, not at any adult. They looked to the children, the baby and Rosacoke, for rescue, relief.

But Rosacoke said, her voice like a blade, "Let Milo be Judas."

Rooster lurched to Milo, grabbed him under the chin. "Cough up them thirty shekels of silver! Yancey, find him a rope to hang hisself with. Sorry scoundrel, I've got him at last!" Milo submitted and Yancey actually started for the rope.

But Emma said, "Sheriff, I meant what I said," and Milo was free, blood-red round his neck.

Rooster said, "Lady, I heard and believe. Your lost boy is good as back in your arms. The reason I've carried on about that snake was— we don't get too many calls for pythons, but boys get lost several times a day. And we generally find them, white or black, Methodist or Baptist. Boys is easy. I think like a boy and I know where to look. It's snakes and dogs that worry my *mind*—they just ain't human. But the closest thing to my *heart* is your boy. He'll be home for supper. Start frying right now." Then he faced his men and solemn heavy authority seemed laid upon him by the falling light. "Now here is the plan. We are hunting separate in two even groups—one with the dogs, one with me. Since Mr. Mustian and his girl are hunting westward (if they are still *hunting*), we'll hunt east and north and since you mentioned it, meet at old Miss Jack Ryden's place. Hawkins, who lives there?"

"Lizards and owls. Some Niggers did after Aunt Jack died, but they claimed it was hexed and left in the night, owing two months' rent."

So Rooster knelt and taking a stick, gouged a map in the ground.

Then he stood. "That's your orders, boys. Don't take no chances. If the dogs strike a trail, Mr. Capps'll fire once. If they find what we're hunting—any one of the three—fire three if you can, if you've got the time. We'll come hauling. And we'll use the same signs if *we* strike first. Remember we are dealing in precious property—a human being and a snake that's as much God's doing as you are. The dog?—poor fellow, shoot the dog on sight." He let that register, then stared at each man. "Anybody that's got other business at home, go now." No one moved. "Right. Anybody that can't take orders from me or Mr. Capps, go too." No one moved. "Then we'll split this way." He consulted his list. "Mr. Capps and the dogs and Deputy Wilson take Ryden, Goins, Thrower, Umphlett and Driver. Me and Deputy Breedlove'll take Mustian, Gupton—they'll be our dogs; they'll smell so good the snake will come to *us*—Stegall and Russell." He removed his hat. "I ain't said much this morning, have I? Let me just say this much before we go. In all my years as elected sheriff, I have *done* some deeds. I have captured several pondsful of moonshine liquor. I have took razors out of crazy Niggers' hands, blood on the blade and a gal cut to ribbons laid dead in the ditch. Just last week I arrested a man that had bit off and swallowed another man's thumb—his wife's boyfriend. So I've had a full life—I'm honored to have it—but this job today is the *height* of my life. And I've got a strong feeling—come on me in the night when I couldn't sleep—that all of us here, every man and boy with a part in this day will end bigger men in the eyes of their loved ones and enemies if they *play* that part the Lord has give them. Also a man from the *Warren Record* will meet us at four p.m. for pictures. So I want us to pause here one last minute and leave with a prayer. It's the least I can do, breaking up a church service. I'm going to call on the one that's got most to gain or lose—Milo, give us a prayer." He reached to touch Milo but Milo stood farther away than he knew—and frowned at first, for a relay of reasons: disbelief, embarrassment, scorn, final ignorance of what to ask. "Don't worry, son. The Lord will provide."

Milo's lips were suddenly separate from his face, red and long and as clearly, firmly lined on his skin as if worked with a blade and intended for silence. But they moved, opened, and this was provided—"Today we are hunting three valuable things that have give some pleasure to several people. My brother Rato is valuable to us. His mad dog Phillip is valuable to him. And Death is valuable to the Provo ladies. Help us to always remember that, all day today. Help us be worthy of what we are hunting. Help us to live with whatever we find."

Rooster said "Amen" and looked to Mr. Capps but thought to himself, "Let this be the day I prove to Kate the man I can be if she lies still and lets me be what I'm meant to be, what the Lord intended—a help to others, to keep their peace." His mouth hung open but no speech followed.

So Mr. Capps said to Emma Mustian, "Lady, I'll need a scent for my dogs. Give me a piece of your lost boy's clothes that ain't been washed."

Emma nodded, turned but thought before going, "What will you do if you don't save Rato? You did not save his sorry father. Save one helpless thing, for me." She pointed Milo to his shoes beside her (the laces unknotted), then vanished inward.

Selma Provo sought Milo's face (which he freely gave), took its ghostly shock. "Leave me," she thought, "what little You've left. At the end of this day bring me Lois and Death, the things he left me."

Rosacoke sought her brother's look. He had not faced her, by light, all day. He did not now. And Rosacoke thought, "Bring Rato back safe. Bring Milo *back* in his old right mind."

Milo looked to the waiting woods. "Let me find Rato, let me find Death, then let me take my ease on some girl."

Macey looked to the sun and its light sucked from him a long high laugh and this, aloud—"Keep it burning, Lord. I'll need it today in them black pines." The light found an unleaved hole in the trees and struck Macey broadside, laughing again. "A-*men*. Thank you, Lord. Prayer is heard. Now save Macey Gupton from the jaws of Death!" He ran to the car and the men could only follow.

Rooster was tired by three o'clock and lonely, having walked alone for more than two hours through empty woods—apparently empty though how could he know what had slid through their net, so loose and feebly cast? Every step now seemed a step away from what this day was meant to be—a gift to Kate in hopes of holding her—a step into tiredness, helpless age, abandonment, the long wait for rest. He suddenly knew an important thing, the thing he had meant to tell Milo this morning after the church service—the shield, safety, to the otherwise deadly advice he had flung out, unasked, unwanted but plainly taken. He called for Milo—one word, the name, not loudly to his right. If his orders were obeyed, Milo was there fifty yards away, and Macey was fifty yards to his left (and the others at equal spaces beyond). But no answer came. Then he broke into a small natural clearing, a pine-needled bowl, shaded but light, and he paused to listen for Milo and Macey. No help came, not so much as the sound of a human foot behind or beyond. They had surely passed him or left and gone home or disobeyed and arranged themselves into better ranks that could work without him, leaving him here with only the rest of his life to face. Then above his head unseen in a tree the nasal click of a squirrel began, certain warning. He braced to listen—warning of what? Up from the earth, from somewhere near came the gentle unhurried displacement of leaves by something that shouldered its way towards him, low and long. He reached for his pistol to summon help—if help was near—but whirling and seeing no visible threat by the roots of trees, he found a rusty whistle in his pocket and blew three times. The sliding silenced and he heard distant Milo passing the call to his right-hand neighbor and him to his—sweet fading music to Rooster Pomeroy, the ring of his unquestioned authority spreading through woods like the hump that will rise through a length of rope from a flickering hand. He was not alone, there was day still ahead.

Yet it took Milo a minute to burst through the trees, crouched to struggle—"Which is it, Sheriff?"

Rooster pointed up. "I heard a squirrel talking, then some sliding on the ground but I don't see nothing. Just another false alarm. Let's all rest a minute. But before they get here, listen to this and don't forget it long as you live. You recollect what I told you this morning?—not to wait but to use every kind of strength you got while you're young and don't *care?*"

"Yes sir and I said I wasn't waiting, remember?"

"That's what worries me, you saying that. You ain't got a Daddy and the one you had never knew this, never acted like he did, so listen to this. This keeps you from harm—" Yancey Breedlove broke in from the left, rifle ready, and then in loud succession from the right, Ballard and Buck—Buck with the pistol he had so far hid. So Rooster said to Milo "Wait" and calmed them.

They laughed and loosened, began to squat and light cigarettes, but Milo stayed up and said "Whereabouts is Macey?"

Yancey said, "Where is he supposed to be?"

"Well, here before you. He was fifty yards closer to the sheriff when we started."

Yancey said, "God Almighty, Sheriff. It's Yancey's day off. I'm a newly wed. Now damned if we ain't lost another moron."

Rooster said, "Son, you don't own that badge. I can rip that off so fast you'll see stars, and what'll you feed that gal on then?—a diet of hot loving?"

Yancey looked at his badge that his wife had shined this very morning and saw his own face. It was smiling at him, black-haired fool. He smiled back and not looking up said "Yes sir."

Rooster said "God," then cupped his mouth and called Macey to the left, then another long "Macey" in a left semi-circle. Ringing silence, then the clicking squirrel now clearly from the west. Rooster stabbed a hand in the general direction, and sliding began in the dead dry leaves, slow as before, on their west flank, northward.

"There's your snake," Buck said.

Ballard Stegall said "That ain't no snake," living in hope.

They listened, it continued. Yancey raised his rifle. "What is it then?—U.S. Highway Number One creeping north to Niagara Falls for a honeymoon?"

Rooster whispered "Wait," walked to the lip of the bowl they were in, drew his own pistol, then beckoned to Yancey and Buck to follow. The three of them spread abreast, guns cocked, Milo and Ballard six feet behind. Ballard plugged his ears. Then a low cedar moved, swayed rhythmically, and above the natural brush of its limbs came a soft steady "*Wooooo*"—moan or threat?

"Can they talk?" Yancey said.

Buck said, "Damned if I know. That woman didn't say."

Rooster said, "Sure they can talk. They talk in the Bible like college professors. Speak to it, Yancey. You finished high school."

Yancey said, "All I studied was Spanish. This bastard's Burmese." He cuddled his rifle in the notch of his shoulder, sighted it dead at the heart of the tree, then said, "Come out if you're aiming to live!"

The "*Woooo*"-ing continued, then dipped into words, "I'm dead already"—both pistols ached—"but I bring you word from the Great Beyond. Woooo."

Rooster said "Shoot" and Yancey fired. The woods took the sound as if they were brass—rang on and on—but nothing moved. In his nerves Yancey merely had topped the tree. "Not you, fool," Rooster said. "I'm speaking to *it*. Shoot your message, I mean. We're listening, ghost."

A long pause, then "Woooo—the snake you are hunting is with you now."

Rooster said "Didn't I tell you?" to Yancey. "Where is he at?"

"Woooo. Above you, beneath you, beside you, behind you."

The row of guns whirled round looking. Milo and Ballard stared into three barrels. Yancey said "Well, it's invisible then."

"Woooo. You're right. It's a *holy* snake from the Great Beyond, a messenger. Prepare to meet it now. Fall on your knees and it will appear with generous blessings for all who kneel."

Ballard's knees dug two deep sockets in the ground. Milo said, "Hell, Ballard, you *want* it to appear?" Ballard half-rose, half-knelt, not sure.

But Rooster knelt and whispered firmly, "Kneel down, boys. The golden rule in this line of work is to not take chances with peculiar cases. Do what your victim tells you to do—within reason, of course." They obeyed, knelt, lowered their guns, and Rooster said, "Right. We're down in the dirt like a bunch of Catholics. Now where's the snake at?"

The cedar shook hard as a woman in labor, then gave a kind of birth of its own—a figure in man's clothes, five-foot-six, its arms stretched towards them, legs hacking wide stiff steps in the ground (clods of dirt coughing back from its heels) and whatever head it bore, hid from them by thin white cloth that hugged its neck (the vague print of features lurking behind). Everybody, kneeling, fixed on the head, but Milo down in the second rank heard the gentle threading through leaves again—not made by those feet, nearer than they. He studied the foreground, then said, "Hold it, Ghost. Excuse me asking but you hadn't noticed that copperhead, have you? Put on your glasses."

Macey fumbled in his pocket, unveiled his face, put on his glasses, studied the ground, bent like lightning to a spot beyond his feet and stood with a copperhead two feet long, salmon pink and brown, lashing his arm. He smiled and came towards them.

Rooster said, "I hope that's a ghost you're *holding*."

"This or this?" Macey said and extended his left hand first—his face cloth had been a pair of ladies' bloomers—then his right with the snake which he waved within a foot of Yancey's nose (they were all, but Milo, still kneeling in shock). Yancey fell back and spat and his rifle struck ground.

Rooster said "That" to the twining snake which rung Macey's arm like an Eastern disease.

"No sir, that's a real snake. Copperhead, Milo?—didn't you say? Just a little old egg-sucking copperhead. Friend to man, eat rats by the pack."

Milo nodded and Rooster said, "Yes but—hold his neck tight— he'll kill you *dead* as any ghost if he takes a mind to bite."

Milo said, "A copperhead isn't no king snake, Macey. I told you that last summer, remember?"

Macey turned his wrist to face his snake. Its snouted head was locked by his clamping fingers, but it fended his gaze with a forked black tongue slick and fast as the girls in Phyllis's tent. Then he looked to Milo. "I forgot," he said. It was offered as both apology and plea.

Yancey stood and pointed to a bare spot beyond. "Fling him down yonder and I'll blast his damn legs off."

Milo stood. "You got a lot of blasting ahead of you then. He hadn't got legs. Mrs. Provo said just pythons did. Didn't you hear her?"

Yancey said, "No, I didn't—she was raving on so—but that explains a lot. That bastard we're hunting is probably way on past Richmond by now, legging it home."

"Burma ain't that way," Rooster said. He pointed east. "And nobody's shooting no more till I say to. That'd be a signal and we ain't caught *squat—*"

Macey said, "Well, *I've* caught something and it's waiting to kill me. *Do* something please."

Rooster thought and said, "Listen, just let him go. There's no other way. Walk yonder ten yards—where we already been—and fling him as far as you can to the south. This is my day to spare things anyhow."

Macey went, drew back and flung the snake. It traveled as stiff as a shut umbrella end over end till it struck a pine and fell and streamed for cover. Then Macey stepped into his bloomers and twisted towards them. He swayed up to Yancey, said, "Hey, big boy. Give me a quarter and I'll strike your *match.*"

Yancey nudged him in his rayon crotch with the rifle. "I'll strike *your* match. Where in the Hell you get them things?"

"Off a Nigger girl."

"That's a lie," Yancey said.

"How come?" Macey said.

"No Nigger gal that thin wears pants."

Milo said, "You know, don't you, Yancey?"

"Damn right I know. I'm the county expert on women's underwear, black, white or red."

Macey said, "Son, you're wrong today. These were give to me ten minutes ago by a gal as black as Moses' butt." He slapped his own butt, slung it out towards Yancey. "She left them anyhow when she heard that whistle. I was way ahead of you all, minding my business, stomping through briars chin-deep when I heard some laughing. I eased up and crept on nearer to the noise till I found me a hole in the briars to peep through. I'm scratched up terrible." He showed his welted arms.

Yancey said "What was it?"

Macey said "What you mean?"

"What you saw through the briars, fool."

"Another hole, fool. Ain't you never been hunting in here before? You have to step high or break your ankle, falling in some gal, Nigger or not." That was meant for Yancey but said to Milo—"Ain't it so, Milo?"

They all looked to Milo and he began to nod, but it drowned in the hot blood rushing to his face. Milo's blushes were as rare as his songs, and this one was doubly scalding for him—he did not understand its secret cause: that he no longer stood with Macey here (in knowledge, experience) but with Yancey, Buck Russell, the worn-out Rooster. Macey seemed shrunk, blotched with stinking dirt, mouth streaming ignorance. "Shut your mouth, Macey," Milo said, looking down. "You don't know what you're talking about."

Macey wavered, swallowed hard—the gristle beak grated up, down in his tightening throat. Abandonment rushed like warm wings against him.

But Yancey said, "Come on. What did you see?"

The story he had made to amuse Milo—the kernel of truth, the cushion of lies—crumbled in his head. Even the words to tell it betrayed him, seemed clearly childish guesses, but Yancey's face waited so he flew blindly on as if through flames, hoping to survive—"A Nigger girl laid out flat in the dirt with her bloomers beside her and this Nigger boy that was giving her—"

"What?" Yancey bored like a drill.

"You know," Macey said.

"No I don't," Yancey said.

Rooster said, "I do—a free driving lesson. Ain't that so, Macey?"

Macey laughed. "That's it. I predict she'll get her license soon. He's a A-1 teacher—I saw that myself." He laughed again tightly, then found he could smile.

Rooster said, "Yes sir, Yancey, you take heed. There's a college education lying free in these woods for a fellow with eyes. You ought to come strolling out here more often."

Yancey said, "Shoot, I'm enrolled in night school in my own house on a Beautyrest mattress, no flies on me and my gal's white."

"Don't knock black," Buck Russell said. "It's a good-wearing color—black don't show marks. 'Learn on black and pay at the hole'—that was my motto when I was still loose. It worked like a charm and all it ever cost me was fifty cents a throw, sometimes a quarter if the gal was dumb or had one eye, but you don't see the mantel when you're poking up the grate. Only trouble I had was the year I got married. I stopped running round oh a month before the wedding—to purify my blood. The Nigger I was punching hadn't never seen a washrag. And luck was with me. I passed my blood test to get the license, and the wedding come off and the honeymoon. We went to Washington—took all I had, October '29 and the stockmarket crashed before we got home. I didn't have no stock of course but poor is *poor*, and for six or seven years we kept from having children—I won't tell you how but it won't much fun. The Lord was just with me—He's mostly been—but I'm getting ahead of my story here. Two or three months after I was married and settling down, I was at the store, standing there talking, and my Nigger gal come walking towards the door, her baby sister with her. I saw right off she was toting a load, was far-gone pregnant but I didn't worry. I never told myself I was her only business, never wanted to be. Well, I went on talking and she come in looking dead ahead and stared at the showcase. You know how they do—ain't got but a nickel and hope if they stare at the glass long enough, it'll melt away and the candy come streaming so all they got to do is just reach out and take it. Then she asked how much were the Mary Janes—do they still make those? pull your teeth right out— and Gip Roland said "A penny a piece." (I well knew that—I paid for many a piece with Mary Janes.) She untied her rag—took another five minutes—and there was a penny. I ain't Santy Claus—a seventeen-year-old gal can live without candy—but there stood her baby sister all eyes and teeth so I said 'Come here, girl'—I was talking to the baby—but Della came over. Now you know who it is—"

Milo said "Della Brame."

Buck Russell nodded. "So I gave her a nickel and she didn't say a word. She bought her sack of candy and went out the door and stood on the steps with her back turned to me. She was already hunch-shouldered, toting her load—used to stand straight as wild poke-weed—and all she was moving was her jaws on that candy. She gummed down the first one and took out the second and tore off the paper and threw it towards the road and then turned around and walked to the door. The door was closed—it was late December—but she knocked on the glass and we all looked up. None of them knew I had ever touched her. I won't a big talker then—you always can tell; the ones that are talking ain't doing much else. But she pointed at me and said 'Mr. Buck' loud enough to hear. I went to her, walked with her far as the road, then she said, 'Buck, how much you paying me for this?'—'This *what?*'—'This youngun,' she said. I said, 'Della, I paid at the hole every time in money or goods and you give a receipt.' She didn't give no receipts but I said it, and she recollected and knew I was right. She just nodded and called her sister's name that was scratching in the dirt, and they walked on home eating Mary Janes. So like I said, black don't show marks. Don't knock black."

Milo said, "Did she have a baby?"

"I guess she did. She took up with Boot sometime that winter, and they've had all that yardful of children."

"But you were Jack's Daddy?—the one that's in prison for killing Ella Grant?"

"Well, he don't look like me, black as Egypt. She could have snagged him from half the men in Afton, white or black. Boys used to come here by *car* to see her when cars were scarce as camels. No, I don't know. I never did ask."

Milo said, "How come?—since you remember everything so clear?"

Buck said, "Because I had changed my ways. Because it won't none of my business to ask."

"And it ain't none of yours, son," Rooster said.

Milo looked down. He had made little parallel ridges of pine straw like furrows as he listened, like a well-tended field. He made his hand a spade or a single claw and canceled that, slow and deliberate.

"Speaking of black," Yancey said, "look yonder."

They turned west to where a Negro girl was flanking them, twenty yards away, looking dead ahead, a small load hid in her far right breast. Macey whispered "That's her," still squatting in her bloomers.

Yancey hollered "Come here."

Macey whispered, "Leave her alone. I want these bloomers for my Mama's birthday!"

She walked on south, no faster, not looking. "You girl, come here."

She stopped in deep shade, half-turned to Yancey. "You hollering at me?"

"I don't see your *sister*. Yeah, come over here."

She faced south again, pointed that way. "My Mama is sick. I'm heading home."

"Well, I'm sick too and I'm a deputy sheriff. You coming or not?" Yancey stood, his rifle downwards, and took a step towards her.

Rooster said, "Yancey, let her go. We got business."

Yancey said, "Maybe I got business with her." Anyhow she turned and was pumping towards him as if she would not stop but pass through Yancey, a new way home.

But she stopped on the lip of the bowl they were in—her right leg thrust on as if not obeying, her bare dusty foot, and the blade of her black shin flashed in the light, violet, gold. ("She has greased her legs," Milo thought, "for some boy. She ain't studying *Mama*.") She drew back the leg and stood to her height which was tall for a girl and which leveled her thin eyes with Yancey's where she stared, not flicking once to his rifle, his badge, the sheriff or Macey in bloomers. No one knew her so no one could use her name to break her gaze which Yancey returned. (Milo thought, "This girl isn't waiting, on Yancey or God. She's doing her own will.") Then Yancey laughed and swept her with his eyes—from her high narrow head, the short hair brown and preened back stiff as wires, held from her skull like wings that, strutting, lifted the corners of her brows, her eyes (so black their whites were diluted brown), her vaulted cheeks, lifted all but her mouth, purple, oval, slit straight as a razor, laid in her face a sideways copy of what Milo could almost see in her fork, downwards, slung from her canted hips.

Because he stood farthest and lowest of all, Milo could see what Yancey could not—that she stood at the edge of a pool of sun flung from behind which seeped through her yellow dress, lighting this private sight for Milo (he looked to the others, no one had seen it, they all stood wrong): her legs were spread and the sun set a perfect hourglass between them, the shape of the seal on a Black Widow spider. The bottom bell rested on earth and rose, bound by her shins, rusty knees, hid thighs to shut in her crotch. Then it swelled again there to the upward half—black bell, black bulb—hid by a single thickness of cloth, by nothing else but as surely there as her tan fingernails, her wiry head. A cloud broke the light. She was solid again but Milo knew, and only Milo. He said to himself, "Let Yancey talk. I got information. Whatever Macey saw, this girl is naked as peeled sweetgum."

Yancey stepped up and asked her "Cat got your tongue?"

Her face was no more than two feet from Yancey's though lower now since he had risen. Her lips split open, her tongue thrust out like Macey's copperhead's and wiggled at Yancey, pink and wet. Yancey drew back a hand.

Rooster said "Yancey."

Yancey said to the girl, "Don't you know who I am?"

She looked down his length—badge, rifle. She touched the badge, left her fingerprint on it. "I see that badge. You say you the sheriff."

"I said I'm a deputy but the sheriff's right yonder." He pointed, not looking.

She lowered the load she had held at her breast, slid it half-behind her—a quart Mason fruit jar full of clear liquid. Her eyes had still not moved off Yancey. "What you call me for?"

"Well, *two* things now." He pointed to her jar. "I was just going to ask you had you lost anything." He pointed to Macey, the milkwhite bloomers.

She would not look. "I ain't lost nothing. What I got to lose?"

"You got a point there—lost it long ago, eh? But you ain't lost no clothes today?"

"I'm dressed, ain't I?"

"Far as I can see. Course I can't see through cloth."

"You telling me to strip off?"

Rooster said "No" and stepped closer to her, pressing Yancey back with one firm hand. He pointed to her jar—"What you carrying there?"

"Some water for my Mama."

Rooster said, "Ain't you got a well? You tote it by the *jar?*"

"My Mama is sick and this is the spring water helps her misery."

"Where's the spring at?"

She looked north. "In yonder."

"And where's your house?" She lifted her chin, hooked it south. "Do I know your Mama?"

"You know Dump Wilson?"

"Yes."

"That's her."

"*Old* Dump Wilson? I thought she was dead."

"She going to be if you don't let me go."

"You sure that's nothing but water?" She nodded. Rooster thought, then reached his hand for the jar. She gave it to him and he gripped the lid to unscrew it, then stopped.

Yancey said, "If that's water I'm Margaret Truman" and he sang three notes. "Let me taste it, Sheriff. I'm thirsty now you mention it." He volunteered a hand.

Rooster said, "I ain't mentioned nothing to *you.*" He turned to Milo, smiled. "Come here, son." Milo came. "Taste this and tell me is it water or not."

Milo slowly unscrewed the lid, sniffed at the rim—(Macey said,

"Look out, your eyebrows are scorching")—then tilted his head and sucked a good inch out, ramming it down with his Adam's apple like an iron pile driver. He rose and his eyes shut, lids clamped as if planning hibernation. Then he looked to the girl, to nobody else. "Water," Milo said. "Nice cool spring water—make old Dump think she's gone to Heaven and hadn't even had to die to get there." He screwed down the lid and handed the jar directly to the girl. "That's a spring and a half."

She said "Thank you, sir" and looked to Rooster.

Rooster said, "Tell Dump I said to get well soon but to go easy on them water treatments. At her age and mine, your bladder gives out, and then where are you?—leaking all night."

She said "Yes sir" and turned to go.

And had gone five steps when Yancey said, "She sure made a damn fool of every man here." He looked at them all. No one agreed or disagreed. They were watching her go, the shock of her wide steps calmed in the shivering halves of her butt. He looked to Milo and by force of will tore his eyes off the girl—"Water, my ass." Milo smiled, turned back to the girl whom he already saw through waves like heat, rising from the pure corn liquor on his belly. Yancey said, "Sheriff, you just going to let her go? Get nothing out of her?—not even where that still is at?" Rooster nodded (he knew where it was, had known for years) so Yancey said to Macey, "Give me them bloomers, fool, and quick!" Macey hopped about rushing out of the bloomers, and Yancey snatched them and followed the girl.

By the time he reached her she was far enough away from him to speak and the others not hear. He touched her elbow. She stopped, not turning, and he stepped round to her face and said, "I know you're lying and if I was sheriff you'd be in trouble up to your bare ass. Here, put these on. Keep the ticks out of it." He stuck out the bloomers—which she accepted, not looking at him (she remembered his looks), not speaking a sound. "Now where's that still?" She was folding the bloomers to a neat handful. She did not speak. "You and your Mama want a friend or a enemy in the sheriff's office?" She met his eyes and pointed north. "Far?" he said. She shook her head. "Niggers?" he said. She nodded. "Your kin?" She nodded. He dug in his pocket, found fifty cents, laid it between her unresisting thumb and the cheap white bloomers. "Buy you some candy." Then he looked to where the others waited—the young ones at least. Rooster and Buck were down again, resting, and Ballard was squatting, but Milo and Macey stood guard towards him, Macey two steps ahead of Milo. Yancey found a dollar bill in his pocket, showed it to the girl, said, "Want to make some money for your poor sick Mama?"

"Doing what?" she said.

"Nothing new to you," he said. "You know what I mean?" She did not answer but did not move so he beckoned to the young boys. Macey looked back to Milo and they came on together though Milo stopped again two steps behind. Yancey said to Macey, "How old are you boys?"

"Fifteen—both of us but I'm the oldest."

"Have you ever played the game of ten toes up and ten toes down? If you ain't it's time."

Macey thought, understood, looked back to Milo. "I ain't," he said. "I'm speaking for myself."

Yancey waited for Milo but he would not answer. "Bashful, huh? Well, everybody's got to dive in sometime, and you know what Mr. Russell just said." He said to the girl "How old are *you?*"

"Eighteen," she said.

"Old enough to be drafted," Yancey said. He looked to her bare feet dug in pine straw. "Your toes just turn up naturally, don't they?" She stared at her toes—the big toe did ride high on its neighbor. Yancey handed the dollar bill to Milo, pointed south to where briars and low cedars set up a shield, said, "Take her down yonder. It's all on me and in years to come think of Yancey Breedlove."

Milo studied the dollar, rubbing with his thumbs as if to test it. He looked up to Macey (looked down in fact, Macey being shorter).

Macey smiled. "I'm game if you are, Milo. Always a first time. Nice cool day. Spring water to drink."

"Perfect conditions," Yancey said. "Just don't lie down on your copperhead."

Macey laughed, searched for Milo's answering eyes. They were down on the dollar which he still was rubbing. Then he raised his thumbs. They were faintly green (from veins beneath, from the light off leaves). Smiling, he held out the bill to Yancey—"Yancey, even Niggers can't pass fake money. Your ink is fading. Come on, Macey." He slowly turned and, Macey following, went towards Rooster, and before he was there said, "Sheriff, what was it you been trying to tell me?"

Rooster looked up from his seat on the ground, saw the boy, thought, said, "Oh nothing new. Nothing you hadn't learned."

Milo shrugged and said, "I'm a terrible learner, terrible memory. Ain't it time to hunt?"

They had walked ten minutes when Rooster said "Yancey's pouting" and stopped. The others stopped too and they all looked back to where Yancey stumbled and kicked his loud way, twenty yards behind. Rooster said, "Yancey, come on and walk with us. We ain't contagious—just smell like we are." Yancey stopped where he was and would not look. They waited awhile. Then Rooster led on, whispering to Milo, "Leave him alone. Maybe he'll recover."

"I hadn't done a thing to Yancey, Sheriff."

"I know you hadn't and I ain't neither—I'm his second Daddy. It's that new wife. Never known it to fail—take a boy like Yancey, a good faithful boy that'll follow you around like a puppydog and work round the clock a week at a time (just so you let him blow steam on Sunday), then hitch him to a girl (nine girls out of ten; hitch him permanent, I mean) and in two weeks' time you can look at his face and you'll barely know him. His eyes will be tired, his neck will look broke. What's happened? I'll tell you. I've thought about it a whole lot lately—his pride is ruined. He's caught what he thought he always wanted, was always hunting, what he thought he was working and saving for, training his hair for, washing and shaving for. And what has he got?—if he's lucky, about a hundred and twenty pounds of curly-headed trouble that won't being hunted but was hunting *him*, a free footwarmer for cold winter evenings and a scuttle to haul his ashes in every Saturday night as the years toll by. He'll strut around for a year or so, acting up, showing off, doing every fool thing that comes his way just to claim back a little of what he's lost, what hurts so bad—the notion that somebody *cherished* him but was running from him for fear, and for fun. He don't of course—get none of it back, won't ever, won't *meant* to. And after a while he'll understand or give up trying. Some never do though—"

Macey said, "Are you talking about Yancey?"

Rooster thought. "I may be. I meant to be."

Milo said "My Daddy too."

Rooster said, "Your Daddy. You remember him? Seems like he died fifty years ago."

"Three years," Milo said, "nearly four. Yes sir, I remember. My memory's in my eyes. Anything I ever *see*, I remember."

Buck Russell said, "That's an awful affliction—good eyes, I mean. Near-sighted, night-blind—only way to live."

"That's me," Macey said.

But Rooster said, "Buck, you have said a mouthful. And it's nearly my motto, has to be the motto of every law man otherwise jails would outnumber churches—then where would we be? Hell on earth. No, I tell you boys, my rule in this—if a razor don't flash or a loaded gun, if the fellow can crawl home somehow or other and not get hisself run over or drowned, then leave him alone. Oh scare him a little—let him think he's bound for the electric chair—but remember he's *some* kind of human being and maybe that beating was what his wife needed, maybe that gal just needed that humping to calm her nerves, maybe that moonshine soothes more pain than all the doctors in Warren County." He looked to the sky, flung an open hand to the visible blue—"Roll on, world!" and waited a moment as if for obedience.

Macey said, "I noticed it was waiting for your permission" and Rooster walked on.

Buck said, "And that's how come we've changed course?"

Rooster said, "Yes, I figured you knew, figured everybody knew but poor old Yancey."

"Knew what?" Macey said.

"Hush, fool," Milo said.

Rooster said, "Knew that liquor still was right in the path we was taking before. Been there long as I've known about liquor—twenty, thirty years—and I pure forgot it. I'd have led you all smack into the boiler if Yancey hadn't dragged that gal over to us and she hadn't said Dump Wilson was her Mama, her Grandma maybe. We used to live near Dump when I was little in a house just two cuts better than hers. Main difference was we had a tin roof—and we had the well. Dump came to us for drinking water, and when my Daddy died my poor Mama worked beside Dump in cotton many a year, right down on her knees like a Nigger in the dirt—I did too and will tomorrow if crime should cease—and some of Dump's kin were running this still even then, her brothers or sons or some of her husbands. I've always spared them since I've been powerful so why lead Yancey—hob-nailed—to their business after all these years? That's how come I said hunt together and led us off here. To the best of my knowledge we are passing it now. It's just about there behind them trees." He pointed east and nobody spoke, but nobody stopped—even Yancey behind, baffled, in pain.

They tramped on silently, watching the ground, the upper trees and soon their minds had separated and they went together but secret and alone with whatever private need they were hunting besides the python, the dog, Rato. They of course found nothing they needed or could use, but every few yards a foot would scuff out something worthless and beautiful—a turtle crazily gouging a hole in a spot of sun to lay more eggs (and first frost due within the month) whom Macey flipped to her back and stranded, stacks of brittle mica that Rooster gathered for Kate's mantelpiece, bleached oyster shells from God-knew-where (the sea two hundred miles away) and the wolfish skull of a murdered weasel which Milo paused and lifted to study.

Its globed brain case was cleanly drilled by a perfect hole—bullet or tooth?—and though every uneaten muscle and nerve had been leeched away by months of rain, it was still so fierce in its rigid sym-metry of fissures, foramina, nerve-paths, arches that it seemed to burn, to radiate, and Milo held it at full arm's length to ease its threat, to focus and calm his blurring eyes (the liquor had struck). Then Macey laughed so he brought it to his nose. The stench of its secret clinging life scalded his nostrils, and he said to himself in his new man's voice but silently, "I am drunk like my Daddy the night he was killed, like most of the nights I remember my Daddy—and God will punish me surer than sunrise. Rato will die some awful death out here alone or Death will strike down on us from above or Lois will tell

Papa what I done and what I have started, what I'm aiming at tonight, what I need so bad"—(he saw it, felt it in his groin, his mouth)—"Will slam in my drunk face. Serves me right!" Tears rushed upward in him and he dared not swallow nor blink his brimmed eyes. He drew back the skull and flung it so hard that, striking a tree, it exploded and sent down a flying squirrel like its sudden ghost, web-legged and red, that glided beyond them to earth and vanished.

Macey pretended to chase it though, needing to run after their long rest, and he ran out of sight beyond the others. Still they could hear him—his heavy feet and occasional grunts, his high-pitched calling for "Rato, Rato. Hot-damn, Rato, where are you *at?* Give me a clue, give me something to go on."

They heard a second voice, lower, answer Macey—"How many? Cash money?"—and they heard Macey halt.

Without breaking step Rooster whispered, "Damned if he ain't stumbled on it after all. All my fault, leading you wrong. Been so long I lost my way. Bear left, boys," and they bore left but too late—Rooster looked back at Yancey.

Yancey had heard and understood. He was aimed like an arrow for the hidden voice that came again—"Cash. How many you want?"

So Rooster took hold and did what he must. He headed too for the voice—whoever—and the puzzled others fell in behind.

The voice was a child and the child was black, a boy maybe seven or eight years old, dressed for Sunday in ragged white, stood in the midst of another small clearing, buried to the calf in Mason jars, Macey before him slack-jawed and staring. Rooster said, "All right, Macey. What you found?"

Macey said, "A parrot—can't say nothing but 'Cash' and 'How many?'"

Yancey had come up even and said, "It's a bootlegger, that's what. The youngest bootlegger south of Washington. I knew he was in here—spring water, Hell!" He turned to Milo—Milo was swaying—then back to the boy. "I reckon that's pure spring water you're selling? Well, take along a jar when you go to jail. It'll taste good there."

The boy said "How many?" to Yancey's badge which the sun was on.

Rooster noticed that, unpinned his own badge and dropped it in a pocket, said "Step back, Yancey" in a firmer voice than the previous time. Then he asked the boy, "Who's your Daddy, boy?" The boy looked down at his dozen jars. "I know you didn't make this by yourself or tote it all here. Is Wilson his name?" No look, no answer. "Are you some kin to old Dump Wilson?"

The boy looked up to the sheriff's pocket—the two pin holes where the badge had been, the bulge where it was—and he made the starting grunt of a speech but halted.

Yancey said, "Maybe you some kin to that gal we saw just a little ways back with one of your jars of healing water?" He turned to Macey—"Or maybe he's the scoundrel that was humping that gal when you caught them, Macey?"

Macey narrowed his eyes to examine the boy. "Could be," he said, "Could very well be"—which the boy sustained in patient mystery.

Yancey said, "Then he's under arrest—statutory rape, carnal knowledge of a female minor. Handcuff him, Sheriff—looks dangerous to me."

The boy's black wrists had been in his pockets. He withdrew them now to take what came though he did not extend them, and Rooster reached down and rung one wrist with thumb and finger, tight as steel for a moment. Then he eased his grip but still held the boy and said, "Who are you, boy? What's your name?" The boy shook his head but took pains to leave his wrist with the sheriff.

Yancey said, "Search him. His pockets are full. Probably got pictures of his whole sorry family—his Mama and his Daddy, his sisters and brothers and that hot bitch Macey saw him hunching. All we need—put them *all* in jail. Ought to been there thirty years ago."

Rooster pointed to the Mason jars. "What you selling? You a snake-oil doctor?"

The boy said "How many?" and pointed also.

Rooster said "Two."

The boy said "Cash money?" Rooster nodded so the boy took two jars and gave them to him, then kept out a hand. "Three dollars cash."

Rooster said "Wait," handed one jar to Yancey, then opened his own, filled the lid full of liquor and finding a match, lit the liquid into flame that even by daylight was clear hard blue. "It's pure," he said. "No lead in this. You and your Daddy run a clean still, don't you?"

The boy said "Cash."

Rooster said "Wait," drank off an inch of his private jar and nodded to Yancey. Yancey opened his, turned up and drank, then passed it to Buck and from Buck to Macey, even to Ballard who wet his lips, and then to Milo.

Milo again drank an inch without pausing, and at once it affected his mind and eyes—his eyes, barely open, seemed heavy magnets towards which each sight—person or tree within his clear half-circle of day—flew helpless and raw to wait for his gradual merciless judgment. So he looked on and waited. Time seemed his to bestow like pardon. He bestowed it, silently, saying to himself Rooster's words to the sky—"Roll on."

Rooster rolled on, shut his jar, asked the boy, "I said was you any kin to Dump Wilson?"

The boy said, "You said 'Cash money' too but I don't see none."

Rooster set his jar between his feet, found his black snap-purse and laid three dollars in the boy's ready hand.

The boy neatly folded the money to a wad the size of a peanut shell, stuffed it in his already bulging pocket and then seemed free, seemed twenty pounds lighter, raked every face with a smile as wide as a piano keyboard, rested on the sheriff. "You the Law, ain't you?" Rooster nodded. "I thought you was. That's how come I didn't say nothing but what Daddy told me. But now you bought it, you guilty as me."

Yancey said, "We ain't bought nothing, boy. We loaning you that to pay the electric bill when we electrocute your sorry Daddy."

Macey said, "Shoot, you behind the times, Yancey. We gas them now. That's cheaper still. You'll have about a dollar left over, boy. Buy your naked gal a new set of bloomers."

Yancey said, "No, we still fry Niggers. Can't gas a Nigger. Niggers don't breathe."

The boy's smile had survived—towards the sheriff, not moving off him. Then Rooster said, "Is that right, boy? Niggers don't breathe?"

The boy broke his smile to gasp twice deeply. "Ain't that what you call breathing?" he said.

Rooster nodded.

Yancey said, "Then we can gas you and save juice. Just fry your Daddy. What else can you do besides breathe?"

"Sing," the boy said. "I can sing and dance. You want to watch me?"

Rooster said, "Wait. Where is your Daddy?"

"Gone to church."

Rooster said "What's his name?"

"I just call him Daddy."

"Where's your still at?"

The boy jerked left and almost pointed to the hidden still, then thought and said "You don't know?"

"I got a good guess."

"That's all I got then. I don't know myself. Get lost every time I come back in these old woods." He stamped both bare feet and went to digging fiercely at his thighs—"Snakes and chiggers, they *live* on Niggers" and as he scratched his feet began a shuffle.

Yancey said, "He asked you where the still's at, boy."

Feet still shuffling, the boy looked steadily left to the woods, balanced on the rim of certain betrayal and—for all he knew—maybe jail or death. Then he looked in order at the ones nearest him in height and age—Macey was looking at the older men, hoping to take his expression from them; Milo's eyes were mostly inward since his second drink but still were drawing the day to them, planning no help only waiting to judge. No help, no hope so he looked to his own feet, and slowly the shuffle became his dance, so powerful it shook him, body and arms, and forced from his mouth his notion of music, a quiet low wail broken by smiles and by odd understandable words ("My *Papa*, my *brother*") which flashed like rags of signal through his song—to decoy, deceive, beguile, claim real distress.

They all watched awhile but as minutes passed and the boy continued to imagine and act his unrepeated patterns of chaos, fresh and desperate, Yancey lost patience and said above the singing, "I'm going to break me up a still" and raised his rifle and feinted east, walking towards the trees where the boy's eyes stayed. Macey followed. Yet the dance went on, faster and louder—Buck Russell even clapped time like gunshots—and as Yancey and Macey reached the edge of trees, Rooster told the boy, "All right, you can stop," but the boy still shook, so louder Rooster said "What's your name?"

The wailing died, the boy drew air to surrender at last, but Milo lurched forward and stopped the boy's mouth with his own flat hand, yelling to the boy's eyes, "Don't tell them nothing. They get your name, that's all they want. You and your Daddy and all your brothers and your naked-assed sister will be *under* the jail or building roads the rest of your life."

Yancey and Macey stopped where they were. Yancey retracted some steps and said, "Goddamn. Don't you recognize a joke?"

With both sudden hands Milo shut the boy's ears. "Don't hear no more. *I've* listened last night and all day today, and every damned word they *say* is lies. You think they are out here hunting your still? You're sadly mistaken and so am I. *I* thought they were helping me hunt my brother and his mad dog and a twenty-foot maneating python snake. They ain't, they *ain't*. They are running their filthy mouths, that's all— running away from their moron wives just so they can roam out here and *lie*—telling me about their sorry lives, the mess they have made on other people, asking me to think the world's like this, that they've come this far—sheriff and deputies, badges and guns, blackjacks and jailkeys—on the sense you could stuff in a crab-louse's heel, asking me to think that God Almighty would leave them living, mean as they are, if He anyway cared. Look at them, would you?" He pointed to each— "A sheriff that can't even serve his wife, limber as beeswax soon's he hits the bed; Buck Russell yonder with a half-Nigger son in Raleigh in prison; Yancey Breedlove; Macey Gupton that I've known all my life—" He tried to spit, nothing came. "They have broke my heart. They've done that much. My brother is dying, a snake worth five hundred dollars is loose with a foaming mad dog, and you know where I'm supposed to be?—riding on top of a girl named Lois—and what are we doing? I'm the only one knows—we are looking, hunting for valuable things. Come *on*." He spoke to the boy and tears poured down his cheeks, "Come hunt with me. I don't know your name and I ain't going to ask." He staggered two steps towards the north, the trees. The boy took a step to obey, follow, but Milo bolted to a low briar thicket and spreading his legs and buckling deep, he wretched at the partial cause of his fury as if it were barbed and hooked to his heart.

Rooster said "Wait" to the boy and the others, set down his jar and walked to Milo who was turned from them. He stood back till Milo's rasping stopped, then leaned and said (from behind, not facing him), "Son, I had you figured for a sport. I take it all back. But I can't blame you. I brought it on myself and the Lord let it fall—telling you this morning in sight of a church to do your will anytime it rose. What I left out, what I ought to told you when you asked me was this—when you start prancing, don't step too high. Keep your feet to the ground else you'll be flinging dirt on your own pretty belly not to mention people's eyes or kicking by mistake. You know what I mean?" He moved up and touched Milo's still-bent neck.

Milo said "Leave me alone" and jerked his head, then was shaken by another harsh rising from his belly.

Rooster said, "Son, you have cut me deep but you don't know what you are saying. I forgive you. Soon as you feel up to walking on, we'll find your brother. He can't be far."

Milo hunkered to the ground above his own mess, shook his head to clear it, then said from the ground, "If you're cut so deep, you ain't up to hunting no more than to humping. Go back to bed, I'll hunt my own brother and when evening comes and I lay a-hold of Lois, I'll have up a hard you'd give your little badge for."

Rooster kicked him and he sat in his mess.

Milo looked up slowly and around and faced him—"Am I under arrest?"

"No, but you will be if you keep on many days like today."

"That leaves me tonight then." Milo stood with difficulty, brushed at the seat and sides of his pants and started north again, not looking back. Rooster let him go—they all let him go—and he went ten yards. Then his right leg sank into a rabbit hole, and he fell completely, not fighting the fall, not sparing his face which dug into dirt. Macey ran towards him but when he passed Rooster, Rooster said "Wait, I'm handling this."

Macey stopped but said, "*Handle* it then. He's nothing but a boy— him and me both."

So Rooster went to Milo and knelt by his head. His eyes were shut but his breath was steady. "Son, are you hurt?"

"I'm dying," Milo said. "Least I feel like I am, wish I was."

Rooster said, "You'll live but listen to me—you better let me send you home in the car and we'll hunt on."

Milo said, "*Home?*—and me drunk as my Daddy ever got? Rooster, you're sick. You're crazy, friend. I'll lie right here till the Lord forgives me."

"We can't wait for *Him.*" Rooster thought a moment. "Listen, here's my plan—first thing I'll do is beg your pardon (I don't know for what but I'm on my knees, begging), then I'll call Yancey here and give him the keys and you and him walk back out to the car and drive to Warrenton and leave that liquor at my house, hear? We'll be hunting and you'll be sobering, and when you get back we'll meet you and Yancey at the old Ryden place." Milo opened one eye but was silent. "You hear what I say?" Milo nodded (his chin plowed dirt). "Do you take my advice?" No nod, no word. Rooster laid a hand on Milo's back—drunk as he was, sick and filthy, emptied for now of his hurt and meanness, it was still the back of a prime dray-horse, as lean of fat as a walnut table. Rooster bent towards his ear and whispered, "You be the chaperone of Yancey—hear?—when he sees my wife. At heart she's younger than him if that's possible. You ready now?" Milo thought, smiled and Rooster turned—"Yancey, come here."

Though they walked out a straighter way than they came (in total silence) and drove in silence at eighty miles an hour, it was still as late as four o'clock when Yancey stopped on the far edge of town by a squat Dutch oven of a house, weathered gray, not a leaf of shade, dead morning glories roasting by the door on a stringwork trellis. Milo looked to test his eyes. They saw clearer now despite the pounding so he turned to Yancey to offer amends, thumbing to the house—"Is that all the house old Rooster can afford? Shoot, that ain't a cage for a sick killdee much less the hot wife I hear he's got."

Yancey killed the motor but left in the keys. Then he unpinned his badge, laid it on the seat and slid out the door. He slammed it and leaned through the window towards Milo. "It ain't Rooster's house. It's

Yancey Breedlove's and you're mighty right—it's every damned cent poor Yancey can afford and his hot new wife is in yonder now, lying on her belly on the dirty daybed reading funny papers and frying in the heat. Well, I'm heading in to turn her over and fry her some on the other side—which'll take me the rest of the afternoon. She's a slow damn cooker but the walls is asbestos so don't you worry, and you tell Rooster that I ain't coming back not today nohow, that here's my badge and my rifle's in the trunk and I wish him luck, and if he wants me back on the force Monday morning, to come around here after eleven a.m.—I'll wake up then—and beg my pardon and offer me at least a five-dollar raise." He drew back, rounded the front of the car, aimed for his house and had reached the porch before Milo could speak.

"What about me and the sheriff's liquor?"

Yancey smiled from the top of the steps. "You such a big man— deliver it yourself. You can drive, can't you?"

"Sure but I hadn't got a driver's license."

"Well, I'm still the Law and I give you permission. Drive on in peace." Yancey waved a hand.

"Yeah, but where am I headed? Where's the sheriff's wife *at?*"

Yancey sniffed at the air, then pointed upwards. "Smell that?" he said. Milo sniffed—some distant burning, rank and stinging. "That's her," Yancey said. "Just a bitch in heat. So follow your nose but don't fall in." He turned and vanished through a rusty screen door.

Milo called "Yancey!" but did not repeat it. The house already seemed derelict and falling. He sat a minute to confirm his solitude, then slid to the wheel, cranked the engine and smiling, sniffed the air a second time before he rolled. He would ask directions from the first passing Negro.

The sheriff's house was no bigger than Yancey's, but it stood on a mild rise of ground, was white and had had some grass till the August drought. Beside it was an open lot deep in weeds, and staked out there near the side of the house was a fat tan cow and a gallon hand-crank ice-cream freezer that the cow was licking. Not a flower in sight except goldenrod, not a clothesline, outside washing machine, freez-erlocker nor any other sign that a woman lived here and waited inside, but when Milo had sat a good three minutes and no face had shown at window or door, he reached to the foot for his Mason jars. As he rose he caught his face in the mirror—streaked with tears—but he said to himself, "I can call it sweat if anybody asks" and did not notice his other dirt. He stepped to the ground and started the climb to porch and door.

He knocked four times and stood back to wait. Nobody came and no sound came through the open windows. He would knock once more but first he tensed his feet in his shoes, alerted his toes to sense vibrations in the soft wood floor. Rock, or so it seemed, bed-rock—floor, house, cow, still air. He turned and heavily walked to the steps and faced the opposite lower houses, equally still. He thought of something he had read in the paper—that a human body is nearest to death the instant before it is forced to yawn. Milo yawned and thought he would shout to the street "Yawn!" but a car scraped round the corner below him, the street caught breath and a black Chevrolet-load of boys tore forwards. He saw at once it was no one he knew nor had seen at school, but seeing him the car slowed and stopped and a squirrel-faced boy maybe eighteen leaned out—"How much you charging, sport?" Milo frowned, not understanding. "For your white lightning, buddy? I can't use *you*."

Milo stared at his jars. "This is nothing but pure spring water," he said, trying to whisper and still make it carry, "and this is the sheriff's house, I warn you." He pointed behind him, then raised that finger to his lips for silence.

"It's also the sheriff's *wife's* house, Ham-hock. When he ain't home she charges two dollars and sometimes—if the wind's blowing right—she'll take it out in trade, don't you know?" The boy wet his index finger loudly and shoved it up Indian-style to the wind. "Just right," he said. "But you got water, huh? Hang on to it then. It puts out fires—and you're smoking already, just standing on her porch." Another boy, hidden, sailed out a high laugh that even struck the cow—she threw up her head, upset her freezer—and the car whined away.

Milo saw himself, in no glass except his own clear mind, jerked sober by a laugh—a grown boy old enough to be a father (could have had a baby more than two years old) yet offering himself to public view on a peaceful Sunday in green army pants, a blue workshirt (both stained and stinking with spew), face filthy, hair matted, waiting in borrowed underwear for a woman he had never laid eyes on before to hand her two jars of bootleg liquor made in the woods by high-hat Negroes—and his brother roaming desperate not five miles away maybe wounded, dead. He walked like a hunting cat to the door, set the jars there in Mrs. Pomeroy's path and was standing to leave when he saw a thing he had previously missed, the day being bright—to his right, hip-level, was a dim orange light the size of a dime. He bent to see it and saw it was a plastic button, lit behind, and beneath it on the wood were these words in pencil—

> *In case of emergency day or night*
> *Press this light*
> *Direct hookup to sheriff's bedroom*
> *Be right with you*
> *Thank you for your cooperation*
> > *Rob Pomeroy*

Milo stood and as clearly as he had just seen his own shameful self, saw Rooster Pomeroy rise in a vision from that bell light as if from a jug upward like fume, shedding hat, pistol, badge, all clothes as he formed and rose to float buck-naked on the Sunday air, pink-skinned, blue-veined, sparsely tufted with limp white hair, a firm low belly deeply dimpled where it shelved above his groin—a shed to guard his prized possessions, a mother brooding on his nest of squabs doomed not to rise, to wither unfledged—and on his round face a helpless smile directly at Milo. Milo smiled back, even pointed to the jars, said to Rooster (but silently), "Two quarts of liquor isn't no emergency, I've set them down and am heading back to help you," but Rooster's smile went frantic and opened—"No, *press* that bell. Son, help me *here*. Son, rescue the Rooster!" Milo laughed aloud, said aloud "Saved by the bell!" licked his broad thumb and jammed the button till the back of the house hummed like a hive and the soles of his feet took the coming steps.

The door swung open before he was ready—he stood too close (six inches from the screen), his actual laugh hung on unfinished at the rims of his mouth—and there stood a woman, more nearly a girl, in a pink bathrobe, huge black eyes eye-level to him for the instant it took her to see Milo pressed close, half-laughing. Then her lips pursed and gasped like a fish for air, then smiled, said "Oh!" One hand opened, reached towards him in greeting. Then she folded to the floor like a well-oiled hinge.

Milo leapt back and said, "Lady, I'm your husband—*from* your husband, I mean. Whatever I am, get up—I'm harmless." He had whispered it fiercely, but if he had shouted she still would have lain in her compact heap—he stepped to the screen and saw she was out, fainted or dead. He turned for help to the empty street, the opposite houses, but the same black car had also turned and was bound down on him, slowly now, intending to stop. So he reached for the china knob of the screen. It opened, he rushed in, straddled the body, took her by the wrists and dragged her back three feet, then slammed the wood door and fell against it. He could hear two things—his pulse in his ears and the same boy's voice from the car outside, "Go easy, sport. She'll grind you to dust," then the same high laugh as the car drove on.

Milo said to himself, "She's ground her last. Now what must I do?"—and in fact no visible atom moved; even her wild black curls were still—"Drive back and hunt up the sheriff and say, 'Sheriff, your wife fell dead at my feet before I could even give her my name. You never told me she had a weak heart'?" Macey's favorite joke clattered through his ears—girl says to boy "Oh, honey, my *heart*;" boy says to girl, "Never mind your heart, hang on to your *hat!*" He said "Lord forgive me," then went to her head and knelt in hope of faint signs of life.

Since he had dragged her she lay nearly straight—only her legs were folded to the right beneath her robe, her face was profiled and her arms were hooped above her head—but she still volunteered no visible breath. If life was there, burning inward—banked—he must hunt it out, hunt pulse or heart. He rocked to his buttocks to brace himself—just a week before in health class at school they had felt their own pulses; it had taken Milo a good while to find his and when suddenly it humped out as if from ambush, he yelled in the room, then laughed with the others but secretly tasted terror for an hour (and since, in memory). Her left wrist was nearer. Still reared back, he took it and turned it till the cords of gristle, the sunk purple veins struck his eyes like a shout. He knelt on though, bent closer, stared and daring a finger, lightly traced the path of a scar, still pink, ruthlessly straight for two full inches through all that tangle like an ideal route, the shortest way. Then his finger probed for the pumping blood. If it was there it shrank from him. Yet her flesh was warm and her joints were free, showed no threat of stiffening. He would strike for the source, seek her heart. He gently laid her wrist on the floor, more gently laid his own straight fingers above her heart on the cloth of her robe and gently pressed.

She whispered "Tom" and her whole trunk shuddered, shoulders buckled inward, rolled left, relaxed—leaving two of Milo's fingers stranded on the slope of her left breast exactly half-bared where her robe had gapped to beyond its crest that was stained the color of one blackberry crushed in milk. Milo shut his eyes. He had seen something new—in person, at least; by touch, at least. Oh of course he had seen magazine photographs—the *National Geographic* at school— and a book Macey bought when their class went to Raleigh for the legislature (women like gourd vines) and then hot Phyllis and her girls at the fair (hot as fruit Jello and about as thrilled) but not a bare *woman* whose name he knew and beneath his own hand the first time out (by the time he had been old enough to remember his mother bathing, the breasts he had nursed had been dug at by Rato and Rosacoke till they hung like bladders at hogkilling, full; and even Lois on Friday night had kept on her shirtwaist, he aiming elsewhere in the time they had). His eyes stayed shut but his fingers stayed still though the bones shivered. She had spoken and moved but was she awake and were her eyes open? That was the next ordeal to meet. He met it, looked. She was still sealed against him, but leaning to see, he shifted balance and laid new weight on his three touching fingers. She murmured again, "Tom, look. I have waited; I have met you at last" and shuddered, rolling back rightward, gown closing slightly.

It had closed over Milo's hand still there and hid it to the wrist in its new resting place, for it did rest now—he had clamped his teeth, tensed his neck but surrendered his whole hand, heel and palm, to the shielding service she seemed to demand, sought in her sleep. He guarded her heart or told himself so, but it beat so far beneath his cupping that he could not filter its thuds from his own. Still the woman was alive and warm, and he—content. He knew that slowly, felt calm rise from his hidden hand to numb all fear but also desire. He was tired (he had slept very little lately, had only just struggled from his first shameful drunk), and this seemed rest—to sit above a sleeping woman, her black hair crowding about his knees, who trusted him enough to sleep, to take his guarding. Thinking of sleep, he fought to stay awake but only half-succeeded. He began to rock above her mildly like a well-anchored boat, and in another minute his mind was blank so that when his thumb of its own accord began to flick across the hump of her breast, it stirred him no more than rubbing a child or the clustered grapes at the head of his bed, walnut and smooth (which even now he would reach back to rub when he could not sleep), and it did not notice her various risings, her nipple's quick budding, the slower strengthening of her heart.

But he rubbed her awake. Her brown eyes clicked open, upward, backward. He did not think to remove his hand nor to stop his thumb. He smiled broadly at her (knowing she saw him upside down and would not notice a gentler greeting), leaned to within eight inches of her face, said, "Lady, my name isn't Tom. Wish it was but it isn't and I am sorry. Believe me, I'm sorry from the bottom of my heart."

She said "Oh!" again and though she was prone, sank deeper even than at the door.

"Well, damn," he said and sat back from her, noticing then what his hand had done, holding it out for thorough inspection, then quickly raising and dropping his brows, pouting his wide amazed lips as he gave it a grin of pride and envy. Then he said, still aloud, "If I'm this ugly, knocking ladies out, I better get me an operation, trade in my face on an easier model. I've certainly sunk this helpless soul—two times now; three times, you're drowned." He thought of remedies—spirits of ammonia—but thought he had done enough already, could hardly afford to ransack the house hunting ammonia. He thought of the jars that waited on the porch. If it cured Dump Wilson's private misery (and drove himself crazy, just two clear inches), then surely if he barely wet her lips, she would come to and welcome him normally, hear his name and simple business?

He went to the door, opened it carefully, checked the street for cars or walkers, then took up the jars and was safe inside. But seeing from there the poor sprawled woman, he thought, "She'll drown if I dose her there. I got to prop her up. Where? Against the wall?" A wall was the only prop in the hall as bare as a blighted chestnut. The bedroom would be that door at the back (the bell had rung there), but her robe still gapped too freely to risk it—Rooster *was* sheriff even if he couldn't stir tapioca with the tools he had). Milo looked directly right—a sitting room, a brown couch and pillows. So he went there and set the jars on a table by a thick white mug, empty of coffee but the spoon still in it, and piled three pillows on an arm of the couch. Then he tipped to the woman, knelt again, lifted her so easily he shivered in surprise, never having lifted a woman before, and took her to the couch and laid her there, arranging her robe in case of visitors. Then he unscrewed Rooster's jar—the fuller one—and licking dried coffee off the spoon from the mug and tilting the jar, dipped out a level portion of liquor. He crowded her gently back with his butt, sat by her waist, raised her head with the crook of his arm and prying her lips with his thumb, poured it through her teeth (her teeth were short, nearly square like a baby's but were white and dry and bit as perfect as the jaws of a trap), then followed it at once with a second spoonful.

She frowned and groaned but her throat slowly swallowed, and her eyes were seared open—again on him where he sat beside her, cradling her head. She stared till the liquor had struck her stomach, then she said, "How come you have dyed your hair?"

He set down the spoon and roughed his hair. "I hadn't," he said. "It was born this color. Maybe the sun has bleached me a little but—"

She shook her head. "It was red as a penny. And you look so *young*."

"Lady, I *am* young but I'm eating and growing. Now let me tell you this but don't be scared—for God's sake don't pass out again (I ain't a doctor)—my name isn't what you think it is."

She raised a quick hand and stopped his mouth, nodding as she said, "I understand. I won't ask questions." Then she sat upright and turned to face him, touched his shoulders with the ends of her fingers, ran down the length of his arms to his hands—they were open. She stopped there. "What are you running from this time, Tom?" Tears large as peas fell on their joined hands.

Milo met her eyes, which was no easy meeting, but he did not answer. He thought, "Two things—she is crazy or drunk. Whichever one, I can see she's in misery deep over her head. You don't get eyes like that from laughing. I owe *somebody* one decent thing to pay for all my mess since Friday. Let it be her. Let me be what she needs." He pressed her hands. "I'm standing still now—and I brought you this." He nodded towards the liquor. She would not take her eyes off him, seemed to be feeding or drinking off him like a famished mare that will not raise her head from water, once found, for any cause other than thunder or lightning. He was neither one so he looked away, inspected the room. "Nice place you got."

That broke her stare. She saw the room she had seen for ten years and wondered again how she had lasted it (Rooster was how—his red heart's blood)—nine feet by fifteen, beaverboard walls the color of liver, low ceiling, one card table with an old radio in the shape of a church window, one green easy chair by the open window as swollen as if it were dying of dropsy (the window curtainless), one ladderback chair with sideposts like spears, a coffee table with lions feet, the couch they were on and on an endtable beside the couch her two wedding presents—from Rooster an electric clock dead accurate that marked time as if it were grinding grist, quiet but endless; and the lamp from her parents. She pointed to that. "*That's* nice," she said. "That's all I like." The base of the lamp was blue mirror glass cut and laid in a winding upward stairs around the pole; the shade was darker blue and was spangled with dozens of gold foil stars, some of them already peeling at the prongs. "Stairway to the stars—get it?" she said.

"Yes," Milo said.

"All the balance could burn down tonight. I wouldn't shed a tear."

Yet more tears fell onto Milo's hands (his hands rode hers now). "You wish that on poor Rooster, do you? Death by fire?—little sleep as he gets?"

"No, I don't," she said. "He has saved my life one time already and may have to again any day. My precious life. That's more than you done."

"You're right," he said. "Still I nursed you when you fainted just now, brought you in here, got you comfortable. I swear I never knew I was such a shock. I'm taking plastic surgery early next week."

She smiled but said, "You still ain't told me what you're running from *now.*"

He knew he must decide—to stand, beg her pardon, say his name and leave or to follow her further, one lie on another, towards whatever gift she would finally ask. But maybe she would ask for something he could give—something painless, harmless, free—so he said, "*You* know, my same old trouble—prancing too high, kicking up mess in somebody's face, then clearing out till the dust can settle."

She said, "I won't ask that somebody's name, but looks like most of the mess hit you." She meant his clothes. She had noticed them.

"Generally does," he said. "That's life."

"Oh it's life," she said, "but it ain't *living.* Take off your clothes. I got to go wash them. You can't go nowhere looking like that. They'll know you right off."

"I hadn't got time—" He paused for her name but it would not come. Rooster had said it once but he had forgot.

"*Make* time," she said. "It won't take long. I can dry them in the oven."

"And I just sit around naked while you do? What if some company walked in and saw me?"

"*Company?*" she said. "Listen, if somebody walks through that door, it'll be Rob or the undertaker to get my body or a ghost out of Hell. That poor door hadn't been knocked in ten years and Rob's poor bell—when it rung just now, I thought it was Judgment. That's why I fainted—that and seeing your face so close, laughing like thirteen years hadn't passed, hadn't pressed you no more than a feather quilt."

"They *hadn't,*" he said and stood before her, leaving her hands. "Thirteen years ago I was nothing but a child. But I have learned things. Thirteen years ago I was lonesome as the moon, but people come to me now." He extended both arms like wings beside him, flapped once silently, rose (on his toes but as if on air), and still drew her eyes though his own looked upward—"People need me now since I'm a man."

His arms stayed up, trembling with the strain, so she stood and began to unbutton his shirt (the two top buttons), then stopped and said, "They always did. You just notice it now but it's nothing you've learned. Don't fool yourself. It's a gift from God." He made a ring of his thumbs and forefingers and lowered it over his head like a halo, rapidly blinking worshipful eyes. She rolled out a laugh like a spool of thread, thin and cutting, which reeled itself in and thickened to a moan. "You got to understand that, believe that," she said. "Believe me, Tom, I have told you before. I know what I say—you have got powers. You could heal the sick, ease troubled minds, draw poison from sores. How come you don't?" She reached to his head where his hands rested now, took one by the wrist and laid it on her own head, bowed, eyes shut.

He waited a moment, allowing what power there might be to flow, then whispered, "Honey, you are welcome to it—all five fingers—but I ought to warn you, it ain't going to work. It won't even cure a fever blister, not to speak of troubled minds."

Yet she stood on beneath its mild weight another minute, eyes still clamped, teeth clenched but rattling. Then he took back his hand, and she opened her eyes, raised her head and said, "My mind is eased. I told you. I told you. I been waiting for this thirteen years, Tom." She held out her own left wrist between them (the wrist where he had hunted her pulse). "Ease this," she said and he did what he had done in her sleep—traced a finger down the route of her scar, down, back. She grasped his hand. "Ease *this*," she said and thrust it to the lapping V of her robe, left it there flat in the trough of her chest. Her eyes shut again, her head rocked back, rolled limp on her shoulders.

He said "Peace."

She said "*Peace*. Tom, give me peace. You owe me that."

Was that her demand, the final gift he was called to give? Final or not, it seemed in his power—in the moment he wondered, it became his desire. His fingers moved of their own accord, honest not stealthy, spread the neck of her robe, took their previous seat above her heart which was also her breast that drooped slightly now because she stood. His hand moved on to lift that droop, then pressed, then rested, waiting for his previous calm to rise. The calm did not.

She said again "Thank you," stood straight and smiled, then stepping sideways, slid from his hand as if from a spear—it hung on an instant—and walked to the door. "Now give me your clothes—keep your underwear—and go take a bath. The bathroom is yonder through our bedroom." She pointed, not looking, towards the back of the hall.

He saw himself again, thought of explaining the mess to his mother and started undoing the rest of his shirt buttons. He carried it to her. She took it, looked away. He untied his shoes, unbuttoned his pants and stood in Rato's underwear, staring out the window at a child in the road—a girl at least ten, maybe eleven, long straw hair, long bones, blue dress, writing with her finger on Rooster's dusty car. Writing what, thinking what, seeing what now as she turned and stared directly at the window he stood behind? He did not retreat but he lowered a hand to cup his groin, harmless as it now seemed, lazed in the heat of the low small room, the afternoon. The woman came, took his pants from the floor and left him alone.

He had never bathed in a tub before, never covered all his body with warm water (never with cold except when he and Macey had swum in creeks or on church picnics at Mason's lake or at his baptizing) so the bath he had drawn had been deep and scalding, and he had lain sunk maybe fifteen minutes, floating his arms, his heavy head, eyes shut (feeling his hair snake clean behind him, feeling through drowned ears the poor woman's steps in the opposite kitchen). He had lain and thought, "I must think about her," but eyes still shut and the water not cooling, he had only managed one thought of her—"Maybe this isn't the sheriff's house" (forgetting the bell); "Poor Rooster, if it isn't"—when he pictured Lois Provo instead. Fully dressed—he had not seen her otherwise. And when he had mildly strained to strip her picture, he had left himself with only her head—he had not seen the rest (having touched what he had touched in darkness), and what he had not seen he could not imagine. So he had opened his eyes, raised his hot neck to study what he could see—his own sunk body. Even to him it seemed carved and pressed from two kinds of lean wood—hands, arms, neck and face (which were bare to the sun all summer in the field) of walnut or cherry and shoulders, chest, belly, legs (which were always covered) of white pine, unstained but haired with tight coils of gold. He had plowed one finger from throat to groin and freed a line of small milky bubbles and looking closer had seen that he wore a whole skin of bubbles, clung to his true skin, to every hair like a loving armor and had thought again, "Things come to *me*," then he swayed himself shoulder to hip to shed them. The bubbles had clung. Only his limber handle had danced—left, right—at the pit of his belly. Hands still floating, he had stared at that, had smiled and said aloud, "Calm down, son. It's still afternoon. I got to find Rato, Phillip and Death before I can think about feeding you—but oats it'll be when nighttime comes! That's a promise, son." Its swaying had already stilled by then—it had lain left and rested, floating in no need of calm or soothing speeches. Drowsed as he was with heat not liquor, he had noticed that, had smiled and spoke again, "This *is* Rooster's house and looks like Rooster's trouble is catching." He had seized it in his fist, gritted his teeth, exhorted it as if it were a coward in battle, "Cephas, arise! We got puddings to stir, wounds to heal, hearts to ease. You got *powers*, son. You can ease the world and the world is waiting—listen!" He had listened and heard two things, out of reach—the chink of the cow's chain among the weeds, the poor woman washing for him in the kitchen. "Cephas, you have only begun to fight!" He had stretched it up to twice its length, then released it suddenly to stand alone as his present and future banner of triumph. It had settled lazily into hot water, floated like the butt of a soft old log half-sunk for years. Then he had felt that his heart barely beat—only twitched in his breast like a frail metal thread stretched thinner, thinner—and had realized with what mind was left that the heat had struck, had secretly drained his once-proud standard, his clear hard mind and was reaching for his heart to silence that.

So he had stood with difficulty, stepped from the high tub and clinging weakly to walls, doors had staggered dripping into the bedroom. He had stopped in the middle and extended his arms, no longer as wings but as boneless props against walls and floor that buckled and heaved, as rudders to right him. But the whirl had begun. Blood had instantly chilled and funneled to his feet, head had roared vacantly, ears had filled with tissue paper above whose crackling he still had heard two solid things but rapidly fleeing—the cow, the woman—and had opened his mouth to ask their help but knowing he was naked, had shielded again his shrinking handle and surrendered alone to what seemed death, a rocking, a leaning, a final fall. But had landed sprawled on the unmade bed which was Rooster Pomeroy's cross to bear and had thought as his last thoughts on entering night, "I am costing Rooster his precious badge, dying here, and my own mother will perish with shame—when I never intended to harm a soul. How come I'm punished, so young and harmless?"

So that when she had laid his clean clothes in the oven, washed her face at the sink and in a hand mirror, arranged her hair, bit color to her lips, she came to the bedroom door and listened, and hearing no noise of water or drying, she pushed the door which was only half-shut, and he struck her across twelve feet of space—the shape of thirteen years' hope and need, waiting simply. She stood on that far, one hand on the door, thinking he would hear or feel her presence and rise, shamed or ready. He did not hear (he was whirling on down), but blinded and weak, he did feel her gaze, accept her hopes and turn them in his mind to a momentary dream—Lois at last, clear in perfect nakedness, waiting on a porch as he moved towards her, answered her smile, extended his open hands to hers and heard her say, "I have been afraid, waiting in the dark. I have kept my promise. Why have you failed? You said you would come to me long before night." He answered, "Night? It is still clear day" but looking up saw it was really night, that the light was from her, her readiness, so he said, "I am sorry. I was tending to duties but now I am here and look, I am ready."

She walked towards the bed, stooping for his flung-off underclothes, and stood by the edge folding them neatly as his dream became his visible force, as his heart restored new blood to his limbs and his sleeping senses crouched to wake so that when he woke he saw two things as clear as his dream but solid and in reach—above him, the woman washed and younger (and though healed, wilder), loosening now the cord of her robe; and on himself cresting up his belly at last like an emblem earned by his youth, his joy, given (by whom? by the clear day itself) for his generous use of healing powers, in this room rare as the unicorn—a ready horn, his one-eyed son, prodigal returned.

He spoke to it first, "Welcome home, old son. I thought you were *gone*. Kill the fatted calf!" Then he looked to her, moving only his eyes, not rising from the sheets—"You be the calf," he said and blushed to the breast bone. "I thought we was both gone, him *and* me. Lady, your tub is a killer but look, I lasted, *we* lasted." He looked down again. They had more than lasted, had come from the bath another size grander, another new man. Then back to her, "I'm too young to die, too pretty and harmless. I must have been spared for a wonderful purpose. Maybe I've got them powers you mentioned—reckon I have?" She nodded but did not smile nor move forward, did not touch the long bared stripe of her body—from crown to sole ten inches wide a map in relief of unknown countries (well, once-known; by night), colored like no other map he had seen: black, white, milky berry, white again, oh black again. Marking whose possessions?—was all that Rooster's, every hill, valley, bottomless gorge? His if he fed and guarded them daily. He could not see all from where he lay but he lay on, prone. "I've almost eased your troubles," he said.

"How do you know I ain't all healed?"

"Eagle eyes," he said—he flickered his eyes, then left them shut—"and various pieces of signal equipment." He raised his arms above his chest, oared them as if taking delicate signals—all of him oared, till he slowly rose from the waist still blind and oared before him till he brushed her arm, slid down to her hand. Then he looked.

"Who are you?" she said.

"I'm a boy," he said.

"I figured that," she said, still not smiling. "No, who are you?"

Now he held both her hands and knelt before her, his knees on the mattress. "Tell me somebody's name you expected."

"You know," she said.

"Well, I'm him," he said. "Just Tom," he said. He gave the mildest pull to her hands, and she gave in smiling, like the side of a dry hill after first rain, that slowly, entirely, having waited thirteen years, accepting the name he had finally offered, a name which seemed no lie to him but the gift he had meant (and now wanted) to give, which any Tom alive—young enough, brave enough—would freely have given.

He did Tom's spadework for half an hour, never dismounting, hardly pausing, and took Tom's pay (Tom and Rooster's)—thirteen years of back pay with interest paid down sweetly in five installments but silently. (Her last words had been "You know," then eyes and mouth sealed and she only breathed.) Then he did pause in saddle, not from exhaustion—body had thirstily obeyed each order, having waited nearly as long as she, and still stood and waited; his belly and groin still cradled a lake, tapped but bottomless. He paused for the heat and lay perfectly still, her as his mat, face in her hair that was wild again, hoping to cool but feeling only—in the ebb of joy—an acid bond of sweat between them. He stiffened his arms, raised his head to see a clock in the room. There was no clock so he guessed the time by the weight of the air—past five o'clock, the desperate minutes before the sun loses, as it threatens not to. Past five o'clock, his prime hunting hours all but gone, and what did he have to show for his day?—a woman beneath him firm as a horse and as ready to run but crazy maybe and without the manners to say even "Thank you" or ask his true name and look to watch his broad back, working. He rose a little higher and looked down his chest, his belly to their joint, thought to himself, "I am firm as a fiddle and lady, I've played you some lovely tunes but I ain't no Tom. I've done Tom's work—and was glad to get it—but I'm somebody else and I want you to know it before I leave to save my brother." Then he saw her face—flushed and wet and so calm that he could not consider blurting his name and claiming his rightful recognition. But her face was so closed—"She is locked in behind them eyes with Tom. This has all been a homecoming party for Tom and I'm not aiming to break up her party so I'll *be* Tom but who the Hell's Tom? I got to find out and I'll dig to find it."

He dug awhile, deeper and slower than before. She bent with the spade and soon her breath was thinning, quickening so he dug on still deeper (she was years and years deep), one stroke faster than her shallow panting till she drew a long breath and spilled over into a string of little moans by slowing and slightly shortening his dig, and when he had her on the verge of blooming, he said in her screened ear, "Tell me if you're happy."

"Mmmm," she said.

"No, say a word. You can whisper, I'll hear you."

"Yes," she said.

"Is it me makes you happy?"

"Yes," she said.

He spaded on but slower. "Me and who else?"

"Just you," she said.

"Just me," he thought and he threw her such a promise from the hip that she hiccuped. "Not sixteen yet and no driver's license but can't I drive? — I'm the driver of the century, pilot and jockey thrown in to boot. Wrong-way Mustian but I've found the way!" He had thought that not said it, and he eased a moment to taste the honey banked in his thighs but soon realized that joy was not knowledge — he was still in the dark — so he started again so slowly so sweetly and whispered, "Just *me?* I ain't that conceited now. Me and who else?"

"Just you," she said.

"Who am I?" he said.

"Silly — you know."

"I don't," he said. "I have hunted for you so long and hard — halfway round the world and back, I have lost my memory."

"That's all you've lost."

"Thank you," he said, "but who am I?"

"Tom," she said.

"And who are you?"

"Kate Pemberton — I was anyhow when I first knew you."

"Where was that?"

"In jail," she said. "Remember now?"

"I'd forgot that too." He was moving still. She was answering in the gap between breaths. "What had you done?" he said.

"It was you," she said. "That child you stole."

He had not intended to lose control, but he was fifteen and all he had was strength not skill so in the silence that followed her words, he dug on in rhythm and before he could open his mouth to laugh, his spade had forced her into bloom, slow but huge, and much to his own surprise, he followed with a sturdy sprout of his own that branched and leaved upward within her into warm white life—to fade and fall with gradual speed, leaving him the sense of loss for a while, the witness of death where delight had stood.

They both were still, his eyes were open, his cheek in her hair, but what he saw was his brother plainly—eight years before, Rato's first day of school, his own second year. He was drawing a ship awhile before lunch when the class door opened on Rato, escaped and in silent tears, searching twenty faces for his brother. The teacher said, "Can I help you, son?" Rato shook his head and went on searching, and he himself laid his head on the desk, praying no one would yell that Rato was his. But hid as he was, he saw Rato and knew from his fumbling hands his distress—stiff new overalls he could not unhook. Milo knew his own duty clearly as now (to stand, claim Rato, lead him to pee), but he left him to stand till the stain began and spread down his leg to his bare foot and watched him turn and leave. And at six years old though he couldn't do buttons, Rato could walk five miles and find home—which he would not leave again for weeks nor speak his brother's name till Christmas—Christmas morning he mumbled "Thank you" for a celluloid statue of Popeye and Milo himself said, "Rato, thank *who?*"—"Thank you, *Milo*" (the *Milo* was whispered).

He was shrunk now and separate so he rolled off and lay ten inches from her, facing the ceiling. His right hand searched the floor by the bed, found her robe and his underwear (Rato's underwear). He wadded it, left his hand on the floor and facing the woman, took her eyes once more and spoke in the voice he thought was harmless. "My name is Milo and, Lady, I'm not but fifteen yet so I'm grateful to you, but this ain't why I'm here at all. The sheriff sent me in with some liquor he found while we were hunting my brother in the woods. Now I got to go back. But I thank you again and I beg your pardon. I lied—but didn't you want me to?" She nodded, smiled. "You knew all along?"

"I knew you *thought* you were lying," she said. "I ain't sure you were. I believe in ghosts. You could still be him—years ago, before I saw him."

"Maybe I am. Hell, I'm several dozen people a day. So people tell

me—my sister, my mother. Always telling me, 'Milo, behave. Act natural. Act your age. You're still a child. Don't act so big—you ain't a
baby. Calm down. Cheer up. Be yourself. Try to change. You're acting more like your Daddy every day.' Who was he? Tell me."

"Your Daddy or Tom?"

"Well, either one. No, Tom, I mean."

"That's too long a story."

"How long?" he said.

"I don't even know the beginning or end, but my part alone takes
thirteen years."

He paused to feel the time again—the heat focused on them by
the black tin roof—and felt slight relief, nothing like a breeze but at
least the news that the day was broken, twenty past five. "Tell me the
first ten minutes," he said. "Then I got to hunt."

"You been hunting," she said, "for the last half-hour. More ways
than one to hunt in this world."

"My brother, I mean."

"You'll find him," she said. She smiled, looked down. "You got a
built-in compass—look."

He looked and he did, of its own accord. "You don't know much
about compasses then—he's pointing due-south. A compass points
north."

"He's pointing to you."

He said, "Do you blame him? Wouldn't you point at me if *you* had
me?"

She rolled to her right side, facing him, nearer. "Yes," she said.

"Then *point*," he said to her side-drooping breasts, her leaning
belly, and threw his dropped hand which laid her flat and pulled him
in one unbroken move to his left side, his knees, then high astride
her—his knees in her arm pits, his tight butt settled in her wiry fork.
Her arms reached out to draw him down. He seized her wrists,
pinned them behind her head to the pillow. "Tell me ten minutes of
your story, please ma'm. Then I'll give you your final treatment and
leave." He freed her arms, rocked back to listen.

She began to tell it to the shaded window. "Thirteen years ago
when I was your age—or one year younger—I was pretty and as for-

ward in my growth as you. I had eyes, I knew it, and boys at school passed me all sorts of notes—poems, drawings. They understood what was happening in me and acted like dogs round a bitch in heat—as best they could at fourteen or fifteen. But I flung them off like summer flies. I was aiming to find my equal in the world, and also I had a job after school so I had no friends and lived to myself. My job was helping my mother and father. They were jailers—my Daddy still is, here, now—and my mother did the cooking and cleaning for the jail, which was also our home. We lived downstairs, the prisoners overhead—what few there were, old drunks asleep or rarely a maniac waiting for a vacancy at the asylum and locked up with us, having no other home or bed to wait in—and what Mother cooked, I delivered on trays—good country vegetables, corn bread, gravy. My Daddy went with me to chaperone or if Daddy's back was bad, a deputy—and though we ran the nicest jail in South Carolina (number-10 cans of red geraniums in every cell window), I hated my life like a snake wrapped round me, choking me, shaming me—young as I was, unseen, untried. So I planned all sorts of ways to escape, but every way involved a man. (All my life I have leaned on men.) I needed a man to claim me, see me. I knew if the right man could ever *see* me, he would rescue me in fifteen minutes—and when I wasn't crying for him, I was praying, telling the Lord I would give Him a year to repay me for His awful mistake or I would take measures. Well, He repaid and in less than a year. One Sunday morning Mother woke me up when breakfast was ready and I woke in tears—straight from peaceful sleep into tears, just seeing my room and thinking of Sunday. Sunday is of course the big day in jails, coming on the heels of Saturday night. Mother said, 'Kate, stop crying. We're lucky.' 'How come?' I said. She said, 'Guess how many men are upstairs.' I said 'Black or white?' 'White,' she said. ''Three,' I said. 'One,' she said, 'but guess what he done.' 'Rape,' I said. She said 'Not that bad.' 'Arson?' I said. 'Kidnaping,' she said, 'and we got the fellow to feed this morning. Happened in your sleep about two a.m. Nice young fellow, neat as a pin. Come on let's go.' All our previous real criminals were black so I was curious but no more than that. Just put on the nearest dress at hand and went—and it wasn't nothing special, at first sight nohow. A young fellow, red-headed, maybe nineteen. But the image of you—that's how come I fainted, today not then. Though even then I thought I had seen him. He looked at you that way, open and grinning like you were the one he was thinking about just the minute before, aching to see, and now here you were—and him with crime on his hands and heart. But as I say I wasn't struck at first, just nodded to him as he said 'Good morning' and studied his hands while Mother talked to him. I'm a student of hands—whole hands not palms. I can tell a person's whole life from his hands, if I can watch them doing several things—handling bread or buttoning their pants or the way they touch theirself, feel their own face."

Not thinking, Milo took his own hands (they had been on her waist, as if to resuscitate) and hid them behind him.

She smiled. "Too late. I've studied them good."

"Tell me what you know."

"I know you don't hate yourself," she said. "That's half the battle."

He looked down and grinned at his standing pride. "Hate that?" he said. "The Lord made that and it's Sunday—praise Him! Tell me what else you know?"

"I was *telling* you the quick of my life. Do you want that or not?"

"You think I need it?"

She looked at all of him. "Yes," she said so he nodded for her to continue and listened. "Mother was asking him his religion. 'Baptist,' he said, 'till I heard about Hell and decided it sounded like more fun than Heaven.' Mother said, 'Hush, you *need* faith now.' He said, 'Lady, I left home at age fourteen and your friend the Lord stayed home when I left—He don't like to travel, that's o.k. with me, but don't ask me to go calling on Him at this late date. *I* got faith but in just two things—the U.S. dollar (silver if possible) and my two hands.' His hands again."

"What had you learned about him by then?"

"That he didn't care whether he lived or died. Not that he hated himself like some that claw at theirselves for a simple scratch or gouge their red eyes or hawk at their gullet like a bone was stuck. No, he just never touched himself at all, kept his hands at rest some inches from him or if he was standing, just slightly hanging like them and his body were total strangers. But he smiled a lot as I already said, and when Mother said she would bring him a Bible, he said, 'Wooo, no! I don't read dirty stories, lady.' She laughed and said, 'Well, how about Kate here reading *to* you? I can send her up when the dishes are washed.' He looked me over—mess that I was—and agreed to that. So I went to him after a while with the Bible, having washed and dressed, and sat on a stool beyond his cell just out of reach. (He had short arms.) I asked him did he have any special requests, meaning Bible verses, but he stared at me and said 'How old are you?' I said 'Fourteen.' He said, 'Old enough. I request you, Kate.' I didn't pay no attention to that—working round a jail you learn to be deaf—but went on and read my favorite part about Jephthah's daughter. You know that, don't you?"

Milo said, "No, I'm going to Hell too."

"Jephthah was a general that promised the Lord if he won a certain battle, he would sacrifice the first thing that came out to meet him when he got home. So the Lord accepted and he won hands down and rode to his house and who came out?—his only child, a girl about my age (my age then), dancing and beating tambourines. Jephthah tore his clothes and gnashed his teeth and said, 'Alas, my daughter, thou has brought me very low, and thou art one of them that trouble me, for I have opened my mouth unto the Lord and I cannot go back.' You see, I know it by heart since then, but that morning I read it and didn't look up till I got to the end where he gives her two months to roam the hills and mourn her virginity and then cuts her throat and burns her for the Lord, keeping his promise, young as she was—'She knew no man.' But at the end I looked and he was crying—not sobbing out loud, just great tears dropping which he did not lift a finger to wipe. I didn't speak but looked back down and commenced to hunt for a happier passage. They are pretty scarce—in *my* Bible at least—but just as I stumbled on Jacob and Rachel, he said, 'Hold on. What was her name?—the dead girl's name.' I didn't know and turned to see. She didn't have a name so I said, 'Poor girl. She's just been Jephthah's daughter countless ages. Let's you and me name her.' I said it for fun—to ease his pain not to be sacrilegious—and started to reeling off modern girls' names. 'Alice, Carol, Phyllis, Mavis.' He hollered, 'Shut up'—woke up the two drunks—and the tears rolled again and this time sobs. I stood up and said I was joking with him, that I didn't know he took the Bible so serious and I turned to go. He looked up—his face all ruined like a child's but he still wouldn't touch it—and begged my pardon and said 'Don't you *know?*' 'Know what?' I said. 'The reason I'm here?' I said, 'I know you've kidnaped something—that's all,' and he broke down again so I really left and left the Bible where he could reach. I have always believed that is how to give, to lay what you're giving in the other one's reach, let him take it or not."

She halted, flickered her moist thighs in Milo's clasp to rouse her blood that had drowsed with his weight. Milo misread her last words, her moving; reached down and upward to accept again, give again their mutual gift. But Kate turned serious eyes back to him, slowly shook her head. "I am offering something different now. Stay still and listen." He nodded, looked down a little embarrassed to show he was hearing but left his one reaching hand in place, a claim postponed, unurged for now.

"So I went to Daddy and asked him the crime. 'Whose?' he said and I didn't know—the boy's name, I mean. Neither did Daddy. The boy wouldn't tell them, and when they searched him, all he had was the two bus tickets and a miniature checkerboard for fun on the road—not a scrap of paper with his name or home. But Daddy knew this much, picked it up talking to various ones—late Saturday night a northbound bus stopped at the station and a man and a child went into the diner. The man bought the child some sweet milk and fried pie but nothing for himself—just sat and watched her eat it like she was magic and would turn it to money or joyful days. I say *her.* The child was a girl about three years old. Then while she was chewing, he excused himself and went to the toilet. Well, the waitress of course had waitress-curiosity and asked the child, 'Is that your Daddy, sugar?' The child kept chewing as calm as a king and said, 'No, just a man that's kidnaping me.' The waitress knew she was pushed for time so she said, 'You sure you know what kidnaping means?' The child said, 'Stealing you while your aunt's asleep.' Then the man walked out of the toilet. Time was up. The bus was loading. Nothing to do but call the Law—which in that town was mainly my Daddy, the sheriff being nobody you could rely on. And Daddy went—introduced himself just as the man bent down to the child to lift her into the bus before him, asked to see some identification. He claimed he didn't have any, and later at the jail when they searched him, he didn't—had two bus tickets (I never asked to where) and a dollar and some change. So Daddy asked his name and he said to Daddy—smiling, I guess, 'Is that what the world is waiting to know?' Then he shut up, wouldn't say another word, not even to hush the child when Daddy commenced to quizzing her. But all she knew was that yes, she was kidnaped; the man had told her so; he was being good to her and she knew his name but couldn't remember. Daddy was deputy as well as jailer, and in his judgment it all smelled funny. He said to the man that in view of not having any name or papers and in view of the awful wave of crime— the Lindbergh baby was just in the past—wouldn't they just spend the night in town and wire back home for identification? The man shook his head so Daddy had to say, 'I will give you one last chance, son. What is your true name and where are you headed?' The man thought awhile and looked round the little knot of people that had ganged to listen. Then he looked to the child that was still in his arms. She was looking at him. He said to her, 'Are you happy with me?' She didn't speak but nodded so he said to Daddy, 'I am somebody that wouldn't harm anything. I am trying to get home with what I love.' Daddy said, 'Son, I for one hope you make it, that you've got the right to, but long as this child claims she is stole, the right ain't yours till you prove it to me.' The man said, 'I ain't no mathematician. I can't prove nothing.' Then he set the child down and she stood by his leg, but he did not touch her or even look down, not one time again. He said, 'If you are taking me, what about her?' Daddy didn't have time to worry about that. The waitress that had called him was standing by, and she volunteered to keep the child till news arrived. And the child went to her, not looking back and the man not watching her go neither till the instant before she passed from sight. Then he spoke towards her back—said, 'Meet me. Promise to meet me please'—but she never turned, never promised nothing, just *went* like her memory had slammed against him."

Milo's upright body shuddered suddenly, from his high chin and neck down through his hot thighs, his one touching hand. She stopped of course and took his apologetic grin. "Excuse me," he said and he looked upward from her to the dim low ceiling, then arched farther back, searching above them. "Must have been an angel flying past."

"Or a lonesome ghost walking on your grave." She smiled a little too.

But Milo was serious. "Don't rush me," he said. "I am too young to die. I have got the best part of my life yet to live."

"What part is that?"

He was still looking backwards in search of the angel. "Being a man, being free to live any way I want, have a wife and children and give them things—little things they need, things they don't need or maybe just live right by myself alone as a rock, no good to nobody, holding back all I have for myself." He rolled his tired head back towards her.

"Too late," she said.

"Too late for what?"

"Holding back. You have give it all already."

"Who to?"

"Well, I can't speak for nobody but me."

"What have I give you that Tom never did?"

"That's what I am trying to tell you, boy."

He closed his eyes, his chin touched his chest, his hands hung loose by his hard damp flanks. "Tell on," he said.

"He stayed with us—in the jail, I mean—for two days, waiting on information. It took two days to find the child's home, but when a Missing Report came in and she fit the description, Daddy and the waitress put her on the bus back south to home, a tag around her neck with her name and destination. I never saw her, being otherwise busy—didn't want to see her. And he never saw her again neither, never asked about her, never mentioned her name no more than if she had powdered to dust when she took that waitress's hand and left him. He talked about other things though—mostly me. He took an interest in me from the start. When I went to see him the second time to take his Sunday dinner, he asked me to sit down and watch him eat—'It'll prove I am human' is what he said. I told him, 'Shoot, everything eats—germs *eat*.' He smiled and said, 'Right, but did you ever hear a germ reciting Scripture?' He handed me the Bible I had left him that morning, open to the Song of Solomon and said 'Hear me.' Then looking at me the way nobody had, way nobody has till an hour ago, he said what he had learned since morning, having used his spare time thinking of me—'Set me as a seal upon thine heart, as a seal upon thine arm: for love is strong as death; jealousy is cruel as the grave: the coals thereof are coals of fire, which hath a most vehement flame.' He stopped a minute then and stared at me, waiting for me to answer somehow, but what do you say to something like that when it comes at you sudden at age fourteen? I was going to say 'I will'—that's what—but he put out a hand to stop me and smiled and went on reciting, 'We have a little sister and she hath no breasts. What shall we do for our sister in the day when she shall be spoken for?' Then we could both laugh a little—I was forward in my growth as I said, but fourteen is fourteen and I was small here."

She touched her breasts that pooled back full but firm, and Milo said, "They must have got a heap of exercise since then."

She tested his face for meanness, found none. "If acting as teethers for a middle-aged man with false teeth anyhow is your idea of exercise, they have." She brushed them again lightly upwards as if in amends for what they had borne. "*He* never touched them, if you're thinking that—never tried. I have tried to recollect all these years if he ever touched me anywhere—with his hands, I mean—but as much as I wish it, I don't think he did. He wasn't shy. He could love you with his eyes hot as most men could with *two* sets of hands. And he kissed me right straight—that first Sunday evening when I come to collect his supper dishes. I had spent so much of the afternoon with him—hearing him recite and then sitting silent, that three feet between us—that Mother said to just grab his dishes and leave. I tried to do that, asked him to shove them through the little trap-door and tried not to face him as I stooped for the tray, but just as I braced to stand, he spoke—he never whispered, never thought about fear. 'Look here,' he said. I looked. Oh tears were standing again in his eyes—his eyes were blue. I knew right then, if I ever doubted, that he had not been stealing that child, not meaning her harm noway, nohow so I said—I whispered—'I know what happened at the bus that night, and I know where the waitress lives that's got the child. I'll go and see about her or take her a message—what shall

I say?' He said, 'Don't move. Don't speak of her again. She was never mine. I been sitting here all afternoon forgetting her.' I could see by his eyes how true *that* was—talk about a seal set on his *heart*; his heart and eyes were coals of fire. But then he shook himself like a boy out of swimming and stood his full height—I was still stooped above his supper tray. 'Stand up,' he said. 'How come?' I said. 'Because you are no good to me down there.' I said, 'Am I any good to you anywhere?' 'You will be,' he said. 'How?' I said. 'The first step is for you to stand up,' he said. So I stood up—I have met two people you could not disobey. 'Now come forward to me.' I stepped forward to him and he kissed me then."

Milo had leaned to her through that last. Now he plugged her mouth with a kiss of his own—a sudden hard attempt to become her dream, her pitiful past. He thrust into her, past teeth towards her gorge, and she let him go but did not meet him nor welcome him so he rose and rested halfway above her, propped on his arms.

"Thank you," she said, but she looked to the wall and brushed her lips with a cleansing hand. "Of course I didn't think of nothing but that—that three or four seconds—the whole next day, sitting in school. I would keep my hand to my lips when I could to hide any sign that might be there, any permanent seal. Oh I know there was nothing—not outward nohow. The boys still joked me at recess and lunch, but what I knew, they would not know for years if ever, ever—that something can rise up in your life where nothing stood before and be a burning angel, that awful, that grand, gutting you like a dry cotton gin with the fire he makes, the fire he is. I don't mean angels in Sunday school pictures with lace on their pants, humming *Silent Night.* I know the Bible—they got flaming swords and will wrestle you all night to change your name. I don't know much but I know an angel when I see one. I have seen two"—she waited a moment but did not look up. "The first one—the one I am telling about—changed my life at least if not my name. (Rob changed that. It's all he's changed.) I went home from school that afternoon and crept past Mother upstairs to him. It was Monday, the day Daddy got word about the child and the man's name, but I didn't know that. He did—Daddy had told him already, that the child was headed home alone and that he would sit with us till a State man came to escort him down to face what he'd done, most likely

tomorrow. So he knew the time was short if I didn't, and the first thing
he said when I walked up to him, right up to the bars (I was still afraid,
sure, but if he meant me harm, well, harm it must be)—he said, 'I told
you last night you could be some good to me, and you took the first step.'
I nodded to that and he said 'Well?—' and waited, not smiling. So I said,
'What is the second step?' He said, 'For you to get your Daddy's keys.'
I said 'No' to that automatically, having lived in jails all my life where
escape is the main terror you have. But he wasn't mad. He just
explained—'I never meant *escape* for a minute. I mean that, Kate'—he
pointed to the narrow cot in his corner. 'I mean you to come up here
to me when they are asleep.' 'What for?' I said. I knew the first half of
what he meant, but what I needed to know was why—why me, why
now, why here and what lay beyond me when he was gone? Well, think
over all the reasons he could give, the reasons any other hot boy would
have given, the lies that he might believe were true—and I've had thirteen years to think—and you won't never come across *his* reason. 'I want
to get me a child,' he said—'Soon.' I thought a whole minute, then I
said 'Am I old enough?' He nodded and then said, 'Go on downstairs
now and do your studying so your Mama and Daddy don't get suspicious, and when you bring my supper, don't even speak, but when they
are sleep, get the key and I'll be here.' I nodded and left and was in sight
of mother before I knew he had still never touched me except our lips.
I had an hour to think before supper. Daddy was asleep on the big divan,
but he had told Mother the news about the man and the child, and she
told me though she had forgot the man's name already—I still hadn't
asked, thinking I had no rights over him. So I thought that through and
decided this—right then while Daddy was nodding in the front room,
I'd get his extra cell key from his desk, and when I took the man his supper, I would hide that key in his folded napkin and leave like he said
before he found it. Then I would not go to him in the night but would
wait till sunup and go to him then. I figured it this way—if he was just
lying to me to escape or just to take my first love and run, then I would
give him his freedom direct, not make him use me to tell his lie. And
I did it all—barely looked at him when I shoved the try in, the key in
the napkin—and when I came down I asked Mother would she please
collect the dishes as I had extra studying to do. Then I went to my

room—I had that much, a room to myself—and I stretched stiff on my back and waited. All night long, not shutting an eye though I cut off the lights—I can think in the dark. I seined every sound from the air like minnows—Mother and Daddy undressing for bed and the sheriff of course roaring up an hour later with a Negro drunk that I thought would ruin any future I had, but after a while the Negro's rich brother came in and bailed him out, and then there was nothing but my Mother's breathing—her lungs were half-eat-up already but we didn't know it. Mother's poor breathing and my heart that swole in my chest like a child, planted already and growing furiously to beat the daybreak. I would try to ease it and soothe time away by saying in my head over and over, 'Nobody ever asked you for nothing that they really needed, could not live without, and may never ask you again in your life. You are giving something you never knew you had, a precious gift to ease his pain.' I said it till I three-fourths believed it and day was creeping at the edge of my window. Then I stood up and went in my bare feet, my long nightgown to take his gift and begin my own. Well, he was gone— oh gone ten minutes, his bed was still warm as my hot hand and all that was left was my Bible open to the page he had learned and this message wrote with a dull pale pencil. '*I have laid here and watched for you all night and now it is day. Why have you failed me that needs you now and will need you always and carry your face on my heart like a seal to the waiting grave?—Tom.*' He had signed it. That was his name, all of it I knew." She halted, face still turned to the wall, eyes unseeing.

Her voice had held firm and clear to the end but Milo almost whispered now. "When did they bring him back?"

"Never."

"Where did they take him?"

"They never touched him no more than I did, never laid eye on him again no more than if he had *been* that angel and gone to God."

"Or a ghost to start with," Milo said. They both shuddered involuntarily, both looked up in sudden panic to the ceiling that shrank back from them as though the room were quickly flooding with unseen life. But the moment passed—threat or blessing unfulfilled. She and Milo could face each other, spared, relieved, a little abandoned and Milo could speak. "So you have waited all this time."

It was not a question but she began to answer. "Not *all* the time. Twice I give up and slashed my veins—the first time, the morning I found his note. But I lived and thought I was saved for a purpose so I waited again. Of course Daddy had to get a new jail—I had ruined him in Gaffney—and we came here and I waited here, not thinking at first that Tom would never find me if he came back to claim what I was saving. When I realized that—that my roots were cut, the one last thread that strung me to Tom: my sorry address, the Gaffney jail—well, I slashed again. And I mean *slashed.* I really tried, not like a movie star that takes a cold butter knife and strokes the bony heel of her hand where blood don't run. That was before blood plasma was invented, and I had the rarest blood type known. Nobody else in Warrenton had it but Rob Pomeroy, and he donated it arm to arm while I was fading—the only thing he ever got in me far enough to matter, but it seemed to give him rights over me so when I lived and he began hanging round me like a wet spell, I looked up and smiled—out of pity pure as mother's milk, and when his Mother died (that had stunted his life) and he come to me the night of her death and said 'Kate, I need you'—I went to him." Kate looked to Milo, studied him till he broke beneath her gaze, leaned to bury his face in the trough of her chest. Then she laid one hand into his hair, pressed him deeper. "How could I know you would come again? Who was I to earn God's notice like that?"

He accepted the force of her hand for a while, exactly as long as his breath held out. Then he surfaced for air, turned aside to speak. "And all that is true?" He could feel the affirming nod of her chin in the crown of his skull so again he whispered—"Then what must I do with what I know, with who I am?"

Kate said, "I couldn't tell you that. I may look old enough to be your Mother but I'm just twenty-seven. What can you learn in twenty-seven years?"

He said "I asked *you*" and rose from beneath her heavy hand to sit again in the natural seat of her hardly used body.

"You can learn to recognize the Lord when He comes—or any messenger He may send."

"But what if you are the messenger boy?" He grinned, downwards. She did not accept his grin nor reflect it. "You can know what message you are bearing, can't you?—not stump in the dark when light would do, when you're *built* out of light?"

The doorbell rang above their heads (Rooster's alarm), and Milo's body showed its own alarm—face flushed, legs tensed, trunk rose from Kate to stand or run, it did not know which. But Kate lay calm, staring back and up at the bell. "It ain't nobody that can harm us worse than we've harmed each other." She looked to Milo. "Climb off please. Let me answer my door."

Milo held in place. "Wait. What does *that* mean?—we have harmed each other? You are changing tunes like a fast piccolo."

"It means whatever time makes it mean." She sat to the side of the ruined bed, then stood naked facing him a final moment, then stooped for her robe, fumbled it on, smiling as she turned towards the open door. "It mainly means I have looked my life in the eye this afternoon—my sorry life—and seen it was happy, very nearly happy. Won't it happy to you?"

Milo nodded, smiled—not to mean Yes or No nor to lie but to speak when spoken to, a lesson he had learned the day he could talk.

Before his smile faded Kate said, "That is the harm—that I never knew till now: all that time I was nearly happy." Then she was gone, leaving "Thank you" behind on the door sill, firm—but nothing else, neither "Leave" nor "Wait."

So he stood to the floor and at once felt the downward weight of his groin. He looked to the tan squab wobbling there. "Thank *you*, old son. You deserve the prize but the day isn't done. Honors come at sundown. Don't fail me yet." Then he looked round the room for signs of his clothes, knew Kate had left them to dry in the kitchen and tipped to the open door to listen—Kate's voice, faint, and an answering man. Milo slowly peeped out towards the sounds, and there on the front porch ten yards away was Kate and a strange young man with a camera, Kate pointing behind her towards the bedroom and Milo, saying "Still there is one job you could do so as not to waste your day entirely. Private job. Take a boy's picture that's in yonder now."

Milo did not pause for fear or understanding. Bare as at birth he crossed the dark hall in one silent step to the opposite kitchen, went straight for the oven door ajar and was in his warm clothes and out the back before Kate and her new man had touched the front screen, even into high weeds beside the house and crouching there before he realized three things: that the man was from the *Warren Record* and had gone to the woods to photograph the hunt but had not found Rooster, that Kate did not even know half his name and that his feet were bare—shoes where he dropped them by Rooster's easy chair.

Through the open windows of the living room, Kate's voice came. "Wait here please sir. I'll see if he's awake. He's my husband's cousin, fifteen years old. Boys like to sleep but he'll be glad—his mother'll be glad, Rob'll be glad—to have his picture. Rob loves him like a son, having none of his own."

The sound of that raised Milo from the weeds to stand for a moment entirely visible while his face and hands worked with the upward rush of desire—to walk to the house again (barefoot, ruined), stand for the picture, say a decent goodbye, leave his name, *say* her name (he had not said it). But what could she ever do with that? Worst of all, how could poor Rooster use it?—a picture of him and the story the photographer would strow like stink over what would be plain (his face like a mirror with a memory, his hands still rank)? Nothing. No use. This much was ended.

He ran for the car and had it rolling silent downhill when Kate walked back to the man and said, "Never mind. Excuse me. He's gone, looks like," and the man left too and Kate saw him out and stood awhile on the bright porch steps—still bright at six—not looking either way, not searching, not waiting, as straight and unshaken as if truly healed, unharmed within while fraction by fraction with a perfect aim Milo's white seed (his shape, his life) flailed upward against the pull of earth towards her ready womb.

Milo thought of Kate—his mind a quick knot of remembered pleasure, astounded pride, shame for himself and her before Rooster and the radiance of someone who gives his gifts as clouds give rain—till he came to the road at the bottom of her hill, cranked the engine, turned right towards the hunt, shook his head at the thinning houses of town and spoke aloud to the empty car, "What in the world did I ever give anybody but trouble?" No answer came but the gnash of the engine, dry steel on steel as though oil never was. So he spoke to the start of the cool air and woods—green shade, failing sun. "Thank you, Lord—I've got a mind that drains. It's what saves my life, with all *I* see." And then it drained in a silent rush, in a tenth of a mile like a tank unplugged. Then it plugged again and began to fill, dim thought on thought, expectation and desire—saving his lost brother, penning the snake, redeeming his face before Rooster and Macey and filling Lois like a trunk with treasure in the oncoming night brim with his proved skill, his undreamt prowess, garlanded prow.

The old car bore him like wings through that, and then as he turned to the dirt side road that flanked the woods before the old Ryden place, while his mind was with Lois, a tire blew beneath him, the car slewed right towards a shallow gully, humped twenty yards over bone-dry trash before he could stop it, look and speak again— "Damn if it ain't night." In the pine-walled road it was nearly night— "Too soon for early October," he thought and leaned to the sky to explain the dark, saw clouds ganging for a storm, leapt out, kicked the right front tire and walked to the car trunk, praying for a spare. It was there, ready, and Milo said again, "Lord, You are fighting on my side today," and bent to the trunk to look for tools as thunder slammed on him from the thickening sky. *"Easy,"* he said—to the sky, the Lord— "I am bare as a baby. Let me fix this tire please before You start."

Among Rooster's mess he found all the tools he needed but a lug wrench. He rocked on his heels, said "Damn" again but felt no despair though he knew this road was empty for the night, not a chance in a thousand of a helping car. Still he scotched the back wheels and took the jack round and on nothing but faith, bent to the strain of jacking the right front—mind drained again, so empty of worry that he paused in mid-job and said to himself, "You ought to been a Nigger, Milo— little as you care. Well, *God* takes care, don't You, God?"

He looked up from hunching above the front bumper and stared a dark man in the dark eyes, close. "Wooo," Milo said. "I was praying for help. You're the fastest answer to prayer I've had." He did not stand but squatted fully and looked to the new man to see all he could—white, middle-sized, in baggy clothes, no luggage in sight, hands hid behind him.

The man said "Am I?" His voice was from Afton, from home anyhow.

"The Lord didn't send me a lug wrench, did He?" Milo smiled but could not see if the man's face replied.

But the man's right hand came out and extended a thin bar of iron. "This help you?" he said.

Milo took it, examined it by eager touch till he found the lug hole, the chisel end. "Well, I didn't know Daniel Boone carved lug wrenches—this ain't the latest model but yes sir, it'll do. I'm much obliged." The man did not speak, stood with empty right hand on his hip. Milo said, "Would you reach in the car please and switch on the lights? Battery's low but these clouds are swarming. I can't see nothing."

The man took a backward step as to obey, then halted, tried to speak but stammered like someone rusty for talk. What he finally said was, "Would this help you any?" and his left hand showed with a small glass lantern which he stooped and lit and held to Milo before the swelling flame could show his own face.

Milo took it, raised the wick, set it by him in the dirt, laughed and said "Whew, don't kerosene stink?"

The man said "Yes."

Milo took his jack handle—"Don't get me wrong. I'm grateful to you"—gave the wheel three more hoists, then moved his lantern round and began with the wrench. He worked with clenched intensity for a minute or two, not thinking of the man nor of courtesy. So at last he said, "You say you live around here?" No answer, no sound. Milo's head rose to see. Where the man had been was just night air. Milo stood, walked round, looked behind the truck—nothing. Then he walked to the midst of the road, looked ahead. Fifty yards ahead a man—his man surely—was walking in the gully on the Ryden side, right arm out like a rudder, a wing, gently slapping the saplings it could reach. Milo thought, "*Go* then if you're in such a rush." Yet the man walked slowly as if slowly knowing he was lost or abandoned. So Milo spoke in his natural voice, knowing sound would carry on the loaded air—"Mister, I thought you were helping *me*."

The man stopped, half-turned, waited awhile, then came back to Milo a little faster than he left, stopping five feet away, partially smiling in the lantern light but mainly puzzled. "I'll help you," he said. "Any way I can. I am just heading home. No rush about that."

Milo said, "Well, good. Keep me company a minute and I'll ride you home. Anyhow you went off and left your stuff—your wrench and your light. Don't never leave a light, hard as they are to find." The man went on half-smiling and nodded.

Milo, having nothing else to say, returned to his wheel. The man followed round to hold the lantern though that was not needed, and Milo worked so hard and fast that he had only one thought, a saying of Papa's—"Everybody's crazy as they can be. Carry a knife and take pity when you can." Then the tire was on, he could lower the jack, hand the man his wrench and say, "You saved my life. Tell me where you're headed and I'll take you to the door."

The man pointed forward the way he had walked, again tried to speak, failed, took a new tack—handed Milo the wrench, said, "You'll need that again before I do."

Milo thanked him, went round to load the tools and bad tire, and when he returned the man had killed the lantern flame and stood in the same spot, staring at Milo, straining to speak. Milo spoke for him—"You look awful tired."

The man nodded rapidly. "You hit it," he said. "You hit it on the *head*," and soft laughing started, stopped in midair, cut down. "I am lost," he said.

"I figured you were. What you trying to find?"

"My home," he said.

"Who are you?"

The man began to laugh again. "That's what I've got to remember first, ain't it?"

Milo said, "It would be a big help." The man only nodded and Milo thought, "I could spend all night with this simple soul" so he said, "I tell you—my own brother's lost somewhere in these woods with a mad dog and a twenty-foot snake and a whole posse's hunting him and I'm late to meet them. Looks like to me the best thing for you is to stroll up this road—if this is your road—till you get your bearings. There's landmarks all up and down, thick as thieves." He took two steps towards the door of the car. "I thank you again and good luck to you." He reached for the handle.

The man didn't move but he struggled to speak. Milo had the door open and was on the running board when clear words came. "You ain't going to leave me now, are you, boy?"

Milo thought, "Let me turn on the lights and see this fool," and he reached for the switch, then thought of Rooster's weak battery and said aloud, "No. But listen, my main duty's to my *own* that's lost. All I can do now is take you with me and maybe you'll find what you're looking for—you know, hunt for birds and you may catch a bear."

"Thank you," the man said and moved for the passenger door, climbed in. Milo slammed his own door, cranked the engine (saying "Lord, let it start"), and they rose from the ditch and drove in darkness twenty-five yards till he lit the lights. From the moment they rolled, he could feel the man's stare on his right profile, and now he turned to meet the gaze, study the stranger. But the dashboard lights of the car were dead, and the man was darker than before.

So Milo did not speak but faced the road and watched what he could—black trees, dead weeds, a scuttling possum—thinking, "Friend, you won't find home by staring at me, won't find nothing in me but my dinner and that's fading fast." It was the first thought of food he had had, and testing his stomach he knew he was starved, thought, "How come Mrs. Pomeroy didn't offer me something?—all that work I did for her—and how am I going to do justice on Lois, weak as a wormy pauper in winter?"

The man said "Stop"—plea not order—and Milo stopped as soon as he could with the brakes he had, their rear end slinging round in the dust like a scrap yard behind. But the man didn't move, only stared on at Milo.

Milo said, "Cap'n, you're full of surprises."

"I'm not but a private," the man said and laughed.

"Well, Private, you recognize where we are?—do, you must have radar, dark as it is." Then Milo strained out through his open window to take his bearings. "Damn," he said, "if I won't lost too. This is where I'm going." He drew in and drove them to the ditch again.

"Where is it?" the man said.

"The old Ryden woods. House is in yonder somewhere. Now we got to find it and a storm coming on." Thunder had gone on griping above them. Milo opened his door, slid quickly to the ground but the man didn't move. Milo said, "Come on and bring your lantern." The man still faced him but did not move. "It was *you* yelled 'Stop.'"

The man said, "I did but I don't know why."

"Well, I can't stand here and answer riddles. Light that light and I'll lead you *somewhere*."

For his own reason the man slid across and used Milo's door, stooped to set down his lantern, fished for matches and bent to obey. As the wooden match bloomed in his hand, he looked up. He said "Who are you?"

"That's one thing I know. I'm Milo the meanest Mustian alive, and whoever you *were*, you're going to be ashes—look at your match."

The match had burned to the man's clasping fingers, lapped at them like a lover's tongue, but the man only studied the flame, then smiled, carried it on to the lantern wick and held the smile as he rose facing Milo—"Lead," he said.

"That's my name—Kindly Light." Milo took the lantern, led off towards trees dark as any grave.

But he was not the guide he promised to be, and within five minutes he thought "I am lost." The path had stopped at a low wall of vines, and now all his lantern showed was thicket—rusty briars, oiled poison oak and deep dry pine straw underfoot as a treacherous mat over holes, sharp rocks (and his feet bare). Still he did not pause, only slowed a little. The man slowed behind him, three steps back. And he went that way not scared but angry till his right foot sank to the ankle in a hole and he lurched forward and the lantern fell. His first thought was of his ankle not fire so he sat and rubbed his foot.

But the man came up, passed him, reached for the lantern, held it above him and looked ahead, his back to Milo and Milo's foot. Then he said "You are lost."

Milo said, "That makes two and one is a cripple."

But the man still showed no concern for Milo. He started ahead and had taken three steps before Milo could recover to speak. "Now who's leaving who?"

The man stopped, turned, raised the lantern enough to show he was smiling. "I am not lost now," he said. "Come on."

Milo stood, hobbled after him to stay with the light, and the man wasn't lost, not if the Ryden place was his goal. In less than three minutes he broke through a final tangle into what clearing remained and stopped on the edge. Milo came up beside him and the man held the lantern out far as he could reach, his straight arm trembling as the feeble light crept to the empty house—broken windows, open door. Not looking to Milo he said "They are sleep."

Milo said "They are dead."

"Dead?" he said. "Who were they? Who am I?" He turned on Milo, exposed his own face to the lantern now, wrenched by mystery, the fear of loss.

Milo stood his ground two feet from the face, studied it slowly. "You're a middle-sized fellow in your early thirties in war surplus clothes with red hair, blue eyes; and if this was your home, you're bound to be a Ryden unless you're an owl or bat or snake. Nothing but Rydens ever lived here till two years ago, then Miss Jack died and the wildlife arrived."

The man turned and moved through the clearing towards the house, stopped a little way short of the steps, did not turn round but said "*Dead*, you say?"

Milo took a step forward, his ankle well now. "Dead—but you ain't alone. There's one Ryden left—Hawkins is hunting these woods tonight; you may see him yet—and *I'm* your cousin. That is if you're sure you're this bunch of Rydens. Miss Jack didn't have but one boy to my knowledge." The man went on to the steps, climbed them, still did not face round though Milo continued, "Of course there are things in the world I don't know."

The man pushed the half-open door fully open, stood on the sill, held his lantern inward. The warm shine lit the front-room windows, and Milo shuddered once against his will. The man said, "Where is her boy living now?"

"He is—" Milo halted, then walked to the foot of the steps himself. The man would not turn so he told it to his back. "I'm sorry to be the one to tell you, but I am your kin and that's better than a stranger—he is six feet under the peaceful ground in the South Pacific. Guam, I guess."

The man never flinched and his arm outstretched with the heavy lantern hung like steel on the air. At last he spoke. "Now tell me his name."

"Tom," Milo said, "—for Thomas, I guess."

The man thought awhile, then shook his head (the general sign for No) and stepped to the center of the bare front room—picked by Hawkins of all that would move or bring ten cents at a rummage sale. He set down the lantern in thick white dust, but his head shook on as he stood and faced the next dark door, to the bedrooms, kitchen.

Milo had followed to the front-door sill and spoke to answer the man's apparent No. "It was Tom all right. I know that much. Papa and Mrs. Provo were speaking of him yesterday."

"Who are they?"

"Jasper Mustian my Granddaddy and Mrs. Selma Provo that's in Warrenton at the fair with her niece and a snake show. Tom was a favorite of Papa's—Papa said—till he run away from home when he was a boy, and Mrs. Provo met him down in Florida. He got there somehow and roomed with her, left owing money though I think she said he give her the snake we are hunting tonight. It's her niece I am mainly waiting for here—she's older than me by several months (I am nearly sixteen; well, nearer than *fifteen*), but that didn't matter to her night before last. She bent to my need like a baby willow—"

The man threw himself on Milo like a train—that huge and black—and when they hit the floor, a pine board split. That was the only sound for a while. They struggled in total silence, Milo losing—the man's hands (he seemed to grow dozens in the dark) like pig-iron bands on Milo's wrists, knees, ankles, neck. Then Milo began to suck breath loudly and above his fear, he managed one thought—"This fool ain't breathing"—and for all the rolling and force of his body, the man breathed no harder than a sleeping child. But he made a large error—he rolled Milo in his grip to one side and Milo freed a hand, grabbed the man's butt—desperate—and found his last hope, the wrench still there. So with final power he clubbed the man's head behind the ear. The man said "No," rolled limp, and Milo rode him—vaulted in an instant to straddle his chest, pin arms with his knees, clamp his wrists to the floor.

Before he could think, Milo saw the man's face—prone beneath him, the lantern light stroked it—and though Milo spent no time around mirrors he knew his own face: it was there on the man, himself asleep, only red-headed, older. So he tensed his pressure on the man's pinned arms and risked one hand to shake the man's chin, saying softly as he shook, "Why must you mistreat your kin-people, sir? They are all you got and you're close kin to me. Look at me now and see yourself." That last he whispered in the man's nearest ear, then sat back and watched him swim up from sleep.

The man said, "How come you didn't kill me?"

"I tried," Milo said. "How come you won't die?" But because the man remained limp beneath him, accepting his victory, Milo smiled down at him. "You were just confused from your long trip, won't you?—thinking clearer now?"

The man waited to answer that, testing for clearness, and though he showed no trace of resistance, Milo's grip never slacked as he started. "All I know is this and I give it to you to beg your pardon. I have got no memory past an hour ago. I was just walking down that road and found you—"

"I never *passed* you," Milo said.

"I can't explain that."

Milo thought a moment, then said, "I can. You ever listen to the radio?" The man seemed to hear but did not answer. "If you listen you've heard of amnesia. Everybody's got amnesia on the radio (grope around for years not knowing their names; feeling for home, kin, recognition; would give their leg for just a piece of paper with their three *initials* much less their name). That's all you've got—a little amnesia. Relax, ride it out. It'll pass in a flash one day and you'll know."

The man's voice rushed in—"Don't confuse me. Let me say what little I *do* know. I was walking in the middle of that dirt road, and if I had a goal or plan, I never knew its name, but it won't worrying me till I found you in trouble and you started the questions."

"How come you had a wrench and a light?"

"That's the least of my worries, I tell you—maybe I'm just some helpful somebody that patrols the roads. No, what worries me now is *not* worrying then—but moving down the road as natural as if I had made it myself. I was headed *home* and if you hadn't stopped me I'd have been there now."

"*You* brought *me* here—remember that?—and I didn't cause Miss Jack to die nor Hawkins to sell her stuff to Niggers."

The man said "Please" and Milo stopped. They were silent awhile, the sky growled on beyond the porch, storm nearer now. The man finally said, "I am here anyhow and all I know—I don't *know*, I *feel*—is I'm waiting for somebody."

"Who isn't?" Milo said. "*I* am."

The man said "Who?"

"I told you once. That's when you come at me."

The man said, "Excuse me. You were crowding me, throwing all them people at me that may be my own flesh and blood, maybe not."

"Well, the girl I'm expecting isn't no flesh of yours whoever you are—won't be none of *mine* after tonight. The fair she travels with is gone already. Her and her aunt are just waiting on Death—the snake's named Death—so I got to give her what I got tonight or bid her goodbye empty-handed in the morning."

"What you got to give?"

"I'll put it this way—Milo (that's me) is riding you now cause you acted so wild, but when the three posses meet here like they should and the hunt is over, Milo aims to sit a better saddle."

"That's what you call giving?"

"What else could I give but my red blood to dying men?—and the war is over."

"And the name?" the man said.

Milo said "What name?"

"Your riding saddle."

"Lois," Milo said, "—an orphan like me (my Daddy's dead), like you too, ain't she?"

The man thought, then looked backward at the lantern and went so still in every nerve that Milo felt the further peace and let his own grip ease a little. When the man turned to him again from the light, the face that had been so grieved and torn seemed smoothed from within like calming water. But he did not smile. He said to Milo, "When will she get here?"

"I was wondering that myself—worrying some. She is hunting with Papa, and all I know is they left a note saying meet here at sundown." Milo's hands left the man's wrists, and he looked round at door and windows to check for surviving traces of day. There were none, not within that thatch of trees and a storm sky yearning like a bride for lightning. Lightning flashed. Thunder answered terrifically. Milo looked on out as the first loud raindrops thunked the tin roof and not turning back, said, "I ought to go find her and find my brother and lead them here. This is going to be hard." He had meant the storm—which crashed in now—but harder than the rain was the blow on his head from the lug wrench gripped in the man's free hands.

What came after, came in two places—in the room itself (bare of all but prone Milo and the kneeling man) and behind shut eyes in Milo's bloody head, a sleeping vision. When he had slumped to his side from the blow and his wet wound glistened even in the dark, the man knelt above him, dabbed in his blood as though blood were money—that rare at least—then rolled him to his stomach to spare his head, decently arranged his arms and legs, rocked back to study— and studied him for what to a living man would have been five minutes (time unmeasured being ghastly, mute as trees that crash in empty woods). Then the man spoke—"Dead. All my life I have meant to kill a man and have been on the lip of killing many—for money, liquor, women, my name—and was always stopped by God or the Law or just going to sleep, and now I've killed my own blood cousin." He wiped the drying wrench on his palm, smelled at the brown blood, tasted it at last with a slow dry tongue. "I am sorry," he said, "but I've sent you to Heaven as pure as this rain"—the rain was torrents—"by keeping you off of my Lois tonight. Surely the Lord will grant me pardon for killing my cousin to save my child that I have not seen in countless years but is set like a seal"—he scoured his heart— "and when I have come, been *sent* to bless her, to ease her life with the gift I have, to give her good for all my wrong?" He was now on his knees, but he stood looking up, head thrust into dark near the sounding roof—"Am I pardoned or not?" No answer came. "Am I *sent* at last to give my gift or must I still roam?"

There was an answer, not in words nor at once, but as the wick of the lantern dried and the white flame struggled, giving less light—none—then a new light as slowly swelled in the room, in Milo's vision. It seeped at first, then flowed, then streamed from the man who stood rock-still till the room was as clear with his light as with day, till the light became warmth, sealed Milo's wound—became heat, became fire—consumed the man's feet, hands, face where he stood, till he no longer stood, neither man nor ghost but a messenger hung in astonished air, then sent to its work.

Yet it left through the door (not the walls as it might), and its infinite progress over porch, down steps calmed the rain to mist so that Milo, drawn from the floor by light, followed stunned but awake in hot dry air as it moved ahead seeing him no more, knowing him no more than hawks know their young years after birth, than light knows the air it rides to earth.

It entered—or assumed into itself—Miss Jack's garden privy. Then the sound came out of dry wood raised on a rusty hinge, and the light began fading—so suddenly that Milo halted five yards away, still having power to consider his safety. Then the light was gone except a blue haze (more heat than light) that clung to the rotten privy boards—as guard or beacon Milo did not know, but he moved on through the black air towards it, right hand blindly extended for its gift till he stood in the privy no larger than a grave (but darker now) and said above the stink half-tamed by age, "I have got your message. Rest easy now. I will bear her whatever gift you send, not touch it myself and will guard it from others. Rest easy now. You have come too far." No answer came. No gift appeared. Even the blue haze had leeched from the wood. His head rolled back to look above.

Death fell on him from the unseen ceiling—at once sank its teeth in the meat of his shoulder, a hundred teeth so delicately used that he did not feel them. But he felt its weight like a dry landslide flinging him to the dirt, its instant first coil whipped round his trunk, both arms inside, then even as he rolled and struggled to his legs to hold his own, stave off a second coil, constriction began in the first coil, gently. And steadily with each breath he sucked, the coil embraced, gained final ground. His hands could not even rise to claw it and thrashing only consumed his scarce wind so he thought, "I will use my final breath." What he yelled was *"Tom"*—to his own surprise but not to the snake's; its aim never faltered and before the cry had left the privy, it had thrown its second coil by the first, the gradual rhythm of death unpausing. Milo could think but he could not speak—mouth gaped open on empty lungs—and his thoughts were rapidly addled by poisons (the trapped wastes of his own suffocation), but he managed this much: "I commenced this hunt with a prayer to be worthy of whatever I found, and I've *found* things—my first drink of liquor, a nice crazy lady that cooled my burning, a spirit returned and a monstrous python strangling me now. Was I worthy of so much in one short day? If not—and I don't have time to decide—I'm sorry and I beg Your pardon, Lord. Take me on now to some better place than a garden-house floor and I'll try to improve. Or considering these unusual events, if You manage one more and release me now from the jaws of Death, I promise You this—" He paused to consider (not wanting even now to commit himself to what he couldn't keep) and found this much he could safely risk—"I will never forget the stuff I have seen and learned today, and if I ever have occasion to use it, I'll use it as free as water in spring." He meant that to be his last thought if not words, but in the last conscious moment he had, a question came—"What *have* I learned and what use *could* I be if this won't the end, my day won't done?" Then through the roaring of death in his ears, he seemed to hear as if whole states away, high frantic barking from dogs, seemed to see clusters of light above him, hear a rifle fire.

The coils relaxed, air found its own way into Milo's chest, his blood gathered speed and vision swam wildly back to his eyes, hearing to his ears. The first sight—lit from flashlights above—was Lois knelt above him, hair and clothes soaked but eyes dry as sand, with one hand prising Death's teeth from his shoulder, laying the plugged head gently to earth but not looking at it, only watching him. And he watched her, not alive enough to smile, but the first sound (above the dogs) was Rooster. "What have you done to deserve this, son?" And other voices clattered near, stunned, disbelieving.

So Milo strained to read their faces—above him in the privy, packed close as wet weeds was the sheriff, Hawkins Ryden, Papa and

Lois (all the rest were huddled at the door, all but Mr. Capps who was chasing his hounds scared by the snake at the end of their trail), and every face but Lois's was blank amazement, all staring at his body down from his head. He tried to lift up and see what they saw, but his strength was still out. Then he tested and found he could speak, softly. "Hadn't you seen boa constrictors before?—little old buggers, ain't poisonous." (It was still around him, still woven round the privy like Christmas garland.)

Lois smiled down. "That isn't no boa constrictor. That's a python." Now he could smile. "I'll remember that."

Papa bent from the waist with no sign of pain—something he had not done in Milo's lifetime. "Son"—he was using his careful voice to prevent bad news—"what have you done?"

In his gratitude Milo almost told them—his lips were parted, he was drawing wind to say, "Rode Rooster's wife till she hollered 'Quit!'"

But Lois herself had looked down by then, seen what the others saw and with her strong hand she lifted his head, said "Look," pointed to his legs in Death's loose grip.

He was buried from thighs to ankles in money, new green dollar bills crisp as beech leaves in fall and drifted as thickly. He cast his eyes up where Rooster's light probed the privy ceiling, and there in the eaves where Tom had vanished (or what Tom became), where Death had waited was a cardboard box on its side, lid open, a few last dollars still waving on the edge.

Lois said, "Where are we and whose is this?" She pointed again but would not touch the money.

Milo moved his head and her hand, towards her. "We are in your rightful home and this is yours." He also tried to point to the money, but his arms were still pinned.

Lois said, "Is it yours to give?"

He said, "It was yours to start with, Lois. I am just passing it on for a friend."

Rooster—nor nobody else—understood them. All he knew to ask was "How much is it?"

Hawkins Ryden horned himself in (a swollen foot in a narrow boot), took one look and said, "I estimate it's ten thousand dollars. If it is, it's the insurance Aunt Jack got for Tommy dying—claimed she never got it, but we knew she had and was too mean to say so, knew it was hid and I've looked under every damn board in that house. Well, here it is and it's every cent mine." He squatted to snatch the first fistful.

Milo kicked up a leg and struck Hawkins in the chest. "Never," he said. "It's *hers*, I told you."

Papa said, "Beg Hawkins' pardon, son. And get up out of that snake and go home. You are talking like a fool because you ain't eat supper."

Rooster said, "*That's* it. I knew I wasn't myself someway. Let's all go eat." Hawkins by now had torn off his shirt, squatted bare to the waist and was knotting the sleeves. Rooster said, "You going swimming before supper, Mr. Ryden?"

"I'm making a sack for my money," Hawkins said. "I am Miss Jack's nearest living kin, and like I said I paid for every crumb she ate for years, and she ate a many a crumb."

Lois had worked through that, not listened—Death's jaws free and Milo raised a little in her arm, she unwound the first coil, faded already of its grand bronze fire (its beauty was its life) and set loose Milo's upper body.

He rose with it now like a steel trap sprung, sat rigid with anger. "Didn't nobody hear what I just said?" he said.

Nobody answered till Macey unseen in the huddle outside yelled "Yes, you are heard."

"Then what must I do to make you believe me?" He was speaking to all the visible faces.

But again Macey answered—"Try telling the truth."

So he looked for Macey to tell it to him—he had asked, no one else—but his look was balked in a thicket of legs. He said "Macey, step here."

Macey's face bloomed between Papa and the sheriff—knee-level to them, eye to eye with Milo and not so much as glancing at the useless snake nor grinning at the girl who cradled his friend but interested only in smiling for Milo to greet him back from his mighty match.

Milo's mouth opened but his mind thought this, "How can I say to a face like that, simple and faithful as a white dinner plate, that the truth I bear was given like it was? It would break his heart—missing out on that." So he said, "Macey, gather this money up for Lois."

Macey's hand went out like a trained bird dog, took a handful. Hawkins closed on his wrist, shut the bloodstream down.

Milo calmly said "Sheriff, help Macey please."

Nobody moved. All stood frozen by Milo's fate—he had lost his mind in his quick ordeal. All but Macey. His fingers spidered in Hawkins' grip, securing his bills.

Milo said, "Sheriff, listen. If I'm not right how come I am *here* and how come three separate posses turned up at the final moment?—because you were *led* to hear what I know. This money is hers, the house, the land—and this stinking hole."

Rooster said, "Son, you are here because I asked you and Yancey to meet me here when you took the stuff to Kate—how was Kate, son?"

"She was fine," Milo said.

"And where is Yancey?"

"He's quit his job."

"No he ain't," Rooster said, "but getting back to you, we all met up in the woods awhile back between here and the road—having missed your brother, the dog, the snake—and when lightning commenced, them two bloodhounds that had been as much good as an old maid with asthma lit after a trail and drug us here in the drenching rain, thinking you was your brother—it was his scent they knew. Well, you won't but we saved you anyhow. You must smell like him is all I can say."

Macey said "He's wearing Rato's underwear."

Milo said "Am I?"

"Yes."

"How do you know?"

"Because when we went swimming week before last, I noticed you had on Rato's drawers. Too small for you."

Milo said "Maybe so" but he did not look.

And Papa said, "Week before *last?* No wonder you've lost what mind you had—swimming at the end of September, God help you."

Milo was already for his final move—against his nature, they had forced it on him. He stood entirely, shedding money, one coil still round him (so he lifted fifty pounds like a fistful of feathers). He put his lips to Rooster's ear, said secretly to him, "I know you can't do your duty at home and up to now that's been your secret, but if you don't do your duty *here* and take this money into your safekeeping till I can get home and talk to Mrs. Provo and prove my truth—well, there's other boys waiting to fill your shoes, fill *all* your shoes."

Rooster stood awhile—Milo still like a kiss at his ear—and then raised a hand to Milo's neck, harshly at first, a seizing claw. Then the pressure eased, rocked the full neck gently, and when Rooster spoke he whispered too, but what he said was "Who ruined your head?" He had only just seen the dried hole there.

Milo said, "Tom Ryden returned. This poor child's Daddy that tried to kill me, then left me alive to do his one good deed."

Rooster nodded slowly. "You going to explain everything to me later on this evening?"

"All I can," Milo said.

"About this money, I mean," Rooster said (they still whispered). "I don't want to know nothing else—you hear?—nothing I can't use in my various duties."

Milo said, "Don't worry. I'll give you your life."

And Rooster released him, used his hands like a swimmer to stroke back Milo and Papa towards the door. He picked two steps through Death's remains till he stood in the midst of the money himself, smiled at Lois, Macey, Hawkins still there on the ground. "You all step back. I'm the only Law till a better Law arrives, and I confiscate all disputed findings till the truth is clear and justice can settle." In one hand he still held the warm pistol that had finished Death.

Macey dropped his handful at once and left. Then Hawkins stood and spoke to the pistol. "You mighty right there's a better Law, and when it hears all Hawk Ryden's been through for Tommy-damn-Ryden and his Mama he deserted, it'll bring me this money on a shining tray and beg me to take it with six per cent interest."

Rooster said, "That very well may be but the duties I *can* do, I'm doing—step aside." Hawkins went and Lois rose at the order, leaving only three in the privy now—Lois and Rooster and Milo by the door, Death at his feet. But Rooster held the only light, and as Lois stood into it, started for the door, he noticed her (something he had not really done before) and with his free hand (he had holstered his gun) touched her bare arm that was damp and cold. "Excuse me, honey. I didn't intend my first word to you to be orders to *leave*. I'm trying to do what I think is best, and killing your snake was part of the best, but I'm sorry that duty laid in my path. I know he was you all's daily bread—the *world* to you—and I'll make it up to you if I ever can."

Lois said, "No need. Thank you just the same. He was not mine even. Some boy that boarded with my Aunt Selma gave him to her when he ran off and left her unpaid, and since she was leaving her husband then, it gave her the idea of traveling with snakes so she took me when my own mother died, and her and me and Death and several dozen snakes (that came and went) traveled together these thirteen years since I was three. But don't you worry. I have had this dream of stopping moving, of sitting *still*, and Death didn't have no part in my dream." She looked down a final time to the dirt, the colorless weight still faintly seething in baffled refusal to accept its end. Then she looked to the door where Milo stood—or wavered in weakness—against banked lights from the others outside. His face was towards her but too dark to read so she did not smile (which was her desire) but looked to Rooster, gave the smile to him. "Maybe I owe you *thanks*," she said. "Maybe you have forced me to find a life."

Rooster said, "Honey, you don't owe me so much as a look—a kindly look in a rainy week. Good lives are lying round thick as seed. But I would take anything you care to give. And I mean it nicely." He still had the light and could see that she looked beyond him to Milo so he took that too and said, "Can you drive a car?"

Lois said "Yes."

"Then will you do me a favor and carry him home?" He thumbed towards Milo. "He's had his day. He needs attention—feed him good, scrub his cut, strap his chest for broken ribs. I'll get most of these boys back to hunting now, and then I'll collect this money and hold it and skin this snake for your aunt to remember Tommy by, and we'll come on to the Mustian place when we've found poor Rato and killed his dog."

Lois nodded. "Who is Tommy?" she said.

Rooster turned to dark Milo who shook his head, then said, "The boy that died a debtor to your aunt." Then he asked Milo, "Son, if you lead this girl to my truck, she'll save your life. Can you walk that far?" Milo nodded. "If you can't we'll tote you."

Milo said, "I could walk to Europe."

Rooster said "I ain't asking that." Then he handed Lois his great flashlight—"We got plenty lights"—and she went on to Milo, and though they did not speak, they walked together through the door, the slack-lipped speechless men and Macey, across the clearing past the house again abandoned and into woods.

At first Milo had walked ahead, Lois holding the light, throwing it ahead between his legs, but she had quickly seen his weakness—his unsteady knees, wandering bare feet—so she moved up beside him, not explaining why, then took a little lead. He permitted that, eased back slightly to take his own time and could see her smooth legs work against the light through briars and branches, fearless, not pausing. Warned as he had been, punished but spared, Milo strained not to think—and managed it awhile. There was only the one place to keep his eyes though—on the ground ahead, Lois's light and the lower third of Lois herself—so his straining failed and he thought one thing, "Her legs are like two tan polished tusks—curving that fine, pledging that strength." Then he looked above to halt that tack, saw only black trees and said to himself, "I have not been with her in woods before." (She had stopped him on Friday night in the open, forced him to work beneath just the stars.) He shook his head sharply to fling that aside but went on looking up (for spiritual safety), feeling his forward path with his feet—till he ran full-face into Lois who had stopped and turned to wait. He drew back as if from scalding iron, said "What's wrong?"

"I was wondering that myself," she said. She kept the light downward, a pool for their feet. "—Wrong with you, I mean."

He said, "Looks like I'm a little tired."

"Tired of what?"

"Not tired *of* nothing but *because* of some things—mainly not getting my sleep last night."

"How come?" she said.

Milo knew she knew—that he had stood a cold blind beggar half the night, chattering at her door, refused as if he were crusty with sores—but he could not say it. "I was worrying about my brother," he said.

"I'm sorry," she said. Her free hand found his wrist in the dark—no fumbling at all—and shackled him with one finger, one thumb.

"That's all right," he said. "You have to worry about your kin. What else have you got?"

She said "Yourself"—he slid from her grip but did not step back. "Milo," she said, "by *sorry* I meant what I did last night, holding you back when you needed me."

"That's all right. I won't really *needing* nohow, just wishing for company. I don't need but three things—food, water, air."

She could tell by his voice that he was not smiling, but the light stayed down—she did not look. "I know that's where you are wrong," she said. "You needed your parents to get here at all. You needed your mother when you were helpless—"

"Boys have been raised by wolves," he said. "A scientific fact."

"—Now you need Lois to take your love and make us a life." Her hand moved out to take him again.

But his wrist was gone—he had shrunk back a step on his silent feet. "Let's go home," he said, "and settle some problems and get your money."

"I don't want money. I want you," she said.

"Lois, I'm a child—ain't you noticed that? Why choose me out of all you've seen, traveling the world? By morning you'll own ten thousand dollars—got with no pains but one dead snake. You could buy you the world's *best* boy. Why me?"

Lois raised the light, not enough to flood him but enough to show her his face again, clearer than since the previous morning—an ordinary face such as crowds the world, with wet straw hair hooked across his forehead, a jaw and lips that could no more lie than tat a lace band and blue eyes that seemed unable to blink—that open, *unclosed*—which calmly bore her study now.

But more than bore—he saw her too by light cast back from his own pale skin and was strongly drawn—against all warnings from the grave, all vows—to study her darkness by his own dark shine till he felt indeed the need she had mentioned, had it rush upon him like hot dry wind. "I must cherish," he thought, "and weigh in my two naked hands each half of her"—for he suddenly saw that she came in halves—her lifting breasts, high cheeks of her tail, the double folded lips of her fork. But while he thought she receded before him—dark hair, dark eyes grew darker, then black like cold stars flinging towards colder space in infinite flight at speeds beyond thought—so he lifted his hand to touch her, halt, reclaim, use the Lois he had known, had his first joy from, who had stood here moments—was it moments?—ago and begged his touch.

She whispered "Wait" and in midair he waited, strove to read in her now lightening face the sight she saw as she studied him—the face that shone beneath his own with a light not his, the face she had loved since before her birth, that rode her dreams (unnamed) each night. When her face was as warm with reflected light as the face she watched, her lips broke back on a helpless smile—greeting and gift. "I have met you," she said, "where I promised I would."

Milo nodded, his hand sank slowly—to his own flank not hers, and the buried probing light within him slowly died. They both stood dark. The flashlight was out, had been out for minutes.

Then she found his hand with her own dry hand—the cool hands of kin, demanding only company. "Where am I?" she said. Her voice was all question but firm, unafraid.

"You were home," he said, "and you'll go back soon. But come on with me to *my* home awhile. One more person's got to take my message."

She did not speak, did not move to lead. The lead was his. Having borne his message to half his mission, he took lead and moved, and in total dark—light dead in her hand—he led her out (hands still joined calmly) through harmless thorns into dripping ferns, then cold pine straw, then the edge of the ditch, the road—moonlight.

When his turning lights struck the windows of the room where the women waited and climbed towards the house, the women went quickly and stood like members of a relay team in the chilling dark to welcome him home—or as if they manned a frail lifeline, flung into water at a faceless victim, fearfully hauling him unknown ashore. Selma waited in the doorway, leaning for support. Emma waited on the porch between door and steps, beneath the light. And Rosacoke was posted on the edge of light at the foot of the steps, waiting while Milo opened his door, slowly felt with his foot for the still-dizzy ground, then stumped down and came towards her ahead of Lois (not slowing for Lois, not looking back) till porch light struck him like a second blow, opened his dry wound, flamed his stains as he passed before her (Lois coming behind) still not slowing. Rosa said to halt him, "Where is Rato? What's wrong with you?" He did not pause an instant for his sister nor even for his mother—"What hurt you, son? Where is Rato, son?"—but moved to the door despite his day as smoothly as if he rode a belt or hovered till he stopped a foot from Selma's face, raised his eyes to hers, waited in silence, his face his message.

"Tom," she said—speaking in wonder but quietly enough for Lois not to hear six feet behind.

He nodded, not meaning to lie, not lying.

Emma came up behind him, examined his wound with a hard gentle finger. "Who hurt you, son? Is Rato alive?"

He nodded, not looking back to his mother.

So Emma, deprived of his new face, went on—"Then come on and let me clean this gash and tell me all you know."

He shook his head No and spoke to Selma. "I got to tell *you* what I seen."

"I know that," she said.

"Death is dead," he said.

"I know that," she said and turned in the door and limped down—but fleet and young—towards Emma's bedroom.

His hand went out to the screen-door handle to open and follow, but his mother's hand on his shoulder held back. "Son, are you sick? I'm your Mama. Look here. Tell me what's going on."

He did not look but opened the screen and took a strong step to leave her grip. "You can come if you won't interrupt," he said, "but nobody else." Then he went towards Selma and Emma went behind, accepting for the first time yet in her life a child's condition, abandoning Lois and Rosa to the dark alone together, cold to each other as the evening air.

*   *   *

In his mother's room Selma already sat on the white iron bed she had lain in to rest (Emma's own big bed was across the room, and Baby Sister slept in it now, deep as drowned), but rest was the least thing she thought of now. She stared to the open door till Milo entered, then her eyes clasped to him as he crossed the room (Emma shut the door, threw the thumb-bolt loudly) and took his place by the mantel that hit him shoulder-high now. Their gaze was mutual—unblinking, unsmiling, broken only by Emma passing between to her low washstand where she poured out the water to deal with wounds, wrung rags, came towards him, saying, "Sit down, son. You are taller than me."

He was, this year, though they neither had noticed, but he did not sit nor acknowledge her further than to lean his head to her side slightly. Then as Emma washed, he spoke at last to Selma. "The first thing I have to tell is a story."

"That is what I can understand," Selma said.

He nodded—or Emma moved his head once for him; in any case Emma said, "Tell the truth, not stories."

"Stories can also be true," he said, still watching only Selma. "See if this story is." She nodded her readiness. He started, speaking low. "Thirteen years ago south of here"—he pointed south, Selma briefly looked—"a young fellow turned up late one night, a Saturday night, in a bus station diner with a child, a girl about three years old. He got her to eating fried pie and milk, then stepped to the bathroom and left her. But not alone. A waitress came up and asked the child was that her Daddy? The child said No, she was being kidnaped so the waitress called the Law and the jailer came. The child held out she was being stolen though she didn't show pain so the jailer asked the man to name himself, tell his destination—gave him every kind chance with the bus cranked to leave, people ganging round—but the man asked the child, 'Are you happy with me?' She nodded she was so the man set her down—he had held her till now—and said to the jailer, 'I am taking this thing that I love to my home.' But the jailer forbade him, said the man must stay till they found his name and the child's rightful parents. The waitress offered to keep the child and the child went to her, not looking back, not telling the man goodbye nor nothing so he said to the child, to her vanishing back—"

"He said, 'Meet me, darling, at home, if you can.'" Selma had said it, raised by the memory—old pain—to stand and suck for air as though the room were filling with water, chin-level, cresting against her dry lips.

Milo nodded—his own nod now (Emma's washing had stopped, she listened in silence). Then when Selma had breath, seemed steady on her feet, he asked her finally "Is that story true?"

"Every word," she said.

"But how do you know those last words he said?"

"She told me then—soon as she came back—and has said them in her sleep many long nights since long past the time she knew his name or recalled his destination for her."

Milo frowned, not deeply but enough for his mother to notice and study—a frown in his eyes as though they were pained by lies like smoke—so Emma said, "*It's* true. She told me last night but who told you?"

He still spoke to Selma and the frown deepened. "I can't tell that but I know—don't I know?"

Selma nodded, took one step forward—hand out towards him—then retracted and let the hand lower itself. "But do you know the rest?"

"I am *knowing* it more than gradually. But you got to tell it."

She sat on the bed again, heavily pressed. "Why?" she said.

"Because I am bearing an overdue message that's burning me, but I can't give it till I know the right party, have perfect proof. Tell me who was that man and who was that child and where are they now and why were they there, running from who?"

"He was Thomas Ryden—called *Tom*, your cousin—and he's buried overseas—in Guam, isn't it, Emma?—and the child was Lois, *is* Lois now beyond that thin door with your own sister. The reason they were caught in Gaffney that night is another story—" Her eyes flew to Emma for refuge, relief.

But "Tell it," he said, unsmiling, merciless.

So she told it to Emma who had heard it before. "*Mrs.* is my stage name—Mrs. Provo. I was born Selma Provo and that's how I'll die, it looks like now. But I had one person that was closer to me than husbands ever get—my sister Edith, younger than me by nearly ten years and pretty from the start. (I was born looking like a parboiled rabbit and still do, don't I?"—she glanced from Emma to the dim mirror above the mantel—"an overworked hundred-and-sixty-pound rabbit.)" She returned to Emma and they swapped quick smiles. Milo did not smile. "Our parents had died when the flu came through in the first World War, and me and her were all each other had. Papa had farmed up in north Florida, and we were raised there—land black as oil and string beans up to your earlobes for sale—but when they died, Edith and me were all but orphans—no brothers, nobody but an old maid great-aunt down in Clearwater. So we went down. I was ten years old, Edith was barely two, but we hunched our shoulders and humped our backs and Aunt Helen laid her boarding house on us to tote till she died. Tote we did—it was tote or starve. Other people think they have seen many wonders, but did you ever see a child of two with only black ringlets to shield her from harm cook three meals a day for seventeen men? And I mean *men*—railroad gangs, circus hands, drummers of every item invented—but that's what Edith had to do sometimes when I was sick or had started to school (I quit school soon, lacking heart to burden Edith). Cook and set table and serve and wash dishes and scrub and sweep and strip dirty beds—well, we did, that's all, and for twelve long years till our great-aunt died at eighty-eight on her two strong feet one Christmas eve out looking at the stars in her backyard. *Hers* I say and *hers* it was, every inch till that night when her heart burst in her and flooded her throat and the place was ours, not because she left a will in our favor but because we were all the people she had. She had outlived the rest—too mean to die. I had thought for years I would shout with joy when that day came and I did—oh privately, just me and Edith back in the kitchen, the boarders still hungry through death and all—but after that slowly as we took over in name and fact, had a few pennies to call our own, I began feeling sad in a fresh new way. I loved Edith still, leaned on her hard as ever—we had held each other up more than twelve years by leaning together like sides of a roof—but being alone with only just her, I saw for the first time how young *I* was—not but twenty-two. I say *alone*—what I mean is, you are not alone till you wake up one morning and the show is *yours* to make or break, nobody older, nobody to run to, nobody to blame, not even one mean tight-kneed aunt, *great*-aunt at that. Here I had worked like an ink-black *black* through my whole childhood, burning my strength and my will to live, my ten-cent hopes, like some kind of coal, soft fast-burning coal. And here I had eaten up all my girlhood, started on my woman-hood—and stood stock-alone, raving hungry—for love, I mean. I had lived without love for twenty-two years. Oh it can be done—to live without love. Right now there's people that do, I guess. There's people that live at the North Pole too—named Eskimoes." She stopped, chuffed three little laughs like balls of smoke, then moved her eyes from Emma to Milo as slow and cautious as if moving a bowl brim-tip with water, as pained and reluctant as a self-named criminal forced towards a judge. She chuffed again. Milo did not smile. "But I was telling about Edith, wasn't I?—my baby sister. It turned out she was worse off than me—for love, I mean. I had had a few years of a mother at least. She had even missed that, recalling only our old aunt and me—and say what you will, nobody that aims to tell the truth will claim two sisters ever get closer than puppies in a litter. I know I said differently a minute ago, but women don't love each other—do they? They weren't meant to. Anyhow Edith was thirteen then—maybe fourteen, I'm poor on figures—and if you are young and are not a peg leg and are looking for love; well, a boarding house is the place to find it—or one of the many substitutes. What she found was a child named Tommy Ryden. I say *child*—he claimed nineteen but if he was seventeen I'm a poor damn judge of what times does to eyes—and I say *found*. I saw her find him. He come in one cool night that January—just after Edith and me were free—January nineteenth, General Lee's birthday; that's how I always remember the date. We still kept the same room, the same big bed, and we had turned in and rolled separate ways when the door knocker knocked. I moaned and said something like, 'Let him sleep out, coming late as this,' but Edith was already up, in her bathrobe, heading down. I said, 'Edith, it isn't Jesus asking for pity.' 'I know that,' she said. But she went anyhow, so straight and unfearing—you could usually scare her by dropping dust—that I got up and stood at the head of the steps to watch her go and be her protection in case of a drunk (it was Saturday night). It wasn't a drunk. I often wished it had been. Drunks are mainly out to hurt themselves. It was Tommy on the porch, age about sixteen with no more baggage than a lightning bolt. She said 'Good evening.' She must have smiled—her back was to me—because he smiled back as if smiling were something he had personally invented, held a patent on. 'It's night,' he said, 'and I beg your pardon but I'm lost and looking for a warm board to lie on.' Edith said 'Who are you?' 'I'm a Christian gentleman from up north,' he said. (Our aunt's porch sign was still by the door—*Room and Board for Christian Men*—and *up north* was North Carolina of course.) Then he said, 'How much will you charge for a bed?' Edith said, 'How much have you got?' 'Nothing,' he said and she stepped back—to shut the door, I thought—but she didn't. She said, 'Then that's what I'll charge' and led him in to the little front room and put him in there with a man that was advertising a show—some circus was coming and he went ahead of it, putting up signs on any bare barn. Well, she turned to leave him in the dark doorway and climb back to me but he said 'Wait.' She waited. He said, 'My name is Tom and I just want to say, however old you get to be, there'll always be one boy named Tom that worships your name.' 'Then my name is Edith,' she said and waited awhile more and turned and dragged herself up towards me as if I was prison gates, cold iron. But I never said one hard word to her—not to ask how much that boy had paid or when he was leaving, least of all how come she had welcomed him in to all we had—our home, after all—with no word of who he was but *Tom*. There have been Toms that cut women's throats in their sleep. This one didn't but he might as well— Edith's, I mean. He had cut her *heart* out by eight the next morn- ing—just by drinking the coffee she poured, saying 'Thank you' for every move she made. (If you ever work in a boarding house, you'll think the word *Thank you* is some foreign thing you learned in a dream, that nobody else ever learned or uses.) All I did was stand and watch. My philosophy was—still is today: if you're anything—man, woman, fox—that's on the run, and there's all grades of hounds, and you see cover yawning in the midst of your path and that cover doesn't show a *Keep Out* sign, then take it and pray it's not a bear's cave or a rattler's hole—though people have lived with snakes before. And Edith was on the run. *I* knew—from me, from our aunt that was barely cold, from her life that was dry as a baked tin can. The worst trouble was—so was he, so was Tom. And from the same thing—no previous soul had loved him enough to say, 'Stand still please. Let me *look* at you,' then look awhile and say, 'Thank you. Yes. I am coming to you. From this time forth you will be my life.' Well, Edith said it before a week passed, but it wasn't what Tom wanted to hear, not then anyhow. He stood still exactly long enough—excuse me, Emma—to sling one baby deep up her like a hook. It hooked and grew—and Tom was long gone, having taken up with his circus roommate—and when I saw it growing, it was too late to act. All I could do was wait, wait with Edith, keep her out of sight, tell her what seemed lies—that Tom would be back like he said he would, would be here now if she knew his address and could get him word. 'Word?' she'd say. 'He doesn't need *word*. He *aimed* to do this and did it and smiled and said, "Pray it's a girl that has your hair." ' I mentioned Edith's baby ringlets? They were long by then, blue as black cockerel feathers swagging down her back. Well, he aimed dead-center. It was nothing but a girl, and you've seen her hair already, both of you—" Selma's voice failed—not a crack nor a frog, just silence when she moved her lips to continue so she waved again with her hand towards the door, towards wherever black-crowned Lois lurked. Emma looked but not Milo. Selma's voice returned. "But his hook went on past the baby still deeper, struck Edith in the heart, and she died while I was bathing the child. I had been the only one with her, you see; done all the work that Edith didn't do—she was cheerful and awake through the whole quick thing—but when I tied the cord and turned with the baby and went to the washstand, Edith said, 'Selma, don't take *her* away.' I didn't look round. I thought she was joking. I said 'Hush up and rest' and went to bathing, saying backwards to Edith, 'This child hasn't cried. That's a good sign, isn't it? She just started breathing as easy as walking—a quiet soul, let's wish her that.' Edith didn't speak. I thought she was asleep and finished my work and wrapped the baby and went back to her, saying 'Name it now.' But she was far deeper down than sleep so I named the child Lois for our own mother, then

called the doctor. Her heart, he said, wasn't big enough to drive a cat
much less a girl through sixteen years of field-hand labor and a secret
child. That was October tenth, sixteen years ago—my God, *today*. It's
Lois's birthday and we all forgot." She looked at last to Milo. "Did you
remember and give her something?"

"I think I have got her the grandest gift, but you hadn't finished
your story yet. Tell to the part I have already told." His previous con-
tinuous frown was deeper, as a guard dog lying at your side will tense
at threats that reach his ears and subside without your notice or care.

"That is the hardest part," Selma said, but she nodded to Milo and
told it to him. "Two months later right after Thanksgiving—when I had
nearly got myself back together and Lois was thriving but I was dreading
the Christmas season—an envelope came addressed to Edith. The first
mail she ever got and too late, postmarked *Wilmington, Delaware*. I
couldn't be sure who it was from, but for three or four days, I couldn't
bear to open it. I held it to the light but could not see through so I laid
it in a drawer till I worked up my grit. It was a Christmas card from
Tommy, saying, '*I have been running the snake show lately. They have
gone on down to winter quarters where I'll join them soon and will trust to
see you, but meanwhile I hope it is time for this—so here is a gift to buy
something with for yourself and anybody else you have by now that I
ought to love.*' The gift was ten dollars. No way to return it—still no
address—and anyhow in 1932 ten dollars was something I'd have taken
from Hitler. So I took it and bought my baby some clothes (a cap for
ears that protruded at first and the rest I put into flowers for Edith). I say
my baby and she seemed to be that from the first bath I gave her—still
seems to be and treats me mostly kindly though she knows her real
mother died at her birth and thinks her father died broken hearted a few
months later, leaving her to me, to take my name. But her father came
sooner than he said he would—Christmas day about suppertime. Imagine how happy a day I had had—alone as a Catholic at a Baptist con-
vention, a three-months' orphan my only company, even my worst class
of boarders—tramps—gone to *some* roost. I was back in the kitchen
warming Lois's milk when a soft knock came. My heart lifted slightly
and I took Lois with me and went to answer, hoping it would be somebody, *something* that I could welcome. It was Tom—who else?—look-

ing five years older, so thin and tired that whatever I had meant to say or feel, I said 'Merry Christmas.' He smiled and bowed and said 'Who is that?' and I handed him Lois—right out the door to the porch where he stood. The second I did it I saw my mistake—the way he took her, held her to him, studied her with no more questions, as natural and happy, as *relieved* as if he had come in a dead-straight line through hails of pain hoping to find this very thing that he had started long months before. I knew from that second I would have to fight to keep her mine, keep her safe from him, make her all the amends she was already due. So I put out my arms to accept her back—not saying 'Come in'—but he came with Lois, not giving her up till we stood in the kitchen and he laid her on the table (she had not whimpered yet) and asked where was Edith. 'What do you mean to do with her?' I said. 'What?' he said. I said, 'What if Edith was to walk in now and say what you know—that this child is yours—and then ask you what future you saw for her?' He thought about that, then answered to Lois—'I'd tell her I wasn't no gypsy,' he said, 'no fortune teller. I *wait* for the future, let it come when it will.' I said, 'How about the past? Can you understand that?' He didn't look at me. He studied that child as if she was Scripture—and she let him study, lay still, serious. Then he turned to me. 'Yes I do,' he said. 'I have killed Edith, ain't I?' 'Yes,' I said and he went back to Lois and stayed there with her like she was his till her milk was ready. I took her then and he watched me feed her, but I couldn't watch him and we didn't speak, barely spoke for two days—not because we were either one *enemies* but maybe because barely knowing each other, we loved and wanted and thought we needed the same one thing—that simple child—and were both working out our plans in silence to win her for good. Well, if Tom had a plan at the end of three days, it was nothing but *wait*. Some roomers turned up towards the end of the week so Tom told me he would head on down to the show's winter quarters and rejoin his snakes. He gave me another ten dollars which I took out of need—and partly pity, my second mistake—and I took his address and promised to write in case of bad trouble. We were on the porch steps before he said what he really felt, what laid my heart open clean as a blade—'Selma, I know you have reasons for grief—so do I—but I want you to know I am finally happy, having this child I made that will love

me, need me all of her life, all of *mine* and mourn me beyond whatever
grave I choose.' I said, 'Tom, don't count too hard on that. You said you
were not a prophet—remember?—and nobody's bound to love anybody else. Half the time, blood runs thinner than water.' He nodded to
that, said 'I well know that—my past life shows how thin blood can
get—but I'll be to her something she cannot fail to love.' 'Oh what will
that be?' I said and laughed, no longer swallowing the bitter taste that
had coated my throat since Edith went. And I laughed on louder, 'And
when will it be?' He did not strike back but when I had calmed, he went
down the steps and turned in the walk and said, 'Don't you see that is all
I need to know, all *I'm* trying to find?' I could not laugh again but I gave
him my back and threw my last bolt, 'Don't fail to send me a postcard—
hear?—when you're something to love. Contact us then and we'll both
come to you through snakes or *snow*. I promise that.' Then he—"

Milo said "Wait." His face that had frowned in gathering doubt
was clenched now in pain, and his calm heart lurched into double
speed—for no reason he knew. But he fought to understand. "How
much of all you have said is true?"

"Every word," Selma said.

And his mother said "*Milo*," meaning to warn him against disre-
spect, seeing him only for what he had been, to now, to her for fifteen
years—her oldest boy yet a boy, a baby. But the boy suffered. She
could see that much—his face white and drawn (all the muscles
drawn *up*), his careless hands that seldom touched himself now
kneading his chest. Emma took him by the shoulder, said, 'Son, now
rest. You have heard enough," and he looked down at her for the first
time since morning, spread his lips to speak but silence came, then
tried to yield to her guiding arm, follow her towards rest.

But Selma said "*Wait*, oh wait, don't move" and put out her own
detaining hand that again hung before her, sealed in air.

He could not move—only his eyes which returned to Selma.
What came after, he read in her face which mirrored slowly, a
moment late, his own pain and fear, her added amazement. What he
felt, more than pain, was pressure—the sense, in the final words
Selma said, that the room around them, above, beneath was suddenly
full, packed with a presence unseen as air but offended, potentially

hurtful, growing and with each ounce of weight demanding from Milo's pressed skull and hear what they could not give—mere truth, plain justice to the unseen nameless rush around him.

Selma felt the same rush but studying Milo and its work in him, she knew its name—Milo's face being finally, fully Tom's from within, Tom's as he always looked on leaving, as though he were drawn, torn, washed away by hateful powers not his own flawed heart, as though your duty was to fling yourself into night and storm to hold his lips one moment from drowning (when you yourself had strangled long since in abandonment). And she felt the demand on her own tired chest, finally knew it was just if not right. Facing the hurt and baffled boy four yards away—and thirteen years and the rest of time— she managed to move her head a little, side to side in the sign for denial. Then at once the full room began to empty, pierced by the final approach of truth. Selma's head moved freely, her lips and voice said "No" clearly. Her hand that had been trapped out to detain now loosened, moved round once in farewell.

And Milo was free, dispossessed, also abandoned, allowed to speak—exhausted and low. "Now tell what is true."

Selma said, "It was true if you leave out Edith. There was never an Edith."

Emma said, "Selma, you lied to me."

Selma smiled, "Emma, I have lied to worse than you."

Emma said, "Then this will have to change my opinion—"

"Hush," Milo said. "Opinions ain't worth the meanest hant in Hell. This evening I have found—been led to find—ten thousand dollars which I got to give justly to the rightful owner." He turned back to Selma. "Tell on," he said. "The pure truth now."

But Emma stepped between them. "You two couldn't tell the truth," she said, "if God walked in that oak door now and said, 'Judgment Day! Sheep here, goats there.'" She turned on Selma—"Making me hear that long story twice because I thought it was pitiful and true and you and that black-headed girl deserved help—why, I couldn't sit through *Gone With the Wind*, and you have the nerve to use my roof as a shed for lies and, pardon my French, a strumpet's den. Get yourself ready and *I'll* drive you to your trailer." Then she turned to Milo.

"I hope you are crazy—I hope to God—because if you ain't, you have grown overnight to be a worse fool and scoundrel than your Daddy and that's fast moving, son. I spent twenty years of my life with a fool— a drunk one at that—who thought the world, meaning me, owed him air, food, blood just because he could smile most women's hearts out. Well, I gave mine once but never again. I'm ugly as a mud fence daubed in misery and I've sinned my share, but one thing I have done with my life—I have *learned* some things, learned you don't use your eyes to judge people by, learned you don't get nothing worth taking home till you've paid hard money of one sort or other, tears, stinking sweat. *Found* ten thousand dollars! Been *led* to find it!" She seized Milo's arm as though it were lethal, must be fought for life. "I reckon you were led by an angel of God and are licensed by Heaven to talk like a fool. But where's the money? I don't see you stooping your back with the load." Not glancing at Selma, she pushed Milo before her towards the door—leaving Baby Sister asleep to guard Selma. "This day is over for *you*, big man. You get upstairs and get in the bed but kneel down first and beg salvation. I ought to call the Law on both of you." She threw the door open on Rooster Pomeroy and light struck his badge, his smiling teeth, a loaded paper bag resting on his holster. (Rosacoke waited in the dim hall behind him—and dimmer behind her, what seemed to be Lois.)

Emma stepped back and tried to say "Speak of the devil," but the shock had her breathless, and the sheriff anyhow was studying Milo. "Son," he said, "what must I do with this money?" He unrolled the greasy mouth of the bag (it had held his lunch) and drew out more cash than his pudgy fist could hold—bills tumbled round his feet and were stirred by the draft.

Milo freed his arm from Emma, stepped back, said "Come in." Rooster entered the bedroom and Rosacoke followed at a sneaking distance. Milo slid Emma's hand off the white doorknob, pushed the door against Rosa. "Not you," he said, "but get Lois ready."

"For what?" Rosa said through the locking door.

"For me, when I call her."

"Who are *you*?" Rosa said.

"Amen," Selma said—or whispered through tears.

But Milo said "Milo," then "Everybody sit."

Selma sat on the bed, Rooster sat in the smallest straight chair in the house (money and hat like a scales on his knees), Milo himself leaned back on the mantel. Only Emma stayed up.

She had found her voice and she turned to the sheriff. "I know I don't have many rights. I have had that ground in my face tonight, but this *is* my bedroom (or was till last night) so before anybody starts another long lie, just tell me one thing—is Rato alive?"

Rooster gestured to the chair nearest Emma (a plushbottomed rocker). "If that's all that's worrying you, sit down," he said. "Lady, *lay* down flat." Emma waited upright so he said to Milo, "You told her about the snake?" Milo nodded. "Then we *know* he's all right. What's left to harm him?—just a little mad dog that loves him like a Daddy, and if by mistake it should snag him with a tooth, they got enough serum on ice in town to cure him of whale bite. No ma'm, I left my men looking for him—his Granddaddy's with them—and they'll be here with him by bedtime sure."

Emma sat and said "Thank you."

Rooster said, "Son, I have counted this money—nine thousand eight hundred eighty-nine dollars. You were talking mighty high in Miss Jack's johnny and of course I knew why—that snake choked round you—but now that you're calm and got your good nature back, tell me all you know. Whose money was this?"

Milo spoke as himself for the first time since dark. "It was what Tommy Ryden got for dying in Guam—ten thousand dollars from Uncle Sam, less eleven dollars Miss Jack spent or lost. But with her dead now, it belongs to—"

"Hold on." Rooster smiled but meant it. "We ain't there yet. Where did you find the money?"

"Where you found me."

"Why were you in there?"

Milo strained to remember.

Rooster read the strain as embarrassment, charged in with help—"Just say 'Call of nature.'"

Milo did not say it, said nothing because he could think of nothing, retained his frown.

"Why were you at the Ryden place at all?"

Milo's frown—no longer of pain but of blankness—deepened further.

"Because I had told you to meet me there—you and that sorry Yancey when you come back from Kate." Rooster waited, no confirmation came though Milo faced him square as Truth on a courthouse. "Ain't that why?"

Emma said, "Son, are you feeling bad?—dizzy maybe? You've got every right to."

Milo said "No," facing each one separately, then staring at the light bulb bare in their midst. "I just do not remember."

Emma stood and moved towards him, laid a gentler hand on his shoulder now. "Come rest," she said and Milo yielded, took a step to obey.

Rooster said—almost whispering, "Just one minute. You claimed this money didn't go to Hawkins, that your black-headed girl was the rightful owner, that you would get me proofs, had a message to give." Then he also rose, approached Milo kindly—"Remember all that?"

Milo said "No," no longer frowning.

Selma said, "Sheriff, the message was given."

"What was it?" Rooster said.

"It was private," Selma said.

Emma nudged Milo another step towards the door. Rooster set his hat on the floor and rose, then he laid on Milo a look of reproach as heavy as mild. "Son," he said, "you have misused me when I trusted you, took you for a man."

Milo faced him, unflinching but too tired to wonder what misuse he meant or defend himself by revealing secret favors he had anyhow forgot or never known of—Kate's life refreshed, her dryness watered, Rooster's name prolonged one generation more.

Rooster opened his palm on the cud of money. "Well, I hope this will make Hawkins Ryden smile. Wonder what he'll do with it?"

"Make misery," Emma said, voice hard as a spike, "or at least not ease the misery he's in—wife and children hanging barefoot and boney on a front porch that won't support a feather bed. It'll be a black sin and I'll always wonder why—but I wonder a lot." She took the doorknob to lead Milo to rest. "Sheriff, find my boy and bring him to me."

"Yes, ma'm," Rooster said and restuffed his bag, bent to take his hat.

Selma said "Wait." They all turned to her—she was white as paper—but she spoke to only Rooster. "You almost spoke of Tommy Ryden this morning. I heard you. I know. How come you stopped?"

Rooster said, "So I wouldn't harm his rest if he's resting somewhere though I doubt he is—all the pain he caused."

"Who to?" Selma said.

"Well, his poor old Mama and Daddy that he left just like they were weeds that could live on air."

Selma said, "Most people do that. That's what Jesus intended—put your hand to the plow and don't never look back."

Rooster nodded to that. "Jesus ought to been shot. But he plowed all right—right through everything he touched."

"Name one thing," Selma said.

"Well, *me*," Rooster said.

"Did you know him?" she said.

"*Know* him? I've lived with him every day of my grown life and slept with his memory at my side every night for thirteen years." (Milo slid from his mother's loose grip and her hand eased on the doorknob to listen.) "No, I never seen him to know who he was, not even a picture though we spent our childhoods three miles apart. The first I remember hearing his name was when he left home in the early Depression. I was already working in the Law—a deputy—and early one morning his Daddy come in to the office and said their boy was lost and would we find him? Boys was getting lost like buttons back then, but I said I'd try and asked Mr. Ryden to describe him please—height, weight, hair, the usual stuff. He thought awhile but he didn't know—didn't know what color his son's eyes were. I thought to myself, 'I'd have got lost too,' but I said, 'Then how will we recognize him?' and he said—no waiting, 'Find the pitifulest girl in every town you try and shake her till she rattles—he'll fall out eventually.' I asked him again how old the boy was. 'About fourteen,' he said. So I said 'Why the pitifulest girl?' 'Because,' he said, 'Tom's hot as a pistol, he's looking for love and aims to spread joy, but nothing but a fool would let him in.' Well, we never found him and I never told this to another breathing soul, but I'll tell you tonight—a little later on, one fool let him in down in Florida, a woman considerably older than him that ran a rooming house. Let him in—excuse me—in more ways than one and had herself a baby as a souvenir, a girl I believe."

"How do you know that?" Selma said, looking only at him.

"Oh the Law kept up with Tommy Ryden—well, not *kept up* but at least a step behind. He was too fast for us—too fast for everything but one Jap bullet, just a little slug of lead."

Selma swallowed that, hard, to preserve a calm face. "What did he ever do but run away from home?"

"Run away from everything else," Rooster said. "But the reason we was *really* hunting him once was, he stole that child he claimed was his—went to see that woman when the child could just walk, acted sweet as ever, give her handsome presents and walked off with that child clean as a cut when the fool wasn't looking, *run* off by bus and got to South Carolina—headed God knows where—till they caught him in Gaffney on the woman's complaint. That's how I knew. But I never told his Mama and his Daddy was dead. The woman raised a yell to the Florida police, and they notified every sheriff in the country. Well, they held him in Gaffney for a day or two till they knew who he was and could ship the child back and extradite him—and he run again, out of jail, out of *sight*. Not before he plowed up another soul though, sitting tight in jail." Rooster stopped, bent his straw hat double, wrung it like a rag.

"Who?" Milo said.

Rooster wouldn't look up, not wanting to hear.

"What soul?" Milo said.

Rooster faced him, said "Kate my wife's"—quietly, all but whispering as though in the midst of a warm room of people—two women, a boy, a sleeping child—a secret was still a matter of tone. Then he smiled and said "But you knew that."

Milo did not nod but did not deny.

"I knew you knew—soon as you said Yancey didn't stay with you. And I must have known Yancey wouldn't stay—must have sent you on purpose. Reckon I did?"

Milo did not nod.

Rooster said, "Thank you. She don't mean harm. She can't help herself and I can't help her—I told you that. Ever try being somebody else? I mean trying to do your job in the dark when the girl you were loving wasn't studying *you*, wasn't living in her body but was hid in her mind with some other face you never even saw? You don't blame me do you?—I mean for sending you in, for my whole life even?" Rooster was smiling—not broadly but fully, clearly, in total surrender, total shame.

Milo did not nod.

"It don't make me nothing but a fool," Rooster said. "Does it, son? Think around a little—there's other fools living. Think—and I think of her every night—of that poor lonesome fool down in Florida."

Selma said, "That's me. Thank you for the thought."

Rooster wheeled on her, at first in relief (that other fools existed), smiling—"*What?*" Then sitting, dumping backwards on his squatty chair in cold astonishment.

Selma nodded. "I am her—that took Tom in every way you mentioned, some you didn't and won that baby that's out yonder now and hung my unused love around her and took his visits twice yearly like *food* till that last visit when he came with the snake—a baby python that he may have stolen—and seeing I didn't flinch from it like a woman, said, 'Selma, never say I left you empty-handed' and handed me the snake, then left in the night with Lois that loved him even harder than me though she doesn't remember."

"Can you prove it?" Rooster said.

"Prove what?" Selma said.

"That you are the foo—that the child is yours and Tom was the Daddy?"

"Look at me," Selma said. "Ain't I proof? Ain't these scars enough?" She laid both palms loud and flat on her forehead, drew them slowly downward over eyes, neck, breast, then abandoned the rest as too ruined to show.

Rooster said, "Lady, you are holding up fine. If you had a *car* that was fifty years old, you'd think it was due to knock on you a little."

"I am forty-one years old," Selma said—and could smile at that. (Even Emma smiled.)

"Proved," Rooster said and ducked in apology. "But what I'll need is legal proof, something Hawkins Ryden can't chew up in court."

Selma said, "I've got stacks of that locked in my trailer in a little strong box—her birth certificate (I didn't lie then), Tom's letters to me and her, and his picture. But I haven't seen the picture since I last saw *him*. It's sealed in a blank envelope, no name." She paused to justify that to herself. "I owe myself *some* favors, don't I?"

Rooster said, "Yes'm. Then the money is yours." He stood and went to her, his stuffed sack extended. Selma's hand hung open, limp at her side. Rooster reached to take it, then paused, remembered— "You know I had to kill your snake?" Selma nodded. "It was *snake* or *boy*"—he pointed to Milo—"so I chose *boy* having no time to think. Maybe if I had—but I saved you the skin, already nailed it to the side of Miss Jack's to cure-out for you, make you shoes for life."

Selma shook her head. "Let Hawkins have it. After thirteen years, what is it to me?—not one scale on it Tom ever touched."

"On you neither," Rooster said and smiled. "Washed by time—like the Luray Caverns!"

Selma also smiled. "Like Kate your wife."

Rooster thought that through, continued smiling, took her limp hand firmly, closed it round the money, said again "It's yours."

Even Milo smiled.

Selma sat on the bed (backwards, not looking, the sack unnoticed in her unnoticed hand) and studied Milo—for *Milo* he was again, only himself, a tired wounded boy, harmless, powerless, abandoned by Tom as finally as she, with less of Tom now in his face and person than most cousins share, however distant. Why had she ever sweated blood over that; why crawled up and down the Eastern seaboard with a ten-cent show and the snake he gave in hopes of seeing him one more time, that one night Tom would stroll in, make amends; why lied to Lois that she was her aunt when she herself had made every *grain* of Lois? Well, all that was over, *done*, thank God. Seventeen years she had worked in that harness. "How did it ever hold me?" she said, astonished, relieved—to Milo and all he had meant tonight.

Milo barely heard and did not understand, but he shrugged and grinned with his eyes shut for rest.

"Thank you," she told him, then left him with her eyes—forever, she thought—and looked to Rooster, held the sack out to him. "No it isn't," she said.

Rooster's face fell open in silent shock, and Emma winced deeply (meaning "Not only strumpet and fool but wasteful"), but Milo gathered new life from the words, the "No" itself—his shoulders, chest, chin filled with sudden strength, his eyes with the last glow of mission, message. "Right," Milo said. "It was never yours. It is Lois's—and has been since Tom Ryden fell and bled to death."

"Lois doesn't know that," Selma said.

"Yes she does. I told her an hour ago—with Death wrapped around me and ten thousand dollars like a blanket of leaves."

Selma said, "But she doesn't know *why* it's hers—and never will. I have spent every minute since I got her back, soothing her Daddy out of her memory (any dreams she had), filling any gaps he left in her with all the love I could find to give, and I'm not about to gouge her up again." Again she offered Rooster the sack, thrust it towards him. He did not move so she turned back to Milo. "It's nothing but money. You take it, son. Make your family happy. I give it to you."

"Thank you," Milo said. "But it's not yours to give."

"Let us be," Selma said. "Open that door please and give me your arm and a ride back to town, and we'll leave your life and live our own. Haven't we earned that much—*me* anyhow, after all my pains?"

Milo said "No."

"Who are *you*?" Selma said. "Who gave you the right to ruin my little life I have made?"

Milo no longer knew but he had the right. He knew that at least, and in two silent steps he stood at the door, hand on the knob, half-turned to open.

Selma stood. "Emma, stop him. Emma, save my baby for me—she is *mine*."

Emma said, "Selma, you have to tell her. I don't understand no more than you—least of all understand my own boy Milo—but Milo's right. Let him tell her, Selma."

"Just give me one reason—what good will it do her? How can she use that ugly news? Emma? Sheriff?"

"As a warning," Emma said.

"Of *what?*" Selma said. She searched every face, even Baby Sister's. They all were thinking. Baby Sister seemed drowned.

Finally Milo said "Of love."

Emma nodded — "Of the ruins love has made."

Rooster nodded — "Of the ruin life is if love has to lie."

Selma settled on Milo. He bore her look but had no further answer — *was* and had been for two days his answer. She shut her eyes, nodded, "You tell her please."

Milo opened the door on the dim deep hall. Lois and Rosa seemed a county away, propped straight as slats on the opposite wall two yards apart. Milo saw only Lois and only Lois moved — when she came forward to him, Rosa kept her own place. It at least was hers.

When Lois stood well into the room and the door was shut, Milo stepped to Selma and took the full sack, then went to Lois — hand's breath from her face — and spoke to her eyes (no one else could have met them), "This is the gift your father left you. He died to get it and meant you to have it. His name was Tom Ryden. The house where you saved my life is your home and this is your mother." He nodded towards Selma.

Lois put out her hand and took the sack as though she had spent her life taking gifts, her unquestioned due but for which she was grateful. Then she said, "I have known that all my life, but it slipped my mind till an hour ago. I will always love — "

Baby Sister said "Wait" and every eye jerked to the corner bed where through cracked eyelids, sleep-roaring ears, she had seen, heard all. Now she rose to her knees in the nest of cover, eyes squinted, lips down. "What in the Sam Hill is love?" she said.

Milo suddenly knew, took two steps towards her, spread smiling lips to tell, warn, delight her, then dropped — silent, senseless — in a heap by her bed.

THREE

If Milo was well he slept without dreaming (or if he dreamed it was only of rest—a walk through shade or stretched in green woods, shielded from day) so now when he woke, he knew he was healed—he had slept that calmly since they laid him here though for only nine hours. Rooster had carried him up in his arms at eight in the night. It was five o'clock now—well before dawn, still dark—but he woke because of a sound not the hour. Someone said his name and before it was finished, his eyes were open—on total dark. His first thought was, "I have not dreamed. I am all right," but the voice spoke again—or asked again, both times the name had been a question: *Milo?* clearly. The voice was near and seemed a young woman's so his second thought was, "I am *deathly* sick. I am dreaming a girl is in my room." He clamped his eyes twice to force them awake, and then he could see—but only dark shapes by the crack of hall light that slid beneath the door. The shape was a girl and the girl seemed Lois—her height, size, long hair streaming, arms and shoulders bare. She stood at the foot of the bed and waited—her question asked. Then Milo thought, "I am not alone. I am sleeping with Rosa who will wake any minute and raise a yell." And he longed to say, "Fool, this ain't a fair. It's a home. Go to bed." But his left hand slid up to test the head-board—the cold carved grapes of his own bed—and his right hand slid across warm sheets to test for Rosa. Rosa was gone if she'd ever been there. Milo said to himself, "Wherever we are and whenever it is, Lois is standing in her slip by my bed." He was fully awake.

Lois asked again—"Milo?" and waited.

Milo thought, "She is not asking after my health. She is offering me the only thanks she knows. Wherever all the others are and however crazy it will be, how can I lie still, not welcome her?" And his left hand moved from the headboard to greet her but rising, brushed his bandaged head (bandaged by his mother after he fainted), the hidden cut like a savage warning. So his hand lay still. He said to himself, "I was nearly killed for *taking* once already. I am meant to give." He did not speak, lay quiet but breathing—not faking sleep—and waited for Lois to understand that, that his service was ended. At last she did, turned, moved to the door, stood a moment half-naked in naked light, then left, shut Milo again in his dark—the deepest dark being what even after Sunday he did not know and warned by his wound (by Death itself) could not learn yet: that givers and takers need not be separate, can be two joined hands locked yet shifting, each becoming the other awhile (if the gift from one hand at least is love—the attempt to accept, forgive, pledge shielding).

He lay a moment in the various darks, satisfied, free to rest again. His eyes shut slowly. Then as if delayed between eyes and mind, that last sight struck him—Lois in the door, having failed to give thanks, turning to leave, maybe for good. And other sights followed in a hot rush within him—Buck Russell watching his black girl leave, not knowing— never knowing—if her rising belly was his first child; Selma Provo accepting Tom's gift of Death, thanking him and rising next day to find him gone forever (with Lois for a while); Lois herself at the age of three leaving Tom by the bus in South Carolina with a promise to meet which could not be kept; Kate Pomeroy feeding Tom the key to freedom and waiting too late on her single bed; Milo himself four years ago at the age of eleven on the Afton store porch one Saturday evening, staring up the road at his staggering father who came towards him smiling (it had seemed a smile), then a truck tore between and halted beyond, and the air where his father should have stood was a hole; even Rato on Saturday vanishing in trees after Death and Phillip—maybe also for good. Milo rose in the bed at the thought of his brother—lost? found? dead?

or trapped in pain? His kin was his duty whatever his wounds, and he flung his bare feet to the cold floorboards, felt his body, found himself still in Rato's drawers, groped towards a chair for the rest of his clothes, then heard down the hall Rosa's door shut gently, footsteps quicker than Rosa's on the steps, heading down, away—Lois surely, dressed and leaving. He found his trousers and shirt, pulled them on, reached the door in a step, stood a last dark moment—head knocking, swimming—and said aloud the thing he had earned for his trouble and care, "What use on earth is a warning from the dead when the dead are at rest?"

No answer came. They were resting at last.

So he opened the door, lurched into the hall, the watery light and tracked Lois, trackless.

He had been so fiercely seized by the chance—the certainty—of loss that he ran without looking past the cracked kitchen door (warm light streaming) through hall, front door and stopped on the porch in what was still night—air chilled and damp—staring uselessly towards the hidden road, thinking, "Gone. Gone. Another one gone. Young as I am, they are *leaving* me."

Emma's voice said "Son."

He wheeled on his mother where she stood in the door, dark against the hall behind her. "What?"

"*Ma'm*," she said.

"Ma'm?" he said.

"Rato is dead."

For an instant he thought she spoke of his father—Rato was also his father's name—and that they had lost his father again, must endure the cut, the long year of healing, again. *How?*Then he saw his mother's hands stiffly extended and went towards them. Her hands were full, not empty for him to fill and comfort. He leaned in the dark to see what she offered—a wad of cloth which he took, held up to the light to examine. A blue shirt torn as if by hate and mottled with emblems of blood like entrails—rust brown shapes of livers, lungs, a great dry heart. It had been his own shirt a year ago, but when he grew, it had passed to Rato—his brother Rato.

He replaced the shirt in his mother's hands, then looked to her face and shook in surprise. Her eyes were strangled with grief again, the thing he had vowed at his father's death to spare her in future. Again he had failed. He could only speak. "Where is he now?"

Her head shook side to side in mystery.

"Then who brought you this and where was it lying?"

She tried to speak, then finding no speech, stabbed with a finger towards the kitchen behind her. Then speech came or hideous noise—"Huunh," the cornered plea for relief.

Milo took his mother's elbow, lifted her the one step into the hall, led her as though she were blind to the kitchen.

The kitchen was the largest room in the house and always the warmest though its walls and floor were applegreen. There were two cook stoves—one electric, one wood—and two broad tables. The one in the center nearer the door was dark wood—the family eating table. The other was by the opposite wall, smaller, lower, covered with red oilcloth for work, and when Milo opened the kitchen door fully, nudged his mother ahead, he looked past the three men at the eating table over what seemed watery space, long time, to the smaller table where Lois sat with Rosacoke facing—Rosa's open palm in Lois's hand, Lois studying it till Milo entered, then meeting his eyes with her eyes blank, not smiling, not frowning but not unkind, only waiting for his eyes to show their need.

And he felt a need like wind upward through him to rush somehow through all the dense space (the hot crowded room, his fool mistakes), seize Lois, take all the thanks she could give, give all she had shown she needed from him, his thanks returned for these brief days—his whole life to come his gift to her.

But before he could so much as show that need and though she stood to receive it, dropping Rosa's hand, he was called back to duty. Two of the men at the big table stood—Rooster and Mr. Favro the preacher (Papa was the third, he stayed in his chair)—and Mr. Favro came to Milo, arms hooped to force unwelcome harbor on him. He accepted duty. His eyes left Lois (she sat again slowly, turned slowly back to Rosa), and took Mr. Favro's stifling embrace, the voice like warm oil ladled on his neck—"Death is dead."

Milo nodded into the hot shoulder—"I know that."

And Rooster said softly to Milo's eyes, "Of course he's dead. Me and Milo killed him."

Mr. Favro had not heard. "It's nothing but a brief postponement now, nothing but a nuisance. You will all be lonesome for a few hard months, then the years will slide and there he'll stand in New Jerusalem—waiting, smiling, clothed in light to welcome you in and show you the ropes—"

Milo drew himself back, stood free to draw breath—not so much as thankfully glancing at Mr. Favro—then reached behind for the shirt his mother held, extended it towards Rooster. "Where did you find this and where is he lying?"

"Somewhere under them peaceful stars." Rooster pointed behind him to the still-dark window—(no one could see stars; they took them on faith, the night having cleared). "After you fell out and I got you in bed, got the ladies easy, I drove back towards the Ryden place and met your Papa coming out of the woods with that bloody shirt and the posse behind him. A bloodhound had found it, running from the snake, and the posse found the hound curled down in a ditch with the shirt in his mouth. Your Papa said he recognized the shirt, and they combed around for another good hour in the dark thick as weeds till all of the flashlights were finally failing and they gave up and struck for the road and met me there. When I seen that shirt I knew the worst so I said to your Papa, 'Come on, Mr. Mustian, I'll ride you home to rest till light. He'll wait till morning. Wherever he lies, he's peaceful now.' Your Papa agreed so I thanked the posse and sent them home. We come on here and your Mama called the preacher and here we've sat. But don't you worry. It'll be morning soon, hasn't failed in *my* lifetime."

"It is morning eternal where Rato is." Mr. Favro slammed in his wedge, first chance. "And Milo, son, if you look at him right, think about the harmless life he lived in the time he had, never bothered a soul—"

"Never spoke to one." Papa said it for himself but aloud, firmly.

"—If you study him, I say; follow his example, he'll shine for you through life's dark nights like the North Star of old to wanderers lost."

Milo said, "Are you speaking of Rato or Jesus?"

"Well, *Rato*," Mr. Favro said, "though the same goes for Jesus."

"Then say again what his example was—Rato's to me."

Mr. Favro looked to Emma for help—it had been her boy—but she stood dumb and dazed against the door. So he faced round to Papa. "Mr. Mustian, what would you say to that?"

Papa said, "I won't the one making claims for Rato. He won't an example of nothing to me. All I knew was, Rato was different. All he needed that other people needed was something to eat. And then all I could do was feed him—or have food standing by ready, don't you know? But Preacher, you're the one with education. If Rato was ever any kind of example, you are the one to know what of."

"Of never hurting things," Mr. Favro said.

Emma said "That's it."

Milo stood a moment alone with himself, not seeing even Lois. Then he said to Mr. Favro, "If morning should come and we go out and find Rato's body lying truly dead—then will be time enough for me to tell you what a lie you've told."

Mr. Favro's eyes flew to Emma for defense. She had barely heard much less understood so he stared at the blank door and yearned in silence for all kinds of rescue.

But Rooster said, "Son, tell *me* what you mean. I may not last till day." He smiled.

Milo thought again alone, then stepped past Mr. Favro, frozen, to the center of the room by the black wood-stove. He looked past Lois, past Rosacoke to the old glass pane (watery as a pool) that hung between him and the butt-end of night—what stars there were, whatever lay waiting in woods to be found—and he spoke to all that. "He was never no example of nothing to nobody—Rato, I mean. And if he's dead now it's a sorry damn sight for us to have to live with—the life he had in his fourteen years. To be born with half the mind most people get; to spend your childhood alone as a hawk (but not hunting nothing, just hanging around); to go to school and never learn to write your own name, never play a game that needed two people; and when you turned twelve and your nature took life of its own accord (grew a mind of its own), just to keep on thinking it was nothing but plumbing; to stand in your life and never look forward to being grown, giving somebody something—their food and their pleasure; to think you would sleep every night of your life like a dog in winter, curled on yourself to save your own little heat, not touching nothing but the ground beneath you or a few cold leaves; nothing to do when morning came but get up and shake and wait out another day, waiting for nothing but the last lay-down, the night you'd die—" Milo turned on Mr. Favro like an enemy. "I know I'm a child but I hadn't stood still. I have *learned* some things, and this is one thing—if Rato's dead he's in Heaven, all right. He's had all the Hell he ever could have earned in four hundred years much less fourteen."

Mr. Favro could only shake his helpless head, but Milo's new tone had called his mother partway back. She kept her place by the open door, but the look she sent him—not anger but loss—washed the preacher aside, straw in a flood. "You never learned that talk from me," Emma said.

"From *me*," Rooster said, "from me and my family and it's every word so." He looked to Milo, smiled again, but Milo had his mother's gaze to bear, could not flinch from that.

"I thought you loved your brother," Emma said.

"*Loved* him?" Milo said—his hands separated like cold steel jaws; the bloody shirt ripped into loud clean halves—"That was my heart tearing in *two*, can't you see?"

Emma shut her eyes, nodded.

So having shown his mother the old heart beneath the hard new hide, Milo turned to Mr. Favro, showed the shirt halves that still seemed to quiver, shriek, bleed.

Mr. Favro studied at a distance, nodded too, then looked to where Papa hunched at the table, cooling his coffee with a thin strip of breath through dry blue lips, not hearing what they said, no longer caring, bolted in age and exhaustion, no hope. Mr. Favro took two steps towards Milo, spoke to him softly. "Now you are the man—not just by default. You'll need all the help you can get, believe me. I'm not *all* fool. So I'll pray for you daily."

Milo said "Thank you," then said "Pray *what*, sir?"

"That the Lord will hand you day by day every gift He held back from poor Rato."

"Don't worry," Milo said. "He's handing already. I'm thankfully taking."

"But don't stop with taking," Mr. Favro said.

"I ain't," Milo said. "I been learning things—but I told you that. These past three nights, these two clear days, I been handing out stuff like the whole Red Cross, like loaves and fishes to people on the hills."

Mr. Favro nodded, showed he could smile, then thought it out slowly. "Everybody isn't waiting out on the hills, and food isn't all they're waiting for."

Milo said, "I know that too, but there's all kinds of food."

Mr. Favro had turned and with slow hand showed what he thought were the nearest needy, waiting now—Papa numb in his age; Emma clubbed again by abandonment, by her helplessness to help (even briefly shield) the few things she loved; even Rooster smiling and round as a clock (his full need a secret to all here but Milo).

Yet Milo turned to Lois. She was not facing him nor listening but was leaning deeply over Rosacoke's palm, speaking softly to her. The inward curve of her back and neck, her black hair spilling forward onto her breasts, the calm of her profile (cleared now of sleep) seemed signs to Milo that she had truly gone beyond needing him, had at last accepted his gift from her father as full final payment of all Milo owed and was already launched on her own free life. But he was not free. He said to himself, "It takes two to say goodbye" and reaching blindly behind, laid the torn shirt halves on the larger table, took a step towards Lois.

Mr. Favro touched him with a hindering hand, said, "Son, there are others here that need you more."

Milo paused but did not face him. "They may, yes sir. They very well may but I never said I was all man yet. *I'm* part-fool too. Anyhow they'll wait. They know I'll come. We all got time. Morning still isn't here." He crossed the remaining way towards Lois, stopped only when his hip nudged her shoulder. She still whispered rapidly to Rosacoke. "Morning," he said.

Lois looked at last, saw his face clear of grief but not being sure of which duty he had chosen (her or his sister), she only half-smiled—"I wish it was"—and looked at the dark still gripped to the pane.

Rosacoke also faced the window, her hand still in Lois's. "Maybe we have had the last day of all. The sun has maybe failed. It'll happen one day—why not today?" When she looked for answer, she looked first to Papa (and all eyes followed), but he was asleep upright in his chair, his wind grating quietly. So Rosa looked to Rooster—"Maybe this is the end?"

But Rooster looked to Milo, answered to him. "Could be I guess. What could *keep* it from being? You've had *your* day. Maybe I've had mine—maybe never will." Milo watched him but did not offer hope so Rooster faced the worst. "*Nothing* to keep this from being the end except I am five miles from my lonesome wife."

"That's no reason at all—" Every eye but Papa's crouched at that, searched wildly for the speaker. It had burst from Mr. Favro like shrapnel from a shell, and once said, it left him as scattered, ruined.

Each sought the face that seemed to him suddenly to offer denial or at worst, protection. Emma looked to Milo's back, was balked; Rooster to his left profile clung there; Rosa to his face that would not face hers. Milo looked to Lois, offering her freely what the others craved.

But again she was back over Rosacoke's palm, studying as though another girl's skin, a child's skin (though already polished, thickened by work) would yield what hope and safety there were—a promised future for someone at least.

But a cry split the house, swift and clean as an axe—one threat realized. Then they all looked to Emma. "Baby Sister is having a dream," she said. "I'll have to go calm her. And Selma just got her poor eyes closed." She looked to Mr. Favro. "Excuse me please. I'll be right back."

"Surely," he said. "But I'd better go too. I've done what I can, what the Lord indicated—fed what little I had to His sheep. Send for me as soon as you know any more." He bowed to Rooster, bowed to Milo, said "Rosacoke—" She looked up and nodded and he vanished past Emma.

"Just a minute," Emma said—to the air he had stirred—"I'll see you out." But he was past hearing or answering so she said to Rooster, "Sheriff, would you excuse me once if I leave you here with these children awhile and try to lie down and wrestle myself somehow before day?"

Rooster stood, said, "Yes'm. I just wish I could help. You have had more than your share to bear, Mrs. Mustian."

"That's all right," she said. "Just find my boy."

Rooster laid his hand in pledge on his heart. "I will find your boy wherever the Lord has left him," he said.

Emma nodded, shut her eyes. "If you don't that's the thing I could not bear." She wavered a moment—blind—put out a hand, found the cold door jamb. Her eyes split open. "Yes I could," she said—to only Milo. He knew that, nodded and she left too, silently closing the door behind him.

There were two sounds left in the kitchen then—Papa's hoarse sleep and Lois's voice into Rosacoke's palm, not so much to Rosa as to herself, discovering lives for others as she spoke. "I am just a beginner at this," Lois said, "but one thing here is plain enough for any child to read." She traced the deep J of Rosa's lifeline—"Looks *carved* in, don't it?"

Rooster took a step to look and Milo leaned forward. Rosa said "Who carved it?"

Lois said, "You. You've been planning your life since the minute you were made."

Milo stood back above them, said "What is her plan?" And Rooster nodded, stood to wait also.

So Lois began to tell it to Milo—looking up from the hand to him not Rosa as though this separate person's life were as urgent to them both as breath, rest, morning. "She has two years of freedom left."

Milo said, "How old is she now? Can you see?"

Lois looked. "Eleven."

Rosa said "He knew that."

Lois said, "Sure he did. He's testing me." She continued to Milo—"Two more years. Then one fall day out walking in the woods, she will see a boy and hand him her life."

Milo said, "What will be his name?"

Lois strained to discover. "It's there, all right. She has chose him already—or had him chose for her—but I can't name him. As I said before, I'm new at the future."

Rosacoke said, "Can I ask something?—why will I lose my freedom to him?"

Lois said—still to Milo not Rosa—"Because you'll love him."

"Why will I love him?"

Lois did not need to study further. "Because you have had the life you've had, are who you are."

Rosacoke said, "Oh I knew that much." She studied Milo—"I ain't been free, wouldn't want to be"—turned again to Lois. "I thought you could find me a better reason." Lois did not look for another reason, only shook her head. "Then tell the rest of my plan," Rosa said.

Lois knew without looking, continued to Milo, "Then she will live in misery for years."

"Why?" Milo said.

"I never promised to explain," Lois said. "—Because it's her plan."

Milo said, "But it isn't her *right*."

"Oh," Lois said, "it'll end, it'll end—the misery, for a while."

"How?" Milo said.

"She will take a baby from the boy, then marry him."

Rosacoke thrust in—it was her life—"You mean, marry and then take a baby from him."

Lois looked back for that, reworked the hand with a firm finger, plowing as if it were a field, then shook her head. "It is planned the way I said it. The child is a boy, will come in July, but you will only be married at Christmas."

Rosacoke counted the months on her fingers. "All right," she said.

But Milo said "Stop," stepped powerfully in, pressed his own flat hand over Rosacoke's, scoured against her like a polishing wheel.

Rooster said "Wait," stepped forward too, stacked his hand palm-up on the others, looked to Lois. "You ain't lying are you?" Lois shook her head. "Because if you are, I'll lock you up *now*, won't wait for day."

"I know too little to lie," Lois said.

"Then look," Rooster said, "Oh *see* please ma'm, if there's any baby here." With his free hand he stabbed at his open palm.

Milo and Rosa were first to look—the hand seemed a baby itself, smooth, chubby. Then Lois bent. It took her eight seconds—(Rosacoke counted silently). "Yes," Lois said.

Milo said "When?"

Rooster left his hand with Lois but looked to Milo. "When?" he said.

Milo thought, then his head shook slightly. He did not know.

But Lois said "June."

Rooster's palm flipped over and became a sudden fist locked on Lois's wrist. "You *know* that?" he said.

"*You* know it," Lois said. "It's been in your hand since you had a hand."

Rooster's hand released her and he studied it hard. As he looked— as they all looked—it slowly cupped of its own accord, preparing for the gift. He smiled down to Lois. "Say it's going to be a boy."

"It is," she said.

"Thank you," Rooster said. "And coming in June! I'll beat you by a month, Rosacoke. Think of that."

"A month and nine years," Lois said. "This *coming* June."

Rooster's mouth fell open, eyes gathered in pain. Then he also counted—backwards from June, not in public like Rosa on his visible fingers but with taps of his tongue on the roof of his mouth. He looked to the window, calculated the remainder of night, then said to Rosacoke, "We've got another hour and I've got to go home and see my wife. She's been by herself all Sunday, all tonight."

"You'll be back," Rosa said and stood in her place.

"Yes I will," Rooster said and he backed from the close group, shoulders hunched inward not to touch anyone, then turned his back on them, moved quickly to the door, opened it, halted, spread heavy silence like fog through the room.

Milo said "What is it?"

Rooster waited, then turned. When he spoke his face was too grave for the question, his voice too hard. He spoke to Milo. "What must I name him?"

Milo took it as gravely as Rooster intended, thought carefully through every chance and duty. "If it was my boy I'd name him Rob."

The news—amends, forgiveness, plea for pardon—took awhile to work through the space to Rooster, but once there, he smiled. "Thank you," he said. "That'll be his name—the new Apple King!—and I'll tell him you chose it." He left more quickly than large men generally manage to leave, but unrushed, unridden, already at peace with the various seeds broadcast in his life and waiting to grow.

But Milo shuddered—once (still for fear) as Rooster vanished, once (in understanding and helplessness) as the front door shut behind him (only its distant click reached the kitchen). Lois did not notice. She had already looked back to Rosacoke's hand, found a new shape there which she struggled to read, but Rosacoke saw him both times and thought he shivered from cold—the room had chilled since Emma left— so she took her hand from Lois, saying, "Thank you but I'll take the rest in surprise" and brushed past Milo who was burning not cold to the squat wood-stove. She took the lid-lifter, raised a lid—fire dying—then went to the woodbox, bent and loaded herself with the little wood left, fed it in, turned to Milo—he had been watching her—and said, "That is all the wood in the house. I'll fix you some breakfast if you get me some wood. You ain't had a meal in—what? two days? Food's all you need."

"It's one thing," he said and moved three steps towards the door to obey—go out to the woodshed coatless in darkness. It was dark that stopped him before he reached the hall—the thought not the fact— and he stopped ashamed, having never feared darkness even as a child (had spent half his life, it seemed to him now, hurling round by night in various games). He did not face round onto Lois or Rosa, and this time Rosa did not see nor understand, only went on finding the pans she would need.

Lois did or at least said to Milo's back, half-laughing, "I'll come and hold the lantern if you'll chop the wood."

At that Milo turned and went swiftly towards Lois, but silently not to break Papa's sleep. Two steps short he extended his right hand flat as a plate and delivered it to her, not forced in her face nor on her own hand but laid on the table beneath her baffled eyes.

She looked at once from his hand to him. "What is that?" she said.

"Hell," he said—he whispered—"it's my right hand. It's what you been finding people's lives in, remember?"

"Oh that—" Lois said as if whole days had passed.

"Yes that," he said and he probed with a finger at the palm's few lines. "It don't look like much of a plan to me, but whatever it is, you are in it—ain't you?" He did force it now, threw it up before her eyes.

Lois would not look, clamped her eyes as if Milo offered fire.

"*Lois,*" he said—he whispered still but with power enough now to etch cold glass—"I am making you a gift so remember your manners. You either got to take it or say why not."

She opened her eyes, on his eyes not his hand. "What gift?" she said.

"My life," he said.

"Why?" she said.

"Because you asked me for it twice in three days. Because I have learned my lesson by now."

"What lesson?" she said.

"That the worst thing of all is not paying your debts—and paying in time; that you got to give people what they need *in time,* not years too late when they've famished and fell."

Lois said, "Milo, who taught you that?"

He rose back to think and the large high kitchen seemed swarmed with his teachers, pressing on him like water in the depths of a pond, on his eyes, eardrums, sunk temples, soft throat—everyone he had seen these two days, three nights—and he forced his lips open to answer at last, say "Everybody did—"

But Papa said loudly, "I'm *one* that didn't, I can tell you that much. I been owing some debts since Hoover come in—Hell, since Woodrow Wilson crept home from Paris and turned to stone." Like stone himself, only half-returned from sleep, he sat up in his chair. "Debts ain't nothing but money—remember—and owing ain't a reason to pay, I've found, unless your debtor's in worse need than you."

"She's in need," Milo said.

"All right," Papa said, "I won't ask why (though if somebody handed me ten thousand dollars, I wouldn't need nothing but a better bed; then I'd sleep six months), and I won't ask why you are buried in debt to a stranger you saw for the first time Friday. I won't say nothing if you'll let me say this—for God's sake pay her back with something she can use, don't stand around offering her your bare-faced hand like hands was rare."

Milo thrust his hand at Papa. "This stands for my life."

"Your *life?*" Papa said. "What use is a life?"

Rosacoke said, "I could use a load of wood."

*   *   *

When they had crossed the pitch-black yard—Milo leading darkly first from his hot need to give, then Lois passing ahead with the lantern from what was her own impatience to receive, then Milo up again by unthinking memory through threatening litter (spiked scraps of iron, split jars, bare roots)—when both had stooped and entered the woodshed and silently hurried, but not touching yet, out of every thread of clothes and stood a moment separate, still and in study in the flame light that rose from the lantern on the ground, what Milo gave and Lois received was this much as least: a hand as tough as a Gladstone bag on her cold left shoulder; then that hand tightening and drawing her forward till she brushed against, then was held full length (though still upright) along a stretch of skin like fine broadcloth (that seamless, warm, dry); then was kissed once on her smiling mouth, hard but dry and quickly, stopping on the surface as a child would kiss an aunt at the start of a visit while looking beyond her at deep woods, a lake or sand for play; then was steered by that hand on the height of her butt towards a dim far corner, half-laid, half-pushed to a cushion of pine bark powdered with age—that much at least Lois thought of as taking (no thought of using). But Milo paused above her on arms as straight as what stood ready beneath to serve, looked at her eyes—only them, nothing lower—and said unsmiling, "I have heard that the saddest thing on earth is to love somebody and they not love back."

"So have I," she said and by smiling fully, forced him to smile, then rocked the heel of her own tough hand in the pit of his neck (where nerves pierce the skull) and drew him forward, welcomed him down, and the rest was giving—pure gift for both, no thought of receipt though receipts poured in so long as they worked, as if fresh joy could flood your thighs, stream down through your legs, drown your heart, gorge throat and brain, offer (even threaten) a new clear life (so long as you moved) and yet roll on, roll past, leave you spared.

It could and did—rolled on, spared them both, left them mildly grateful. Then though they still touched, lay as joy had left them, they quickly grew separate—at first with the distance of brother and sister close but ignorant of one another; then like strangers in a crowded room, burdened by nearness; then farther still till at last when Milo's body fell back he fell like a fledgling from a narrow nest, a pear from an overweighted tree, still faintly aware of gratitude but forgetful already of to whom or why and mainly free, mainly grateful for that.

Yet relieved as he was to have paid in full, he could still not accept his joy to be free, not face this final assault by the hound that had sought him since his father's death but closely, fiercely all weekend — that people depart (undetained by love, unprepared for their journey) and we watch them go and they do not return.

So he half-rose and looked for Lois's face. It was turned away. He gently hauled it round till her eyes met his and their lips mirrored smiles. Then again he showed her his open hand. "Look and see if you ain't there," he said.

This time she looked, no longer afraid of her certain absence, wishing in fact that there might at least be a shallow trace of her life in his, some sign of her passing, and she turned the hand all angles to the light — nothing, no sign, his whole life so plainly illegible that she could not have guessed so much as his name, not to speak of their mutual fate to meet, touch twice, exchange sweet gifts, discover blood kin. "I am not," she said and she shut his hand like a quiet door, returned it to his thigh stretched separate beyond her.

Milo said "Why not?" quite seriously.

"You didn't plan for me, that's all."

"Who have I planned for?" He spoke gravely now in need again but of foresight, vision, *news*, not a simple girl — "And where will I go?"

"Nobody else knows that but you."

He did not answer — agree or deny. He was turned away, his face to the light.

"Do *you?*" she said.

"Yes," he said. He spoke to the light. "I have got two plans — one old as my hand, one I just now made. The old plan was for me to live on here and work like a mill from day to dark every day but Christmas doing what my Daddy did (my sorry Daddy, the days he could walk), what Papa does now tired as he is — raise eight acres of neck-high tobacco, plant the seed in March under muslin beds (seed that make mustard seed look like cannon balls), lose half my plants to frost and blue mold, then transplant the rest in early May and nurse it all summer like a millionaire's baby—losing half again to wet weather, dry weather, worms, blight, maybe all to a five-minute hail storm one evening; pulling leaves in late July, tacking them in barns hot as biscuit ovens till they kill out gold; then hauling them to town to a tin-top building and watching bone-tired some fast-talking stranger frown at it—not feel it—give you fifty cents a pound like he's Jesus healing wounds. Hell, I don't even *smoke*. But in my old plan, I die doing that year after year." He halted but did not turn his head.

"Nothing else?" Lois said.

"What else?" Milo said.

She said, "Well—fun, a little enjoyment. Don't you plan to laugh any, take any vacations, rest up between years? Won't there be somebody to lighten your load?"

"Mama will cook what meals I eat. Rosa will wash and iron my clothes till she starts that life you promised her."

Lois waited for him to continue, to hope, but he lay on silent and that silence mixed with the chill of the dark clasped her—the heat of their moving gone—so that when she spoke she also shuddered. "I was speaking of a wife." She touched him, unintending—her hand at the small of his cooling back.

He turned to face her. "Oh sure," he said, "maybe two years from now, maybe three if I'm lazy, I'll pick out one of those girls I've known since I first went to school—Nancy Gunter or Sarah King or Sissie Abbott if she'll shut up—and we'll drive to town every Saturday night and chew earlobes in the dark theater and after a year or so of that, get married, live up in the room I sleep in now." He stopped, having reached another blank end.

"You mean that to sound like fun?"

"Well," he said, then waited to think—"I never claimed to be a comedian. But I'll get home for a while most nights or for dinner at least, and then I can saw me off a slice of fun—if that's what you mean, what you and me was slicing a minute ago but better than that, on warm bed sheets."

"That wasn't all I meant."

"Me neither. I'm flogging myself too hard. Children are bound to come rolling in, and I guess giving them their Santa Claus will be some pleasure—and raising them up till they take their own growth." He paused still facing Lois and smiled to break her stare. "Doesn't that sound like fun to you?" She did not answer nor reflect his smile. "Well, it's what nine-tenths of the humans born since God said 'Adam!' have thought was a life, planned out for themselves—all my people, my Mama, my Daddy (it was what strangled him), Rosacoke if you foretold truly. It was *my* old plan."

"What's the new one?" she said.

"It depends."

"On what?" she said, hope again in her voice (though against her will).

"On Rato really being dead," he said.

"If he is?—" she said.

"I'm leaving at daybreak."

"*Leaving?*" she said. "Leaving Rato's body for a posse to find? Leaving your mother and sister to scratch like me and my—mother. You are all that's left."

"Papa's left."

"For exactly three years."

"You seen his hand?"

"I seen his eyes."

Milo thought awhile. "I'm leaving still and I'll tell you why—any world where Rato Mustian dies bloody for saving a dog that wouldn't bring a dime in a catfood factory, any world where—" He stopped. All his kin ganged before his eyes, living, dead (and he knew more dead than the average boy)—all his friends, enemies, speaking acquaintances—and all seemed ruined in various degrees: hobbled or addled or stove-in deeply. He spoke again to clear his sight. "Any world like that is in serious need of somebody's help. I volunteer."

"Why?"

"To change some things."

"How?" Lois said.

"By telling what I know, the things I have learned these past three days. My learning's just started but I've learned some things."

Lois said, "Start with me. Tell me please now."

He turned again from her to the lantern—flame as steady as hammered iron—and waited tensely for his knowledge to gather, the wounds and visions of three clear days to narrow in the gap between his eyes behind his skull, transform into words. And he clamped his eyes to force the conversion, but only colors came—the reds and purples of his own thick blood as it thinned in his eyelids, received the light—no word, not one. His heart clenched hotly and to spare it danger, he faced round violently onto Lois, forced his throat to speak (eyes still shut). "Everybody has got to—" Again he was refused, not permitted to say what all the others—his mother, Rosa, Mr. Favro, Selma, even Rooster, even Macey—would have rushed to offer, and his throat was locked silent as if by a hand or a coarse wool throttle. So he hung there darkly above dark Lois—only his back receiving light now, and what the light showed was only his back, curved like a vine that flails for grip, the next foothold on food and life.

Lois touched him gently on his tight ringed throat. His eyes split open but his head shook fiercely and her hand fell back. "No," he said, "I have not learned nothing. I have just seen things that passed and are gone." He waited for strength to drive to the next—"But I'm going too. This isn't my place. I have got to find rest."

"You are just fifteen."

He nodded. "Fifteen, but I've lived more lives than most men at fifty. Time isn't what wears people out. There's Niggers round here—in sound of my voice—that can bend their back and pick cotton faster than you can dance (and sing while they do) but are well past a hundred and can picture slavery clear as I can Rato. Look at your Daddy—"

She looked, half-hoping, to the lantern—simple light.

"He was younger than me by a year when he left, fourteen years old and already finished, finished here, ground down. He had had his share of the local day, and he either had to go or die in his tracks in Ryden dirt—ground *fine* as dirt—had to find some life, a few more days, a little rest."

"What did he ever find?"

Milo studied Lois beside and below him, at his mercy entirely. "You," he said.

Her eyes shut, head shook No three times. Then she waited, then asked, "What good on earth was so much running for that little rest?"

Milo turned her question like a weapon on himself. "I never said I was running from a fight. I'm running towards my life and I'm game to wrestle every step of the way. What I won't do, *can't* do is stand in my tracks—my ancestors' tracks—and be whipped dry, dead but can't lie down for sixty more years."

"You *could*," Lois said. "You could die in a ditch. But at least you've *got* tracks. How many people have? And where was my father taking me that time? Where did he beg me to promise to meet him?—not in cold midair."

Milo looked to his feet as if testing their power, then answered her first question not her last—"I could but I won't"—and stood in a perfect thrust, went to his clothes and dressed in the light, his back to Lois.

So she watched his back.

Then he went to the dark rear end of the shed, quietly gathered an armload of wood—the fresh pine quarters he had split on Friday just before supper, before the fair, with Rato watching.

In the short time it took him, Lois stood and dressed too, thinking he meant to return to the house (and her to her mother), hand Rosa the wood, eat the food she fried and begin his life—the old first life in his old home here.

But when his arms were full, he walked unseeing past her—she was stroking her hair into place with her hand—and stopped at the open door of the shed, set the wood down there, stood, clapped his hands to shake off bark and looked to the sky.

The sky had faded though only a little—to the sharpest eye—from black to deep gray so that when Milo faced round on Lois, she saw him clearly by two lights now (gray sky behind, lantern on his face) as she had only seen him in deep dark before (Friday night in the field by the fair and this passing night in the Ryden woods), the image of her oldest memory—her father, her final promise to him, to meet, keep faith—the message given, gift delivered.

Milo said "I am going." His hand flapped mildly against his side. He turned, took a step.

Lois said, "The wood. You forgot Rosa's wood."

Milo stopped beyond the door, half-faced her again. "No I didn't. She'll come looking soon and it'll be here. It ain't going nowhere."

Lois said "Are you?"

"Yes."

"Where?"

He pointed away from the still-dim house towards his own dim left as though a clear destination lay there, enduring his journey. Then he seemed to smile fully (though she only guessed that) and said, "You still never said your plan."

"That one," she said. She pointed his way.

"All right," he said, "but you got to come now, leave all—clothes, money, your new belongings. We are hunting not hauling."

"I know that," she said and went towards him, past lantern and wood into still-paler air—the sky at least; the ground was black so they both looked downward to choose their way, and though Lois kept her hand near his, he did not take it till he suddenly stopped on the edge of the yard ten yards from the field, the woods beyond. Then he found her fingers, took hold to stop her, but she had seen only just after him the dark shapes ahead that broke from the pines and entered the field and moved their way—a high hunched form that came on slowly and, slightly ahead as if clearing a path, a low form that hugged the darkest furrows.

Lois said "Who?"

Milo said "God knows" and the cold wrapped wound behind his ear fried out like a brand. He dropped Lois's hand—or freed it, not so much abandoning as leaving her ready for what this was should it come to claim her, renouncing his claim. Then he started again, also entered the field—Lois one step behind—to face what shape, what claim bore down.

Nothing but Phillip and Rato behind—bare to the waist, maybe five pounds nearer the bone than before—but safe, spared and there so sudden, unquestionably as to silence Milo, fling him back on his heels, Phillip prancing around him, wetly panting.

So Lois spoke, pointing first to Phillip. "Is Phillip safe?"

Rato said, "Always was. Nothing but worms and he's cured of that, found the grass he needed hunting you all's snake."

"That's dead," Lois said.

Rato said "I'm sorry."

"Thank you," Lois said. "Where'd you lose your shirt?"

"In a fight with a fox."

"But you're live," she said. "That's all that counts."

Rato said "We're live," thinking she included Phillip, and as Phillip had already streaked towards the house, Rato nodded to Lois and followed his dog, past Milo as though Milo were air, a piece of the day.

But Milo turned and watched him go. He could see him now, even Phillip far ahead—light had swelled that much in that brief meeting—the back of the house, Phillip skipping the steps, waiting Rato on the porch, Rato moving on slowly, knowing the house and its contents would wait, the house seeming washed by the new light, home. So Milo followed with a longer stride—Lois fell in behind— and in eight long steps, he was near enough to Rato to touch, shield, cover his bare cold back (a black rake of claws had dug the lean meat, had abruptly halted at the spine, postponed).

But Rato turned, faced Milo, grinned. "Morning," he said.

"Morning," Milo said. Then they both looked up to the lifting sky—Lois followed their eyes—and found they were right. It was morning (clear, cloudless, the oldest gift), would be morning oh six hours yet.

A CHAIN OF LOVE

They had observed Papa's birthday with a freezer of cream even if it was the dead of winter, and they had given him a Morris chair that was not brand-new but was what he had always wanted. The next morning he was sick, and nobody could figure the connection between such nice hand-turned cream that Rato almost froze to death making and a tired heart which was what he had according to Dr. Sledge. Papa said "Tired of what?" and refused to go to any hospital. He said he would die at home if it was his time, but the family saw it different so they took him to Raleigh in Milo's car—pulled out the back seat that hadn't been out since Milo married the Abbott girl and spread a pallet and laid him there on pillows with his head resting on the hand-painted one off the settee, the gray felt pillow from Natural Bridge, Virginia that he brought Pauline his wife six years before she died, off that two-day excursion he took with the County Agent to the model peanut farms around Suffolk.

Much as she wanted to, Mama couldn't stay with Papa then. (Mama was his daughter-in-law.) She made him a half a gallon of boiled custard as he asked her to, to take along, and she rode down to Raleigh with them, but she had to come back with Milo in the evening. It worried her not being able to stay when staying was her duty, but they were having a Children's Day at the church that coming Sunday—mainly because the Christmas pageant had fallen through when John Arthur Bobbitt passed around German measles

223

like a dish of cool figs at the first rehearsal—and since she had organized the Sunbeams single-handed, she couldn't leave them then
right on the verge of public performance. So they took Rosacoke and
Rato along to sit for the first days till Mama could come back herself.
Dr. Sledge said there was no need to take on a full-time nurse with
two strong grandchildren dying to sit with him anyhow.

And there wasn't. From the minute Papa had his attack, there was
never a question of Rosacoke going if Papa had to go—no question of
wanting to go—and in fact she almost liked the idea. There was just
one thing made her think twice about it, which was missing one Saturday night with Wesley. Wesley Beavers was Rosacoke's boyfriend
even if Mama didn't like the idea of her riding in to town with a boy
two years older every Saturday night to the show and sitting with him
afterwards in his car—Rato there on the porch in the pitch dark looking—and telling him goodbye without a word. That was the best part
of any week, telling Wesley goodbye the way she did when he pulled
his Pontiac up in the yard under the pecan tree, and if it was fall, nuts
would hit the car every now and then like enemy bullets to make
them laugh or if it was spring, all those little rain frogs would be
singing-out over behind the creek and then for a minute calming as if
they had all died together or had just stopped to catch their breath.
But Wesley would be there when she got back, and anyhow going to
the hospital would give her a chance to lay out of school for a week,
and it would give her extra time with Papa that she liked to be with.
Rosacoke's Papa was her grandfather. Her own father was dead, run
over by a green pick-up truck one Saturday evening late a long time
ago, almost before she could remember.

But Rato could remember. Rato had seen a lot of things die. He
was named for their father—Horatio Junior Mustian—and he was the
next-to-oldest boy, nearly eighteen. He didn't mind staying with Papa
either. He didn't go to school, hadn't gone in four years, so he didn't
have the pleasure of laying out the way Rosacoke did, but seeing all
the people would be enough for Rato. Not that he liked people so
much. You could hardly get him to speak to anybody, but if you left
him alone he would take what pleasure he needed, just standing
there taller than anybody else and thinner and watching them.

Dr. Sledge had called on ahead, and they didn't have any trouble getting Papa in the hospital. He even had the refusal of a big corner room with a private bath, but it cost twelve dollars a day. Papa said there was no use trying the good will of Blue Cross Hospital Insurance so he took a ten-dollar room standing empty across the hall, and they wheeled him in on a rolling table pushed by a Negro who said he was Snowball Mason and turned out to be from Warren County too, up around Sixpound, which made Papa feel at home right away and limber enough to flip easy onto the bed in all the clothes he insisted on riding in. But before he could get his breath good, in came a nurse who slid around the bed on her stumpy legs as smooth and speedy as if she was on roller skates with dyed black hair screwed up and bouncing around her ears. She called Papa "darling" as if she had known him all her life and struggled to get him in one of those little night shirts the hospital furnished free without showing everything he had to the whole group. Everybody laughed except Rosacoke who had undressed Papa before and could do it in the dark. She gritted her teeth and finally the nurse got him fixed and stepped back to look as if she had just made him out of thin air. Milo said, "Papa, if you have somebody that peppy around you all the time, you won't be tired long." The nurse smiled and told Papa she would be seeing lots of him in the daytime and then left. Milo laughed at the "lots" and said, "That's what I'm afraid of, Papa—you getting out of hand down here," but Rosacoke said she could manage fine and wasn't exactly a moper herself and Papa agreed to that.

Soon as the nurse got out—after coming back once to get a hairpin she dropped on the bed—they began inspecting the room. There was a good big sink where Rosacoke could rinse out her underwear that she hadn't brought much of and Rato's socks. (Anywhere Rato went he just took the clothes on his back.) And Mama liked the view out the window right over the ambulance entrance where you could see every soul that came in sick. She called Rato's attention to it, and the two of them looked out awhile, but it was getting on towards four o'clock, and much as she wanted to stay and see what Snowball was serving for supper, she told Milo they would have to go. She couldn't stand to ride at night.

Practically before the others left the building, Rosacoke and Rato and Papa had made their sleeping arrangements and were settled. There was one easy chair Rosacoke could sleep in, and since Rato couldn't see stretching out on the floor with his bones, he shoved in another chair out of the parlor down the hall. That dyed-haired nurse saw him do it. She gave him a look that would have dropped anybody but Rato dead in his tracks and said, "You camping out or something, Big Boy?" Rato said, "No'm. Setting with my Papa." Then he went off roaming and the first thing Rosacoke did was open her grip and spread out her toilet articles all over the glass-top bureau. They were all she had brought except for two dresses and a copy of *Hit Parade Tunes and Lyrics* so she could get in some good singing if there was a radio and there was—over Papa's bed, two stations. And at the last minute Mama had stuck in what was left of the saltwater taffy Aunt Oma sent from Virginia Beach that summer. It seemed like a good idea—nurses hung around a patient who had his own candy like Grant around Richmond, Mama said—so she took a piece and gave one to Papa and began to paint her face, trying it out. Papa gummed his candy and watched in the mirror. Mama would have jerked a knot in her if she could have seen the sight Rosacoke was making of herself but Papa smiled. He had always said Rosacoke looked like an actor, and since the only picture show he ever saw was *Birth of a Nation*— and that was forty years ago in the old Warrenton Opera House with a four-piece band in accompaniment—then it must have been Lillian Gish he thought Rosacoke looked like. And she did a little that winter—not as small but thin all the same though beginning to grow, with a heart-shaped face and long yellow hair and blue eyes. That was what Rosacoke liked the best about her face, the eyes. They were big and it was hard to say where the blues left off and the whites began because everything there was more or less blue, and out the far corner of her left eye came this little vein close under the skin that always seemed to Rosacoke to be emptying off some of all that blue, carrying it down to her pale cheek.

But she couldn't stand there staring at herself all the time—she wasn't that good looking and she knew it already—so after the doctors began to ease up with the visits on the second day, Rosacoke got a little tired. That is, till the Volunteer Worker from the Ladies' Guild came in in a pink smock and asked if maybe they wouldn't want some magazines or a deck of cards maybe? She had a pushcart with her full of razor blades and magazines and things, and all Rosacoke had to do was look at Papa, and he—so happy with a lady visitor—pointed to his black leather purse on the table. The best thing she bought was a deck of Bicycle Playing Cards, and Mama would have jerked another knot if she could have seen Rosacoke right in Papa's bed, teaching him to play Honeymoon Bridge and Fish which she had learned awhile back from town girls on rainy days at little recess. But she never mentioned Slap Jack, her favorite game. She knew in advance Papa would get excited waiting for a Jack to turn up and maybe have a stroke or something so they stuck to quiet games which Papa took to easily, and you could have knocked Rosacoke off the bed with a feather when *he* started teaching her and Rato to play Setback, playing the extra hand himself.

They could count on the cards keeping them busy till Sunday, but they would have to do something with them then. Mama had said she would come down on Sunday to sit her turn with Papa. Milo would bring her after Children's Day. Milo was her oldest boy and he pretty well ran the farm alone with what help Rato could give him. He would probably have to bring Sissie along for the ride even if Papa couldn't stand her. Sissie was Milo's new wife. Just try leaving Sissie anywhere.

The doctors didn't tell Papa what was wrong with him, and he didn't tell them but one thing either which was that he wanted to die at home. He told them they had been mighty nice to him and he appreciated it, but he couldn't think of anything worse than dying away from home. They said they would take care of that and for him to rest till they told him to stop and they would send Dr. Sledge a full report. And Papa didn't worry. He had left it in their hands, and if a doctor had walked in one morning and said he had come to saw his head off, Papa would have just laid his neck out on the pillow where the doctor could get at it. But the doctors didn't bother him for much of his time, and taking them at their word, he slept the best part of every day. That was when Rato would roam the halls, never saying "p-turkey" to anybody, just looking around. And when Rosacoke could see Papa was asleep good, she would tip over and listen to his chest to make sure his heart was beating regular before she would walk across the hall to the corner room, the one they had offered Papa. It was still empty. The door stayed open all the time, and she didn't see any reason for not going in. There was reason *for* going—the view out the window of that room, a white statue of Jesus standing beside the hospital, holding his head bowed down and spreading his hands by his side. His chest was bare and a cloth was hanging over his right shoulder. Rosacoke couldn't see his face too well, but she knew it, clear, from the day they brought Papa in. It was the kindest face she had ever seen. She was sure of that. And she went to that empty room more than once to look out at him and recollect his face the way she knew it was.

But that didn't go on long because on the third day Rato came in from sitting in the hall all morning and said they had just now put some fellow in that empty room. Rosacoke was sorry to hear it. It meant she wouldn't get to go over there in the afternoon any more but she didn't say that. She would rather have died than tell Rato how much time she spent there, looking out a window. Papa wanted to know who it was that could take a twelve-dollar room, and Rato said it was a big man. Papa was disappointed too. He had got it figured there was something wrong with that room, lying empty three days or more. Rato said the man's wife and boy were with him—"I expect it was his boy. Looked like he was anyhow. The man hisself didn't look a bit sick. Walked in on his own steam, talking and laughing." Rosacoke wanted to know if they were rich, but Rato couldn't say, said he didn't know. You couldn't ever tell about Rato though, how much he knew. He wasn't anybody's fool. He just liked the idea of not telling all he knew. Keeping a few secrets was everything Rato had. So Rosacoke said, "Well, he's getting a beautiful room" and then walked over and buttoned Papa's night shirt. She made him stay buttoned square up to the neck all the time because she couldn't stand to look at his old chest. Papa said he was hot as a mink in Africa and that his chest had been that hairy ever since he shaved it to be Maid of Honor in the womanless wedding Delight Church put on when he was seventeen years old.

The night before, when the lights were out but they were still awake, Papa asked Rato to name the best thing he had seen since arriving, and Rato said, "That old lady with all the cards in the big ward down the hall." Rosacoke said, "What sort of cards?" "Every sort there is—Mother's Day, Valentine, Birthday, Christmas . . ." Papa said, "Get-Well cards?" "She ain't going to get well. She's too old." Rosacoke said "How old?" and Rato said, "What's the oldest thing you know?" She thought and said "God." "Well, she's something similar to that." Rosacoke and Papa laughed but Rato said, "I'm telling the truth. Go take a look if you get the chance. She sleeps all the time." Then they went to sleep but Rosacoke knew he was telling the truth, and anyhow he spoke of his doings so seldom she thought she would take his advice. So the afternoon the man took the twelve-dollar room, she went down while Papa was nodding, and at first it looked the way Rato promised. There was a lady older than God in the bed by the door (saving her a walk past nine other beds), covered to the chin and flat as a plank with no pillow under her head, just steel-colored hair laid wild on the sheets. Rosacoke stepped close enough to see her eyes were shut, and thinking the lady was asleep, she looked up towards a sunburst of greeting cards fanned on the wall over the bed, but she hadn't looked fifteen seconds when the lady shot bolt-upright and spoke in a voice like a fingernail scraping down a dry blackboard—"Praise my Jesus." Rosacoke said, "Yes'm" and the lady smiled and said, "Step here, honey, and take a seat and I'll tell you how I got saved at age eighty-one in the midst of a meeting of two hundred people. Then I'll show you my cards—sent by my Sunday school class and my many friends"—and commenced scratching her hair. But Rosacoke said, "No thank you, ma'm" and walked out quicker than she came. She went a few feet outside the door and stopped and thought, "I ought to be ashamed, getting her hopes up. I ought to go back and let her talk." Then she heard the lady's voice scraping on to the empty air so she said to herself, "If I went for five minutes, I'd be there all afternoon, hearing about her cards. Papa is *my* duty." And anyhow she didn't like the lady. It was fine for your friends to send you cards, but that was no reason to organize a show as if you were the only person in the hospital with that many friends and all of them with nothing in the world to do but sit down and write you cards all day. She thought that out and then headed for Papa.

She was walking down the mile-long hall when she saw him—not right at first. At first she was too busy looking at people laid back with their doors open. She didn't know a one of them, not even their faces the way Rato did. The only thing she knew was Snowball Mason in one room, talking to some old man that looked so small in his little outing pajamas with his legs hanging off the bed no more than an inch from the floor like thin dry tan gourds swinging in a wind on somebody's back porch somewhere. Snowball saw her and remembered her as being from Warren County and bowed. She stopped to talk but she happened to look towards the left, and there he was—Wesley—sitting way down across from Papa's door, dressed to the ears and watching the floor the way he always did, not studying people. Still he had come sixty miles to see her so she whispered to Snowball she had to go and went to meet Wesley, holding back from running and trying not to look as if she had seen a ghost which was close to what she had seen, considering this was the last hope she had. He hadn't seen her yet and she could surprise him. She hadn't really missed him so much till now, but when she got nearer she knew how sorry she would be to miss this Saturday with him, and she speeded her steps but kept them quiet. She was almost on him and he put his hands across his eyes—it would be Wesley all over to go to sleep waiting for her—so she came up to him and smiled and said, "Good afternoon, Mr. Beavers, is there something I can do for you?"

But it wasn't Wesley at all. It was somebody she hadn't ever seen before, somebody who didn't really look very much like Wesley when she thought about it. It took whoever it was a little while to realize she was speaking to him, and when he looked up he looked sad and nearly as young as Rosacoke. He looked a little blank too, the way everybody does when you have called them by the wrong name and they don't want you to know it. In a minute he said, "Oh no ma'm, thank you." "No ma'm"—as if Rosacoke was some kind of nurse.

It just about killed her to have done that like some big hussy. The only thing left to say was "Excuse me," and she almost didn't get that out before shutting Papa's door behind her, the hot blood knocking in her ears. Papa was still asleep but Rato was standing by the window, having some Nabs and a Pepsi for dinner, and when she could speak she said would he please peep out and see who that was sitting in the hall. As if Rato had ever peeped in his life. He had done plenty of looking but no peeping so he just pulled open the door as if he was headed for dinner and gave the boy a look. Before he got the door closed good, he said, "Nobody but that man's boy from across the hall. That man they moved in today." Rosacoke said "Thank you" and later on that afternoon she wondered if since he looked like Wesley, that boy could say goodbye like Wesley could.

If they didn't do anything else, those people across the hall at least gave Papa something to think about. They kept their door shut all the time except when somebody was going or coming, and even then they were usually too quick for Rato to get a good enough look to report anything. Something was bound to be wrong though because of all the nurses and doctors hanging around and the way that boy looked whenever he walked out in the hall for a few minutes. Rato reported he saw the man's wife once. He said she was real pretty and looked like she was toting the burden of the world on her shoulders. Even Rato could tell that. So Papa couldn't help asking Snowball the next time he got a chance what was wrong with that man. Snowball said he didn't know and if he did he wouldn't be allowed to say and that made Papa mad. He knew Snowball spent about two-thirds of his time in the man's room, taking bedpans in and out, and he told Snowball at the top of his voice, "That white coat you got on has gone to your head." Rosacoke could have crawled under the bed, but there was no stopping Papa once he got started. You just pretended hadn't a thing happened and he would quiet down. She could tell it got Snowball's goat though and she was sorry. He walked out of Papa's room with his ice-cream coat hanging off him as if somebody had unstarched it.

But that evening when it was time for him to go home, Snowball came back in. He didn't have his white coat on, and that meant he was off duty. He had on his sheepish grin, trying to show he had come on a little social call to see how Papa was making out, but Rosacoke knew right off he had come to apologize to Papa who was taking a nap so she shook Papa and said Snowball wanted to speak to him. Papa raised up blinking and said "Good evening, Snow," and Rosacoke couldn't help smiling at how Snowball turned into a snake doctor, dripping up and down around Papa. He said he just wondered how Mr. Mustian was coming on this afternoon, and did they have any old newspapers he could take home to start fires with? Papa said he was tolerable and hadn't looked at a newspaper since the jimsonweeds took over the Government. What he meant was the Republicans, and he said, "The bad thing about jimsonweeds, Snow, is they reseeds theyselves."

Snowball hadn't come in on his own time to hear that though, and it didn't take him long to work his way to Papa's bed and lean over a lot closer than Papa liked for anybody to get to him and say it the same way he would have told a secret. "Mr. Mustian, they fixing to take out that gentleman's lung."

"What you talking about?"

"That Mr. Ledwell yonder in the room across the hall. He got a eating-cancer. That's what I hear his nurse say. But don't tell nobody. I just thought you might want to know so soons I found out . . ."

"A eating-cancer? That's what it is?"

"They don't seem to be no doubt about it. I done already shaved his chest for surgery. He taking his operation in the morning at eight."

Papa wanted to know, "Is he going to live, Snowball?"

"Can't say, Mr. Mustian. He spit the first blood today, and alls I know is they ain't many lives past that. They ain't many. And if they lives you almost wish they hadn't. That's how bad they gets before it's over."

And Papa remembered that was the way it was with Mr. Jack Rooker who swelled up to twice his natural size and smelled a long time before he died. "I can recollect sitting on the porch in the evening and hearing Jack Rooker screaming clean across two tobacco fields, screaming for his oldest boys to just let him rest because there won't nothing nobody could do for him, not nothing. And I'd say to Pauline, 'Pauline, it don't look like Jack Rooker is ever going to die, does it?'" But that was a long time ago when Papa was a lot younger and a lot farther away from dying himself. That was why he could feel so for Jack Rooker back then. It had just seemed as if Jack Rooker was going through something wouldn't anybody else ever have to go through again.

Snowball was nodding his head up and down, saying, "I know. Yes sir, I know," but Rosacoke could tell he had made his peace with Papa and was ready to leave so she stopped Papa from running on about Jack Rooker and told him it was time for Snowball to go home. Papa thanked Snowball for coming in, as if he had never been mad a minute, and said he would count on him keeping them posted on all that happened to that fellow across the hall.

Rosacoke followed Snowball out. "Snowball, what's that man's name again?"

"Mr. Ledwell."

"Is he really going to die, you think?"

"Yes'm, I believe he is. But Miss Rosacoke, you don't have to worry yourself none about that. You ain't going to see him."

"I know that. I just wondered though. I didn't even remember his name."

Snowball said he would be stepping along and would see her in the morning. But Rosacoke didn't hear from him till way in the next afternoon. Papa was taking his nap and she was almost asleep herself when Snowball peeped in and seeing Papa was asleep, whispered that the gentleman across the hall was back from his operation.

"How did it come out, Snow?"

"They tell me he doing right well, Miss Rosacoke."

"Has he waked up yet?"

"No'm, he lying in yonder under his oxygen tent, running on about all sorts of foolishness like a baby. He be in some pain when he do come to though."

"Are his people doing all right?"

"They holding up right well. That's his two sisters with his wife and his boy. They setting there looking at him and waiting to see."

She thanked Snowball for letting them know and said she would tell Papa when he woke up. After Snowball left she stepped into the hall herself. The door over there was closed, and for the first time it said "No visitors." She wanted to wait until somebody opened it. Then she could at least hear the man breathing, if he was still breathing. But there wasn't a sound coming through that oak door thick as her fist, and she wasn't going to be caught snooping like Rato so she went back in to where Papa was awake, spreading a game of Solitaire which that dyed-haired nurse had taught him to play. That was *all* she had done for him.

Since they were away from home, they went to bed around ten o'clock. That is they cut out the lights, and Rosacoke would step in the closet and undress with the door half shut. The first evening she had shut it all the way, and Papa told her there was no use to be so worried about him seeing her as he had seen her stripstrod naked two or three hundred times before she was old enough to walk, but she kept up the practice, and when she was in her nightgown, she would step out and kiss Papa and tell Rato "Sleep tight" and settle in her easy chair under a blanket. Then they would talk a little about the day and home till the talk ran down of its own accord though Papa was liable to go on another hour in the dark about things he remembered. But it would all be quiet soon enough, and Rato would be the first to sleep. After Rosacoke's eyes had opened full to the dark, she could look over and see her brother stretched sideways in his chair, still dressed, with his long hands caught between his drawn-up knees and his head rolled back on his great thin neck and his mouth fallen open. Most people seemed to be somebody else when they were asleep. But not Rato. Rato went to sleep the way you expected he would, like himself who had stopped looking for a while. Then Papa would fall off, sometimes right in the middle of what he was remembering, and Rosacoke could see him too, but he was different—sweeter and with white hair that seemed in the night to be growing into the white pillow his dark leather head rested on, holding him there forever.

After Papa slept Rosacoke was supposed to but she couldn't this night. She kept thinking about it, the man and his boy. Papa had forgotten all about Mr. Ledwell. She hadn't told him anything about the operation, and she had asked Snowball not to tell him either. She didn't want Papa to start back thinking and talking about that poor man and asking questions and sending Rato out to see what he could. She had it all to herself now. Snowball had told her Mr. Ledwell's boy was staying there with him through the nights. Mr. Ledwell had made the boy promise him that before he would go to the operating room, and the boy would be over there now, awake maybe with his father that was dying and she here on her chair trying to sleep with her Papa and Rato, her Papa turned into something else in the night.

Still she might have gone on to sleep if she hadn't thought of Wesley. If she was at home she could go to sleep knowing she would see Wesley at seven-thirty in the morning. He drove the schoolbus and went nearly four miles out of his way on the state's gas to pick her up first so they could talk alone a few minutes before they looked up and saw all those Gupton children in the road, knocking together in the cold and piling on the bus not saying a word with purple splotches like thick cobwebs down their legs that came from standing by an open fire, Mama said, and in winter afternoons Wesley would put her out last into the cold white yard that would be nearly dark by five, and she would walk on towards the light that was coming already from the kitchen windows, steamed on the inside like panes of ice stretched thin on frames. And huddled there she thought how Wesley had said they would go to Warrenton this coming Saturday for a traveling show sponsored by the Lions Club—an exact copy of the Florida State Electric Chair with some poor dummy strapped in it, waiting for the end. Wesley was interested in anything mechanical, and she would have gone with him (no charge for admission the paper said, just a chance to help the Club's Blind Fund) if that was how he wanted to pass time—striking up friends with the owner of the chair whoever it was and talking till time to head back home. But that would have been all right with Rosacoke. She would have waited and been glad if she had got the chance, but she wouldn't now and like as not Wesley would take Willie Duke Aycock which was what Willie Duke had waited for all her life. That was just Wesley. Let her miss school even two days at hog killing and he practically forgot her.

It was thinking all this that kept Rosacoke from going on to sleep. She tried once or twice to empty her head the way she could sometimes at home by closing her eyes and thinking way out in front of her, but she couldn't manage that tonight so she listened till she heard slow breathing from Rato and Papa. Then she got up in her bare feet and felt for the closet door and took down her robe from a hook and put it on. It was peach-colored chenille. She had made it herself and it had been honorable mention at the 4-H Fall Dress

Revue in the Warren County Armory. She took her shoes in her hand and opened the door. The hall was empty and the only light was the one at the nurse's desk, and that was so white, shining into both ends of the long hall and against the white charts hanging in tiers. The two night nurses were gone or she could have talked to them. She hadn't ever talked to them, but they seemed nice enough not to mind if she did want to talk. She guessed they were out giving sleeping pills so she walked towards the big ward to pass time.

It was dark down there and all these sounds came out to meet her a long time before she got to the door like some kind of Hell she was hearing from a long way away—a little moan strained out through old dry lips and the grating of each private snore as it tore its way up the throats of the ones who were already asleep. Rosacoke stopped in the open door. The nurses were not there. Nobody seemed to be walking in the dark anyhow. All she could really see was, close to the door, an old woman set up in bed, bent all over on herself and scratching at her hair real slow. But she knew the others were there, and she knew there ought to be something you could do for such people, something you could say even in the dark that would make them know why you were standing there looking—not because you were well yourself and just trying to walk yourself to sleep but because you felt for them, because you hadn't ever been that sick or that old or that alone before in all your life and because you wished they hadn't been either. You couldn't stand there and say to the whole room out loud, "Could I bring you all some ice water or something?" because they probably wouldn't want that anyhow, and even if they did the first ones would be thirsty again and pitching in their hot sheets before you could make it around the room. You would be there all night, and it would be like trying to fill up No-Bottom Pond if it was ever to get empty. So she turned in the open door and saw one nurse back at the desk and walked in that direction, stopping to look at the flowers waiting outside the room of an old man who said they breathed up too much good air at night.

She was some way off when she saw the man's boy. There was no doubt about it being him this time and she was not surprised. The boy walked fast towards the desk, his shirt open down the front, the white tails sweeping behind him in the light of the one lamp and his chest deep brown almost as if he had worked in the field but you knew he hadn't. When he got to the nurse he shut his eyes and said, "My father's nurse says please call Dr. Davis and tell him to come now. It's serious." His voice was low and fast but Rosacoke heard him. The nurse took her time staring at a list of numbers under the glass on her desk before she called. She told whoever she talked to that Mr. Ledwell had taken a turn for the worse. Then she stood and walked to his room. The boy went close behind her so she stopped at the door and said "Wait out here." When she shut the door it stirred enough breeze to lift his shirttail again. He was that close and without stepping back he stood awhile looking. Then he sat by the door where Rosacoke had seen him that first awful time.

She looked on at it from the dark end of the hall (she was not walking by him in her robe even if it had won honorable mention), but she saw him plain because a table was by his chair and he had switched on a small study lamp that lighted his tired face. His chin hung on his hand like dead weight on delicate scales and his eyes were shut. Rosacoke knew if he looked towards the dark he might see her—at least her face—and she pressed to the blackest wall and watched from there. For a long time he was still. No noise came through his father's door. Then clear as day a woman's voice spoke in the open ward, "I have asked and asked for salt on my dinner"—spoke it twice, not changing a word. Some other voice said "Hush" and the boy faced right and looked. Rosacoke didn't know if he saw her or not (maybe he was just seeing dark) but she saw him—his eyes, far off as she was, and they were the saddest eyes in the world to Rosacoke, that pulled hard at her and called on her or just on the dark to do something soon. But she didn't. She couldn't after the mistake of that first time. She shuddered in the hard waves that flushed over her whole body and locked her there in the shadow. Once she put out her hand and her foot and took one small step towards the boy whose head had dropped onto his folded arms, but the bleached light struck her robe, and she dropped back the way one of those rain snails does that is feeling its path, damp and tender, across the long grass till you touch its gentle horns, and it draws itself back, hurt and afraid, into a tight piece you would never guess could think or move or feel, even.

She couldn't have said how long she stood there, getting so tired she knew how it felt to be dead, before the doctor they called came in. He didn't have a tie on, and sleep was in his eyes. He saw the boy and touched him and said something, and they both walked into the room. Before they shut the door a sound like a mad child catching at his breath after crying ran out behind them to where Rosacoke was. She didn't know what was happening, but the boy's father might be dying. She knew that much. She felt almost sure that if the man died they would make some kind of public announcement. But he didn't die and she had waited so long she was nearly asleep. The hall she had to walk through back to Papa's was as quiet now as a winter night in an attic room when you could look out the window and see a sky, cold and hard as a worn plow point shining with the moon. All those people in the ward were asleep or maybe they had given up trying and waited. It seemed as if when you waited at night for something—maybe you didn't know what—the only thing happened was, time made noise in a clock somewhere way off.

It was the next morning that Rosacoke made up her mind. If Mr. Ledwell had lived through the night, she was going to call on him and his family. It was the only thing to do, the only Christian thing to do—to go over there and introduce yourself and ask if there was anything you could do to help such as setting up at night. The way she felt she might have gone over that morning if the room hadn't been so quiet. She hadn't seen a soul come or go since she woke up. She didn't know how Mr. Ledwell was getting along after everything that happened the night before. She didn't know if he had lived out the night. All she could do was wait for Snowball to tell her. She wasn't going to ask Rato to do any more looking for her after the last time.

Snowball was late coming by that morning, but he got there finally and called her out in the hall to talk. He said Mr. Ledwell had a relapse the night before, and they thought he was passing away, but he pulled through unexpectedly. "He not going to last though, Miss Rosacoke. The day nurse tell me he full of the cancer. It's a matter of days, they say, and he know that hisself so all of us try to keep his spirits up. He ain't a old man. I old enough to be his Daddy. He resting right easy this morning, but he was bad sick last night. In fact he was dead for a few minutes before the doctor come and brought him around. They does that right often now you know."

That made Rosacoke think of the day the Phelps boy fell off the dam at Fleming's Mill backwards into twenty feet of water, and three men who were fishing dived in in all their clothes and found his body face-down on the bottom and dragged it out, the mouth hanging open in one corner as if a finger was pulling it down. He had stayed under water four or five minutes, and his chest and wrists were still. They said he was dead as a hammer for half an hour till one man pumped air in him and he belched black mud and began to moan through his teeth. But what Rosacoke always wondered was, where did they go if they died for a while—Mr. Ledwell and the drowned Phelps boy—and if you were to ask them, could they tell you where they had been and what it was like there or had they just been to sleep? She had heard that somebody asked the Phelps boy when he got well enough to go back to school what dying was like, and he said he couldn't tell because it was a secret between him and his Jesus. Mama had said that was all you could expect out of a Phelps anyhow—that she wouldn't ask him if you paid her cash money and that you couldn't just suppose he had gone to Heaven and if he hadn't, you could be sure he wouldn't admit going elsewhere. (She had smiled but she meant it. She had never had a kind word for that branch of Phelpses since they bootlegged their way to big money some years before.) But not everybody felt the way Mama did. A church of Foot-Washing Baptists up towards South Hill heard about it and invited the boy up to testify but he wouldn't go. And from then on Rosacoke had watched him as if he was something not quite natural that had maybe seen Hell with his own eyes and had lived to tell the tale—or not tell it—and she had followed after him at little recess, hiding where he couldn't notice her so she could watch his face close up and see if his wonderful experience had made him any different. As it turned out it had. He was the quietest thing you could imagine, and his eyes danced all the time as if he was remembering and you couldn't ever know what, not ever.

By the time Rosacoke thought that, Snowball had to leave, but before he went she asked what he thought about her going over to see Mr. Ledwell and his family.

"It couldn't do no harm I can think of, Miss Rosacoke, if you don't stay but a little while. He can't talk much with his one lung, but he be happy to have a visitor. You wait though till he get a little of his strength back from last night."

She nodded Yes but she hadn't planned to pay her visit that morning anyhow. She had made up her mind not to go over there till she could take something with her. She might be from Afton, N.C., but she knew better than to go butting into some man's sickroom, to a man on his deathbed, without an expression of her sympathy. And it had to be flowers. There was that much she could do for Mr. Ledwell because he didn't have friends. He and his family had moved to Raleigh less than six months ago. Snowball had found out the Ledwells were from Baltimore. But of course there wasn't a flower for sale anywhere in the hospital, and anyhow it wasn't cut flowers Rosacoke had in mind. She got a dime from Papa by saying it was time she sent Mama word as to how they were getting along. Then she hunted down one of the Volunteers and bought two cards with the Capitol on them. She wrote one to Mama.

Dear Mama,

We like it here alot. I hope you and Baby Sister, Milo and Sissie are all O.K. Papa and I are getting plenty rest. Rato is the one taking exercise. When you come down here would you bring some of your altheas if they have bloomed yet?

Yours truly
Rosacoke Mustian

She wrote the other one to Wesley Beavers.

Dear Wesley,

How are you getting along? I am fine but miss you alot. Do you miss me? When you go to see the Florida Electric Chair think of how much I would like to be there. If you see Willie Duke Aycock tell her I said hello. I hope to see you Monday early.

Your friend,
Rosacoke

Then she mailed them and waited and hoped the altheas had bloomed. Mama had got an idea out of *Life* magazine that you could force things to flower in winter, and she had dug up an althea bush and set it in a tub and put it in the kitchen by the stove and dared it not to bloom. If it had she would gladly pick a handful of oily purple flowers that bruised if you touched them and hold them in her big lap the whole way to Raleigh on Sunday.

And Sunday came before Rosacoke was ready. She woke up early enough (Rato saw to that—he could wake the dead just tying his shoes), but she took her time getting washed and dressed, straightening the room and hiding things away. She didn't expect the family till after dinner so it was nearly noon before she set Papa up and lathered his face and started to shave him. She had finished one side without a nick, singing as she worked—the radio was on to the final hymn at Tabernacle Baptist Church—when the door burst open, and there was Baby Sister and Mama close behind her with flowers. Baby Sister said "Here I am." Rosacoke got her breath and said, "Blow me down. We sure didn't look for you early as this. Mama, I thought you had Children's Day to get behind you before you could leave."

Mama kissed her and touched Papa's wrist. "I did. But once I pulled the Sunbeams through 'Come and Sing Some Happy Happy Song,' I felt like I could leave so we didn't stay to hear Bracey Overby end it with Taps. I know he did all right though. I hope he did—he practiced till he was pale anyhow. Then after leaving church like Indians in the middle of everything to get here early of course some Negroes drove up at the house just as we was starting—some of those curious Marmaduke Negroes with red hair. Well, they had heard about Baby Sister, and they had this skinny baby and wanted her to blow down his throat." (Negroes were always doing that. A child who had never seen its father could cure sore throat by breathing on it.) "It's a awful thing but Baby Sister enjoys it—don't you?—and I can't deny her any powers she may have, especially on Sunday." (Nobody had denied Baby Sister—six years old and big for the name—anything she wanted since she was born six months to the day after her father died. Even the nurses didn't try. Mama marched her in past a dozen signs that plainly said *No Children Under*

12 and Baby Sister in Sweetheart Pink and nobody uttered a sound.) All through her story Mama looked around, and when she was done she said "Where is Rato?"

Rosacoke said, "Patrolling, I guess. He'll show up for dinner," and before she could wonder where were Milo and Sissie, they strolled in from parking the car. Milo kissed Rosacoke and said, "Wesley sent you that." Mama said, "No he didn't. We haven't seen Wesley." Then he laughed and kissed Papa—"Miss Betty Upchurch sent you that, but I don't tickle as good as her." (Miss Betty was a crazy old widow with whiskers that he teased Papa about.) Everybody laughed except Sissie. When they quieted down Sissie said "Good morning" and showed her teeth and settled back to looking as if a Mack truck had hit her head-on so Milo explained it to Papa. "Sissie will be off the air today. She's mad—woke up mad but didn't find reasons till we were leaving home. Then she found two good ones. One was she had to shell butter beans all the way up here because Mama didn't read the directions and froze her damn beans in the shell. The other thing was she had to sit on the back seat to do it because Mama and Baby Sister had spoke to sit up front with me and the heater. Well, she sat back there shelling, and when she finished—it took her an hour and we were on the outskirts of Raleigh—she lowered the glass on her side, intending to empty out the hulls, but Baby Sister said, 'Shut that pneumonia hole,' and Sissie got flustered and threw out the beans instead. Mama capped the climax by laughing, and Sissie ain't spoke a word since except just now." He turned to Sissie who was already staring out the window—"Say something, Doll Baby. Turn over a new leaf." She wouldn't even look so Milo laughed and that did seal her. It was a good thing. Nobody could make Papa madder than Sissie when she started running her mouth.

Mama frowned at Milo and said, "Everybody calm down. We got half a day to get through in this matchbox." She meant Papa's room that was ten by twelve. Then she went to the bureau and while Rosacoke scraped chairs around, she took off her hat and her white ear bobs and combed her hair and put on a hair net and slipped off her shoes. She went to the chair where Rato slept—in her stocking feet—and said, "Rosacoke, get me my bed shoes out of my grip." Rosacoke got them.

Then Mama settled back and blew one time with relief. She had come to stay and she had brought three things with her—dinner for seven in a cardboard suit box, her grip, and enough altheas to fill a zinc tub. She made it plain right away that Rosacoke would go on home with Milo and Sissie and Baby Sister but Rato would stay on to help her with Papa. Milo said he planned on leaving between eight and nine o'clock. (What he had in mind was to pacify Sissie by taking her to supper at the Chinese café she liked so much and then going on to a Sunday picture. But he didn't tell Mama that.) And Rosacoke couldn't object to leaving. In some ways she would be glad to get home, and Milo's plans would give her time to pay her visit to Mr. Ledwell, time to do all she wanted to do, all she thought she could do—to step over when she had seen her family and pay her respects and give them the flowers that would say better than she could how much she felt for Mr. Ledwell, dying in this strange place away from his friends and his home, and for his people who were waiting.

So she had that day with her family (Rato appeared long enough for dinner), and the day went fine except for three things. One thing was Sissie but nobody ever looked for Sissie to act decent. Another thing was, after they had eaten the dinner Mama packed, Papa reached over to his bedside table and pulled out the playing cards. Rosacoke had taken pains to hide them way back in the drawer, but Papa pulled them out in full view and set up a game of Solitaire and looked at Mama and grinned. She made a short remark about it appeared to her Papa was learning fancy tricks in his old age. Papa said couldn't he teach her a few games, and she drew up in her chair and said she had gone nearly fifty years—seven of them as a deaconess in Delight Baptist Church— without knowing one playing card from the other, and she guessed she could live on in ignorance the rest of the time. But she didn't stop Papa. He just stopped offering to teach her and lay there the rest of the afternoon, dealing out hands of Solitaire till he was blue in the face. He played right on through the nap everybody took after dinner. You couldn't have stopped him with dynamite. The third thing was after their naps. When they all woke up it was nearly three-thirty and the natural light was dim. Rosacoke stood up to switch on the bulb, but Milo said "No don't," and even closed the blinds. Then he went to Papa and

pointed at his necktie and said, "Watch this. Pretty soon it'll start lighting up." It was something he had got that week by mail, and he claimed
it would say "Kiss Me In The Dark!" when the room got dim enough,
but they waited and the only thing the tie did was shine pale green all
over. Rosacoke was glad he didn't get it working but Papa was disappointed. He asked Milo to leave the tie with him so he could test it in
total darkness and show it around to the nurses, but Milo said he was
intending to wear it to some crop-dusting movies at the high school that
coming Thursday.

In a few more minutes it was five o'clock, and Milo started his plans
by saying he and Sissie were going for a little ride and for Rosacoke to
be packed for home by nine. Then he got Sissie up and into her coat
and they left. Whenever Milo left a place things always quieted down.
Papa went back to his Solitaire, and Mama crocheted on a tablecloth
that she said would be Rosacoke's wedding present if the thread didn't
rot beforehand. Even Baby Sister, who had pestered all afternoon to
make up for Sissie being on strike, was worn out and sat still, sucking
her thumb, so in the quiet room Rosacoke took down her grip and
packed in almost everything. But she kept out her only clean dress and
took it down to the nurses' utility closet and pressed it and put it on. She
had washed it in the hall bathtub the night before. When she came back
to the room, nobody paid her any mind. They thought she was just getting ready to go home. She washed her hands and face and stood in
front of the mirror, combing her hair and working up her nerve. She
turned her back to Mama and put on a little lipstick and rouge to keep
from looking so pale. Then she took the altheas up out of the water
Mama set them in and dried the stems with a clean towel and wrapped
tissue paper around them. Mama said, "You are dressing too soon," and
Rosacoke said, "I reckon I am," but before anybody had seen her good,
she slipped out the door in her yellow dress, holding the flowers. She
had tied a white card to them. Snowball had got it for her the day before.
It said "From a Friend Across the Hall."

She took three steps and stopped and stood in front of the oak door,
taller than she would ever be, that said "Ledwell." Behind it was
where Mr. Ledwell was and his people that she didn't know, where he

had laid down that first day Rato saw him talking and laughing, where he had gone out from to take his operation, and where it was not his home. Rosacoke was nervous but she told herself she looked as good as she could, and she had the altheas in her hands to hide the shaking. She knocked on the door and she must have knocked too soft because nobody came. She knocked again and put her ear to the wood. There were dim sounds coming from the other side so she pushed the door open a little, but the room was dark and quiet as an open field at night with only the sky, and she was drawing back to leave when the moving light of candles caught her, streaming from a part of the room she couldn't see into, drawing her on. So she went inside and pressed the door silent behind her and stood up against it, waiting till her eyes had opened enough to halfway see. There were five or six people in the room. Mr. Ledwell was a ridge on the bed that the sheets rose and fell over in gullies like after a rain, and his boy was by his head, holding one of the candles. In the yellow light the boy looked a way Wesley Beavers might never look, and the same light fell through a clear tent that covered his father's head and chest. A little of it fell on three ladies off in a corner, kneeling on the hard floor, and on a man standing near the bed by a table with two candles on it. He was all in black and falling from his neck was a narrow band of purple cloth with fine gold crosses at the ends. He was talking in words Rosacoke didn't know, almost singing in a voice that was low and far away because he was old with white hair and was looking down, but finally he looked up at Mr. Ledwell's boy, and the two of them pulled the tent back off him. Rosacoke knew he was alive. She could hear the air sucking into his throat, and his eyes were open on the boy and on the yellow candle.

The old man in black moved his hands in the air three times carefully, wide and long over Mr. Ledwell. Then he took a piece of cotton and waited for Mr. Ledwell to shut his eyes. He wiped the cotton over the lids, and they were shining for a second, wet and slick under the light before Mr. Ledwell opened them again and turned them back to the boy. The boy rolled his father's head to one side and then to the other while the old man touched the cotton to the ears that looked cold, and all the time Mr. Ledwell was trying not to take his eyes off the boy as if that sad face in the soft light that came and went was what kept him from dying, and except for that same soft light, the walls of the room would have disappeared and the ceiling, and Rosacoke could have walked out through where the window had been that she used to stand by. It seemed to be time for her to leave anyhow. She didn't know how long this would go on. She didn't know what it was. She only knew they were getting Mr. Ledwell ready to die in their own way, and she had taken the first step to leave when the boy's face turned and saw her through all that dark. His face changed for a minute, and you might have thought he smiled if you hadn't known that couldn't have happened now, not on his face. That was why Rosacoke didn't leave. He had looked at her as if he knew why she was there, almost as if he would have needed her if there had been time. But the old man touched Mr. Ledwell's lips, and Mr. Ledwell strained his head off the pillow and sucked at the cotton before the old man could pull it back. He thought they were giving him something to drink. And it went on that way over his hand that had to be pulled out from under the cover and his feet that seemed to be tallow you could gouge a line in with your fingernail. When they finished with his head, they put the tent back over him, and Rosacoke couldn't hear his breathing quite so loud. From his feet the old man walked back to his head. He put a black wood cross that had Jesus, white and small, nailed on it into Mr. Ledwell's hand. Then he shook a fine mist of water over him and made the sign again, and Rosacoke heard words she could understand. The old man told Mr. Ledwell to say, "Thy will be done." Mr. Ledwell nodded his head and his eyes opened. He took his hand and tapped on the inside of the clear tent. When his boy looked at him, his voice came up in pieces—but Rosacoke heard him plain—"Don't forget to give Jack Rowan one of those puppies." The boy said he wouldn't forget. Mr. Ledwell looked easier and when the old man reached under the tent to take the cross and Jesus away from him, he nodded his head over and over as he turned the cross loose.

The old man went over to speak to the lady who must have been Mr. Ledwell's wife. She was still on her knees, and she never took her face out of her hands. That was when Rosacoke left. They might switch on the light, and there she would be looking on at this dying which was the most private thing in the world. She had stayed that long because the boy had looked at her, but he might have forgotten by now. He had never looked again. A chair was by the door. She laid her flowers there. In the light somebody might see them and be glad that whoever it was stepped over to bring them, stepped over without saying a word.

She waited in the hall for the sound of his dying because he had seemed so ready, but it didn't come—nobody came or went but a colored girl, pushing a cartload of supper towards the ward—so she had to walk back into Papa's room, dreading questions. The room was dim though and still with only the light over Papa's bed that shined on his hair and the cards spread out on his knees. But he was just turning them over now, not really playing, and when Rosacoke shut the door, he looked and put one finger to his mouth and pointed towards Baby Sister, asleep at last in Mama's lap, and Mama nodding. Rosacoke thought she was safe and halfway smiled and leaned on the door, waiting for breath. But Papa stared at her and then tried to whisper—"You are leaving me, ain't you?"—and Mama jerked awake. It took her a while to get her bearings, but finally she said, "Where in the world have you been with Papa's flowers?" Rosacoke said, "To see a friend." Papa said, "I didn't want no flowers. Who is your friend?" She said "Mr. Ledwell" but Papa didn't show recollection. Mr. Ledwell hadn't crossed his mind since the operation, but just to say something he asked was the man coming on all right? Rosacoke said, "He ain't doing so good, Papa" and to Mama who had never had a secret, never wanted one, "Mama, please don't ask me who that is because I don't know."

Then she went to her grip and turned her back on the room and began packing in the things she had left till last. She was almost done when Rato walked in. Nobody had seen Rato since dinner. He walked in and said it the way he might walk in the kitchen and drop a load of wood in the box—"That man over yonder is dead. Ain't been five minutes." Mama said she was always sorry to hear of any death, and Rato said if they left the door cracked open they could see the man because a nurse had already called the undertaker to come after the body. But Rosacoke faced him and said "No" and said it so Rato wouldn't dare to crack the door one inch. He just left fast and slammed it behind him.

But Baby Sister slept through it all, and Mama didn't speak for fear of disturbing her so the room was still again. To keep her hands busy Rosacoke rearranged the few little things in her grip, but she stood sideways to look at Papa and have him fill her mind. Papa had his cards that he went back to, but he dealt them slow because he was thinking. He was so old himself you couldn't expect him to be too sad. Lately he always said he knew so many more dead men than live ones that there wasn't a soul left who could call him by his first name. And that was the truth. That was what took the edge off death for Papa—grieving over so many people, so many of his friends, burying so much love with each one of them till he had buried them all (everybody he had nearly) and pretty nearly all his love, and death didn't hold fear for him any more. It wasn't as if he didn't know where he was going or what it would be like when he got there. He just trusted and he hoped for one thing, he tried to see to one last thing—for a minute he stopped his card playing and asked Mama could he die at home, and Mama told him he could.

That was what made Rosacoke think so long about Mr. Ledwell who had died in that dark room. She wouldn't be able to go to his funeral, wouldn't even be asked. But that wasn't so bad. She had done what she could, being away from home, hadn't she, and didn't she know his name at least and hadn't he died not cut up or shot or run over but almost in his sleep with his wife and his boy there, and with all that beautiful dying song, hadn't he surely died sanctified? If he had to die wasn't that as good a way as any, leaving his living picture back here in that boy? But she hadn't ever seen him alive really. She hadn't ever told him or any of his kind—out loud—that she felt for them. She hadn't ever said it so loud she could hear her own voice—that Rosacoke Mustian was sorry to see it happen. That was why she spoke at last. She had been quiet so long, and now her slow lean voice cut through all the dark in the room. "It don't seem right," she said. "It just don't seem right. It seem like I had got to know him real well." And her words hung in the room for a long time—longer than it took Papa to pick the cards up off the bed and lay them without a sound in the drawer, longer even than it would have taken Rosacoke to say goodbye to Wesley if it had been Saturday night and she had been at home.

A LONG
AND HAPPY LIFE

ONE

Just with his body and from inside like a snake, leaning that black motorcycle side to side, cutting in and out of the slow line of cars to get there first, staring due-north through goggles towards Mount Moriah and switching coon tails in everybody's face was Wesley Beavers, and laid against his back like sleep, spraddle-legged on the sheepskin seat behind him was Rosacoke Mustian who was maybe his girl and who had given up looking into the wind and trying to nod at every sad car in the line, and when he even speeded up and passed the truck (lent for the afternoon by Mr. Isaac Alston and driven by Sammy his man, hauling one pine box and one black boy dressed in all he could borrow, set up in a ladder-back chair with flowers banked round him and a foot on the box to steady it)—when he even passed that, Rosacoke said once into his back "Don't" and rested in humiliation, not thinking but with her hands on his hips for dear life and her white blouse blown out behind her like a banner in defeat.

It was because Wesley was a motorcycle man since his discharge (or would be, come Monday) and wouldn't have brought her in a car if fire had fallen in balls on every side. He had intended taking her to the picnic that way, and when Mildred Sutton died having her baby without a husband and Rosacoke felt compelled to go to the funeral first and asked Wesley please to take her, he said he would, but he saw no reason to change to a car for a Negro funeral. Rosacoke had to get there and couldn't walk three miles in dust and couldn't risk him going on ahead so she didn't argue but pulled her skirt up over her knees for all to see and put her hat in the saddlebag and climbed on.

Riding like that she didn't see the land they passed through—nothing new or strange but what she had passed every day of her life almost, except for the very beginning and some summer days when she had left for 4-H camp at White Lake or to stay with Aunt Oma in Newport News or to set with somebody in the hospital, like Papa before he died. But the land was there, waiting.

The road passed a little way from the Mustians' porch, and if you came up their driveway and turned left, you would be at the Afton store and the paving soon, and that took you on to Warrenton where she worked. But they turned right today and the road narrowed as it went till it was only wide enough for one thing going one way—a car or a truck or a mule and wagon—and it being July, whatever passed, even the smallest foot, ground more dirt to dust that rose several times every hour of the day and occasionally—invisibly—at night and lingered awhile and at sunset hung like fog and if there was no breeze, settled back on whatever was there to receive it—Rosacoke and Mama and Rato and Milo walking to church, if it had been a first Sunday and ten years ago before Milo got his driving license—but settling mostly on Negro children aiming home in a slow line, carrying blackberries they had picked to eat (and if you stopped and said, "How much you asking for your berries?" they would be so surprised and shy and forget the price their mother told them to say if anybody stopped, and hand them over, bucket and all, for whatever you wanted to give, and all the dust you raised would be on those berries when you got home). It settled on leaves too—on dogwood and hickory and thin pine and holly and now and then a sycamore and on Mr. Isaac Alston's cherry trees that huddled around the pond he had made for the hot air to pass over, choked and tan till there would come a rain—trees he had set out as switches twelve years ago on his seventieth birthday and poured fish in the water smaller than the eye could see and claimed he would live to sit in that cool cherry shade and pull out the dim descendants of those first minnows. And he might, as the Alstons didn't die under ninety.

What Alstons *had* died were the things they came to, after trees—
the recent ones, overflowed from the family graves and laid out on
this side of Delight Baptist Church, looking shorter than anybody
would have guessed, with people around them that never had family
graves to begin with—Rosacoke's Papa (who was her grandfather and
who by the time he died had completely forgotten Miss Pauline his
wife and asked to be buried beside his mother and then forgot to tell
them where his mother was) and Miss Pauline, the size of a dressed
rabbit, and Rosacoke's own father who was no Baptist (who wasn't
much of anything) and whose grave had sunk into the ground. The
graves went towards the church, taking grass with them, and then
the white sand began that had been hauled in from a creek bed. The
church stood in the sand under two oak trees, wooden and bleached
and square as a gun-shell box, daring people not to come. The Mustians went and even Wesley Beavers, with *his* name.

But it wasn't where they were going now so they passed by, and the
graves and Delight Church and the sand and the two long picnic
tables turned to the woods that Milo and Rosacoke and Rato had run
in as children with Mildred Sutton and any other Negroes she
brought along (that had scattered now, to Baltimore mostly). The
woods began by the road and went back farther than Rosacoke or
even the boys had ever gone, not because they were scared but
because they got tired—the woods went on that long, and every leaf
of them belonged to Mr. Isaac Alston. Once Rosacoke and Mildred
packed them a dinner and said to themselves, "We will walk till we
come to an open field where somebody is growing something." So
they walked on slowly in a straight line through the cool damp air
under trees where sun never came but only this green light the mush-
rooms grew by. When they had walked an hour, they were breathing
in air that nothing but possums and owls had breathed before, and
snakes if snakes breathed. Mildred didn't like the idea but Rosacoke
kept going, and Mildred came on behind, looking mostly *up*, checking on the sky to still be there and to see what snakes were studying
down on them. Then they came to an open field the size of a circus
ring where there were no trees but only bitter old briars and broomstraw the color of Milo's beard that was just then arriving. They sat on

the edge of that to eat their biscuits and syrup and for Mildred to rest her feet, but Rosacoke thought and decided they couldn't stop here as it wasn't a field where anybody had *meant* to grow anything. (Nothing ate broomstraw but mules and mules only ate it if they thought it was something you valued.) So they stood up to go, and Mildred's mouth fell open and said "Great God A-mighty" because there was one deer behind them in the trees for quicker than it took to say if it had horns. But its eyes were black and it had looked at them. When its last sound had gone, Rosacoke said, "Don't let's go no farther" and Mildred said "All right." They were not afraid of any deer, but if those woods offered things like that, that would take the time to look at you, when you had only walked an hour, where *would* they end, and what would be growing in any field they found on the other side, and who would be tending it there? So they came out, taking their time, proving they hadn't given up for fear, and when they got to the road, Mildred spoke for the first time since calling on God to see that deer— "Rosacoke, it's time for me some supper"—and they parted. It was no more time for supper than it was for snow, but Mildred meant to get home quick and unload that deer on somebody—his streak he made through the trees and the sound of his horn feet in the old leaves and his eyes staring on through all those biscuits at what they did, and waiting.

If Rosacoke had looked up from Wesley's back at the woods, she might have remembered that day and how it was only nine years ago and here she was headed to bury that same Mildred, and was that black-eyed deer still waiting, and did *he* belong to Mr. Isaac?—that deer? But she didn't look up and she didn't remember. If you were with Wesley Beavers, what good was remembering? You couldn't tell him what you remembered. He said he lived in the present, and that meant that maybe when he went a hundred and thirty miles from home to spend three years in the U.S. Navy, lounging around in a tight uniform fixing radios and not moving a step out of Norfolk, Virginia (or so he said) except to come home a few weekends, maybe he seldom thought of her. Not the way she thought of him anyhow— wondering every night if she was his, hoping she was, even when he didn't write for weeks and then sent sassy post cards. But he had been home a civilian three days now, and tomorrow he was headed back to Norfolk to sell motorcycles with a friend of his, and she didn't know a thing she hadn't known for years—which was that he still came to get her Saturday night and took her to a place called Danceland and danced with every woman there in succession so fast he seemed to be ten Wesleys or a dozen, swarming, and then rode her home and kissed her good night for an hour, without a question or a word.

She thought that through once. It was the deepest thinking she could manage on a motorcycle with dust running up her legs, and she was just changing to something new—that at last Wesley had found the vehicle he was meant for (being with Wesley had always been like being on a motorcycle)—when she felt the shift of his shoulders under her cheek and his hips under her hands. The way he moved she slackened her grip for a second. It was too much like holding your eye through the lid while it turns, smooth in the socket but easy to ruin.

She looked up and they were at Mount Moriah Church where they meant to be, and Wesley was turning in, not slowing up at all but gouging a great rut in the dusty yard. He stuck out a leg and his black ankle boots plowed a little way, and that halted them under the one low tree. The coon tails relaxed but Wesley kept the motor going, racing it with twitches of his hand, listening as if he expected it to speak, till Rosacoke said in his ear, "Hush your noise, Wesley."

"Don't it sound funny to you?"

"No," she said. So he let the motor die, and in the astonished quiet where every bird had surrendered to Wesley's roar, the only sound was that truck and the cars coming on behind, rumbling like distant buffaloes, with Mildred. "Get down, Wesley. They'll all be here in a minute." Wesley swung off the seat and watched while Rosacoke got herself down. Now they were still, the heat settled back on them, and they both shook their heads under the burden. But they didn't speak. They had given up talking about it long ago. Rosacoke took out her handkerchief and wiped her face before the sweat could streak the dust. She looked in the round mirror on the handlebars and combed out her hair that had the wind in it still after the ride. With the black tree behind her, you could see the dust fly up around her head from out of her hair, and in the round mirror it outlined her with a sudden halo. Even Wesley noticed that. Then she put on her hat and said, "We didn't need to come *that* quick" and took off towards the church, sinking through the thin crust of ground with her high heels. When she had walked ten yards alone and her white shoes were tan, she turned and said, "*Come* on, Wesley. Let's don't be standing around staring when they get here."

"Well, I'm going to work on this motor awhile to make sure we can get out when we want to. I'll be in there in a little bit. You just save me a seat by the window."

She only blushed—all she ever did now when Wesley let her down (which pretty nearly kept her blushing non-stop)—and said, "Don't go playing that harp" (the harmonica was another thing he had taken up in the Navy) and climbed the steps. She stopped at the top and looked back towards the road. That way, Wesley saw her and thought how far she had come in three years to being this—tall almost as he was, maybe five-foot-nine, and her skin pale as candles laid close on her long bones, and what wind there was, twitching at her hair pulled to the back of her neck, falling down long and dry and the color of straw from under her level hat, stopping below her shoulders where your hand would have been if you had been holding her and dancing with her, close (the only way Wesley danced since his discharge). Then his eyes moved on. And every time he passed below her swinging hair—looking—he got onto women he knew in Norfolk or at the beach and how they smelled, twisting in the dark, and how their smell stayed on him now he didn't recollect their names or how they looked though he had labored in them whole nights of his life and the feel of them was on his fingers like oil, real as if they were by him now under that tree, calling him Junior with their hands working and him starting and them crying "Sweet Jesus!" to him in the night.

But suddenly a bird sang in the tree over Wesley's head, holding up its one clear voice like a deed in the scorching day, and Rosacoke looked at Wesley as if he might have done it—that song—looking clear through him and all he thought, it seemed, shaking her head at what she saw. But Wesley was twenty-two years old his last birthday, and what was so wrong, he wanted to know, with thinking all those things?—

except maybe they didn't fit Rosacoke, not the way she was now, new and changed since the times three years ago when they went in to shows in Warrenton and drove nearly home and stopped and spent an hour or longer telling each other good night with the windows misted up, sitting under a tree with pecans falling on the car to make them laugh. Those other women, he had touched and claimed whenever he needed to, but how much of Rosacoke had he touched? Knowing her all that time, how much of her could he see whenever his eyes were closed? How much of her could he claim?—her standing on church steps in Sunday white, straining to see where Mildred was—how much of that could he just walk up and ask for and get?

He might have tried to find out if she hadn't turned and vanished in the dark church, not meaning to roll her hips but letting loose all the power she had there (which was enough to grind rocks) and showing, last thing, her white ankles flexing firm on her heels, and Jesus, he was back in Norfolk sure as the sun poured down. And it did—all over Wesley Beavers from head to foot which was half the trouble. So to change the subject he took out his cycle tools and tightened screws that were tighter already than God ever meant them to be.

Rosacoke remembered in the vestibule that she hadn't been here since the day she slipped off with Mildred and came to the meeting where Aunt Mannie Mayfield stood at age eighty and named the fathers of all her children, far as she could recall. Rosacoke looked round now and the same three things to notice were there—a bell rope hanging from the steeple for anybody to pull, and a gray paper hornets' nest (built in the window by mistake during the war but deserted now far as the eye could see though nobody would tear it down for fear one hornet might be there still, getting older and meaner), and by the open door to the auditorium, a paper bag nailed to the wall with a note saying, *Kindly Leave Gum Here.* She took one deep breath—as if it was the last she would get all afternoon—and went in, and the hot air came out to meet her like a member.

It looked empty—just a choir at the back around a piano and a pulpit in front of that and on the side a stove and then hard seats enough for a hundred people though it would hold half again that many for anything special like a funeral, but it gave no signs of a funeral today. There was not a flower in sight—they were coming with Mildred in the truck—and nobody had thought to come ahead and open the windows. There were six long windows and Rosacoke picked the back one on the left to open and sit by. She went towards it up the bare aisle, and when she got to the pew, the church wasn't empty at all—there was Landon Allgood laid out asleep, the size of a dry cornstalk, breathing heavy, one arm hanging off the bench to the floor and his shirt buttoned right to the neck. He lived alone in a one-room house a little beyond the church and dug graves for white folks, and his trouble was, he took paregoric when he could get it which was mostly on Saturday and then seldom made it home. You were liable to find him anywhere Sunday morning, asleep. One Christmas before Rosacoke was born, he fell down in the public road, and who-ever found him next morning had to carry him to Rocky Mount Hos-pital and have all his toes cut off that had frozen solid in his shoes. That was why, to this day, his shoes turned up at the ends. Rosacoke didn't know how long he had been there or whether he was ready to leave, but she knew he ought to go before the others came as he wasn't dressed for a funeral so she said "Landon." (She wasn't scared of Landon. She had gone in the store herself and bought him bottles of paregoric with his quarters when she was little and nobody would sell him another drop.) She said "Landon, wake up." But he slept on. "Landon, this is Miss Rosacoke. You get up from there."

He was ready. He opened his eyes and said, "Good morning, Miss Rosacoke" just as if he had met her in the road on the way to work.

"It's afternoon, Landon, and will you please get up and go home?"

"Yes'm," he said, sitting up, noticing he was in church and smiling, "Here I am again." Then "What you doing here, Miss Rosacoke?"

"They are burying Mildred."

"What's wrong with Mildred?"

"She died."

"Well, I do say." He got to his feet and put on his cap and tipped it to her and headed as best he could for the door by the choir that led out back. Rosacoke went on into the pew and raised the window. When Landon got to the door—he even had his hand on the knob—he turned and said, "I'm some kin to Mildred, ain't I?"

"Her uncle I guess."

"Yes'm, that's it." Then he could leave.

The church sat sideways to Wesley's tree and the road, and Rosacoke could stay by her window and see what happened in the yard. Landon wasn't ten feet out the back when the truck turned in, having a little trouble with the ruts Wesley made and bringing twelve cars behind it, each one paler with dust than the one before and all packed full. The cars unloaded in order and the first two women were Mildred's mother Mary and Mildred's sister Estelle who had stayed at home when all the others scattered because of her health which was poor from the night Manson Hargrove shot her at a dance, both barrels in the chest. (She lived though—shooting Estelle's bosom was like shooting a feather bed.) Then came the little boys that belonged to most anybody. They were brought to help carry the flowers, but when they swarmed out and saw Wesley, they took off towards him and stood in a tight dark ring, staring out at his cycle like the Chariot of God that could fly. But Wesley had stopped his tinkering when Mildred arrived. He answered one or two questions the boys asked—"What do it burn?" and he told them "Coal"—and then nodded good afternoon to Mary and shut up and leaned against the tree. Somebody called out, "You boys come get these flowers." They went over and took up the wreaths and brought them towards the church, and the one in front wore roses around his neck like a horse that has won and can smile.

Mary and Estelle stood by the truck, looking, and that boy kept his eyes and his foot flat on the box as if it was his and nobody was getting it. Then the other women came up, silent. One of them—Aunt Mannie Mayfield who had walked four miles to get there and was so old she didn't remember a soul now she *was* there—hugged Mary and said what seemed to be a signal, and they climbed the steps—two girls nearly lifting Aunt Mannie who could walk any distance but *up* and who would be next. But the men stayed by the truck, and when the flowers had gone, that boy leaned over and shoved the box to the end, and Sammy and three others took it (to say they had, any two could have carried it alone). They stood a minute with it on their shoulders, taking their bearings. Somebody laughed high and clear. The preacher turned to the church and all the men followed.

Rosacoke saw that and thought every minute Wesley would break loose and take his seat beside her. But he didn't, not even when the yard was empty, and when she heard Mary and Estelle leading the others in, she had to take her eyes off him and stand and nod to the people as they passed and call them by name—the family taking the front pew and sitting as if something pressed them and the others filling in behind, leaving Rosacoke her empty pew at the back, and all standing up—except the ones with babies—till the box was laid on two sawhorses in front of the pulpit, and a boy laid flowers on the lid over what he reckoned was Mildred's face—one design, the Bleeding Heart that Rosacoke sent at Mary's request (white carnations with roses for blood at the center, which would take some time to pay for). When that was done five women stood in various pews and walked to the choir. The piano started and stopped and for a second there was just Bessie Williams' voice slicing through the heat with six high words, calling the others to follow. It was "Precious Name, Show Me Your Face," and it was Jesus they were singing to—meaning it, looking up at the roof to hornets' nests and spiders as if it might all roll away and show them what they asked to see. But the song ended and Rev. Mingie thanked the ladies and said Mrs. Ransom had composed the obituary and would read it now. Mrs. Ransom stood where she was, smiling, and turned to face Mary and Estelle and read off the paper she held, "Miss Mildred Sutton was born in 1936 in the bed where she died. Her mother is Mary Sutton of this community, and her father was Wallace Sutton, whereabouts unknown, but who worked some years for the Highway and before that, said he fought in France and got gassed and buried alive and was never the same again. She had a brother and three sisters, and they are living in Baltimore and Philadelphia—except Estelle who is with us here—and are unable to come but have sent telegrams of their grief which will be read later. She grew up all around here and worked in cotton for Mr. Isaac Alston and went to school off and on till she started cooking for the Drakes and tending to their children that she loved like they were hers. She worked for them nearly two years, and they would surely be here today if they were not vacationing up at Willoughby Beach. Mildred aimed to go with them right to the last and then wasn't able. She stayed here and died not far from her twenty-first birthday. Her favorite tune was 'Annie Laurie' which she learned from Miss Rosacoke Mustian who is with us today, representing the white friends, and I will sing it now at her mother's request." And standing where she was, she sang it through alone, not to any tune Rosacoke had ever heard but making it on the air as she went, knowing Mildred would never object to that.

Then the preacher read the telegrams. They were all very much like the one from Alec her brother—"Thinking today of little sister and sorry the car is broke." That seemed sufficient reason. Everybody nodded their heads and one or two said "Amen."

Rosacoke sat through that, trying to see past flapping fans to the box. Every once in awhile somebody would turn to see was she there and, seeing her, smile as though the whole afternoon would fold under if she didn't watch it with her familiar face (the way a boy three rows ahead watched her, holding her in his gaze like some new thing, untried, that might go up in smoke any minute). It was that hot inside and her mind worked slowly back through spring water and shade till she was almost in the night with Wesley, but the voice came at her faintly where she was—"Miss Rosacoke, will you kindly view the body?" It was the preacher standing by her, and she turned from the window—"Now?"

"Yes'm, she is ready." They had uncovered Mildred and they wanted Rosacoke to see her first. Mama had warned her this would happen, but there didn't seem to be a way out. She stood up, hoping the preacher would walk with her (and he did, a few feet behind), and went to the box, setting her eyes on the pulpit behind it so she wouldn't see Mildred the whole way.

They had laid Mildred in a pink nightgown that tied at the throat and had belonged to the lady she cooked for, but she had shrunk to nothing this last week as if her life was so much weight, and the gown was half empty. She never had much bosom—Estelle got most of that and when they were twelve, Rosacoke told her, "Mildred, why don't you buy some stuffing? Your bosoms look like fried eggs"—and the ones she had, swollen uselessly now, were settled on her arms that lay straight down her sides and left her hands out of sight that were her good feature. Sometime during the ride her body had twisted to the left, and her profile crushed bitterly into the pillow. Whoever took off the lid had left her alone. Rosacoke wondered if she should move her back for all to see. She looked at the preacher and nearly asked if that was what he meant her to do. But she thought and turned and walked to her seat down the middle aisle with her eyes to the ground, passing through everybody waiting to look, feeling stronger with her part done and Mildred turned to the wall where nobody would see.

And so was Wesley turned away. He was squatting on the ground, and his shoes were sunk in the dust, but he was polishing every spoke in the wheels of that machine as if he never again intended driving it over anything but velvet rugs. The congregation lined up to view Mildred, and Rosacoke had time to think, "Tomorrow he will ride it to Norfolk and take his new job and sell motorcycles for maybe the rest of his life, but he can't leave it alone for one hour and sit by me through this service."

And he polished on with his arms moving slow as if they moved through clear thick oil. At times he would rock back on his heels to study what he had done, and his sides would move above his belt to show he was breathing deep—the only way he gave in to the heat. When he was satisfied he stood and cleaned his hands on a rag and his arms to where his sleeves were rolled. But it was grease he was wiping, not sweat. He was somebody who could shine a whole motorcycle in the month of July and not sweat, and his dark hair (still cut for the Navy, stopping high on his neck) was dry. It didn't seem natural and when he leaned against his tree and stared at the ground, he looked to Rosacoke as cool as one November day six years ago, and she thought about that day, so clear and cool—the first she saw of Wesley. He lived three miles from her, and all her life she heard about the Beavers but never saw one till that day—a Saturday—when she went out in Mr. Isaac's woods to pick up pecans off the ground. It was too early for that though—the leaves were gone but the nuts hung on, waiting for a wind, and there was no wind this day—so she was heading home with mighty little in her bucket, going slow, just calling it a walk now, when she looked ahead, and in one tall tree that the path bent round was a boy, spreading his arms between the branches and bracing his feet like he was the eagle on money. It was a pecan tree and she walked straight up under it and said, "Boy, shake me down some nuts." Not saying a word he gripped the branches tighter and rocked the fork he stood in, and nuts fell on her like hail by the hundred till she yelled out to stop or else her skull would crack. He stopped and she picked up all the pecans she could carry, thinking the whole time he would climb down and help her, but he stayed up there and when she looked at him once or twice, he wasn't even watching her — just braced on his long legs that rose in blue overalls to his low waist and his narrow chest and bare white neck and his hair that was brown and still cut for the summer, high above his ears by somebody at home, and his eyes that stared straight out at sights nobody else in Warren County was seeing unless they were up a pecan tree.

"What are you looking at?" she asked him.

"Smoke."

She looked but the sky looked clear to her. "Don't you want to share out these pecans?" — as if bushels of them weren't lying all around her.

"I don't much like them."

"Well, what are you doing up that tree then?"

"Waiting, I guess."

"Who for?"

"Just waiting."

"Who are you?"

"Wesley" — as if he was the only Wesley ever made.

"Don't you want to know who I am?"

"Who are you?"

"Rosacoke Mustian — how old are you?"

"Going on sixteen."

"That's old enough to get your driving license. My brother Milo and me slept in the same bed till he got his driving license, and then Mama said he would have to move."

He smiled at that and she saw the smile was as close to victory as she was coming that day so she said, "Thank you for shaking the tree" and went on home and didn't see him again for nearly a year, but she thought of him in the evenings long as those nuts lasted — him caring for nothing but the smoke she couldn't see, wondering if there was fire somewhere, waiting.

Through that the line went on past Mildred. Some of them—the young ones mostly—skipped by her fast as they could and took a little look and jerked away, and Jimmy Jenkins fell out in the aisle on his way to sit down because he held his eyes shut till he was past Mildred (to keep from having her to remember). A good many took their time though and were sorry her head had turned, but nobody reached in to set her straight, and when Minnie Foot held her baby up to see and he dropped his pacifier in the box, they considered that pacifier gone for good—except the baby who commenced to moan and would have cried if Minnie hadn't sat down in time and unbuttoned and nursed him off to sleep so deep he didn't hear Sarah Fitts when she saw Mildred and wailed "Sweet Jesus" at the sight, but the name went out to Wesley wherever he was (out the window and facing the church but not seeing it, not studying the funeral), and he looked up quick and smiled—maybe at Rosacoke, maybe at the whole hot church—and still smiling, straddled his cycle in a long high leap like a deer and plunged downward on the starter like that same deer striking the earth and turned loose a roar that tore through the grove and the whole afternoon like dry cloth ripped without warning and Wesley was gone.

Rosacoke saw it that way, that slowly. After her remembering she had turned from the window to watch the last ones pass Mildred and to get ready for the testimonials that would be next, but when Sarah released her "Jesus," Rosacoke looked out to Wesley again to see what he would do about *that*, saying to herself, "That is one something he has got to notice." So she saw it from the beginning—his leap—seeing the deer in him as he started and with him still smiling, something even stronger when he reared on his black boots with the calf of his leg thrusting backwards through his trousers to turn loose the noise. She could see that and not think once what he had done or wonder would he come back. She could even turn and watch Mary and Estelle being led to take their last look and breaking down and taking everybody in the church with them into tears except Rosacoke who had as much right as anybody, knowing Mildred so long. But she didn't cry because suddenly the sound of Wesley's cycle stopped—he had taken it up the road a quarter of a mile beyond the church and now surely he would be circling round and coming back to wait. And sure enough he began again and bore down on the church like an arrow for their hearts till every face turned to Rosacoke, wondering couldn't *she* stop his fuss, but she looked straight ahead, not seeing him when the noise got louder and loudest of all and fell away quick as it had come. That little staring boy three rows ahead slapped his leg and said out loud "Mama, he *gone.*" Wesley had passed her by. He was headed for the concrete road, she guessed, and the twenty miles to Mason's Lake and the picnic and everybody there.

"Supposing he is gone for good," she said to herself. "Supposing I never lay eyes on him again," and that made her wonder what she would have left, what there would be that she could take out and hold or pass around and say, "This is what I got from knowing somebody named Wesley Beavers."

There were these many things—a handful of paper in a drawer at home that was the letters and postal cards he had sent her. (He didn't write much and when he did, it was like getting a court order, so distant and confusing that you wondered for days what he meant by some sentence he meant nothing by and wound up wishing he hadn't written at all or wanting to call him up, long distance, wherever he was and say, "Wesley, I would like to read you this one sentence you wrote" and then read him his own words, "We went to Ocean View last Saturday and met some folks at a eating stand, and they asked us why we didn't come on and go skinny-dipping by moonlight so we did and had a pretty good time and stayed there till Monday morning early," and afterwards ask him, "Wesley, will you tell me what sort of folks you would meet at a hotdog stand, and what is *skinny-dipping* please?" But how could you just pick up the phone and pay good money to say that when all he would answer was, "What are *you* worried about?") Besides the letters there was one picture of him—a grinning one in uniform—and a poem she wrote for a What I Am Seeking in an Ideal Mate Contest (but never sent in as it got out of hand) and a sailor cap he gave her at her request. (She could have bought it for a dollar at any Army-Navy store. She wore it once when he came home, hoping he would take a few photos of her but of course he didn't, and finally she *gave* him the only likeness he had of her, all but forced it on him as a birthday present—Rosacoke Mustian from the neck up, tinted, and looking less like herself than anybody you could imagine.)

That much, then, but wasn't that much left of everybody she ever knew who was gone for good?—the rusty snuff cans that kept turning up around the yard as signs of her Papa, and even the collars of every dog she ever had, and a 1937 New Jersey license plate that hung on the back porch to this day—the one thing she knew that was left of her own blood father who found it the evening she was born, lost on the highway, and brought it home drunk as a monkey and nailed it up over the waterbucket and said, "Will everybody please recall this is the year my daughter was born"—that one thing and nothing else, not a picture, not a thread, no more than if he had been swept away by the Holy Ghost, bag and baggage, in a pillar of fire instead of drunk and taken at dusk by a pickup truck he never saw but walked straight into as if it was a place to rest.

So would there be more than that of Wesley?—anything besides that first November day and a lot of Saturday nights and this last afternoon with him vanishing in a roar and dust? It came to her—what he had said the night before when he was quiet and she asked him if, when he was in the Navy, he looked much at her picture. "Sometimes," he said. "Why?" she said and he said, "Because I would forget what you looked like" and then laughed. Thinking about it though, she reckoned he meant it, laugh and all. He had known her seven years nearly, and when he went that far from home, sometimes he forgot her face. But what was so bad about that? Rosacoke herself when she went to 4-H camp in the summers (and that was for only eight days) would lie on her cot at night, thinking, and suddenly one of them—Mama or Rato or Milo or Papa—would be walking around in her thoughts with no more face than a cheese has got. She would strain to recollect the features and even try to draw out a face in the air with her finger, but sometimes it wouldn't come till she got back home and looked. Funny how when you could remember every mole on President Roosevelt's face and see Andy Gump clear as if he had ever breathed, still you couldn't call up a face you had spent your whole life with. But it never was Wesley she forgot even when he was no more to her than the farthest Arab on burning sands.

There would be the way he looked. And wouldn't that be with her always?—whoever she would meet, wherever she would go even in her sleep—the sight of his face up a tree amongst pecans or down from the tree six years and turned to what he was this afternoon but holding in him all the time that younger Wesley, unchanged and hard at the core, untouched and maybe untouchable but enough like an unlabeled seed, dry and rattling in her hand, to keep her wondering from now on if he might not have gone on growing—that first Wesley—and learned a way to look at people that didn't make them feel ten thousand miles away and to think about something but the U.S. Navy and motorcycles and to talk to people when they talked to him and say whatever he meant and stand still—supposing he had learned all that before it was too late, wouldn't he have made a lovely sight, and then if someday he had ever had to go, couldn't he have left something suitable behind him such as a child that would bear his funny name but have his face and be half hers and answer when she called?

It was the one thing left of Mildred (once they lidded that box again)—her child that had lived God only knew how, dark and hard in the orange crate they lined with white and laid him in, his back curved inwards and his spidery arms and legs twisting inwards to his navel as if something was winding him up with a key or as if he didn't know he was already born and had killed his mother and that there was nothing to call him but Doctor Sledge as no father came forward to tell what his real name was—hard dry little fellow with nothing to go on but half his mother's blood and maybe her looks and the way she used to talk held inside him in case he lived, waiting.

The preacher was waiting too now they had got Mary and Estelle away from Mildred and set them down again. He had intended to have the testifying next, but he could see Rosacoke was studying something besides the funeral so he went ahead and gave his remarks that were supposed to be the last thing before they shut the box— about all of us being raised from the grave including Mildred, but not a word about that live baby no more than if Mildred had died of sore throat. He watched Rosacoke the whole time to see when she would look round and be ready, but she looked on out the window through every word, even the prayer, and when he came to the end of all he could do, he had to say quietly to the back row, "Miss Rosacoke, we all know Mildred thought a heap of you, and it seem like you thought a heap of her"—a lot of people said "Amen"—"and I wonder is there any testifying you could do for her now?" His voice carried and Rosacoke looked round slow and blank as if he had called her from the edge of sleep. To help her out he went on, "If you can find anything in your heart to say, we would be mighty glad." Everybody was watching her. She nodded her head. She had meant to think out in advance what was best to say, but nothing about this afternoon had gone as she intended. She bit at her upper lip because of the heat and stood up and said, "I hadn't seen much of Mildred lately, but we always observed each other's birthday, her and me, and the other evening I thought to myself, 'It is nearly Mildred's twenty-first birthday' so I walked down to her place after supper, and nobody was there except the turkey. I didn't know till the next afternoon they had carried her away. There I was just wanting to give her a pair of stockings and wish her a long and happy life and she was already gone."

That was what she could find in her heart. She wondered if there ought not to be more, but if there was, it was covered now by other things. She sat down and before anybody could thank her, she thought what seemed to be the truth right then—"Everybody I know is gone." In the stifling air she went as cold all over as a pane of glass and took up her pocketbook and pressed her hat safe on her head and walked straight out of church—not from grief, not shedding a tear—but stopping the funeral dead while everybody watched her out of sight and Mrs. Ransom said "She is overcome" and punched Sammy her son at the end of her row and told her, "Sammy, go see what ails that child."

Sammy went and there was Rosacoke on the middle step, hanging onto her hat as if a storm was due, the sun laying her shadow backwards to the door and her just staring down the road. Not wanting to scare her by speaking, Sammy struck a match on his shoe and lit a cigarette. She looked around—just her dry eyes—and said, "Sammy, aren't you burning up in all that wool?" (He was in dark blue—the one man she had seen all day dressed like he knew what a funeral was.)

"If you needing to go somewhere, Miss Rosacoke, Sammy can take you." He said it as gentle as if it was the hospital she might need.

She hesitated as if she was thinking of a map and was on the verge of saying something distant such as—"Buffalo." "I don't reckon so, Sammy. I may have to go home and I can walk that."

"In this heat?"

"I have played baseball in worse than this and so have you," she said. Then thinking what she had done by walking out on the testifying, she said, "I don't intend to ruin Mildred's funeral any further by taking *you* away. Go on back in and tell Mary I'm sorry I can't stay, but I got to locate Wesley."

"No telling where he, Miss Rosacoke, with that machine between his legs."

"No. But I'll be saying goodbye to you, Sammy."

"Yes'm." And she walked into the yard and towards the road in her high heels that were not meant for standing in, much less walking. Sammy finished his cigarette and saw her vanish at the first turn. He was the age of her oldest brother Milo, and this was the first day he had ever called her *Miss* Rosacoke—nothing else to call her, the way she looked, though they played many games of baseball together before Mr. Isaac hired him—her and Milo and Rato (and Mildred and Mildred's sister Baby Lou at shortstop). He had driven the truck today and carried a fourth of the box, and it was generally guessed he was the one might tell the world what the rightful name of Mildred's baby was so he went back to where they had given up waiting. Bessie Williams was singing "Come Thee Disconsolate" which by now Rosacoke couldn't hear.

She walked in the middle of the road, looking down. Wherever the dust was thick there would be the track of Wesley's cycle printed like a message to her. Seeing that, she would speed up a little and sad as she felt, smile and think, "What do I think I am—an Indian nosing out a deer?" But she would come to long stretches where the dust had blown away, and there would be nothing but the baked red ground that took no more sign of Wesley than if he had flown every now and then. The smile would fade and she would walk even faster to get to the next deep dust till her legs, from the knee down nearly, were streaked with the red and her shoes were fit for nothing but burning. She could see that but she said right out to the trees around her, "I will see him if I have to walk to Norfolk." That thought clogged through her chest and mouth till she gasped for every breath she got, and everything else was choked—Mildred, the heat, her shoes—leaving nothing but Wesley hanging up in her, not speaking a word, and her at the worst she had ever been. She couldn't cry. She couldn't speak. But she thought, "I have spent six years thinking of Wesley Beavers day and night, giving him things he didn't want, writing him letters he barely answered, and now I am trailing him like a dog and him at Mason's Lake, I know, cooling off. I will stop walking when I get home and rest in the swing, and I hope he sells motorcycles till he drops."

She was coming to Mr. Isaac's woods where the deer had been so long ago for her and Mildred, and Wesley's tracks that hadn't showed for awhile showed again—not straight but twisting over the road from ditch to ditch. She said, "If that is his idea of fun, I'm glad I'm walking," and she looked up at the woods and decided to step in and take their shade till she was cool again.

Between the road and the woods was a narrow gully from the last rain. She took off her shoes and held her hat and jumped it and landed right away in deep moss that was cool with damp from God-knew-where. She took a look in both empty directions and decided to go on barefooted so she struck inwards a little from the road, and when it was nearly out of sight, she turned and walked on parallel to the narrow dust she could see through the trees. She was still in hollering distance if anybody was to pass that needed hollering at. Working indoors all summer the way she had, her feet were tender, and she yielded to them with pouts and little hunches of her shoulders when a stick cracked under her or a rock pressed up from the ground, and the sight of an old blacksnake stopped her dead till he raised up as if to speak and she beat him to it—"Well, old brother, which way are *you* headed?" and he went looping off slow over a log and on deeper in the trees. That kept her looking at the ground from then on, but once when she stopped to breathe, there was a red cardinal staring at her from the same bent tree she and Mildred had called a horse and ridden a thousand miles. She couldn't think how a cardinal sang, but any bird will answer you once, however you sound, so she whistled three notes, and he answered just to show her the right way. She told

him "Thank you" and tried it his way, but he had given all he meant
to give and sat there and swelled up. "What are you looking so biggity
about?" she asked him. "You look like every cardinal *I* ever saw." He
headed on too for the heart of the woods—north—and if he wanted,
he could make Virginia by dark. She called after him, "You better stay
in North Carolina, boy. You are the official bird here." Then she wondered, "Why don't I follow him and see where *he* leaves me?" But
what reason was there to take off barefooted after a bird?—unless he
was aiming for the spring. The spring would be reason enough. She
looked back to the road but the dust lay still. Nobody was going anywhere or coming back so she struck deeper for the spring with that
bird singing before her as if his heart would burst.

The only path to the spring was two tracks the width apart of Mr.
Isaac's truck wheels, left from the days when nobody but he and a few
wild children knew it was there. She followed on, picking her way
through glossy poison oak, and when she came to the spring (the bird
wasn't there, he was halfway to Virginia), it was only a wet circle in
the leaves, choked with whatever had fallen from the trees since Mr.
Isaac's last stroke. (It had been his private spring that he kept clean
long as he could, not for drinking purposes but to cool his feet.)
Rosacoke laid down her shoes and hat and bent over and put her
hands in where the leaves were wettest—slowly, hoping there wasn't a
lizard around—and lifted them out till there was a basin of brown
water the size of the evening sun and cold as winter ever got. Looking
in it, trying to see her face, she thought of the evening they found this
spring—her and her brothers and maybe five Negroes. They had
chased all the way from home, hollering some game back and forth
till Milo who was leading stopped and raised up his hand like an
Indian brave. They halted in a ragged line behind him, and before
they could speak, they saw what he had seen—Mr. Isaac there
through the darkening leaves, his trousers rolled high and pure cold
water ringing round his little bird ankles and him not noticing the
children at all or where the sun had got to but staring ahead, thinking. He looked up once in their direction—maybe he couldn't see—
but he never spoke a word, not to say "Go on" or "Come here," and
directly they all whirled round and started home, circling him wide,

leaving him to whatever it was made him look like that. Afterwards, some scorching days they would come and look at the spring and think how cool it was, but seeing Mr. Isaac that once was all they needed. Not a one of them would have waded in if they had been blazing bright from the waist down. Rosacoke had drunk from it though on the day they saw the deer (she had remembered the deer), checking first to see had Mr. Isaac waded lately, then bending over and touching the water with nothing but her lips. She had told Mildred, "Come on. He ain't been here today and it's run clean," but Mildred said, "I don't care if he ain't been here in a month. I can wait. That ain't mouth water no more."

It would be mouth water now—rising up clean for nobody but Rosacoke. Everybody else had forgotten or was long past needing cool feet and drinks of water. She took her seat in the shade on ground that sun hadn't touched since the trees were bare, and she thought of washing her dusty feet. The broiling day was above her, but her feet were deep in moss, and damp was creeping through her dress. "Let the spring run clean," she thought. "I am cool enough the way I am. It will take time but time is the one thing left of *this* day, and when it is clean I can drink. Maybe some water is all I need."

And maybe while the spring ran clean, she could find the broom-straw field. Surely the deer was there and even if she failed to see him, wouldn't he still see her?—peeping through the cluttered woods with his black eyes, watching every step she took, twitching his tail in fright, and not remembering that other summer day, not connecting this changed tall girl with the other one he had seen, not wondering where the black girl was, not caring, not needing—only water, grass, the moss to lie in and the strength of his four legs to save his life. But wasn't it far to walk? Hadn't it taken them an hour to get there, and even if the deer was to kneel and eat from her hand, who would there be to cry "Great God A-mighty" the way Mildred had?—to show it was the one wonderful thing she ever saw, the one surprise. Her baby was no surprise. Rosacoke had met her in the frozen road last February when they were both working and hadn't met for some time. They agreed on how cold it was and wouldn't they be glad to see summer. That seemed all they had to say till Mildred moved to go, and her old black coat swung open—there was her chest flat under a shrunk-up pink sweater that hugged tight to the hard new belly stuck in her skirt like a coconut shell. Rosacoke asked her, "Mildred, what in the world is that?"

"Nothing but a baby," she said and smiled and shut her coat.

"Whose baby?"

"Well, several have asked me not to say."

"Is it somebody from around here?"

"Bound to be."

"And you haven't tried to throw it?"

"What I want to throw him for, Rosacoke?"

"Won't nobody marry you?"

"Some of them say they studying about it. Ain't no hurry. Just so he come with a name."

"Why on earth did you do it, Mildred?"

"I don't hardly know."

"Well, are you glad?"

"Don't look like *glad* got nothing to do with it. He coming whether I glad or not"—and said goodbye and walked away home. Rosacoke had stood in the road, shivering, to watch her out of sight. She went with her thin wrists held to her sides, not swinging, and her fine hands clenched, and when she was gone round the first bend (not looking back once), she was gone for good. Rosacoke never saw her again—not alive, not her face. Mama had said, "I don't want you going to Mildred's another time till they get a Daddy for that baby. The way she's been messing around, they're going to have trouble finding one, and there's liable to be some cutting before they do." Rosacoke had stayed away, not because of what Mama said but because that one cold afternoon was the end of whatever Mildred she had known before. Now Mildred knew things Rosacoke didn't know, things she had learned just lying still in the dark, taking her child from somebody she couldn't see, and what could you say to that new Mildred, her load growing in her every second without a name, sucking blind at her life till his time came and he tore out and killed her and left himself with nothing on earth but a black mouth to feed and the hot air to howl in?

"And here I have walked out on her burying because of Wesley Beavers and his popping machine," she said and stood up at the sound of his name. It was her first thought of Wesley since seeing that bird and it startled her. She said it again — just the name — to test herself. But the name came easy now, not with so much rising in her chest. This was the way she worked — let Wesley pull one of his tricks or go back to Norfolk from a leave and she would nearly die with grief or anger till she could think of something big enough to take her mind off how he looked, not smiling, not answering when she called. Not everything was big enough, only things that had no connection with Wesley such as people telling sad stories or going to walk where Wesley had never been. Sometimes nothing big enough would come, and then there was nothing to do but hope each night the next day would be better, and usually it would (though she had to keep her eyes off pecan trees and not hear rain frogs beyond the creek at night or harmonica music). She would go on that way and finally be all right and free and bothered by nothing but, sometimes, the thought, "How can I say I love somebody who can leave and not worry me no more than this?" — till he came home again, bringing his face like a chain to loop around her neck.

Now with Mildred on her mind, she was free, and from sitting awhile she was cooler. She looked into the spring. It was working but it wouldn't be clear before night. "I will just rinse off my feet," she thought, "and go home and stir up some Kool-Ade and set in the swing and think of what to do for that baby to make up for how I acted today."

She pulled her dress high above her knees and sat again by the edge of the spring and not being able to see the bottom, stuck in her red feet slowly, saying, "If there's water moccasins down there, they are welcome to *these* feet." But her feet sank into cold mud, and brown clouds wreathed the shank of each white leg. She pulled her dress even higher and showed — to herself, to any passing bird — the tender blue inside her thighs that had barely seen the light all summer. Seemed a pity — even to her — having that firmness and keeping it hid (unless she went to Ocean View and showed it to every sailor on the sand). "Well, you're saving it, honey, till the right time comes," she said, breaking the silence above her where the birds had quieted—she wondered when, not noticing them so long. Then she saw the mess she was making of the spring and thought, "I'd be ashamed if I didn't know it would purify a thousand times before anybody needs it again."

But she was wrong. A dim rustling broke the quiet between her and the road, and gradually it turned to somebody's footsteps bearing down on the cracking sticks towards her. "Everybody I know is picnicking or burying," she thought, "and no stranger is catching me like this." She grabbed up her shoes and ran twenty yards to hide behind a cedar. The steps came on and she peeped out. Whoever it was hadn't appeared but there lay her hat by the spring big as a road sign and no hope of getting it now because it was a man that was coming—his shape moved on through the leaves but not his face, not yet.

It was Wesley who broke into sight, stroking through the branches like a swimmer with his head held down and his ankle boots turning in the soft ground till he was beside the spring and shaking his head to see how muddy it was. Rosacoke strained to see on him some sign of where he had been and why he was here, but all she could tell was that, wherever he had gone, he had combed his hair—a fresh part marched across his head like a chalk line—and that he was almost standing on her hat, and what would he do when he saw it? But he looked down for a long time, working his tongue in his mouth as if the next thing to do was spit in the spring and complete the mess, and Rosacoke's hat might as well have been air.

When he moved it was a step backward to leave, and Rosacoke hoped he would step on her hat—then she could speak—but he missed the hat and turned to the road. She took the last chance and stepped out and said, "Wesley, what do *you* know about this spring?"

He reached with both hands for his black belt as if guns were hanging there for such emergencies and hitched up his trousers—"I know somebody has stirred Hell out of it."

"That was me," she said. "I was just rinsing off my feet when I heard you coming—except I didn't know it was you. I figured you was picnicking by now."

He smiled and took another look at the spring and frowned. She walked towards him, holding her shoes. "I don't stir it up *every* day, Wesley. I don't strike out home in the dust every day either." She bent down for her hat—he never moved his foot an inch. "I was watching you from behind that cedar, wondering when you would notice my hat."

"I didn't know it was yours," he said.

"Good thing it wasn't a rabbit trap or you'd have lost a leg." She set it on her tangled hair. "I'll have my name painted on it real big so you won't fail to know me next time." Then she dried her feet with the palm of her hand and put on her shoes.

"You ready for this picnic?" he said.

She looked to see where the sun had got to. It was well past three o'clock. "I had given up on the picnic, Wesley. Anyhow, by the time we got there everybody would be gone."

"Suits me," he said. "There'll just be that much more water to swim in. But Milo will be there, you know, and your Mama said she would save me some chicken."

"Well, I can't go looking like the Tarbaby. You will have to stop at home and let me change my clothes."

"No need," he said. "Everybody will look like Tarbabies by the time we get there," and he took her hand and started for the road. They were nearly at the cycle, and Rosacoke had stood it long as she could—"You haven't said a word about where you tore off to or what I was doing at the spring."

"I went home to get something I forgot, and you said you was cooling off."

"I don't normally walk a mile on a July day to soak my feet."

"If you will hush up, we can ride twenty miles, and you can soak everything you've got."

"I have soaked sufficient, thank you. I have also changed clothes three times today—going on four—and I wouldn't peel off again to bathe in the River Jordan."

"Well, it's nothing but Mason's Lake we're going to, and you can sit on the bank and watch me execute a few Navy dives."

He was already on the cycle and waiting for her, but there was one more thing to ask. "Wesley, how did you know about Mr. Isaac's spring?"

"Somebody showed it to me a long time ago."

"Who?"

"One of my old girl friends." He laughed as if it wasn't so but it was—and laughed on in Rosacoke's head above the roar while she climbed on and laughed still when she laid against his back like sleep, wondering only who that old girl was till they were halfway to the lake and she changed to remembering Mildred. "They are burying Mildred Sutton now. If I had not forgot, I would be there where my duty lies—not *here* anyhow, hanging onto somebody I don't know, streaking off towards a good time, straddling all the horsepower Wesley Beavers owns."

Milo sighted them first of anybody from where he stood at the top of the tin sliding board, slicking back his hair and detaining behind him a whole line of children while he decided whether he would try it head-first (and risk rupturing a thing or two) or just his normal way. From the top he could see where the highway bent by the lake, and when Wesley and Rosacoke made the turn and were near enough to notice him, his problem was solved—he flipped belly-down on the wet slide and hollered "Here come Rosa" and waved with one hand and held his nose with the other and shot head to toe out of sight in the muddy lake. A cannon sound rose up behind him. (He was twenty-four years old, and Sissie his wife was as pregnant as women ever got.)

Wesley had seen Milo and stopped by the water. He laughed again with his goggles turned to the spot where Milo sank and said, "I bet there ain't a scrap of skin left on either side of Milo," but behind the goggles he was skimming the whole lake to see who was floating, even while he helped Rosacoke down. She was looking too. They were looking for the same floater, and Willie Duke Aycock was nowhere in sight.

Milo surfaced and stood up in the shallow end near them, every hair on him (the color of broomstraw) curling downward to the lake like streams. He grabbed his groin and moaned, laughing, "Good thing Sissie is already served. *I'm* finished." Then he rearranged everything inside his trunks and said, "Wesley-son, I don't advise you to try no belly-sliding, else you might deprive Rosa of a lovely future."

Rosacoke said "Milo *behave!*" But she smiled and Baby Sister came out to meet them, trailing a string of little wet girls—mostly Guptons.

"You just missed the baptizing," Baby Sister said. "I have baptized every one of these children today—some of them more than once."

"I'm glad you got them before they passed on," Wesley said, walking already towards the bathhouse, taking off his shirt as he went. "They look like cholera chickens right now." The Guptons just eyed him, not understanding—yellow and nosy and slick as peeled squirrels with hard round stomachs poking through their bathing suits and tan hair roping round their eyes raw and wide from so much dipping.

"You two don't look so good yourselves," Baby Sister said and huffed off towards what was left of the Pepsi-Colas, leaving the Guptons hanging in blistering sun.

Rosacoke called after her "Where is Mama?"

"Nursing Sissie over yonder in the shade."

The shade was behind the bathhouse under a close knot of pines that was all Mr. Mason had left, bulldozing his lake, and the remainder of Delight Church's picnic was mostly spread out there—on Rosacoke's right nearest the water, Mr. Isaac Alston in the black leather chair he went everywhere in (that he had barely left since his last stroke), staring at the swimmers and waiting for Sammy to come back with the truck. His collar was undone and there was that line drawn straight through the middle of him—one side moving and one side still—and beyond him was Rosacoke's Mama on a wool blanket, fanning Milo's Sissie who was leaning back, white as fat meat, on a pine with her eyes shut and her hands folded on her belly, not expecting to live, and a little way out of the trees in a pack of their own, a number of Guptons in chalk blue, all exactly alike, set up in the sand straight from the waist as hinges, shoving gnats off their bony legs and lean as if they had never eaten all they could hold (though they had just eaten half a picnic).

Rosacoke was not swimming and Mama had already seen her so she knew there was nothing to do but head for the shade and on her way, speak greetings to Mr. Isaac. That was her duty, as he had been good to them. But bad as she felt, she couldn't face telling him who she was—whose daughter (he never knew lately until you explained and then seldom showed any thanks for your effort). She lowered her head not to see him and bore to the left and circled towards Mama, dusty as she was and blown (with the feel of wind from the ride still working in the roots of her hair), but Mama called to her from ten yards away, "How was the funeral?" so she detoured a little to speak to Marise Gupton who was Willie Duke Aycock's sister and had been in grammar school with her but looked a hundred years older from giving Macey Gupton the children Baby Sister had dipped. When she got to Marise, Marise looked up with no more pleasure or recognition than Mr. Isaac would have showed and let her begin the talking. All she could think to say was, "Marise, have you been swimming yet?"

"I ain't swam once since my first baby," she said, and her fourth baby who was her first boy and three months old, named Frederick, cried from a wad of blankets on the ground behind her. (Macey her husband was sleeping beside him. He was Milo's age and he couldn't swim.) Marise frowned up to Rosacoke at the noise, but she reached back and took him and laid him on one shoulder. He was hid in a heavy knit suit and a cap that covered his ears (all blue to match his family), and crying so hard, he looked like a fired cook-stove.

Rosacoke said, "Don't you reckon he's *frying*, Marise?"

Marise said "No" and that seemed the end of what they could say as Marise was opening her dress with her left hand. Before she was open completely, Frederick rolled down his head and his jaws commenced working. His wet mouth was seeking her breast through blue cotton cloth. "Just *wait*," she said, a little harsh—to him, not Rosacoke. But Rosacoke waited too, not speaking, and Frederick found what he needed. Marise didn't talk either but watched her baby—number four—pulling hard at her life. In a little, still sucking with his eyes shut tight, he halfway smiled, and Marise gave him a quick little smile in return—her first of the day. Rosacoke might just as well have been in Egypt (and very nearly felt she was) so she looked on ahead and went towards Mama.

Mama said, "How come you didn't speak to Mr. Isaac?" and before she could answer, "You look like you rode in on a circular saw" and kept on fanning Sissie.

Rosacoke said, "If that's what you call a motorcycle, I *did*."

Sissie barely opened her eyes and said, "I wish somebody had took me motorcycle riding on a rocky road five months ago, and I wouldn't be this sick today."

"What's wrong with Sissie?"

"Not a thing," Mama said, "except she had already eat her Brunswick stew when Milo announced about old Mr. Gupton losing his teeth. But there was no way on earth to have told her any sooner. Mr. Gupton was the last man to stir the stew before they served it up, and he had been carrying his teeth in his shirt pocket to rest his gums. Well, everybody had commenced eating their portion except Mr. Gupton, and Milo noticed him frowning hard and feeling his pockets and looking on the ground all round the pot so Milo went over and asked him was anything wrong, and he said, 'I have mislaid my teeth.' *Mislaid!* There he had been leaning over twenty gallons of delicious stew for a solid hour, and where were his teeth *bound* to be? Well, not in the stew it turned out, but nobody knew that till some time later when one of the children found them, unbroken, over by the wood-pile where he had dropped them picking up wood. But as I say, Sissie had eat hers and collapsed at the false news long before the teeth appeared, and here she's laid ever since, me fanning her like a fool." Then Mama thought again of what she had waited all afternoon to hear—"How was the funeral?"

"Mama, it wasn't a picture show."

"I know that. I just thought somebody might have shouted."

"Maybe they did. I didn't stay to the end."

"Why not?" But Mama broke off—"Look at Wesley."

Wesley had run from the bathhouse and taken the high-dive steps three at a time and up-ended down through the air like a mistake at first, rowing with his legs and calling "Milo" as he went (for Milo to laugh), but then his legs rose back in a pause and his arms cut down before him till he was a bare white tree (the air was that clear) long enough for Rosacoke to draw one breath while he went under slow— not a sound, not a drop and what began as a joke for Milo's sake didn't end as a joke.

"He can dive all right," Mama said. "Reckon he has touched bottom by now," and at that Wesley shot up, holding a handful of bottom overhead as proof, the black mud streaming down his arm.

"If he's been on the bottom, he's eat-up with leeches," Sissie said. "I told Milo if he got a leech on him, he wasn't coming near *me*."

"Wesley is too speedy for any leech to take hold of," Mama said. Rosacoke said "Amen" to that.

"I can't speak for the leeches," Sissie said, "but Willie Duke Aycock has took hold already." (Willie Duke had had her eyes on Wesley since the seventh grade when she grew up overnight several months before anybody else, and there she was paddling out to him and Milo now, moving into the deepest part with no more swimming ability than a window weight, so low in the water nobody could tell if she had on a stitch of clothes and churning hard to stay on top.)

"She can't keep it up long," Rosacoke said.

"Honey, she's got God's own water wings inside her brassiere," Sissie said. (And Sissie was right. Willie Duke had won a Dairy Queen Contest the summer before, and the public remarks on her victory were embarrassing to all.)

"Well, I don't notice Milo swimming away from her," Rosacoke said, at which Milo and Wesley grabbed Willie Duke and sank without a trace.

People in the lake began circling the spot where the three went down, and Rosacoke stood up where she was, shading her eyes in hopes of a sign. Mama said, "They have been under long enough," and Baby Sister was running for the lifeguard when they appeared at the shallow end, carrying Willie Duke like a sack of meal to dry land and laying her down. Then they charged back and swam the whole lake twice, length and breadth—Milo thrashing like a hay baler— before they raced up to the shade and shook water on everybody's clothes and lit the two cigars Milo had in Sissie's bag.

There was a leech, yellow and slick, sucked to Wesley's leg. Nobody saw it till Sissie yelled. It was the last blow of the day for Sissie. She just folded up like a flower and lay back, swallowing loud. Mama stopped her fanning to look, and Milo of course made the first comment—"That leech is having *him* a picnic now"—and Wesley showed he wasn't too happy by stamping his foot. But Rosacoke sat up on her knees, and the leech, being almost on Wesley's hip, was level with her eyes, about the size of her little finger, holding on with both its ends and pulling hard at Wesley's life. She touched the end that was the mouth and it crouched deeper inward.

Mama said, "Don't pull it off, Rosa, or Wesley will bleed to death."

And Milo said, "If we just leave him alone, he can get enough to last till the next church outing, and Wesley will never miss it."

Wesley said, "Milo, if you are so interested in feeding animals, I'll turn him over to you just as soon as I get him off," and he took the cigar and tried to burn the leech's head, but his hand shook and he burnt his leg. "Rosa, you do it," he said and handed the cigar to her. She blew off the ashes and touched the mouth. It flapped loose and dangled a second before the tail let go, and when it hit the sand, it hunched off, not waiting, in three measuring steps towards the water before Mama got it with her shoe and buried it deep till there was no sign left but Wesley's blood still streaming. Rosacoke gave him a handkerchief to hold on the bite, and he wore it round his leg like a garter.

Then everybody could calm back down, talking a little about nothing till the talking died and Baby Sister wandered back and said she was tired and flopped in the sand and sang the Doxology (her favorite song), and when they felt the low late sun pressing so heavy through the pines, sleep seemed the next natural thing. Milo and Wesley stretched out in their bathing suits—hair and all laid right in the sand—and Rosacoke propped against the other side of Sissie's tree, and they slept off and on (except Mama who could never bat an eye till the sun went down) until Macey Gupton yelled his three girls in, and the yell woke up Baby Sister who was hungry and said so (who was also twelve years old, with every crumb she ate turning to arms and legs). Mama tried to hush her but she woke up Wesley who was hungry too and who shook Milo's foot and said, "Milo, why don't you ask that question you was talking about in the lake?"

Milo came to and asked it. "Mama, what have you got in the way of something to eat?"

"Enough for us six," she said, "and we'll eat it when the five thousand leave." (She meant the Guptons. She couldn't fill them up.)

But it was already past five. The lake had emptied of everything but one old man (not on the picnic) asleep in his inner tube, rocking with the water while it slowed down and woke him up, and the only clue to this being a pleasure lake was the high dive quivering and the temporary-looking slide, and up in the shade the picnic was drifting away. The signal for leaving was when Mr. Isaac's Sammy came back from the funeral with his blue suit still on and drove the truck right to Mr. Isaac's feet and buttoned his collar and lifted him in and loaded on the chair and nodded his head towards Rosacoke. She nodded back and Sammy drove off, and Milo said, "That is the nigger killed Mildred Sutton."

Rosacoke said, "You can't prove that."

Milo said, "No'm, and your friend Mildred couldn't neither. If you back up into a circular saw, you can't name what tooth cuts you first."

Rosacoke swallowed hard but she didn't answer that. Nobody did. They looked off towards the Guptons for relief. The Guptons were all lying down except Marise, but they swatted gnats to show they were not asleep. What they were really doing was *lingering* to find out the Mustians' plans—every few minutes a head would rise up and peep around in case an invitation was on the way. That got Milo's goat and when Frederick cried again, Milo said loud enough for Marise to hear, "What that baby needs is a bust in the mouth!"

Wesley said, "That's what they all need."

Mama said "Hush!"

And Sissie said, "He's *had* it twice already since noon. Don't make her pull it out again."

So finally with nobody saying a word about free supper, the Guptons had to leave. Macey stood and said "Let's go eat" and waved silly to Milo and led off towards the truck. The others straggled on and when they were loaded in, Baby Sister said "O.K. Mama." Mama looked around. The Gupton truck hadn't moved but she guessed it was safe, and she pulled out the stew and chicken and a whole box of eggs (deviled before breakfast) that nobody but Milo would touch.

The Guptons still didn't move—maybe their engine was flooded—but the Mustians were deep in eating (even Sissie) when Mama looked up and said "Oh Lord." Willie Duke Aycock had appeared from the bathhouse door and was heading their way. (The Guptons of course were riding her home. Her family hadn't come.) She stopped at a little distance and spoke nice to Mama and called Rosacoke's name like an item in a sick list and asked if she could speak to Wesley a minute.

Milo said, "Go get her, son," and Wesley went out to meet her with a silly grin that Willie Duke matched as if it was their secret. And she stood right there facing the whole group and whispered to him with her tiny mouth. Her wet hair was plaited so tight it stretched her eyebrows up in surprise, and her high nose bone came beaking white through the red skin, and she had on the kind of doll-baby dress she would wear to a funeral (if it was hot enough) — the short sleeves puffing high on her strong arms and the hem striking her just above the wrinkled knees.

Rosacoke didn't speak a word. She swallowed once or twice more and then set down her supper, not wanting another bite. All she had eaten hung in her stomach like a fist. Milo said "*Sick* her, Rosa!"

"Shut up," she said and he did.

When Willie Duke stopped whispering and went to the truck and Wesley came grinning back to take up his eating, Rosacoke couldn't look at him, but she frowned to silence Milo who was swelling with curiosity before her eyes. Wesley ate on, not alluding once to Willie Duke's brazen visit, and everybody else was looking at the ground, picking at little roots and straws. Finally Milo had to speak — "How many more you got, Wesley?"

"More what?" Wesley said, knowing very well *what.*

"Women trailing you? I bet they're strung up the road from here to Norfolk right now, waiting for you to pass."

Sissie said, "Milo just wishes he had a few, Wesley," but Wesley didn't say "Yes" or "No." And Rosacoke didn't make a sound. The trouble with Wesley was, he never denied anything.

Milo said, "How do you know I ain't got a whole stable full?"

"Well, if you have, Sissie's got the key to the stable now, big boy," Sissie said and patted her belly that was the key.

Mama said they all ought to be struck dumb, talking that way around Baby Sister — around *anybody.*

"We are just joking, Mama, and nobody asked you to tune in," Milo said.

"I'm *not* tuned in, thank you, sir. I was thinking about your brother and how he would have enjoyed this day." It was the first thought of Rato anybody had had for several weeks and they paused for it.

Milo said, "He's happy as a baby right where he is and getting all he can eat." (Rato had been in the Army four months, as a messenger boy. He had got tired of working for Milo—taking his orders in the field—so early in April he hitched down to Raleigh and found the place and said he had come to join. They asked him what branch did he want to be in and he said *"Calvary."* They said there hadn't been any cavalry for ten years and how about the Infantry? He asked if that was a walking-soldier, and they said "Yes" but if he didn't mind carrying messages, he could so he said "All right.")

"I wasn't worried about him eating," Mama said. "I was just regretting he missed the funeral—off there in Oklahoma carrying messages on a Sunday hot as this. Rato knew Mildred good as you all did, and I reckon her funeral was big as any he will ever get the chance to see."

"Why didn't *you* go then and write him a description?" Rosacoke said, seeing only that Mama was hoping to hear about the funeral now, not seeing that Mama was thinking of Rato too.

"Because my duty was with my own."

"Deviling eggs for Milo to choke over? Is that what you call your own? And fanning the flies off Sissie Abbott's belly? And keeping Baby Sister out of deep water? I'm glad you are sure of what's yours and what ain't." That came out of Rosacoke in a high, breaking voice she seldom used—that always scared her when it came. The skin of her face stretched back towards her ears and all the color left. And Milo winked at Wesley.

Mama said the natural thing. "I don't know what you are acting so grand about. You said yourself you didn't stay to the end."

"No, I did not and do you want to know why? Because Wesley wouldn't sit with me but stayed outside polishing his machine and in the midst of everything, cranked up and went for a ride. I thought he had left me for good and I ran out."

Milo said, "Rosa, you can't get upset everytime Wesley leaves for a minute. All us tomcats got to make our rounds."

Wesley smiled a little but Rosacoke said, "Milo, you have turned out to be one of the sorriest people I know."

"Thank you, ma'm. What about your friend Wesley here?"

"I don't know about my friend Wesley. I don't know what he is planning from one minute to the next. I don't even know my place in that line of women you say is strung from here to Norfolk."

Milo turned to Wesley—Wesley was lying on his back looking at the tree—"Wesley, what is Rosacoke's place in your string of ladies? As I am her oldest brother, I have the right to ask." Wesley lay on as if he hadn't heard. Then he rolled over suddenly, flinging sand from the back of his head, and looked hard at Rosacoke's chest, not smiling but as if there was a number on her somewhere that would tell her place in line. It took him awhile, looking at all of her except her eyes, and when he opened his mouth to speak, Rosacoke jumped up and ran for the lake in her bare feet.

Mama said, "What have you done to her, Wesley?"

"Not a thing, Mrs. Mustian. I ain't said a word. She's been acting funny all day."

"It's her battery," Milo said. "Her battery needs charging. You know how to charge up an old battery, don't you, Wesley?"

Mama ignored him and said, "That child has had a sadder day than any of you know."

"Sad over what?" Milo said.

"That funeral."

Sissie said she hadn't noticed *Mama* pouring soothing oil on any-body, and Milo said, "No use being sad about that funeral. I knew Mildred just as long as Rosa, and she didn't get nothing but what she asked for, messing around. Nothing happens to people that they don't ask for."

Mama said, "Well, I am asking you to take me home—that is the sorriest thing you have said all day, and the sun is going down. That child won't but twenty years old and she died suffering." She took the box of supper right out of Milo's lap and shut it and said, "Baby Sister, help me fold up this blanket." There was nothing for Sissie and Milo and Wesley to do but get off the blanket and think of heading home.

Rosacoke had taken her seat on a bench by the bathhouse with her back turned, and Wesley went down that way, not saying if he meant to speak to Rosa—maybe just to change his clothes. When he had gone a little way, Mama called to him, "Wesley, are you going to ease that child?"

"Yes'm," he said. "I'll try."

"Will you bring her home then and not go scaring her with your machine?"

"Yes'm," he said. "I will." And Mama and them left without Milo even putting his trousers on—Sissie carried them over her arm—and whatever last words he wanted to yell at Wesley got stopped by the look in Mama's eye.

All Rosacoke was seeing from the bench was pine trees across the lake on a low hill and two mules eating through clover with short slow steps towards each other. Somewhere on top of the hurting, she thought up a rule. "Give two mules a hill to stand on and time to rest and like as not by dark they will end up side by side, maybe eight inches apart from head to tail, facing different ways." It wasn't always true but thinking it filled the time till Wesley came from the shade and stood behind her and put one thick hand over her eyes and thinking he had come like a panther, asked her who it was.

"You are Wesley," she said, "but that don't tell me why you act the way you do."

"Because I am Wesley," he said and sat beside her, still in his bathing suit.

The sun was behind the pines and the mules now, shining through their trunks and legs to lay the last red light flat on the empty lake. The light would last another hour, but the heat was lifting already, and Rosacoke saw a breeze beginning in the tails of those two mules. "Here comes a breeze," she said and they both watched it. It worked across the lake—too feeble to mark the water—and played out by ruffling the hem of her dress and parting the curled hair of Wesley's legs. They were the only people left at the lake except Mr. Mason who owned it. He was on guard in the cool-drink stand as hard as if it was noon and the lake was thick with screaming people.

Wesley laid his hand above her knee. "Let's go swimming before it's night."

"What am I going to swim in?—my skin? This dirty dress is all I've got."

"You could rent one over there at the drink stand."

"I wouldn't put on a public bathing suit if I *never* touched water again. Anyway, why are you so anxious about me swimming? I thought you got a bellyful of underwater sports with Willie Duke."

"No I didn't," he said and laughed.

"Didn't what?"

"Didn't get a bellyful."

That made her thigh tighten under his hand, and she looked away to keep from answering. So Wesley stood up and waded out to where the water was deep enough to lie down and then swam backwards to the diving board with his head out just enough to keep his eyes on her. It was his finest stroke and she wasn't seeing a bit of it, but when he twisted round and rose and grabbed the ladder to the board—she saw that, him rising up by the strength of his right hand, not using his feet at all and hitching his red trunks that the water pulled at. (Even the skin below his waist was brown.)

Then he dived one lovely dive after another—not joking now for Milo's sake but serious and careful as if there was a prize to win at sunset—and she watched him (not knowing if that was what he wanted, not being able to help herself). Once she narrowed her eyes to see only him, and once while he rested a minute, she focused on the hill beyond and those two mules that only had a short green space between them now. Then Wesley split down through the green with his red suit, blurred and silent and too quick to catch.

Before he surfaced, somebody spoke to Rosacoke. "Young lady, what kin is that boy to you?" It was Mr. Mason who owned the lake. He had shut up the cool-drink stand and was there by the bench with his felt hat on, hot as it was.

"No kin," Rosacoke said. "I just came with him. We are the left-overs of Delight Church picnic." She looked back to Wesley who was pretending not to notice Mr. Mason. "He has just got out of the Navy— that boy—and looks like he's trying to recall every dive he ever learned."

"Yes ma'm, it do," Mr. Mason said, "but I wish he won't doing it on my time. I mean, I'm a preacher and I got to go home, and the law says he can't be diving when I ain't watching. He can swim a heap better than me I know—I ain't been under since I was baptized—but you all's church has paid me to lifeguard every one of you, and long as he dives, I got to guard. And I didn't charge but nineteen cents a head for all you Delight folks."

Maybe Wesley was hearing every word—he wasn't that far away—

but just then he strolled off the end of the board and cut a string of flips in the air as if to show Mr. Mason *one* somebody was getting his nineteen cents' worth. That time he stayed under extra long, and when he came up way over on the mule side, Rosacoke said, "Wesley, Mr. Mason has got to go home." Wesley pinched his nostrils and waved Mr. Mason goodbye.

That seemed to please Mr. Mason. He laughed and told Rosacoke, "Lady, I'm going to leave him alone and deputize you a lifeguard. He is your personal responsibility from now on." He took off his hat and took out his watch and said, "It is six-thirty and I am preaching in a hour. What must I preach on, lady?"

"Well, if you don't know by now," she said, "I'm glad I haven't got to listen." But she smiled a little.

And he wasn't offended—"What I mean to say is, you give me your favorite text, and that's what I'll preach on."

Rosacoke said, "'Then Jesus asked him what is thy name and he said Legion.'"

"Yes ma'm," he said, "that is a humdinger" (which wasn't the same as committing himself to use it). Then he said he felt sure they had enjoyed their day and to come back any time it was hot and he left.

So Rosacoke and Wesley were there alone with nothing else breathing even but those two mules and what few birds were hidden on the hill that sang again in the cool and whatever it was that sent up those few bubbles from the deepest bottom of the lake. There was an acre or more of water between them (Wesley was still on the mule side, up to his waist), but they saw each other clear. They had had little separate seeings all day—his sight of her at the church that threw his mind to all those Norfolk women and her seeing him out the window, rubbing his machine or stroking through bushes to the spring or vanishing under the lake with Willie Duke Aycock in his hands—but this was the first time they had both looked, together. Wesley had his own reasons and she had hers and both of them wondered was there a reason to move on now past looking, to something else.

Wesley found a reason first. "Rosa," he called and the name spread flat on the lake and came to her loud, "have you got anything I can drink?"

"What do you mean?"

"I mean I am thirsty."

"Well, you are standing in several thousand gallons of spring water."

He took that as a joke and lay down and swam straight towards her over the lake that had been brown in the sun but was green with the sun gone down—the water flat green and pieces of bright plant the swimmers stirred up ragged on the surface and Wesley's arms pale green when they cut the water and his whole body for a moment green when he walked up the narrow sand and stood by the bench and looked again. She smiled, not knowing why, and turned away. Her hair had darkened like the water, and turning, it fell across her shoulder in slow water curves down the skin of her white neck to the groove along her back that was damp. He saw that. She said, "The drink stand is closed." He nodded and walked off to the bathhouse, and she figured they were going home now so she walked back to the pine shade and got her shoes that Mama had brushed and left there and went down to the motorcycle and stood. Wesley came out with nothing on but his shirt over his red trunks and no sign of trousers anywhere.

"Who stole your trousers?" she said.

He didn't answer that. He just said "Come here" and waved her to him. There was nothing to do but go, and when she got there he took her hand and started off round the lake away from the motorcycle.

"Aren't we going home?" she said. "I mean, Mr. Mason has shut it up and all—maybe we ought to go."

"Maybe I can find some drinking water up in them trees," he said.

"Wesley, there is plenty of drinking water at every service station between here and home. Why have we got to go tearing through some strange somebody's bushes? I have had a plenty of that already today."

"Hush up, Rosa," he said. She hushed and he held up the barbed wire, and she crawled under onto the hill with the mules. One yellow hair of hers caught in the wire, and Wesley took it and wrapped it round and round his finger.

"Is that mine?" she asked, stroking her head.

"It's mine now."

"Well, you can have it. The sun has bleached me out till I look like a hussy."

"What do you know about a hussy?"

"I know you don't have to go to Norfolk, Virginia to find one."

"What do you mean?"

"You know who I mean."

"If it's Willie Duke Aycock you mean—she will be in Norfolk tomorrow along with them other hussies you mentioned."

That was like a glass of ice water thrown on her, but she held back and only said, "What is she going up there for?"—thinking it was just a shopping trip to buy some of those clothes nobody but Willie Duke wore.

"She's got a job."

"Doing what?"

"Curling hair."

"What does she know about curling hair with that mess *she's* got?"

"I don't know but she's moving up, bag and baggage."

"What was she asking you about then?"

"She wanted to know would I ride her up."

Rosacoke took her hand out of his. "On that motorcycle?"

"Yes."

"Then she is crazier than I thought she was"—they were climbing the hill all this time, looking ahead to where the trees began—"Are you taking her?"

"I don't know yet."

"When will you know?"

"By the time I'm home tonight." He took her hand again to show that was all he was saying about Willie Duke and to lead her into the trees.

They walked through briars and switches of trees and poison oak (and Wesley bare to every danger from the hip down) with their eyes to the ground as if a deep well of water might open at their feet any minute. But when the trees were thick enough to make it dark and when, looking back, she couldn't see the mules, Rosacoke said, "Wesley, you and me both are going to catch poison oak which Milo would never stop laughing at, and you aren't going to find any water before night."

"Maybe it ain't water I'm looking for," he said.

"I don't notice any gold dust lying around—what are you hunting?"

There was an oak tree on Wesley's right that was bare around the roots. He took her there and sat in a little low grass. She clung to his hand but stayed on her feet and said, "Night will come and catch us here, and we will get scratched to pieces stumbling out." But the light that filtered through the trees fell on Wesley's face, and when she studied him again—him looking up at her serious as if he was George Washington and had never smiled—and when he pulled once more on her hand, she sat down with him. A piece of her white dress settled over his brown legs and covered the pouting little mouth where the leech had been, and she asked him something she had wondered all afternoon—"How come you are so brown even under the belt of your bathing suit?"

He folded his suit back to the danger point and said "From skinny-dipping."

"You never told me what that is."

"It's swimming naked."

"Where?"

"Anywhere you can find a private beach and somebody to swim with you."

"Who do you find?"

"People ain't hard to find."

"Women you mean?"

"Ain't you asked your share of questions?" he said and lifted her hair and hid under it long enough to kiss her neck.

She drew back a little, finally sick from all the afternoon, and said, "Wesley, I am sorry and I know it maybe isn't none of my business, but I have sat in Afton on my behind for the best part of three years making up questions I needed to hear you answer, and here you are answering me like I was a doll baby that didn't need nothing but a nipple in her mouth."

He didn't speak and when she turned to him, he was just looking at his feet that were almost gone in the dark. For awhile the only noise was a whippoorwill starting up for the night, but Rosacoke watched Wesley through that silence, thinking if he looked up, she would know all she needed, but he didn't look up and she said something she had practiced over and over for a time like this—"There are some people that look you in the eyes every second they are with you like you were in a building with some windows dark and some windows lit, and they had to look in every window hard to find out where you were. Wesley, I have got more from *hitchhikers* than I have from you—just old men with cardboard suitcases and cold tough wrists showing at the end of their sleeves, flagging down rides in the dust, shy like they didn't have the right to ask you for air to breathe, much less a ride, and I would pass them in a bus maybe, and they would look up and maybe it wasn't me they were looking at, but I'd think it was and I'd get more from them in three seconds than you have given me in three whole years."

He didn't even answer that. He hadn't seen that every question she asked was aimed for the one she couldn't ask, which was did he love her or didn't he, and if he did, what about those women Milo mentioned and he didn't deny, and if he didn't, why had he kept her going this many years and why was he riding her up and down on a brandnew motorcycle and why did he have her under this tree, maybe miles from drinking water and the night coming down?

He didn't answer but when she was quiet he commenced to show her why. For awhile he did what he generally did around her face and lips and her white neck. And she let him go till he took heart and moved to what was underneath, trying for what he had never tried before. Then with her hand she held him back and said, "Is that all you want out of me?"

"That's right much," he said. And if he had let her think a minute and look, he might have won, but he said one more thing. "If you are thinking about Mildred's trouble, you ain't got that to worry about. You'll be all right. That's why I left the funeral—to go home and get what will make it all right for me and you."

"No, Wesley," she said. Then she said, "It is nearly dark" and stood up and asked him to take her home.

"Rosa," he said, "you know I am going to Norfolk again. You *know* that don't you?"

"I know that," she said. She took a step to leave.

"—And that maybe I'm riding Willie Duke up there?"

"Wesley, you can ride Willie Duke to Africa and back if she's what you're looking for. Just make sure she don't have Mildred's trouble." So Wesley gave up and followed her out of the woods—her leading because she had on shoes and could cut the path—and when they got to the hill, it was almost night. All they could see was the mules outlined against the lake below, resting now and as close as Rosacoke guessed they would be. Wesley saw them and said "Congratulations, mules."

At the bathhouse Rosacoke kept going to the cycle, and Wesley turned in to put on his pants. But there were no lights in there, and Rosacoke could see up at the eaves the glow he made with a match or two before he stamped his foot and came towards the cycle with his pants and boots in his arms. She said, "Do you mean to ride home naked?"

"Hell no," he said, "but I ain't hopping around another minute in yonder where it's dark and snaky." He switched on the headlight and stood in its narrow beam and stepped out of that red suit into his trousers with nothing but a flapping shirt tail to hide him, and Rosacoke turned her face though he didn't ask her to.

Then not stopping once he took her home round twenty miles of deadly curves hard as he could, and she held him tight to save her life. When they were almost there she squeezed for him to slow down and said to stop on the road and not turn in as Mama might be in bed. He did that much—stopped where she said by a sycamore tree and turned off the noise and raised his goggles and waited for her to do the talking or the moving. She got down and took what was hers in the saddlebags, and seeing the house was all dark but one door light the moths beat on, she asked him to shine his light to the door so she could see her way. He did that too and she walked down the beam a yard or so before she turned and tried to say what needed saying. "Wesley—"

"What?" he said—but from behind the light where she couldn't see.

And what she couldn't see, she wasn't speaking to—"Have a good trip."

"All right," he said and she walked on to the house and at the porch, stood under the light and waved with her hat to show she was safe. For a minute there was no noise but rain frogs singing out behind the creek. Then the cycle roared and the light turned back to the road and he was gone.

Rosacoke wondered would she ever sleep.

WHEN he was gone three weeks and no word came, she sent this letter to him.

August 18

Dear Wesley,

How are the motorcycles? Cool I hope. And how are you? Sleeping better than us I hope. All the ponds around here have dried up and nobody in the house but Baby Sister has shut an eye for three nights now. We are treating each other like razor blades. If there doesn't come a storm soon or a breeze, I will be compelled to take a bus to some cooler spot. Such as Canada. (Is that cool?) My bedroom of course is in the eaves of the house under that black tin roof that soaks up the sun all day and turns it loose at night like this was winter and it was doing me a favor. My bed feels like a steam pressing machine by the time I crawl in. Last night by 1 a.m. I was worn out from rolling around so I went downstairs and stretched out on the floor—under the kitchen table so Milo wouldn't step on me in the dark, going for his drinks of water. The floor wasn't any cooling board but I had managed to snooze off for a good half hour when here comes Sissie tripping down in the pitch black to get her a dish of Jello (which is what she craves). I heard her coming (I reckon they heard her for miles) and knowing how scarey she is and not wanting her to have the baby right there, I stood up to announce my presence but before I could say a word, she had the light on and her head in the ice box, spooning out Jello. Well what could I do then? I figured speaking would be the worst thing so I kept standing there by the stove, big as a road machine but trying to shrink, and Sissie was on her second dish before she turned around and saw me. That was it. She held onto the baby—don't ask me how. Cherry Jello went everywhere. Mama was there in a flash and Milo with the gun, thinking there had been an attack. Sissie calmed down right easy—for her—but not before it was sunup and the chickens who had heard the noise were clucking around the back-porch in case anybody felt like feeding them. So what point was there in going to bed? None. Mama just cooked breakfast and we sat there and stared at each other like enemies. Before we had even washed dishes, the sun was hot enough to blister paint and I had to go to Warrenton and spend the day putting through telephone calls between people who talked about how hot it was. Guess what a lovely day I had. I would never have got through it if I hadn't plugged in by mistake to some Purvis man telling his fancy woman it was all off and her saying, "That's what you think!"

But the heat doesn't bother you, does it? I wonder why. Low blood, I guess. Have you ever had it tested? Being in the Navy, you must have.

I will stop now as Milo said he would walk with me to Mary Sutton's to take some clothes for Mildred's baby—not much I'm afraid, with Sissie laying claim on everything here. The baby is living. I don't know why but maybe he does. The baby, I mean. All I have talked about is me and my foolishness but nobody here has done a thing except sweat since you left. I say left—looks like you left three years ago and aren't coming back.

Goodnight Wesley. It has just now thundered in the west. Maybe it is going to rain.

Love to you from,
Rosacoke

For that, in two weeks' time, he sent her a giant post card of a baby with a sailor hat on in a baby carriage, hugging a strip-naked celluloid doll and sucking on a rubber pacifier. The caption said, *I Am A Sucker For Entertainment,* and Wesley said,

Hello Rosa, I hope you have cooled off a little bit by now. From the heat I mean. Yes we are having it hot here too but it don't keep me from sleeping when I get in the bed. That doesn't happen regular as summer is the big season on motorcycles and when I am not closing a sale I am generally out at Ocean View where I have friends and can take me a relaxing dip. That is where I am writing you this card from. I would

write you a letter but I am no author. I know Milo is having a hard time
waiting out Sissie's baby. Tell him Wesley said Ocean View is the place
for Tired Rabbits.

—And it stopped there. He had crowded it exactly full of his big writing, and there was no room left to sign his name or say "Yours truly" or any other word that gives you away.

Rosacoke waited awhile, wondering if she had the right, and then said,

September 15

Dear Wesley,

 It doesn't seem like a fair exchange—me writing letters and you writing cards—but here I am anyhow because it is Sunday and I can't think of anything else to do. I can't think of anything else but you. (You are no author but I am a poet.) Seriously Wesley, there are alot of questions playing on my mind. They have been playing there six years nearly and tonight I feel like asking them.

 Wesley, I want to know are we in love? And if we are, how come you to act the way you do—tearing off to Norfolk after a motorcycle job when you could have stayed back here with your own folks, including me? And not even trying to answer me when I write but telling me about relaxing with your friends at Ocean View and not saying who—just leaving me to wonder if it's Willie Duke Aycock you're riding around or some other body I've never seen. Wesley, that is no way to treat even a dog—well it's one way but it don't make the dog too happy.

 I think I have held up my end pretty well and I am wondering if it isn't time you took up your share of the load or else told me to lay mine down and get on home to Mama. So I am asking you what do you want me to do? All I am asking you to do is say. What have I ever refused you but that one thing you asked me to do last time you were here—when I was nearly wild with thinking about poor Mildred and the way I ran out on her funeral to hunt you down—and what right did you have to ask for that when you never moved your mouth one time to say "I love you" or make the smallest promise?

 I know this isn't no letter for a girl to write but when you have sat in

silence six whole years waiting for somebody you love to speak—and
you don't know why you love them or even what you want them to say,
just so it's soothing—then it comes a time when you have to speak your-
self to prove you are there. I just spoke. And I'm right here.

> *Goodnight to you Wesley,*
> *from Rosacoke*

His answer to that was,

> *September 25*

Dear Rosa,
You are getting out of my depth now. We can talk about it when I
come home. I hope that will be real soon as the rush season here is
petering out.
I haven't got any news fit to tell.

> *Good luck until I see you again,*
> *Wesley*

So she waited, not writing to Wesley again (not putting thoughts to
paper anyhow) and not having word from him—but working her way
through six days every week and staying home evenings to watch
Milo's Sissie swell tighter and to hear Mama read out Rato's cards
from Oklahoma (saying he had visited one more Indian village and
had his picture made with another full-dressed Chief) and sitting
through church on the first Sunday morning and not telling anybody
what she was waiting for. (Nobody asked. Everybody knew.) And
along with the motorcycle season, the hot days petered out, and the
nights came sooner like threats and struck colder and lasted longer till
soon she was rising up for work in half-dark nearly (and stepping to
the window in her shimmy for one long look through the yard, thinking some new sight might have sprung up in her sleep to cheer her
through the day, but all that was ever there was a little broomstraw
and the empty road and dogwood trees that were giving up summer
day by day, crouched in the dawn with leaves already black and red
like fires that were smothering slow). And the first Saturday evening
in November when she was rocking in the front-porch swing, Milo

came home and said to her, "Rosacoke, all your cares are ended. Willie Duke Aycock has got a rich boy friend, and she don't know who Wesley Beavers *is.*"

Rosacoke kept rocking but she said, "What do you mean?"

"I mean it ain't been an hour since Willie Duke landed unexpected in her Daddy's pasture in a private airplane owned and piloted by a Norfolk fellow who's *compelled* to be in love—nothing but love could make a airplane land in Aycock's pasture!"

Rosacoke laughed. "How long did it take to dream that up?"

"Honest to God, Rosa, it's *so.* I won't a witness but I just seen her Mama at the store buying canned oysters for a big fry, and she said the family ain't calmed down yet, much less the cow. She said when that plane touched ground, every tit on the cow stood out like pot legs and *gave.*"

But once Rosacoke believed him she didn't smile the way he hoped. She stood up and said, "I better go set the table" and walked towards the house.

Milo stopped her. "What ails you, Rosa? You got the world's most worried-looking mind. Willie ain't dropped no atom bombs. You ought to be grinning wide."

"How come?"

"Don't this mean Wesley is your private property now?"

"Ask *Wesley* that."

"*You* ask him. Wesley come home in that little airplane too." He beamed to be telling her that at last.

She turned full to the house and said, "Is that the truth?"

"It's what Mrs. Aycock said."

She didn't look at him again. She went in and set the table but didn't sit down to supper, saying she wasn't hungry but meaning she didn't want to hear them laugh at Willie Duke's flight and tell her to dress up quick before Wesley came. She did change clothes—but nothing fancy, nothing but the pale blue dress and the sweater she wore any evening when she had worked all day—and she sat back out in the swing and rocked a little with both heels dug in the white ground to keep her rocking so slow she could always see the road. What light there was came slant and low in the rising cool and

touched a power line of new copper wire in separate places, making it
seem to float between the poles towards both ends of the road. A dead
maple leaf curled down to her lap. She ground it in her hand and
wondered where it fell from (the tree she swung in being oak), and a
spider lowered to her by one strand of silk, trying again to fill the air
with unbroken thread, and beyond the road two crows called out
unseen from the white sycamore that was bare already and straight as
Wesley's diving. A distant rifle cracked and the crows shut up.
"Mighty late to be hunting," she thought and counted to twelve, and
one crow signaled to start again. Then the dark came in. A light went
on in the house, and there was Mama at the dining-room window,
ironing. (She would stand there till bedtime. Then Milo would tell
her, "All right, pack up or you'll have the Ku Klux on me for working
my Mama so late.") But the road stayed black and nothing came or
went, not even lightning bugs. (Every lightning bug was dead. There
had been the first real frost the night before.)

And it frosted Saturday night. Rosacoke knew because she didn't
sleep but stared out her window every hour or so to the road till finally
by the moon she could see frost creeping towards her — gathering first
on weeds low down near the road, locking them white till morning
and pausing awhile but starting again and pulling on slow up the yard
like hands, gripping its way from one patch of grass to the next and
(nearer the house, when the grass gave out) from rocks to dead roots
to the roof of Milo's car. Then it silvered that and reached for the
house, and Rosacoke fell back and slept.

TWO

But Sunday was bright again and the frost was dew when she woke up, and the road was full of black children creeping towards Mount Moriah, trying their white breaths on the morning air, and carloads of white folks she knew but couldn't see, bound for Delight. Her clock said half-past ten and the house was quiet. They had gone on and left her. But when she tore downstairs to the kitchen, there was Milo dressed to the neck, eating syrup. "Oh," she said, "I thought I would have to walk this morning."

Milo tested her face to see what he should say. "Mama went on with Baby Sister. She said to let you sleep if that was how you felt."

Rosacoke looked in his shaving mirror over the stove. "I may *look* dead but I'm not."

"Well, Sissie ain't feeling good either. She's laid out upstairs so you can set with her."

"Milo, I'm *going*. Sissie will be all right and if she commences having babies, Delight Church will hear it. Just cool me some coffee and I'll get dressed right now."

So she dressed the best she could on such short notice and took a deep breath, and they headed off in a hurry (but not fast enough to ease her mind). When they flew past Mr. Isaac's, Rosacoke looked up through the thinning pecan grove to the house and—to break the quiet, to calm herself—said the first thing she thought, "Mr. Isaac's truck is still there. Reckon he's too sick for church?"

"Not if he's live," Milo said, and they went on by the pond and skidded the final curve, and there was Delight stood up in the morning sun with little fellows weaving round it in games and little clumps of men on this side near the graves, making clouds as they smoked through the last few minutes of air. From the curve Rosacoke looked towards the men, knowing she was safe and couldn't see a face from so far off, but after they pulled in the yard and every man turned to watch and one little boy screamed "Rosey-Coke!" (which was what boys called her), she couldn't look again. She looked to the graves where her father was sinking steady. But she didn't notice that. She could only see Milo searching with his eyes for anybody special in the crowd. She trembled to think what he might say any moment, and she said in the voice that scared her, "Don't tell me what you see." Then she got out alone and walked on straight to the church past all those men, seeing nothing but white sand under her feet. And nobody called her name. She went in just that fast and took her place four pews from the front on Mama's left.

"Have you eat?" Mama said.

"Yes'm," she said and turned to the pulpit and meant to look ahead for one full hour, but Baby Sister faced the people, and Mama twisted round periodically to watch every soul come in and report it. Rosacoke would nod her head at the news, but she kept looking forward till Mama couldn't stand it any longer and punched her and said "*Hot dog!*" and she had to look—because in marched Willie Duke Aycock, grinning like she wouldn't be *Aycock* long, with her new friend that she set up front for all to see (and all tried except Rosacoke who read up the hymns in advance, but he had a little head, and nothing much was visible but his Hawaiian shirt with the long open collar laid out on his round shoulders. Mama said, "He must not have counted on church when he packed"). The big surprise though was all the Aycocks strutting on behind. Mama said, "They ain't been to church since the drive-in opened." (A drive-in movie had opened across the field from their front porch, and all summer long on Saturdays they sat in the cool and watched every movement from sundown through the last

newsreel, which left them too tired for church—and ashamed to come
to the picnic. They didn't hear a sound of course—of the movies—but
in no time after the opening, Ida their youngest had learned lip reading and could tell them every word.) By the time they had all settled in
round the friend, it was going on eleven, and out the windows were the
sounds of men coming unseen to join their folks, grinding cigarettes in
sand and scraping their shoes on the concrete steps and having what
they hoped was one last cough. When they came in the back and scattered down the rows (bringing cool air with them that raised the flesh
on Rosacoke's neck), even Mama didn't turn. But Baby Sister saw
them all and didn't speak a name, not even Milo's when he took his
place by Mama on the aisle. Rosacoke could feel him turned towards
her, but she didn't meet his eyes, thinking, "Whatever he knows I don't
want to hear." Then the preacher and the choir ladies came in and sat.
Everybody quieted except Mama (who said what everybody thought),
"Mr. Isaac ain't here. He must be bad off," and not knowing who was
behind her and with no way left to find out, Rosacoke thought, "How
will I get through this hour alone with nothing to look at but three
white walls and a black pulpit and a preacher and ten choir ladies and
the back of Willie Duke Aycock's neck?—not a flower or a picture in
sight and nothing to think of but Wesley Beavers and whether he is ten
yards away or three whole miles and why he isn't here by me."

The preacher stood up and called for the hymn, and while the
hymnals were rustling, the side door opened by the choir, and Mr.
Isaac's Sammy walked in with the black leather chair. He nodded to
the people in general, and they nodded back in relief, and he set the
chair where it belonged by the front of the Amen Corner, half to the
preacher, half to the people. Then he went out and everybody waited,
not standing, till he came again—Mr. Isaac in his arms like a baby
with a tan suit on and a white shirt pinned at the neck with gold,
holding Sammy's shoulder with his live left arm (his right arm slack
in the sleeve and that leg) and his face half live and half dead, with a
smile set permanent by two hard strokes on the half that turned to the
people when Sammy set him gentle in the chair and knelt to arrange
his little bird legs. Then Sammy stood and whispered some message
in the live ear and sat down himself on a pew by the chair. And the

singing began, with Baby Sister leading them all to a long "Amen," low but sure.

So she had Mr. Isaac to watch through that long hour—the still half at least to take her mind off whatever people were behind her—and she started by thinking back quick as she could to the way he scared them when they were children, not by meaning any harm but by stopping his truck in the road whenever he saw them and calling out "Come here, girl" (or "boy"—he never said names). They would creep towards him and stand back a little from the truck, making arcs on the dust with their toes till he said, "Whose girl are you?" (meaning who was their mother), and they would say "Emma Mustian's." He would say "Are you sure?" and when they nodded, hand them horehound candy out the window to eat with the blue lint of his shirt pocket stuck in it and then drive away, not smiling once. But the permanent smile was on him now, tame as something made with needle and thread, that didn't have a place in the ways she remembered him—like the day he stopped in the road and not smiling once asked Milo, "How old are you, boy?" Milo told him "Thirteen" and he said, "If you rub turpentine on your thighs, it'll make hair grow" (Milo tried it and nearly perished with the stinging) or before that even, the day they found his spring—her and Milo and Mildred and the others, coming on him sudden in the woods with his ankles in water and the look on his face showing he wasn't there behind it that made them turn and leave without waiting for candy—and the evening her Daddy was killed and Mr. Isaac came and stood on the porch and handed her Mama fifty dollars, saying, "He is far better off" (which was true) and the day he came to see her Papa in the hospital and Papa, just rambling, said, "How come you never got married?" and Mr. Isaac said "Nobody asked me" and smiled but soon fell back into looking the way that covered his heart like a shield and kept you guessing what he was thinking of—his age? (which was eighty-two now) or his health? or all the money he owned in land and trees which he didn't spend and which, since he never married, would go to Marina his sister who cooked his food but was too old herself to offer him love and care?—the only thing that loved him being Sammy his man who had grown from the lean black boy that drove him on the land in a truck to the man who carried him now in his arms.

She stopped her thinking for the second hymn. (Willie Duke's friend more than did his share of that.) Then she bowed her head for the prayer, but once the preacher was underway, thanking God for everything green but weeds, Marise Gupton's Frederick tuned up to cry from the back of the church. Rosacoke and Mama looked quick to Milo to stop him from mentioning busts in the mouth, but Marise stopped the crying and Milo just smiled and they all bowed again. The prayer went on about doctors and nurses and beds of affliction, and Rosacoke looked to Mr. Isaac. She had to. He was somebody that didn't know Wesley, except by name. His head was up and the dead right eye was open, bearing straight to the opposite wall, but Sammy was bowed like everybody round him. Towards the end of the prayer, Mr. Isaac's live hand flickered on the arm of the chair and tapped Sammy's knee one time. Sammy didn't look up (though the live side faced him) and the hand tapped again. Sammy knew and, still bowed, reached in his pocket and took out two pieces of horehound candy that would keep him happy till the end. Mr. Isaac put one in his mouth and hid the spare in his hand, and Rosacoke looked all round (except behind) to see had anybody else watched that. Everybody was bowed, including Baby Sister who took prayer serious to be so young, and Rosacoke said to herself, "I have seen it alone so maybe the day isn't wasted."

Thinking that kept her fairly calm through collection and the sermon and the final hymn—right to the last few words the preacher spoke. He looked at the people and smiled and said, "We are happy, I know, to welcome old members who are with us today from the great cities where they work, and I know we will all want to greet our visitor who descended last night from the clouds!" Then he spoke a benediction and before it was out of his mouth, Willie Duke shot her friend through the side door like something too delicate to meet. Rosacoke thought, "At least I have got out of speaking to Willie," and Mama said to her, "Come on and speak to Mr. Isaac." (A dozen people were waiting already to shake his hand.)

Rosacoke said, "Mama, don't bother him today" and faced the people that were streaming out. Wesley wasn't there. Those visitors from the clouds were nothing but Willie Duke Aycock and her friend so Rosacoke followed Mama, and they stood their turn to greet Mr. Isaac.

He was still in his chair with Sammy behind him now, and when people spoke he didn't speak back or hold out his live hand that was clenched in his lap but bobbed his chin and let the half-smile do the rest till he saw Rosacoke. She came up in line before Mama and said, "Good morning, Mr. Isaac. I hope you are feeling all right."

He tilted his eyes to her face and studied it, still as before. Then he spoke in the voice that was left. "Whose girl are you?"

She held back a moment and said "Emma Mustian's," not sure that was what he meant, and pointed at Mama behind her. But he looked to his clenched live hand, and it opened enough for them both to see the one piece of candy that had hid there since the prayer, damp and soft. Then he clenched it again and looked back at her. No one had seen it but them—not even Sammy—so he matched, on the live side of his face, that lasting smile. Rosacoke smiled too and thinking he finally knew her, told him goodbye and went on quick out the front before Mama caught her and started commenting, and there of course all but blocking the door stood Willie Duke and her friend.

Willie said, "Rosa, come meet my aviator." Rosacoke looked at him. "Rosacoke Mustian, this is Heywood Betts, my boy friend who flew me down."

Rosacoke shook his hand and said, "How do you do."

He said, "Good morning, I'm fine but scrap metal is my work—flying's just a hobby."

Willie Duke waved at some Gupton girls in the yard—her nieces—and said (not looking at Rosacoke), "I kind of thought Wesley would be here today, not being home in so long."

Rosacoke said "Did you?" and looked round as if she had just noticed his absence.

Heywood Betts said, "Maybe he's laid up after our pasture landing."

"Shoot," Willie Duke said, "nothing don't bother Wesley, does it, Rosa?"

"Not much."

Heywood laughed. "He looked plenty bothered yesterday when you talked me out of landing at Warrenton airport."

Willie Duke said, "Nothing don't bother Wesley. He just didn't have his sweet thing to show off like I do you"—and squeezed Heywood tight.

Rosacoke looked towards the car where her people were waiting and then towards the sun. "Sure is bright," she said. "I better be getting on home. When are you all leaving?"

Willie Duke said, "Me and Heywood's definitely leaving this afternoon. But I ain't sure about Wesley. He's took Monday off so maybe he's leaving and maybe he's not.

"Well, happy landing," Rosacoke said and went to the car for the little trip home. Milo drove it fast as he could, and nobody spoke, not even when they passed Mr. Isaac's stripped cherry trees and his pond again that had shrunk in the sun but was so hard-blue it seemed you could walk on the surface like Jesus and not sink. But when they were home and climbed out slowly, Mama put her arm round Rosacoke's waist and forced their eyes to meet—"Rosa, go rest a little. You don't have to eat." That hit Rosacoke like something filthy across her mouth, and she ran out of Mama's arms to wash her hands for dinner.

And everything went all right for awhile at dinner. There was a lot of laughing about Willie Duke's man. Mama said, "*He's* rich. He didn't give a cent when the plate was passed," and Milo said, "Well, rich or poor, Willie Duke has sure took hold—and in the right place." But Rosacoke almost welcomed that. There were worse things now than Willie Duke Aycock, and it looked as if the family knew her feelings and were honoring them—even Milo—till Sissie finished all she could hold. Sissie had come down to dinner late and hadn't heard the news about church so she blurted out, "I thought you would ask Wesley to dinner, Rosa."

Rosacoke looked at her plate.

Milo said, "Hell-fire, Sissie. How are we going to ask him—by homing pigeon?"

"I'm sorry," Sissie said. "I just thought he would be at church and come home with you all—specially since your mother stayed up half the night cooking this mighty spread."

Mama said slowly, "Sissie, Wesley, as you could tell from his name if you had thought, is not a Baptist."

Milo said, "No, but he put in pretty good attendance long as he was interested in the Baptists he knew."

Mama said, "I hope he was at the Methodists' with his mother. That's where he belonged."

Rosacoke spoke for the first time. "Looks like to me all this isn't any of you all's business."

"Listen, Weeping Willow," Milo said, "if you could see the way you look—pale as ashes right this minute—you'd agree it was time somebody took a hickory stick to Wesley Beavers and made him behave."

"Well, don't let that somebody be you," Rosacoke said. "I can take care of my own business."

"Yes, and you've made a piss-poor job of it, honey. He landed here Saturday evening. You ain't seen him for what?—two months? You still ain't seen him and he's setting on his own front porch, not three miles from this oak table."

"All right," Rosacoke said, "tell me one magic word and I'll have him here, dressed for marriage, in ten seconds flat if that's what you want."

"Magic ain't what you need."

"What is it then? God knows I've tried."

Sissie, not meaning harm, had started it all so she poked Milo and said "Hush up."

But Milo was rolling. "What you need is a little bit of Sissie's method." He turned to Sissie and grinned, and she shoved back her chair and left the room. He called after her, "Sissie, come tell Rosa what your uncle said was the way to get old Milo."

Sissie hollered from the living room, "Milo, I got you *honest* and my uncle didn't tell me nothing."

So Milo sang it himself—

> *Pull up your petticoat, pull down your drawers,*
> *Give him one look at old Santy Claus.*

Mama said, "Milo, leave my table," and Rosacoke ran up the stairs to her room.

Half the room was covered with yellow sun so the first thing she did was pull the shades, and when she had made it dark as she could, she stepped to the middle of the floor and commenced taking off her dress. She checked every button for safety and tested a seam and stepped to the high wardrobe to hang it there in the darkest corner as if she was burying it. She unstrapped her wrist watch and stepped to the mantel and laid it there (but she kept her eyes off the propped-up picture) and kicked off her shoes and, still standing, peeled down her stockings and held them against a shaded window for flaws. Then she fell on her bed and cried over Wesley for the first time in her life. But the tears gave out and the anger, and behind them there was nothing. Plain nothing. She couldn't think. As a girl, when she was sad, she would shut her eyes and cast her mind to the future, thinking what a month from then would be like or when she was old, and she tried that now. But she couldn't. She couldn't think what an *hour* from then might be or the next day (which was Monday and work), much less a month or twenty-five years. She turned on her back and stared at the yellow goat's head stained on the ceiling. Her Papa told her it came from him keeping goats in the attic that peed. But he was joking. Everybody she knew was always joking. So she said it out loud, "What must I do about Wesley Beavers? And that's no joke." It was the second time she had asked the question, and the only answer anyone had offered was Milo's jingle that clattered behind her eyes right now. Milo was the closest kin she had that was grown (Rato being grown from the neck down, only), and he had sung that to her.

To cover his song she listened to the only sound in the house that reached her room—Baby Sister on the porch, putting paper dolls through her favorite story at the top of her voice. There was a daughter-doll who worked and one evening came home to tell her mother she had lice. The mother-doll said, "My own flesh and blood and you have lice!" It was the worst thing Baby Sister knew of. Rosacoke thought she would lean out the window and tell Baby Sister to talk a little quieter please or hum a tune, but her own door opened and Mama walked in, knocking down coat hangers as she came.

Rosacoke raised up and squinted to try and show she had been asleep. "Mama, I have asked everybody to knock before they enter."

"Don't make me mad," Mama said, "before I have spoke a word. I walked up fourteen steps to talk to you."

"What about?"

"I wanted to show you this old picture I found when I was cleaning out Papa's chest." Rosacoke gave her a look that meant couldn't it wait, but Mama raised one shade a little and came and stood by the bed. Rosacoke took the stiff tan photograph. It was two boys in pitiful long low-belted summer clothes on a pier with a wrought-iron rail behind them and, beyond that, water. The oldest boy might have been ten, and he had on white knee-stockings. His hair seemed blond and covered half his forehead like a bowl. His eyes were wise and full of white, and his mouth cut through his face in one perfectly straight line. He didn't frown but he didn't smile. He just held on tight as if he had something grand to give but the camera wasn't getting it—not that day. The boy who held his hand was smaller—maybe seven— and laughing with his mouth open wide. He had laughed till his face was blurred and the one sure thing about him was an American flag in his right hand and even that was flapping.

Rosacoke said, "Who is it of?"

"The biggest one is your Daddy."

"Well, Lord," she said and turned it over. There was her father's name and "Ocean View, July 1915." "I never saw him so clear before," she said.

Mama still stood up. "I didn't believe there was a likeness of him in the world, and then I come across this. It must have been the time your Papa took them all to water for the day. It was the one trip he ever gave them, and it ended awful because he put a five-dollar bill in his shoe in case of emergency and then walked ten miles up and down the sand. About leaving time, emergencies arose—one was your Daddy wanting a plaster of Paris statue of Mutt and Jeff—and when Papa took off his shoe for the money, it was just little soggy pieces. He had wore it out! He talked about that for thirty years."

Rosacoke kept looking at the picture. "Did you know Daddy then?"

Mama said, "Good as I ever did" and sat on the bed. "I don't mean to say we passed any time together—we was nothing but babies—but I used to see him sometime at church, and at Sunday school picnics he generally wound up eating on us. He never did like Miss Pauline's cooking, and chicken pies was all she brought to picnics." She held out her hand for the picture. "The funny thing though is, this is how I always *recall* him (whenever I recall)—looking like this, I mean. So young and serious—not like he got to be. If he would have stayed this way, he'd be here right this minute. But Rosa, he changed. Folks all have to change, I know, but he didn't have no more will power than a flying squirrel. He didn't have nothing but the way he looked, and I never asked for nothing else, not in 1930 nohow. Then when the money got scarce as hens' back teeth and his drunks commenced coming so close they were one long drunk and he was sleeping nights wherever he dropped in fields or by the road—I took all that like a bluefaced fool. I never asked him once to change a thing till it was too late and he had filled me up with four big babies and himself to the brim with bootleg liquor and then walked into a pickup truck." She rubbed the picture on her dress for dust. "But like I said, I don't recall him that last way and I'm thankful."

Rosacoke said, "Who is the other boy?" (not bringing up her only recollection which was of that last way).

"I've been wondering too but I can't see his face. Maybe it was some little fellow they met that day and never saw again. Looks like he's hollering something, don't it?"

"Yes'm," she said. "Wonder what it was?"

But Mama was through with the picture. She thought it had served the purpose she meant it for, and she went to the mantel and propped it by the one of Wesley in uniform. "I'll leave it here awhile so you can see it good. It'll be yours someday anyhow. None of the others wouldn't want it. That's why I didn't show it when I found it." Then she turned and said what she came to say. "Rosa, *he* ain't coming so why don't you get some good fresh air?"

Rosacoke faced the wall. "*He* ain't what I'm waiting for."

"Don't lie to me. What else is there but Judgment Day?"

"A heap of things, Mama." But she didn't name one. She lay in misery, wishing the Lord would strike her mother dumb, and far off a drone began and bore down nearer like some motorcycle leaning round curves to get to what it wants or like an arrow for her heart. She jumped off the bed and threw up the window and strained to see the road, but Baby Sister was dancing in the yard, pointing to the sky and screaming before the noise completely drowned her, "It's Willie, Rosacoke—make haste, it's Willie in the air!" And the shadow of Willie's fellow's plane, little as it was, swept over the yard and stirred the biggest oaks before it vanished north. When the drone passed over, Baby Sister was crying, "There's *three* folks in that plane!" And Mama said "There they go."

Rosacoke looked back to the mantel and the pictures and the mirror. "And here goes Rosacoke," she said. She put on a green winter dress and old easy shoes and didn't comb her hair that was tangled from misery. Her black Kodak was beside the photograph of her father with half a roll of summer pictures in it. She took it up and said, "I'm going to walk to Mary's. I told her I would take a picture of Mildred's baby to send to his aunts and uncles." Mama went over and spread up the bed and Rosacoke opened the door.

"You'll freeze like that," Mama said. So Rosacoke took out her raincoat and a scarf like silk, and Mama said, "Walk easy down them steps. Milo and Sissie said they needed naps. You know what their naps are like—and Sissie big as a fifty-cent balloon."

Rosacoke heard that. She took off her shoes and shot past where Sissie and Milo were and on down the steps. In the downstairs hall she could hear Baby Sister through the porch door. That paper-doll mother was still mirating at her own flesh and blood having lice. Rosacoke smiled and thought, "That is the one funny thing since Heywood Betts and his Honolulu shirt." But thinking of him and Willie—and whoever else flew with them back to Norfolk—put her deep again in the misery she was running from so she stepped in her shoes and ran on—out the back and almost down the steps before she knew she was thirsty. She came up again to the porch where Milo had left the well-water he drew after dinner. She took one look at the 1937 New Jersey license her father nailed over the bucket, and she drank one dipper of water so cold every muscle in her throat gripped tight to stop her swallowing. But she swallowed and the new cold inside her seemed to ease the way she felt. She said, "I will just walk peaceful to Mary's and not think about a thing," and she started, walking quickly down the steps again and straight on ahead through four dead acres of purple cotton stalks and into a little pine woods that had one path. She walked with her head just level, not looking up where the plane had been or at anything else that would cause her to think. But Mary's was a mile from the Mustians', and a mile is right far to think about nothing.

Still she walked every step of that mile, and it was nearly four o'clock when she came to the end of the pines where Mary's was—three wood rooms and a roof, washed by the rain to no color at all, narrow and pointed sharp up from the packed white ground like a bone the sun sucked out when nothing else would grow. The only things that moved were brown smoke crawling from the chimney and a turkey that saw her at once. Rosacoke stopped and said "Mary" as the turkey was famous for temper. He gave a cocked look with his raw red head and stepped away to let her pass. Mary hadn't answered so Rosacoke climbed the steps and said again "Mary" and opened the door. That was the big low room where Mary slept, but there was no noise, only dark and the smell of kerosene. Maybe they were all at afternoon church. Rosacoke went in, thinking she would leave a note to say she tried, but the only paper in sight was magazine pages nailed to the wall to keep out wind. Then she looked at the feather bed. In the middle of it four pillows were boxed together like a nest, and there was Mildred's baby laid on his back on thick newspapers with fists clenched tight to his ears. His head had twisted to the left, half buried in the white pillow slip. The one cotton blanket was around his feet where he had kicked it, and his dress which was all he wore had worked up high on his chest, leaving him bare to the chill of the day. Rosacoke went over to him, thinking this meant Mary was somewhere near and she should wait. When she saw the baby was deep asleep, she bent low enough to hear him breathe. His lips were shut and he breathed from all over—from the awful top of his head where the skull left off and the dark skin throbbed at anybody's mercy and from his arched belly and the navel knobbing out almost as far as what was underneath where the bud of him being a boy crouched on the loaded sack and rose and fell with the rest of him. He didn't seem cold but Rosacoke thought she should cover him. She pulled at his dress to get it down and raised the blanket gently from around his feet. It was enough to jar his sleep. He grunted high in his nose with his eyes still

shut and oared with his feet at the blanket and picked at his dress with
one slow hand. Rosacoke stood back—to keep him from seeing her if
he woke—and prayed he wouldn't wake. His legs slowed down and the
grunts, and for a minute he seemed asleep. Then he turned his head
and opened his eyes on Rosacoke, and the scream he gave split out from
whatever awful place he went to when he slept—describing it clear and
wordless as a knife. Rosacoke thought of ways to quiet him, but they all
meant picking him up—him screaming and naked again and her a
stranger. He stared straight at her though, and even if he didn't see, she
couldn't let him howl so again she pulled down his dress and reached
under his head and back to lift him up, but he belched and thick yellow milk spewed down his neck into her hand. She jerked her hand as
if it was scalded and flung the milk in clots on the floor and wiped her
fingers quickly on Mary's bed. The screaming went on, but choked now
and full. Rosacoke looked at the child and said, "Baby, *I* ain't what you
need" and ran to the porch to try once more for Mary. This time Mary
answered. "Here come Mary," she said, coming to the house from the
privy, not smiling, taking her time.

Rosacoke said, "Come *on* then and help this baby."

"What you done to Mildred's baby, Miss Rosa?"

"Not a thing—but he's sick."

"He ain't sick, Miss Rosa. He just passing the time of day."

"Well, I went in to take his picture and he woke up."

"And you picked him up, didn't you, when I done just now fed
him?" She still hadn't smiled.

"I was trying to hush him, Mary. Don't get mad."

"Yes'm. He threw up his dinner, didn't he?"

"Yes."

Mary bent down for a leaf that lay on the spotless ground and studied it in her hand long enough for the turkey to creep up behind her,
but she heard him and ran in his face—"Go on, sir!"—and he hobbled off. The screaming went on inside, a little tired now but steady,
and Rosacoke frowned. Mary came slow up the steps, holding her
straight back and said, "He throws up regular. I don't know if he can
grow, not keeping hold of his nourishment no better."

"Go stop his crying, Mary."

"What you so scared of crying for? He come here crying and he be crying when I ain't here to hush him. He got his right to cry, Miss Rosa, and why ain't you used to babies by now?" Then she smiled and went in the door and said, "Come in, Miss Rosa. I'll get him clean and you take his picture."

But Rosacoke couldn't go back. She looked at the drained evening sky. "It's too dark now, I think. I better come back next Sunday."

Mary stopped in her tracks—"Yes'm, if that's what you think"—and Rosacoke went towards the pines. On the edge Mary called her back and gave her the Kodak she had left. Mary said, "They tell me Mr. Wesley got him a airplane."

"Who is *they*, Mary?"

"Estelle saw Mr. Wesley in the road last night, and he say he got him a eight-cylinder airplane to come home in and he was taking it to Norfolk this evening and to watch out for him in the sky."

"That won't Wesley's airplane, Mary. He just hitched a ride in it, and they have already gone back."

"Yes'm. How is he coming on, Miss Rosa?"

"I reckon he's fine. I ain't laid eyes on him since the funeral."

"Yes'm," Mary said, seeing how Rosacoke looked (though she held back half the misery from her face), seeing that was all she ought to say and watching Rosacoke head home again and stop and take another look at the sky.

"I'm going to see his Mama, Mary. Reckon she can tell me what I've done wrong?"

All Mary said was, "Step along fast, Miss Rosa, else night will catch you"—which the night was bound to do as the Beavers lived a good two miles further on, facing the road with their back to the woods that started at Mary's. She could walk home first and take the car and go by the road (it was three miles by the road), but that would mean explaining a lot to Mama and talking her way out of supper. If she walked on now through the woods, she could get to the Beavers' as they finished eating and do her talking and call for Milo to carry her home. So she crossed Mary's yard the other way, not seeing Mary still in the door, and passed into trees that gradually shielded out the baby's crying.

She had gone more than halfway before she was no longer running from Mildred's baby, and the trees had thinned to the place
where a fire had been in the early spring, charring the sparse pines
and opening the ground to the sky. She stopped there and wondered
what she was running *to*—as if Wesley's mother knew how Wesley
felt—and she thought of turning back. What could she say that the
Beavers would understand? But turning back would put her in pitch
dark in a little so she said to herself, "I will just walk on and ask the
Beavers real nonchalant to let me use their phone and call Milo to
pick me up. If they want to talk to me then, let *them* decide what to
say." She took her breath to go, and a light wind in her face brought
two things out to meet her—low on the trees a hawk with his tan
wings locked to ride the air for hours (if the air would hold and the
ground offer things to hunt) and his black eyes surely on her where
she stood and clear against the sky, his iron beak, parting and meeting
as he wheeled but giving no hawk sound—only shivering pieces of
what seemed music riding under him that came and went with the
breeze as if it was meant for nothing but the hawk to hear, as if it was
made by the day for the hawk to travel with and help his hunting—yet
frail and high for a killing bird and so faint and fleeting that Rosacoke
strained on her toes to hear it better and cupped her ear, but the hawk
saw that and his fine-boned wings met under him in a thrust so long
and slow that Rosacoke wondered if they wouldn't touch *her*—his
wings—and her lips fell open to greet him, but he was leaving, taking
the music with him and the wind. She turned to watch him go and
wanted to speak to call him back, but her lips moved silent as his
beak. You could joke with a cardinal all day long, but what did you say
to something like a hawk?—nothing that a hawk would answer so she
just went on, helped by the breeze that pushed from behind her now,
not practicing things she could say to the Beavers nor the way she
would try to look, but searching her mind to name what pieces of
music the hawk carried with him and wondering what had made
them. But the memory was fainter already than the music, and it
hung in her mind, unfinished and alone, spreading its curious sadness over whatever troubles she had, burying them deeper than feeling and frowning, leaving her free for this short space in evening air

that was warm for early November with the last light clung to the slope of her cheek where colorless down, too soft to see in the day, swirled up to her temple and the coarse yellow hair laid back on the flickering wind and her legs pumped on through weeds that were dead already from the frosts but still were green and straight—free to go on or back while she took the last few steps that put her nearly in sight of the Beavers'. Then the wind turned round once more, and the music was on it, close and whole. Now there was no going back because it was Wesley, sure as war would come, playing his Navy harmonica when she had counted on him being in Norfolk or at least headed north in Willie Duke's plane.

The Beavers' house sat back from the road at a slant and in a white dirt clearing but with the trees reaching round on three sides like arms to the road. When Rosacoke came to the end of the trees, she could have seen the side of the house, but she circled just out of sight till she was almost at the road. Then she turned and there was the porch, fifty yards away, and the three steps and on the top step, Wesley's youngest brother Claude, sitting on his hands, looking to where Wesley was, hearing the music.

Wesley was on his feet at the corner of the porch nearest Rosacoke, leaning one shoulder on the last post, facing the road but looking down. From the trees Rosacoke could see three-fourths of him—the dark blue trousers he had worn all summer, the loose white shirt, his hair lighter from the sun at Ocean View—all but his face. He covered most of that with his hands that quivered tight on the harmonica till the music stopped for awhile. Then one hand opened and it started again— not songs or tunes and like nothing she had known since she was a girl and heard old Negroes blowing harps as if they remembered Africa and had been grand kings or like Milo that summer he grew up (when his beard arrived, the color of broomstraw) and went past telling her his business and every evening sat in the dusk after supper before he would leave the house, whistling out his secrets in tunes she never understood and planning back of his eyes what he would do with the night when it fell altogether (which would be to walk three miles to see an Abbott girl who was older than him—and an orphan that lived with her uncle—and was taking him in dark tobacco barns, teaching him things too early that some folks never learn). Anyhow, it was nothing *she* had ever sung to him—something else he learned away from home, maybe in the Navy. ("But if the Navy is sad as that," she thought, "why do folks join it of their own free will?")

In all she could see—the yard, the house, his brother, him, the trees beyond—his hands were the only moving things. The wind had died completely, his brother watched him as still as she did, and Wesley himself was still as a blind man when his guide suddenly leaves him, embedded upright in the gray air like a fish in winter, frozen in the graceful act, locked in the ice and staring up with flat bitter eyes—far out as anything can be and come back. But his hands *did* move—them and the music—to show he could leave any minute if leaving was what he wanted. (How could she know what he wanted?) And his brother spoke—or moved his mouth. Like that boy in the picture with her father (him on the left, holding up like a lily the American flag, speaking silence to the wind), she couldn't make out the sound but Wesley could. He took down his hands and looked at his brother and laughed and said "No" to whatever the question was, and they talked on awhile, too quiet for her to hear but with enough laughing to make Wesley roll his head so she could see. "He just don't know," she thought. "He don't know how he looks." Then the talking stopped and Claude went in the house. Wesley hesitated a minute, knocking the harmonica on his hand and looking to the road as if Rosacoke, unseen, had made him think of leaving. "There ought to be a way," she thought. "There ought to be some way you could hold him there. Anybody who looks like that—you ought to give them anything you have. Anything you have and they want *bad* enough." So she went on towards him and thought of nothing but that.

And from the moment she broke through the trees, he watched her come, stepping long as she always did, not showing a thing he hadn't seen a thousand times before. She was watching the ground which meant she was deciding the first word to say, and that meant Wesley didn't have any cause for worry. Not meaning to play but for something to do, he raised the harmonica again, and when she got to the steps and looked up at him, he smiled from behind his hands.

"I heard you playing," she said and pointed behind her to the woods.

"I have been to Mary's to take that baby's picture, but he was scared of me, and I thought I would just take a walk to here—it being so warm—and call up Milo to come get me. A half a mile back I heard you playing. But I didn't know it was you. I thought you were air-borne by now." She grinned and his answering laugh whined through the harmonica and made her say, "If you managed everything good as you manage a harp, wouldn't none of your friends ever be upset."

"I never studied it," he said, "—harp-playing, I mean. Just what I picked up in Norfolk."

"That's where I reckoned you were tonight—else I wouldn't be standing here."

"I got tomorrow off," he said.

"There were three folks in that plane going back."

"I know that," he said. "I surrendered my seat to Willie's Mama. Anyhow, I won't riding back with Heywood Betts. He drives a airplane about as good as I tap-dance. I been laid up airsick till this evening."

"Have you? Mary said Estelle saw you in the road last night."

"Yes she did," he said and tightened his lips, not as if he had made a joke but as if he had ridden that track as far as he intended and wouldn't she like to throw the switch?

"Well, can I use the phone?" she said. "I better be calling Milo so they won't think I have died."

"I can carry you home."

"Thank you but my stomach hasn't been real easy lately, and I won't trust it to a motorcycle ride tonight."

"The motorcycle is in Norfolk. You didn't think I brought it down here in a airplane, did you?"

"Do me a favor," she said. "Say *Rosacoke.*"

"Why?"

"Just say it please."

He said "Rosacoke" like an answer for a doctor that asked to see his tonsils.

"Thank you," she said. "That is my name. I bet you ain't said it since late July."

"I don't walk around talking to trees and shrubs like some folks if that's what you mean."

"That's not what I mean but never mind. You are Wesley—is that still right?"

"Unless the Law has changed it and not notified *me.*"

"I was just checking. I know such a few facts about you and your doings that sometimes I wonder if I even know your right name."

"Yes ma'm. You can rest easy on that. It's Wesley all right and is Wesley riding you home or ain't he?—because if he is, he will have to get the keys."

"If nobody else is wanting the car, I'd thank you," she said, thinking her last chance might be coming, thinking she might find the way to give him whatever he wanted to calm him down—thinking she knew what he wanted. She would do her best but maybe Wesley didn't want anything she had, not any more. "He must give a sign first," she said to herself and when he went for the keys, she made up what the sign would be. There were two ways Wesley could turn when they got to the road, and the way he turned would be the sign. If he went right— that was the bad road but the quickest—they would ride all the way past dead open fields and be at Rosacoke's in no time. But if he turned left—that was the long circle way that would take them first through an arched mile of trees and then past Mount Moriah and Mr. Isaac's bottomless woods where the spring was and the deer had been and, beyond, Delight Church and the pond and the Mustians'.

Wesley came out of the backyard in the tan Pontiac with no lights on and waited while she got in. It was full night but they coasted down the drive in darkness like thieves and stopped when they came to the road. Then Wesley turned on the bright lights, and the car headed left slow as if it turned itself. That was the sign and Rosacoke waited for what would come after. But they ran through the darkest mile in silence with Wesley gripping both hands to the wheel and watching the road like foreign country and Rosacoke catching little glimpses of him in the dashboard light as he passed up every chance to slow down or stop—ruts and holes and even the hidden turn-in that had been his favorite stopping place when she first knew him, where they had sat many an hour other nights (not talking much, to be sure, not needing talk then), and on past Mount Moriah, lit up and full of black singing, and when that died behind them and they commenced the first long curve of Mr.

Isaac's woods, Rosacoke said, "I might as well be behind you on the motorcycle for all the talking we have done."

"What do you want to say?"

"Wesley, you are at least half of this trouble, and you said you would *talk*. In that last letter you said I was getting you out of your writing depth and hadn't we better talk when you got home."

"I don't remember everything I say in letters."

"Well, I sure to God do. I learn them by heart just trying to figure out what you mean."

"God A-mighty, Rosa, I don't mean *nothing* by them. I just say whatever—" but they had pulled round that first curve, and the head-lights shot forward unblocked. Wesley said "Sweet Jesus" and Rosacoke said "Stop" because their light struck a deer the moment it flung from the woods on the right, broadside to them in the air with its hair still red for summer and the white brush of its tail high and stiff, holding in the leap for the time it took to see them coming, then heaving its head and twisting the leap back on itself to where it started in the dark—before they could speak again. But when it was gone (from their eyes, not their minds) with crashing enough for a herd, Wesley stopped where they were and said, "He is the first one I ever seen try it."

"Try what?"

"Try to get his does across the road to water, I guess. It ain't too late for that."

"Was it a buck then?"

"Didn't you see his horns?"

"I guess I did—he was so sudden." They sat on, still, a moment. Then Wesley reached for the gears, and quick as gunfire Rosacoke said, "I saw one once before way behind Mr. Isaac's spring—Mildred and me, nine years ago. It wouldn't have been this same one, would it?"

"Not hardly," he said and the car didn't move.

"What water would he be taking them to—the spring?"

"Not hardly—that'll be clogged up—but there's creeks all back in there if you go far enough."

Those were the most peaceful words they had said since late July. Rosacoke took them as one more sign and saw a way to keep them going. "Reckon will he try to cross them over again?"

"I reckon so if he don't see no more lights for awhile. He's watching us right now from somewhere back there, waiting till we go."

"Pity we can't see them cross," she said.

"He may not try again right here, but we can wait up yonder in the tracks to the spring if you ain't in a hurry."

She knew Mama and Milo would already be standing on their heads with worry, but she said, "I can wait. All I got to do is go to work at nine o'clock in the morning."

Wesley turned off the lights and when his eyes had set to the dark, there was a little moon to show him the grown-over tracks just ahead that used to lead Mr. Isaac to his spring. He eased the car towards them and backed in to face the road. He pulled up the brake and lowered his window and leaned his arms on the top of the wheel and pressed his forehead on the glass to see the trees beyond the road and whatever they held. Rosacoke reckoned that was a temporary position—that in a minute he would move in as far as she let him. To pass the time she looked ahead too, but not the way Wesley did. He *only* waited—nothing else crossed his mind but seeing that deer and how many does he would have. Rosacoke thought, "Him and that deer are something similar. Not but a few things wait like they do. Most things are busy hunting"—she thought that last so clearly she couldn't swear to not saying it. But if she said it Wesley just waited harder. He didn't move. So she closed her eyes for the next thinking to begin, but a picture came instead—of that cool November day seven years ago and the path and the pecan tree with Wesley up it like an eagle shaking down nuts at her request, not hungry enough to want them himself—old enough though to want *her* (other boys that young had wanted her) but not even caring enough to ask her name, much less for anything better, just waiting nicely till she left him alone with what he could see from the fork he stood in, sweeping nearly all Warren County with his eyes and telling her he saw smoke to make her leave—and him so hard to leave even then with the threat of being grown hung on him like thunder. With her eyes still closed she ran through all her time with Wesley till finally she could say to herself, "Mama lived with my Daddy fifteen years and took his babies and his drunks, and now she don't recall him but as a little serious boy in a picture. That is the way I recollect Wesley—like that first November day. Every other way is like that—him waiting for something to happen to *him*, daring somebody to do something nice such as come up and touch him just so he could say, 'Why in the world did you do *that?*' and hold on tight till whoever bothered him vanished—and nothing about him since has ever surprised me. I knew from the first, young as I was, what was coming. Take a child like Mildred's—you can look at him and say if he is a pretty or ugly *child*. You can't see what he will look like when he is grown though. But that first time—wasn't Wesley standing plain as day in a clear shadow of his grown man's body that sat out around him like a boundary he had to fill? *I* saw it and young as I was, I saw there wasn't no room for Rosacoke Mustian in what *that* boy would turn out to be. So he went on filling out his boundary lines and getting the face I knew he would, and while he was getting it, he came to me all those times and I let him have me to kiss and touch, and I said to myself, 'He has changed and this is love.' But all those times I was no more to him than water to a boat— just a thing he was using to get somewhere on, to get *grown* so he could tear off to Norfolk, Virginia and the U.S. Navy and every hot hussy that would stretch out under him and tell him 'Yes' where I said 'No.' And just because of that Rosacoke went out of his mind completely. I knew from the first it would happen, but that didn't make no difference. I hoped he would change but he didn't change, and *that* didn't make no difference." She said it out loud—"Wesley, do you reckon on ever changing any?"

He didn't look round. He whispered gently as if he was asking a favor, "Rosa, no deer is going to walk in on a round-table discussion of Wesley Beavers' personality."

"Yes sir," she said but she had thought all she needed to think. She had made herself see what she had to do. So she waited—not to see the deer and his does but knowing if they crossed to water, they would be her chance to save Wesley from running off again. She waited by staring at her dark lap and her hands that lay flat and nearly unseen on her flanks.

And they crossed—the deer, a little above where the buck had showed before. She didn't see their first steps or hear them, so dainty on the packed road, till she felt Wesley's whole body stiffen forward—

not by him touching her but through the springs of the seat. She looked to where his brow pressed hard on the glass and turned herself along his gaze to where she caught them the moment they sank into Mr. Isaac's woods—three deer moving careful as clock wheels so close together she couldn't see which was the buck and was leading. But they drew her on behind them. Wesley felt that too (he had seen them longer than she), and he strained so hard to see their last that she whispered, "There's safety glass between them and you, Wesley, and you are about to poke your head right through it." But when the deer were gone, Wesley gave no sign of taking the chance they offered. He only said, "Now you have seen two does getting led to water" and reached for the key to crank the motor.

Rosacoke laid her hand on his wrist. "Since it's a warm night how come we don't wait and walk in behind them and see is it the spring they are after?"

He looked at her hand, not her, and saw what she meant, "If you want to," he said, "but we ain't coming near that buck."

"If we went gentle maybe we could."

Wesley reached in the back seat for a flashlight and opened his door. He came to her side and stood while she got out. They walked a few loud steps through weeds that were dead from the frosts and then struck into the trees with hands at their sides, separate and not swinging till they walked so close their fingers brushed and their hands went together so natural you couldn't say who took whose. Then the walking was quiet because there was pine straw under their feet and darker because they were under black pines and Wesley didn't once switch on his light. It was early November and the snakes were gone. They knew the path. And they both knew where they were headed— which wasn't to the spring because when they came to the spring and Rosacoke held back on his hand (thinking she should mention deer) and whispered "Are they there?" Wesley just breathed out through his nose to show he had laughed (he was too dark to see), and Rosacoke said, "Throw your light on the spring and see is it clean," but he led her on where the path gave way to the thickness of leaves and soft old logs that powdered beneath their feet and the deer passed out of their minds completely, and Rosacoke thought of nothing but "Where will we stop?" till a briar bush stopped them. Wesley was one step ahead when the briars took hold, and Rosacoke walked up against him. That was when the light came on (Wesley must have done it but without a sound) and showed them piece of a broomstraw field. Wesley pulled out of the bush, and the light went off without them seeing each other. They walked on hip-deep in straw another few yards before any sound was made. Rosacoke said, "Don't let's go no farther" and they stopped again. "Listen," she said.

They listened awhile. Then he said "Listen to what?"

"I thought we might hear them," she said. "It was a field like this where Mildred and me saw that other deer."

"It wasn't this field," he said.

"How come it wasn't?"

"This is my private field. Mr. Isaac don't know he owns this field. Don't *nobody* know this field but me."

"I never knew it," she said, "and I been walking these woods my whole life."

"You know it now."

She said "Yes I do" but she couldn't see it. She couldn't see at all. She thought she was facing Wesley though nothing but her seemed to breathe, and she thought they were standing on level ground. Her left hand was still in those other hard fingers, but when she offered her right hand, she only touched straw that sighed. She drew back in sudden terror and said to herself, "I don't even know this is Wesley. I have not laid eyes on his face since we left the car." So she spoke again, calm as she could—"Would you switch on the light so I can see your field?"

"You ain't aiming to take no pictures, are you?" He was facing her and he sounded like Wesley, but from that minute on, she wouldn't have sworn just who she was giving up to.

"I left my Kodak in the car," she said. "It don't work at night."

"Then if you don't need no light, I surely don't," he said and took her other hand and pulled her gentle under him to the ground. The straw lay down where they were and stood up wherever they weren't, and Rosacoke reached behind her head to grip her hands in its dryness. The last clear thought she had was, "If it was light it would all be the color of Milo's beard."

But Wesley didn't need any light. He started above her and even if the sun had poured all over him, she couldn't have seen the one thing she needed to see, which was down to where he was locked already at the center of what she had started, where he was maybe alone or, worse than that, keeping company in the dark with whatever pictures his mind threw up—of some other place he would rather be or some girl he knew that was better. But he didn't speak to tell her *where* he was. He only moved and even that was a way he never had moved in all the evenings she had known him—from inside the way he did everything but planned this time fine as any geared wheel, slow at first and smooth as your eyeball under the lid, no harder than rocking a chair and touching her only in that new place, but soon taking heart and oaring her as if he was nothing but the loveliest boat on earth and she was the sea that took him where he had to go, and then multiplying into what seemed a dozen boys swarming on her with that many hands and mouths and that many high little whines coming up to their lips that were nothing like words till the end when they came so close they broke out in one long "Yes," and what he had made, so careful, fell in like ruins on them both, and all she had left was her hands full of broomstraw and one boy again, dead-weight on her body, who whispered to her softer than ever, "I thank you, Mae" (which wasn't any part of her name) and not knowing what he had said, rolled off her and straightaway threw his flashlight on the sky. The beam rose up unstopped and she turned away to keep him from seeing the things he had done to her face—the look he had left there. But he didn't notice. All the light went up and he studied that awhile. Then he said, "Did you know this light won't never stop flying?" She didn't answer so he laid the back of his hand on some part of her that was dry as peach-skin still and said, "There ain't a thing to block it. It'll be flinging on when you and me are olden times."

But now that their moving had stopped, the chill of the night set in, and Rosacoke shuddered beneath his hand before she said, "Is that something else you learned in the Navy?"

"Yes'm," he said. "Ain't I a good learner?" And with his hand he asked again for what she had given so free before but she held him back.

"Why?" he said, thinking naturally he had the right.

"I got to go home."

"What you got at home that's half as good as what I got right here?" He pulled her hand through the dark to where he was ready.

But her hand was dead in his. She drew it away and he heard her stand. "If you aren't carrying me back, I will have to walk, but since you know these woods so good, please lend me your flashlight."

He threw the beam on her face and said "Sweet Jesus" to what he saw—which was no Rosacoke he had seen before. She looked straight down at his light, not seeing him behind it, not hiding any more. Then she opened her mouth, thinking only if she could speak, the hate on her face would break into something gentler like regret. But all she could do was hunch her shoulders, and if Wesley in the Navy had sometimes forgot how she looked, he wouldn't forget again.

"Are you all right?" he said.

"I'm all right," she said and started for the road.

Wesley had some dressing to do before he could follow so Rosacoke walked to the edge where the briars began and waited while he caught up behind her with the light. When he was two steps away and the light spread round her feet, she moved on again, not slowing once and with every step, her front leg striding from her raincoat just beyond his light as if she couldn't bear *its* touch either. Wesley let her go that way till the path widened out where the spring should be. Then he came up beside her and said, "How about us stopping a minute to see is the deer been stirring the spring?" and he laid his arm along her back.

"You ain't studying deer," she said and ran on to the car.

Not knowing whether she would wait or walk on home, Wesley took his time. He walked to the spring and shined his light down in it. The deer hadn't passed that way, hadn't stopped anyhow. The vines were in place. The water was clear and the bottom was clean—most likely since the day of Mildred's funeral. But there was one broken stick, half in, half out. The underwater half was furred with tan sediment, and on the black half above was a single ugly moth, the color of the sediment. It was still—the moth—and Wesley knelt to touch it and see was it dead, but it took a little bothered flight and settled on the stick again. It had lasted two frosts so he let it sleep, and since he was kneeling he bent all the way and laid his mouth to the spring and drew three swallows of water. Then he stood and said to himself, "It will run on clean another two weeks. Then the leaves will take over."

He had taken his time because he thought he knew what Rosacoke's trouble was and—if she had waited—how to ease her. And when he got to the car, she had waited. She had also straightened her hair, but her face was the same so he drove that last little way in silence. Not a frog was left in the pond nor a dryfly in the trees, and the nearest noise was the singing at Mount Moriah (if they were still singing), but that was behind them now, and Rosacoke gave no sign of wanting the talk she asked for before. She watched the road. But Wesley had one thing to say which he thought was gentle and which he thought she needed, and when he turned in the Mustians' drive, he stopped under their big pecan tree and said it. "Rosa, you got to remember that the way you feel is a natural thing after what we done. It'll pass on off in a little, and you'll feel good as you ever did. I guarantee that. And if we was to do it again sometime, it wouldn't last nearly as long—you feeling sad, I mean, about what we done."

"*We* ain't done nothing, Wesley—" She might have explained if they hadn't heard the front door slam. The porch light was off but what they saw was bound to be Milo coming towards them. He stopped halfway, just looking at the car, and Rosacoke said, "I got to go. He's worried about me."

"He ain't worried now," Wesley said. "He knows this car." And Rosacoke might have believed him and sat awhile if Sissie inside hadn't just then switched on the light and stepped on the porch and stood. The light didn't reach out quite to the car, but it struck along Milo's back—him facing them with his hands at his sides, working, and his head all dark but his hair lit up.

"I'm going," she said and opened her door. She was out on the ground before he could move, and she whispered, "Now leave here fast. Milo is mad at you anyhow, and I don't want him seeing your face."

"Well, are you all right?"

"I'm all right. I was just mistaken. But so were you—my name hasn't never been Mae." And before he could open his mouth, she had walked off towards Milo, standing with the light against his hair (his hair the color it was). When she came close enough to show her face, *he* would know why she looked the way she did. He wouldn't speak of it to her or sing his advice again. He would just walk in behind her. But later in the night (in bed when he got chilly) wouldn't he roll over on Sissie his wife and tell her what he knew? Which would make four people that knew—Rosacoke herself and Wesley Beavers and Milo her brother and Sissie Abbot his wife who was big as a fifty-cent balloon.

MONDAY afternoon was clear and cold, and Wesley hitched himself to Norfolk, not seeing Rosacoke again. But that weekend he sent this letter.

November 10

Dear Rosa,

It is way past time good boys was all in the bed but I am still up so will just write a line to say I'm back on the job. (I was last week, I mean, which don't signify I'll be there tomorrow if I wake up feeling like I expect to.) Also I am writing to know wouldn't you like to come up here Thanksgiving if you get any time off? The reason I ask is I won't be coming home again before Xmas as the only time I have off is Thanksgiving and some folks I know are throwing a big party that weekend. A lot of my friends have left for good. That's what living in a Navy town means. But there is enough left to keep the ball rolling so why don't you come on up for the holidays? You could stay at your Aunt Oma's or I could get you a room in the boarding house where I stay—that would suit me better.

What's suiting me right now though is my bed that's waiting so good night Rosa. Say hello to everybody for me. I'm sorry I didn't see Milo. What did you mean about him being mad at me? I'm hoping I'll hear from you soon and see you in a little. Hoping also you have got over your blues from last Sunday evening, I am

Yours for a good night's sleep,
Wesley

Two evenings later when Rosacoke came home from work, Baby Sister ran out to meet her. She said, "Guess where you got a letter from?" But Rosacoke didn't ask. She walked straight to the living room and spoke to Milo who was nodding but who woke up to watch her read the letter. It was propped on the mantel, but Rosacoke waited, warming her hands at the stove. When she finally looked and saw Wesley's writing, she took it and started upstairs. Baby Sister said, "You don't have to go in the freezer to read it!" (meaning there were no fires lit upstairs), but Rosacoke went and turned on the one ceiling light and lay on her bed with the letter in her hand, wishing she never had to open it, knowing—whatever it said—it would call on her for some awful answer. When she read his first line, she knew what the answer was and wrote it out then.

November 12

Dear Wesley,

No my blues are not over. What makes you think they ought to be? Everybody in the world doesn't feel the same as you. I don't think I have ever felt the same as you about anything except the weather—even then you don't sweat when it's hot—and sure thing I don't feel like spending my little Thanksgiving on a Greyhound bus bumping back and forth to Norfolk so I can tag behind you to a party full of folks I don't know and wouldn't want to know if I met them, including Mae. Anyhow Mama and Aunt Oma are not on speaking terms so I couldn't stay there and thank you very much but I won't be boarding at your place either. I have been deer-hunting once already and once was enough for me.

Sincerely,
Rosacoke

She addressed it and stood it on her own mantel by the picture of her father as a boy—where the one of Wesley had been. But she didn't seal it. Her habit was to let letters cool overnight and read them one more time in the morning. And in the morning she tore it up, not because what she said was wrong but because maybe she should wait. How could you just say "No" that way after waiting six years to say "Yes"?

She waited five days but nothing changed really—not for her, not inside—so on Saturday night she sat down in the kitchen to write again, not thinking what she would finally say or how, not knowing how she really felt, but thinking maybe things might change the way Wesley said if she just wrote the news of that bad week and put Wesley's name at the top.

November 16

Dear Wesley,

Thanking you for your letter that I'm sorry to take so long to answer but we are having a right busy week here, especially as Sissie has been having her baby on and off for the last two nights and all day today. No seriously, she started up Friday evening—yesterday. She was three days overdue yesterday. And those three days have been a real experience for all of us—the evenings anyway with nothing to do but sit and watch Milo trying to cheer up Sissie. We got through the first two evenings somehow till Milo finally said he was tired and took Sissie off to sleep (they have been sleeping downstairs in Mama's room for ten days in case of emergency) and we started last night as usual—Sissie had spent most of the day lying down but rose up at sunset to eat with us. When we got through that I volunteered to wash dishes and the others went on in the living room. I took my time in the kitchen but when I couldn't find another thing to wash, I joined them. Baby Sister was just finishing her part of the entertainment—a description of her wedding plans (age 12, just dreaming). She had got as far as the music arrangements. All the music she wants is "Kiss of Fire" and alot of Gupton children laying down pine cones in her path. I sat down and took up my knitting (I am knitting Sissie a bed jacket) which was the signal for Milo to make his remark about what a dangerous thing it was making Sissie a bed jacket because once Sissie got down didn't we know how hard it would be ever to get her up? (The truth. Last winter she reacted to roseola like it was pellagra.) We laughed some at that, even Sissie who had been more sensitive than usual lately (setting a new world's record). Then there was a lull and everybody stared at their own lap, glad of a few minutes peace. But it didn't last. Sissie gave a little moan and lurched in her chair to show the baby had just rearranged itself. Milo said, "Is he traveling again?" (Milo knows it's a boy) and Mama said, "He must be hungry" and stood up and said she would serve the dessert now—we had all been too full after supper. So she went off and came back with cherry Jello which we have eaten right much of lately, it being what Sissie craves — lucky she craves something cheap — and while we were eating that, somebody knocked on the door. It was Macey Gupton and Arnold his brother (the bachelor with no palate that you may never have seen — they don't show him off much). Macey and Mama are both deacons at Delight and they are the committee to select the gift the church will give Mr. Isaac at the Christmas pageant when he retires as Chairman of the Board of Deacons and Macey had come by to say he was driving up to Raleigh on Saturday and would get the gift if they could decide what it ought to be. Milo met them at the door and invited them in like prodigal sons — so happy to see anybody that might bring Sissie cheerful relief, much less Macey Gupton who had sat by and seen Marise have baby after baby like puppies. So they came in and took their seats. Arnold took a rocker as far out from everybody as he could get — it was like having Rato back. They had Jello and then everybody commenced asking what to get Mr. Isaac. Macey said didn't we think it ought to be something useful? There was discussion on that but nobody came up with anything that would be any real use to Mr. Isaac in his condition. Milo said, "Get him a wife. That is what he has needed all these years" — and asked Arnold if that wasn't so. Arnold just grinned and kept on rocking but Macey said he was serious and was thinking of something big like a wheel chair to replace that leather one Sammy totes. Milo said, "Hold on. What does a rolling chair cost?" Macey said, "Alot but we could collect a little from every member." Milo said, "Do you realize, Macey, that if Mr. Isaac wanted a rolling chair, he could buy a sterling silver one easy as you and I can buy a cigar?" Mama said that was the truth and that she thought it would upset Mr. Isaac to spend so much on him now so late in life. Milo said, "Yes and do you know what he'd rather have than anything you could give him? — a sack of horehound candy." Everybody laughed, knowing it was true — it is what we give him every Christmas — and seeing he had hit a snag with his rolling chair, Macey changed the subject. He looked over at Sissie ramrodded in her chair (nobody had looked at her since the Guptons arrived) and said, "Well when is it going to be?" Sissie said, "It ought to been three days ago." Mama said that was just the doctor's guess — that

it would come when it got ready. And Milo said, "Ready or not, he better hurry up. He's got to make room for the other nine." He asked Sissie
if that wasn't so. She said it could be if he would do the having. Macey
said children were like socks—you couldn't have too many and if you
did you could have a rummage sale with the surplus—but he wondered
if they hadn't started right late. Milo said, "No. I timed it beautiful. He
is coming just in time for the pageant." (This year is Sissie's turn to be
Mary and Milo keeps saying she can use their boy for Jesus.) But Sissie
said, "Kiss my foot. You are not timing this baby and don't be a fool
about Christmas. Even if I have this baby and am well enough to be
Mary, I am not taking it out in the December night at age six weeks to
be Baby Jesus or anybody else." Macey looked back at her and said,
"Smile, honey. You haven't got nothing to worry about. You are built
very much like Marise and Marise has babies like a Indian-lady." I had
been watching Sissie through the whole discussion and I knew the end
of the rope was coming soon. Well it came right then—Sissie stood up
quicker than she had done anything for weeks and said, "I may be big as
a house but Marise Gupton is one thing I am not" and then walked out
and on upstairs before any of us could stop her, stairs being the last
thing she should have climbed. Mama and Milo went up behind her,
leaving me and Baby Sister alone with the Guptons to smooth over
Sissie's performance. I said a few excusing things such as "Poor Sissie,
her nerves are skinned bare with waiting" but my heart wasn't in it and
naturally Macey felt uneasy at touching off the scene. He sat there pecking his teeth and listening to hear Sissie bellow and Arnold just rocked
faster and faster till he rocked up nerve to say he was sleepy and how
come they didn't leave? Macey looked like he wanted to—by the nearest
exit—but he felt compelled to stay till somebody came down and
reported on Sissie so we sat on in silence till Milo arrived to say she was
resting though not speaking, which would do her good, and for everybody to sit still and we could play a little Setback. Everybody sat and
Milo was getting out the card table when Mama came in. He asked her,
"Has she had it?" Mama took a look at the card table and said, "No
and playing cards under her isn't going to make it come easier." But
Milo went on setting up the table and then looked round. I could see
right away what the next problem would be. Milo said, "Arnold, can

you play?" Arnold said "Yes" and Milo said, "Who is going to hold the
fourth hand?" Baby Sister volunteered but Mama said, "No ma'm. Sit
still." So Milo looked at me and rather than let the evening fall through
any further, I said I would. Well we played. Milo and I were partners
against the Guptons and I wish you could have seen us. Arnold cheated
like we were playing for lives which of course meant they won time after
time but that didn't matter. We were just helping the clock go round and
when it had gone to about 9:30, I could see Milo was tired of playing.
He asked Mama (who had sat there and smiled at Arnold's cheating
like it was a judgment on us all) if she wasn't planning to serve something to our company? She said there wasn't a thing but more Jello
though it would be a different flavor. Arnold asked if she had a few cold
biscuits and some syrup but there wasn't a biscuit in the house so everybody took Jello and just as we started eating, Macey said we ought to get
back to deciding on Mr. Isaac's gift. Milo said, "First let me just see does
Sissie want some of this" and went to the foot of the steps and hollered
to her. We all listened and there was no answer so Milo, instead of
climbing the stairs like a human being, said louder, "Sissie, do you
want to come down and eat some nice Jello with us?" From behind
closed doors, Sissie said "No"—loud. Milo turned round to rejoin us
but just as he stepped in the door, Sissie followed her "No" with a yell
that turned into "Mama"—she mostly calls Mama Mrs. Mustian. Milo
went white and said "Mama, you go." Mama said "Come on, Rosa"
and I followed her, knowing I could be no help. Sissie was lying there
scared to death and crying easy so as not to upset whatever would happen next. Mama sat down by her and started soothing and told me to
call Dr. Sledge and tell him the waters had broke (if you know what
that means). I went down to call and Milo was waiting at the steps to
know was Sissie dead. I told him live and then called Dr. Sledge and
told him what Mama said. He asked me alot of questions but I couldn't
answer any of them and he said in that case, he would be out as soon as
he could. Milo had gone upstairs while I was on the phone and when I
hung up, Macey was standing behind me. He had heard what I said
and just wanted to tell me it was nothing to worry about. I said I was
glad to hear it and hoped everything would be over soon, meaning that
as a hint for him and Arnold to leave, but he said, "Sometimes it don't

come for a day or so after this"—and walked back in the living room to
wait for Milo. I knew I would be all thumbs upstairs so I followed
Macey and took a seat. Macey of course wanted to discuss having
babies and how Marise did it but Baby Sister was right there on the
piano bench which put a damper on him. It wasn't till he gave up trying
though that we all missed Arnold. He was gone from his rocker and
didn't answer when Macey called his name so Macey went looking for
him and came back in a little to say he was sitting out in their truck in
the cold—scared and saying he wouldn't come back in. "He'll freeze
solid out there," I said and Macey said, "Yes I'm fixing to take him home
but I'll come right back in case you all need any help from an Old
Hand." There was nothing to say but "All right." Macey was looking forward to a Setting-Up more than I was, especially as I was the one person
present who had to work Saturday morning but anyhow he went on off
to put Arnold to sleep and Baby Sister said why didn't she and I make
some candy so we did that—fudge, and before we got it in the refrigerator, Dr. Sledge came. He examined Sissie and said exactly what Macey
had said—nothing bad had happened and things had more or less
started but they might not end for a day or more. He sat awhile with
Sissie to ease her mind. Then he came down and we gave him some of
our candy and while he was eating it, Macey returned, bringing best
wishes from Marise. Dr. Sledge asked Macey what was he doing here
and Macey said he had come for the Setting-Up. Dr. Sledge said, "I
thought you had enough of those at your place" and he and Macey
commenced expert talk about when it would come. Dr. Sledge said he
had no idea it would be before morning and he would just have to leave
and see a few people that were bad off. Then he asked me to step out
and call Milo and when Milo came down, he repeated all that to him.
Milo of course wasn't happy at him leaving but Dr. Sledge said there
wasn't a thing he could do for Sissie till pains started and when they
did, there would be plenty of time for him to get here. So Milo resigned
himself and said, "Macey, you'll stay with me, won't you?" Macey said
"Sure" and Dr. Sledge went up to say a few soothing things to Sissie
before he left. I wish he had said a few more to Milo because the minute
he walked out the door, Milo commenced twitching—and not a thing to
worry about with Sissie resting easy and Mama sitting beside her, know-

ing all she knew about babies—but he got worse and worse till Macey
said, "What we ought to do is just get Mary Sutton to come spend the
night." (She has midwifed all her life and helped all of us get born.)
That suited Milo fine so he and Macey took off by foot to get Mary, not
saying a word to Mama or Sissie. Things were quiet the whole long time
they were gone but when they came back, Mary was with them and she
had brought Mildred's baby with her (Estelle not being home to keep
him). She had put blankets in a cardboard box and laid him in that
and when she got to our place, she set the box down near the woodstove
in the kitchen and went upstairs to see Sissie. Just having Mary in
the house seemed to settle Milo's nerves and he and Macey took seats in
the living room and went on talking. Baby Sister and I stayed in the
kitchen. By then it was nearly midnight and things being so relieved
with Mary here, I was thinking mostly of how soon working time would
come and Baby Sister was getting wall-eyed from lack of sleep so I
told her to go on in Mama's room and stretch out there and I would join
her in a little. (She was scared of going upstairs where Sissie was.) She
asked me to wake her up when it came which I promised to do and then
she went, leaving me in the kitchen with nothing but Mildred's baby
and him doing nothing but breathing in his sleep, laid back in his box,
the color of Mildred. (They are just calling him Sledge. I still haven't
heard what the last name is, if any.) And sitting at the kitchen table
with the room so warm and no noise but what laughing came through
from Milo and Macey, I nodded off and didn't wake up till after 2 a.m.
when Mary tipped in to feed Sledge. He hadn't cried. She had just
waked him up and given him the bottle and he was half-done when I
came to. Mary said Sissie was asleep and Milo and Macey were nodding in the living room so why didn't I go on to bed? I watched her put
Sledge down and then I went in Mama's room with Baby Sister and
slept like death till Mama shook me at 6:30. She beckoned me into the
kitchen and asked me was I going to work? I said, "Not if you need me
here" and she said there wouldn't be a thing I could do now that Mary
was here so I told her to stretch out by Baby Sister and gather her
strength (she hadn't shut her eyes all night) and then I tipped upstairs
to dress, past Milo and Macey who were nodding stiff-necked in chairs,
but when I came down again, Mama was frying me some breakfast. I

wasn't hungry but I didn't mention it. It would have just started Mama
arguing and waked up Sledge. He was sleeping sound when I left—the
picture of Mildred, already the picture—and it wasn't till I left that I
knew how glad I was to leave and not have to sit there all day, waiting
for Sissie to go off like a dynamite cap. Well I worked hard through the
morning and didn't get to call up home till lunch. Baby Sister answered
and said there was no news yet and none in sight so I didn't call again
but waited till I could get home and see for myself and when Mr. Cole-
man let me out on the road at six, I could see there was some sort of news
to hear as every light in the house was burning and every chimney smoking and Dr. Sledge's car was there and when I got closer I could see the
fire from one cigarette on the porch. It was Milo standing in the cold. I
walked up to him and said, "What is the news?" He said, "All I know is,
it started at one o'clock and hasn't got no better since." It is 9:20 p.m. as
I am writing this sentence and things have gotten worse and worse with
Sissie yelling closer and closer together till now I don't know when she
finds time to breathe. It seems alot to ask her to bear, her being a raw
nerve all her life. And it isn't easy on any of us—not now it isn't.
Mama and Mary—at least they are upstairs with the doctor working
but Baby Sister and I are just sitting here in the kitchen and have been
since six. Nobody wanted a mouthful to eat so I have been writing on
and on to you and Baby Sister has been rocking Mildred's baby and
singing him songs like he was hers (I know she wishes he was and the
way he lets her handle him, maybe he wishes so too) and Milo just pen-
etrates back and forth through the house—and out in the yard when
the yelling gets extra bad. (He has always said, nothing happens to people that they haven't asked for. Well he asked for a boy but I don't guess
he bargained for so much noise.) Awhile ago he asked me what would
calm nerves. I told him a dose of ammonia but he took camphor and got
no relief and has gone back out somewhere. I am wishing Macey was
here with him (he has gone to Raleigh for Mr. Isaac's mystery-gift)
because Milo is the one with the burden now. Mama is pouring the
ether to Sissie so fast she doesn't know what is happening. I don't
guess she does though the way she sounds through plaster walls lets
everybody know she is not having fun. Even Mildred's baby can
hear her. He is tuning up to cry this minute, meaning hunger, so I will

stop and fix his milk. Baby Sister drops him like a hot potato when he cries.

It is later now and right much has happened since I broke off. The main thing is, I was holding Sledge when Mama came down to find Milo. I hadn't seen Mama since breakfast but I knew the worst right away. I said he was outdoors so she stepped to the porch and called him. He must have come running because I could hear him panting in the hall. Mama told him, "It never even breathed" and he broke down. Then they went up to Sissie but I couldn't follow—mostly because I had Sledge still to feed. He seems to take to me now so I stuck with him. He is the picture of Mildred. But I told you that.

This means I won't be accepting your Thanksgiving invitation—not that I am needed here but I couldn't leave after this. Things will have to be quiet awhile.

Thank you Wesley, and excuse me now please,

Rosacoke

When the letter was done she felt she had stayed away as long as she could, that her duty was to go upstairs and speak her regrets. She stood and smoothed her hair and rinsed her hands at the sink, but before she went she tipped to the stove to check on Sledge in his box. She reckoned he was asleep, having eaten just lately, but in case he wasn't she stopped where he wouldn't see her. And he wasn't. He was fumbling quietly with his dark hands at his eyes against the light. She stood a long time, watching, trying to picture his face as a boy's or a man's, but his features were closed on themselves like tight brown buds on a mystery-tree in spring. All she could see was Mildred that last cold day in the road, and it seemed to her she was more use here than upstairs talking to people that were each other's comfort so she took Sledge instead and sat back down and laid him in the groove of her lap, hoping she could make him smile one time and then go to sleep. She did a few quiet jokes with her face and hands to please him, but he only stared with his black eyes grave and his lips crouched cautious against her, and soon she gave up trying and commenced to sway her legs and hum low, and he twisted to the left and buried his face in her thigh and slid off to sleep. She waited. Then when it seemed safe she shifted one leg and rolled him back towards her, and he smiled at last as if in his sleep he saw better jokes than what she could offer. But that was all right. That was enough. And she sat still, hearing his steady sighing till she was nodding herself with her hands beneath his head.

Then Mary came to the door. "You done changed your mind about Sledge, ain't you, Miss Rosa?"

"No. He has changed his mind about me."

"Yes'm, he sure is. He don't let many hold him that way. He is a *shoulder* baby." She stepped towards Rosacoke and lowered her voice — "Well, give him here and you go on upstairs. I don't want him keeping you from your folks. Miss Sissie is sleep but Mr. Milo is setting by hisself in the front bedroom."

So Rosacoke passed Sledge to Mary and was almost at the door when the question came to her. "Mary, what is that baby's name? — Mildred's baby."

Mary looked to the box. "I expect it's Ransom, Miss Rosa, but they ain't said nothing about *feeding* him."

Then Rosacoke went out and up the cold stairs, shivering. The door was shut where Sissie was, and she went on to the front room that was Papa's before he died. She knocked lightly there. Somebody made an answering sound and she opened on darkness. (Papa had never let them wire his room for light.) She said, "Who is in here?"

Milo said, "Me and this baby."

She had suspected that. She stood on in the door, seeing nothing, feeling nothing but the warmth of the room leaking past her, and finally she said, "Could I bring you a lamp or something?"

"No."

"Well, I'll be saying good night then, I guess." She stood a little longer, wondering what else she could say to a pitch-dark room. But he hadn't asked for anything else. He hadn't even said "Step in," and anyhow he was *Milo* and she hadn't been close to Milo for years, not since Sissie Abbott took hold and taught him whatever it was that changed him from a serious boy to the fool who sang her the Santa Claus jingle not two weeks ago. Then she closed the door and went to her own room across the hall. She took off her clothes in the dark and stretched out to rest. But she didn't sleep. She heard a man's footsteps leave Sissie's room and go downstairs and a car driving off. That would be Dr. Sledge. Then Mama came out and went to Milo and asked was he setting up all night? He said "Yes" and Mama said, "Son, I have got to rest. How come you don't go set in yonder with Sissie? I'll send Mary in here." Milo said, "Did Sissie tell you to ask me that?" Mama said "Yes" and he said "Get Mary first" so Mama went down and sent Mary up, and then there was the sound of Milo walking past Rosacoke's door towards Sissie Abbott. When Rosacoke had heard that she said to herself, "They will all get over this soon. Wasn't that a child they never saw alive or called by name? It was God's own will and Christmas is coming. Just *sleep*." Then she slept.

Sunday afternoon when it was time, Mama and the preacher were upstairs with Sissie who was not resigned, and Milo was shut in Papa's room. He had been there since Mary left that morning. He had seen two people all day—Mama and Macey Gupton—and he had spoken twice. (When Mama took him breakfast he said, "Get Macey and ask him will he go to Warrenton for the casket." Macey did that and after dinner when Mama had ironed him a shirt and taken in his clothes and asked was he ready, he said "In a little.") But Rosacoke was ready. She had been ready since ten o'clock when Mama came to her in the kitchen and said, "You have got to go speak to Sissie" so she went and just by opening the door, shook Sissie out of sleep. Sissie said, "You woke me up." Rosacoke said, "I am sorry for that too," and Sissie cried, not hiding her face but staring at the ceiling. Rosacoke had seen Sissie do a number of things but not cry silent so she went to the steps and called Mama. Then she went to her room and dressed in what black she had and waited for three o'clock.

At three she stepped on the porch to make a last arrangement with Macey who stood in the yard. She walked to the steps and said, "Macey, will you carry the casket?" He said that would be an honor but was Milo ready? She said "I hope so" and Macey laid his hat on the steps and went towards the door but was stopped by the preacher coming out and Baby Sister and Milo and, behind them, Mama who would stay with Sissie. (None of Sissie's people knew. It was how she wanted it.) Milo had the casket in his arms. It looked about the size of a package you could mail.

Macey said, "Milo, let Macey tote that."

But Milo said, "Thank you, no. I will," and they went to the car. Milo and the preacher sat in back. Rosacoke and Baby Sister sat in front with Macey who would drive.

Macey said "Ready?"

Milo said "Yes" and they cranked up and rolled to the road and turned right. Just before the house passed out of sight, Rosacoke looked back, and Mama still stood in the door, her black dress against the black hall behind her, and her white arms bare, surely cold. Rosacoke turned to the road and knowing they would ride in silence, chose that sight of Mama to fill her mind through the slow half-mile to Mr. Isaac's when she looked again—at the day this time. She thought, "It is the kind of day nobody wanted"—still and gray and low but so clear the wrenched, bare cherries looked gouged on the pond with some hard point—and she wondered, "Does Mr. Isaac know of this?" But she didn't speak aloud—there was nothing he could do with the news—so they passed him too, and none of them looked at each other, and since the pines were next, Rosacoke didn't think again but watched the road. A wind began and kept up the rest of the way—nothing serious but strong enough to twist little cones of dust in gullies and when they could see Delight, to sway Landon Allgood, the one person waiting, black by the grave he had dug.

Nobody else came. Nobody else knew (except what Negroes passed on the road and stared), and there was nothing but a few words said at the grave. What could they say but his name (which was Horatio Mustian the third)? Then Milo and Macey did the lowering. Landon put on his cap and came forward to shovel, giving off sweet paregoric like his natural scent, and they all headed back for the car—the men and Baby Sister first and Rosacoke falling in last. But before she had gone ten feet, Landon said, "Miss Rosa"—she stopped and he took off his cap—"I am mighty sorry for you."

She studied him a moment, wondering what he thought he was burying. She pointed half behind her and said, "It was *Milo's* boy."

"Yes'm," Landon said and stepped back to his work, and she went on to the others and they went home. Nobody had cried and what Rosacoke had noticed most was the new red dirt Landon threw on her father to fill his sinking.

And nobody cried riding home or during the supper they ate without speaking or, after Milo went up to Sissie (to sleep on a cot by her bed), during the long evening in the front room with Mama writing Rato the news and Baby Sister acting her paper dolls through flesh-and-blood stories till finally they all turned in. So Monday, seeing no real job at home, Rosacoke went to work and sent Wesley her long letter by Special Delivery without even looking to know what it said, knowing she hadn't faced up to Wesley yet—what he had done and wanted to do—but having in the death for awhile one thing big enough to hold her mind off whatever troubles she had. And the death worked in her like a drug, not making her sad but numbing the day while she worked and the cold ride home that night.

She was late getting home Tuesday night. It had rained all morning and in the afternoon turned cold, and the roads froze too slick for speed. It was nearly six-thirty when she walked up the yard to the house, and Mama met her at the door, saying, "Where have you been? You are too late now and I wish you had never worked today. Milo has broke our hearts. Directly you left this morning he drove off. He didn't say a word about where, and he left me with every bit of Sissie to handle and me thinking all day long he had gone off somewhere drinking like your Daddy. Well, nobody here laid eyes on him till a hour ago when he come in so quiet I didn't hear him. I was cooking our supper but Baby Sister was in the front room yonder. She had come home from school and dragged out some naked baby doll and was mothering that—singing to it. He went in there and just set by the fire. In a little Baby Sister took it in her head to go upstairs and ask Sissie could she have a few clothes to dress up that naked doll. She didn't mean harm but Sissie started crying and called for me. I didn't hear her but Milo did and tore upstairs, and when he saw the trouble, he grabbed up all the baby clothes he could find and said he couldn't pass another night with them things here and was taking them to Mildred Sutton's baby. Sissie couldn't stop him so she hollered, 'Yes, take every *stitch*. They are no use to me no more. The woman you get to have your other babies can buy her own mess or let all ten run naked.' Well, I heard *that* and caught Milo at the door and told him them things was too little for Sledge but I couldn't stop him. He was gone. He is still gone and hasn't eat a mouthful this whole day, and I don't know is he drinking or not."

Rosacoke said, "Give me the flashlight and I will go find him."

"I can't let you go in the dark," Mama said. "I was just getting ready to call up Macey and ask him to go."

But Rosacoke said, "Don't call in the Guptons for any more Mustian business." So Mama gave her the flashlight, and she went out towards Mary's. It was colder already and the sky was clouded. What moon there would be hadn't risen, but as long as she walked through open fields, she could see without light, and when she came to the black pines, she tried to walk in darkness—she knew every inch of the way and she wasn't scared—but the path was loud with frozen leaves and a briar caught at her leg so she switched on the light and walked in its yellow circle till she came out at Mary's. The only light at Mary's was shining from the kitchen where an oil lamp burned. Rosacoke flashed her beam round the yard to check for the turkey that was roosting high. Then she went to the front and knocked.

Mary came with a lamp and said, "Miss Rosa, it's *you*" and stepped on the porch and shut the door. "Miss Rosa, he is here and I think he is better now, but when he come I didn't know *what* would happen. He must have crept in while I was back in the kitchen because when I heard a noise in the front room and went to the door to see, he was *there*, just standing over Mildred's baby, staring down wild at all them clothes he had throwed on the bed. Child, I thought he was crazy, and I didn't do nothing but tip on back to the kitchen and get me a knife. I flung open that kitchen door, and I said, 'Sweet Jesus, come in here and help me.' Then I went back to do my duty, but he had eased and looked like hisself and was setting down by that baby, and when I said 'Good evening,' he just said, 'Mary, please cook me some eggs.' I said, 'Yessir, Mr. Milo, and you come talk to me while I fix them,' and he is eating right now in the kitchen."

"Well, let me go see him."

"Yes'm, but Miss Rosa, is he *give* us all them clothes?"

"They are his to give."

"Yes'm," Mary said and led her in. The first thing the lamp struck was Sledge, lying back amongst his new clothes.

Rosacoke said, "Ain't it too cold for him, Mary?"

Mary said, "I reckon it is" but kept on towards the kitchen and opened the door. The warm air met them and Mary said, "Look, Mr. Milo, we got us some company."

Milo looked up and said "Yes" and ate another mouthful and then said "Sit down, Rosa" like the house was his.

Mary said, "Yes, Miss Rosa, let me cook your supper."

Rosacoke said no, she wouldn't eat, but she took the other chair at the table, facing Milo with only a lamp between them, and Mary left. Milo didn't speak again or look up—just ate—and Rosacoke was quiet too. But she watched him (what she could see in the warm lamp-light—his forehead pale as hers though he spent every day in the weather and his eyes like hers but his hair the color that, now she noticed, was one more thing their father had left)—and with all his three days' misery, he seemed for the only time in years like the first Milo she had run after, hundreds of miles through Mr. Isaac's woods, laughing, before Sissie Abbot gave him secrets, before he got his driving license even, when his beard was just arriving and they would sleep together in the same big bed if company came and she would rest easy all night and wake before sunup and turn towards Milo beside her and wait till the first gray light carved out his face on the pillow and then woke up the birds that sang. Still it *wasn't* that first Milo—not after these days—but something changed, and she didn't know to what nor what new secret he kept there in his misery. But she had sat long enough, and she thought she should speak. She said, "Milo, if you want me to—"

He broke her off—"I am not taking them clothes back."

"Milo," she said, "them clothes are yours to give, and I didn't walk all this way to get them back."

Milo looked up. He had finished eating. "Well, why *are* you here?"

"I just came to say that if you want me to—" But she stopped again and frowned at the opening door where Mary stood with Sledge in her arms, the image of Mildred and awake.

Mary didn't see the frown. "You all just go on talking," she said. "It's chilly in yonder so I'll feed him where it's warm if Mr. Milo don't mind."

Rosacoke looked to Milo, thinking this was more than he would bear. But Milo said "Go ahead" and watched Mary walk to the stove and begin heating milk.

Rosacoke thought, "He is better than I reckoned" and stretched out her arms and said, "Mary, let me feed him. He has taken to me lately."

Mary said "All right" and came on to hand him over, but Milo shoved back his chair and stood and laid about a dollar on the table and said, "I got to go. Rosa, are you coming with me?"

Rosacoke put down her arms. "I'm coming," she said, still looking at Sledge and Mary and seeing why Milo had to leave. Then she stood too.

In the door Milo turned—"I'm much obliged, Mary. That money is for my supper."

Mary said, "You paid for them eggs many times with that stack of clothes but we thank you, sir" and Milo left.

Rosacoke said, "Excuse me rushing, Mary."

And Mary said, "Go where you are needed."

So Rosacoke followed Milo. He was walking slow and she caught him just in the pines and switched on her light to help him see, but he speeded up and walked six feet ahead till they came to the field of cotton stalks. From there they could see the house and the light where Sissie was. Milo stopped and turned on Rosacoke. She switched off her light, knowing he spoke best in the dark, and he said, "What were you trying to tell me?"

"—That I will lay out of work if you want company."

"That would be mighty nice," he said and took a few steps towards Sissie's light, but before she followed he stopped again and faced her. "Sissie's awake," he said.

She said "Yes" and caught her breath to say what she knew was her duty—to ease him and lead him home—but in what moon there was, he was still too nearly that first Milo so she waited.

He waited too but when he spoke he said, "Go in the house to

Sissie and Mama and say Milo is out yonder but he ain't coming in unless they give their word not to speak about clothes or baby again."

She said she would—it was all she could say, all he asked for—and went to tell Mama and Sissie. Mama said, "This house is one-third his. Tell him to just come on and rest," and Sissie said, "Yes do, but the baby was one-half mine."

Rosacoke went back and signaled from the porch with her light. Milo came on and when he got to the steps, she said, "They say come in but Milo, the baby was one-half Sissie's."

"Making the other half Milo's," he said and stood in the dark, not climbing the steps. Then he said, "Did Sissie tell you to say that?"

"Yes."

"But you didn't have to, did you?"

She couldn't answer that and he walked by her up the steps and into the house. She went in a little later and heard him in Mama's room. He was meaning to sleep there without saying good night to Mama and Sissie upstairs. Rosacoke went to the door—he had shut the door—and said through it, "I'll see you in the morning, hear?"

In awhile he said "O.K."

She went up and stopped at Sissie's door and told them he was home safe and sleeping downstairs and that she wasn't working tomorrow. Then she went to her own dark room in hopes of sleep. But she lay in the cold awake, not feeling Sissie in the next room awake—seeing only Milo's face at Mary's and hearing him break down Saturday night in the hall. She heard him over and over—*Milo* who was asking only her to share his burden—and she pictured the baby (that she never saw alive or called by name) till the baby was almost hers. Then the burden bore down on her hot through the dark. She took it and cried and it smothered her to sleep.

She slept till somebody's hand woke her in the clear early morning. It was Mama bending over and whispering fast, "Get up. Milo is up already and wanting to go. He wouldn't eat with me and Baby Sister but said he would wait in the yard for you so come on and feed him." Rosacoke raised up and stared out the window. He was standing halfway to the road with his back to the house, but the day was so bright against him she could see his hands at his sides that opened and shut on themselves and, beyond him, one white sycamore straight as diving. She threw back the cover but Mama said, "Let me say one thing—Sissie don't know I am speaking to you and wouldn't want me to if she did, but I have sat by her three whole days, and I know how she feels." Rosacoke stared on at the yard. "He is your brother, I know—he is also *my* oldest boy—but that don't make him ours. He belongs to Sissie Abbott, like it or not, and what has he said to her since the funeral except 'Good night'?"

"What are you asking me?"

"I don't know what to ask you. If it was just me I wouldn't say nothing but, 'Ride with him to Atlanta, *Georgia* if he wants to, just don't let him take up drinking'—he is too close kin to his Daddy for that—but Rosa, there is Sissie lying yonder—" She whispered that but she pointed to the far wall.

Rosacoke looked to the wall with sudden fear as if Sissie herself had broke through plaster and stood before them. She said, "Listen here, Mama. Milo is an adult man that is old enough to know his mind. He has called on me for help. He may *be* Sissie's but Sissie can't help him flat on her back, and anyhow I have known him a good deal longer than Sissie Abbott so what do you want me to do?— say 'No' when he needs company?"

Mama only said, "Go with him today if he wants to go but keep him off liquor, and if there comes a time—Rosa, *make* a time—say to him, 'Milo, Sissie needs you bad.' "

Rosacoke nodded to make Mama leave. Then she dressed and went down past Sissie's shut door. She called up the man she worked for and asked to have a few days off because of death. He of course said "Yes" but hoped she could come back soon. She said she would try but things were in right bad shape. That left her free for Milo to use however he needed so she went to the door and called his name. He turned where he was—just his face—and she waved him in, but he stood, his fingers still working at his sides. She waited in the cold and thought, "Mama and Sissie are upstairs listening, and now maybe he won't come after what I said last night." Then she went to the kitchen and began cooking on faith, and soon he was there, stopped in the door, looking to test her face. She knew and turned full to him—the way he looked had lasted the night—and said "Come in."

He came and sat quiet at the table while she cooked, and they ate in quiet till he said, "Did you sleep good?"

"It took awhile but yes, I managed all right."

"That's good"—he stood and went to the window—"because I was thinking we could take us a trip today, it being so bright."

"Where to?"

"Well, if we went to Raleigh, we could get Mr. Isaac's Christmas candy."

Before she could answer, Mama's footsteps passed in the hall overhead so she said, "Don't you reckon we ought to stay closer-by than Raleigh?"

He turned to her. "Look—are you sticking with me or not?"

She looked and said "Yes."

"Let's go then."

She scraped their dishes and left them in the sink and said, "I'll get my coat."

"Where from?"

"My room."

"All right, but come straight back."

She went up and got it and came down quiet past Sissie's door. Milo was waiting in the hall, and they went towards the front together. But Rosacoke stopped in the door. "Don't you reckon we ought to say where we are going?"

"You ain't expecting no Registered Mail, are you?"

"No."

"Then let's go."

They went through the yard with their backs to the house, not speaking, and just at the car they heard a knock behind them. Milo didn't wait but Rosacoke turned to the house, knowing where to look, and there was Mama in the window of Papa's old room upstairs. She hadn't raised the glass to speak and she didn't knock twice, but her knuckle rested on the pane it had struck. Rosacoke thought of the dishes she had left and opened her mouth to explain, but Milo cranked up and when Mama saw the smoke of his exhaust, she nodded so Rosacoke just gave a little wave towards the house. Then she got in and they rolled down to the road and, still quiet, headed left for the paving and the store. Milo stopped at the store. There was nobody in sight but some trucks were already there. He said, "Step in please and get the mail." She went, seeing he didn't want to answer folks' questions, and the only letter was one that had just then come from Norfolk. She took it to the car, and Milo drove off while she read to herself,

November 18

Dear Rosa,

I just got home from work and found your letter lying on my floor with them Special Delivery stamps all over it. They really had me scared for a minute! But I have recovered and want to say I was mighty sorry to hear about Milo and Sissie's bad luck. I had been looking forward to seeing their baby at Christmas as Milo told me last summer it would come in time to be in the show at Delight and him and me counted on being Wise Men with Rato if he comes home. Maybe you will think it is a little funny that I am not sending Milo a sympathy card or anything and am just writing to you but you never said what you meant that night about Milo being mad at me so I don't know where I stand and sure don't know why he was mad unless he has X-ray vision through trees at night. Anyhow I have always thought a whole lot of Milo and his foolishness and I hope whatever he was holding against me has blown over and that you will pass my sympathy on to him and Sissie. Sissie must be extra-let-down, toting it through all that hot weather so tell her too I am sorry.

I am also sorry you won't be coming for Thanksgiving with me and my friends because I reckon what you need more than anything now is a little cheering up but I see what you mean about staying home awhile till the coast is clear. When it is though and you feel the need of a change, come on up here. Just give me fair warning! And speaking of the coast being clear—I hope you aren't having any more old or new worries about our deer hunt and that the coast is all clear there too. Is it? Time enough has passed so it ought to be. I am stopping now to get this on the train.

Good night Rosa from your friend,
Wesley

She folded it carefully and thinking she would never read it again, sealed the flap with what glue was left. Then she laid it in her lap with

the writing down and looked at the flat road before them. She didn't
know what she had read. Her mind was like a bowl brimmed with one
numbing thing—Milo's burden he had asked her to share—and what
Wesley said was oil on the surface of that, waiting. But looking ahead
she could feel Milo throw curious looks towards her so to stave off questions, she faced the window at her right, and if it was the letter Milo
wondered about, he took her meaning and drove on quietly till he had
to speak—"Do you reckon Sissie meant what she said last night?"

"I wasn't there to hear her."

He waited almost a mile to answer. "She said I could get me somebody else to take my children from now-on-out. Reckon she meant that?"

"I can't speak for Sissie," she said, still turned to the window.

"Well, thank you ma'm for trying," he said, but he left her alone with
her burden, whatever it was, while he went on, watching both sides of
the road for anything cheerful to mention. It took awhile to find such
a thing, but when he did he took the chance and pointed past
Rosacoke's face to the window—"Have you eat any pecans this year?"

She said "No," not seeing.

"I thought you was a great nut collector." He slowed down a little.

"That was in olden times."

"Well, we can get us some right now." He stopped on the shoulder
of the road and said "See yonder?"

She looked gradually, at nothing strange, at things she had passed
every November of her life and not seen, things that had waited—the
rusty bank thrown up by the road and gullied by rain and, beyond in
the sun, a prostrate field where nothing stood straight, only corn with
unused ears black from frost and stalks exhausted the color of broomstraw, beat to the ground as if boys had swarmed through with sickles,
hacking, and farther back, one mule still where he stood except for
his breath wreathing white on the bark of a tree that rose up over him
straight and forked into limbs with nuts by the hundred and twitched
on the sky like nerves because a boy stood in the fork in blue overalls
and rocked. Then Wesley's meaning sunk through her mind like lead.

But before she could swallow her awful gorge and speak, Milo
jerked at her arm and said, "Come help me shake down some pecans."

"Milo, we better go home."

"What's the trouble?"

"Nothing. You ought to be home with Sissie."

"Sissie don't want to see me now, and Rosa, you said you was sticking with me."

She turned from the window to her lap, but the letter was there so she faced Milo suddenly—that first Milo, not changed. "I ain't studying Sissie, Milo. Take me *home*." He didn't answer that and with nowhere else to hide her face, she turned to the window again and the boy rocking yonder in the tree, and Milo took her home round miles of deadly curves not slowing once, staring only forward in mystery and anger with not one word for Rosacoke who could feel Wesley's burden grow in her every inch of the way, nameless and blind.

At home Milo stopped sudden in the road, and the tan dust from his wheels rolled past them. Rosacoke sat for a moment, facing the house but not seeing where they were, and Milo didn't move to help her out. He sat with his feet nervous on the gas and his hand on the gearshift and his eyes forward, and when he had waited sufficient, he said "You are home."

She looked and said, "I am home" but not as if being home was a comfort. Then she opened her door and left him, and before she could get through the yard to the porch, he had turned and roared off the way they came. But she didn't see him go or hear his noise. She was listening to hear some sound inside her maybe, but all she could hear was her feet in the crust of the ground and—when she went in and climbed the steps easy, hoping to pass unnoticed—the thud of her heart in her ears like wet dirt slapped with a spade.

Mama stood ready at the top by Sissie's door. "Where is Milo?"

Rosacoke looked behind her and pointed with the letter in her hand as if he was there on the steps. "Gone to Raleigh—to get Mr. Isaac some candy."

"I thought you was riding with him."

"No'm, he just took me to the post office."

"You *said* you was riding with him, didn't you?"

"Mama, *Milo* is all right. Just let me go."

"Are you sick or something?"

"I'm not feeling *good*."

"Well, do you want a aspirin?"

"I don't want nothing but quiet, thank you, ma'm," and she went to her room and shut herself in and sat on the bed and not taking off her coat, said to herself, "I have asked time off for death so I can't work today. I have got to just sit here and think." But when she had closed her eyes, she was seized by a shaking that started at the back of her neck and flushed down through her. At first she thought, "I will build me a fire," but the shaking went on and she dug both hands in her thighs and clenched her jaws and thought, "The room is not this cold," but that didn't calm her so she slackened her jaws and gave in to it and it rattled her teeth and passed on off.

When she was steady again she opened her eyes on the mantel and the picture there of her father and not having thought, took paper and pencil and wrote,

Dear Wesley,

No it is not clear—the coast you are talking about—and if you are a human being you will come here now and do your duty.

But she couldn't say more than that. She couldn't even say that and be sure, not yet. So she waited, managing in desperation to sleep through most of the day—through Mama peeping in to check and Dr. Sledge's visit to Sissie and what little cooking was done, waking three or four times and lifting the shade to stare across the road at naked trees but forcing herself unconscious again till finally at night a car turned in and woke her and she watched Milo come through the dark with candy in his hand and heard him climb to Sissie and say good evening to Sissie and Mama and sit with them, not speaking, and then in a little heard Mama step out and shut their door and Sissie say something Rosacoke couldn't hear and Milo answer her low and them talk on like that till they faded out and Rosacoke thought, "I have failed Milo and drove him back on Sissie, and they have gone to sleep"—which was somewhere *she* didn't go that night again.

Or many other nights that came after, though she took any chance to tire herself—working through weekdays hard as she could (working

Thanksgiving at her own request) and in evenings at home, washing clothes, for instance, that were clean already and ironing till everybody but Mama was asleep and she would appear in her nightgown to say "Rosacoke, that's enough," and Rosacoke would climb to lie-out one more night between cold sheets with nothing but black ceiling to look towards or if there was moon, its glare on the floor boards and the unlit tin stove and the mantel and with nothing to hear but, inside her chest like her own fierce pulse, the thoughts she could speak to nobody—not to Mama or Baby Sister or her own dark walls (for fear Sissie Abbott next door might know) or even by mail to Wesley until she was sure.

It was a month's time and a Sunday afternoon before she was sure. Milo had carried Mama and Baby Sister to Delight to make plans for the Christmas pageant, leaving only Sissie and Rosacoke at home. Rosacoke had kept up a fire in her room most of the day and stayed there, but about five o'clock she thought of Sissie downstairs alone and felt guilty and went down to her. Sissie was shut in the front room with the stove broiling high, and when Rosacoke came in she barely spoke, just went on flipping some magazine to the end. Rosacoke commenced reading too but in a little Sissie stood and went to the window and looked at the half-dark and said, "Isn't it time they was home?"

Rosacoke looked out. "I guess it is."

"Wonder what is holding them up?"

Rosacoke said, "I can't imagine." (She knew very well but she wouldn't say.)

"Well, I bet they are trying to find a Mary since I backed out. Your Mama said she didn't see no way to keep from offering it to Willie Duke Aycock when she gets home from Norfolk—unless they call on Marise Gupton and she is pregnant again."

Just to speak, Rosacoke said, "*Willie* will be a sight."

But Sissie took it wrong and turned on her. "You didn't expect *me* to go through with it, did you?"

Rosacoke said "No'm, I didn't" and Sissie cried a little, quiet and turned to the window. She had cried a good deal that month, but Rosacoke still couldn't watch her so she stepped to the hall and took a coat and not saying where she was going, went out and walked down the yard. By the time she reached the road, she had forgot Sissie. She turned right and looking down and saying to herself, "Pretty soon I have got to *think*," she walked on in dust till the dark was broken by the silly hoot of guineas in trees which meant she was at Mr. Isaac's.

She faced the house and the pecan grove, hoping it would give her several minutes' thinking, and yes, there was one light coming dim through curtains from the downstairs parlor. She thought, "They are all in there with the light," and she pictured them—Mr. Isaac nodding already since Sammy had fed him, and Miss Marina queer for the winter, tuned to whatever station came strongest on the radio, and Sammy maybe waiting for word to take Mr. Isaac in his arms and put him to bed—and when she had finished with them, she walked on another little way before the glow of car lights showed beyond the bend in the road. That would be Milo and Mama so she ran off the road down a slope, and when the car had passed and dust had sifted back over her, the guineas broke in again. She looked towards their noise—she was almost at the pond—and behind the pond in trees, she could just make them out on the sky, huddled in black knots from the cold. She wondered what was after them before real night and for something to do, went on in hopes of finding the trouble. She stopped at the pond. She had not really seen it since summer drought—not close—and she walked out on the short pier, her feet on the boards sounding far. By what light was left she could only see that the pond had filled its banks with recent rain and swamped the rotten boat staked by the pier and that it was gray, but the guineas kept up their noise, and Rosacoke said to herself, "It must be a hawk that is troubling them."

Then the weight of her own trouble spewed hot up through her chest and throat into her mouth. She gripped hard against it but it prized her teeth open and forced her to say out loud at last, "What am I going to do?" No answer came so she shut her eyes and, locked and blind, brought up in a rush, "Wesley Beavers tinkered with me six long years, wanting nothing but his pleasure, and when he finally took it dishonest and collected the sight of me in a broomstraw field, giving all I had, to mix in his mind with the sight of every cheap woman that has said 'Yes' to him, what did he hand me in return but this new burden that he knows nothing about? And if he turns up home for Christmas, won't he count on having me time and again, free as water? And if I was to tell him the trouble he has put me in, wouldn't he just sneak off to Norfolk by night and rejoin the Navy and sail for—Japan—and leave me not one soul to speak to and nothing to do but bow my head and sit home with Sissie Abbott staring and Mama maybe crying out of sight and Baby Sister playing her flesh-and-blood games and Milo joking to cheer me up while I wait for this child to take its time and come, bearing Wesley's face and ways but not his name?" Then she looked to the trees across the pond and took breath and said again, "What must I do?"

Like an answer, a piece of yellow light showed slowly in the trees near the ground, moving towards her. Against the black she couldn't see what made the light or was bringing it, but by its color and swing, she guessed it was a lantern, and nobody toting a lantern was up to mischief so she stood on and soon heard feet in the leaves. When the light had reached the far edge of the pond, whoever held it stopped for a little and then said gently across the water, "Who is that yonder on the pier?" It was Sammy Ransom's voice.

"Nobody but Rosacoke, Sammy."

"Good evening, Miss Rosa. I'll come speak to you."

He walked round the pond to where she waited and set his lantern on the pier. Its warm light struck along the barrel of the gun he held. "What you fishing for here so late?"

"Nothing much. I was just walking on the road and heard the guineas fussing and came down here to investigate."

"Yes, ma'm. That's what I was just now doing myself. Miss Marina heard them in the house and sent me out here, saying it was a hawk."

"That's what I thought."

"No ma'm. Most hawks is sleep by now. I don't know what ails them fool guineas. Just old age, I reckon."

"How is Mr. Isaac, Sammy?"

"Not doing so good, Miss Rosa. Look like it's his mind now. He just rambles round inside hisself and don't know who me and Miss Marina *is* half the time."

"Do you reckon he can go to Delight next Sunday for the pageant?"

"Yes ma'm. If he live."

"Well, they are planning to give him a present."

"Yes ma'm. What sort of present?"

"A rolling chair, I believe."

"He don't need no rolling chair long as Sammy's around."

"I know that but Macey Gupton was the buyer."

"Yes ma'm. Well, we'll be there to get it if the Lord be willing."
Then he thought to say, "Are you in the show this time, Miss Rosa?"

"No, not me."

"I remembers you from last year. Reckon will Mr. Wesley be in it
again?"

"I don't know, Sammy. I don't even know if he is coming home."

"Don't you? Miss Rosa, I thought it was near-about time for you all
to get married."

"No."

"Well, when is your plans for?"

"There are not any plans."

"Lord, Miss Rosa, I thought you had a *good* hold of him."

She waited in silence for the answer to give him, trusting it would
come directly. But no answer came. She could not know yet how his
one word *hold* had struck her mind dumb or what it would show her,
in time. She could only say to herself, "I have known Sammy Ransom
all my life—he has played baseball on our team—so I know he meant
no harm by that."

And to save her from speaking at all, a door slammed up at the
house. They looked and there stood Miss Marina in the back-porch
light, facing them. She could not see the lantern, but she beckoned
now and then with her arm, and Sammy said, "Miss Rosa, I would
ride you home, but you see they need me yonder." Rosacoke nodded
and he took the lantern and said "Good night" and started for the
house. She watched him go five yards, his right side in warm light
and the shotgun dark on the left, and she thought for the first time in
her life, "I cannot walk home in this dark" so she called out
"Sammy—" not knowing what she would ask though for months she
had had one thing to ask him.

He turned in his tracks. "Ma'm?"

But she asked what she needed most now. "I was wondering could you spare me that lantern just to get home with?"

"Oh yes'm. You take it."

She went on to him and took it and said, "I am much obliged to you" and headed for the road and home with the lantern in her clenched right hand, swinging close to her side, casting light upwards to her face sometimes and her eyes that didn't really see the road but were staring inward at what Sammy Ransom had showed her (not knowing what he did)—a Sunday evening in early November and her having been led on past a hawk by the curious sound to stop in trees at the edge of a clearing and look across a gap through falling night to Wesley Beavers, locked alone with his own wishes in the music he made on a harp with his mouth and moving hands that caused her to say to herself, "There ought to be some way you could hold him there" and then go forward to try a way.

At home she set the lantern on the porch and went by the kitchen where they all were eating to write this letter in her room—

December 15

Dear Wesley,

I guess you will be wondering when you see this how come I have waited so long and am turning up now so close to Christmas. The reason is, you asked me something I didn't know a sure answer to but now I do. The coast or whatever you want to call it is not clear and I thought you better know that before your Christmas vacation begins in case you want to change your plans some way. (I haven't heard anybody speak of your plans for coming. You say other things in your letters but you don't say you will come.) I mean, maybe you won't want to come here now. Well what I want you to know is, I have thought this all out and I am not glad but I can't blame you if you don't show up, as it is me I hold responsible, and what I have done, I reckon I can live with. That is the news from

Rosacoke

—which she couldn't mail. She waited.

THREE

The Sunday morning before Christmas (Christmas being Wednesday that year), Milo left Mama and Rosacoke cooking dinner and Sissie lying down upstairs and drove to Warrenton to meet Rato who had set out by bus from Fort Sill, Oklahoma two days previous and had ridden upright through four states, barely closing his eyes, to get home—not because after nine months away he wanted so much to see his people or to leave camp awhile and certainly not to be in a Baptist pageant but in order to pass out the gifts he had bought with his own money and to show the family in person his Expert Marksman badge and the uniform he meant to wear for the next thirty years if the U.S. Army would let him.

When Milo was gone Mama set Baby Sister as the lookout. She squatted at the dining-room window and stared to the road through the dull cold day till an hour had passed and dinner was ready on the stove. Then a car came in sight with two people in it and turned towards the house. Baby Sister hollered "Here is Rato!" and threw herself out the door to meet him. Mama left the kitchen just as fast, not putting on a coat, and they got to him halfway down the yard. He had never been much on kissing, but he let Mama touch him on the cheek and gave Baby Sister his free hand to pull towards the door where Rosacoke stood (the other hand held his duffle bag). When he was almost at her, he set down the bag and pulled his hand out of

Baby Sister's and stopped—not looking Rosacoke in the eye but grinning from under his overseas cap (the only clothes on him not wrinkled like paper from the ride).

Rosacoke didn't speak at first or smile. She was studying Rato with something like fear, and thinking back. He had come between her and Milo in age, and Mama had named him Horatio Junior for his father before she could see what was plain soon enough—that the mind he got would never make any sort of man. He had grown up mostly of his own accord, running sometimes with Milo and her and Negroes and taking what candy Mr. Isaac offered but seldom laughing and never being close to a soul or asking a favor. Still, he had *been* there all her life until last April. He had sat by her on cold school buses till he turned fourteen and stopped school completely and she met Wesley Beavers, and after that he had spent every Saturday night looking on from the porch at her and Wesley in the yard saying goodbye slowly. He had gone with her to the Raleigh hospital that week they sat with Papa before he died. And always, if he was nothing else, he had been one thing she could count on not to change, which was what she looked now to know—covering his face with her eyes (long yellow face rocked forward on his neck). But nine months of Army had taught him nothing new—thirty more years wouldn't either— and he had her father's name. So she held out her hand and smiled and said, "Merry Christmas, Rato. You have put on weight."

He said "Army food" and gave her his cool fingers to hold a little.

They all stepped into the hall and Rato stood again, not knowing where to set his bag. He never had a permanent room in the house but penetrated back and forth, stretching out wherever there was nobody else, and now Mama said, "Son, while me and Rosa's getting up dinner, you go to Papa's old room and put on your own clothes."

He looked at his wrinkles. "Thank you, no'm. These ain't mine but they are all I got."

Milo said, "What in the Hell you got that bag stuffed with then?— a woman?"

Baby Sister said, "Looks like Santa Claus to me."

Rato said, "That's what it is."

And Mama said, "Well, eat like you are but some of us will have to press that uniform before tonight," and she and Rosacoke went to lay out the food. Milo went upstairs to tell Sissie he was home, and Rato dropped his bag again and dangled in the hall with Baby Sister staring at him speechless. Mama called "Ready." Then Sissie crept down ahead of Milo. She spoke Rato's name and he spoke hers and said, "I have eat just peanuts since Friday" and stepped to the table before the others.

At the table Mama called on Rato for grace. There was considerable time while he searched for words, and Rosacoke thought, "That is mistake number one. After eight months away he's forgot," and Mama had opened her mouth to say it herself when Rato shot out, "Lord, I thank you for dinner."

They waited awhile for "Amen" but it never came so they looked up gradually and unfolded napkins and commenced passing bowls. They knew there was no point asking Rato about his trip or the Army—he had never made a satisfying answer in his life—but Mama couldn't pass up his grace without comment. "You all must not have much religious activities at camp, do you, son?"

Rato was red from his effort. He said "No'm," taking biscuits to butter.

And at first that seemed to stop other questions, but Milo thought and saw his chance—"What about them talks on women the chaplain gives?" Rato grinned at his plate and chewed and Milo kept on. "I certainly hope you have been attending *them*." Rato still didn't speak though Mama was watching him. Milo said "Have you, Rato?"

Sissie for a change raised eyebrows over the table to Rosacoke, meaning "*Brother* is closer kin than *husband*. You stop him," and Rosacoke said "All right, Milo."

Mama said "Yes, stop" but she was curious now, and when there had been quiet eating for a little, she said, "Are they some kind of marriage talks, son?"

"I don't know'm. I ain't heard one."

Milo said, "Well, you have missed a golden opportunity, I'm sure."

"*I* don't know," Mama said. "Some folks don't want to get married, do they, son?"

Rato nodded. "I'm one of *them*."

And Mama had to make a new start. "Son, do you all have a chaplain just for the Baptists or does everybody get the same one?"

"I ain't seen a Baptist since April. Just Catholics."

"Well, you will see some tonight."

"How come?"

"Because we are retiring Mr. Isaac from the Deacons tonight."

"Is he still alive?"

Milo said "Sort of."

Baby Sister said, "We are also having the pageant and you are in it."

"No I ain't." (Every year since he grew too big for a Shepherd, he had begun by refusing his part.)

Milo said, "Yes you are. Me and you's Wise Men."

Sissie said, "Who is the third?" and when Milo and Mama stared at her, she saw her mistake and bolted a mouthful of food for the first time that day.

But her question hung above them plain as the swinging light so Rosacoke laid her hands on the table. She pushed back her chair and stood and took the empty biscuit plate. Only Rato looked at her but she looked at Sissie and said, "The third one is Wesley if he comes in time." Then she went to the kitchen and stayed there longer than it generally takes for biscuits.

When she was gone Mama said soft to Milo "Is he come?"

"He's here. I seen him at the store just now when we passed."

"Well, I called up his mother yesterday to see was he coming for the pageant. She said she just didn't know his plans so I told her we would practice this afternoon and to tell Wesley if he come. Has Willie Duke come?"

"Oh yes. That scrap-iron fool flew her in last night."

Rato said, "Is *she* in the show?"

"Looks that way," Mama said but with Sissie there she didn't name Willie Duke's part.

Rato of course didn't know what they meant, talking low, but he had finished eating, and as Rosacoke stepped back through the door, he looked to her and said "When is Christmas?"

She smiled and said "Wednesday" and sat down.

"How come you ask?" Mama said.

But Rato was on his feet and out to the hall and back with his duffle bag. He stooped to open it. "Because I have brought you all presents from the PX. Everything is real cheap there."

Mama said, "That's fine, son. But wait till Wednesday."

He just said "No'm" and brought out six boxes. They were all very much the same size and in white paper with no name tags, but Rato weighed each box in his hand, trying to know them by touch. Finally he passed one to Baby Sister, and while the others watched his sorting, she opened it. At first it seemed like a red plastic sack, but she found a valve and blew, and directly it was a toy elephant with black eyes that rolled behind celluloid. She thought to herself it was a very strange gift for a twelve-year-old, but all she said was "Thank you, Rato."

He said "That's O.K." and stayed on the floor, but everybody else turned to Baby Sister, stuck with her blown-up elephant, wondering where to set it. Mama laughed a little and the others followed, even Sissie, so Rato looked to see why. When he saw the toy he jumped to Baby Sister's chair and grabbed it from her. "This here ain't yours," he said. "It's a baby toy" and he put it to his burning face and bit off the valve with his teeth. The elephant shriveled to a sack again, and Rato stuffed it deep out of sight. Then he rocked on his heels and studied the five boxes left. "Listen," he said, "I bought this stuff way before Thanksgiving so I don't know what is what." That was as much as he had said at one time ever in his life, and he started refilling his bag. The others tried but they couldn't help staring at Sissie. Sissie for a change held up. But that was the end of eating. Mama stood and said, "That's all right, son. Take your time. Christmas will be here too soon as it is. You and Milo just go in the front room and set. By the time me and Rosa wash dishes, we will have to get on to Delight and practice."

Rato said "Who is *we*?"

"You all that's in the pageant and me that's managing it."

Rato said, "Are you in it, Rosa?"

"No. I had my chance last year, remember?"

He said "Yes" and dinner broke up. Sissie went back upstairs to continue resting. Milo and Rato went to the front room to wait for Mama—Baby Sister followed in case Milo told jokes—and Rosacoke and Mama washed dishes.

In the kitchen when the last dish was dried, Rosacoke hung two wet towels on a line by the window and stood, looking sideways to the empty road, her face the color of the day. Mama saw her and knew she had put off speaking long as she could, that she had to find a way now to offer blind help. But Rosa was Rosa (her strangest child). She would have to study out what to say so she wiped round the sink and washed her hands and slipped on the narrow gold ring she always removed before working. When that was done Rosacoke was still locked at the glass. Mama walked up behind and not touching her, said, "Rosa, you have barely laughed since summer ended. I don't know why exactly but even if you *are* my own flesh and blood, I ain't going to ask the trouble. I just want to say, if you got any business that needs telling—well, I am your Mama." She stopped to take breath but Rosacoke didn't turn. "And another thing, if there is some person in that pageant you don't want to see, just stay here tonight. I will understand." (She didn't understand. She hadn't guessed what the real burden was.) Rosacoke stayed facing the road and Mama walked to the door to leave. At the door she tried again. "Did you hear me, Rosa?" Rosacoke nodded one time and Mama went out.

But all Rosacoke had heard was the last, which worked in her mind as she saw Milo lead the others to the car and drive off to Delight. After they vanished she said to herself, "Even if I do feel like crawling underground, I will not sit here tonight and moan with Sissie Abbott. Mr. Isaac may die any day. He has been good to us, and I mean to pay my respects with everybody else, including Wesley Beavers." She had halfway turned to get her church dress and iron it when she caught in the side of her eye a cloud of dust at the far curve of the road. She had to look. It was nothing but Macey Gupton's truck headed for the practice (he was Joseph and was hauling Mr. Isaac's gift-chair on the back, held down by his wormy daughters that were Angels), but when it was gone Rosacoke couldn't leave the window. She had to stand and take the sight of whatever cars passed by.

And the awful car she expected came soon enough—the Beavers' tan Pontiac moving fast as if it was late, twitching to dodge great rocks and with one person in it who suddenly knew where he was and slowed at the Mustian drive almost to a stop but not seeing any sign of life to call him in (*some* reason of his own), rolled on by scratching his wheels. Rosacoke pressed her face to the cold pane and watched to the end. Then she could think, "That is all the proof I need," and the thought, being what she had waited to know, came almost like relief. She had not seen a face or enough to swear who was driving but she knew. She also knew she could not attend any evening service—Mr. Isaac dying or not. But what she *could* do came to her next. "I will walk over now and take him his candy and tell Sammy I can't be there tonight."

She went to Mama's room and found the candy where Milo had left it. She wrapped it like Rato's things in tissue paper. Then she climbed the stairs to comb her hair and get her coat—she had dressed that morning for Rato's arrival. On the way down she stopped by Sissie's door and spoke through it. "Are you all right?" Sissie said she was. "Well, I am just going to step to Mr. Isaac's—hear?—and give him our candy." Sissie said not to mind her so Rosacoke went on.

She went the back way—off the road through a half-mile of bare woods. Near as they were, she didn't really know these woods (Milo had warned her long ago—to keep her from always trailing him—that somewhere in here was a place named Snake's Mouth where all snakes for miles got born, and the story had served his purpose till she was too old to explore), and looking down she walked through pine straw and waiting briars fast as she could, not because she was scared but because after watching the tan car fade, she didn't mean to stay in silence longer than she could help, even if Sammy Ransom was the only thing to talk to. Still, it took much longer than she hoped, and when she broke out of trees at last on the edge of the grove with the naked road on her left and Mr. Isaac's before her, she all but ran the hundred yards to the porch, and the pounding of her feet on dead earth flushed waves of screaming guineas into pecan limbs. The porch was not much help. The soft boards gave under her weight like carpet. The only thing moving was a dirty rocking chair, and the truck was nowhere in sight. She gripped the package and pulled with her chest for breath. Then she said, "Sweet Jesus, let *somebody* be here" and knocked.

And Sammy came, clean in blue work clothes, looking glad to see her. He stopped on the sill with the screen door between them. "How are you, Miss Rosa?"

She couldn't speak at first but she blinked her eyes and smiled. "Kicking, but not high, Sammy."

"You look a little pale, sure enough. I hope you improves by Christmas. Can I help you, please ma'm?"

She showed him the package in her hand. "Sammy, I won't be going to Delight this evening to honor Mr. Isaac with the rest. I got to stay home with Milo's Sissie so I brought him his candy. It's from all of us though."

"He be glad to see that, Miss Rosa. He and Miss Marina eat up all they had last Friday, and I ain't been able to leave him to get no more. But he don't understand that and yesterday evening after I got him in the bed, I left him for just ten minutes, and he worked himself to the edge and commenced rummaging in his table drawer till he found one of them little cakes of hotel soap that he got twenty years ago—in Richmond, I reckon—and Miss Rosa, he *eat* about half of it before I come back and saw lather foaming round his mouth. (He is mixed up, you see—thinking about nothing but hisself all day.) But it didn't seem to hurt him none so I just wiped him off and didn't tell him no better. Yes ma'm, he be glad of this and so is Sammy." But he stood on in the door, blocking her way.

So she had to ask. "Well, if he is all right now, reckon could I speak to him a minute?"

Sammy smiled and lowered his voice and peeped behind him. "Yes ma'm. I was just holding off to let Miss Marina hide. She don't see folks in the winter." Then she stepped back and Rosacoke passed.

She had been in the house maybe forty-five minutes of her life, but she knew right away it was all the same, the way it had been every Christmas-visit since she could remember—the dark low hall, broad floor boards stretching to the back (bare and polished from the little walking since Miss Marina threw out the rugs, saying "Moth hotels!"), green curtains drawn across the four room doors (Miss Marina hiding back of one), the rose love seat and the tired, preserving air that held it all from one year to the next, unchanged and clean and stifling as a July night. The one new thing was hung by the parlor door—a calendar for the present year (with a picture of a new Buick car and the sea behind), turned to December with each day circled through the twenty-first. Sammy saw Rosacoke notice that—"Miss Marina is counting off the days to Christmas"—and led her to the far door on the left, saying, "Stand here, please ma'm, while I get him fixed. I got him in the bed, resting up for this evening."

She thought, "I have never been in this room. It is the last place on earth Mr. Isaac in his right mind would ask me," and she said, "Sammy, don't bother him now. *You* give him this."

"Oh no'm. He be glad of company. It's the only thing he glad of now. He might not know you though," and he went through the curtain, but Rosacoke could hear every sound. Sammy said, "Set up, Mr. Isaac. I got you a guest," and there was heaving of the bed as he propped the old man on pillows. Mr. Isaac bore it quiet as a sack of seed, but when Sammy had finished and headed for the door to get Rosacoke, Mr. Isaac tapped on wood and Sammy went back. Rosacoke could hear him hawking at his throat and finally his whisper, "Brush my hair" so Sammy poured water to damp his head and brushed him and said "Now you ready" and called Rosacoke.

She stepped through and saw first thing on the opposite wall three pictures of people—the only one she knew being Franklin D. Roosevelt, torn off *Life* magazine, tacked up, crisp and curled and happy, over a bureau that lacked a mirror and had nothing on it but dust from the road and a tortoise-shell hairbrush. The rest of the room was just that bare—her eyes passed over a low washstand with a pitcher and bowl and the black leather chair and one wide window and a long rusty wall till she found Mr. Isaac in bed way round on her left, too far to see his pictures. She went three steps towards him, and Sammy said, "This is your friend Rosacoke, Mr. Isaac."

She was not his friend. She had never been more to him than one of Emma Mustian's dusty children in the road—the one that had grown up bringing him every Christmas the horehound candy her Mama bought to offer in partial thanks for the fifty dollars he gave when the children's Daddy was killed—but facing him now she knew she was right to come. He filled her mind already with something but bitter dread—set up on white pillows in a white flannel nightshirt with spotted hands flat on white sheets and still, for all Sammy's pains, looking dirty because his face had yellowed too deep to fade now and the hair above was streaked like old piano keys.

She went the rest of the way and held out the package. He looked at her offering hand and at her—the dead smile on the right side of his face but both sides blank as paper—and to Sammy beside her. Sammy said, "Take your present and thank Miss Rosa." He turned to his own hands before him and stared as though he would move them invisibly, by sight. Then his live hand commenced a flutter on the sheet like a learning bird in hopes of flight and reached out slowly to Rosacoke.

When his fingers had the package, she said, "Merry Christmas, Mr. Isaac. I hope you have many more."

But he didn't speak and his face didn't show even recognition. He carried his hand back halfway and held it at seeing distance, studying what he had. Sammy spoke though—"You want me to open it for you?"—and before Mr. Isaac could nod, took it and tore off the paper. "Look here, Mr. Isaac, you got you some horehound again. Ain't you glad?" The old man looked at the candy and then to Rosacoke for a long try at remembering, but if he knew her or why she had brought him this or was thankful, he gave no sign. Sammy said, "I told you, Miss Rosa" and broke the bag and laid two sticks of candy in Mr. Isaac's hand. The hand shut on them like a trap. Sammy said, "Miss Rosa, take a chair" and fetched her one with a horsehair bottom and set it near the bed.

She had no reason to stay (no reason she could mention), but what else could she do?—walk back through those woods again? or up the road where whoever passed could see her alone? and pull herself upstairs and feed her stove and sit on the bed with Sissie sealed in next door, needing comfort? and feel, one mile down the road, everybody she knew at Delight (Milo and Wesley and Macey quizzing Rato about women and joking with Landon Allgood—drunk but trying to sweep—and Baby Sister bossing Guptons and Mama pleading every two minutes, "You all *please* behave")? So she said, "Well, I *will* stay awhile" and pulled back the chair and sat and turned to Sammy, hoping he would talk.

He said, "You say you got to set with Miss Sissie this evening—how is she, Miss Rosa?"

"Dr. Sledge says she is all right—her *body*. It will take her some time yet to stop grieving though."

"Yes ma'm. It was a boy, won't it?"

"Yes."

"What was his name?"

"Rato."

"Named after Mr. Rato?"

"Rato was our Daddy's name."

"Yes ma'm."

Rosacoke turned to Mr. Isaac then, thinking he might help her change the subject, but he was only watching his shut hand and Sammy began again. "Well, I hope she gets her a new one soon."

"Sissie you mean?" but she didn't face Sammy.

"Yes ma'm."

"I don't know if she could stand it again."

"Yes ma'm. Don't look like folks been having much luck this year, does it?—Mildred Sutton, she died, and now Miss Sissie's boy." He waited but Rosacoke still didn't turn. "Is you seen Mildred's baby, Miss Rosa?"

"Yes."

"Don't he take after Mildred? I seen him last week. Estelle had him at Mount Moriah, and I seen him just from a distance. First time."

Rosacoke had looked for comfort from Sammy, but with what he said her heart was wild again, and she had tensed her legs to stand and leave when Mr. Isaac came to life. He turned far as he could and tried to whisper to Sammy, "Who is her Mama?"

Sammy said, "Miss Emma Mustian. This is Rosacoke." And Mr. Isaac nodded. He didn't look at her or smile, just opened his hand and carried one stick of candy to his mouth.

Rosacoke had stayed to see that, and once it was done Sammy said, "Will you set here, Miss Rosa, while I go fix his medicine?"

She could only say "Yes" and Sammy went. Mr. Isaac watched him go and as his steps died out towards the kitchen, stared at the curtain, wondering maybe was that the last of Sammy. Rosacoke wanted to set him at ease, but he didn't look at her. He went back to his hand and took the next stick of candy and crammed the room with the noise of eating as if he was grinding teeth to powder. Rosacoke had to stop him. She said, "Mr. Isaac, I hear you are going to church this evening." But he didn't stop. He chewed to the end and swallowed, and she thought he hadn't heard. Then he turned on her—his eyes— and he started, "I—I can't die. If you was to shoot me, I wouldn't die. So I don't pray." He pointed to a spot on the bare floor between them—"I—I—I don't pray no more than that dog does yonder."

There was not any dog. There hadn't been a dog for fifteen years. There was only—out the wide window—high black trees stuck up on the far edge of the pond where woods began (where the deer was and the spring and the broomstraw field) and nearer, crawling cherries and water, hard on the surface but swarmed with cold slow-blooded fish, locking the rotten boat by the rotting pier, and there was no sound of Sammy coming so Rosacoke got to her feet and walked to the wall and the pictures. She had saved them to look at if she needed—the ones she had not recognized, tintypes in round walnut frames on each side of Roosevelt, a lady about her age and a man about fifty. At first sight she knew the lady. It was Mr. Isaac's mother (Miss Marina, even crazy, was her image), and the man was his father—stern and bald, screwed to the chair he sat in, one empty sleeve pinned up at his shoulder. He had given an arm in the War. (Mr. Isaac had told her years ago when he met her one day in the road and asked for the hundredth time who was her Mama. She had said "Emma Mustian" and then asked who was his Daddy. He had told her, "Dead—died at ninety and his last words were, 'I do not understand.' But Cas was his name. He fought at Vicksburg and lost his arm and didn't eat nothing for forty days till him and his men caught rats." She had said, "No wonder he died" and had gone on home, Mr. Isaac laughing behind her.) Recollecting that was a help and she turned to the bed. "Mr. Isaac, is this your Daddy here?"

His hand was on his yellow hair—just smoothing—and he kept that up as he strained his eyes to the wall and said, "Papa told me I would be bald as him but I ain't."

That helped a little too. (He was right. He had never lost a strand—

except what was in his brush—and the sight of it now brought her the memory of when Milo was ten and came in one morning from the store with what Mama sent for, plus a nickel. Mama asked where he got it, and he said, "I was coming out the store, and Mr. Isaac was setting on the steps in the shade, and he said to me, 'Boy, I will give you a nickel to scratch my head.'") And when that had run through her mind like spring water, she felt she could sit again for as long as Sammy was gone and she was needed. She went to the chair, stepping careful not to jar what little calm she had made, and when she sat, knocking came from the front of the house. At first she wondered was it Miss Marina and had Sammy heard. But his footsteps passed from the kitchen to the front and opened the door. For all the quiet she still couldn't hear who was there or what Sammy mumbled till he spoke up at last—"Step on in. She's watching Mr. Isaac for me"—and led somebody towards her. She didn't face the door or stand. She faced Mr. Isaac and when Sammy drew back the curtain, cold air struck her neck and Wesley spoke her name. Her legs thrust up and twisted her round to see where he stood, his face like a weapon against her.

With the breath she had she said, "Why have you trailed me here?"

Sammy brought him on by the arm, and Rosacoke backed till the bed stopped her. Nothing was between them but the dead air her chest refused. Wesley said, "Your Mama sent me home to get you, and Sissie said you was here. You will, Willie Duke has eloped by air with Heywood Betts to Daytona Beach, and you got to be in the show tonight so come on with me to practice." He smiled and Sammy Ransom smiled behind him.

Rosacoke would have run—she had already whimpered, cornered and wild, in the roof of her mouth—but something touched her coat from behind, and she flung backwards to see what it was. It was Mr. Isaac. He had slid to the edge and reached for the candy and knocked the broken bag against her back with his liverish hand and was smiling on both sides of his face, his old teeth parted, the stink of his age leaking through them. There was nowhere better to turn so Rosacoke stared on and shuddered. Then he lifted the candy towards her and whispered, "Give this to the children."

She frowned hard and Sammy came forward—"What children,

Mr. Isaac? This is *your* Christmas present"—and took the candy from him.

But Mr. Isaac pointed to Rosacoke, "That is for the *children*," and Rosacoke ran past Sammy and Wesley with their grins, through the curtain, past Miss Marina hiding, to the door and the porch, towards the road, headed God-knew-where, but away from Wesley Beavers who didn't *know* and who wouldn't care—hair and coat like old flags behind, legs pumping noise from her belly through her nose to drown his nearing steps (low sick whines like nothing she had made in her life, that her teeth couldn't stanch).

Her breath lasted halfway to the road, and terror took her another few yards before Wesley came close enough to touch her shoulder lightly. That touch—asking, not clutching—sent tiredness through her like a killing shock. She ran beyond his hand. Then she stopped. He was somewhere behind her. She didn't know how far. She didn't care. She just had to rest. Her head slumped towards the ground as if she would never look up, and hair fell over her face. Then he touched her again. She was too numb to feel anything but weight so his right hand stayed on her shoulder as he came round in front and rocked her chin towards him. (He had never done such a thing in daylight before.) Her skin was paler than usual, and her eyes wouldn't meet him though they were dry as sand. But those were the only signs—why should he understand those? He said, "Sweet Jesus, what ails you, Rosa?"

She drew her chin back towards the ground. "Nothing you can cure." Her voice was like a croupy child's.

"Tell me what's your trouble."

"If you don't know by now—"

"I don't know nothing except you are acting mighty strange for Christmas." He slid his hand down her arm and took her cold fingers—she let them go like something not hers—and said, "Come on now, Rosa. We got to go practice. Everybody is waiting. We'll have a *good* time."

She shook her head, meaning No, and shut her eyes.

"Rosa, Willie Duke has eloped and you got to take her part, else your Mama's show will fold up."

Her eyes stayed shut. "Marise can do it."

He laughed. "Then you ain't seen Marise lately."

She shook her head again but her eyes opened.

"Marise can't be in no Christmas show *this* year. She is swole-up with baby-number-five the size of that house yonder." He pointed to Mr. Isaac's and Rosacoke turned her head to see. Sammy Ransom stood on the porch. He had run that far with Wesley and waited to know if he was needed. Wesley hollered, "It's all right, Sammy." Sammy smiled and waved and went in.

Rosacoke said "No it ain't," not meaning to speak, feeling it slip up her throat.

"What ain't?" Wesley said and reached to take her other hand.

But she stepped back. Her hands twitched a time or two, and to calm them she smoothed one side of her hair. Then both arms went straight at her sides and the fingers clenched. "Marise Gupton ain't the only one working on a baby." Her voice was almost natural, just tired.

"Who are you speaking of?"

"I am speaking of me."

He didn't come to her so they stood a long minute like that, stiller than they had ever been, four feet of day between them. Wesley was downhill from her and lower, facing the yellow house (the pecans, the guineas, Miss Marina peeping) but seeing only Rosacoke in his head—the way she had looked that November evening by flashlight in broomstraw, the way she looked now, almost the same, just tireder. But Rosacoke stared past his head (his hair grown dark and long for winter) and stopped her eyes on the road that was empty. She said one thought to herself as a test—"Wonder have many other women told him this?"—and she waited for the hurt but it didn't come. Her mind was empty as the road. She was numb to Wesley Beavers for the first time in eight years, numb as a sleeping leg.

But Wesley was not, not now if he had ever been. He said slow and careful, "Understand what I say—you don't know nobody but me, do you, Rosa?"

She said "No," not looking.

He took a long deep breath and let it out. "Well, come on then. We got to go practice." His car was up by the house, and he wandered towards it, not taking her hand as he went. He had to think and he was trying, the only way he knew—by draining his eyes and his mind of everything and waiting till an answer rose to the surface. He had gone ten yards before he knew he was walking alone so he stopped and twisted one foot in dirt. Rosacoke heard that and turned her head a little. He said "Rosa?" and started again for the car. And she came on behind. It would be somewhere to rest.

They rode without speaking, separate. Wesley's hands hung from the top of the wheel, and his forehead leaned almost to the glass—his eyes flat and blind—not to see Rosacoke till he knew how to speak whatever he decided. Rosacoke's hands were palm-up, dead, on knees that had gapped apart to let her eyes bore through to the floor. So both of them failed to notice the one thing that might have helped— rare as lightning in late December, a high white heron in the pond shallows, down for the night on its late way south, neck for a moment curved lovely as an axe handle to follow their passing, then thrust in water for the food it had lacked since morning. But in no time the church had swung into view and still Wesley didn't know. He glanced at Rosacoke—she hadn't seen where they were—and drove on a ways with the woods around them, to wait for what he must do and the words to speak it in.

Then the words came to him, and he pulled off the road. Rosacoke thought she was there and reached for the door handle, but he had stopped by the tracks that led to Mr. Isaac's spring. Far as she could see, only briars and frozen weeds stretched into thickening pines, and Wesley's eyes were pressed against her face, waiting for something from her. He said, "Rosa, how come you ain't told me sooner?" His voice was almost happy. It was the beginning of his offer.

But she said, "Take me to Delight please."

"We got to talk some, Rosa."

She said, "I don't owe you two words," but still he looked and gave no signs of moving. So she made one try to save herself the walk— "Am I riding to Delight or have I got to go by foot?"

He would have to finish what he had begun, but he saw she could not listen now. He knew she was tired and that seemed reason enough. Anyhow, he had never begged anybody for anything, and he didn't know how to start at age twenty-two. He said, "You are on your way" and faced the rear window and turned in Mr. Isaac's old tracks and drove her back slowly, guessing she only needed time to calm herself and listen. He stopped fifty yards from the church by Milo's car near the graves. Rosacoke looked up again—at creek sand now, like snow, and the square white building—and she thought, "How in the world can I troop in yonder, smiling, and practice this part for tonight, knowing all I know?"

In her wait Wesley reckoned he saw another chance. He said, "Rosa, why ain't you told me before now?"

She faced her window. "What good would that have done?"

"It would have saved wear and tear on your nerves. You look right peaked." He sounded as if he was smiling—"And if I had had warning, I could have spoke to Heywood Betts, and we could have flew off with him and Willie to Daytona Beach for Christmas!"

She said, "I have not been sleeping much. Don't joke with me."

He said "I ain't" and when she moved to get out, he laid a hand on her wrist and looked to the church to see was anybody watching. "Listen here. We will drive to South Carolina tonight when the show is over. To Dillon. That's where everybody goes—you ain't got to wait for a license there. Then we can head on to Myrtle Beach if it ain't too cold and collect a few shells and get back here on Christmas Eve. O.K.?"

She left his hand in place, thinking it meant nothing now, but she said, "I am not *everybody*. I am just the cause of this baby. It is mine and I am having it on my own."

"Not a *hundred* per cent yours, it ain't. Not if what you say about knowing nobody but me is *so*."

"It's so."

"Then we got to go to Dillon this evening." It was that simple to him.

She shook her head and gave him the first reason that came—"It would break Mama's heart."

"It'll break a heap louder if her first live grand-baby comes here lacking a name."

"Hers ain't all that will break."

"No, I reckon not. I ain't exactly glad it happened this way myself, but it don't upset my plans too much. I mean, I have paid up my debts. Every penny I make from here on out is mine. We can live. Anyhow, we done this together and—"

She knew she could not bear the end of that, whatever it would be. They hadn't done *nothing* together. She stepped to the ground and went on towards the church. Wesley watched her go three yards. Then he got out himself, intending to catch up beside her, but the sound of him coming quickened her walk so he followed at the distance she chose—not understanding, hoping he just had to wait.

And she would have gone in ahead as she meant to if halfway across the grove, she hadn't heard the choir door open, rusty, at the side and seen Landon Allgood tip down the steps and head across her path, weaving enough to show his condition and dressed for summer but with both arms full of holly—thorned leaves and berries that shined at her clean through the grove like cardinals hunched against Landon from the weather. She wondered, "What does he need with holly like that?" (It was plain he was taking off some of Mama's best decorations. Greens like that only grew deep in Mr. Isaac's woods, and the youngest boys had spent all yesterday gathering them.) But she had no idea of asking, and she stepped along faster not to meet him. He hadn't noticed her and she thought she was safe till Wesley called out from behind, "You look like a holly bush, Landon," and Landon stopped to lift his cap but seeing his arms were loaded, smiled and came on. Rosacoke told herself, "There is no way not to speak now—him this near and Christmas on Wednesday" so she stopped too, and Wesley reached her the same time as Landon. She said "Good afternoon, Landon," trying just to answer his grin and overlook the holly.

But Wesley said, "Where are you taking all them greens?" He was grinning like Landon. He took this meeting as a sign.

"They is just some little Christmas greens for Mary, Mr. Wesley." (Mary Sutton was his sister.) "She say she would give me my dinner if I find her some Christmas greens."

"Well, you sure found some grand ones, didn't you?"

"Yes sir, I did. I don't know who she decorating for except that baby, and it don't know holly from horses' harness."

"I don't reckon so. How old is it, Landon?" He didn't need to know. It was just the next thing to say.

"I don't know, sir. It won't walking last Tuesday though."

Rosacoke had to speak. "His name is Sledge and he come in late July."

"Was it that long ago?" Wesley said, glad she had offered *something*, and she nodded, looking off.

Landon said, "What you asking me, Mr. Wesley?" He had not kept up.

But to stop Wesley's answer Rosacoke said, "I got to go practice, Landon. Let me just give you this." She felt for her purse but it was at home.

Wesley said, "What you hunting, Rosa?"

She didn't say, so Landon told him. "Sometimes she give me a dollar for my medicine I needs."

"—But I haven't got it now," she said. "I am sorry. Come by the house on Wednesday."

That was all right with Landon, but Wesley said "Here's your dollar" and reached for his money.

Rosacoke said, "*I'll* give it to him Wednesday."

"You maybe won't be here Wednesday."

"Where am I going," she said.

He smiled, not seeing she had not asked a question, and Landon looked back and forth between them, confused. But Wesley had already pulled out two old dollars. He stuffed them in Landon's pocket. "That'll cure a heap of toothaches," he said.

"Many-a-one," Landon said, bowing deep on his holly. "Thank you, sir. Thank you, Miss Rosa." Then as if it was his gift for them, he nodded to the side. Rosacoke knew where to look. "I been spreading new dirt on Mr. Rato where he sinking."

And there through the grove was her father under raw new dirt, changed to dirt himself after thirteen years, who had changed one time before—from the boy her Mama recollected, in white knee-stockings so solemn on a pier at Ocean View, to the drunk who killed himself one Saturday evening by mistake (like everything else he did) and left behind a tan photograph and four blood children (Milo with his hair, and Rato Junior with his silly name but no mind, and her with one or two awful memories, and Baby Sister working in Mama when he died)—and was sinking now by his Papa and Mama and his first grand-baby that would also have had his name if it had breathed, and someday might have passed it on. She said "Thank you, Landon" and in the church the piano started (that hadn't been tuned in memory), seeping through the walls as if from underwater, too faint to call a tune.

Landon said, "I wish you all a happy Christmas and many more to come" and started for the road and Mary's, and Rosacoke started for the church. But Wesley held her—his hand on her shoulder, not so gentle now. "You know I am serious, don't you?" She didn't pull away but she made no sign and she didn't look. "Well, I am. And you got all evening to think it over. Tell me tonight." He lifted his hand and she walked on but he didn't follow. He stood where she left him, waiting to know would she look back one time at least, wondering what had turned her against him, yet seeing how little her picture had changed since summer—her high legs lifting her on over sand like snow crust, working from her hips like stainless rods, steady and lovely (even now, toting their new burden) as if she was walking towards a prize.

She got to the steps and climbed and at the top, in the door, turned and not knowing why, not thinking, looked back the way she had come—the car and the graves and her sorry father, then a little careful, still testing, to Wesley Beavers for the first time since Mr. Isaac's, looking down on him and thinking, the moment she met his eyes, "I am free"—a way she had seldom felt since the November day eight years ago when he rained down pecans at her request, the way she had felt for maybe ten minutes that other November evening when she struck out for Mary's—after the hawk passed over and the music—as if her life was hers, till the wind turned and the music came back and pulled her through briars and roots to the Beavers' clearing where she could see Wesley on the porch, leaning on a post over his brother, his hair still light from the beach, his white sleeves rolled above dark hands that shaped the music, and his face not smiling no more than the hawk— sealed off with his private pictures, not seeing her, needing nothing he didn't have, but happy. Now everything was different. The distance between them—the space—was half what it was that evening. Now

Wesley was flat on his feet with his arms pinned to his sides. His wrists had faded white and showed from the sleeves of his sailor jacket (he had grown some in the Navy), and his face was offered up towards her like a plate—with nothing on it she wanted, not any more. She told herself, "Well, I held him. I tried and I held him. I caused him this bad afternoon, and maybe I have ruined his Christmas and I am sorry. But I reckon he has learned one thing he never would have guessed on his own—that it is very lonely, donating things to people that they don't need or even want—and he will be all right in awhile. He has paid up his debts. He can live. He hasn't got to take no share of this load I brought on myself. I am free from him. God knows I am free." She thought it was her right to think that, and if he had come on then when a final No seemed simple as breathing, she would have said it and saved him waiting till night. But the piano, that had strummed on alone under what she thought, crept into the first of a tune, and all at once there was a girl's voice, riding out pure as spring water. Rosacoke knew it and went in towards it, and Wesley followed in a little. It was Baby Sister. She was practicing "Joy to the World."

And she sang it that evening after they retired Mr. Isaac and gave him his chair and Sammy wiped his eyes and set him in it by the Amen Corner and Mama at the back switched off the lights and the pageant members took their stations unseen and most of the coughing calmed into waiting breath and the preacher recited in the dark, "And there were in the same country Shepherds abiding in the field, keeping watch over their flock by night. And lo, the Angel of the Lord came upon them, and the glory of the Lord shone round about them and they were sore afraid. And the Angel said unto them, 'Fear not, for behold, I bring you good tidings of great joy which shall be to all people.'"

She started it back in the Sunday school rooms out of sight, and the first words didn't carry, but she came on closer till soon every sound was cutting the pitch-black air like a new plow point, reaching some eighty people. Then she moved into sight—to join her song—through a door up front at the side, trailing behind her a swarm of humming girls, mostly Guptons, in cheesecloth veils with trembling candles that were all the light in the church. They were meant to be

Messenger Angels, and Baby Sister's song was meant for the Shepherds, and when she was at the pulpit and the girls closed in around her, there they were—Moulton Ayscue and John Arthur Bobbitt and Bracey Overby, stretched on the floor in flannel bathrobes with peeled sticks beside them. At the touch of light they sprang up afraid and crouched with quivering arms while she finished—

> *Let every heart*
> *Prepare him room*
> *And heaven and nature sing.*

Then the preacher went on. "And it came to pass as the Angels were gone away from them into heaven, the Shepherds said one to another"—and Bracey said, "Let us now go even unto Bethlehem and see this thing which is come to pass, which the Lord hath made known unto us."

But Baby Sister's girls were the light. They couldn't go away so they led the Shepherds slowly to the choir where Macey Gupton stood as Joseph and Rosacoke sat as Mary and Frederick Gupton, eight months old, rested in a basket set on legs, as Baby Jesus. The Shepherds stopped in front of him, and Mama at the back switched on the overhead star and the Angels circled behind. When the flames had steadied in their hands, a ring of light crept past Rosacoke and Frederick till it reached the two front pews and the Amen Corner where Mr. Isaac was. The Shepherds knelt in the center of that ring. Each one laid a hand on the manger that rocked with the weight, and John Arthur Bobbitt commenced to nod his head. On his third nod the Shepherds sang ragged and thin,

> *Away in a manger,*
> *No crib for a bed,*
> *The little Lord Jesus*
> *Laid down His sweet head.*

They had been warned at practice to sing low enough and not scare the baby, and the way they started there seemed no danger, but still Rosacoke leaned over to see how he was. His head was turned away and a fist was against his ear—that was all she could see—but he seemed asleep, seemed safe, so she looked beyond the boys and followed the weakening light to its edge, and there was Mr. Isaac, ten yards away, dim. (Sammy was somewhere dark beside him.)

He had had a long full day—a full week, eating that cake of soap—and even in the dimness she could see his face was not calm yet. His face was *all* she could see, and silver spokes in the wheels of his chair, but she looked on awhile till she reckoned she saw other things, things she needed to see just then—that his eyes were set towards her, looking a way she had not seen before, not the blank look of his strokes or the old shielded way but unsatisfied, wondering, as if he might turn any minute and jerk Sammy's sleeve and try to whisper, "I do not understand" and point at her. She said to herself, "I ought to beg his pardon—acting so wild this afternoon, confusing him like this. What I will do is, go back to see him Christmas day if it's fair and tell him, 'Mr. Isaac, I have come to beg your pardon for my actions last Sunday. You have always been good to us, and I've felt mighty bad, running out on you like that, so I know you will understand when I say I am not myself these days. I am toting more load than is easy alone, if you know what I mean.'" She kept on staring and she wondered, "What will he say to that? When my Daddy was killed he drove to the house after dark and sent in for Mama and waited on the porch till she came and gave her fifty dollars, saying, 'Emma, he is far better off.'"

He waited through her thinking, still as he was that time they found his spring and him cooling in it—her and Milo and Rato and Mildred Sutton. The candlelight trembled on his face—the Guptons were fidgeting—but she knew his look hadn't changed, that he did not understand, and looking inward till she couldn't see him at all, she told herself, "I can't just beg his pardon and not say *why* I acted wild. So what on earth can I do?—stand by his stale bed and point out his side window past the pond and say loud enough for him to hear (and Miss Marina up the hall), 'What I mean, Mr. Isaac is, one evening early last month I followed some deer in your woods. I thought they were headed for the spring but they weren't, and then I came to a broomstraw field you may not have seen and laid down under a boy I know that was with me. I have known him quite awhile—eight years last month. (I met him when we was just children in your woods, where there's a pecan tree that the path bends round.) Anyhow, that night I offered this boy what I reckoned he needed to hold him. I looked on it as giving. But it wasn't like no kind of giving *I* ever saw. I just laid back still in the dark— I couldn't see him—and he did what he had to do, and I was the one got caught with what *he* gave. His burden is swelling up in me right this minute without no name but Mustian. Oh, I *held* the boy. But I don't want him now. All this time I have lived on the hope he would change some day before it was too late and come home and calm down and learn how to talk to me and maybe even listen, and we would have a long life together—him and me—and be happy sometimes and get us children that would look like him and have his name and answer when we called. I just hoped that. But he hasn't changed. He said he would ride me to Dillon tonight and take me to Norfolk after Christmas to spend my life shut up in a rented room while he sells motorcycles to fools—me waiting out my baby sick as a dog, eating Post Toasties and strong pork liver which would be all he could afford and pressing his shirts and staring out a window in my spare time at concrete roads and folks that look like they hate each other. He offered me that. But that isn't *changing*—not the way I hoped—so what I have done, I will sit home and pay for. I am not glad, you understand, but I ain't asking him to share what trouble I brought on myself.'"

Then Mr. Isaac moved and Rosacoke saw him again. His head turned from her and bowed and his lips parted, whispering to the dark where Sammy was, and since it fulfilled her thought, she halfway expected his hand to point her way, but Sammy's hand stretched out— just his hand—and covered Mr. Isaac's for a second. Then the live fingers flicked to his mouth, and he faced her again and ground his jaws one time, looking almost satisfied. He was cracking candy under the music, and when he had swallowed, Sammy leaned forward out of the dark to wipe his chin with a handkerchief. Rosacoke saw first thing that Sammy was wearing the blue wool suit he had worn to Mildred's funeral, and with his face held there before her, she strained to draw out some sign that would prove his part in Mildred's baby, but he finished his wiping too soon and gave a quick look towards her and smiled with his eyes to show he knew before leaning back.

And Rosacoke knew she could not speak a word of what she had thought, not to Mr. Isaac. Saying it to him would mean telling Sammy—Sammy in the dark with all he knew—and anyhow what good was that news to him?—age eighty-two, claiming he couldn't die but dead already in half his body, the other half shielded as always, hoping to live on to ninety and equal his father, and not understanding, after all this time not knowing half *she* knew. So she thought, "He don't even know me. He has not known me all these years—not my name. He can't know me now in this costume, and I reckon he is far better off."

The Shepherds were coming to the middle of their song. Nearer the goal, their hands gripped tighter on the basket, and their voices washed strong over Frederick to Rosacoke and brought her back—

> *The cattle are lowing,*
> *The poor baby wakes,*
> *But little Lord Jesus*
> *No crying He makes.*

She had not thought of Frederick since the Shepherds began, and a chill of fright twitched at the roots of her hair. She said to herself, "I have not done my duty," and slowly, testing, her eyes worked down. But Macey behind her had shifted, and his great shadow hid the baby. She reckoned he was safe though, and she looked out straight before her over the Shepherds to the back of the church. Mama was supposed to be there, waiting to turn on lights at the end, but the back was dark as the night outside, and she narrowed her eyes to find her. What she found was four black figures against the wall—one that was Mama and three together in robes that were Milo and Rato and Wesley Beavers. When the Shepherds finished, the Wise Men would come.

And the Shepherds were curving onwards—

> *Be near us, Lord Jesus,*
> *We ask Thee to stay*
> *Close by us forever*
> *And love us, we pray—*

so for somewhere to look, hoping to rest her mind on something calm, Rosacoke bent forward over the basket. She could not see till her face was nearly at the rim. But Frederick had been seeing her. With the Shepherds singing at his left and his Daddy standing over him and his three blood sisters giving off the light, still he had set his eyes on her. She couldn't know why or for how long, but she was glad a little, and at first he seemed peaceful as if he knew who he saw, as if in all his secret thoughts there was anyhow no fear—serious but peaceful, wrapped loose in a Gupton-blue blanket with bare arms free and only his fingers moving as if a slow breeze lifted them one by one. He didn't seem cold but Rosacoke thought she could cover him better, and she put out a hand. He watched it come and when it touched, his eyes coiled against her and his fingers clamped and his lips spread to a slow black hole. Rosacoke drew back her hand and her face and thought in a rush, "Now I must wait while he makes up his mind to cry or be calm." The Shepherds saw him too, threatening to break up their song, and they lowered their voices in hope—

> Bless all the dear children
> In Thy tender care—

but Frederick gave no hope of blessing. He hung fire before their eyes, every muscle in his body cocked against Rosacoke but *waiting* as if he would give her this last chance to offer what he needed before he called on the church at large. She could see that but she couldn't move. She didn't know a thing to offer, and she said to herself, "I certainly don't have much luck with babies." Then she looked up again—to the dim front pew where she reckoned Marise would be—and her eyes asked desperate for help. Marise was there all right, settled around her hard new belly, tireder already than Mr. Isaac and staring at her family performing—the ones standing up, Macey and the girls. She couldn't see Frederick in his basket, but he had nursed her dry an hour before and swallowed ten drops of paregoric so her mind was at ease about him, and she didn't even notice Rosacoke.

The Shepherds crept on to the end—

and take us to heaven
To dwell with Thee there.

Then they lifted their hands off the manger that rocked again and they stood, and Frederick turned to them, suddenly seeming calmer. But the Shepherds were finished. They were leaving. They ducked their heads to Frederick as a bow and filed to the rear of the choir and picked up candles from a chair and took fire from the Angels, adding that much to the light. When they were gone Frederick lay on through the quiet, still turned to the side, and he lay through the preacher's voice, "Now when Jesus was born in Bethlehem of Judaea in the days of Herod the King, behold, there came Wise Men from the east to Jerusalem, saying, 'Where is he that is born King of the Jews? for we have seen his star in the east and are come to worship him' . . . and lo, the star which they saw in the east went before them till it came and stood over where the young child was," and when the Wise Men began their song, the distant voices seemed to calm him more than anything had—

We three kings of Orient are
Bearing gifts we traverse afar . . .

His fingers went loose again and his stiff legs bent a little, but he didn't look back to Rosacoke, and that was for the best because at those first words, the cords of her chest took hold of her heart and a frown spread from her eyes. She was seeing the far dark wall. They were still at the back in darkness—the three men. They would sing one verse together. Then they would light their candles and come forward separate, offering separate verses. But before they moved, dim as they were, the sight of them deepened Rosacoke's frown, and when Mama struck a match and held it to a candle, then Rosacoke was worse. But that first candle was Rato's—it lit only *his* face—and as he began his verse and his march, she felt a little ease. He couldn't sing—nobody expected him to—but he knew his words, and he moaned them in time to his long, shaking steps, looking down as he came.

> *Born a babe on Bethlehem's plain,*
> *Gold I bring to crown Him again—*
> *King forever, ceasing never*
> *Over us all to reign.*

That much brought him almost to the choir, and the dark two at the back sent him on as they joined in the chorus—

> *O star of wonder, star of night,*
> *Star with royal beauty bright,*
> *Westward leading, still proceeding,*
> *Guide us to the perfect light.*

He came till his toes knocked hard on the first step of the choir, and looking only down, he bowed low enough to set a brass bowl on the floor by the basket. It represented gold, his gift. Then he unbent upwards and stepped to one side and rocked his face onto Rosacoke. She met his great yellow eyes and thought it was the first time in clear memory he had *faced* her so she smoothed her frown the best she could and tried to match his simple unrecognizing graveness. Then she waited while he searched her face, wondering, "Why is he staring at me like this? Have I changed that much since supper?" And feeling as she did—so low—she reckoned that was right. Maybe nobody knew her at all. Maybe nobody in all those dark pews saw what she thought they were seeing. Maybe what they saw was changed too far to know—not by a blue cambric costume but by what she had done that night seven weeks ago, by what she was *making* that grew in her body this instant not ten inches from her heart, twisted on itself in the dark, using her blood for its own. Maybe that face was showing through hers for all to see—shapeless, blind, nameless face. Needing some kind of answer she looked to Mr. Isaac. But if he knew her the secret would die with him. *Sammy* knew. Sammy saw both faces, surely—her old first face and this new one, working under it—but Sammy was out of sight. And Guptons, Aycocks, Smileys, Riggans, Overbys, Mama and Milo and Wesley himself, and Frederick if he would turn back and face her—what were they all seeing, what did they *know* from the way she looked? And supposing she stood up now right under that star and testified, "I am Rosacoke Mustian and the reason I look so changed tonight is because I am working on a baby that I made by mistake and am feeding right now with my blood against my better wishes—but a baby I am meaning to *have* and give my Daddy's name to if it lives and is a boy, one I will try to raise happy, and I'd thank you for helping me any way you can"—what would they say to that? They would not believe her at first, and in time, when they did, they would turn their heads and never speak a word, much less offer help, and Mama's heart would break. She looked up at Rato again. His eyes were still on her so—silent, with her lips—she said "Hello, Rato" and tried to smile, but the smile didn't come and Rato didn't answer, just looked down again as if what he had seen would last him a long time yet.

The only thing like an answer came from the back. Mama struck another match and lit up Milo and he started forwards. *He* was singing though he didn't know the meaning of half he sang, didn't care—

> *Frankincense to offer have I.*
> *Incense owns a Deity nigh—*

and he walked so fast he reached the choir with two lines to sing—

> *Prayer and praising all men raising,*
> *Worship Him, God on high.*

Then all three began the chorus, and Milo bowed to give his gift. What he laid by the basket was nothing to him but a cheap jewel box he had won on a gas-station punchboard six years before (he had never smelled incense in his life), and Macey, that he looked at first when he rose, was nothing but Macey-dressed-funny and the same for Rato and Shepherds and Angels and his sister Rosa and, at first, even Frederick. As he grinned at them all (he crossed his eyes at Baby Sister), they could see he was making up jokes to tell when the show was over—all except Rosacoke. She didn't see him, not at first, not his face. She had not really faced Milo since the nineteenth of November, the morning she promised to stick with him, when they struck out for Raleigh and she got Wesley's letter and read it and when she understood—stopped by that dead field and that pecan tree—went back on her word and told Milo to take her home, leaving him his whole burden. So she looked down at Frederick when the chorus began, but Frederick was studying Milo or maybe the fire in his hand, and as he looked Milo must have made some crazy face—Frederick oared with both legs and though he didn't smile, he held up a hand. Rosacoke could see—anybody could have seen—that the hand was for Milo, and still singing, Milo put out his free hand, and Frederick took one dark finger and closed on it and drew it towards his mouth. Rosacoke had to look up then, and what she saw was almost that first Milo, the one who could tear her heart, and the look that grew on him was awful to her—not a frown but the way he had looked that night in Mary's kitchen—and she had to change it. She had to draw Frederick's attention to herself. She reached in the basket and commenced arranging the blanket, and Frederick turned her way as she hoped, letting go of Milo's finger. That was all she intended but Frederick meant more, and when she took back her hands, he whimpered once—not loud—and huddled in readiness. Rosacoke didn't move. She braced herself for what would come next, but behind her Macey had seen everything. He bent to her ear—"Rosa, pick him up. He's fixing to yell." She heard him (everybody heard him for yards and stiffened) but she didn't move. She shook her head and said just with her lips, "Frederick, I ain't what you need"—and to herself, recalling the last time she said such a thing, "I guess I can't run this time." The chorus stopped. Milo stepped aside and Rosacoke looked to the back.

And she couldn't—couldn't run. Mama struck the last match and held it out. The candle caught fire and Wesley Beavers had a sudden face that he was bringing on, a black bandanna hiding his hair, a black robe crossed at his neck—

> *Myrrh is mine, its bitter perfume*
> *Breathes a life of gathering gloom.*

The frown cut deeper into her eyes, and Frederick whimpered stronger than before. She thought, "Take a-hold, Rosacoke. You are *free,*" and she tried to turn to Frederick, but Wesley, coming slow, was six steps away, and what she saw held her locked—just his face borne forward on a candle through eighty people towards her, swarmed with warning of the ruins and lives he would make—

> *Sorrowing, sighing, bleeding, dying,*
> *Sealed in the stone-cold tomb.*

Her head rolled back and her lips fell open as if she would greet some killing bird, but anybody watching—her Mama and Milo, even Marise Gupton, even Rato—saw her suck one breath in pain.

Then Wesley was at the basket, looking down, his verse finished. He stooped to place his gift (a covered butter dish) and stood for the chorus, and as it began he looked over Frederick to Rosacoke—offering his face, his real gift, the only gift he always gave, without even knowing, but it pressed against her now through six feet of air like a knife held waiting on her skin—his eyes which had seen her that awful way in the broomstraw field (her secret and then her hate), which had seen other women (God knew how many) laid back like her but giving him things she could not even guess, and under the bandanna his ears that had heard those women say "Yes," and then his mouth that had never moved once to make the word "love," not to her anyhow. He was not frowning but he was not glad—she could see that plain—just waiting. He had trapped himself and then done what he saw as his duty— *offered* his duty—and now he waited for her. Before she could shake her head and set him free, a voice cut up through the chorus. It was Frederick at last and Macey who could only see Rosacoke's shivering back, bent to whisper, "Hand him here. I'm his Daddy, Rosa."

She was at her worst. She knew it. And she found the strength to try that—to try handing Frederick on—not because it would save the show but to save herself from running or screaming. Somehow she got both hands in the basket and under Frederick, and she leaned to take his weight. The minute he was in the air, his crying stopped. Rosacoke knew she could not lay him back, not yet, and she knew how strange it would look if she gave him to Macey now so she brought him on to the groove of her lap. He was too long to lie there straight, but his legs jack-

knifed till he fit, and his head weighed back in her hands. He probed
once easy with his feet at her belly, but he seemed content and Rosacoke
said to herself, "Look at Frederick. Think about Frederick." And she
thought, slow, to fill time, "You are named Frederick Gupton. You are
Marise Gupton's fourth baby, and I think you are eight months old which
means you were born last April. You are long for your age, seems like,
but most of your length is in your neck. You sure got the Gupton
neck—long as most folks' leg—and your *eyes* are your Daddy's and your
flapping ears. But you got Marise's black hair, poor thing—straight as
walking canes. You look about as much like Baby Jesus as Rato does."

But he wasn't studying her. He was using her hands as something to
roll his head on, limber as an owl, and take his bearings, and Rosacoke
let him look but she didn't follow his eyes. It was hard enough, watching him switch that face onto various ones, quick as a whip and solemn,
and waiting till it came her turn. For some time though he stayed on
the Wise Men. They were singing their last to the star—

> *Westward leading, still proceeding,*
> *Guide us to the perfect light—*

and when they were done, Baby Sister and her Angels stepped closer
forward and began "Silent Night," very loud. But they didn't interest
Frederick and after they sang two lines, he looked to Rosacoke and put
up his arms to her and strained his head off her knees till he flushed
bright red. At first she thought, "Frederick, I ain't who you think I am"
(meaning she was not Marise). But his hands stayed up, twitching, and
his head still strained so Rosacoke bent down and touched her cheek
to his—his was warmer—and when she rose she could smell something
strange. Trying to name it she only saw Landon Allgood in her mind,
laid out at Mount Moriah in late July or digging a grave five weeks ago
or just now heading for Mary's to eat, with half Mama's holly as payment, and Christmas coming which would be the anniversary of his
toes. She bent again, not as far. Then she knew what it was—Frederick was the source. He was fragrant with paregoric—his breath—and
by all rights he never should have waked (even now his eyes were
tired). But his hands were reaching. He meant her to take him up—

there was no doubting that and Rosacoke recalled Mary saying how
Sledge was a *shoulder* baby so she gave in to Frederick and lifted him
to her shoulder, thinking, "He can face his Daddy now and feel at home
and sleep, I hope." But he didn't stay there ten seconds. The Angels still
didn't hold him, not even their lights, and his head rolled down to her
chest, heavy on his neck as five pounds of seed. She thought, "Thank
the Lord. He is sleepy" and raised his head with her hand. He was not
too sleepy to show he didn't want that. His head came down again—
wandered slower this time—so Rosacoke left him to take his will, and
looking over people to the back where her Mama was dark, she canceled her sight and fixed her mind on Frederick's weight (that grew
every second) and his heat that crept through blanket and costume into
her cold side, and soon she was far from him and then farther—from
herself and Delight Baptist Church and everybody in it, her mind
roaming empty and freer than it had been since the first time she saw
the deer in broad daylight at the edge of the broomstraw ring, half hid
in trees but watching, waiting (till Mildred said "Great God A-mighty"),
then going, loud in the leaves.

It didn't last much longer than the deer—her blank roaming. The
Angels paused at the end of their first verse, and as they took breath
the new sound Frederick made brought her back. He had worked his
head to her chest, and he was chewing the cloth just over her heart—
not wild or fast or shape (he had three teeth) but wet and steady as if
he had all night, had years of time and the trust of food someday and
could gnaw his way through granite rock, not to speak of cambric and
her white skin, to get what he reckoned was his. Her chest shrank
inwards from his mouth. She pushed his head away as if his spit could
scald, and she thought, "I am not who he *thinks* I am." But before she
could shift him to a safe position, she had to look up and halfway play
her part in the show. The Angels had come to—

> *Darkness flies, all is light.*
> *Shepherds hear the Angels sing—*

and that was a sign for the Shepherds to move. They stepped from
behind the Angels and Macey and down the two choir steps, and they

knelt again at the basket, not touching it this time. They were the reason Rosacoke looked up. It was her part to nod at them and try to smile. She did nod, accepting their praise for the baby, and she tried to smile to show she knew each one—Moulton Ayscue, John Arthur Bobbitt, Bracey Overby—had known them all their lives, but they didn't return her acquaintance, didn't smile, only bobbed their chins and turned to Frederick, where he was.

He was back at her chest, one hand pressing hard enough to flush out his blood and his open mouth laid on the peak of her breast. But his jaws were moving slower and his eyes were shut. Rosacoke saw him, where he wanted to be, and waited a little and then gave in—"If that's all it takes to help you rest, go ahead."

He went ahead, lowering himself deeper into sleep with every pull of his jaws—every pull weaker than the last—his breaths coming farther and farther apart, strained like sighs through his nose, and his eyelids heavy enough to stay down for hours. Rosacoke wondered was he dreaming yet—at first his shut face offered no sign. She asked herself, "Reckon what does he dream when he dreams?" and while the Angels finished a verse, she studied him and tried to guess. "Maybe he dreams about getting born last April in Marise and Macey's iron bed, coming out easy as an Indian baby but howling till they got him washed and turned him loose on Marise's breast. Or maybe he can see further back than April"—she counted back in her mind—"maybe he recalls being made one evening in late July when it had been hot all day and the night was no help, and Macey was twisting in the bed, wringing wet, and then there come up a cooling storm, and when it passed and the rain frogs commenced outside, he felt relief and touched Marise and came down on her in the dark, and she took what he gave for her fourth burden, without even seeing him."

When she finished that, Frederick's jaws had stopped, and his fingers had eased against her. She lowered the hand that held his Gupton neck—to cradle him better. His head settled in her arms as if she was his natural rest, and his whole face rolled towards her. Rolling, he flared out his ears even further and pressed out his hair stiff on her sleeve, and she thought again, "If Baby Jesus looked like you—poor Mary," but then she noticed his life, where it beat hid and awful in each bare temple and—visible, blue—in hot veins of his eyelids and his standing ears, filling him sure as an unlabeled seed with all he would be, the ruins he would make and the lives. "Wonder could he dream about that?" she thought, "—about growing up and someday (standing in a field or up a pecan tree) seeing a girl that he felt for and testing till he knew it was love and speaking his offer and taking her home and then one evening, making on her some child that would have his name and signs of him and the girl all in its face—maybe even signs of Marise and Macey? Wonder could he be dreaming that right now?"

But he offered no answer and the Angels came to—

> *See the eastern Wise Men bring*
> *Gifts and homage to our King—*

and the Wise Men stepped back to kneel with the Shepherds. Rosacoke's part was to look up and nod to them but she couldn't. She looked on at Frederick and went on guessing, to calm herself—"Wonder is he dreaming about *me*, and does he know who I am?" But that was no calming thought, no help. "He don't know me from Adam. Of course he don't. He has not laid eyes on me since late July at Mason's Lake when I was not myself, grieving for Mildred. If he has thought about me for three seconds even, he thinks I am just Marise that can drop my babies like a mangy hound and flip out my bosoms in public to stop them yelling." She looked up to her right, needing somebody to *know* her and nod their acquaintance, but all she met was Mr. Isaac awake in his chair, still not understanding, and Sammy dark beside him and at the back her Mama dark as the night outside, and in the front pew Marise staring tired across her to Macey, and Rato and Milo her own blood brothers, five feet away, not facing her—not one soul to own they knew her.

She looked to Wesley. There was nowhere else to look. He was kneeling tall back of John Arthur Bobbitt with his face and his eyes on her, having offered his duty and with nothing to do but wait for her answer so he could plan his life, still not frowning but not glad, smiling no more than her father when he was a boy before he changed, in a tan photograph on a pier by the ocean with another boy blurred beside him. She stayed facing him. He held her like a chain. Then she drew one breath, hard, and said what she suddenly knew—to herself—what he had showed her, "Wesley knows me. After all Wesley knows me." And she knew that was her answer, for all it meant, the answer she would have to give when the pageant was over and Wesley drove her home and stopped in the yard and made his offer again—"Are we riding to Dillon tonight?"—because it was her duty, for all it would mean.

But also it was her wish. She saw that too. She faced that now and she spoke it as a trial to her mind—her answer. But once she had said it, even silent, it boiled up in her like cold spring water through leaves, rising low from her belly till it filled her chest and throat and spilled up into her mouth and beat against her teeth. She had to speak it or drown, and who could she speak to but Frederick Gupton in her arms asleep? She bent again and touched his ear with her lips and said it to him, barely whispered it—"Yes"—and wished him, silent, a long happy life. When she rose his face was still towards her, breathing out Landon every breath. He seemed the safest thing still, seemed shut for the night, so while they sang the last verse around her (Baby Sister climbing through the rest pure as day), she looked on at him, and under her eyes his lips commenced to move, just the corners at first, slow as if they were pulled like tides by the moon, as if he might wake to end some dream, but his eyes didn't open, didn't flicker, and his lips pulled on till at last he had made what was almost a smile, for his own reasons and for no more than three seconds but as if, even in his sleep, he knew of love.

GOOD HEARTS

FOR

MARCIA DRAKE BENNETT

AND

PAUL CLIFFORD BENNETT, JR.

ROSA WESLEY

Rosa reached out and switched off the last light. Then she said "I hope we both sleep safe." It was what she said many nights at this point. It meant what it said. But also, and often without her knowing, it also meant *Sleep please, nothing else.*

Wesley gave his usual answer, "Anything you say, lady. Good night."

They both always entered sleep on their backs, so they lay flat now and waited for their eyes to adjust to the dark—dim slats of street light on the ceiling and a glow on their skin like the shine of phosphorus on underwater life. Neither one of them was thinking. They'd each worked a normal full-day, had a light supper, watched two hours of dumb television, and expected the same tomorrow. Now they were each exhausted and empty, normally tired—no panic or sudden waves of despair.

You though, if you'd been transparent there, would have seen an apparently young married couple. Both of them looked young because they'd mostly avoided fat and because the dark conceals small furrows. They looked married because of the ease in one another's nearness, the benign neglect which permits two bodies so warm and fine to resist quick union.

In fact Rosa and Wesley Beavers had been married twenty-eight years that month, a wedding forced on them by pregnancy after years of old-time country courtship. Beyond a hurried wedding, the outcome of that accident was Horatio, their grown son who lived half the state away—an only child, kind to his parents but mostly helpless in emergency. And their visible ease with one another's bodies was also misleading, a dangerous illusion shared by Rosa.

She thought they were aging but content (she was forty-eight). So nothing now stood between her and sleep, and in fifteen seconds she'd said her short prayer and was walking through the first light dream of the evening.

In the dream she was standing in a big room of people. None of them wore her family's faces or even her friends'. But she knew them all and knew they wanted her. Somebody in the farthest back circle raised a hand, as if she was the teacher, and said "Please Rosa, recite us a poem." And she did. In real life when she was fourteen to twenty, she wrote lots of poems. They were long gone now, since she burned her diaries and scrapbooks the first time Wesley vanished from home. But in tonight's dream, one of the best poems suddenly swam up in her mind; and she said it straight through,

> I ought to try to say what you gave me—
> Didn't we know the darkest brightness that can be?

Even in the dream, she knew when the poem was written and for whom—Wesley when he'd finished high school. He had signed up for three years in the Navy, and gone straight off during the Korean War where actual local boys were dying. It had been Rosa's way to say what she hoped they'd accomplished (and by then they hadn't ever touched completely; she meant just the hope). So the dream was happy, and it led her on into deeper sleep and the chance of more stories as good as that.

Wesley though, at fifty, was in real pain. It had been part of him all his adult life, a way of walking into a day with a sense of happy blessing only to come up at four p.m. with his nose flat against a blank wall of defeat. Nowhere to go, no way back, no other human to turn to for help, nothing more awful than now except the risk of death. When those ambushes happened, he could never say why. So he blamed nobody but himself.

Tonight lying here at the end of a decent work-day toward the end of the year (it was the third week in December), Wesley had lain down thinking he might join his wife for the slow close fun that would lead to long sleep. But now he was faced with Rosa's polite refusal or at least her hope of separate rest. Well, he always respected her. He hadn't forced himself on her for maybe twenty years. He granted that she mostly joined when he needed her and with a nice cooperation that might not be enthusiasm but was surely not grudging.

So he said to himself over and over "This is just one night, not the end of the earth. Get calm and wait." And though he was not one for regular prayers, he also said a short sentence, "Thank you for everything good that happened, that we didn't do ourselves. Help us to do more." He was even surprised when he felt himself slide off the ledge into sleep. And it deepened pleasantly for almost an hour till the first dream started.

In it Wesley was a boy again, maybe sixteen. He was standing bare in a room full of strangers. He didn't feel naked, though there was a big mirror on the wall in which he could see his whole body. Young as he was, he was already proud of it. He'd seen enough other boys in the baseball-practice showers to know that, in Warren County anyhow, nobody had made a finer body than he. It seemed well fixed to manufacture strong good children any day. It sure God *meant* to, in every cell. But when he faced the strangers around him, their eyes were glassy. And they shook their heads as if to say "Anybody with nothing but this to offer should quit right now and not crowd the world." Yet he knew they didn't have the right to kill him. He'd have to hang around, crowding up space with himself—a failure he couldn't repair.

In the dream, Wesley understood he was dreaming. So he tried to wake up by rocking his whole body back and forth and yelling his name. He could see that clearly from overhead—his thrashing body, his loud mouth. But he didn't come to, and Rosa didn't hear him or feel his panic. He truly was balked and he sank on deeper into more and more dreams the whole night ahead.

If you'd kept watching though what you'd have seen through every hour was the same fine couple, enhanced by darkness. Whatever your rate of attraction to bodies, you might well have thought you'd seldom been given a chance to watch people any gentler than these on the eyes and ears (neither one of them snored or scratched, and even in dreams their breathing was calm). You might have chosen to stay on till daylight revealed their faces and their eyes opened finally, of course their best features. And once you'd seen eyes so clear and keen (so ready to know you like a trusted friend), you might have wished you could go on watching their moves and words—learning their luck, washed in a steady stream of deeds from hearts as good as any you've met unless you meet more saints than most.

When the clock rang though at half past six in winter dark, Rosa and Wesley were there alone. For all the strange night, the clashing dreams, they both looked calm as children who'd stroked through steady rest toward a welcome dawn and the day's first words.

Wesley silenced the clock and rubbed at his eyes.

Rosa switched on her lamp and looked his way. "Sleep good?"

He lied. "Good as ever."

With all the signs of their age plain to see, they'd come through again as what they'd been most days of their lives—people worth watching and hoping to know.

By sundown Wesley's dream and what caused it had driven a man strong as him to leave for parts unknown, with no word to Rosa.

The second night Rosa sat down alone at a kitchen table to think on paper, hoping to crack or at least describe this big new mystery that had struck so hard.

ROSA'S DIARY

It's almost the shortest day of the year, and it ends in an hour. But I'm sure you aren't coming back tonight either, so I'm beginning to write this page. If there's a midnight tomorrow in Raleigh, N.C. and I live through the day to write a second page, then I may have made myself a place I can come to and run and yell in at night. It will be an account of what I did all the time you were gone, if you ever come back. If you decide to, and I decide to stand here and join you, then you're bound to grin and say "Of course you thought it was a good idea. All your ideas about me are good and have been for thirty-odd years. But no, I won't be needing it now."

We had the office Christmas party today. Everybody had got their final exams finished and the grades turned in. So for the four thousandth eon, Jean and I cooked the annual St. Nick Picnic and trucked in with it. I brought a ton of fried-chicken knuckles, and Jean brought one of her football-field size congealed salads—the dark colored ones with mysterious ingredients that you've always been suspicious of. But not those world-traveled PhDs. They shoveled it in by the square yard. Every inch of it went too, while I had several baskets of chicken knuckles left to bring home and freeze. In all the years of those celebrations, we've never had such a turn-out.

Maybe everybody's poor and hungry. Or a Christian again. Anyhow nobody had a foaming fit or struck anybody else, though the usual dozen aren't speaking to each other and popped their necks out of joint trying to be sure their enemies knew they weren't smiling *their* way. That much went according to plan and was a reward.

I got the usual gifts of whorehouse bath-products and paperclip holders with moron-smile faces. And I tried hard to look grateful, even when I know they're bought by wives who wish the old secretary would just go on and retire if not die. The surprises this year were a pair of tickets to a February concert from my chairman and a *pint* of Chanel No. 5 from the youngest professor.

He must think I've got more influence than I do. But he's shy enough to vaporize if you meet his face. I happen to know his salary wouldn't keep a widow in black ink, and I didn't know he'd noticed there were women on earth. So when I saw that lifetime supply of French sweetener, I gave him a hug that set him back years. He may not speak again before spring. Bless his heart.

I've got it on right now, the perfume, and am laying down a fog all round the dinner table where I'm writing. A big nose-fiesta for me and Roger and that one mouse you still haven't caught. He just negotiated the far corner at ninety m.p.h., flashing me a grin before he managed his vanishing trick.

Roger was gentlemanly as usual. He crept farther and farther from me till he could tactfully retreat to the kitchen and his old basket with the new cedar pillow you bought. Otherwise he's put his usual emergency plan into effect. He eats twice the amount of his dry chow. I think when he doesn't see you for twenty-four hours, he decides to try to swell up till he fills however much of the world it takes to bring him back up against your dry knee and he knows he's back where he

—Belongs. The phone rang just then and jogged my hand. I thought it was sure to be Horace, but there was just live silence. I first thought "Good, this is going to be my first obscene phone-call since I was forty." You remember the boy that called here eight years ago on my fortieth birthday by happy coincidence, saying he was taking a consumer poll and would I tell him what size cup I wore in brassieres, and I told him they didn't cup all that much anymore, and why wasn't he doing his homework on a weeknight?

But the silence lasted. I stopped asking questions and set in to wait it out. I think the person took at least one breath, and I guessed it was a man. In ninety more seconds he kept his peace. I thought I could hear his arm move to hang up. But then this voice—man, woman's, talking bat's—said "Never you doubt I watch you by the instant. Others may be fooled. I've got the damned *facts.*"

Then I hung up. Now I'll try to go on to bed, trusting it wasn't you. Whatever else I've accused you of all these years, it was never cheap tricks or mental illness. If I plan to sleep, I'm also going to need to assume it wasn't anybody with a long clean knife and our address. Mine anyhow.

The honest balance at the end of this second day seems to be this. You left the shop two evenings ago and went on somewhere else. Nobody down there claims to have seen you since, and they've never lied to me before. I've looked in your usual places and don't find any note or cash advance. I've got plenty money, as you well know, so that's no concern. And I don't feel the pure terror I felt when you did this same thing for four days when Horace was born and shorter times since. I'm not running for police chief or anything else that bold, but for the first time in my life at about ten o'clock tonight, I said out loud to the room and Roger, "Rosa, you can stand alone."

You said fairly recently that you were not a real prop for me, and I called you wrong. Maybe you were right. Maybe you're giving me a chance to test it. I wouldn't have asked it of you, not now—least of all with Christmas at the door and me having to go to Mama's and explain your absence, if you're still absent Christmas. But there again, those were my plans not yours.

I trust you're alive, Wesley. Safe and indoors and that, whatever's wrong enough to drive you off, it will heal itself in the night. Or you'll call me tomorrow and say what it is and let me try to change it. I can't claim I've loved you longer than anybody else above ground, but I have loved you harder. Every doctor on television says love is supposed to change as any two people walk forward together through more than junior-high dates. I can look at you still, as recently as last Sunday when you were nodding in your chair by the football game, and know why I've wanted to be in reach of you for all but the first thirteen years of my life.

Every picture of you in this house is standing in place, not turned face-down or hidden in drawers. I see you this instant and want you back, strong as ever. Say your prayers, be good to your body, sleep deep. I've got one consolation in knowing you're not a drunk. I can trust you not to be sleeping in gutters. But also I can't blame your absence on liquor. What you've done, you've done clearheaded.

I know, I've gone on more than a page. You always said the worst thing about me was how I loved words, how I talked my way to victory in every fight we had. I know that's true and I'm sorry. I know I've driven you further back into silence to the place where, to get my attention and make your point, you practically have to walk out one dawn and slash my tires. Or slide through those slim tall trapdoors in the outside world that you've always known how to find with your nails and that gladly close behind you. Please reappear.

Christmas Eve and no word. I just talked to Horace. They're staying in Charlotte this year, you remember, with the Mama-in-Law. So he called all bent down with guilt and apology. I told him I was fine, which is not but three-fourths a lie. I told him Christmas was sad enough without him taking on further reasons for misery. I was hoping he wouldn't, but you know what he did next—ask after you. I planned to lie there too, but my mouth wouldn't do it. It just plunged on and told the whole truth. I said you'd been gone since right after eating a big normal breakfast on the eighteenth.

He asked had I checked your sock drawer for notes, remembering the times from his childhood. (Was it two or three times you left back then? I've honestly forgotten.)

I told him I'd about worn your socks out but no, not a word.

Horace said "In that case I'm leaving this minute. I'll see you in three hours."

I almost let him. The thought of seeing my son *alone*, without that wife, for one more time seemed sweet in the mind. But I told him I wouldn't sit still for him to run out on his promise. Just act like the well-brought-up child he is and not go strowing his sad family's mess around the outside world like hog shit down near another man's creek. Not that his mother-in-law's squatty house constitutes the world exactly, but the one sure thing that would wreck me now would be knowing half-strangers are pitying Horace. Or me and you. Or you.

Wesley, you were always so slow to speak up for yourself that it took me long years to realize how I mowed you down time after time with all my orations and grand epistles. Of course I *didn't* mow you down. I never really won. You'd just tuck your square chin, nod, walk on off, and do your will in your own sweet time. But I wish I'd had the fairness to see years sooner how I shut you out of my own calculations and thought I was Miss Country Genius and Judge.

I can plead that I got it from my mother. Our father was so good to watch but so weak, and Mama just got stronger and harder till she thought she knew more than Justice Holmes or John-the-damn-Baptist and the mixed choir of saints. So I naturally kept my eyes on her. I'd have rather watched Daddy, but he was mostly gone—drunk laid out under some cool low tree. And what I learned was "Men are meant to be loved and not trusted." Or "served not loved."

I know I loved you—God knows you heard me moan it enough—and women my age just learned from birth that service was what our hands were for. Hands, eyes, titties, bladders, all. I thought I was going to want to serve you till we'd both worn to dust and blown on away or at least been tucked underground by Horace with one granite stone saying both our names till an H-bomb dissolved it. With all my new education and self-respect, I still think so more often than not.

You think otherwise. So your absence seems to say. Unless you're kidnaped by Shiite Muslims and rushing toward Beirut right this minute with your wrists bound bloody and your eyes tight-blinded.

Forgive me please. Don't let my busy imagination jack this private trouble way past its true size. But isn't that part of what's so strange now? People not one bit grander than us, just broke-down retired old Jews on vacation or sailors on leave with pimples and toilet-paper patches on their chin can step round a corner or sit in the wrong chair and—woom!—be pitiful stars on the news, the urgent business of presidents, popes, and assorted kings.

Of course, all of us matter to God that much. Poor God. Poor us. How can things weak as us bear so much care? If I let myself really dwell on it, it's likely to burn me right to the sockets. You asked me two or three years ago why I'd just quietly given up on church. I wasn't that sure I had, till you noticed. But now I see why. I really don't want to matter as much as church says I do. Reminds me too much of me as a girl, me gazing at you like you were the Holy Ghost in blue jeans with tongues aflame and angels behind you stretched east and west towards dawn and dark. Idolatry.

Am I punished now for that? Are you telling me finally, you and God, to lay off the worship? I quit though, Wesley, some years ago now. It was how we got back at ease together once Horace had packed up for college and gone. You noticed it; you said so. One night you dropped a raw egg on the stove, right down in the eye, and left me to scrounge out the awful glue. I said "Goddamn it! You're a permanent mess." In an instant I was ready to beg your pardon.

But you laughed hard and said "Exactly. I was hoping you'd learn."

You *are* a mess. You were set down here to stir things around. I am a stuck-up missionary nurse sent to press and fold and hide mess in drawers. We had one child, sadder than we two combined. Together we made up my favorite team. Now we're strown round the map like Esso stations, and I hate it worse than anything yet. Christmas Eve and eleven o'clock!

This is meant to be the best hour on earth, long year after year. Stop, sit still, and wait—there, hear the Boy coming. Hold your arms out to greet Him.

I can't speak for you, your arms tonight. Mine are here in my lap. I am sick with shame for my big share, whatever it is, in this wreck we're in.

I broke off there and called your mother. I knew if you'd kept to your old customs, you'd have called her by now. I also knew she'd keep her own counsel unless I pried. I chose not to pry, and she chose not to tell.

She wished me a very nice day of rest. She said she was warm and dry, thank Jesus. She thanked me for my "little thoughtful thing." I knew she'd already forgot what it was—five pounds of chocolate, already rushed down her throat. She said "I'm right here alone as a handsaw."

I didn't know quite how alone a saw was, but I said "I know it and I'm sorry as you."

She finally laughed. I hadn't heard her laugh in years. Then she said "I'm happy, Rosacoke. Get that straight."

I'll try, all night. I hope you've found the Salvation Army and have put your order in for turkey and dressing. Or I hope you are by some kind soul that means to give you Christmas without signing on for a whole life with you. I mean to get up at day with the sun and drive to Afton and face my mother. She let me know by mail late as yesterday that you and I are looked for, us and all other souls bearing one small drop of her strong blood through the fields of the world—*Come hither and feed!*

I slept last night, to my great surprise. That's bound to mean you did. I pray for the same on us both, now and always. Sleep, dark brown rest and no dreams of day.

Christmas night, 10:30. I got back from home sooner than I expected, and tired as I am, I'll turn to this in hopes of burning myself all the way down to the gutters. Who but me wouldn't be cold white ashes after a day full as this? But you know my nerves *eat* trouble. They're standing on end down my whole body this minute, playing "Reveille" on those little Yankee Doodle flutes that etch glass.

And I got up before the sun, finished wrapping the presents for home, fried me a big breakfast, enjoyed every bite of it, watched the Bethlehem, Judea service on t.v., took Roger for a stroll round the block among all the children with their new realistic toy implements of destruction, then settled Roger in with a day's supplies. At the whiff of me leaving too, he started that puppydog trembling that comes nearer to breaking my heart than most human signals.

Horace called up just as I was heading out the door at 8:30, so I laid back five minutes to let him put in enough writhing to stoke his shame. He said he'd rather be with you and me than any thirty of the Lomaxes.

I said "Me too."

And that made him worse.

Finally I had to say "Son, I truly don't want you here. We've had enough Christmases together to last us till Heaven. I'm beginning to realize I love a little freedom. I'll call you collect the next time I'm blue. But don't hold your breath."

It shocked him badly. I thought he was about to hang up in my face. But then he said "Promise me you're lying."

I waited and said "Of course I am. Come down early in the New Year—by yourself if you can—when everybody's not blue as indigo. I'll cook you exactly what your heart desires."

He accepted and I ran.

All the way up home though, I knew I hadn't lied. I didn't want to see him and least of all Priscilla. Horace turned out as satisfactorily as we have any reason to expect, and I'd write him a good job reference tomorrow, but till I get a lot older than now, I won't be needing many days of his time.

You though. The nearer I got to Afton, the more I felt the shape of your body being cut out of me like a live paperdoll—a shape that was leaving me with less than I need to live on. Once I got on past Louisburg and people gave out and God took over, I got worse by the mile. In ways I'll never understand, you are so personally involved in that one stretch of pines and oaks, the white sandy soil, that blond broomstraw that looks like it's growing from buried Viking giants (their beards, chests, and crotches), the way the sky huddles down and cups the land like a pale blue dome that seems to be promising to protect it forever. The way you can come round a long curve of road through woods and slowly build up the expectation that—yonder just the instant you break out into view of that halfway hid rock up yonder—a fourteen-year-old boy, a little old for his age, is going to rise up from sitting on that rock, wave you down, step up to your window, motion you to open it, and then without saying anything but your name reach out and hand you a folded slip of paper that, when you read it, says either "You can stop now, Child. You've finished. And you've won perfect rest" or "Stop. You have failed. Step out of this car, leave your keys on the seat, head straight for those trees, and brace your face. Your punishment begins"— both in God's handwriting, tall straight black ink.

I've always know the boy's face will be yours, the face you had the day I found you. The one I tried to earn for so long till it vanished behind what the years did to you. You and me and everybody else but my good mother.

I was into Mama's road drying my cheeks with the back of my

hand when I caught sight of her standing straight by the door. You recall how she always knows when I'm due. No air-traffic boss can foretell arrivals like my Emma Mustian. I was a few minutes late, so she'd got a little chilled. I could see her flinch once, and someway that scared me much worse than finding you gone the other night. The thought that my mother might ever go underground, agreeing to die, still won't run through me without hard snags and bloody cuts.

Nobody was there yet but her and Rato. When was the last time you saw Rato?—two or three years? My next-older brother has genuinely got younger. For a few years there around forty, his face looked like it might crackle all over the way a white cup will. But it didn't. Whatever clouds blow through that mind, they blew on away and left him calm as a good April evening.

He could be that boy on the road too—Rato, the boy that hands you news from God. In fact I remember thinking, just before I met you, that Rato might stand up at the supper table some night or when everybody was ready for bed and say "I know you thought I was human, your son and brother, but no. I'm an actual angel and I've noticed some things. Get ready to hear me." I don't think I'd have been the only one that halfway expected it.

Mama says he stays indoors with her from Thanksgiving through the middle of March and does every possible chore for her. But let the first leaf show on a tree, and Rato's off to roam the woods from dawn till dark like when all of us were young. "I might just as well not be here," she said. She doesn't know what he can be doing out there. I wondered if he might not have a big profitable liquor still, and Mama said "He does seem to have his own pocket change."

When I climbed the steps to Mama and kissed her cold cheek, Rato was suddenly there behind her in that scary way he has of condensing out of nowhere.

I said "Merry Christmas."

He looked me over closely and said "Let me see your passport." You know how he's always liked spy movies and used to claim he was a spy but wouldn't say who for.

I said my credentials were out in my car with the presents if he'd please go get it all, which he did.

After that it went very much like a normal Christmas visit. Milo and Sissie drove up from Henderson while Mama and I were putting dinner on the table. With how Milo's acted in recent years (leaving the farm for a truck dealership and neglecting Mama), I wondered if the eldest brother would appear. But they did, grinning like they still lived upstairs and helped the family through thick and thin.

It was Mama's usual light lunch—the turkey with cornbread dressing and cranberry sauce, country ham, corn pudding, snaps and little butterbeans she'd put up last July, spiced peaches, cold crisp watermelon-rind pickle, macaroni and cheese, creamed potatoes and gravy, then her own angelfood cake and ambrosia. Every mouthful made the only way, from the naked pot upward by hand. I hadn't eaten with her since the Fourth of July, and it was a real shock to my tongue—that many kind flavors, all happening at once like good deeds intended for me. Whenever I compliment her on it, she just says "It's the only way I know to cook. I know they've got a lot of fine speedy things now, but I haven't got the time to read all those instructions they put on the boxes, and anyhow my glasses are generally lost." Even when she and Rato are there right alone, she turns out three of those meals a day—every one of them simple and appropriate as the original patent-model Last Supper.

The only new strange thing was that nobody mentioned you till after dinner. It was four o'clock and we were halfway through opening presents in the front room when Sissie as usual finally stepped in it. She picked up your present, dangled it toward me, and said "Am I going to be the first one to ask if Wesley is alive?"

Milo laughed. "I *knew* you would."

Even Mama had somehow held back, so I'd made it a game to help me through the day—who could keep quiet the longest and not ask Rosa the oldest question, "Where's Wesley?" At first it hadn't seemed that hard to do. But by the time Sissie blundered ahead, I was ready and relieved.

I said "I very much hope he's alive and well. His body at least has not been found. He left for work several days ago and kept on going."

Sissie had to ask "Is he still up to that?"

"Still?" I said. "It's happened a time or two in twenty-eight years. I don't call that an everyday event."

Sissie said "Thank God it's something Milo never tried."

Milo stood up and said to my face "Too true, too right. That's why Milo is no more living back of *these* two eyes than Tyrone Power." He rubbed both eyes with his hard thumbs like Milo was gone and his eyes didn't matter. In a second—whoever he was—he was gone out the back door toward the woods. That was my old trick, bolting dinner when my feelings got bruised.

Sissie said "He'll be back before dark. He's scared of dark." Then she begged my pardon. Sissie learned the secret of family diplomacy in early childhood—say everything you think, *then* apologize. You get the best of both worlds.

As always I excused her. But my own nerve was up, so I told Mama I'd get some air myself and would be back directly.

She said "You haven't opened my present yet."

I told her I'd save the best for last.

And I went to Milo like a heat-seeking rocket. All I had to do was walk double-time. I knew where he'd be, the path he'd take.

He heard me coming in the thick dry leaves and slowed down his pace, though he never turned to face me.

When I got up behind him, I didn't try to speak and he didn't either. I think we'd have circled the globe like that if I finally hadn't said "Can we sit down a minute?"

Milo said "I didn't know *we* were doing this."

I said "I need you."

He thought that over for what seemed a mile. Then finally we came in sight of the saddle tree, the one bent down by a snowstorm years ago but kept on living. He suddenly turned back, grabbed me round the waist, and sat me up on the saddle easy as if I was still a lightweight skeeter. He sat on the ground three paces beyond me, found my eyes, and said "What do you need?"

I told him I'd never been worse than now, that you were gone with no word of why.

He wanted to know what I had done wrong?

I was mad at once and said so. Why did he think, first pop, I was wrong?

He said "Wesley's two years younger than me and gone. No man in his fifties will push off from home if he's got a home."

I said "Then you're way too far out of touch. Wesley hasn't said one hard word to me in the last five years."

Milo said "Him leaving is a sermon, commencement address, and the twenty-third damned psalm all together. Check his last words. What's the last thing he said?"

I tried to remember. The last real act of yours I could see is how you put your straw hat on once your father was buried and went to the car, not waiting for me. The last unusual words were maybe two years before when we'd made nice love and were resting. You said "For a Baptist missionary, Rosa, you can sure damn *dance*."

Milo shook his head. "No, the morning he left. Did he say he'd call you or see you or what?"

I said I'd gone back upstairs to dress.

"So you didn't speak at all? No wonder he's gone."

I asked him what we had left to say after so many mornings? "What can Sissie tell *you* that she hasn't said ten zillion times?"

"—Some mess she's just now heard on t.v. or a secret chuckle from our honeymoon."

I told him I bet that was one long laugh.

He said "Well, it wasn't Jackie Gleason, but then you and Wesley aren't the only food for laughter. Me and Sissie have had our pretty moments too."

I told him I was glad. I didn't say it was a bigger surprise than you leaving. If I knew the answer wasn't bound to be you, I'd have thought deep and told him the next-closest truth—that Milo Mustian my oldest brother was the most important person on earth to me. As it was I said Wesley was the name that came to me when anybody mentioned a boy's name and love or happiness.

Milo said he understood me.

I said I thought my family in general looked down on Wesley.

Milo stood up and came over toward me. Those eyes he got from Mama were big bowls of water that looked like tears. He was facing the ground, but he said "Rose, I don't look down on anybody. A man'd have to be digging fast toward Peking to be farther down than me."

I took both his wrists and pulled his eyes up to meet me again.

The tears had drained on away, no sign of water. He said "You and me ought not to have give up on each other."

I said "Maybe not." Then I kept on looking. He kept on moving back faster and faster till soon he was too much like the brother I'd known so well and trusted. Then I finally bent down enough to kiss him. He's of course my brother, though I don't think I'd ever kissed him outright before—just dry cheek brushes. It ended in no time.

But it got Milo's attention. He didn't try to force anything else on me, not from that direction. But he said "Oh Rose, why in God's poor name did I let all these strangers in on us?"

You know how, anytime things have gone bad between you and me, Milo has blamed himself for introducing us. The hundred times I've told him the way we really met—me sighting you in the woods up a tree—are just waste breath.

He wanted to know if you had abused me?

I told him absolutely not. I said there were times I could imagine you murdering me frankly with a gun or a quick knife but never with meanness or poison. And I said I'd always figured I could stop you cold if you came at me violent.

Then he wanted to know if we had "given up on the bedroom"? He put it exactly that way. All those t.v. sex seminars have got to him.

"Not given up," I said. "But it never did seem like the answer to anything between me and Wesley. It was always more like the question itself. How come we wanted that out of each other and went for it at such different rates and times?"

He told me more than I'd ever wanted to know about Sissie and him. How she'd pretty well cut him off at the spring years ago, which I figured. How he'd found a willing ample girl at that Farm Bureau motel-weekend he spent up here studying soy beans right after the Vietnam war (the time he came out and barbecued chicken for us). How he wanted to set her up in a house in Florida and find his way to pull out of here and eventually be an orange-grove worker near Orlando with her. Her name was Spain, I seem to remember—her first name, a redhead, Spain Russell. Milo thinks she's still down there, and he still thinks he knows her phone number but has never tried to call it again. He said it out to me like a lesson I'd someday need—area code so and so, dot dot dot dot dot dot dot.

I smiled and said "Thank you."

He turned to head home, back to Mama's (I keep calling it *home*). Before the trees gave out completely, he looked back at me, took both my elbows, kissed my forehead, and said "You ever get tired of being this lonesome—Christ knows, *I* do—you call me collect. We could both pick oranges another twenty, thirty years. Then we'd be right there in retirement heaven. We could drop in our tracks. They've got boys in white coats roaming the streets day and night, to shovel you up for the incinerators."

I thought it was the foolishest proposal I'd ever heard but also the kindest and, right then, welcomest. If you get to read this ever, don't be mad or jealous. And don't even mention it to Milo or me. It means too much to either one of us. Just remember *old* Milo—the one that was better than you and me both for sweet open-heartedness and eyes like the temple altar of God, incense coals fanned red by troops of angel wings. That boy's still hid somewhere way down in this scorched old man, fifty-two years old and worn to the threads.

Back at the house Sissie and Rato were watching t.v. from opposite sides of the kitchen, and Mama was ironing the latest gift wrappings to save for next year. She's got a little deafer in the last twelve months, so I had a short second when I came through the door before she saw me. She's seventy-three years old and seriously she doesn't look in any important way a bit different from how she's looked ever since I remember. And that goes back to 1939, me two years old staring from the baby bed at that same face beyond me, the hair a little darker, otherwise the same—my perpetual moon, always at the full.

What does that make you? Women aren't supposed to say this anymore, but doesn't it make you the sun? Aren't you the power I've moved around and because of? In those eleven or twelve years when Horace needed more or less all of me, I guess I was his sun or—again—his moon. Maybe I was getting power from you and shining it on to him. But surely Mama didn't get one amp of power from my poor father. So was I wrong all that time? Was all my strength mine? Did I just imagine you?

How much of whatever you and I made through these past thirty years was sex?—just the big force of God working through us to make a new relay of people? Is it what went wrong between us, the reason you're gone? Did my body stop being something you wanted? But surely you noticed, back when we were young, that age and change waited for us too and that neither one of them was fun or lovely? Nothing is much sillier than t.v. doctors saying "Age is beautiful." What?—speckled old hands and slack jaws, loose thighs, and thick toenails? About as beautiful as dog-do in August on a sizzling road.

I know this much at least, that you'd turned away from me slowly but more and more. You were always courteous about it—but the fact is, you turned. It hasn't been all that hard for me to bear. I've been able to think it was a natural movement of time, working in both of us. But I can't help seeing all these old couples on t.v. saying they've never been happier with their bodies than now, when their children are grown and gone, and they can be alone in the house together. Not that you and I are old, but we turned out not to know what to do alone together. That was one fault at least, and I bear at least fifty percent of the blame.

Neither one of our bodies looks as good as it did back when they were the things that brought us toward each other. Not one single cell, outside or in, is the same as when we met and drew at each other. But in me at least the cells of my mind still look for you. When I walked back into this house tonight just awhile after dark, I prayed you would be in sight in here waiting again. In *sight*, Wesley. But no, here were all the pictures and the big statues of you my memory has carved in all the corners but not you—no part of you I could touch.

Where are you? If you're not with Horace or your mother, then you're not with anybody I know. If you had any private friends, I don't know when you saw them. Except for basketball games at the Coliseum with Ray, you haven't been out of here one long evening in years. No successful tomcat ever stayed home good as you.

Any mechanic good as you could get a job for the asking at any crossroads on the moon. So you could be working, and paid fairly, anywhere. But for all your Navy cruises, I can't imagine you living outside the south. You always said Yankees all look like they've taken a serious laxative and are bound for the head. For all I know, you may just be on the other side of town. Or in Durham.

You may be laughing with some younger woman, way better built than Rosa now and with new eyes fixed on your every blink like Rosa's once were. She may be spooning you constant streams of nourishment your bones have craved and that I stopped giving or never knew how to make. But Wesley, you never said you needed that. It was all I could do to get you to ask for supper if I got home late.

But now I'm clawing at my own eyes and lips. I never was that good at manure eating, mine or others'. It starts my eye watering, and I'm not going to try tears on you, even in writing. Words were what I used to try to drown you with. As much as any Holy Roller at an August revival, I've had the permanent gift of tongues. And now here again are all these *words*. They're for me—you well know—much as you. They're to keep my mind from melting in the heat of all I think and wonder about. You may not ever have to read one word, but they're helping me put one foot down firmly and then the other— without yet needing to scramble and run.

I won't try further to picture you this minute where you are, alone in a motel watching football with no more company than a cold pizza-box or with some better person. I didn't try to call or see your mother for fear you might be there with her, though I knew you wouldn't be. *Knew?* What's left that I know now?—not you, never did. Whatever I thought.

Last night of the year. Jean and Hal invited me to their New Year's Eve party. Like a fool I went. One reason was, I'd already begun to feel what I know you'll feel if you ever read me this far—that I'm talking on way too long about feelings. It was always my failing, and I'm at it again.

I will therefore try to concentrate more on actions, things I do that might be worth reading about. In which case, this whole project will probably end a day or two into the New Year. That still hasn't chimed in yet. It's not but 11:30.

I said I was a fool to go to Jean's party and oh was I. Hal works in the Research Triangle for one of the big microchip outfits, you recall.

So the place was full of PhDs in Physics, Engineering, and Math plus
their wives, and some of them were doctors too. Talk about practical
knowledge! If I'd had a flat tire in the yard, I doubt if there'd have
been one volunteer to help fix it. But it would at least have given us
something in common to talk about. I got Jean aside after the first
awful hour and asked her what she found to talk about—you know
Jean is no stronger than us in the I.Q. department. She said "Try sex
or food, movies sometimes work, no t.v. except sports. And don't
admit it if you're a Christian or a Democrat."

There were a couple of single men that got within firing range of
the whites of my eyes, then saw I was old enough to be their aunt if
not their mother and retreated. A few of the wives seemed pitiful and
came over saying they heard I worked with Jean, and wasn't I fine to
have made something of myself and learned the English language,
implying of course I'd come from the briarpatch and white-trash roots
in general?

I told them my people were clearing and improving this land
when theirs were still selling scissors in Sevastopol, and that mine
were the people that invented the English language and handed it to
Shakespeare, ready to use. I overheard more things I knew were gram-
matical errors at that party than in any two months at home with our
families.

You know I *didn't* say any of the above, just gnawed a big hole in
the side of my cheek and told Jean I'd be around to help her wash
glasses late tomorrow morning, but that now I had to get my horse-
and-wagon on home before midnight. You and I never celebrated a
New Year in public, and I'm not going to make an exception this time
just because you're invisible.

All the holidays that are important for me happen within ten days
of each other—our anniversary and Christmas and tonight, except for
Easter. I can still actually feel the old year dragging out the door and
the young one drawing nigh with barely a sound. I'm not even going
to switch on t.v. and watch the ball drop on Times Square. I'm going
to wash my face for bed. With any luck at all I'll have said my prayers,
mostly touching on you, and will be deep asleep for the fireworks and
tears and auld lang syne at midnight.

Jean asked me, as I was leaving on the doorstep, when I was finally getting mad with you? She thinks I'm holding back anger that's killing me and blocking me getting on with my new life.

I asked her who was anger going to hurt but me and the crockery? And I told her I didn't feel the need for a new life—that I hadn't minded the old one, not more than most people.

She said "Ro, that's a sad damned lie."

It made me mad. I said "You're drunk. Go on back in with your smart funmakers. They like your brand of jokes more than me."

Even in the weak porchlight, I could see her go white. So I begged her pardon.

But Jean said "Ro, I *said* 'Get mad.'" (You recall she took that course in Conflict Resolution.)

I said "You can't even guess what you're asking for. Rosacoke *mad* is more than you and any six psychology degrees could begin to tie down." I didn't know what I meant, but it felt true to say.

She cried next of course.

And I left her standing.

She'll be on the phone at midnight now to beg my pardon and wish us grand new heights of mature-woman friendship in the office and elsewhere this whole coming year.

I may not answer.

I did. This is January 18th, nearly three weeks gone. I was in bed dark but still awake and saying my prayers when fireworks started at the end of the street, and the bedside phone nearly rang off the table. In the silent instant before I answered, I thought it was you not Jean, and then I couldn't speak.

So a strange voice said "Home early, I see."

In the disappointment—and somehow relief—that it wasn't you, I blurted out "*Late.*"

It said "never too late." Then I think it laughed.

I say *it* because by then it seemed so much like a thing, an expensive new machine for scaring victims in the pitchblack dark. Then it hung up hard.

For a minute I prayed it had really been you, that you finally cared enough to check, even mean as that. Then unfortunately I got sensible. I told myself I'd been lucky till now, that I'd finally started getting my share of crank calls after years of nothing but a hot teenager. By the time the fireworks played out, I was truly asleep—the kind of sleep where you keep on thinking "I'm wide awake here. I'm wasting good dark."

I had a long dream about Roger. He had turned into an old Boston bull-terrier. You were gone and I knew I was meant to take care of him, but I kept forgetting to feed him. He was awfully weak and thinning down daily. The neighbors kept trying to remind me to feed him. Then in two or three weeks when I finally got to it, he was too frail to eat. His legs were dissolving to dry little stumps. I tried to force food down his throat with my fist. He still refused and his teeth grazed my skin.

Then I woke up slowly. At first I thought it had to be you, and I tried to be glad. I was on my back on my side of the bed. My arms were up and around a man who had just now started rooting at me. It was hard to believe you'd start like that after so long away, and my hands kept finding clothes wherever I touched—he was dressed in something like coveralls. In all his pockets he wore big objects that pressed in painfully. It dawned on me then that he had to be armed, that those were weapons. Then I knew it wasn't you. He was clean to the smell and not really cruel in the way he moved, not yet anyhow.

So dazed as I was, it took me another thirty seconds to tell myself "You are being raped, Rose. Now what do you do?"

I thought if I screamed or started to fight, he'd do nothing but kill me. I thought he might well do that anyhow once he was finished. But the thing is, I stood it as long as I could. What kept me lying there was a strange curiosity. The man was trying to talk while he moved, like a speech he'd memorized way back in school for this one moment, if the moment ever came. At first I thought if I just heard his speech, then I'd understand and could talk him down. But all I got was his main word *help.* If he said *help* once, he said it fifty times.

The lower half of his body was working, but it felt more like a dry bumping duty he had to accomplish than any kind of fun or meanness to me. Wesley, forgive me—I felt like laughing. Then again I was scared cold, and I made one mighty roll with my hips.

He hit the floor loud.

I thought "All right. I'll be dead in two seconds." I was calm as you.

But he stood on up. In the streetlight coming weak through the blinds, I could partly see the side of his face—a full-grown serious strange adult, no hungry boy. His hair was still combed, and he seemed to be thinking.

I knew my time was flying by fast. But for some odd reason, what I thought of was Rato. I thought how he would not understand this—how once I was dead, then nobody else on earth would try to answer Rato's questions. He'd be left thinking I'd been murdered by somebody crazy or mad at me, not by a man fired up with a fury he could only try to drown in *women*. Then I thought "You sound like Jean or a t.v. psychiatrist. Save your damned life." So I sat straight up and said "Get out of here. I'll give you one minute."

He stood on still, then turned to face me.

That way, the light was shining toward me. He could see me but his own face was dark. Whatever he saw, whatever he believed, whatever he'd *accomplished*, he said "Please thank me."

I'd better admit that I think I obeyed. I knew I didn't mean it, but the memory of it fouls my mouth.

He was still near enough to hear me, but at least he didn't answer. He bent down slowly to pick up something he'd dropped on the floor, then faced me one long last time. Then he was out the kitchen door, that he closed firm behind him.

I lay back down with both my hands up beside my head, both open and dry. I tried to think of plans for the rest of my life. It seemed important to plan everything now, carefully as possible. I would say a short prayer to be alive, then get up, strip this linen, start it washing, then bathe myself, dress, and *get out of here*. To my continuing surprise, it all felt like a list of things I could do. But beyond the washing and leaving, I couldn't plan. So I stood up in the dark and stripped the bed.

I'd locked the back door (that I'd overlooked—his easy way in), and the washing machine was underway before I thought "Police. I'm destroying my evidence." I opened the washer to stop the water. Then I knew I'd been right. This was my business now. The last thing I needed was to open a hole on the swarm of crows that waited to fly at my eyes and mouth if I touched the phone. I shucked my pants and added them to the sheets, touching them only in two tiny places at the waistband. Then I went to our bathroom.

I remember a movie that nobody else seemed to see in the early sixties, called *Something Wild* with Carroll Baker. She was a girl that got raped in a park while she was walking home from school in her neat uniform. After the man finished with her, she straightened herself up and continued home. Her mother called to her in the hall and asked was she O.K.? She said "Yes ma'm" and went on upstairs. In the bathroom she undressed slowly, then sat down on the tile floor by the commode, took her mother's big sewing-scissors, cut her slip and pants into slow narrow strips, and flushed them away. The sight of her cutting so neat and quiet broke my heart to watch, the first time and now. Then she took a long bath.

I turned on the faucets and made myself examine my gown. It was no more wrinkled than after a normal night's sleep, and there was no sign of stain or damp. But I didn't touch my body, didn't look closer than was necessary to tell I wasn't bleeding.

And I was deep in a tub of hot water before I asked out loud "Now have you been raped?" In legal terms, I guess I'll never know. But after three weeks of thinking it through—and oh I've thought it through, in, out, up, down, back, and forth—I can sure God say this much. I've been used, hard, for some stranger's own secret need or mission. He picked me to prove some blunt point on, and he left me without the least clue of what he meant—whether he proved it or whether I stopped him.

And was he a stranger? One of my tough problems has been the thought that he must have known me. Surely nobody would pick a name out of a phonebook for such a personal deed. Anyhow the name in the book is yours. Was he a boy from the college? He looked older than that. But with forty years of good nutrition, some American eighteen-year-olds look thirty.

Since he left me, I've read two books on the subject and several articles. And I know that a number of raped women feel like they caused it to happen, that they drew the punishment down on them for any number of reasons. Honest to Christ, I don't. I know I haven't hurt anybody consciously, not any remotely sane man. And I'm not aware of knowing any lunatics. I know I haven't done anything that deserved punishment on the scale I received in those maybe ninety seconds he groveled down in me. Then and since.

I gave up writing here three weeks ago, which speaks for itself. I took a bath a lot longer than Carroll Baker's. I forget how many times I drained and refilled the tub. I dressed in street clothes—no shoes—and lay down in Horace's room on his high single bed. I tried to pray and discovered God was nowhere to be found, not by me. By then it was no more than two a.m. No hope of daylight before nearly seven. So I clamped my teeth, pulled up the afghan that Mama made Horace, and composed my hands to wait out the time. If I'd had any hint on earth of your whereabouts, Wesley, I'd have choked down handfuls of pride and come to you through crushed glass if need be.

Yet I doubt I could have told you. One reason I could start back writing here is, I've given up on you.

Bronnie, at the shop, finally called me two days ago and asked one more time if I'd heard hide or hair of you.

I had to say no.

He said "Mrs. Beavers, excuse my language. But Wesley's the best damned mechanic since Henry Ford, still I got to fill his place. If he does turn up, please God let me know—I'll try to hire him back. But you know I can't promise."

From that minute on I believed you were gone. With God hid from me and you nowhere I could reach in time, I knew there were just two hopes on earth. I had one son, no farther off than Charlotte. He was no tower of strength and anyhow I probably couldn't tell him, just huddle up near him till something better dawned. But then a little snag, that I'd felt before in my mind, stopped me cold—maybe you were with Horace. It didn't seem like you to hide down there that close to Pris, but maybe Horace at least knew more than he'd said all the times he'd called—so concerned and shamed. So I wouldn't press Horace, not till I had to.

Then who but my mother? I had a whole nother week of time off. I'd drive back up there and sit by her, take walks with Rato. The fact that she hadn't asked about you Christmas made her seem like even more of a chance than before. The hope kept me lying there still and covered till daylight started. I'd told myself I could call her at daylight. At maybe five a.m. a car stopped in the street exactly in front of the house and waited two minutes, long enough for me to seize up in a shudder that threatened my teeth. I was frozen down. If it had been that same man, with two more, I'd have stayed there frozen while they did their business. But then it roared off. And I managed sleep, of all strange things.

The telephone woke me awhile after day, maybe seven-thirty. I still couldn't face our room, so I ran to the kitchen and answered. And at first there was a silence that scared me. I thought of course it was my last guest.

But then a man's voice said "Rosacoke?" No man in Raleigh had called me that in twenty years, so I knew I was safe to that extent.

I said "Yes sir."

And he said "Hey." Then he seemed to say "It sounds like her anyhow" and drop the receiver. I was near to guessing I knew the voice, some man kin to me.

But a woman's voice came on. "Rosa, is that you?"

I said something like "I think I believe so."

She said "Make up your mind and let me know. Rosa's mother called to say 'Happy New Year' to her. If she's not there, I'll save my money."

Honestly, Wesley, I don't think Jesus in person could have been more welcome. My mother doesn't call me more than once in three years, and then it's just to tell bad news—some more dead kin.

I said "Oh Mama, it's Rosa—yes *ma'm*. I just didn't recognize Rato's voice."

She said "This foolishness is his idea. He woke up early saying 'Call Rosacoke.' Said he had a bad dream about you in the night, said he'd pay for the call. You're all right, ain't you?"

The fact that my mentally underpar brother had dreamed the painful truth about me and was worried—that was a sweet consolation already. But the fact that my old realistic mother couldn't imagine me being any less than all right was almost certainly what saved my life. But I'd known she could save me; she had before now. I said "Yes ma'm, I'm truly all right." And then I hated myself and burst out crying. It wasn't really sobs but a block in my throat that shut me up for the next long seconds.

Eventually Mama said "You need me with you?"

Too quick I said "No, no. I'm fine."

Mama said "I think you're telling a lie—and on New Year's morning."

So I said "What if I wanted to come up there and hang out around you and Rato and my old room?"

Mama said "I'd remind you that room is near about a glacier. But it's your home, Rosa—you want it, we got it."

I said "Anything you need from Raleigh?"

She thought a second and said "Is there a Stuckey's Candy Store anywhere along your road?"

I said "Oh yes."

She said "Then bring me and Rato a pound of those pralines. They're good for his eyes, so he claims."

I said "And they don't exactly harm yours, do they?"

She laughed, which is always a shock from her, and said "All right, make it five pounds. I'll reimburse you."

I said "I think I can underwrite that much harmless pleasure." Then I told her I'd be seeing them in late morning. I got my mouth and face ready, then went to the kitchen and fixed the only breakfast I could eat—a cup of tea and part of a slice of dry toast. Then I got the sheets out of the drier and went outside and put them in the garbage, the only real percale all-cotton sheets we had left.

Nowhere in the backyard was there any sign of footprints. The place at least had not been damaged. There was just the big hole in the air that man had made when he slammed through me.

Then I tackled our bedroom—I had to, to pack. It seemed like a place that might have been hurt beyond healing, though nothing was out of place except that little throwrug at your side of the bed. The man had skewed it when he hit the floor. I straightened that slowly, and since my hands obeyed so calmly, I wondered for the first time if this whole thing was a New Year's dream.

Now that I'd washed the sheets, my gown and pants, there wasn't a shred of evidence the naked eye could see. And I wasn't going to ask the S.B.I. to come in with their microscopes and tweezers. The only conclusion I could come to right then was *Yes old Rose, you were hit maybe harder than even you know. The enemy was a human male, not a demon. You will very likely never have to meet him again above ground. You don't yet know what he did to you, but nothing seems to be badly torn. What's burned is your mind; hunt something for that.*

So I called Jean's house. Hal answered and said she was out at the garbage cans. I told him not to bother her, just to thank her again for last night and to say I'd been called to my mother's on unexpected family business. I'd be back well before term began.

Hal got confidential in tone and wanted to know what had gone wrong last night.

I told him that Rose had never been much of a party girl at her best and that now I was way under normal.

He said "Do you want us to help you find Wesley? I know some good detectives right here in town. With computers and government taxes and so on, people can't just vanish easy like they used to. Wesley's probably already laid down a trail of canceled checks and charge-card receipts. If you let me approach the right people, I think I can help maybe more than you know."

I thanked him but said I'd always respected your occasional need to just vamoose. I said I meant to give you room. You'd speak up when you had something to say.

Hal started whispering then. "Tell me to shut my damned mouth if you want to, but did Wesley find out something you didn't want him to know?"

Finally something had made me really mad. I said "Hal Gillam, I'm not a secret poisoner or a millionaire dealer in blackmarket babies."

Hal said "I understand but you know these days women are trying all sorts of things that used to be male property. More than eighty percent of modern divorces are initiated by the wife or the wife's new behavior."

I said "My behavior is the same as it's been. And one thing I'm still nuts about is promptitude. I need to get on the road now for home.

Tell Jean what I said." I left him standing with his seminar hat on, that early in the day. Hal has taken more courses than Jean. He's living proof that there's such a thing as pulling your bootstraps so hard your mind just vanishes down in the soles.

I loaded up my bag and Roger and left by nine a.m. The highway was empty as if there'd been a nuclear attack and atomized everybody but me, an old boxer dog, and everything but concrete, trees, and empty houses. Occasionally an ancient black woman would be strolling on the edge of the pavement with a tall walking stick. I'd wave and she'd stop, turn, and watch me out of sight. But you don't see anything like the number of Negro shacks you used to, those tall little huts the wind blew through. A lot of them have just collapsed back into the earth, and the grandchildren have bought themselves "double-wide mobile homes" with decorator-pink shutters and a little packed dirt yard with not a hope of a flower. Well, they're dry anyhow and warmer than before.

But the balance of everybody under sixty has moved up north to stand on desperate street corners, I guess. In all the sixty miles, I didn't see a soul under sixty years old. And pretty fast I worked up the idea that maybe God had finally punished all the descendants of Indian killers and slave owners by making young blacks vanish, that He'd driven them all to Detroit and Harlem (does He think that's a reward?) and left old ladies to guard this gorgeous land down here. Who did that make me then? I never decided.

But thinking about it, I held up through the ninety minutes alone. All the reading I've done says that rape victims first go through a bad stage of hating their own bodies. I felt exhausted that morning. I've faced numerous other New Year's Days with a lot more to hope for. But I knew I was right to be going home and changing my scenery.

I didn't hate my body or anything about me. Maybe it was because I moved so fast to clear out the evidence that I really didn't know what had happened to my body and still don't. I think though that what worked, and is still working, in me is the sense that my man was out to harm my *mind*. My body was just something he was knocking at, hoping to find my mind and bruise it, plow it up and leave the picture of him in the middle of my mind and life for the rest of the time I'm given. And he may have managed that.

But what I'm planning is that the memory is just of embarrassment, nothing worse — the embarrassment of having a dog get excited in your presence and start humping your leg with somebody else watching. That may be a serious lie, but how am I going on if I believe worse than that and let it press on me? then he *will* have hurt my mind.

What began to hurt, then and there as I came in sight of home country, was all that part of me that's grown toward you and into you. Even if we were married in a j.p.'s office at nine-thirty in the morning, we both knew it was *till death did us part*. I'd come through what could have turned into death just the night before, and I prayed you weren't dead or anywhere near it.

But if not, why the hell weren't you here beside me? Then I could be in our house, *our* home, and not streaking back to my mama — me a forty-eight-year-old woman with nothing more natural to run to than my mother. Why the hell weren't you there a hand's breadth away from me last night to save me from that? At what point in all our years together have I ever shirked anything you asked for? I would die for you every instant of the day, and you damned well know it — and don't forget, I am writing this three weeks after a lunatic fouled me head to foot and in your bed, Wesley, in a house we both paid for but that's in your name and that you left a month ago with no word of warning.

At ten-thirty on the stroke, I nosed into the old dirt track up to Mama's. You'd think red dirt couldn't hold in place against trucks and every act of God's weather for so many years, but every deep cut and bump that I memorized as a child is still there waiting to hurt you again. I don't want to sound spoiled, but since Rato had dreamed about me so conveniently the night before, I did think he or Mama might be there to meet me. But I left my things and Roger in the car and went inside to see what was what. The house was empty as home in a nightmare. That was when the willies hit me.

I stood in that cold hall, calling both their names at the top of my voice. I felt convinced that the man from last night and every other body that had ever dreamt of harming me was hid just yonder behind the room doors. Then I all but flew out the back.

Mama, as I told you, is more than a little deaf. I had to go round the edge of the woodshed before I could see her or she hear me. But oh she was back there, chopping wood at her age for that little cook-stove she keeps in the kitchen and won't throw out.

I went up close enough for her eyes to see me, and she stopped long enough to take a thorough look. For the only time yet, I thought what a lot of assaulted women seem to think—"She can *tell*. She's going to mention it, and then I'll truly die." (Even now I wouldn't be surprised if some friend's face goes all scared, and I look down and there's a wet stain of blood in my lap.)

But Mama just said "I do this to keep my arms in practice. I doubt the Law'll let you put a woman in the poorhouse when she still chops every stick of her own wood." She smiles a lot more than earlier in life, and now she let loose a beamer that about knocked me over and made me realize one of the stranger things about recent history—how much Emma Mustian, this plain country woman with a tenth-grade education and never more than five thousand dollars cash-money, looks like the Queen Mother of England. Just get her one of those ostrich-plume hats and a satin purse with a modest diamond clasp (say, a hundred small stones), and she could change the Guard this afternoon and not get arrested.

I said "This may be the best day of my life."

Mama looked at the sky, thinking I meant the weather. "I'm grateful to be here to see it," she said. "I don't know if I grade it that high in history though."

I laughed and said "Let me finish that for you."

She said "You haven't touched an axe this century. Go back in the house and make you some coffee."

I nodded. "All right. But where is Rato? I thought he did these heavy jobs for you."

Mama looked toward the back pines, then took a strong heave at her next slab of wood. "Rosa, your brother moves mysteriously. What I ask him, he does. But he's got his own burdens, so I don't ask much. He wandered on off after you said you'd come. I think he's ashamed I told you he was worried. He wouldn't want to be accused of caring, you know, for anything sorry as his next-younger sister. He woke me up though in the dark, about five, and asked could he crawl in the bed with me. It'd been so many centuries since a man asked to join me in linens that I said "Get warm." So I lay there quiet by my baby son—what? fifty years old—and waited for his message. Finally he got up his nerve and told me a terrible dream he had about you."

I asked her at once not to tell me please.

She said "He took care of that. He swore me silent." Then she studied me again, longer than before. "I'm proud to see he was wrong to worry. You look some stronger than you did Christmas day, a little tired around here." She touched her own eyes.

"I went to Jean Gillam's New Year's party last night."

"Wesley didn't go with you?"

"Wesley's still missing."

By then she'd gathered an armload of wood, and I stooped to help her. When we turned toward the house, she said "I've been scared to death for you, Rosa."

"Why scared?" I said.

"I know what Wesley meant to you."

I said "He's been gone more than a week. I might have thought I'd cave in too. I guess you're not my mother for nothing."

She gave her old loud hiss at foolishness. We'd got to the back steps. She took the first two, then faltered an instant. I thought she'd fall. But she got her own balance and said "Plan to break. Say when you're going to do it, and choose who you want to watch you." Then she set her wood in the old box on the porch and went to the kitchen.

My mind wouldn't let me believe I'd heard her right. I dumped my own wood though and followed her in.

I walked around the house and let Roger out of the car. You know how the country surprises him. The number of new things coming at his eyes and nose all at once gets him too excited.

He stood there among chickens, the woods, squirrels, and the way-off noise from a chainsaw. He looked up at me like "You expect me to manage all this?"

I said "Go to it" and waved him off.

He gave me one more slow look, like "I refuse to take responsibility when something breaks." Then he trucked off slow toward the nearest trees. His left hip is getting worse by the week.

Inside, Mama had already started cooking the big midday meal she turns out for just her and Rato. Today it was going to be the traditional blackeyed peas and hog jowl (a little pork roast really, baked in vinegar), stewed okra and tomatoes that she'd canned, little lacey pones of fried cornbread, buttermilk, and a lemon meringue pie.

She tried to involve me in the easy first rounds of the preparations, but soon it was plain that my own three decades of experience in our kitchen still hadn't earned me senior rights here. My hands just will not move like hers.

Finally she said "Don't you need a little rest after your trip? I'll call you when Rato turns up."

So I went toward the living room and stretched out on the old tufted leather nap-couch. And again she was right. I slept without trying.

At twelve-thirty Mama and Rato watch their one soap opera, "The Young and the Restless" (the one you call "The Hung and the Breast-less"). What holds them is the fact that the actors let the producers make them look so much worse than real people do, what with the wigs and eyeshadow and the uniform Dupont stainless teeth. They keep waiting for some actor to just refuse and walk on the screen one day looking normal and nice like somebody you might know, and they only invest a half-hour a day. They say when you've seen the first half, you can guess the second. Anyhow it moves about as fast as an uphill glacier. You can watch three weeks and they won't even have finished the dinner they started a month ago—otherwise it *is* all very lifelike, provided your income is a quarter-million dollars and you believe amnesia is an epidemic like Hong Kong flu. Then Mama and Rato eat their big meal in the kitchen where, winter and summer, desert plants would thrive. They keep the wood stove fired that high.

I stripped down to my blouse and slacks and joined them.

Rato said his peculiar grace (you remember, "O Lord, I thank you for dinner" or whatever meal he specifies). They both served themselves bounteous helpings and struck in. I did the best I could. Rato wouldn't notice if nobody else above ground ever ate another crumb, but it's one of the main beats Mama patrols.

That day though she didn't say a word. She just kept up a closer watch than usual, even for her.

The feel of her eyes prowling my cheek hurt at first. Then after I warned myself to bear it, it began to seem normal and even strengthening. So much so that when Mama finally said "Rato, tell her your dream," I said "Wait. I'll tell you what *happened*."

And I actually told them. I didn't go into every detail of the man's movements against me or the condition of the laundry, but I let them know that a totally strange man broke into our house just the night before and tried to harm me in my own bed.

Mama's eyes stayed on me through every word. But when I'd finished, the first thing she said was not to me. She said "See, son, your dream was wrong."

Rato said "You don't know all my dream. I told you she was hurt. I didn't tell all."

I had to laugh. Here I'd confided what was maybe the worst secret of my life, and all I'd triggered was the usual wrangle.

But Mama came back to me. "You seen a doctor?"

I couldn't admit I hadn't thought of a doctor, not to that moment. I nodded. "I'm all right."

She asked me his name.

I said "Doctor Gattis."

"No, the rogue," she said. All criminals that aren't *murderers* are *rogues* to my mother.

"I said he was a stranger."

"But they caught him?" she said.

I had to tell her they hadn't.

"And may not," she said, "short-handed as they are." With television, Mama and Rato know as much about life on a big-city police force as any old cop.

I said "I didn't call the police and don't plan to. The man fled the scene with no real damage, to me or the house. I don't want my name blazed around Raleigh, every sick fool ringing me day and night."

Through it, Rato had sat very quietly. I looked over toward him to check at least. And oh dear Christ, his eyes were full. Next to you and Milo, Rato's always had keys to all my hearts. So I stood and went toward him.

But he waved me off. And when I kept coming, he bolted upright and ran out. The next thing I heard was the back door slamming.

Mama said "He don't understand this, Rosa."

I said "I hope you don't think I do."

"I didn't say that. I see you're here so I guess you're lost. I hope some way I can help you out."

I told her she'd taught me all I knew. It wasn't really true but I don't plan to write her and change the claim. She understands me.

When we'd washed the dishes and got them all put away for the four millionth time, I mentioned Rato not being back. I thought she'd said he spent the winters indoors all day, and that day was cooler than usual.

Mama said "He spends a night out ever so often, not when it's quite as cold as this. I worry some but it don't seem to hurt him. He was always tough but thirty years in the Army turned him into something that can take what comes."

"Except his sister," I said.

"Ma'm?"

"Except me, what's happened to me. That's spooked him."

Not till then did Mama turn, drying her hands slowly. "Let me just say this—you told him wrong. You said that man tried to *harm* you. That shied him. That's what scared Rato off."

Again I all but laughed. "Mama, I was telling the plain truth. You don't seriously think a rapist means well, do you? I thought it would help us all to get it out at the start of my visit so we don't bumble around in the dark knocking each other down in ignorance."

Mama nodded yes but she said "You shouldn't have said *hurt*."

I couldn't believe her. "I can't tell a thirty-year Army veteran that one other person in this world just might intend to hurt somebody?"

"But it was you that got hurt, Rosa. Anybody else, even me, he wouldn't have flinched. You are something he's made a whole life out of."

Then I did laugh.

But late in the afternoon, when I had managed a long cold nap up in my old room, Rato still hadn't come back. Mama was in the front room reading her daily devotional and *The News and Observer*. Reading is the only surprise for me in her present life. When I caught her at it, she almost apologized for taking a quiet half-hour in a chair, and I realized she'd never had time for it till the last one of us was gone—the last one needing care. I told her to sit still. I was going out to get a breath of air.

Again for the first time, she didn't rise up to be sure I was dressed for my Arctic expedition. I left her looking back at the thin little book, following prayers with her silent dry lips.

I wasn't sure I was hunting Rato, and I knew I could never guess where he'd be. He'd never had personal favorites in *places*, unlike me and Milo. At least he'd never said so. But it dawned on me that I hadn't seen black Mary Sutton in years—the mother of Mildred, my friend that died of the bastard baby shortly before you and I got married. Mary had always been good to me, even if she was tough as whit-leather.

She even gave me the best advice of anybody in the early days when you were the one big problem on my mind. She said if I needed you, then *hold* you in whatever way it took. I've sometimes wondered if I didn't arrange to get pregnant with Horace because of Mary's advice. I know I conceived him within an hour of hearing Mary say to *hold* you.

Now I didn't even know if she was alive. But her ancient shack had stood in a clearing half a mile in the woods north of home, about midway between our place and yours. So I struck off in that direction hoping Roger would find me but he never did. Maybe he was with Rato. Most dumb beasts are.

The path was still clean, and in a minute I was passing big trees that I'd known as switches, individual rocks with shapes I remembered, and the old smells of evergreen and sweet rotting leaves that all came together to remind me of nearly the first half of my life. Some of the memories were sad—our dumb premarital struggles that kept me roaming the woods or trekking to your house with head in hand—but most of them went farther back than you to a happy childhood. And by the time I broke out in the clearing, I was calmer than I'd been in twenty-four hours at least.

The shack was still there. The ferocious tom-turkey that had always patrolled the place was nowhere in sight, and there was no smoke from the old rock chimney. But nothing else was different. The house was balanced pretty much where it had always been, on the absolute verge of collapse. And the boards had got more than ever like bones or driftwood, leached out nearly white till the whole thing seemed like a miracle of how long a shelter could last just because it was needed. Somebody had to be in it; otherwise it would have blown right to dust. I went up and knocked. No answer for what seemed a month.

Then it opened half an inch. The room behind it was dark, and the day itself was running down, so I could barely see a face.

But I guessed it was Mary, and I risked her name.

The face stepped back and opened the door another two inches.

A blast of hot air struck me. I realized she was saving precious heat, and I rushed to step in. By the time my eyes had adjusted to the dark room, the person had gone to a far corner and stood against the wall.

And it was Mary. She said "Mr. Rato told me he seen you."

"When?—this afternoon? I'm hunting him."

"Ain't you going to speak to me?" Mary grinned, then quickly covered her teeth (or the empty gums).

I said "Excuse me, Mary. You surprised me at the door. Had to get my bearings."

"You been here before. Is it that long ago?"

I told her "At least twenty-eight years."

Mary said "Seem like last Sunday to me."

I looked round for changes. The only thing missing, that I recalled, was the cardboard box she'd kept Mildred's baby in—long taffy-colored bastard Sledge with the serious eyes. You remember he went to the pen ten years ago for killing a girl in Petersburg? I asked about him.

"Sledge own a big car-wash. Doing real fine. Don't send me no money."

I'll probably never know if she was lying. I did ask "Where is he?"

Not missing a lick, Mary said "Newport News." I know Virginia's a peculiar and stuck-up state, but even there can a man go from the pen straight to owning a car-wash in that short a time? I left it right there.

But Mary reached behind her, found a picture frame on a table, walked farther forward, and waved it at me.

I thought at first the man was Billy Dee Williams, the black movie-star—same mustache, same finger-waved hair. But Mary's picture was plainly homemade, a little blurred and faded. I looked for Mildred's likeness somewhere on him, maybe in the eyes. But no, he was just a light-complected man with an empty face. Maybe Sledge, maybe not. Why should I doubt her? I asked did she have a picture of Mildred?

Mary pointed to the dark wall behind where she'd stood. Dim as it was, I made out a whole spray of dime-store brass frames. She said "You sent it to me after Mildred passed."

I'd forgotten. It was one I took with that huge box-Kodak Rato sent me from the PX in Fort Sill, Oklahoma. And amazingly, for my skills, it was clear as something from *Life* magazine. Mildred was walking in the road near Delight Church. Milo was driving me to the store. I told him to stop for Mildred. He grumbled but did. By then Mildred and I had gone past the childhood friendship we had. I guess she was nervous about the racial stuff that was already rumbling. Back then I was way too blind or dumb to understand how strange it must have felt for her—her best little girl-friend now a grown white lady. But she smiled and posed, frowning broadside. The frown was at the sun, not me. One picture came out clear, and I sent it to Mary right after you and I moved to Raleigh. How much else of my life—good clear memories—have I sent off and long since forgot? So I asked could I look at the other pictures?

Mary was in my path to the wall, frowning. But then she smiled and stepped aside. She said "You caught me."

I asked "In what?" But I went to the wall, and there were several old pictures of me (all high-school pictures with sweater and pearls and those extra teeth I always seem to have in pictures). I knew I hadn't given them to Mildred or Mary. So I was baffled—much more so when I looked down low, and there was a framed newspaper clipping from *The Warren Record* of December 1957 reporting our marriage in Dillon, S.C. And a dog-eared announcement, in my handwriting, of Horace's birth. I was speechless. Why had Mary collected all these, and where from, and why had she first tried to hide them?

She said "Now you caught him."

"Milo?" I asked. I couldn't think who else might have herded up this little Rosacoke collection in a hot Negro shack deep back in the woods.

Mary shook her head. "I ain't seen Milo since way before you. This is Rato's place. He begged me for it."

I said "Mary, I don't understand."

She said "Rato came down here ten or twelve years ago with two pictures of you. He wanted to know could I buy him some frames, if he give me the money? I told him he went to town more than me. But he said no, he didn't want nobody else to know his business. He give me two dollars, and it was a long time before he come back. I had his frames though and handed them to him. He sat down yonder at the table and put the pictures behind glass, took him best part of an hour. It wasn't till then that he asked me could he hang them up right here? I asked him what in the world for? I mean, I knew you—Mildred thought you were *something*. But I didn't have no call to spread you out up here like my lost darling baby-girl. Rato just said 'I'm asking you nice. Rosacoke is the person I miss in the world. I don't want everybody asking questions about me and her, if I keep them at home. Down here, I can know in my mind where she is. I can walk down and see her and you anytime.' I didn't want to laugh, but it did seem peculiar. So I chuckled. And Rato smiled. But he said 'Mary, your damned walls are naked.' So I told him 'Sure, hang all you want.' And in later years he brought all the rest—the rest of the pictures and that baby card, yours and Mr. Wesley's boy. I bought some more frames, and he still comes to see them. Never says what he's doing, never goes right up to the wall and studies them but sits out here in the chair. And *I* know. Rosa, your face give that poor boy *satisfaction*. Don't laugh at him now. Don't tell him I told you."

I told her I wouldn't think of such a thing. But I did ask had he been down here today? When she said no, I thanked her for the news, said I was home with Mama for a few days' rest and had to run now but that I'd come back for longer toward the end of my stay.

Mary followed me to the door, watched me halfway across the clearing and then called my name in her strong voice. When I looked back she said "You got a secret, ain't you?"

I tried to laugh. But then I had to say "Should have known I couldn't hide it."

"Not from me anyhow. I knowed you too long." Mary smiled again and said "You know where I'm at, all day and all night." Then she shut her frail door.

Secrets *on* secrets—my thrilling life.

That was the start of my country rest. At least it gave me another kind of surprise, to spread on top of New Year's night and sweeten it maybe. Maybe. Milo had been the brother I leaned to when we were children. He was so good to watch, still or moving. And being four years older, he could show me signals of the world up ahead where he was already. Rato, with his peculiar mind, was somebody who lived with us a good many nights but said about two hundred words a year—really. The rest of the time, he was off God-knew-where.

For all I knew he was climbing tall pines and launching out high with nothing but his long arms and gliding all day in the summer sun. I knew that, after Mama, I was the person in the family he paid any attention to. Every once in a while, he would bring me something— a cut finger to bandage or a rock he'd found in the riverbed.

Seriously, one day he brought me a big damned rock the size of a coffee can, hauled it upstairs, sat it on the floor by my bed, and said "I brought you this because I knew you'd want it."

I thanked him and said I could use it for a doorstop. Rato just kept staring at my eyes hoping I'd understand, I guess.

When I didn't, he finally said "It's because it looks like you." I started to say I was deeply insulted.

But I looked again and yes, there was the line of a nice girl's face on one side of the rock. I thought he meant he had found it natural, carved by the water.

Then he said "It *had* the face when I first saw it but hid down deep. I gouged it some with another rock to find it better." I thanked him and thought for the thousandth time my next-oldest brother was bound to be from Space. But it never dawned on me I was something he thought about when I wasn't there.

Even now it still didn't matter a lot. Coming on top of you leaving and New Year's night, it was one more case, that I didn't need, of how sadly little I know about men—what they truly think in those calm-looking minds, what they really will ask for, if they'd ever really ask for all they want.

I mean you of course. Once my father was dead and Milo married Sissie, you were the only man I wondered about and needed to know. And now you've taken your secret and gone. Call up, Wesley—collect if you need to—or come to the backyard just close enough for me to hear your voice and tell me, finally tell me exactly what you need that I didn't give. What final straw broke our camel's back? It was bound to be from me, right? Who else did you know long enough and hard enough to let them fail you so bad you had to leave?

I know that sounds like Ms. Door-mat of the Ages. I know I'd be drummed out of any woman's-rights club, the biggest traitor of all to my sex. But as much as it's caused me years of pain, I cannot truthfully sit here and claim I'd have changed it any way if I could—my feeling for you. Hard as it was to do, in those days at home—surrounded by our old places—I made myself think back to how it was and where it must have come from in my mind and heart.

First, obviously, it had to come from God. Even if I don't go to church more than twice a year, I'm enough of a Christian still to believe that a woman's feelings for her man and vice versa are put deep into her and him by the Maker. And not just to insure that we multiply and tend to the Earth (haven't we done a grand job of that?). Way past the drive to multiply, for me, has been the way I've seen God's image in you much more often than in myself or any six ministers in vestments and rings.

I mentioned the danger of idolatry here awhile back. It's a danger I haven't always avoided. More than once at important times, you've been a bigger sun in my sky than God Himself. We've both suffered for it. But even when I've kept my worship in balance, I've known that you at your best were just stamped out in God's image and you *showed* it. That's why I was glad for long years to serve you.

After God, I learned it next from my father. Has anybody ever figured out why a big percentage of America's truly lovable men are drunks? Not the kind you see on t.v. now, drinking a few too many martinis over a business lunch or an extra bottle of champagne late on a wonderful candlelit night but the concentrated kind that buys a cheap pint of antifreeze bourbon, goes in a white room with one naked light bulb hung from a wire, sits down in a straight chair at a table painted green, and drinks and drinks till he pours to the ground like the last tan drop, then stands up, scrubs his eyes, and starts again.

My father was nobody's genius, I know. He wasn't even that good a farmer before he took to the bottle in earnest. *His* father kept us alive till Milo could take over when he was sixteen. But from the time I can remember, little flashes from age three or four, my poor father's is the face smiling down at me and drawing me toward it. I know from my years with my own son that Mama had to have spent endless gentle hours stooped over me doing every task I needed. So why is it I don't have one single grateful memory of her, not until I'm at least thirteen? All I remember from her in my childhood is hard words and switchings, which has got to be miserably unfair.

Calm-headed now, I calculate my father can't have spent a whole hour doing hard jobs for me. He very likely never even saw my butt dirty, much less had to wipe it. Like I said though, his face was what I learned to love on. Half of what I did awake was to try and please that face that could beam like the gorgeous sun at Morehead City on a warm spring dawn. Oh it could beam and *did,* now and then in my presence but so seldom that I was never sure if I'd caused it or of how to cause it again. So I told him over and over I loved him.

He'd say "Sweet Rosie, I may love you," but he drank on deeper in the bottle till all he aimed at was one great bottle that could drown him forever till he walked up the road that one particular sweet summer evening and stepped out into Duke Simpson's truck speeding hell-for-leather to a church fishfry with a twenty-five-pound tub of iced coleslaw and a peck of cornbread.

Then there was you in the mile-high fork of that pecan tree the Sunday I found you for the first time ever, thirty-five years ago. I tried to talk at you up there against the glare. You were fixed on something way out past me, that I couldn't spot and you wouldn't speak of—"Smoke," you said. You were watching smoke. I was watching fire.

Everything I've loved in my entire life, I've loved then and there on the spot that instant I caught sight of it. My mind says *"There"* and my heart says *"Hold it."* From that hour on, I held you, Wesley. Or sure God tried to. And thought I'd more or less succeeded till Christmas week when that same smoke you've always watched closed around and hid you, from my sight at least.

Be alive, old friend. Sleep deep. Come home.

WESLEY

Wesley is still the kind of man people watch. Even children will stop their urgent business to watch him pass. Though he's fifty he hasn't gained more than ten pounds since his Navy days. His auburn hair is still strong and dark, and his eyes are firm as ever—barely blinking. People always used to praise him as sexy. He'd grin and shrug. But he never refused the tribute due a power he prized in others as much as himself. Before his marriage at twenty-two, he "used himself" (as he thinks of it now) with nineteen women and three men. He still has a clear list of the names and a detailed memory of the circumstances of all those partners with whom he was sober.

Nobody mentions *sexy* much now except occasional women in bars, and he spends very little time in bars. But a good many people still like to touch him. He has noticed how—in shopping malls even—if he sits down on a bench to rest and watch the world, some child is likely to spot him, run up, and (before it can think) grab his legs around the knees or lay a damp head on his broad thigh, smiling. If he lays his hand right in his own crotch, within two minutes at least one woman or man will pause to look. A surprising number will circle back for a second glimpse.

The fact gives him no special pleasure; it's just one more peculiar thing he knows about himself. He stirs that kind of need in others, that curious trust. The men he works with, and the office girls, are often compelled to frisk him with quick fingers when he passes—little good-luck samples of his force and sweetness, his palpable goodness.

His goodness is his power, which he's never understood. Despite eyes hot as a diving hawk, Wesley has never intentionally harmed a living soul. Better, he has done several thousand acts of kindness unknown to anyone but him and his object. Several dozen of them qualify as really good deeds (he sent a cousin's son halfway through college, and even Rosa never missed the first dollar), and the goodness shines through his broad skull and eyes like blood through your hand in a flashlight beam. That light, combined with his clear regular features and his color and odor, are what people try to reach inside him.

Wesley has generally walked away from that—though with occasional women, even after his marriage, he's stood still long enough to let them express their full intention. But never for more than an hour or so; the other times he vanished were not for women. And though he never mentioned those hours to Rosa, he never once thought of them as cheating. He can enjoy the various facilities and stunts of his God-given body. He can share those bounties on a short-term basis with, every now and then, a clean kind soul that seems in need.

But he's felt no compulsion to crawl on his knees up a dim church aisle the next Sunday morning groaning in shame and eating tears. It's been his plan since the dawn he was married to go to his grave with the same good woman he met as a boy—the woman that asked for his hand, both arms, and the rest of his life. He's always known that Rosa understood. He's even repeated that pledge more than once on nights through the years when he knew repetition was what Rosa craved. *Forsaking all others till death do us part*—even if it was no part at all of the quick civil wedding he paid for in Dillon.

So Wesley was all but as shocked as she when, in late December, he found himself leave work one afternoon, stop by the bank, and draw two hundred dollars from the stainless-steel computer treasury (they'd kept money separate since Rosa went to work). Then he nosed through traffic to interstate 40 and didn't stop for coffee till five hours later on the far outskirts of Asheville in chill black mountains.

*   *   *

The waitress said "You look like a man that's been cut at the bone. Let me bring you what's good."

Wesley laughed. "My bone's all here. I just took a look—pink and pretty as ever. But sure, bring me everything you think I need."

It was two chicken-fried steaks, something he'd never have ordered for himself. He took a long look at the battered gray meat, searched the waitress's wide blue eyes, and said "I must look tore up bad. But if you say so, I'll gum those down."

She nodded. "You do. Then streak it to Nashville. Don't stop till you're safe in a chain-locked room."

He obeyed her to the T—ate both steaks, heavy enough for wolves; ate a slab of peach pie with peach ice cream, filled his thermos with coffee. And did not stop till he locked the chain on room 1211 of the Parthenon Motel in Nashville itself.

Then in no more light than leaked through his window from the life-sized reinforced-concrete model of the Greek Parthenon, across the road there in a park flat as Texas, Wesley sat on the broad bed and wept cold tears.

He could not say what had flung him this far. It was nothing he could touch, no word he had said or heard from Rosa. No trouble with his son, none at the shop. And he'd lost all memory of last night's dream. He'd just been working that last afternoon and reached for a metric tool from his bench when his hard right hand stopped in midair. Those clear five fingers seemed no more *his* than the car he was tuning. They paralyzed completely and would not draw back when his mind called them in. An instant's panic, then the hand hit his side, and blood recommenced.

But in another minute a voice in his head said "Death is what you just reached for." He laughed out loud, then realized the voice was not his. Wesley had no truck with brands of religion that deal in voices and unknown tongues. Still he couldn't shake the certainty that what he'd heard was a version of God's word, a true special message. What did it mean?

Wesley's own father had died at fifty-six. And once Wesley passed fifty, he realized it wouldn't be long before he'd close in on his father's goal-line. But that hadn't seemed to set him back. Except for steady low-grade prostate misery, a common cross of middle-aged men, his body generally worked like always. Not that he did anything special for it in the way of diet or exercise.

With a few exceptions from magazines and television, Rosa cooked pretty much what they'd grown up eating (with bring-home pizza or fried chicken maybe once in ten days). Wesley was convinced that any man over twenty who was jogging in the road or pumping weights at the YMCA with Baptist organists and hair-designers was ruining his joints and exhausting his chances at that night's sex.

Wesley cared about sex. He couldn't have discussed it for more than ten seconds, wouldn't have given you a key to that urgent private room if he'd been a poet and doctor combined. But from his early discovery of the unimaginable treasure installed just south of his belly, he had been a desert saint of desire and performance. By now he had spent thousands of hours of his life far out on the tether spun by his ample well-made genital. Rosa had been the partner of at least half of those times (the others were with himself and virtual strangers)—generally willing and sporty, though less than eager for the repetitions his mind required. He thought of it always as fire and light, he knew it kept him alert and young, he suspected he'd done more good that way than with ten years' gifts to the damned Red Cross or Community Chest.

So he turned to it now, high up in Nashville by the Parthenon's shine. Even after his wedding, masturbation had been at least half his sex life. Good as Rosa could be if he got her attention, nobody knew the exact rate and grip as well as he. In five quiet minutes in a locked storage room or a clean toilet, he could take himself to the true outer limit, glide in that glare, and come back strong and calm and ready for hours more of work. A whole morning's defeat could be glazed and soothed off that easily and cheaply. And he never needed the aids that so many of his friends laughed about—magazines, head-movies, dreams about strangers. He even had a rule that he couldn't imagine sex with any person who hadn't, in actual life, given him sexual permission. Anything else would have been rape by Wesley's rules.

But that first night in Nashville alone, he labored a quarter-hour with no result but exhaustion. His body seemed willing but the mind wouldn't focus down to that white final moment of laser light that triggered reward. Finally his need was so real that he chose a face off television and worked himself through a quick tale of access to her body—a girl in a parking lot at dusk, he helped her with her groceries, she asked him into the back seat beside her, and from there on (as night fell down on them slow) he gave every service she dreamed of and more. The eventual hard knots of semen tore out of him like dry barbed-wire and pelted his chest with the sour stench of humiliation. But they let him sleep, half-dressed on the covers.

He'd remembered to hang the *Do Not Disturb* sign outside, so it was nearly noon when he woke. His hands and chest were still crusty; his hair was damp and moldy. But he kept the habit of a lifetime and, before he went to the shower, he cleaned his teeth with his tongue, smoothed at his hair, buttoned his trousers, and lay back to pray. Most days he leaned on the Lord's Prayer, with just the added names of his family and a few friends, any particular problems of the coming day. That one morning he tried to state his problem and request specific help. He said "Merciful Lord, I am one scared man. If You've told me I'm bound to die soon, then let me face around and take my due on home ground with my kin. If I misunderstood whoever spoke to me in my head yesterday, or if it was the Devil, still lead me back home now and show me how to act."

But he lived in that same airless room days longer, right through Christmas. He didn't behave like a frightened or depressed man. He kept his curtains open all day, he joked with the maids and waitresses, he drove downtown several nights and went to the movies or to bars near the original Grand Ole Opry auditorium. He struck up conversations with numerous women, but none of them rang back to his voice with the sound he needed to hear—the chime of his mother's old cutglass ice-cream bowl. So midnight after midnight he returned to the motel, renewed his reservation, honored his cock, and tried to sleep.

Many times he picked up the phone and tried to call Rosa, his mother, the man he worked for. He even rang Rosa's line eleven times on Christmas afternoon, but of course she was gone and the phone bell sounded like dying cries from a virgin child left hungry and lonesome in a big dark field. If she'd answered though what in God's name could he say?

So he stayed close in his room, talking to nobody but the black man that brought him the one room-service meal he ate all day (a hot turkey sandwich on untoasted white bread with cool tan gravy and a sad little white-paper cup of warm cranberries). That night he took his first steps of the day—just out and around the parking-lot. He didn't have the energy, not to mention the heart, to walk two hundred yards and see the Parthenon all high and bright. Three other cars were parked near his—the only other guests tonight and all with license plates from the upper midwest, retired old couples fleeing Minnesota snow toward the Florida sun (or new grandchildren on down the line).

By the time he got back to his room that same awful night, Wesley knew this much. He was not as afraid of the actual death that awaited him as he was of being dead at heart now, of having been dead the past twenty years. As a boy he had dreamed of a world in which his own life meant a good deal. He'd been seven or eight years too young to serve in the Second War. But the war had given him the vision of boys mattering outside their own houses, their own mothers' hearts. One single boy—Eddie Steer from near Manson—had been a fighter pilot, won two or three medals, and got his big picture in the Warrenton paper and several store windows. That one face alone (broad, grinning, blond-haired) had meant a world to Wesley in what it said about where plain American boys could go, what they could bring back, and what it would mean to the people they knew and rank silent strangers.

When he'd pitch baseball at John Graham High and head back to class from a victory game, he could glance at every face around him (younger boys, teachers, the tipsy damned principal, not to mention girls) and get an even bigger idea of life—he would not only matter here and now to a small-town school, but one year soon he'd matter to a crowd. Always, even after now, there would be crowds of people calling Wesley's name in genuine need and with thanks to give him. In particular there would be one fine woman, loyal for life and keeping her looks, plus three or four children that would grow up polite and count for something and tend to him and their mother in old age.

Rosa had volunteered, hard and steady when they were both in high school (she was two years behind him), to be the woman. And she had been interesting—the smartest, best-talking girl he'd seen outside the movies and no pain at all to watch, with her long live yellow hair and blue eyes that were the only ones in the world steady enough to stare his own down. But then he'd joined the Navy to begin his big life, sailing out of Norfolk.

It had been a grand hitch. He had missed seeing guns fired at real human foes (since they'd sent him in the opposite direction from Korea); but he'd been to Gibraltar, Naples, Rome, and watched wild horses from the rail of his ship as they flanked the sandy bright Azores. Four of his nineteen women spoke no more English than it took to make change; their moans in the dark were a universal tongue. And it lured him on in his faith that he—this one lean boy— would soon do something the world would love, and discover it had always yearned for.

Nobody'd ever known a word of this. Wesley hadn't mentioned it, not because he doubted his mission and his power but again because words wouldn't support him. Rosa had dreams enough to bypass the damned Queen, and couldn't she evermore hang them out to see?— bright in the air before her till her own eyes burned and Wesley wanted nothing as much as her, her entire body in the clasp of his hands and her secrets touched.

Frustrated as she made him feel, when every dream had to be hers to the letter and go exactly her way, he consoled himself when pregnancy trapped them in a premature marriage that his wife anyhow was well-endowed in mind and body and was going far too. So maybe their strengths could join together. Together they could amount to something, which was more than you could say for anybody else in either of their families since man left the caves.

That was the lie that poisoned all the rest—that he and Rosa would thrive together. Sure as rat bane it poisoned them both, their pitiful son, and the roof on their heads. Once married, they lived in Norfolk for two years—Wesley selling and fixing motorcycles. Then Rosa pressed down powerfully, and they came with the baby to Raleigh and dug in there. Dug bottomless graves. Wesley had decent jobs all the time—always somebody else's best mechanic—and Rosa had improved herself with courses, starting at the YMCA and moving on to N.C. State till she'd got her respectable job typing for a building full of college English teachers (no two of which were smart enough to change a sparkplug). They made enough money to pay a mortgage, run two cars, and put Horace halfway through college till the poor boy decided he'd already learned more than any living teacher and dropped out (with no offer to refund any money to his parents).

But money had never been it—not for Wesley, not the prize he was after. Money was something you took in with one hand and passed out with the other, something that might help oil you forward but was never your goal. And what it was had died of suffocation or disappointment before their son could spell *hippopotamus*.

It was hopeless of course and had always been. It was a dream Wesley had made from the sight of his own good face in mirrors and the things riled women said about his soul and body. Surely God didn't build such towers to burn? Surely they were meant to be true lighthouses, guiding others to joy—or safety at least. What Wesley saw now though (and he spent a good part of the nights reading the Gideon Bible in his room) was the fact that had stove him up. He was meant to have lighted his own light. The tower and the spiral ladder were provided, the mirror was polished in place, he had never lit the fire.

Wesley didn't think it out in those exact terms. But they came close as any to what he felt. He had been created a special soul. If nobody else but his mother had known it, then he at least had. And the way Rosa hunted him, she must have known too. Yet they never asked him to do anymore than sit still and let them twine him in vines strong enough to lock elephants. And soon he'd consented. And now it was too late.

At Judgment Day a few women might stand up and mention a nice quick generous time he'd showed them. Rosa might testify to how much information and poetry she'd got from studying his face. Horace might say his dad had never denied him any reasonable thing he wanted. His various bosses would be forced to say Wesley Beavers could repair the *Titanic* after all this time under miles of water with his eyes blindfolded. But when God got to Wesley himself, Wesley would have to say "Your honor, I just didn't understand. I wasn't smart enough. I thought You'd done it all. I waited too late for You to start me." He wouldn't expect or ask for mercy, and he had no reason to think he'd get it.

So why not pick up the phone, tell Rosa he was on his way home, and hit the road now? (it was the last afternoon of the year). Because in his mind now, Rosa was the cause. She'd fed him the main lie— how grand he was—and had devoted the past thirty-odd years to blinding his eyes to outside duties. As women went, she was nearly first-rate. But now he felt certain he never should have married. Damned if he'd swallow the little pride left and let Rosa lead him blind to the grave. Where else though? And who with?

All his life Wesley had surprised himself by how much he liked loneliness. Three-fourths of his boyhood was spent alone or with dogs in the woods. That was when he formed his conviction of a kinship with all of life. He never spoke it out to anybody. But by the time he was fourteen, he was convinced forever that natural living objects were all aware and wished him well. He suspected them of powers of communication, different from his own but aimed at him. When he was alone he stood a chance of hearing them—short clear sentences about courage and generosity, their own demands for respect.

So another of the big mistakes of maturity was letting too many people into all the rooms of his life, then leaving the wild country for cities where even the finest ear couldn't begin to hear natural signals, even birds couldn't sing. That was another reason sex had stayed so important in Wesley's mind. It was the last line he kept to the secret world where angels spoke in silence and brought their gifts back and forth in relays—self-respect (for your body's power), the sight of your goodness in other creatures' eyes, and oh the chance to make those other creatures happy as you and as ready to shine.

So New Year's Eve in Nashville, Wesley decided to celebrate by going downstairs to the motel bar and seeing what happened. He had spoken to nobody yet but maids and waitresses and desk clerks, the occasional drunk. There was bound to be a New Year's crowd gathered. Let whoever was there set the course for his next outward move; he'd gamble that far. Resting and thinking and reading the scripture had shown him nothing but how balked he was, what a sad cold corpse.

The bar was crammed at ten o'clock. As he plowed his way through the swarm, a man put a drum major's paper hat on Wesley's head. He wore it as far as the mirror, saw it looked about as appropriate as a toupee on a moose, and handed it to the nearest woman.

More nearly a girl. She was barely five feet high with baby-fine blond hair. And she was dressed all in pink wool that made her seem nested, a safe young rabbit almost asleep. What kept Wesley from laughing was her eyes. He'd never seen deep brown eyes on a blond before, and these eyes were big enough and serious enough to stop a hot bull.

She thanked him for the hat, then dropped it on the floor, and went back to her glass—one of those foaming milkshake contraptions that Wesley scorned as "candy drinks."

He ordered straight bourbon and asked her if she had a name.

She said she had till some fool stole it from her. She meant the husband she'd recently left. Her maiden name was Joyce Wilson. She had married Tim Hunsucker but would soon be Wilson again. "Just call me Wilson now," she said.

So Wesley called her Wilson all that night and the rest of the time he knew her.

She was twenty-six years old, a radiology technician at Vanderbilt Hospital; and when after an hour of noise and two more drinks, Wesley asked her to come to his room, she laughed. "Hold on, Pop. My mother said there'd be geezers like you."

It hurt Wesley, which he showed as fury. Women had called him a good many things but never old. He emptied his glass in one long swallow, gave a silent bow, turned his back, and left her. He headed for the parking lot and his car—surely some place in town had to have better company—but halfway there he decided "Hell, you *are* a damned pop. Go watch t.v."

*   *   *

And he was lying on his bed, watching the Times Square mob of soused fools all dreaming better luck, when his phone rang and nearly threw him to the floor (it hadn't rung once since he'd been there).

She said "This is Wilson and I'm still downstairs."

Wesley said "Happy New Year from here then. I'm too feeble to climb back down."

"How about me climbing up?"

He said "You sure you're twenty-six?"

"And a half."

"Then suit yourself."

Once he'd hung up, his first thought was to run. To lie here and wait for her was plainly risking adultery. And Wesley felt that by his own lights, he'd never committed adultery. There was no way he could be locked in this tight a space with that fine a woman and not try to eat her. And being this far, this long away from home, it would be a real cut in his promise to Rosa—it might open out before him like a permanent road and he never go back. He thought it through for several minutes, and Wilson still hadn't knocked. She'd probably lost her nerve. So he turned out his light, switched off the television, and lay still and quiet. He even napped.

He was anyhow dreaming of an almost endless fall down a black-glass chute that led to the end of the universe when somebody tapped the door. He rose in the dark, zipped his fly, and opened on Wilson.

In the half-dark of the hall, she looked smaller and younger. Twenty-six, a year younger than Horace—Wesley could easily be her father. He said "You ought to be somewhere better."

"You too," she said. "Look at pitiful you, holed up on the road while the old year ends. You're asking to die of a bad broke heart."

Wesley nodded. "I am."

"I ain't going to let you." She stepped in past him, went to the toilet, and shut herself in.

He locked the door, smoothed up the bed, and sat in one of the two easy chairs. Only then did he see that he had no bottle, not even a Coke.

Wilson took a long time in absolute silence. But when she came out, she looked even better—some mysterious work around her eyes and cheek hollows. She laid her big purse on the floor by the chair and sat down slowly. Then she studied his eyes for what seemed the better part of two or three hours. Finally she laughed. "Now tell me I've picked the Louisville Slasher. You're wanted for fourteen women and a dog, all headless but grinning in Dempster Dumpsters from here to Ohio."

Wesley nodded. "You got him." No trace of a smile.

She waited that out. "Can I have your autograph, darling?"

He said "Can't write. Never finished first grade. I'm mainly pitiful, is what I am. Dangerous of course."

Wilson said "I'm sure you are. But tell me this—what's the thing you've done that you're sorriest for?"

"I can tell that," he said. "I've thought that through. I killed myself at age twenty-two."

"To be dead that long, you smell good from here."

Wesley said, "Old Spice. It purifies."

"Tell me more," Wilson said.

"I was one fine boy. God had plans for me. I was meant to spread joy. People smiled at my face on more than two continents. Then I let my high-school sweetheart trap me and that ended that."

"How?"

"You've heard about marriage! It's not exactly *freedom*. Both of my feet been nailed to the floor since 1957, Christmas week."

Wilson asked "Where was that?"

"Dillon, South Carolina—our shotgun wedding. We've lived in Virginia and North Carolina ever since, Raleigh most years."

"Then you've done a powerful ripping-loose job, to get those feet tore up and brought west."

Wesley said "That was easy. But now I'm stuck here."

"How's that?" Wilson's legs had curled up beneath her, and a shawl-necked sweater nestled her breasts like the duty it most enjoyed (more than warmth).

Wesley fought a great rush of need to hold her, to drown his eyes and mouth in her neck—the lovely deep bowl at the pit of her neck, lilac-colored and warm from a distance. Not a mark on her visible skin anywhere, from damage or age. And no cheap whorehouse make-up or smells. Just a whole grown woman that trusted her gifts. "I'm scared," he said. "I've ruined so much. I'm scared if I move, I'll crush something else."

"What's left?"

"My wife."

"She know you're here?"

"No ma'm," Wesley said. "She's worried to death."

Wilson asked "Do you love her?"

"I must not," he said. He'd discovered it that moment. Cruel as it seems, and whether it was true or not, Wesley's sudden doubt set free that instant in Raleigh the one living man who meant to harm Rosacoke's own body (Raleigh time was an hour ahead of Nashville).

Wilson said "Be sure. Cause if you love her, I'm clearing out this minute. I'm no kind of thief." When Wesley didn't speak for a minute, she reached for her purse and gathered to stand.

"No God," he said, and waved her down.

"No what?"

"Don't go."

Wilson said "Why not?"

"I'd probably die—be found by the maid on this sour bed with my clean hands folded and my eyes rolled back. Ruin her whole new year."

"It *might* set her back." From that instant on, Wilson's body—with no special knowledge from her—hurled millions of fine silk threads toward Wesley, grappling cables too frail to catch moths but, coming as steady and fast as they did, sufficient to draw him in and helpless. In a while she checked her watch and said "Happy New Year, sport, six minutes ago." They'd heard the noise outside but not noticed.

It seemed to Wesley he was back on the rails, that something (surely this small girl here) had lifted his capsized old engine and set it square and firm on the track. Rusted maybe but stoked again and aimed. His heart filled so full and fast with thanks that he had no choice—if he meant to keep breathing—but to stand now, hold out his right hand, and say "Let me thank you please."

"How would you manage that?"

"I'll know," he said, "if you give me time."

Wilson thought a moment, then took his hand, rose up beneath him, and said "I've got till six a.m. day after tomorrow."

They used it all. Wesley had long since gone past the starved-bunny leap-on-roll-off tactics of famished youth. Most of the first night in fact, he never hardened stiff. In the early hours, that worried him—more for Wilson's sake than his own. But when he eventually apologized, she said "Man, I'm as happy as a bee gargling honey. You have learned some things about women, let me tell you."

So Wesley took heart, got up and turned off the one bathroom light, then came back and worked on, chiefly for Wilson's benefit. Finally a little before three, a big tunnel opened in the black dark above him. And Wesley saw that his luck was renewed. He had a fresh chance to give somebody the thing they'd missed—their body worshiped (Rosa had long since declined to accept that).

He turned then to Wilson with new intent. His faculties pointed to a white-hot focus. He entered her body and let her know how one grown man could search a woman from crown to toe and use each atom of her precious skin—or so it seemed to Wesley (he also sank in a flood of pleasure that threatened to kill, that strong and fast).

At first it frightened Wilson. She'd known a few boys, a few grown men but nothing like this. This fellow was in it for something even she couldn't guess. And while he didn't exactly hurt her—she could feel how steadily he tried to honor her—there was something more than a little scary in being at the mercy of someone this big and strong who seemed to need precisely *her* and *now*. It felt like a need that couldn't be fed, not permanently ever. A need that could swamp any boat ever built, not to mention her cute little spanking-bright rowboat.

But after that, they both managed sleep. By the time daylight woke Wesley, six hundred miles east Rosacoke was climbing the track to her mother's. And he did think of Rosa in the first conscious moments—with a sudden rush of thanks for the times they'd laughed, several million jokes between them (mostly started by Rosa). This afternoon he would somehow call her and find words to say all the questions he felt. Not that he suffered bad guilt about the night, or about Wilson sleeping here bare beside him, but that he couldn't imagine beginning a year without letting Rosa know Wesley was alive, remembering her, and planning on her always if she still cared to know him. He didn't think about it beyond that point—Wilson stirred awake.

Wesley naturally wanted to continue where they'd stopped in darkness.

But Wilson was firm. She wrapped strong arms across her chest and said "I'm black and blue now, buddy. I need me some aspirin and a quart of hot coffee."

That trusting banter was almost as good. They showered together like brother and sister (that might need to spend several weeks in jail) and went downstairs to eat breakfast for six.

From then on they lived in Wilson's trailer. It was brand-new and she owned it outright. It was parked in old cedars on the edge of a big pasture that belonged to her brother on the Franklin road thirty minutes from town. She had bought it with the money from her second divorce. The son of a bitch had beat her badly, then repented of his meanness—Tim Hunsucker, a pitiful drunk (her failing till now: drunks had somehow impressed her but never again). And when she left him, he'd come to her begging—let him set her up in a nice dry place to show his regret. It took her no more than fifteen seconds to tell him where he could buy a new trailer, to her specifications, and where they could park it.

Wesley took to it at once. It was more like living on a ship than anything he'd tried since the Navy. Space was at a premium, so you didn't save any junk that might not matter in the next three days. And even if the built-in furnishings were ugly and looked like they'd melt if one match was struck, you could all but hose it out when it got dirty. Not like a house with brick foundations, where decades of dirt silt up and multiply under your feet. And the rooms were so small you could make a real impression on them. In a bigger space your actions might lose themselves in the excess air before they reached their target.

In the first few days, while Wilson worked, Wesley went to town, bought a minimum of clothes, and cruised the countryside thinking.

He had set a date—January 11th, his dead father's birthday—to decide on his future. To return to Raleigh and his old home, or Raleigh and not Rosa, or to stay here with Wilson, or some fourth place. The happier he felt with Wilson, the more he knew that Raleigh and Rosa were all but surely where God meant him to go.

He'd make a pledge there (Rosa had made them recite the Baptist marriage vows, just between themselves, the week after they finished their civil ceremony); and Wesley never broke sober sane promises he could keep. What if he went to Rosa, explained to her as best he could what had scared him, and asked her to join him in pulling up stakes and going somewhere new—that they both could like and start over in, getting old wrongs right? What place though and what were the old wrongs and what would *right* be? And how would Rosa replace in his heart the things he'd be giving up if he gave up nights like these with Wilson?

After supper on the twelfth, he discussed it with Wilson. She asked if he'd thought anymore about hunting a job? Up till then he'd been living on credit cards. Her question hit Wesley wrong at first, but he held in his temper and told her that he'd be deciding two days from then what his whole future was.

She looked down steadily at her wine and then said "I'm glad you warned me. It'll be my future partly too."

"How's that?"

"Jesus, boy, I've brought you right to the core of my life. I've set you up like the big Buddha here. If you don't want any part of my gifts, then give me the satisfaction at least of running you off the lot like a dog. Don't get up in two days and say 'So long.'"

Wesley smiled. "Run me off. That'd make it so easy. And it's what I deserve."

Wilson shook her head hard, and her eyes filled up. Till that one moment in all their time, she'd been dry as a boy.

Wesley said "No, really. I abandoned my wife. I cheated with you. I've sat here for days now letting you serve me like a coal-black slave. I haven't so much as washed a cup."

Wilson said "You've made me feel like a *soul*."

Wesley laughed. "Beg your pardon?"

"You've made me feel like something that mattered for more than flat-fucking."

He frowned. "Words like that ruin your face."

She smiled. "See, every other man I've know has all but begged me to talk dirty to him."

"I like words too much. My wife taught me that."

Wilson said "Whatever else, you're a gentleman."

Wesley thanked her but stood. "What's your vote say? Which road do I take?"

"You told me you didn't love your wife. I've leaned on that."

Wesley said "Stop. I'm not saying you're a liar, but I don't recall saying any such thing. Maybe you just gathered it from my general actions — I couldn't blame you. But I know I haven't thrown the word *love* around. Don't think for a minute I understand love enough to use it that freely."

Wilson waited a moment, then smiled. "Do you like her?"

"Better than anybody."

It hurt Wilson bad. She waited to ask "Then why are you here?"

"I'd run out of hope."

She said "You haven't exactly come to the hope chest. I've tried two times to kill myself."

"That's what I mean," he said. "I've got hope to bring." Standing in the midst of Wilson's private paid-for living room, Wesley believed himself. Even more, he felt fulfilled for the first time in years in his life's old aim — other people's happiness, caused by him.

Next morning he stopped at the cleanest garage between Wilson's and town; and in half an hour, he had a decent job repairing foreign automobiles. When he got his first check at the end of the week, he would send half of it to Rosa with word of his whereabouts and what he planned. As he walked from the garage back to his car, he caught his face in the outside mirror by the driver's door. He had never spent a whole ten minutes of his life in studying his face, but he held still now long enough to think "This boy'll live."

※   ※   ※

The next Monday night when he'd put his check in a new account, Wesley sat down at Wilson's dining table and wrote to his wife.

January 20, 1986

Dear Rosa,

I'm alive and sorry I couldn't tell you sooner. Nobody harmed me. I just spooked that one afternoon driving home from work and wound up in Nashville, Tennessee for no good reason except that a waitress in a truckstop mentioned Nashville. I appreciate you not reporting me to the Law. Nobody has stopped and questioned me. That's not all I'm thankful to you for.

Rosa, I don't know how much of this is about you. What it got down to was, I was a dead man. Everything I had ever loved to do, everything in me that I ever respected, seemed long gone. After we got married you were the only person I could test myself against. Your face would tell me whether I mattered in the world or not. But with all the years and your new life, I couldn't read much news off of you. That doesn't have to be even half your fault. Don't punish yourself too much.

Not to hurt you but so you will be free to act your own way from here on in, I need to say that I am living with a woman that works as a radiologist at the Vanderbilt University Hospital here. I didn't meet her till well after I got to town. She wasn't my destination, no part of it. But she doesn't smoke at all or drink to excess and for now is keeping me fed and safe.

What it means for me and you in the long run, I can't say. If you want to act against me with the Law, I won't stop you. But now that I've told you this much, I certainly can't expect you not to seek help and company of your own from wherever you find it. It hurts me a lot to come out and put that in writing all of a sudden. But I'm aiming to be fair, and I figure that's fair—mean as it feels.

I've got a decent-paying job and will be sending you half of my pay every week. That will take care of my share of the house expenses. If I've calculated wrong or if there's anything else unusual I should know about, say so. I want to be fair, like I told you.

Rosa, you have given me your whole life up to now, I realize. I've never been sure I asked you for that much, even when we were children and couldn't begin to guess how long time would be. But I sure God know you gave it and gave it from a full heart without stinting. I hope you aren't looking back now and thinking Wesley just took and took and never tried to give. I did try and a lot of the time I wanted to try. It's just that one day in December something in me gave up wanting to try any of the old stuff in the old place.

I don't feel like I never want to see you again. It may work out that way. You may want it that way. But for now I've got to do what I'm doing.

I'll let Horace and my mother know as much of this as they need to know. You can tell or not tell everybody else. I think about you a good many times a day, especially when I'm laughing. We were better at that than anything else, remember?

> *Love still and always,*
> *Wesley*

By the time he finished that and sealed it, his watch said a little past one in the morning. Wilson had been asleep two hours. Wesley felt like going to the little guest-bedroom (the size of a steamer trunk) and sleeping just that one night alone on top of the cover. He brushed his teeth, not facing his own mirrored eyes anymore than was necessary. Then he went to the cubicle and lay down quietly. In under two minutes he'd amazed himself with tears in his eyes. Too tired to ask why or for what, he dried them deep in the hard rubber pillow and seized his shoulders in both broad hands. But in his still head, the voice said "Now you'll never sleep again." It seemed too true to doubt or regret.

Then Wilson came in and sat by his waist. Silent as they were, his tears had waked her. She knew not to mention them. She said "I wasn't all that deep asleep. I'd have welcomed you, son."

"I felt like I ought to be in here tonight."

"What's wrong with tonight?"

Wesley didn't want to tell her, but he had to be fair. The one thing he didn't mean to do this time was tell a real lie. He said "I just now wrote my wife the truth."

"Which is what?" Wilson asked.

"That I'm staying put here with you for now."

"You sure about that?"

"If you'll have me," he said.

"You know I will. I've said it before."

"You never said *why* though. I doubt I believe you."

Wilson waited a minute, then struck him hard beneath the ribs.

Wesley flinched and rolled to his back, face upward. "You'll have me dialing that number for help, a beat-up male."

Dark as it was, Wilson kept her face grim. "I'll keep on beating too, long as you spit on my deep feelings. You've already given me more than I've had in twenty-six years, from anybody else."

"Tell me one thing," he said. He couldn't believe her but needed to.

"You know I can't talk. You're the good one with words."

Wesley said "Christ Jesus, that's a new damned note." And because by then her face touched his shoulder, he fell straight down into sleep like a stone.

Wilson couldn't let him go off unassured. So there, on a cheap bed wide as a plank and hard as the road, she stripped them both with two swift hands. Then boarding his long body low at the knees, she bent and set her mouth to say in a silent prowl up and down his limbs, his hard torso, the sweet white bowl of his thrusting hips, that no one man of all she'd known (and she'd known some) had come anywhere near matching the way he made her know she mattered on the crowded ground like a rare snow leopard or the shining dove.

Wesley lay flat still and let her speak, meeting her silence every three or four minutes with honest thanks—aloud in words—and more hot tears. Dark as it was, he knew he was climbing again and upward in her strong light.

ROSA'S DIARY

When I got back from Mary's that afternoon, Roger was worn out asleep on the porch. When I spoke to him, he looked up a second. But I doubt he recognized me — he was that tired. So he must have been out trekking with Rato after all. Inside, I saw right away that Rato had beat me home and was watching television in the front room with Mama. Poor as they are, they keep that one room hot as Brazil. They could start a rubber plantation in their spare time.

So of course Mama dozes through most of their programs, but Rato sits upright believing every word. I thought my nerves were still not safe alone and that I should sit with them, but by then my lack of sleep was clubbing me down. I said my New Year's party had wiped me out, so I was going upstairs to rest. I'd be down in time to help with supper.

Mama said she'd made up my bed this morning and lit the oil burner, but she followed me up the steep steps anyhow.

And the room was preserved as perfectly as the Wright Brothers' bicycle shop in the Smithsonian. Anything I've ever owned (and haven't burned or taken to Raleigh) is up there right now, and Mama dusts it all. I don't think it's any kind of shrine to me like that spread of pictures at Mary's house. No, in Mama's mind it's just a real living part of her house. The person that used to stay there may be back any minute, so it needs to be clean and ready for occupancy. And isn't Mama right after all? After nearly thirty years, hadn't I just this minute climbed up there, in serious need of a familiar safe place?

Her pale strained face seemed to say that much and a good deal more. I dreaded what she'd ask when she finally spoke, so I stretched out fast with my face to the wall.

She took her time spreading the afghan over me and then sat by my feet. "Are you too sick to talk?"

I didn't meet her face, but I said "No ma'm. I'm just dead tired."

She said "You are telling me two different things. First, that a man broke in your house this morning and raped you. Second, that there's nothing wrong but you lost your beauty sleep. Even you wouldn't come all this way for a nap."

I had to laugh. "I'm very much afraid you're right. It hasn't hit me yet though. I dread when it will. But now I'm telling you the absolute truth—I'm three-fourths asleep."

Mama said "Have you checked yourself real good?"

I told her I wasn't bruised or bleeding.

"Did you get you that 'day-after' pill?"

It's something else she's learned about on television, a pill to neatly flush out any child you may have conceived in a rape—that easy.

I told her I hadn't.

"Then tomorrow you need to go get one of those. Drive to Henderson and see Dr. Drake. He's kind and smart and he'll *talk* to you." (There are no doctors left in all Warren County. Imagine that. In our childhood there were four white and at least one black. Not enough money up there now, I guess.)

I told her I was past that worry, thank God.

It surprised her. She said she menstruated till she was almost sixty.

The last thing I remember saying was "I won't envy you that."

I woke up in the dark praying. Something must have scared me toward the end of my nap because I was out of breath and praying hard for safety. At first I thought I could hear somebody working in the kitchen, but then the house went quiet again. I suspected they'd let me sleep through supper, and now I had a long night to face alone.

It didn't seem possible. If it had come to that, I'd have no choice but to stumble down and crawl in with Mama.

But no, I couldn't start sleeping with my forebears. Mama couldn't come back to Raleigh with me. So I couldn't use her now like a shield, however strong she was. I lay flat out then facing the ceiling—trusting it was there (it was too black to see) and planned my future.

My husband was gone, probably alive but maybe gone for good. My son was married to a social climber and gone forever. My other kin were too old, too strange, or too tied down to help. What it was, was me and a middle-aged boxer dog against the world. And the world that night seemed mainly to consist of one man—surely real, surely nothing I'd dreamed up for fun—that had apparently meant to harm me.

But the fact was, he hadn't done serious damage. I knew enough about my body to know that no, he hadn't even bruised me. My mind might turn out to be a little jostled, but the rest was intact.

The scary thing was, he was still on the loose in Raleigh, N.C. He was somebody I could cross up with at the grocery store smiling. Or he could be back in my bedroom any night he chose, next time with maybe no intention to run.

That sent a chill through me like I hadn't felt till then. More than my body, he had raped my *place*. I'd blinded myself to the worst he'd done. With Wesley gone, the thing I needed most in the world was a safe place to be. And all I had was a strong dry house with a hole stove through it by, for all I knew, a lunatic. A hole he could use to go and come at will. What was the answer to that? Nothing I could think of. So I lay there shivering hard in the dark.

Then at the foot of the steps a voice said "You still up there?" At first it sounded so much like my father that I was scared worse than ever. Rato, like Horace, is named for Daddy. But it had never crossed my mind that he bore him any likeness. It was so close though, I couldn't reply.

He said "Rosacoke."

And I said "Yes sir."

He said "I'm nothing but your next-to-oldest brother." Still he started to climb.

Rato had switched on the light at the bottom of the steps. So by the time he got there, I could see a little of him. And he did look young. He never has had much of a beard, you know, and now he's begun to soften in the jaw and neck. But in most men that just makes them look like their mother. Rato looks more and more like his early self, the one that hung around my childhood like an occasionally friendly but mostly wild yearling—the one whose thoughts were no more likely than a deer's or a colt's to be on any subject you might share. Now he stood in the midst of the door and waited.

I said "Step in here and sit down a minute." I turned on my little weak bedside lamp.

He said "She took your chair away" (you recall he will not call her *Mama*).

I told him I hadn't been using it a lot.

He said "That wasn't enough of a reason. This room is still yours."

I said "Old darling, I'm glad you think so. I may be needing it any year now."

Rato shook his head hard. "Don't ever come back here."

"Why? It's home."

He said "It's the most unprogressive spot on earth."

It hadn't occurred to me that progress mattered much to Rato and I laughed.

He shut me up with a strong palm outward. "This county used to be rich and famous. Old Nat Macon, the Speaker of the House of Representatives under Thomas Jefferson, was from right up the road. The Alstons and Eatons had several hundred slaves each. And look at all those grand homes in Warrenton. Now though it's nothing but fallow fields and Mexican migrant workers in whatever fields are working and miserable Negroes on welfare—did you ever think our family would quit farming and go to selling trucks? I could have killed Milo when he quit."

The fact that Rato even knew history existed was a lightning bolt. But I passed over it and told him "Be merciful. Milo was tired."

"Hell, I'm tired. The *world's* tired. That's a piss-poor excuse. Everybody's meant to work till they vanish."

In spite of his thirty years in the Army, I'd never thought of Rato as that hard a laborer. But I didn't mention it. I just said "I feel like I'm doing my part."

He nodded. "You are. I want to come join you."

I must not have heard him or understood. Anyhow I didn't answer.

So he walked on forward and sat on the absolute edge of the bed beside my feet. "I asked could I come live with you."

I said "You know I may still have a husband."

Rato said "I doubt it, not after this long. I'd leave if he came back."

Something deep down in my heart spread open. I wanted Rato with me. But that would be theft from my mother. I said "What would Mama do without you?"

He said "She's wanted me gone for years."

"That can't be true."

"She wants me married."

I laughed again. "When was the last time she mentioned marriage?"

"Two weeks ago when she had a heart spell."

"What exactly did she say?"

"She said 'Son, I'm going to be dead soon now. Get you somebody.'"

I couldn't doubt that but I said "She didn't mean leave her now, not out in the sticks alone with her angina."

"She does everything that's done around here. I can't even drive."

I said "No but you're on hand. You're company."

Rato said "I'm about as much company as the ceiling."

It was true and also the closest he'd ever come to a joke or to showing any sense of what he might mean to others. So I was amazed but I said "She wouldn't be safe."

He said "You sure God ain't. Somebody's out to ruin you, and he knows where you sleep."

If that's not the scariest sentence anybody could dread to hear, I don't know what would be. Even with Rato there in the room, cold fear slapped up against my teeth. Foolish as it sounds, it hadn't really creased my mind till then—how open to harm I was in that house. I had gone through life thinking the worst that could happen was feelings, some resentment from you or Horace. All the wars on the edge of my life, all the crimes in the next block over, hadn't convinced me of the fact that one or two people in every handful are ready to kill you or pare your face to the slick wet bone and pass on forward. By then I guess my eyes had watered. The little light showed it.

Rato said "Now ask me to join you."

I tried to gather my wits and protect Mama, but he'd caught me in the quick, and I couldn't deny it. I said "For a week or so, sure. Till I get new locks. We can take Mama with us."

"I won't go then," he said.

"Don't be mean, Rato. Why not?"

"Because of Wesley. If he turns up one night and finds just me, it'll be all right. I'll pack in two minutes and climb on the bus. But let Wesley find Mama with that heavy-duty heating pad and all the rest of her rheumatism stuff, and he's liable to look in the window and run."

There seemed to be a sizable truth in that. Old-lady equipment has always tended to shy you. Remember when I bought that cream for the liver spots on my hands? You'd barely go in the bathroom for the whole next week. But who could I get to stay here with Mama? Milo and Sissie might stay a few days but not a long stint. Any special arrangements would mean explaining something incredible to the world—that Rato was going somewhere. *Why? Well, his sister got herself raped in Raleigh the other day; and she needs a bodyguard.*

But I said "Thank you, sir. I'll make us a way."

And Rato cut loose a smile so broad it burned out whatever dark was left in the room.

That was the night of the first day of the year. I stayed on through the first three days, trying the best I could to fit into their quiet ways. What I always forget about my mother and brother is how much like animals they are. I don't mean I feel like any kind of human superior to them, but I sure Lord feel different. They move through their days like self-respecting horses, taking a lot of careful time with things you and I hurry through like eating three meals or arranging to sit in a chair to watch the television news.

At first it made me jittery to watch their slowness—*For Christ-in-Heaven's sake, you don't need to take four minutes to butter that one slice of bread!* But I told myself to hold back. And even with the immediate worries I had, in a couple of days I'd gotten a good deal calmer myself just from adjusting to their rates. Rato and I didn't speak again of any plan to take him to Raleigh, and I didn't plan ways to break it to Mama.

She and I spent a lot of time alone in the same room together, drying dishes for instance. But she never again mentioned the rape or the morning-after pill and never mentioned you. I couldn't decide if she was being tactful and yielding to my maturity or, what I suspected was more likely, that she was too old now to care all that much about her children's lives. She wishes us well but secretly prays we won't tell her too much. She's got other thoughts and we don't need to know what those are yet (I mean is it all just death and regret or some brand of happy relief?).

So it was a big surprise to me when, on the second night as I was undressing in my room, Mama heaved herself upstairs and sat on the foot of my bed and said "I want to ask Rato to go back with you. Is that all right?"

I admitted at once it was fine by me, but what was she going to do for help?

She kept her face serious. "You don't think Rato's a whole lot of help, do you?"

"He's protection," I said. "And company."

"I've got a good rifle and your granddaddy's pistol. My hearing's not what it was. But if they just give me a minute's warning, I could hold off a big squad of rogues. And company! Rato hasn't said five hundred words to me in all his grown life. Don't forget, he was the only one of my four children that refused to breast feed." Finally she laughed.

I told her no, I'd never heard that.

She laughed "No ma'm, after four weeks passed, he rolled down off my nipple one night and never came back."

"Didn't he get hungry?"

"He did, by dawn, and it's lucky I had some bottles left over from Milo's last feedings because when I offered Rato this beat-up old tittie again, he spasmed out stiff as a board in my arms and wouldn't come near me."

I said "You're joking. That can't be true."

She raised her flat right hand, an oath. "Never again—four weeks old and swore off."

"What's wrong with him, Mama?" I'd never quite asked it plain before.

"I know the whole world's always thought he's backward. Your granddaddy used to say 'Nothing wrong with Rato but he's a little backward in coming forward.' Even the Army never pushed him past corporal. I'm just his mother and no great scholar myself, but I've always thought Rato was smarter than the rest of us put together. He figured out at one-month-old exactly what he wanted in life, and he's calmly gone about getting it and doing it from that day forward."

It seemed honest enough for a mother's explanation, so I thought I'd risk a little more. "Mama, do I mean anything special to Rato?"

"You're his sister."

"Beyond that, I mean."

She waited and studied me slowly. "If you're meaning any of this mess they talk about on television—brothers and sisters, fathers and daughters." Her frown was as deep as I'd seen it.

So I laughed. "Calm down. I meant no such thing. I just wondered if there was anything I ought to know before he comes to Raleigh, if he's coming."

"He's coming if you ask him. He's aching to get out of here. I've known that ever since the Army turned him loose and he couldn't get a job anywhere round here. But special? No, I can't think of nothing. He loves his privacy but you know that. He eats all of anything you set before him. Sleeps nine hours every night that comes. He'll tell you every detail of every dream he has the next morning at breakfast. And that's all he'll tell you from that mind of his, night or day. Otherwise, he's as much trouble as your Roger or any other good dog—none at all. You do have to get used to him being there. His soul takes up a lot of room in a house, like having a hot brown racehorse in your sitting room. He's kind to be sure and housebroke and clean. But he's thinking his own thoughts night and day, and Rato's thoughts are the last thing you'll ever guess."

I nodded. "And what happens up here if you fall off that stepladder you're always climbing and break an ankle or have a little heart spell? You want to come with us?"

Mama shook her head hard. "First of all, I'll be fine. Second, if I'm not, whatever happens will be something I'm responsible for. Plenty of women older than me are out in the country here working full days with no better company than squirrels in the yard. Nobody's been killed since the Civil War"—she still says *Silver War*.

I suspected that wasn't quite true, but then I couldn't think of any exceptions—not white ones anyhow. So I thanked her as sincerely as I ever had (and she's been one of my two main receptacles of thanks since birth).

She surprised me again. She said "Besides, you may be doing me a favor. Here lately I've been wondering what lonesome *is*. I haven't been alone ever in my whole life—oh, a few little minutes in childhood. Maybe I can finally fulfill myself."

I hoped she wasn't serious, but I wasn't going to be the first one to laugh.

Then, thank God, she did—a low easy chuckle.

That was the Thursday, as I said. On the Friday evening I phoned Milo in Henderson to let him know the temporary arrangements. Rato was coming to Raleigh with me. Mama would be out here alone. I could tell right off that the news upset him. Milo has always dreaded change. He rightly wanted to know who would be taking care of Mama. I told him the whole thing was her idea (not quite the full truth), that he was not more than forty minutes from her, and that I could get there in exactly an hour. Milo said "The world can end in under an hour, once it starts ending."

I thanked him for the warning.

Then he got mad. He said "Why the hell have you got to upset the whole damned family's applecart now just because your husband has flown the coop?"

It wasn't till then that I realized he didn't know a thing about my New Year's night. I thought Mama might have tipped him off somehow. So I chewed on the lining of my cheek awhile, then went on and gave him a short true account. At the end I was proud of telling the whole story with not one tear or even a frog.

Milo let me finish the whole thing without interrupting. Then he waited a good long time. Finally he said "Have you all finished supper?"

I said yes, an hour ago.

So he asked could he come and take me to ride?

It sounded so old-fashioned, I'm afraid I laughed.

Milo said "I'm glad somebody thinks it's funny. Please show me how."

I told him to come on.

It was deep dark and freezing when Milo got there, but a ride was still what he had in mind. He pecked me on the cheek and made polite greetings to Mama and Rato. Then he said "Rosa and me need to catch up on some business. We'll be riding around."

Mama said she hoped his car heater was working.

He reminded her that few people ever asked for a heater when *his* heart was present.

She said "That was true, oh, thirty years back."

Milo didn't try to trump her but took my elbow and led me out. At the door, Roger made a big play to go with us. But Milo said "This is going to be dog business enough without you, son. Go eat a Gaines-burger and trim your nails" (on Mama's bare pine floors, Roger sounds like Fred Astaire in ski boots).

At first it was like so many dozen nights from childhood and just after. Then it had seemed like Milo wanted nothing but me dark and an arm's length away on a car seat saying nothing till he asked me to—and us forging on in the old pickup like there were no oceans and we might pull into Peking or Lhasa for breakfast tomorrow. Plenty of nights he never asked a single question, and never once did he try anything funny (in all our lives, he never has—though there have been times I more than half wanted him to). For years I'd been honored just to be there waiting to be asked and to think I was some kind of help, whether or not he ever said so.

Wesley, before I found you that first day, Milo had after all been my first sight of glory. He was my brother, that could drive me crazy ten times a day, but also now and then he was a mirror of the angels. Anybody as fine-looking as Milo and you both were when young is bound to know it, bound to realize that their faces and bodies are gifts of God to help other people bear their days. I can look back at photos of me then and see I wasn't all that much of an eyesore myself, but you and Milo were better. No question at all you were heaven-sent blessings. And Milo came first in my acquaintance.

But once we'd threaded through Warrenton and were on the Macon road, he said "I guess I better hear it."

And again I had to laugh at how *my* assault—my big recent chance at a personal tragedy—had become my family's property. I said "Milo, it's not the end of the earth or even of Rosa. Some fool desperado couldn't get through New Year's on his own resources and had to come banging on mine. I threw him out before he got really danger-ous." I realized it wasn't all that true a description, but Milo's attitude had forced it on me. Maybe it would help us both.

He asked "Was it somebody you know?"

I said "Sugar, it was so dark and late, it might have been *you*. No, I don't know but I seriously doubt it."

"None of Wesley's friends?"

I said "Wesley is gone and Wesley is strange in all sorts of ways, I'll grant you, but he'd never send anybody to harm me."

Milo said "I didn't mean that."

I said "Good" which helped clear the air.

But we were halfway to Vaughan before he could finally say "Rosa, you've got me confused. Everything I hear and read tells me that rape is the worst thing that can happen to a woman."

I had to stop him. I asked "What is it?"

"Ma'm?"

"Rape—what is rape?"

Milo turned to me slowly like I'd gone wild right then on the seat beside him. "Rosa, grow up. Every four-year-old knows what rape is."

I said "I honestly don't think I do, not anymore. Tell me what you think."

"It's when a guy holds down a woman against her will and comes inside her body."

"All right," I said. "That's what I mean. It was a man. He held me down long as he could, and against my will, but I'm not sure he came—not inside me at least."

"What did the doctors say?"

"They didn't. I haven't told anybody but my own family—Mama, Rato, you."

"You didn't call the Law?"

"Milo, the Law was the last thing I needed. You know how famed for gentleness they are."

"Then it's too late," he said. "You'll never know his name."

"I wasn't wanting to call up and thank him," I said. "He can stay unknown."

Milo said "*He* knows who he is. He knows where you are—"

"—And how to find me next time. I've been through this. Don't bother to scare me. It's why I'm taking Rato back to Raleigh."

"Rato's about as much use to you as a French-speaking flea."

"Rato's who I've got. Nobody else offered."

Milo said "I never got a chance."

I thanked him. "But you've got a wife and a job."

"You could stay with us."

"Thank you again but I own my house. I can't leave that. My Christmas vacation ends next Monday, and anyhow you know Sissie and I couldn't go half-a-day without starting the Great Sister-in-Law Massacre of 1986."

We had turned around by then and were halfway back to Mama's. But Milo slowed the car and pulled off the road in a wide spot in the pines. He lowered his window an inch, and cold air was quick to hit us. But he looked me over carefully. "Rose, I'm as sorry as I've ever been on this earth."

"For what?" I asked him.

"That this hit you."

I smiled. "It did. But thank you."

Milo shook his head. "What can I do to make it up?"

For one quick instant I wanted to say "Just run with me now, hard and fast far from here. You and me like in childhood, us two together forsaking the rest." But you know I didn't. Too much else, too many more, had come in between us and had their claims. I said "You and Sissie come see us soon. Meanwhile, keep a good eye on Mama out here." When I reached over to touch his face, his whole left cheek was wet with tears.

I thought I knew the answer but I asked anyhow. "What's the real trouble, Milo?" I figured it would be something about Sissie, his sad old marriage.

But he waited a good while, gnawing on the heel of his hand. Then he said "None of it was supposed to turn out this way, was it?" It seemed like a genuine urgent question.

I had to say, "What's *it*, Milo?"

"Jesus," he said, "—our lives, all these awful futures."

For a boy born to dirt-farm every day of his life, Milo always had more dreams even than me. I figured they'd died long since though. He hadn't mentioned them, to me at least, since he was sixteen. I thought he'd just agreed to die from the neck up like the rest of us. I mean, how long can you sell pickup trucks and dream about truth and light?

So I told him I thought we'd done fair enough. We all had our health, good jobs, good dry roofs over our heads, kitchens full of the latest. None of us had served any time behind bars.

He suddenly struck the steering wheel with both fists. "Tell the truth, goddammit! Your marriage is finally ruined. Mine's been a cold junkyard since day one. Your son is a pitiful poor excuse for a new generation. Sissie and I got scared and quit after one dead baby. Now we're all bearing down into late middle age. Death could strike any minute, and what would any of us have to show? A few thousand paychecks, an unretired mortgage—damned little else."

I said "Who do we know that ever had more? Look at our people."

He looked out the windshield like they might have been in the woods all around us. Finally he said "You and I are bad enough, but our people are too pitiful to think about."

I said "Milo, I had dreams too. And I know neither one of us has made it to the White House yet. But we're middle aged now, not dead and gone. We may have thirty more years to live through. If we bend double in pain this early, I don't see how we'll make it to the end."

He said he wasn't sure he wanted to make it.

I said in that case I was sorry I loved him—I'd try to withdraw.

Milo said "Please don't. I count on you."

I nodded again and we went back to Mama's.

Wesley, one thing I want to do right now is break down and bawl. But every time I get my body fixed to do it, somebody walks up that I've loved always and breaks down *before* me. I'm left running to get the cool compresses. Am I going to have to make reservations, say, thirty days ahead? Please book me in, if you have any pull—one big howling whitetrash breakdown.

It's Friday night now, January 24th. When I got home from work, your letter was waiting on the hall table. Rato had laid it there on top of a stack of junk, and at first I didn't recognize your hand. It had been a lot of years since I'd seen that much of your writing in one place. And a Nashville address wasn't quite what I was expecting. I'd somehow got used to the idea you were closer by than that, like the east edge of town with your hair parted on the opposite side maybe. But when the name itself bore in on me, there in the upper left-hand corner of the envelope, I went straight up to our room to read it. Once I was on that bed, I couldn't. I had to go in the bathroom, lock the door, and sit down before I could even cut it open.

You haven't left me a whole lot to say. You've even made it all but impossible for me to go on aiming this diary at you, like you'll ever read it. But it's too soon to make any rash decisions, I guess. I'll try to go on living the way I always have and hope that time will clear a path day by day, the way it usually has.

When I've got my thoughts together, when I've *got* some thoughts at all, I'll draft a letter to you here and then decide whether to mail it. After that I'll try to decide whether there's any point in keeping this sad record alive.

January 26, 1986

Dear Wesley,

I'm relieved to know that you're alive and working, and I thank you for the check. I've done all right with everything but the mortgage, so this is a real help.

I won't pretend to understand any of the rest of what you say, about why you left your home and family and job or how you are living with somebody else in the face of the vows you and I made to one another personally twenty-eight years ago (from the week that you left). That is not to say that I believe I've been anywhere near a perfect wife or to blame you with not being a better husband than I could have dreamed of most days up till the day you left this last time.

I just want to say that I don't think I was living in a cloud, and I thought we were anyhow doing as well as any two people I've watched in all our same time.

If there is any one thing, or any twenty, that I can change to put us back together in better shape, please let me know what it would be. The way I feel now, there's not much I wouldn't do to fix us.

A lot has happened here since you left. If and when we meet again, I can tell you as much as you want to know. In the meantime I will try to hold on in the hope that the good things we had will come clear again in your mind, clear enough to blank out whatever and whoever else may be blinding you now.

Love,
Rosacoke

I mailed it and a month has gone by in silence here—just two notes from Wesley with checks, all on time and honest as far as I know. Precious few words in the notes, no more real news of him or his new friend (if she's still there). And no whisper of a hint that I should ever expect to see him alive, in this world anyhow.

I can see—looking back through this in the past few days, debating whether or not to recommence it—that I haven't said a word about how much it has hurt me. A stranger finding this in the twenty-first century at some flea market or yard sale might be excused for thinking that this marriage broke in two after nearly three decades without hard pain on either side.

I can't speak for Wesley's side of course. But me, I hurt so much right this minute—two months after the last time I saw him—that if you could hook my hand up to a circuit that ran on nothing but pain for fuel, you'd have an arc that blazed in the night like phosphorus you throw off a bridge in the river, phosphorus enough to burn till Judgment.

I really did think I had got past that. Not that I've suffered nearly as much as some people I know. But I have had my father's death to live through and my grandfather's, all mine and Wesley's long courtship miseries, the agony about Horace when he was conceived and I was deciding whether or not to get married, and then the normal hourly pains of a wife-and-mother's trip through all but thirty years.

So I guess I'd fallen back on unearned pride, the belief that I was too strong to be hurt by anything but Wesley's death or maybe Horace's (I hate to sound unloving of my only child, but I'm trying to be honest first). All the more surprising then, how bad off I am now — even this long after the event. You'd have thought a rape, if it was a rape, would have hurt deeper. Certainly all the articles and television prophets claim so.

But right this evening — the night of Valentine's Day — all I feel like is the grown woman who wasn't good enough to keep her place in the heart and mind of the only person alive on earth that she hoped to please and hold to the grave. Was that so foolish of me? Did I stumble this blind into this harsh a punishment? I am a strong unusually healthy woman for my middle age. With the example of my mother's strength in front of me, I can imagine staying on upright with my feelings intact for at least another thirty years. How in the world am I going to do it? And why should I want to?

—Just to go on typing neat letters for a university English Department and bringing home a check that would insult a woman much dumber than me? Or fielding the phone calls of a son who checks in every Sunday night, in duty not enthusiasm? Or cooking two meals a day for my dear extraplanetary brother till he and I both have lost the teeth to eat with and the eyes to see a plate?

This evening, a month after he left Wesley's first letter waiting in the hall for me, Rato asked me about it for the first time. We'd finished our supper and were watching the end of the national news. The last story had been about hungry children in South Carolina (of course — why is it never Boston or Ann Arbor, Michigan?). And when he leaned forward to switch it off before *P.M. Magazine*, which Rato calls *B.M. Magazine*, he said "Poor old world."

And I said "Poor old me." I was just tired, nothing much worse than usual. Get me tired and you've got self-pity on your hands.

That must have given Rato the opening. He came to me over by the dishwasher and put his left hand on my shoulder from behind.

It almost scared me out of my skin. I don't think Rato has touched me more than twice in our lives. I'm afraid I jumped back, put my hand up to my face like a shield, and said "Jesus!"

Rato takes the name of Jesus very seriously and hates more than anything the way people use it today as an all-purpose substitute for "Shit!" in polite company. Rato said "I'm sorry. But don't say that, please ma'm. He don't need it."

I had to laugh and beg his pardon. I explained it by saying my thoughts were miles away and he'd surprised me, that was all.

Rato gave it a few seconds to settle through his mind and then said "I know you're sad. I've been waiting for you to tell me."

"Tell you what?" I asked, though I certainly knew.

"Where Wesley is at."

I asked "Will you drink another cup of coffee?"

He said "I wouldn't sleep till Thursday-week, but I'll watch you drink it till you turn beige and faint."

So I poured a mugful and went back to the table and Rato joined me. I said "He's in Nashville, Tennessee with a working woman. He's got a good job and no plans for home."

"Is he crazy or sick?"

I smiled and said "Thank you. Neither one, he says. He says it had got to where his life felt dead. He doesn't blame me."

Rato said "Sure he does. You're the one he's left."

"That's a big help. Thank you."

He said "No, it's true. And you know it."

"I'm not sure I did, not in that hard a way. But all right, what am I meant to do with the news?"

Rato had gone past the point of timidity now, and he strode right ahead. He thought he knew his ground. "You need to know what I've known all my life—how to live by yourself."

"I don't want to. Nobody else does either."

Rato said "That's a lie. There's a few other people in the world with sense."

"And good sense means everybody holing up, alone as bones, and banging on their bare walls for company till they finally wear out and die with no heirs? How would you arrange for the human race to continue?"

He smiled. "I wouldn't. I think the sooner we give up the ridiculous job we've made and turn the earth over to dolphins and penguins, the better off God and the universe will be."

"I thought it was *all* God's plan."

Rato said "When was the last time you asked God how He liked it?"

"I'm not in all that regular touch with Him."

Rato said "I am."

Coming from Rato, it didn't seem crazy or scary but the simple truth. I'd waited for it all my life. And I said "What am I meant to do then?"

Rato said "Whoa, you're jumping over a few steps here. I'm not saying your whole life has been wrong or wasted."

I said "No, you're the one in the family who came closest to persuading me to marry Wesley back when I was pregnant and in such bad trouble."

He nodded. "I remember. And I don't take it back. There's nothing wrong with Wesley."

"Then it's all my fault," I said.

Rato shook his big head. "It's nobody's fault but the whole human race, except me and a few dozen others that know."

"The priests and nuns and weirdos?" I asked.

"And Ratos." Luckily he was able to smile.

"And what is it that you all know?"

"—What you and Wesley are just finding out. What you call *love* is something that can't last many years past high school, and then where are you?"

I told him you were where we'd been for at least twenty years, two people sharing a roof and a bed with a lot of mutual company and comfort, a son to raise between them, some real good times.

Rato said "And now this awful bad one."

I said "All right but, since we couldn't foresee this, were we still supposed to dry up and stay home frozen in childhood just out of fear of thirty-years-hence?"

Rato said "I didn't freeze."

I said "What did you do?" I'd never before asked him the first ques-
tion about the life in his head and had never heard anybody ask him.
For all I knew, he might stand up now and walk back to Mama's. But
I felt like he'd at least given me the right.

He said "I've had the best life of anybody I've watched" (I already
knew Mama agreed with him). And that seemed the end. He grinned
to guarantee it.

I said "I'm glad to know you. Tell me what was good."

Rato asked me if I didn't think that called for a hot fudge sundae?
One of the main joys of his life in Raleigh is the old fudge maker you
gave Horace a century ago, that made his pimples so much worse.
Rato keeps fudge steaming round the clock. And it's all I can do to
convince him that, if I followed him scoop for scoop, I'd be bigger
than Two-Ton Tessie tomorrow (he never gains an ounce). I told him
to be my guest, which he proceeded to do. But once he had a platter
of several million calories before him (he arranges them very artisti-
cally with the walnuts and cherries), he was ready to fill me in on his
life. "This is America, right? Land of the free? I've been the only free
man that you, or anybody else, knows."

I asked how was that?

Rato leaned far forward and tapped me hard twice right between
the eyes. "Use your bean, sweet thing. I don't owe a cent, in cash or
love, to any live soul. I've had twenty years in the world's greatest
Army, and I've seen half the sights worth seeing on earth. Plus I estimate I had all the pleasures a man's skin can feel. I can still walk into
any PX on any continent and buy the world's finest goods for next-to-
nothing prices—cameras or cars. And I've got a lavish pension and
that big veteran's hospital in Durham, when the time comes and parts
start falling off of me. All that and never once, not one single time,
has nobody ever turned to me with hurt eyes and said 'Rato, you have
cut me to the quick, and I can't forgive you. I'm leaving *out* of here.'"
He downed a big spoonful of fudge. "If that's not freedom and a
happy life, then I *am* the half-wit you've all thought I was."

I said "I never did and you know it. But let me ask you this. Haven't
you missed not having a regular mate through the long days and
nights and no children to watch grow up through the years?"

"No ma'm, not a minute. I swear my Bible oath." And he swore it right there with that flat palm the size of a paddle for the biggest rowboat.

I said "Excuse me, Rato. But to me it looks like a desert life — the diet for a damned horned toad or gila monster."

Rato said "That's because you're brainwashed. You believed in movies and songs and t.v. Somehow I knew it was all popsicles, cold sugar and water and then a dry stick."

"What told you that?"

"Maybe Jesus in the night."

I had to say "Rato, now *you* spare Jesus."

"No," he said, "I may be serious. Something told me to go my way."

"When and where?"

"Long before I was grown. Something out in the woods. I could talk to trees. They'd answer me back."

I had to smile. "We were scared of that."

He shook his head. "Get serious, Rosa. I was a perfectly real child with a working mind. I just didn't want to run with you and Milo and make all that noise. I wanted to be by myself, be still, and listen."

"So you listened to trees and they said what?"

"Not words. I didn't mean that. I'm not a damned simpleton or Walt-damned-Disney. I mean they taught me things about living on my own, finding my own nourishment in my own ground — not leaning and leeching on other poor souls."

"You had Phillip, your old dog. You leaned on Phillip."

"No, I didn't. We also talked to each other a lot, laughed a lot. But it wasn't leaning. I knew Phillip couldn't outlast me. I knew he'd die before he was fifteen and he did."

"And you grieved for him, I remember."

Rato nodded. "I did. Not ever again."

I couldn't stop myself. I had to say "Wouldn't you grieve for me?"

He said "Where are you going?"

"Nowhere tonight. Or I very much hope not. But you know I've got to go someday, and lots of women die younger than I am now. Wouldn't you mind that?"

Rato had finished dessert by then. He didn't have anything else to face but me. So he faced me, not blinking till it almost hurt. He said "Rosa, you could get cruel here in a minute."

But I kept going. I told him I'd been down to Mary's house while I was home.

He said "She told me."

I told him I was honored to see his pictures of me.

He looked miserable as a turtle jerked screaming out of his shell. Finally he said "Those are souvenirs."

I nodded. "Everybody's got souvenirs. Mine are all around me here. I'm glad you've found your place."

He said "Mary's good to me."

I said "She gets lonesome."

So he saw his chance at last to laugh. "You don't have to be lonesome to like Rato."

I told him I'd understood that right along. If I'd offered him a whole nother sundae, he'd have eaten it.

I had gone on to sleep with very little trouble, thinking only that the biggest surprise of the last two months had not been desertion or rape but hearing Rato say his skin had *felt every pleasure.* I'd just thought Rato's idea of pleasure was endless sundaes or, at the most, daylight on his hair. Was there any way to ask him more about that without opening too weird a door on too big a room?

Then at ten minutes past two in the morning, the phone rang by my bed. I answered it first-pop and the one voice in the world I'd prayed never to hear again said "I hope you've had a nice rest."

Some awful bred-in courtesy—plus grogginess—made me say "Yes, thank you."

So he knew he had the right woman. Then he said "I may be needing to check that soon."

And I hung up.

He may be there still.

I lay back a good while, wide awake as a scalded child. For the first quarter-hour I tried to pray. Prayer had been some help to me in childhood and the early years of marriage. It really had seemed to do what Jesus promises in the Gospels, change things. Jesus says "Ask and it shall be given." But as Wesley and I got older and began quietly to go our separate ways and our son went on down a third way of his own, I must have begun to think prayer changed precious little. I mean, I've asked for a thousand pains to turn aside, and to the best of my knowledge I've yet to turn one.

Of course it had begun to dawn on me lately that when Jesus said "It shall be given," he didn't quite say what *it* was. He didn't say it was the exact thing you asked for—money or healing or that your lazy son pass his algebra test. Maybe it's just peace of heart, the peace of knowing you've talked to the center of things and He or It has said "No" or "Not now."

Anyhow I lay there trying again to talk it over with the center. I did have one big request—that I not be killed in my own bed or maimed. Otherwise I asked for the strength to see this whole business through. And by *whole business* I meant everything that's hit me since the end of the year, the end of what I had thought was the rest of my life.

Toward the end of what I had to say, a patch of nerves the size of a half-dollar in my right shoulder began to sizzle like bacon. I thought "That's not too promising an answer" so I said "Amen" and stopped. What was left but to wake up Rato, make a gallon of coffee, and wait for day with every light in the house blazing? I knew it was weakness. I knew my mother wouldn't have done it. She'd have crept downstairs and got the butcher knife and lain in her dark sheets waiting, not asking another soul to bear her trouble, least of all her pitiful husband or her four children drowned in the sleep they needed. But I was Rosa. And Rosa stood up then, put on yesterday's dress, and went to Rato's door.

For somebody private as Rato, it's always strange to me that he sleeps with his door open. But he does. And anywhere within twenty feet of his door feels and sounds like the path to a stable. Again I don't mean to say Rato is some kind of dumb beast but that he doesn't put the usual human brakes on the sounds his body wants to make—snores, belches, and long speeches in the night. I've more than once, since he's been here, heard him sit up in bed and say a whole paragraph of sentences—all clear in their wording and a lot more correct in grammar than he is when awake. In the night I always promise myself I will remember and understand him better. But then I don't. So whatever message he's sent me turns out to be in vain one more time.

Now I waited at the door a minute for some sound that he was asleep or not. But there was nothing coming through but a silence so deep it scared me. I called Rato's name more than once, no answer. I stepped on forward in the pitchblack till my knees bumped his mattress, and then I bent down to feel in the sheets. They were cold and empty and I froze. It seemed like any second a bat the size of a big dog would flap down from the ceiling and claw my eyes. I even covered my face with my hands and called "Rato" loud. But there was no answer.

And speaking of dogs, there hadn't been a peep out of Roger anymore than there had been at New Year's. As a watchdog he's roughly in the Helen Keller class. He either sleeps through enemy visits, or they throw him a soup bone that buys him off. From the upstairs hall, I even called his name too. Still nothing.

Two possibilities. Stay upstairs, call the police, and wait till they arrived creating a mob scene in the neighborhood for no cause probably. Or risk going downstairs and trying to act like a normal grown person. From the top of the steps I couldn't see or hear anything unusual. I always left on a lamp in the front hall for just such emergencies, and it was burning calmly.

So down I went. From the dining room I could see that the kitchen was brightly lit. I had heard how intruders sometimes cook themselves whole meals before leaving. I also knew it was where burglars always go first on breaking in since it's where people keep the *cutting* equipment. Knives are the second most popular thing they steal, after firearms. I picked up a heavy brass candlestick and pushed open the swinging door. And of course there was Rato fully dressed eating Cheerios with extra raisins and honey.

He said "Good morning" like it was.

I said "Don't apologize. You have only scared ten years off my life."

He said "Thank me then. That's ten years less in the Old Folks' Home not knowing who you are."

I thanked him and asked what he was doing having breakfast in the middle of the night?

He said "I was getting my strength up to deal with that creep on the phone." It wasn't till then that I noticed how, sure enough, he did have a respectable butcher knife and the biggest hammer out by his plate.

I asked how he knew about my call.

Rato said "Not a lot of calls at two in the morning are legal, are they?"

I asked "Rato, who is it?"—not imagining he knew.

He said "Lady, I'm a stranger here myself. They're not hunting me."

I asked was he scared?

He said "You forget I served in Berlin in the early sixties."

So I had. Not that I thought Rato had personally been eyeball to eyeball with Khrushchev at the Berlin wall, but he did have a point. I thanked him for reminding me.

"What did he say?"

"He asked me if I'd been resting. When I said 'Yes' he said he might have to end that soon."

"He just meant tonight," Rato said, "—were you sleeping tonight? He knew he could ruin that and he has. That's all he can do now with me here. He gets his little pitiful pleasure from that."

I said "He seems to watch me. He's bound to know you're here."

"Sure he does," Rato said. "Why else would he call tonight? If I wasn't here, he'd have just come without calling. Now all he can get is a telephone thrill. Tomorrow we'll get the company to put one of those tracers on the phone. Next time he dials you, bam—he's behind bars."

What my brother learned in the Army and on television continues to surprise and amuse me. I was impressed and grateful but felt the need to cool him down a little too. "Remember though I've never reported any break-in here at the house, so we can't mention that to the phone company or anybody else."

"Don't need to. Just tell the latest truth—you've been getting a bunch of sick calls. You're losing precious sleep and you want them to stop."

Rato was getting more excited than seemed like a good idea for the hour, so I went to work to calm him down and get us both back upstairs. The usual way to do that is to start remembering our childhood good times together—like the day when he, black Mildred, and I started digging to China deep in the woods where the earth was softer. I told him the whole story again this time, and he enjoyed it as always. Especially the part were Mildred and I give up and quit at supper time. But Milo finally has to go find Rato long after dark and bring him home to bed. He had succeeded in digging himself in knee-deep at least.

Still when I stood up and said "I'm going to go stretch out on top of the covers and get a little more rest before time for work," Rato just shook his head and said he'd stay on down here an hour or so longer.

"You sleep all you can," he said. "Be sure I'm your guard."

I'd no more than pulled up a quilt, touched my head to the pillow, and smiled to think how well my weird brother's visit was turning out, and then I was sunk deep as I'd been in many long years.

Today during lunch hour I did go downtown to the phone company and sign the necessary papers that license them to put a machine on my phone which might catch a nuisance caller. I didn't have to swear (but almost) that if and when they caught somebody, then I'd prosecute. My old dread is that it'll turn out to be somebody I know, some student from school or some old friend of Horace's. Or, pray God no, some friend of Wesley's that knew he was leaving and thought the friend might pick up the slack. It'll be Monday before they can install the tracer, but Rato's looking forward and will be here to let the installer in. At least he's got me doing things, not sitting still waiting for things to be done to me. That can't be bad.

The one thing Rato hasn't mentioned doing yet is buying a pistol. I wondered about myself, before he came. Oddly enough, Wesley would never keep firearms here, saying that if anybody broke in the house ahead of us, they'd just kill us with it when we walked in—which still sounds sensible to me. But I suspect Rato feels differently. I won't deal with that, yea or nay, till he brings it up though.

It's now March 12th, 1986. Two weeks have passed since then, and wouldn't you know it? The minute we installed the tracer, the phone went quiet and has barely rung once. More than ever I think the culprit was somebody who lives near enough to know what the traffic in and out of this house means. But like most Raleigh citizens these days, I don't know the neighborhood well enough to guess who's who. There is a big rowdy houseful of fraternity boys three blocks north, but somehow I think I'm dealing with something besides being rowdy and spring panty-raids.

What else to mention? Life otherwise has been very quiet. Rato spends his days apparently happy to be shut up in this house with the television and all my old detective novels. I've never known him to read before, but he's knocking them back now like popcorn—sometimes two a day. Occasionally he and Roger go for a fast walk around the block, and I've tried to suggest that we go to a movie some night or out to a restaurant or even to a mall, just so Rato can stroll a little and see some new faces. To the best of my knowledge, he hasn't met a new soul in Raleigh. Or since he left for the Army for that matter. But I honestly begin to believe that he's happiest when I leave him to do exactly what he's doing, what he's always said he wants to do. Of course on almost all the weekends, we drive up to Afton and buy two boxes of pralines and check on Mama.

We generally go early on Saturday afternoon, after I've folded the laundry and laid in the week's groceries. She's always there to meet us smiling but not panting with her tongue hanging out for hunger and joy to see her beloved offspring. I think it's begun to sink in, even with Rato, that our mother's relieved to be there alone—nobody to cook for, nobody leaning on her mind even as silent as Rato. It's even surprised her. I can see her working overtime to convince us she's glad we remembered her and turned up one more time.

She tries to make her new duties sound like chores—that she's taken on the nursery class again at Sunday school and has good stories from there every week, that her new young friend down the road (a Limer woman) has started gadding her about to shop in centers as much as an hour away where she even broke down and bought one new dress. It's navy blue to be sure—the same basic model she's worn for sixty years, and she wears it with those same pearl earbobs she must have found in the pyramids. But it *is* brand new and two inches shorter than anything she's worn since leaving high school, so that all but qualifies as a *People* magazine cover-story.

They even came to Raleigh one day last week and didn't even try to call us, just got their feet worked over by the last old chiropodist in existence—their ingrown toenails trimmed and their corns whittled. Mama said "It killed me to spend twenty dollars on feet as ugly as these, but it sure was worth it. These ten toes think they died last week and waked up in Heaven." Her feet have always been her personal crucifixion.

We usually spend Saturday night there, and I make Rato chop a week's supply of firewood (not an easy thing; he thinks Mama needs the exercise). I check on her oil and groceries and touch up anything she's short on. I snoop around the house for fire risks and other dangers. But I seldom find any. She didn't run the place all those years, and raise four children plus a drunk and a cantankerous father-in-law, on harum scarum principles. She sees me checking behind her and never tries to stop me, though I can tell she's amused.

The only real difference is, she's losing weight. Mama's never been really fat, whatever she's said, but she's surely always been well-upholstered. Those layers are quietly peeling off her now. I've asked her about it. She says "Rosa, your mother is an *old* woman. If people don't die in their seventies from bad hearts or kidneys, then you'll begin to notice how they just start vanishing into thin air. It can take another twenty years, but they're on the way. After a while you can all but read the newspaper through their hand. I think it's kind of pretty. Just get used to it anyhow and don't worry me about eating. I eat everything I want. And everytime I think about it, I take that vitamin pill you gave me for insurance."

I know she's right and I believe her. I also know if anything happened to her right now, on top of all this other, it might be the straw that brings my poor old camel right down. (If Mama saw me writing this of course she'd say that the biggest shame I could bring her, as a mother, would be just that—not being strong enough to bear her death.) But late on the Sunday evenings when we pull out of the drive and leave her standing up alone there on that porch—that's always been swarming with people before, people that she *brought into the*

world—and that big body now shrunk in like a dryfly, then my cal-
lused heart hurts a good halfway down the road to Raleigh.

Rato never speaks of it. It's not that I think he's hard-hearted. I just
think he can discard parts of the world that don't directly press on
him, the way I manage to disregard the starving masses of Ethiopia. I
suspect Rato thinks he lives with me now, and I'm his main concern.
And maybe he's right. Maybe one of my big mistakes has been dilut-
ing my feelings by trying to care too much about too many things.

Anyhow I've got no real complaints against him so far. He's as
quiet as a bale of cotton. He lives as neat as a snake, no mess of any
kind behind him. And he's as easy to feed as a baby. If I let him take
his walks when the need strikes and give him control of the television
at nights, then he's the easiest-to-please friend I ever had. And why
not another thirty-odd years of it?

Even down into my early womanhood, in Afton and Warrenton
and all out in the surrounding county, there were dozens of couples
stranger than me and Rato—old brothers that had been together
since the cradle with nothing but a Negro woman or man that came
in to wash and cook for them (that much at least and who knew what
else?). Old-maid daughters and their fathers. Lots of bachelor brothers and spinster sisters.

Everybody thought they were doing fine. I never remember one
word of unkind rumor or criticism against them. This whole idea that
the purpose of the human heart is to make hot love on the even nights
and think about it in a warm sweat on the odd nights is sadly lacking
in imagination, to me anyhow. I think those old Victorian Baptists
were a lot smarter and sure God more tolerant than us with all our
smart ideas and laws that say this one can't touch that one—no no no!

It was just a more sensible time, I guess, back then before Americans got this present idea that life without a richly contented marital
love-life is worse than being staked down to the jailhouse floor in a
banana republic in the worst month of summer with roaches big as
pancakes. People, even in my childhood, used to be trusted to find
their own nourishment like dogs in the woods—the right brand of
grass or herbs to eat that would heal their pain.

If you didn't want to set up in the babymaking business, fine—just take your favorite sister or brother or parent and set you up a house-hold in a nice cool oak-grove and live till you both had your fill and quit. And if either one of you decided to reach out and touch the other one—well, who'd ever know what the response would be and who the hell's business was it anyhow?

When did marriage get to seeming so unrealistically important? Maybe when big families broke up and there was nothing to life but Rosa and Wesley and poor little Horace, no deep cushion of aunts and uncles and cousins around you to help absorb all the million daily shocks of life. Nobody but your sworn wedded mate. And good luck, by the way, when your mate decides he's been dead from the neck-up or waist-down ever since he met you, or two weeks after the honeymoon (if you ever had one, which Rosa and Wesley didn't).

If you arranged in the fifties to be a pioneer career-woman, then you'll have that wheel to push your new-found energies against. But who arranged for that? Not me. I type letters, mimeograph exams, Xerox everything from Shakespeare sonnets to directions for jumping a stalled battery. It's hardly soul food though, believe you me. I could quit tomorrow and, except for the salary, not miss an instant of it ever again.

But even with Wesley sticking by his share of the mortgage, I couldn't begin to think of quitting work. So I'm expected to spend another twenty-odd years at a keyboard typing other people's thoughts eight hours a day just so I can come home and sleep warm and dry in a house that no longer has anything to offer me but protection—and in fact has already failed at that. *Expected by who?*

God is something I guess I've pretty much left out of this diary. And out of my life more and more in recent years. Even in adoles-cence, when a lot of the boys got religious, I could quietly take it or leave it. I mean I've never considered for ten seconds being an atheist. I'm sure there's a divine being that created it all, me included, and is watching me and it sympathetically at least—however many babies get born with their bellies outside their skin and with tumors the size of children's beach buckets. In my experience though He sure to goodness keeps His own counsel.

Maybe I've just been too involved in my own thoughts and hopes

to take the time to learn to sit in silence long enough to hear His version of what comes next, any questions He may have of me. When I
found out I was pregnant in 1957—and me no more married than
Mother Teresa—I tried to pray, as I said. Well, I got as much answer
as if I'd prayed to rocks in the road. A direct answer that is, in words or
music. Then at the last minute I had to stand in for the Virgin Mary
in Mama's Christmas pageant at Delight Church (with Wesley as
third Wise Man), and the sight of real live little Frederick Gupton
tuning up to holler there in my lap—and wasn't *he* my answer? *Rosa,
help this present needy child. And all other children placed in your
care.* So I picked up Frederick and married you and had Horatio
"Horace" Beavers and our long life together.

Since then though I've barely said a prayer. During bad times I
have occasionally said "Take me where I ought to go" and then just
waited to see where my feet went next. But very little else. And look
where the feet have landed.

So that's been my philosophy here these past months since Wesley
left and I got slammed down. I don't know any other way to act. I
guess I could try going back to church, meeting the new minister, and
seeing if he has any help to offer. But church too long ago lost its
shine for me. Even Wesley kept going to services longer than I did.
And when Horace got into his teen years, he went through a deep
time of needing to be religious. I'd find him on his knees in his own
room, praying for whatever little sins he imagined he'd committed (or
so I guessed—I never asked and I doubt he ever saw me at the door).
It touched me at the time, but it never made me want to follow suit.

The real problem was, I worshiped Wesley—didn't I? I've said here
somewhere else how I learned to love men's faces from watching, first,
my father, then Milo, and then Wesley. Needless to say, I hadn't ever
really touched my father and Milo—their secret bodies, I mean (though
I'm not sure it would have been the world's biggest sin and crime; it
might have helped me love Wesley better and more sensibly).

So when Wesley and I finally got down to serious business, I just
started transferring everything I'd ever felt about God and Jesus onto
one human boy from down the road. Wesley's good frank face, his
mysterious eyes, and everything strong and lovely and sad in his long

clean body—for me, all that just turned into God and Christ and Heaven. And when we brought our separate bodies together and made them one (and they did become one—I can take a solemn oath, even here now alone—more times than a few in all our years), then I had even more of a reason for thinking one *man* was the whole point of life—my life anyhow.

It didn't have all that much to do with personal fulfillment, actual orgasms, or any of that woman's-seminar stuff you hear on t.v. I sure never counted the number of orgasms I had in Wesley's presence and with his assistance—maybe not more than a hundred. What it pertained to mainly was my own deep happiness, my best satisfaction. Being bare, with Wesley bare and striving in me—it just came to mean I had a big purpose, secret, known to no one but him, still the thing that justified my life. My tiredness and boredom, my failure to be the kind of woman I'd been as a girl—somebody admired by her family, her teachers, and the damned county paper for general neatness and excellence.

It wasn't that I grew up like some girls I knew to become a common whore and sex-junkie. Some smart decent girls from near us in the country—girls that I've laughed and primed tobacco with—had themselves six children by the time they were twenty-five just because they couldn't stop their bodies from climbing aboard Spencer Scott or some other hot-eyed boy with straight teeth and a nice mole there to the left of his right eye.

Me—I can look at most men, and sex will be the last thing I see and want. It was just—just!—that Wesley didn't do anything for maybe the first ten years I knew him but go on getting grander in my mind (in the night, bare inside me). He seemed more and more like Rosa's only goal. Love Wesley, serve him, give Wesley all you've got.

Then about the time Horace began to have a pre-teenage life of his own outside my kitchen, and I left the house and got me a job, I began to suspect Wesley didn't need me all that much either. He sure never told me otherwise at least. He'd roll over on me several nights a week and kindly but silently gouge down in me the same as before. But it wasn't the same.

Either I'd changed somehow and had less to give him or that, however hard Wesley dug down in me, he couldn't anymore find the stuff he'd found—the sweet and nourishing best heart of Rosa, that had fueled him on through so much trouble.

Maybe that's when he left last Christmas week. It's anyhow all he left me with. And what it brings me down to, here and now, is the least helpful thing imaginable—*me*.

I am all I've got. And it's some kind of lonesome in here where I live, where I'm nailed up lonesome with the little bit Rosa knows and dreams of still. Wesley talks about feeling dead. When he first wrote it, I laughed bitterly just to read the one word—what on earth could he mean?

But now I think I understand perfectly well and agree. I can easily imagine, a year or so from now, just being one of those hollowed-out women that goes to an office job five days a week, types thousands of words a day, files the product, then slides back home on a slick conveyer belt to drink cheap vodka and watch television till two in the morning, then four hours' sleep. Then eventual retirement, with a farewell luncheon (baked chicken, Waldorf salad, and a gold-plated pen and pencil set to write your thrilling memoirs with), and twenty more years in a grimy cheap apartment watching t.v. and thinking how fast time had run and worn you out.

Join the human race, Rosa. Be a normal cold uncomplaining zombie. You had nearly fifty years awake as a woman with feelings in every damned cell—more feeling than any two average others. It's begun to cool now. Little nerves are dying off from exhaustion and old age. Thank your stars and shut up. Lie down and just rest. The human race mainly consists of citizens such as you—people that had a nice few years of life, then consumed the fuel (like natural hair-color before you go gray), and are marking cold time till death stops by one night and says "Now." Two mornings later there's your obituary in *The News and Observer*, three inches long. Some old boss of yours says "Dear old girl" and kisses his wife an instant longer as he leaves for work. Some English major from way-back-when (now a forty-five-year-old advertising man) says "Old Ms. Beavers, she was one feisty lady." And that'll be *it*, except for God—whatever He thinks and awards you in Heaven.

It will after all be the first day of spring in no time now, if the world lasts till spring and Rosa's here to greet it. Some little cell hid deep down in me may still be breathing, may still sprout green if daylight strikes it.

Do. Amaze me. Sprout and thrive.

WESLEY

Like every dream Wesley ever had, this one was real as a normal day. That was why, all his life, he'd counted on dreams to help him onward. His were never foolish or dumb. Even the ones that left him nervous, especially them, were gritty as newsreels. So when this one started outside Nashville just before sunrise, his mind braced itself for whatever would come. From the start though it promised to be long and happy.

The girl was maybe seventeen years old. He must have been somewhere near that age himself since it seemed very natural that they should sit here together, near the surf but warm and dry. He was not in the Navy yet. Or at least he wasn't in uniform, just starched khaki pants and a polo shirt. They were both barefooted. She wore a pale dress. Otherwise all Wesley saw was her eyes. They were fixed right on him in a way that, in any other girl, would have been odd or dirty. And for once that seemed sufficient to him. His hands stayed calm on the sand between them. His mind didn't think of moving elsewhere, to hide in the dunes or even to touch a girl as fine as this.

So he stayed on, peaceful in her nearness and glad at least to find one girl that could watch him and yet not draw on his strength or stroke his body with those eyes, strong as the moon at full. He remembered his mother's training enough to think he ought to say some kind of thanks.

But when he tried it, just the first few words, the girl smiled, touched her silent mouth, and shook her head. So it was perfect, right?—the day, the place, his mind, the company.

No, he needed to know her name. Unbelievable as she was, she didn't seem strange—no haloes or organ music. He even wondered why he couldn't relax and let her just be here. If her name came to him in time, then good. If not, well, there must be worse fates than a happy life with a flawless Jane Doe. Still in another minute of watching, he felt his mouth go to work without him. Over the surf, he heard his own voice say "My name's Wesley."

The girl waited, then laughed. "Of course it is. That ocean's the Atlantic too."

He actually blushed. "Have I lost my mind?"

"How so?"

Wesley said "Beg your pardon if this makes you mad but who are you?"

It wasn't anger on her face but surprise, then maybe regret. She said "This is like soap operas—amnesia. I'm Rosacoke."

Soon after that he woke up in Nashville. As always, he was alert at once. So he knew his surroundings—the master bedroom of Wilson's trailer, her sleeping body beside him.

The sounds from Wilson began to reach him. Nothing you could tape-record or describe, except maybe the rush of blood through her skin or the growth of her hair. Maybe the solemn push of her kindness against the whole world, the big steady trust she'd offered from the start to a strange man old enough to be her father.

In another ten seconds, that was all Wesley knew. The strange dream was gone. Superstitious as he was, he had to gamble that he was lying on the edge of a lucky day—treading the warm and buoyant knowledge that a woman this good would join him in a moment.

He also knew it was the first day of spring. The sky was still dark, the air in the trailer was still dry and crisp, and Wilson's flank—a thumb's reach from him—was chill to the touch. But Wesley's heart lifted at the thought. Content as he'd been in recent months, winter had kept a thick film on his eyes. The past two weeks though, the sky had arched up higher at the spine. The light was healthier, stronger, and seemed surer of lasting. More than ever before in his life, Wesley took the annual blessing of the day as confirmation of the rightness of his place. The sun itself was confirming his choice to be here now, beside this girl.

He lay absolutely still, not touching her, and watched the porthole above her shoulder. Behind the thick curtain it would still show daylight in the instant day broke. From the shine of his watch, he knew it would be another few minutes. Whatever came after that—the first glow that said dark had ended again—he'd wait for day.

In the wait Wesley said his usual prayer, asking God to give special care to the leaders of the world and to his own family. He named them as always—starting with the president, then his mother, his wife in Raleigh, Horace his son and Horace's wife Pris, this woman asleep with him now, and his own sorry self. In prayers, since the day he'd run from home, he thought of himself as sorry and sinful.

Unlike Rosa he'd never really doubted that the world itself, not to mention his loved ones, was held in shape and suspended from harm partly by his prayers. Once in the Navy he'd got in an argument with a Catholic from Providence, Rhode Island. Wesley had attacked the idea of nuns and monks—grown strong people (that could have been farming or painting ships) sitting idle in monkeries and convents, not even plowing or childbearing.

The Catholic had let out a stream of profane abuse more startling than any southern brand; but then he'd said "You ought to fall on your hillbilly knees now, Reb, and thank your stars those sisters *are* praying. If they weren't locked up—peaceful and pure—praying for your spotted ass, God would long since have melted your shit to tar."

And ever since, Wesley had agreed and joined his own daily voice to the silent choir of all those pale pimply ladies kneeling on stone floors behind blinds and bars.

And as he got to the end of it, the porthole gradually glowed. One more weekday, a whole nother spring. It didn't seem sacrilegious in the least to roll with the next breath up against Wilson and start, with his right hand, to rousing her. They had half an hour before the

alarm, sufficient time to honor the occasion—spring and its goodness—and both their good bodies.

Wilson mumbled "I need my sleep now, Wesley."

He laughed. "You slept like a puppy on drugs." He knew. He'd
waked up twice to pee, and every time Wilson had been thoroughly
drowned. His hand went out again, gentler this time. She let him
work and in another half-minute he began to think he'd won. The old
moist findings of his blind hands—perpetually the same, miracu-
lously new—lured him down that dark hall in his mind that led to
perfect repayment, entire reward. Today like all other days, it seemed
incredible that so much could be got for so little—no money, no hard
work, no pain, just mutual patience and courtesy, *permission*.

Without a single word suddenly Wilson was bolt upright in the
sheets, then standing, then pounding the linoleum toward the bathroom door.

For a few seconds Wesley could hope she was fitting in one of her
several brands of sex gear (he still knew less about birth control than
the average high-school boy). But really he knew better. And then the
shower came on. Oh Jesus, she'd started the day without him.

She was one of those modern kids that can spend a whole morning
in the shower, so Wesley knew he was high and dry. Mad enough to
turn the trailer over and leave but still hot and hard as a wombat, he
rolled to his back, threw off the cover, and tried to love himself. In the
dim light he could see enough of his cock to admire. It was straight
and stiff as stainless steel, the hair was still dark—no wrinkles or gray
or other sign of age.

But oh the old bright focus was gone. With all the thick spit of
morning in a hand trained for forty-five years, his mind couldn't help
him. That one mad girl, by turning aside, had the strength to cut Wesley's power at the source. In twenty more seconds he'd lost his will.
What he hated most was the fact she'd won. And he didn't know why.
How had he harmed her? He was gentle as a pet. He'd only meant to
give her the best he knew.

By the time she was ready to show her face, he had made fresh coffee
and was half-dressed, drinking it. Wilson walked the length of the

kitchenette silent on her pink chenille scuffs and found her own cup. When she'd sugared it precisely, she joined him at the table in the living-room corner. She looked young and fine, in her white slacks and figured smock for work, not a hair out of place.

But Wesley's mind couldn't think what to say. He couldn't smile either. He stared out the one big window and said "First day of spring."

Wilson said "Don't I know."

That came as a surprise. He felt even madder. Finally he could say "Then what did I do wrong?"

Wilson looked baffled. "Nothing. When?"

"Don't be childish, Wilson. I'm too big for that. You goddamned well know when I mean."

"At dawn in the bed? What *you* planned to do? It just didn't happen to be *Wilson's* plan. You hadn't asked Wilson."

Wesley said "I hadn't understood you took written applications. Is that the new procedure?"

She laughed a little but then she got earnest. "It may need to be. I been thinking it over. The problem is, Wesley, you need more than me—of sex anyhow. All men seem to, the ones I've known."

"And you've known a cast of thousands, I'm sure."

"Don't be mean now. You were no virgin boy."

"No ma'm. I'm married. You're shacked up—remember?—with a long-married father in a field near Nashville in a mobile home ugly as a mule with mumps. It's adultery, lady. You're a tax-paying grown-up and you're sharing the crime."

Wilson finally asked "You know that too?"

"Yes ma'm, from the start. I'm a Christian boy."

She took a good minute to blow and drink her coffee. Then she had the strength to face him, eyes to eyes. "Then let's end the crime."

Wesley asked "What's your plan?"

"Well, there's two," she said. She had plainly thought through it. "Either you get divorced or we split up."

He said "And either one's fine by you?"

"Maybe so. At first I hoped for plan A. Here lately though I've got some questions." The seriousness invading her face was aging her fast.

She suddenly looked like somebody's wife, some teenage boy's mother lowering the gate.

Wesley hated to watch but he had to push on and know where he stood. He said "Let's hear every question you got." He never thought he'd be in a place like this—some young girl holding his life in her fingers and turning it over like a frog in a lab (in the Navy he signed up for an improve-your-mind biology course till they had to cut frogs, and then he quit—not seeing the point).

Wilson said "Let's wait till we're home this evening. It's early. We're mad. I'm not thinking plain."

Wesley shook his head. "There may not be an evening. This ain't my home, not yet anyhow. And I ain't mad. Tell me now or never."

She felt the knife-edge of hurt in his *home*. And she heard the sweep of his ultimatum in *now or never*, but she held her temper. "We're way apart in age. You know a lot I just don't know yet. You've raised a family. I've yet to have mine. You won't want to go through that again surely."

"I never said so."

Wilson said "You want to discuss it?"

Wesley said "The discussion can wait. I just meant I hadn't ruled kids out."

"But a marriage would need to come first," Wilson said. "You haven't really mentioned a word about divorcing Rosa."

The sound of Rosa's name in another woman's mouth, even this far away, still shocked Wesley. It even surprised him to realize Wilson knew it—her name, his loyal wife's name. Had he just let it slip or had she read his mail? He wouldn't fight that now. He might need it later. He said "I don't know I'm getting a divorce."

"Then how can you ask for this much of me?"

"Because you've given it, Wilson—open-handed till just now. You've give it by the *ton*."

"—In hopes of much more. You don't think I want to be 'shacked-up,' as you say, for the rest of my young life, do you?"

Wesley said "I thought you were burned bad as me. I didn't know you were rushing back to nobody's damned altar."

"I'm not, no. But we've been together nearly three months now, and I'm thinking it's time we knew what we mean."

Wesley said "I've been meaning I'm *happy.*"

Wilson smiled naturally, then pushed it aside. "I'm saying I'm not, I guess. Not now anymore. I just can't keep talking about it this morning. I'll be glad to go right on after work, but now I've got to run."

"You do that," he said. "I may be here."

When Wilson had put on her coat and was ready to leave for the hospital, she stopped by the table. Wesley wasn't due in as early as she and was still drinking coffee and watching the news. She didn't say a word but waited behind him and then bent slowly to kiss Wesley's head—the crown of his skull, still densely covered.

Wesley waited too. But then he leaned back on the pressure of her mouth.

She stayed there to meet him and waited for help—some opening word.

He couldn't find a word though, so he had to let her leave.

All that day at work Wilson thought of nothing but the evening, what she'd say when they sat down finally to talk their way through this mean log-jam. As she X-rayed her fourth patient of the morning—a handsome and valiant twelve-year-old boy with leukemia and a possible broken arm (from school basketball)—she had the closest thing to a vision in her life. Behind this child's threatened nearly transparent skin, as if her own eyes were X-ray, she saw the young Wesley. Though Wilson didn't know it, he was the same boy Rosa had seen in actual flesh, up a pecan tree all but forty years ago gazing off at smoke. The simple condensation on earth of God's love of things, sent for all to see and honor as they could.

Wilson saw it now in those same terms, almost those words. It made her think she would be a big fool to lose Wesley now. Thickened though he was with flesh and years and boredom, the present man who asked for her body—her steady companionship—was as good a soul as she'd ever get a chance at, the only one so far to promise to use her. Stand him beside the rest of the men she'd been through till now, he shone like a torch on a dark hill at midnight.

She'd read enough in women's magazines to know such thinking was old-fashioned and dangerous. It had landed her mother in a marriage as fruitful as frozen sand. But the chance had never come Wilson's way before. She'd about given up hope of that brand of luck, a run at someone genuinely this fine. Calm and grown-up and gentle and *there*. If she drew back now, in fear or self-love, she felt convinced she'd be cursed for life. Meanness, hot hands, hard dirty mouths, blind cocks poking at her in dry cold dark. Sixty more years in howling solitude, strapped down to a relay of pitiful failures till she herself was one more failed woman—grinning too much from a face that looked like a burnt-out trailer, missing a few back teeth and dye-haired, begging all passers for any kind handout.

As the boy with the hurt arm left her room, Wilson heard herself say the sudden kind of sentence she never said—the kind of thing technicians learn not to say. She offered hope. She said "You'll live to be a strong old man." No sooner had it passed her lips than she thought "Damn. That's a lie." But as quick again, she knew the whole truth. She had been shown the future and licensed to tell him. So she sent him a big smile—"I know I'm right."

The boy's name was Travis—Travis Todd. He stopped and stood straight upright in the door. He turned her promise over in his mind, one more claim in the thousand he'd heard since learning of his affliction. Then quick as Wilson said it, Travis knew to believe her. Never having met an angel before, he nonetheless accepted the message. He said "You sure I can hold you to that?"

"Absolutely."

"Where you live?"

"Out the Franklin road—Route 4, Box 40. Big doublewide mobile home on high cinder-blocks. Ugly as a mule with mumps, my friend says, but warm and dry. Stop by any time."

Travis gave a deep laugh, which was startling for his age. "In about sixty-five years I'll be there, you watch. Have a big supper ready. I like everything but liver."

It fueled Wilson's day right through till five. And all the way home, she bore traffic gladly.

But Wesley wasn't there and wasn't there at bedtime.

                                                    *   *   *

He'd worked till after six on a BMW that belonged to a man who taught Law at Vanderbilt, a man maybe ten years younger than Wesley but single and sporty. He was one of the scarce customers that liked to watch Wesley work and talked to him like an equal. Wesley had soon figured out from his well-fit clothes and slow needy eyes that the fellow had to be queer, but that had just got Wesley interested. From his first days in the Navy in Norfolk, he had been a steady queer target—sailors in general were, back then.

Nobody seemed to know whether it was the tight uniforms or their tendency to be knee-walking drunk on shoreleave or the fact that— being generally so horny by the time their feet touched firm ground—they were liable to say yes to the first offer they got for a good meal, some warmth and comfort, some kind of personal attention, and relief. At first it had shocked hell out of Wesley, even hearing the older sailors discuss it as calm as they did. He had said right off that if a man ever touched him below the waist, he believed his skin would crawl right off his bones and head for home if he didn't kill the guy first. Or both.

But neither one had happened. He'd been out at a beer joint at Ocean View one Saturday night when the girls were extra awful. They were the kind you couldn't imagine handling, even with the recommended sack on their head. And he might have known, from the bathroom wall, he was in strange country. Over the urinal in neat handwriting, it said *Blow job $5.00. With lipstick $7.50.* After reading that Wesley was ready to thumb on back to base. But when he had paused long enough to button up all those complicated sailor-buttons and then walked back out into the big dark room, a normal-looking guy in a Harris-tweed jacket walked right up and handed him an open giant-sized can of beer. Wesley had grinned and said "How do I know this ain't poisoned?"

In dead earnest the guy said "You don't," took the can back, drank a long swig, and returned it to Wesley.

So Wesley laughed and said "Now how do I know *you* ain't poison?"

The guy said "Oh *I* am. I'm as queer as Uncle Harry's hatband. But I don't think it's catching unfortunately."

The guy looked about as queer as General MacArthur, so Wesley waited awhile to laugh. Finally he did. Then he drank the beer, felt calm, and a half-hour later was sitting in the guy's room at a swanky beach motel five miles farther south with a magic-fingers mattress and a framed picture of James Dean on the bureau (Dean had got killed just a few weeks before, so surely the picture didn't come with the room).

There they switched to harder stuff, the first bourbon of Wesley's young life. It tasted scarey but he never showed it, never got drunk, never passed out anyhow, never reached a point where he lost control of his will. It surprised him more than his host, who had hoped for at least some signs of slackening. What Wesley was mainly conscious of was that a series of fences in his mind just silently fell down in lovely slow motion, like in a horserace movie, as the guy tried to jump them. Wesley watched it all from as far away as the guy himself—and both of them watched smilingly. Finally Wesley was naked as a peeled tadpole and stretched out grinning in the cool dry sheets. The guy kept his own briefs on but joined him enthusiastically for all the rest, the remainder of darkness and a fair part of dawn.

Wesley's later memory was that he'd lain on his back looking down through the hours as, by dim light that filtered through a crack in the bathroom door, the guy prowled and grazed over Wesley's body like something gentle but almost starved. Wesley estimated that he'd met the guy's every hope and need; the guy had anyhow kept saying "Incredible. Absolutely incredible." Wesley also knew that he personally had never been more thoroughly or skillfully pleased and honored than by that particular stranger's hands, that tireless mouth.

What he didn't remember was that, toward day, he'd gathered the guy—a smaller man than Wesley—into both his arms and held him near while the guy moaned and kicked toward his own destination in his own quick hands. Then they slept an hour. Then Wesley woke up entirely sober, and dressed, and left for base. He'd long since forgot the guy's name or home but could still hear his grateful moan toward daylight and see his dazed grin as Wesley waved goodbye and said again "Thanks."

The rest of his years in the Navy, Wesley had been with two other men. One was a five-hour stand in St. Tropez, France with a cheerful French picture-painter that didn't speak one single word of English (which proved no problem). One was a long cool weekend in Baltimore, completely indoors like something in a test tube but safe and with peaceful background music (the guy was an English teacher). Neither was as strangely peaceful and kind as the one near Norfolk, but both were still good enough to keep Wesley from joining his working mates through the years in their meaner queer jokes. There'd been no reason, in his years with Rosa, to turn back to men. The roar of his early manhood had cooled enough to let him focus fine again.

And women were the natural target of his aim—the harbor of his trip. It was mainly with women that he'd sometimes get the chime he aimed for and worked to hear, that thirty or forty seconds at the end when you've come on off and you know you've showed her your own big secret and witnessed hers. All it is, is everybody's same average secret—a sweaty thrill, eyes clenched, and some panting (though a good deal nicer than baseball for instance). But *average* doesn't mean that it's not worth striving for, not worth any decent form of chase.

Tonight though, March 1986, he'd toiled through a day with the gall on his neck of Wilson's refusal, her problems to discuss in one more session like those Rosacoke had made him dread—"What *you* don't notice, what *I* have to bear." So when the law professor pulled up in a cab to collect his car, Wesley went out to meet him with an open-faced grin.

They discussed the repairs, seven hundred dollars worth, in considerable detail (the fellow knew a lot more about cars than Wesley had guessed). Then the welcome fact of spring, then the lengthening days. Then Wesley had noticed what he'd noticed so often when queers came at him, the man's quick check for a wedding ring. Wesley had never worn one despite Rosa's urging. And when he caught the look, he frankly extended his left hand and spread it. "Nope. No more."

The professor said "Let me buy you a drink."

Wesley said "Thanks, doctor. I'm dirty as a dog."

"My friends call me Stanley, and I've got a shower." The absolute centers of his eyes were empty as some old open well in the country with a magnet buried deep in its heart, the kind of dark you could fall in forever.

Wesley saw that and heard him asking—dignified, brushed and

combed but asking. When had anybody last asked for Wesley? Fifteen years maybe, more like twenty. So it cost Wesley little to say "I hope your water heater's set on high."

Stanley said "Old Faithful. Vesuvius."

Wesley said "All *right*" and felt two whole skins of deadness slough off him. He had no idea what would break next. Going with this guy just meant *going*, one good drink of liquor at the absolute least. Not going back to Wilson's yet, that was the main thing. Wesley was running his own life again, which was two-thirds the reason he was out here at all in middle Tennessee—as poor an excuse for human habitation as he'd run up on in a traveled life.

So he followed Stanley ten quick minutes in his own car—a condo spacious enough for four, every wall hung with antique maps. Wesley took a long shower and, to his surprise, stepped readily into the clean jeans and shirt laid out on the bed by his old work clothes. Stanley was Wesley's exact size and was nowhere in sight. That by itself was the first surprise—he'd fully expected to be interrupted in the midst of his shower with a new bar of soap, some corny reason. Wesley whispered to the mirror "This dude *is* a lawyer." Then dressed and combed, he went out to find him.

Stanley had already poured two bourbons on the rocks big as baptismal pools and was waiting in the den. "You look like a bourbon man."

Wesley laughed. "I'm not a drinking man. But sure, tonight bourbon sounds like the ticket."

Stanley said "You celebrating something tonight?"

Wesley thought it out, then laughed and said "Abandonment."

"You or somebody else?"

"Let's just say both and quit while we're grinning." Wesley chose a deep white chair facing Stanley and managed not to panic when the cushion swallowed him.

With the born lawyer's deference to private rights, Stanley nodded, then raised his glass in a toast and settled in his chair.

They drank bourbon for three quarters of an hour and listened to Barbra Streisand records in chronological order. Or so Stan said. Stan loved her but Wesley had always thought her outsized nose acted like a megaphone at unexpected wrong places in songs. So he didn't mention that, to him, they sounded more like whooping and hollering than actual music. He just kept thinking "That girl's mighty lonesome. Somebody go squeeze her." But it wouldn't be him; he was glad to sit quiet in a safe clean house and be his own man.

By the end of the Barbra stack, Stanley had worked his way through all the basic questions about Wesley's past—a good legal work-up, Wesley could tell.

And Wesley had answered honestly, amused to be asked. Everything—his parents, the Navy, Rosa, Horace, his jobs, his flight, right up to Wilson and this morning's quarrel. Nobody he could think of had ever taken that close a personal interest in the surface of his actions, not even Rosa. One more thing about these fellows, he thought—they can make a straight man feel dignified in a way few women even aim at. Since they aren't trying you out for the role of Prince Valiant or nest builder and daddy, they can afford to notice the more here-and-now parts of your life, like your hobbies. And they can sure, without ever mentioning it, make your face and body feel important again—more even than women in bars, who are much less concerned with sex here and now than in watching men spin at the end of their string.

Also Wesley had finished his third straight drink. He set down the glass and patrolled the inside lining of his skull to check was he drunk. Soft on the surface and his skin was beginning to burn all over but no, not drunk. And when Stan rose to refill the glass, Wesley said "No sir, you sit back down."

More than a little startled, Stan obeyed.

Wesley saw the perplexity and laughed. "Whoa. I ain't the Nashville Strangler. I just meant I've got to drive home eventually. If I stop now, I ought to be ready in an hour or so. If you got plans, go right on your way—I can sit out there in my car till I'm ready."

Stanley said "Not a plan in the world. Stay put. How would a two-inch filet mignon sound, about half an hour from now?"

Wesley waited to be sure firm ground was still under him. Then he met those eyes head-on and said "I bet it'll sound like my favorite hymn. But Stan, let me tell you—I'm an old ladies' man; you'd be wasting money." He sat forward quickly and his eyes stayed clear.

They didn't do business this fast in law school; the need for lawyers would quit if they did. So Stan said "Can you wait while I pour some bourbon?"

Wesley said "Am I that hard to lose—old gator like me?"

That relaxed Stan some. He sat back and said "You're a breath of fresh air."

"*Fresh* I'm not but thanks for the compliment. I've just been a sailor and a strongly-built man for most of my years. I've met a few guys that liked my faculties, and I didn't see any cause to start slugging or call in a preacher and strike out for Hell. I'll be honest with you—I took two or three of them up on the deal, and I won't lie and say my life got twisted. I thanked them all; they were gentlemen—though whether they were Christians or not, I can't say."

Stan smiled. "Episcopalians."

"Are you one too?"

"A Whiskeypalian?—no, God and I called it quits years back."

Wesley said "You still believe in Him and all though? I mean, you like pretty things too much to be an atheist." He looked round the room again—maps, books, antique chairs, a black statue of God's head and neck (or somebody bearded and equally solemn).

Stan smiled again. "Never heard it put that way. No, I guess you're right. But the church ships men like me off in flames, every Sunday on schedule."

Wesley said "Me too. If church calls the shots, I'll be in the sub-sub-basement of Hell. God's name though is Mercy; I heard that in vacation Bible school before I was ten. The lady that told me was a smart old maid; she'd read the Bible through three times, so I bank on that."

"You go every Sunday?"

Wesley said "Lord no, maybe once in two years and then just a funeral or wedding or such."

Stanley said "Then you think all the Bible is right?"

"I guess you don't."

"Saint Paul is the block in the road for me."

Wesley said "Which is he?"

"You know, all the letters—Thessalonians, Corinthians, the laws against everything—women, hair, gays."

Wesley said "I got Saint Paul's number way back when. See, he never met Jesus like Peter and them. So he had to pedal extra hard to make up for that. And me, I'm happier than most grown men; but couldn't you fellows let us have *gay* back? We haven't got all that many words left."

"But you just said you've gone with men."

For a moment it seemed Wesley couldn't remember. Then he said "That was back before steam."

"Never too late again."

Wesley said "*Me*? I'm old as your daddy, stringy and gray."

"More like a brother. You're doing all right." Stan smiled and left to refill his glass two whole rooms away.

Alone, Wesley shut his eyes and at once saw himself upright on a prairie, though he'd never been any place west of Kentucky. He saw no other live human being. He was in khaki pants and the dark blue sweater he'd won in high school; it seemed to be winter. The sky was tin gray and a cold hard wind blew through his dry hair and left his skin tight and sad—how sad? He sat on, blinded, and wondered at the vision till he knew again what he'd felt this morning, with Wilson at sunrise. Every pore in his skin was yearning for touch, some human brand of courteous service with a few quiet jokes. His own shut mind spoke silently "This skin is lonesome, son."

Stanley was back. He went to his chair, set his drink on the table but stayed upright; Wesley's face had changed in the absence. Stan said "You sure you need to leave?"

That somehow shook Wesley; he felt caught out. An instant later he felt a sick guilt, though guilt was as rare in Wesley as Spanish. Every minute he stayed on here was a lie to this kind gentleman, a regular customer. But the way it came when he finally spoke was "What would a fellow, not forty like you, see in me? You can do far better on the downtown market."

Stan said "AIDS."

Wesley said "Beg your pardon?" (he'd of course heard the word; but as late as that spring, it was still not a term on everybody's lips).

"The plague," Stan said. "Anybody like me on the downtown market is begging to die. A clean straight man with standards like yours and eyes that dark with a human I.Q. is a spring in the desert—simple as that."

The candor brought Wesley back down fast. He pulled in his gut, thrust his chin forward, and then said "Doctor, you got me wrong. I was all but a virgin till late December. For going on thirty years, I'd been with one woman—give or take a misstep. But here since New Year's I've been, like I said, with a Nashville girl that has had two husbands and isn't a tramp but is no nun either. I haven't been tested so I can't guarantee I'm not strowing death every time I grin."

Stanley smiled. "You've got a big grin, I agree. But everybody says now that smiles don't spread it or sneezes and coughs, just contaminated body fluids in the blood."

"And you gay fellows are dropping like doves."

Stan smiled. "Many thanks—for the doves anyhow; most people say *flies*. So far I've just lost one old friend—died in New York six weeks ago, his brain reamed out by a cat parasite that almost every child's had and thrown off. In the first few weeks, he kept calling me and saying that maybe a trip down here would bring his strength back. I hemmed and hawed and he got the point. Or had gone past knowing my number and name."

Wesley's head was clearing by the minute now; he sat well forward so his voice could keep low and still be heard. "And you still brought a strange crossroads mechanic back to this handsome spread and hoped he'd help you? Christ Jesus, Stan." Wesley didn't sit back but stayed there nearer.

Stanley stayed deep in his chair. "You found your woman, knowing she'd been around. Am I all that strange?"

Wesley said "You're the one with the well-trained mind, so don't hesitate to say I'm wrong. But here this minute now, for the first clear time, I feel like the world's in for some grade of Hell worse than we've ever seen, and I've seen whores in North Africa eat *out* with maggots—I mean blind maggots boiling in sores—and them still selling their ass half-price. Something right now, since you mentioned your friend, just speaks down in me and says we'll be there in a New York minute."

Stanley said "Worse" and waited to drink, then said "And it may outlast us both."

Wesley sat back, heavy as if struck down. One thing about him had outlasted time—Stan mentioned his eyes; they'd stayed that keen, no glasses ever. From there, ten feet away, he saw Stanley's birthmark—the first time yet. It was almost down in the collar of his shirt, the color of walnut and hen-egg size. And seeing it there did less for Wesley than the sight of a mile-high bird on columns of heat in a summer day. But he thought "He's despised that mark all his life. I can reach out and touch him, right there on the place. It won't cost me a thin red cent. He might just be my brother or cousin; he won't misread me. I can do that much." Wesley didn't think why and he stood up to do it.

But Stan held his palm up. "You know you got to eat. Let's cook those steaks."

Wesley said "You may not believe me now; but country as I am, I eat steak rare."

Stanley said "I believe you. Come and tell me when it's done."

Wesley said "That's easy. Just listen up close, then when it barely stops mooing—"

They ate at nine with a bottle of California burgundy and talked like members of the same old family—long quiet minutes with the clink of silver, then brief remarks on food or weather or the world and local news. Then they went to the den again and watched the first half of *Gone with the Wind* on television. At the end, when Scarlett tried to eat the radish but threw it up and then vowed endurance for her and hers, the camera flew back; the music swelled up, and Wesley's eyes opened (he had snoozed off and on). He said what he always thought at that point "If Scarlett O'Hara had been Jeff Davis, we'd be free now."

Stan was from small-town northern Ohio so he withheld comment, but he was tired too. He got to his feet and said "Are you welcome at home tonight?"

The word *home* almost made Wesley flinch, and he said "—Welcome to a razor fight."

So Stanley offered two simple choices—sleep with him in the king-sized bed or alone in the guestroom, small but clean. He also said "Either place, you're safe—I don't sleepwalk or haven't yet."

Wesley smiled. "Don't worry. I got my brass knucks." He didn't of course but it helped him to say so.

In the guest bathroom Stan laid out towels, a new toothbrush still sealed in a box, and a clean black comb; then went his own way.

Wesley focused his mind the best he could on the here and now—this well-kept place and its kind proprietor. Imagine keeping a back-stock of toothbrushes; this man had to be desperate or a saint. In under ten minutes Wesley shucked his clothes and, naked as ever, was asleep on the wine before he finished the whole Lord's Prayer. From somewhere farther off than Mars, he thought he heard Stan's voice say "Night." He knew he should answer and he earnestly tried, but no words came—just deep brown rest.

Sometime after three though his eyes clicked open, wide awake. Stan had left on a light far back in the house; it crept round the half-shut door and told Wesley where he was. Thoroughly sober, he asked himself was this a mistake? Would anybody hear about this and mis-read him? To hell with anybody; he was now his own boss. So he lay on easy and listened to the space. Was Stan up walking; was that what had waked him? Nothing but the normal sounds of a building break-ing apart by millimeters. Should he rise now, dress, and creep on out? If Stan woke up, he could just say thanks. But where would he go this late?—not to Wilson's and risk finding her with somebody else or locked in with all her deadbolts and chains.

The thing that bothered Wesley most, lying there quiet, was the sense that any instant now the black net would close on his face and mouth—the terrible sadness he'd known here lately. If that should land on him now, God help him; could he stand it alone? Till now he'd never had to. *Head it off.* How? Leaving meant riding around in the dark or find-ing an all-night cafe open or renting a room in some motel.

He stood up quietly and put on everything but his shoes. Then he took one pillow and the heavy spread and walked up the hall to Stan-ley's door. It was fully open and the sounds that came were all but snores—good. Wesley crept on in to the foot of the high bed and laid his covers on the floor beneath it. Fine—he'd managed without wak-ing Stan. But when he knelt, both knees cracked like rifles. He winced in the dark but covered himself.

Then Stan said "Is that where you really want to be?"

"Absolutely. Thank you."

"And you're feeling all right?"

Wesley said "No I'm a miserable worm."

Stanley said "I'd apologize for all that bourbon but you're twenty-one."

Wesley nodded in the dark. "You've been good to me."

"Anything I can help with?"

"Thanks again, no sir." Wesley waited a long time. "Unless you're some brand of angel in disguise."

"It's really that bad?"

"Yes. I'm scared."

Stan said "Not of me. Forget it."

Wesley said "I'm not scared of you, just my whole life. I'm a man with too many problems here now. You don't need to know everything, not yet. See, I've been a boy with no more troubles than a rock in the road, but lately the rock's been learning to worry."

Stan said "Isn't this about normal for the course, men past forty? I'm moving in on it, not many yards behind."

"And you're this lonesome here alone. Doesn't this lonesome life get you down?"

Stan waited to think. "No more than yours, I guess. It's just a real life—same troubles, different names."

"You never been married?"

Stanley laughed. "That was one disaster I somehow missed."

Wesley said "It's got its points."

"Like what?"

A real wait and then Wesley laughed. "I'll think of one soon." Another wait and then Wesley asked "Ever think you'd just as soon *pass* on the rest of it, sit it out?"

"Not but once a minute," Stan said. Then he said "Say your prayers."

Coming from a lawyer, that raised a laugh but Wesley obeyed. And when he'd finished he was worse than before. He got up, went to the single window, and tried to look west toward Wilson's trailer. Whatever he expected, he got no strong transmission through the dark. If she missed him, Wilson was blasting no wail. He even faced round the opposite way—Rosa his wife. Nothing again.

In his whole life till now, had it ever been worse? He'd torn up every root of his past and run, and now where was he all these months later? Great God, in a room with a lonesome lawyer trained to the ears and hungry for men when men were illegal and might well now be poison and death. Another fine life. Wesley stepped closer to the window blinds and tilted them wider. In the thin starlight he could see a stretch of thick grass below. Grand!—if he jumped to die, he'd land in soft grass.

Stan understood from that far away. He said "We could get up and drink some milk. Or I could lie down there near you, in sight. Would that help any?"

At once Wesley said "You get your sleep. You'll need it tomorrow." And then in the silence, he thought of lying under sheets next to Stan—not touching but there. The thought wouldn't work; he was aimed at women. And even though, years ago, his firm brown hide had not been allergic to any well-meaning earthly touch, women were the only real magic for Wesley, in the visible world (he hoped to see God, though he'd never realized it).

So asking for help from a grown man this late in life seemed stranger than trying to understand your bird dog by learning to bark. He actually shook his head and smiled, then quietly counted Stanley's breathing. Under the numbers he kept on thinking of Stanley's life, guessing at its particular trials. Another pitiful fool like himself, old enough to have good sense but down in the dust still grappling for food.

Every audible voice in Wesley's world had told him to run from any such nearness—or stand and fight it. But here again he'd come this close. No one could see; no one would know. So what did he feel? The count of Stan's breath had got to three hundred. Stan was plainly out but Wesley kept thinking.

What did he feel? He tried to think a clear path back to his times with men—like silent wrestling in a dark sack not quite big enough—but no feeling came. Past pleasure is gone as fast as pain; in his own way he knew that and thought *Thank God*. Why would anybody ever reach out again, if all the good past could still be enjoyed?

Wesley's count was up around four-eighty-five when a voice in his mind again spoke clearly—"Nobody you love will pay for this." Till then he hadn't really known such a worry—or owned up to it. But whatever spoke the calm assurance spread down on him like a warm blanket, and he sank on into the same deep solitude as Stanley beyond him.

Between then and daylight Wesley watched a long dream—a world where nobody ever touched again, for bodily pleasure or in hopes of a child, never again from birth to death. All were locked in permanent transparent armor as tight as natural skin so that everybody still looked normal but could never step free. That way they were safe, and though it kept them from talking or smiling or eating their meals, the world kept on otherwise the same. The sight didn't wake him, so he rested till sunup—one more whole day and Wesley still upright.

When Wesley got to the trailer that evening, Wilson wasn't in. But the bed was unmade from the night before, so he knew she'd slept here and would no doubt be back. When she still wasn't in by dark, he broke out the fifth of bourbon he hadn't touched in weeks and poured a stiff drink. In his life till then, Wesley probably hadn't drunk ten ounces alone. And he promised himself it wouldn't be a habit. But tonight it felt like a useful companion. It got him through the televised news and the first dumb hour of comedy.

Then he thought he heard a car pull up. He waited for a hand on the door. But nothing, false alarm. Five minutes later he pulled his hand back from the telephone, dialing Rosa's number. Why be mean to her just to soothe his nerves? But then he dialed Stanley. Three rings, four—what on earth would he say if Stan answered? He couldn't go there two nights in a row. He hung up fast.

Three hard hours, the most time alone that Wesley'd had since Christmas week before he met Wilson. The worst time maybe of his life till then. But he took it sitting down, knowing that was the way— not twiddling or running. At eleven o'clock he finally said a prayer. Still seated firmly in the La-Z-Boy rocker, he said "Lord, I quit. *I* don't know how." He stayed in place, head back and eyes shut. He hoped he could weep and bleed off the pressure. But too many dry-eyed years stretched behind him to make tears easy. So he tried press-ups on the arms of the chair, imagining he'd lost the use of his legs.

Like Willis Shearin, the old shortstop on his high-school team, who'd been in a carwreck; his spine had been crushed. He couldn't feel anything below his two nipples and not one cell in his legs or feet worked. Not for motion at least, though they sent pain through him like squirrels through a maze. After a minute of such self-deception, Wesley felt panic seize him. *Stop this right now or you'll scream pretty soon.*

But he didn't. He went on pressing up faster and faster, his legs *were* dead, pain raced through his trunk like squirrels on an interstate. Now his lungs wouldn't work. He tried to scream but no air came. Nothing to do but work on alone. When he'd done a strong dozen more press-ups, a car stopped. Then the car door slammed—no doubt this time.

Then Wilson stood there, still in her work clothes, her work badge on. Her face was tired and two shades paler, but oh she looked fine. He'd forgot how fine. He was still pressing up. So he paused in midair.

"You lost it?" she asked.

"Yes, lady. I'm a sad lonesome cripple. I've lost my legs." To Wesley's amazement, tears sprang up. He flopped back down in the chair and laughed.

Wilson held her ground by the door, ready to turn and leave. But it was her home. So she came on toward him and sat in a straight chair. "You look all right otherwise. What hit you?"

Wesley forced himself not to wipe his eyes. He said "Nothing really. I was just exercising. You caught me at it."

"But you're crying too."

"I been missing you."

She smiled and sang a little bar of music to match their rhyme. But then she went grim again. "You let yourself in here knowing I was gone?"

"I did, yes ma'm. You hadn't changed the locks."

Wilson thought, then nodded. "Fair enough."

"I took a night off. I think you know why."

Wilson asked "How many more of those you planning to take?"

Wesley said "Can't say. It depends on a lot."

"Then you better head out now for good. I can't have no part-time man, let me tell you. I've told you already—I'm all or nothing."

"I understand that. But maybe we could talk?"

Wilson said "There's not a whole hell of a lot to say, if you don't want to be here."

"I never said that. I said I'm somebody with a lot of trouble to get through. That shouldn't be news to anybody near me."

Wilson said "It's not. But we'd agreed to talk last night, I thought. I came here and waited and you never showed. So guess how I felt— guilty as sin."

Wesley said "You weren't. Shame on you."

"Want to say where you went?"

He said "No ma'm, I don't. It was not to hurt you or make you guilty."

"Won't you want to know where I've gone, if I ever fail you?"

"Wilson, if we ever make each other the big promise, then sure. Till—and if—we do, you can plan your life however you need to."

"And that won't hurt you?"

"Sure it will. I'm a person, not a stainless-steel wrench. But when I left my wife three months ago, I gave up my rights to make such a claim—on her or anybody."

"You like this life?" She waved around her. "Us here, like this?"

"I loved it, yes ma'm, till yesterday morning. I thought we were fine. It was you changed the tune."

Wilson said "I had to. I waited too long."

"But you let me think you enjoyed my body. It was one big part of what I loved about us. Women need to understand that about men."

"And vice versa. Women need different things, this one at least."

Wesley nodded. "I've watched television—I think I know. And I mean, I haven't brought you home any Cold Duck or cut flowers for candlelight dinners, but I've done all I could imagine to let you know you've been a big help to me at this time of life."

Wilson nodded but still couldn't make herself smile. "Everything but the one last promise I need."

"To move here finally and marry you?"

"That's just about it."

Watching her still face, expectant as a dry field in a hot day, Wesley suddenly knew his answer. The last two days had formed it in his mind with no help from him. He said it straight out. "I'd be glad to stay on like this indefinitely, like the life we had till yesterday anyhow. But if what you're calling for is divorce and a wedding, then I can't help you right now. In the first place, a North Carolina divorce takes a year's genuine separation. In the second place, after so many years of goodness, I owe my wife at least a face-to-face visit to tell her my plans and see to her future. I need to see my son. I've got a few things back there that matter to me; I'd need to rent a truck and bring them here."

Wilson waited to be sure he was finished. "Then can't you say you plan to do all that and set a firm date?"

Again he knew the answer. After the early evening panic, it was cooler than he'd guessed. "No, Wilson, I can't."

She could meet his eyes, but she couldn't find words.

Finally he said "You want me to pack?"

She looked at her watch, honestly unsure. It was too close to midnight to throw him out, and she didn't know if she wanted to risk a second night in a dark field alone. So she said "It's too late to find a motel. Stay in the little room and then go tomorrow."

Wesley thought again of calling Stanley but then decided no. That could have its own troubles big as any here. He knew it would be hard to sleep separate from her, but he had no choice. She was offering a kindness. He couldn't make waves now and try to swamp her. He thanked her and stood up. "You sleepy?"

"Ought to be—I worked a double shift—but no, I'm not."

"Me neither. We could watch a movie."

They wound up making a bushel of popcorn and watching *The Three Stooges' Greatest Hits.* The ninety minutes of head-bonking farce eventually broke through their mutual blues and had them finally laughing like children. Still at the end Wilson stood up quickly, washed the empty bowl, and went to her room. Not so much as "Good night."

Not till he went to the tiny guest-cubicle did Wesley realize that his clothes were Stanley's. He'd put them off and back on at work without thinking. Wilson hadn't mentioned them; had she noticed the difference? Was it some secret plan of Stan's this morning—to let him wear them knowing he'd have to call and bring them back? Never mind; he could leave them on the porch some day at noon and just abandon his own to Stanley.

He laid them neatly on the one folding chair and, naked, climbed in the narrow cot. The wall between him and Wilson was cardboard; he could all but hear her breathing, then sleeping. He nearly prayed that she change heart and join him or call him at least. But it seemed unfair to try to set God against her. So he blessed them both and again all his family and this time Stanley. Then he waited for sleep.

It didn't arrive. Instead came a long wave of pictures of Rosa. Still not recalling his earlier dream, Wesley would no more have bet on that than on late snow. But here came a chain of memories of Rosa, all clear silent pictures. All moving backward more or less through the years from this past December to the first real meeting with her he remembered (not the one she remembered, with him up the tree, but almost two entire years later at Warrenton in school with her stumbling into the football fieldhouse by mistake—looking for the home ec. building—and seeing him upright there in his jock).

Wesley had quickly covered his crotch with big hands, but Rosa held her ground in the dim doorway and said "I always catch you wrong."

He'd said "Lady, ain't nobody *caught* me yet. When she does, it'll be the rightest catch of her life."

And she'd said "Stuck up" but apparently believed him and set out to catch his soul and body then and there.

What waylaid him tonight, in the time it took, was the discovery of Rosa's early beauty. That child had been special—and not just her long straw hair and blue eyes so big they threatened to fall right out of her face but the power she gave off steady as voltage. There were some boys who did not see it at all. More than one of them made fun of her for being a solemn sort of Pilgrim mother and smarter than any three of them. But Wesley saw past that plainly to her real power and felt it from the start.

That first day when she said "Stuck up," he went straight over to her—still in his wet jock—and said "Take me down a whole notch then, lady. See if you can."

She'd said "Shoot, Bo, I got better plans" and walked off pretending not to know his name or anyhow not to be already dreaming his face and voice four nights a week, her entire future, the thing she intended every day of her life (once that life began, which now it could).

Could Wesley use that at all, here and now in this spot? Unlike Rosa and every other woman he'd known, he couldn't linger long in memory for its own sake. Memory had to tell him something he could bring on forward and make work now for good sense and present help. It was one thing to realize your wife had been special thirty-odd years ago; what good was that now?

He didn't know a lot about archaeology, but he suspected he was stuck on a kind of ancient dig—sweeping off layers of sand or barnacles, hoping to find a firm core left in an old thing he'd honored and used but that now was near ruined (by him, he granted). Could he find anything deep down in it that he still felt a present need to know and tend? Or sound fiscal practice—why in the world walk off for good from an investment as big and long-standing as his and Rosacoke's?

Only if it gave him new life again. Only if the core of the dug-up statue still showed enough of its old strength and draw. How could he gauge that from this far away? Was it time now to hit the road back east and check out the air? Would Rosa even see him, much less take him back if he wanted to come? Should he get up right now, go to a pay phone and call her up, ask permission to visit? Should he wait till daylight and then write a short note asking the same? It was his own house too. He still paid half the mortgage every month. Why the hell not drive up and unlock the door?

By then Wesley had thought his way through the hours till his watch said two in the morning. So much reasoning, on top of the outlay with Stanley and Wilson, had finally sapped him. If he hadn't already been laid out flat on a decent mattress, he'd have fallen far from a dangerous height and crushed every bone. As it was, he slept like a child—that desperate, sucking up every instant of sleep like the food of life itself and hope.

But the next afternoon Wesley packed up his few duds at Wilson's, took her out for supper at Bar-B-Cutie, didn't say a word about sadness or permanence, kept her smiling, and delivered her safe to the trailer at ten.

Wilson didn't say "Come in" or ask another question or flinch even once.

Wesley honored her style and stood up outside the driver's door as she walked away. He waited till she found her key, stepped inside, and lit the porch light. She didn't look back to smile or wave, but he waved once and heard her lock the door inside before he drove off.

On the way into town, he waited for the hurt to start. Apparently something real had ended, some way toward life. But all he could feel for Wilson was thanks. So what if she'd slammed him hard this week?—back at the start of this new year, she'd shown him again how much he could mean; how good he could feel in the right arms saying the few right words. If he'd found Wilson easy as that, in a downtown motel lounge stuffed with drunks and hookers, then wasn't there all the more reason to hope life still had Wesley Beavers in mind with some better women?

For old time's sake he went back in to the same motel and had a drink in the lounge, all but empty tonight. Nobody looked his way; nobody came over. And when he ordered the second drink, he thought he'd finish that and, if nobody good had turned up, he'd rent a room upstairs and sleep again in the place where he'd started this new life.

But the drink ran out and nobody came, and Wesley couldn't make himself register here. He paid his tab, walked out, and wove a careful way through traffic across the street and a block ahead to the reinforced concrete Parthenon. Wesley knew very little about the original building or Athens or Greece or the virgin goddess of wisdom herself, gray-eyed helmeted daughter of Zeus with owl and spear.

But he had good eyes and an ample but wary supply of awe. And this full-scale replica of the great temple—brought down from its native granite mountain and westward five thousand miles to be set up on a green flat lawn in Nashville, floodlit now on an early spring evening—was sufficient to confirm the gradual happiness that had crept back through him these past twelve weeks.

He was more than half sober, but he wanted somehow to express his gratitude. He'd never been all that good in the past at offering thanks when thanks were due for life's better times. He didn't want to let this night go by without a way to speak what he felt—that Wesley Beavers was *coming through*; that whatever person or place lay before him, Wesley now believed it was all for the best. He knew he'd, some way, tie it all up and make it work from now to the grave—a long way off with him an old man.

With that grand building glowing above him the color of honey on a purple sky, those high bronze doors like gates to Heaven (or surely not Hell), he suddenly regretted how bad he'd been in the seventh damned grade when Miss Jennie Alston made them memorize poems, and he'd hung back and mumbled smiling nonsense to deceive her. Something like the one about World War I, "In Flanders Field," seemed the ticket here tonight (it had always moved Miss Jennie to tears; and she was as tough as a lightwood knot)—

> *To you from failing hands we throw the torch;*
> *Be yours to hold it high!*

But he couldn't say the rest. So he waited five minutes in the far rim of trees, queers, and whores circling round him in cars with their windows rolled down. And finally he knew it, a way to speak.

Wesley climbed straight up the steps toward the doors (three times his height), slow as any actor to the stage or killer to the gallows. He turned toward the floodlights. Then blinded by glare and what may have been tears, he said the thing he knew by heart "The Lord is my shepherd. I shall not want"—all the way through to "I shall dwell in the house of the Lord forever."

He faced back and wondered if in any useful way an imitation concrete temple like this was a house of the Lord. But he didn't feel wrong in his general purpose or the text of his thanks. He touched the flank of the nearest pillar and then kissed the hand. As he stepped back down to the warm damp grass, from one of the dark circling cars came the clear noise of two hands clapping and a whistling cheer. He bowed and grinned to whoever praised him.

While Wesley was sleeping peacefully that same night on the east edge of Nashville in a mom-and-pop motel called *Quo Vadis*, Rosa woke up in Raleigh, crept downstairs in her blue nightgown, and wrote this letter that she mailed the next morning.

March 22, 1986

Dear Wesley,

It has been over two months since I wrote to you last time. In the meanwhile you've been loyal with the checks but of course no news. I've had a lot of news here too, that I've kept to myself. Every woman I've talked to says I'd be a big fool to break down now and start talking to you again.

But the simple fact is you're about the only friend I've had since I grew up, and just in the last week I've felt more and more like if I can't talk to you then I'll likely bust. I've long since gone past being mad at you or constantly asking why? What I mainly feel now is how much I miss you.

Maybe one of your problems here was the way we had got to being like two old dogs in the same yard bumping up against each other at feeding time and curling up together in the cold night for warmth, not much else. Maybe it's not enough to live like dogs, even after nearly thirty years. Still it was a lot more than most people have, to my eyes anyhow. And I'm aching, buddy.

So here is some backdated news from Raleigh, N.C. It's sent by way of filling you in on friends and family, not as a set of warnings or threats or even prayers.

On New Year's Eve I got home early from a party at Jean and Hal's and turned straight in. A few hours later a completely strange (I think) man broke in, found me upstairs in our old bed, and was hacking on me before I really woke up. — With his body, I mean, not any kind of knife.

My mind ran through all the possibilities. Was it maybe you? Any-how when I couldn't stand it an instant longer, I tried to throw him and succeeded. At that point of course he could have bent back down and strangled or stabbed me. But after he paused to look, he ran. Since then I've had a weird phone call or two, a couple of stopped cars outside at four in the morning, but nothing worse.

For good reasons of my own, I didn't call the police. And I still haven't told anybody but Mama, Rato, and Milo. Rato then volun-teered to move up here awhile and live with me—which is what he's been doing ever since, to my considerable relief. We have worked out a right good arrangement.

And Mama, even at her age, seems none the worse for staying out there in the country alone. Your mother does the same and thrives on it. Maybe we'll all have to eventually. I'm thinking it'll be time soon now to get Rato moved on back to the country before he gets too used to city life. We've had one of those phone taps on the line for weeks now, and no other weirdos have called, so I begin to feel like I may be safe again.

Otherwise that's about it, no more big events. I haven't so much as had a date and don't especially want to. I don't say that to punish you. I'm assuming you're still there with your new friend, and I guess I can try to stand straight here and pull my collar up neat and wish you luck with whoever helps you onward. It's either that or "Screw you, you vicious ungrateful thieving hound," isn't it? And since I don't remember ever saying that word in public before, I won't start now. Also I don't really feel it—not yet, not more than one or two minutes a day most weeks.

I'm trusting you haven't run up against anything as rough as I did. (Do men, outside prison anyhow, ever get raped?) Now that I've written this far, I can look back and wonder why and whether or not I'll mail it. I don't honestly think I'm asking for pity or to make you feel guilty—I know you are not to blame. I really do think it's what I said first, that I can't help believing we were each other's oldest closest friends. And I just want my few friends to know the best and worst about me.

So now you know the worst. "The best is yet to be." Or so I'm leaning on. I don't even try to think back to the last time I was thoroughly happy, for more than two minutes. But then they never guaranteed joy,

right? Anytime I feel like throwing my head back and howling at the
moon, I can flip on the evening news and watch a few thousand
Ethiopian children starve in the comfort of my all-electric clean formica
kitchen or another whole block of houses in Beirut crumble to dust with
all hands aboard.

You ever do the same?

Want to be pen pals? You know my address.

> *An old friend,*
> *Rosa*

Two days later at lunch time, Wilson stopped by the service station and delivered the letter (the only address Rosa had for Wesley was the trailer).

He thanked her and offered to buy her a Coke.

Wilson flashed her best smile but said she had plans.

Wesley asked "You all right?"

She said "Bet on it."

Wesley laughed and told her if anybody came around offering odds, he'd take her tip. And she roared off. So he bought himself a drink, sat down in the Volvo he was fixing, and read the letter. Much as he disliked reading, he didn't budge till he got to the sentence where Rosa exonerated him of all responsibility for her rape. He'd read all he could for the moment at least. He folded the letter, hid it in his pocket, and stepped back out into full sunlight. In another minute he walked over to the Exxon sign by the road and flopped down there on the ground at its base.

His boss, a kind old giant named Buster, shambled over. "That gal must of sawed you off at the knees."

Wesley said "She'd like to but no, not today she didn't." He stopped there, hoping Buster would leave. What he needed this minute was time to crank his brain; it had stalled just now. He was blank as if a crowbar had leaned from the lowest cloud and struck him.

Instead Buster pulled out his thirty-eighth Kool of the day and lit it. "You need some time off?"

Wesley thought "That's bound to be God" (meaning Buster's offer). His brain caught fire. He said "Thank you, yes."

"You'll be leaving town?" Buster vaguely knew Wesley had ties in Carolina.

"Very likely, yes."

Buster said "All right. Draw a week's advance pay. If your business takes longer than that, call and tell me. You're as good a mechanic as I've ever known, and I'd sure hate to lose you. Can you work through till six?"

Wesley had worked for good bosses before, but nobody else ever went far as this. He reached up for Buster's right hand, shook it, then let Buster help him to his feet. Then Wesley said "Nobody ever out-bid you. If there's any way on God's earth I can live here, you'll see me in a week. If not, I'll repay you."

Buster said "A deal."

Just after six Wesley drove to the Quo Vadis Motel, showered and shaved again, and paid his bill. As he walked out of the office, he thought "I should have called Wilson and let her know." He could go back now and do it on the pay phone; she'd be home. But what could he tell her for sure? And since *sure* was all she wanted to hear from him, then he had nothing for her. He drove on to the first gas station, filled up, checked his oil and tires, and wove his slow way to the interstate eastward.

As he came off the ramp into speeding traffic, the clock said 7:05 p.m. There was still a weak wash of lilac in the sky low down near the ground. With any luck at all, from God and the humans and this car beneath him, Wesley ought to be home before Rosa woke up. He thought the clear word *home*, then changed it to *there*, then changed it once more to *Rosa's house*. Wherever, he was moving. It didn't feel bad. If he got tired he'd stop and sleep a few hours or days or weeks. Nobody expected him, free as a bird.

Then Wesley thought again *Rosa*. Raped in his bed in the house he'd deserted not three weeks before, a woman who'd done him not one bad turn in nearly forty years—not purposely at least. He suddenly felt responsible. His abandonment of the woman he'd promised to guard had set the world free to turn on her with its own vile plans. He'd said more than once to boys at work that if his wife should ever get raped, he doubted he'd want to touch her again.

It hadn't crossed his mind that he'd be the cause, that his own fear of death and a cold soft peter might flush him off his sworn place strong at Rosa's side and leave her open to any hungry boy with the power of hate. Now it struck Wesley with the weight of a cold steel office-safe dropped on his head from a building at dawn. Blame and guilt were not Wesley's suit. He could accept blame whenever he saw he'd caused a fault, but then he wouldn't spend five minutes howling. He'd concentrate on finding the way to prevent a repeat.

He was on the western rim of the mountains when he saw that the only hope this time was to park up next to Rosa again and literally shield her. Rato was all right for short spells of duty. But Rato had never sworn to stay for long years of this. And anyhow Rato's pitiful brain couldn't handle something complicated as a felon in the shrubbery, not to mention the bed.

Was Wesley ready for that much again? Had a little more than three months out on the road been enough to revive him and strengthen his soul to stay the remainder of a life with Rosa? And if he could, then what about her? She'd written that letter not a whole week ago, warm and open. But one letter wasn't face-to-face forever.

He replayed his memory of the first nights with Wilson, the bones of his mind truly pulverized by thanks for her goodness. The strength she restored to his arms and legs that truly had been at the door of death. The picture was still bright and dark enough in memory, still rank enough with odor, to bring him quickly to readiness here on a black highway with trucks roaring past him the size of bombers at the near speed of sound. No fourteen-year-old kid in bed in the distant cabins beyond him on the highway, locked in with inflamed *Hustler* girls to the sounds of Mama downstairs in the kitchen scraping dishes for the sink, was primed more hopefully than he was now.

As Wesley entered the long slow first mountain-climb then, he set his automatic pilot for sixty, opened his jeans, gently freed his cock from the clean tight drawers, and met its need as only he knew it— grinning at the cheap but complicated thrill. He hadn't done this since leaving the Navy, he was almost sure.

As he got near the ridge, of the rise and his joy, he thought "If women knew how many grown men are out here stroking their lonesome dicks—and all but losing control of their cars just past the speed limit—they'd stay home baking those good cakes and pies, not risking their necks on personal fulfillment."

When he came, he bent low over the wheel to watch the seed bloom up in his fist by green panel light—the beautiful calm that spread up through him from heels to head like cream in coffee. Then he cleaned himself with a warm bandanna, turned on the radio, and sang for ten miles—Kenny Rogers, sad and sweet.

> *You took a fine time to leave me, Lucille—*
> *Four hungry children and crops in the field.*

Since Wesley had never had a moment's uncertainty about his own gender, he imagined he was Lucille trucking back home toward four wormy kids and one sorry man. She was glad to oblige, having had her break in motel lounges and mobile-home beds under willing hot souls. She almost figured she could see it through now, all the long years ahead till death did her part.

By the time he reached the downward side of that broad crest, Wesley guessed he'd accepted the pull of fate. He knew anyhow that he barely held the wheel. The car was taking itself and him where they needed to go, which was Rosa's house—goddammit still his.

At a little before midnight on the near side of Asheville, Wesley pulled off finally to eat a little supper. He'd waited through a lot of hungry hours to get to this particular stop, the place where back in December a waitress had sent him to Nashville. He knew she couldn't be working tonight, but the first thing he saw when he entered the hot glare was her busy body in the far corner serving a family of six. He went toward her and asked if one of her tables was vacant.

She said "Number four" and pointed but gave no sign of recognition.

That cut him down a little, but he sat anyhow and studied the old menu.

When she got free in three minutes, she came with iced water and a sudden big smile. "How was Nashville, old son?"

Wesley grinned. "You remember?"

"Forget *you*, boy? I often forget my own name and number, but a good-looking man late at night—not me. I got a big file of faces in here" (she reached through her pink spun-sugar bouffant and tapped her skull hard). "Gives me a lot of fun. Course I don't tell Sam."

"Sam's your husband?"

"Never mind. Sam's the adult man that thinks he owns my butt. He's kidding himself but I don't aim to tell him; I enjoy his laugh. I asked you a question though—how was your trip?"

"Very fine," Wesley said. "What the doctor prescribed."

"You look healed," she said. "Well, no extra charge."

"You from Nashville yourself?"

She said "Oh no. Never even been there. That night you slouched in here looking dead, I just thought Nashville had to be your place. I've always thought it had to be Heaven. How was Opry Land?"

Wesley told her "The best," though he hadn't gone near it.

She didn't press for details. She said "How hungry are you?"

"Enough to eat a polecat."

"Ever tried it?" she asked.

"In my sweet boyhood."

"They're not what they used to be," she said, "—not nearly. Want me to bring what you need again?"

He remembered she'd ordered for him before. "Sure. But no chicken-fried steaks this time."

She stepped back and frowned. "Did I say you needed anything strong as that?"

"No, I grant you. I just feel different tonight."

"I can see that, I told you. Leave it to me."

Twenty minutes later—five songs on the juke box—she came back with barbecued chicken, boiled rice, string beans, a salad, and a basket of Parker House rolls. Wesley told her it was perfect. And it proved to be.

When he'd also finished the lemon pie and drunk more coffee, her work slacked off again. She joined him in the booth and lit a cigarette. "You headed *back* somewhere big, ain't you?"

"My wife." He nodded. "In Raleigh, still waiting. So I trust."

"Whose idea was leaving?"

Wesley said "Mine."

"She's waiting then."

He laughed and asked "You ever been wrong?"

She laughed "Oh sure but just about me. Everybody else is a plain open book."

"You made mistakes of your own then, have you?"

She said "First, you need to know my name—I've got one: Joretta Robbins. Second, Joretta tore off and left too—a man good as you and for awful reasons. We'd had a girl baby lovely as *day*. She took sick early though, pernicious leukemia. Finally one morning in the midst of her bath—me treating her gentle as a day-old kitten—I broke her leg just drying her off. In three more weeks she died, blue as ink. I watched every minute of a sight worse than World War III, let me tell you. Then I left. Morehead City, right down on the coast, views of the sky that would crank your heart on the meanest day. I left it all. And Cliff J. Robbins, a concrete mixer—sweetest damned man old God ever made. I bet he's waiting on me right now. Last person I talked to from home said he was. Said 'Cliff still acts like you're the last woman alive for him.'"

"How far back was that?"

"Three, four years."

"You gone that long?"

Joretta said "Five years this next month."

"What would make you go back?"

"A sign," she said. "Some big sign, big enough to read at least. Like the one I gave you to Nashville back when."

Wesley thought that through. Then he sat back and faced her. She was no big beauty. But if somebody ordered him here and now to stay beside her for the rest of his life, he wouldn't feel tempted to blow his brains out. So yes, he was sure. He grinned and said "Go call Cliff up right now."

Jo looked at her watch. "It's way too late. He's early-to-bed."

"I very much doubt he'll mind waking up."

She finished her cigarette and watched Wesley through his last swallows of coffee. "Got time for more coffee?"

"Better take time," Wesley said. "I'll be driving till dawn."

So Jo stood up. One sincere moan escaped her mouth as the hips accepted her weight again. Then she brought him a fresh cup and stepped out of sight with no more words.

Wesley played more songs and finished his coffee, no more sight of Jo. But when he rose to pay his check, she appeared from the back and met him at the register. He handed her a ten-dollar bill, said "Many thanks," and told her he hoped she'd take his advice.

She nodded, made his change, then faced him grinning. "I just now did."

"You reach old Cliff?"

"Didn't take but two rings."

"And he wanted you back?"

Jo said "Hold on. We didn't go that far."

"What did he say then?"

"I guess I asked him what he'd had for supper. It was fried bluefish, homemade coleslaw, cornbread, and sliced tomatoes. He always was a good cook; most fishermen are. I asked him where he got decent tomatoes this time of year. Cliff said he never claimed they were decent." Her eyes didn't mist up or anything dramatic. She reached forward though to the penny-mint bucket and handed Wesley two mints in bright tinfoil. "On the house. Drive careful."

Wesley smiled "I can take you on as far east as Raleigh."

Jo said "Thanks. You've done enough for now. You give me your address; I'll keep you posted. I'll also put you in my famous prayers."

"What's famous about them?"

"They work," she said. "I don't burden God more than once or twice a year, so He responds by giving what I ask."

"Except your daughter's life."

Jo coiled back quickly. That had finally struck her. But she kept her voice calm. "I'm not sure this is your business, son, but I never prayed for my daughter's life. I know God's will when it's that bold to read."

Wesley unwrapped one of the mints and ate it. Then he said "I appreciate you telling me. I'm glad I've known you. I'll hope to meet again."

By then Jo had warmed back a little. She stepped round to walk him out the door. In the dark parking lot she extended her hand. "I think you're doing a good thing here."

Wesley thanked her but said "I'm trying to mend something good I broke. Or that time broke for me. That's no big deal."

"No, it is," she said. "Most breakers just run."

He suddenly saw how short she was, maybe five foot tall. He leaned way down till his mouth met her head; then he kissed her once through the sugared pink hair.

As Wesley drove off, Jo never waved. But she watched his lights till they joined the highway and melted into a fast swarm of red, all headed east. She wondered if he'd saved her life or ruined it. For that matter, what had she done to him?

ROSA WESLEY
RATO WAVE

Wesley waited at the corner till twenty minutes after the light went on in Rosa's bedroom. Then he knocked at the front door. Usually she'd finished her shower and was downstairs cooking in twenty minutes. But now there was a long wait. He knocked again.

When the white door finally opened, it was Rato, fully dressed but his hair uncombed like he'd weathered a big blast seconds ago. As Wesley dawned on him, he took three steps back and looked upstairs. His face went red, he couldn't speak, he pointed with his long right fingers—up.

Wesley said "I was hoping to find you, Ace."

Rato burst out grinning. He'd always liked Wesley. Wesley had more sense than Milo or Rosa and got more fun out of life. So he came on forward again and whispered "You want to surprise her or what?"

Wesley said "What you think?"

Telling Rato to think was generally a mistake. He tended to take you seriously.

After twenty seconds Wesley said "She still upstairs?"

Rato nodded. "Go on."

"No, tell you what. You step on up there and gently say 'Wesley's downstairs to see you.'"

Rato said "It's your house. I'm just the boarder."

So Wesley stepped past him, went to the foot of the stairs, and looked up.

Rosa was there, dressed and ready on the top step. Surely she'd heard them.

He said "Morning, lady."

She took a long look. Then she turned and moved quickly toward their room.

When she didn't reappear in another minute, Wesley climbed on up and stopped at the door. He tapped on the frame.

Rosa said "It's your room."

He said "I left it."

"It sounds like you're back."

Wesley couldn't see her from there. He stepped in and she was over by the mirror at the far end in shade. Her eyes, thank God, were dry. Otherwise, she looked like the person he'd remembered. The rape anyhow hadn't marked her face. The bed was still unmade; he couldn't sit there. He wanted to do only right natural things, things he could feel were sincerely true and that Rosa could accept. So he didn't rush to hug her. He took a few steps and stopped by the chest of drawers. "I didn't plan this."

Rosa finally laughed—thank Jesus, laughed. "No, planning was never your longest suit."

"So I don't have any big speech ready."

"Me either," she said. "You come for your things?"

"I come to see you."

"I'd have sent you a photo and spared you the trip."

"Don't be mean yet."

Rosa said "I'm sorry."

"And don't start apologizing. That's my part."

Rosa suddenly frowned and her hand went up. "First thing—I'm hungry. Could we eat breakfast first?" All her life, she'd been a breakfast hound.

Wesley smiled. "Me too," though food was the last thing on his tired mind.

She said "Go take a hot shower, why don't you? Then meet us downstairs."

He said "I'll wash my face, brush my hair. Just coffee for me." When she stepped on past him, he smelled her strongly—just clean skin and soap, as old a smell as any in his mind except the one from his mother's deep breast.

In a while when Wesley joined them in the kitchen, Rato was frying boiled potatoes from the night before. He'd already browned a half-pound of bacon, made a tall stack of toast. The eggs were waiting. Rosa was almost done with the coffee. He sat at the table quietly to watch. They left him alone like he was nothing new. And for those few minutes, Wesley felt he was absolutely right—to be exactly here, this morning. No question it could last as long as he lasted. Even Rato's presence seemed hopeful. Why hadn't they brought him down here before, their own brand of Martian since Horace had turned out so disappointing? Had the man that raped Rosa touched this room? Could any place, this peaceful now, have held such a creature? A hard shudder tore up Wesley's spine.

Rosa saw it. She looked back and said "You need coffee now, am I right?"

"Nothing too desperate. But if it comes in five seconds, it might save a life."

Rato said "And how many eggs, what way?"

Rosa told Rato that Wesley just wanted coffee.

But Rato looked so baffled, Wesley changed his order. "Just scramble ten or twelve, if everybody wants them."

Rosa said "Suits me."

Rato resumed beaming and in another five minutes he had a large platter before them—firm moist eggs, crisp browned potatoes, and perfect bacon.

Rosa had taken her old seat at the far end opposite Wesley. When they all were seated, she said "Rato, you did it. Please bless it for us."

Rato's blessings had always been family treats—never ritual prayers but spontaneous entirely unpredictable responses.

As always it took him awhile. Then he said "God, You certainly kept this one up Your sleeve. But thank You all the same."

When Rosa's eyes opened, Wesley's were on hers smiling. So she laughed. The two men checked one another and joined her. Then they all ate ravenously.

When Rosa left at eight, Wesley sat on drinking coffee while Rato scraped dishes. One thing about Rato, you never had to worry in his presence about small talk; Rato sometimes went months without an idle word. So Wesley could slump back in his exhaustion and wonder just how much longer he had to pretend to be awake and human.

Finally Rato started the dishwasher and came over to sit. The first thing he said was "If you'll run me down to the bus station, I can be out of here before noon."

Wesley said "Hold it, boy. Cool your jets down fast."

Rato smiled. "I'm about as much use as a spare dick at the convent."

Wesley couldn't remember what joke that came from. He wasn't even sure it was a joke or where Rato would have learned about nuns and convents. But he smiled and said "Rato, there's still mysteries here way up to my chin—if not overhead. I may not be here more than today. Rosa and I haven't said ten words about past or future. You've been her lifeline. Don't leave her yet."

"You ain't back for good?"

Wesley said "You know not to count on me. Look what I just done three months ago."

"You're sitting here now. You look good here."

"I'd look good drinking coffee on the moon in an astronaut suit. I'm a nice-looking fellow, Rato—or so most people tell me. It's still half my trouble. People think I'm happy since I look so calm."

"What's made you unhappy? Rosa still don't know."

Wesley shook his head. "No, I told her by mail. I felt dead as this damned table-wood." He pounded once on the rock-maple top.

Rato said "This table is *live*. It's nothing but zillions of atoms all hopping like disco dancers on speed with miles of space between each one—barely seeing each other, they're moving so fast and far apart, all singing their song."

Wesley nodded. Was Rato on speed? Had a few weeks in town pressed some button in him that nobody else had ever found before? Now his old simple-minded brother-in-law knew physics. Well, no doubt the Army had taught the corporal more than the family counted on. "All right. That's me then too. Or was in December. I was dancing in space—couldn't hear the damned music, couldn't see my partner. And if I was singing, it was 'Help me home. I'm a sad lost boy.'"

"So you lit out for Nashville?"

"Not at first, not Nashville. I just left work the shortest day of the year. I thought I was headed here but wound up twelve hours later in Nashville in a motel room."

"You had a woman there."

Wesley said "Rosa tell you I was living with a woman?"

"She mentioned it, I think."

"I met a young woman well after I got there. She kept me awhile and was good to me. But she sure God wasn't what made me leave here, not by a long shot."

"You'd stopped loving Rosa?"

Wesley said "You ever loved a woman in your life?" He'd wondered before. Now he felt the right to ask.

Rato said "I screwed a good many in Germany mostly and Oklahoma, a good few Indians; they sure are warm. But *love?*—I still love Rosa a lot."

"I mean, loved her so hard and steady you just want to touch her all night every night of your life, and give her kids, and save her body from all grades of harm."

Rato grinned. "That's love?"

"When you're young anyhow. For me it was."

Rato laughed. "No sir. Thank God, I been spared."

Wesley said "I pity you. Sweetest thing yet, that feeling I had when I first knew Rosa in high school at home."

"We all thought you were running from her hard."

"I thought so too. I joined the Navy thinking so. But Rosa had some kind of grip on my mind."

Rato said "We all thought you didn't give a damn. Thought she just shotgunned you."

Wesley smiled. "That happened, no way to deny it. It was Rosa's plan to start a baby and slow me down—you know, get my attention. Well, news of a baby with half my blood got my notice all right. But if Rosa had been patient, it wouldn't have taken a baby to stop me. She was already bigger in my mind than any ten others. With all the women I had in a big Navy town, Rosa was the real magic to me. I could get some Norfolk girl twisting in the dark, perfuming the room like a fleet whorehouse, and keep her rolling till daylight stopped us. Rosacoke though was the sight I'd see whenever I got back alone and still. I'd ride my motorcycle out to the beach on winter Sundays—anytime after those nights with girls—and take five-mile walks up the sand toward New York City. The cold salt air and seagulls yelling and all that water, powerful as God, would clean my mind and body out. What would be left was Rosa's face and strong blue eyes set on me, begging for my life. Looking back now I'd have given it to her of my own free will if she'd left me alone and trusted her strength. I still wish she had. She pushed me though and triggered the baby, and we fell in on marriage like a trapdoor. Half our trouble now—that we didn't have time to start life right."

Rato said "Don't waste all that on me. I don't understand. Save your breath for Rosa. She'll want to know. I've always thought Rosa knew more than most folks. But here since you left, she's been dumb as me. Everything I ask her, she says she don't know. I give up asking and just tried to guard her."

Wesley said "And I thank you. I owe you a lot."

Rato said "You can buy me a radio then."

It stunned Wesley but he grinned and said "Sure. What brand you want?"

"Oh, a Sony, I guess. Something big and loud. I like grand opera."

"From Nashville, you mean?"

"Hell, no. Hillbilly music grinds my *teeth* down. I mean that stuff from New York and Europe."

Wesley said "You understand it?"

"I'm not in it for the words. I can tell when they're mad and when they're peaceful. That's all you need to know. Mostly they're mad."

Wesley said "And the women sound mostly like they're about to jump off cliffs."

Rato nodded. "They are. Big as they are, they're in terrible trouble." He waited, looked down, and then asked "You know the reason I'm down here at all—in your house, I mean?"

"My wife being raped? Rosa wrote me about that but not till last week. It's what brought me back."

Rato said "I figured you didn't know sooner. Couldn't imagine you'd know and stay gone. I guess it was right hard on her. I knew it was coming, see. Dreamed about it the night it happened. Got Mama to call her up the next morning, and sure enough I'd been right all night. So Rosa come right on home that day and stayed awhile with us. Then I come back with her and been here ever since."

Wesley asked "How much has it changed her?"

"I'm no big authority on women. But I've been right surprised. Everything you see on t.v. says they're supposed to go wild and hate themselves and all men forever, once somebody grabs them. Rosa's been different there like everywhere else. If it's tore anything up, it's her mind and down so deep I haven't seen it yet. She's still good to me like she's always been. What's deeper than that, you'll have to test yourself."

Wesley wondered if he wanted that test, but he didn't say so to Rato now. In fact, he wondered if it was fair to go on asking Rato any-thing—truthful answers poured from Rato at the touch; it hardly seemed right. Still he had to keep going, to cover as much ground as possible before Rosa came home at dusk and they faced one another. He said "Then the police never knew about this? She never told a soul but you?"

"Me and Mama and Milo. Now you. Why call the cops? They never catch nobody—not in real life, not once the guy's run. And all they'd have wanted was her drawers to sniff. I think she was right."

Wesley said "Maybe so. Still the fool's running loose, and he knows where she lives."

Rato said "I kept him off till now you're back."

Wesley said "For today. We'll see about the rest."

Rato asked "You want to stay? Ain't that why you're back?"

"I doubt I know yet. I'm here because she wrote me about the damned rape. I feel like I caused it."

Rato nodded. "You may."

From Rato, a mind that plain and clear, it cut like a blade. Wesley honored his right to cut that deep. "You think I caused it?"

"Understand I'm no judge but my guess is, you promised the Lord and all her friends and family to guard Rosa's body. They trusted you at your word and looked other places. Twenty-eight years later your eyes flicked off her. You didn't tell us. That left her in danger, and the Devil saw his chance."

Wesley said "You sure you believe in the Devil?"

"I'm a man, ain't I?" Rato said. "Of course I do. Ain't you felt the damned Devil fermenting in your soul?—when you'd be scrounging some clean girl's body just to ease your mind or not giving all your bi-weekly pay to a child you'd see on the street, cold and hungry? If you don't believe in the Devil, I doubt you've got good eyes."

Wesley laughed. "Where you been all my life, son? I needed you."

Rato said "Just waiting. You never asked me."

"Should I stay here now?"

"Depends on what you want," Rato said. "If it's just to protect Rosa, I can do that good as you—maybe better. I got infantry training. All you learned was to keep boats floating."

Wesley said "What else should I want?"

"You're the one got married, not me. Can't help you. Maybe you want what she gave you back when, years ago on that beach in Norfolk. What happened to that?"

Wesley said "Oh Lord Jesus, *time.*"

"Then it ain't Rosa's fault. Don't punish her for time."

"I'm not," Wesley said.

"What the hell were these last three months then? If you'd stayed here beating her all night long every night of three months with a bull-hide whip, you couldn't have hurt her worse than you did. Plus that goddamned maniac breaking in and bruising her there in the tender part of her body and mind. I'd skin his face one cell at a time with absolute pleasure if I knew his name."

Wesley hadn't seen any man care that much about anything but Negroes in the past thirty years. He knew his own flesh ought to be cringing at the thought of what Rosa had borne in these same walls. Was it a sign of how far he'd drifted from his old first love?—that now he could think through that painful night and not force her down to the police station to pore through volumes of felon shots and find the exact face for him to hunt and skin? What he felt was sadness at an old friend's pain and considerable shame at his own desertion of family duty.

The evening to come would tell what Rosa felt, and that might settle all other questions here—staying or leaving again or whatever. Suddenly Wesley's exhaustion hit him, a fifty-year-old man with no wink of sleep in twenty-six hours. His head almost fell forward to the table.

Rato saw it and told him "You're dead."

"I told you that."

"I mean here and now. Go on up and sleep."

Wesley said "You got everything covered, Ace?"

"I'll spend my day like I always do. Don't worry about me. Got my own set of keys."

Wesley said "Good night" and was almost halfway up the stairs when the next reality struck him firmly. He walked back down, stood in the kitchen door, and said "You be using your bed today?"

"Not till midnight, no."

"Can I sleep in your room?"

"Sure, clean sheets two days ago. But you got your own bed."

Wesley said "Not yet. That's some while off."

One more thing Rato didn't understand, though he said "Be my guest."

When Wesley came to it was four-fifteen, and the light outside was beginning to fade. He had an hour and a half at least before Rosa would be home, but he wanted to be entirely ready. So he got up to wash, shave, and dress. His things were still outside in the car. He slipped on his old clothes and started downstairs. Halfway he heard two voices in the kitchen—Rato's plainly and another man's. The man seemed to be in the process of leaving, so Wesley went on quick out the front door and got his grocery bag of clothes. When he turned back to the house, he could see a tall man, black-haired and straight, walking out of the back drive toward the nearest cross-street. Maybe twenty-five years old, thirty at the most—nobody Wesley recognized.

He ducked his head through the kitchen door to let Rato know he was up now and planning to dress.

Rato was sitting again at the table, watching a cheap black television comedy and already laughing hard. He said "Sleep good?"

"Like the *road*. I haven't slept that deep since 1950. Was somebody in here with you just now?"

"I go bowl a few games most afternoons up yonder at the college. A friend walked me home from the bowling alley. I give him a Coke. You don't mind, do you?"

"Not if he's a friend of yours."

Rato said "He's new but I guess he's all right. Doesn't have much to say."

Wesley asked "He know me or Rosa?—a student at the college?"

"No," Rato said. "Hasn't got another real friend in town or so he says. Tries to buy me stuff to eat at the bowling alley—fried pork-rinds, that sick sort of mess."

Wesley said "Watch your step. Can't trust folks here like you can in the country."

Rato laughed. "Country is the last place I trust anybody, country and *home*. I notice you left it soon as you could. Now go get clean. I'll stay on guard."

So Wesley went. Neither one of them had the trace of a guess that Rato's friend was the man who had been here New Year's night.

When Rosa pulled in at six, Wesley had washed his car, then himself, then dressed in clean old clothes, and was quiet in the living room reading *The Raleigh Times*. She unloaded a few groceries in the kitchen, talked a little with Rato about the day's events, stepped up to her bathroom, and combed her hair.

Then she went down to Wesley. All day at work she'd dreaded this moment—first, the chance that he'd be gone again when she got here; second, the almost harder possibility that he'd have stayed and would need talking to. She'd held herself back from thinking what to say. As she stepped over the threshold now, she silently asked the Holy Ghost to guide her speech. But her eyes stayed open, so she saw Wesley rise in place to meet her, no sign of worry on his plain broad features but no smile either.

He said "Hard day?"

"Do I look it? May be."

"No, you look all right. I just meant I'd taken *my* day easy and was feeling guilty."

"Did you sleep off your trip?"

"Pretty well, I think. Course I doubt I'll have insomnia tonight." He returned to his chair.

But Rosa couldn't sit, couldn't make herself rest till she knew one thing. She finally said "You staying for supper? You staying at all?"

"I'd be real grateful for supper," he said. "After that, I guess you'll want to discuss it."

"You're the one that left."

Wesley nodded. "I did—and told you why, the best I could in that first letter. None of it's your fault."

"Sure it was, half at least."

"But things have changed since—what you wrote me about, your New Year's and all."

Rosa sat at last but far from Wesley. "That was not your doing."

"It sure God *was*. Don't forgive me too easy. If I'd been here like I vowed to be, no man would have come anywhere near the door— much less touched you."

Rosa said "That's not the reason I told you, to make you guilty. It turned out you were just my last friend on earth. I'd kept quiet so long, I had to tell somebody. That make any sense?"

"Good sense. Thank you, ma'm." Wesley stood in place; he couldn't think why.

Rosa said "How's it changed me, in your eyes now?"

"None at all, I guess. You look fine from here."

She smiled. "That's a flattering distance though."

Wesley didn't move to shorten it. He said "Go on now and get it all out."

Rosa asked "What?"

"Your feelings about me, how mad you must be. I've been a damned scoundrel. Punish me now. I volunteer." He even extended his hands at his side, not quite in surrender but plainly at her mercy.

Rosa laughed at first but kept on looking, straight at his eyes. They were what she had loved most of all in the world, above ground or under. What she'd lived to serve. Through all these sad weeks, she'd not doubted that. To have them here now—deep and dark as ever, this unblinking steady, this easy to meet—and not to know whether they were offered for good or on some sort of loan was harder than everything else so far. She said "I'm not mad, not one iota. I just want to hear if you mean to stay. It won't take any big panel discussion."

Wesley said "Watch my lips." He touched his dry lips, then moved them slowly to make clear sounds. "I'm here to ask you that same question. You want me to stay?"

Rosa said "Please sir, till I'm dead anyhow."

"No problem," he said.

In the few more seconds they could each bear to sit and meet the other's eyes, they wondered what on earth they meant? Had they only told two more kind lies after decades of kindness that had brought them to this?

Whatever would prove to be the truth days or weeks from now, they'd left Rato home to thaw pizza and had taken themselves to their old favorite place—the Canton Restaurant on Hillsboro Street with roomy private booths. They'd talked about their families in Warren County, the little they'd each heard from Horace lately, how surprisingly different Rato seemed up here in town (what must he have been like in Germany?), some postponed repair work the house was needing.

Then out of the blue, Wesley poured out the full story of Wilson and his weeks with her.

At first Rosa had wanted to stop him (it was coming too fast and painful for her), but something told her she would need the information eventually, and now might be the last time Wesley would easily part with so much of the truth. She'd already used up the rape; so she had nothing to give in return, nothing to balance Wilson. She did tell him about finding Rato's little shrine to her at Mary's house and about Milo's unexpected warm kindness. But before she finished with those, she was sorry. They seemed like childish efforts at making Wesley jealous, when all she was hunting was sizable fresh news.

Still Wesley listened carefully, not drifting off. When she seemed finished, he asked if she was ready for him to run her on home?

She asked "Me? Aren't you coming too?"

He said "Rosa, I'm not trying to be cute here. I just want to give you every fair opportunity to get real honest and turn against the son of a bitch that left you Christmas week to sink or swim."

She thanked him again, laughed, and finally said "Believe me, I've tried. It's not in my heart. At least I can't find it. Let's go home to sleep."

ROSA WESLEY
RATO WAVE

It was only nine-thirty when they drove into the yard, but Rato was already gone from downstairs. The light in his bedroom was on, but his door was shut. And when Rosa called through the door to see if he was all right, Rato only said "Yes but wore out."

She told him that she and Wesley weren't ready for bed, if he'd like to come back down and watch television.

But Rato said "Like I told you, I'm beat."

So she left him alone, and she and Wesley went to the living room to watch a tired comedy on the big set. Wesley drank a beer; Rosa had ginger ale. In a quarter-hour he had slid into his old ease here. For moments at a time, she could do the same. Then she'd remember herself—the nightmare pain of the past few months—and doubt all this. By the time the show ended, Rosa was even wondering if she could manage to sleep beside this man, much less with him. Could she ever want him again?

Somehow Wesley felt her doubts through the air. After they'd watched the first part of the eleven o'clock news (just the standard murders), bedtime was inevitable. But he knew he must wait for Rosa's instructions.

Finally she stood up and said "Remember, I work tomorrow. And you haven't slept in a bed for two nights." For an instant she extended a hand to draw him up, but then she dropped it. She hoped he hadn't noticed, but of course he had.

So Wesley was honest when he said "I can sleep right here on this sofa, no problem." There were two upstairs bedrooms, none down.

Rosacoke said "You can if you want to." She took a step away, then looked back a moment, then spoke to the rug. "In my mind, you still live upstairs."

So he rose, said "Thank you, ma'm," and followed her up.

To have watched them undress would have looked like always, from the outside. The only exterior difference was that they moved entirely in the light of a single bulb from the bathroom and that maybe they hurried a little. They both were keyed up and scared. Neither of them knew exactly what they wanted to happen in the next half-hour.

Wesley was not sexually excited. In fact, as he stripped, his skin showed the innocent early-spring whiteness of a soft boy. Still the nearness of an attractive woman had never failed to rouse him in the past, not once. Would it now?

Rosa didn't feel the revulsion that some raped women report at the sight of the next naked man (in fact the coal black of Wesley's pubic hair against the white of his skin was a nice sight; and his penis looked familiar and entirely harmless, unchanged by its trip). So their fear was of something deeper than sex—maybe of finding that one or the other had changed in an unexpected secret way that only their coming nearness would trigger now fiercely, some bawling mouth of hunger or rage.

In a short clean gown, Rosa went toward the bathroom to wash her face and teeth. When she shut the door and sat to take a last pee, she shut her eyes to say a silent prayer. As usual, at really hard corners, nothing wise or even right would come to her mind. She finally just said a silent "Help," flushed the toilet, and stood.

Walking back through the door, through their dim old bedroom toward the man she'd lived with all her grown years, she felt suddenly and for the first time precisely like a bride. She couldn't help meeting Wesley's eyes and smiling.

He smiled back slowly and turned on the reading lamp by his hand. He was still upright on the far side of the bed in his white jockey shorts. He'd lost four or five pounds in Nashville clearly.

Rosa felt sad to see it—couldn't that woman cook? But she also couldn't help thinking how much better he looked, how much more nearly like the first lean Wesley.

When he'd stood long enough to read her smile, Wesley also grinned and began to count "One, Two, Three." On "One" he'd taken the tip of the bedspread and begun to pull it back.

Rosa joined him on "Two." By "Four" they both climbed into cool sheets.

And by "Six," Wesley suddenly shook with a chill. He lay on his back, hands stretched down beside him; and hard shudders racked him.

Rosa lay down quickly, rolled to face him, and watched for a while. Then sooner than she'd planned, her hand had to touch him in the center of his chest. Her courage and then her foolishness began to amaze her—this man had left her without one word for a whole long winter and now, with spring, had walked back in. What she maybe ought to do was stand up now and speak all her mind. It had been nearly thirty years since she'd done as much. Didn't she at least owe that much honesty to the pain she'd borne, that one bad night? But she didn't say a word.

Wesley shuddered harder.

So Rosa pulled back and also lay flat.

But Wesley said "Oh no, don't quit" and laughed in a whisper. "I'm fine. I'm just tremendously tired and ashamed." By then he had calmed.

So she faced him again. But this time she held back for him to touch her.

He turned off the lamp and reached to her shoulder, waiting for his palm to warm to her own old usual warmth. When it did, he kissed her lightly once. But then his hand wouldn't start slowly down-ward. He couldn't think why. It was like she'd suddenly changed as a punishment. Lying in easy reach beside him, still she'd become a child again, lovely and warm but young and forbidden—not fouled by the rape but a possible victim all the same and fragile.

Rosa thought that of course. In another long minute she rolled back, faced the ceiling, and said "I'm as sorry as I can possibly be." She meant she was sorry for what she saw as their present dilemma — Wesley back and at hand but unable to want her, she wanting him too much to do justice to the pain that lay just behind them, still unforgiven. That revelation had come too soon, before they'd worked through all their other questions.

Wesley understood her but still couldn't say why he'd drawn back. Again he felt she was once more a virgin. And all those years ago — a real virgin — she'd lured him on her, when she thought she had lost him for good. As she seemed just now to have tried to draw him again. Was he finally taking the chance at refusal that he'd lost — what? — twenty-eight years ago? Well, now he was diving far below his own power to breathe. He said "I feel like we're back at the start, nothing worse than that."

Rosa said "Start of what?"

"Knowing each other — you and me, back when."

Rosa said "That well may be the thing that saves us."

"If we get it right this time."

Rosa asked "Where'd we go wrong, Wesley? I really don't know. I haven't known since the day you left."

"Honest to God? Was it just me then?"

"Oh I'm not claiming either one of us was perfect or any of our marriage. I do claim though that, until I got home that evening and you didn't appear, I never suspected we could end for good — not till death anyhow. What was seriously wrong? Better tell me now in case there's time left."

Wesley asked "Do you want there to be?"

"I think maybe so. If we start off innocent again, like you say. But also knowing what we both want and need, both knowing each other and paying attention. Horace is thoroughly gone from us now, Rato'll leave any minute we say, we'll be here alone together for the first time since those few months we had at the start before Horace landed. We might well get another thirty, forty years. We'd need to pay *attention*, Wesley, every minute."

"I may not can do that," Wesley said. "Every minute sounds a lot more like you than me. I honestly believe you could manage new innocence. Poor Wesley, though—he's too dirty, Rose. He's got spots and bruises that won't scrub off. I thought part of what marriage meant was just that—you could look past the grease marks and trust each other's love and promise. You could even ignore the traces of some other person's body—their stray hairs, scraps of their fingernails. And you didn't have to keep prancing around each other with cards and flowers. You knew where you stood and could lean on that."

Rosa said, "All right. But remember one thing—what you're describing is what a man wants. Women are somehow scareder than that."

"I guess so, yes. I'd have to grant that. But you know how soon Wesley starts feeling foolish with the Hallmark love poems and Whitman's candy hearts."

Rosa finally laughed and turned where she was, without moving closer, to see Wesley's face. It took awhile for her eyes to find him in the deep dark night. When the line of his forehead and nose showed at last, his mouth was moving in very slow breaths. He'd plunged into sleep backward like a child powerless to last. That far anyhow, she guessed they were safe—that trusting in one another, that free. She still hadn't asked him the final question—how had he *died* the day he left her?

Here now beside her he was clearly alive. Even fifteen inches there beyond, he broadcast powerfully every fresh odor he'd ever broadcast—all clean and his own, like no other man's she'd ever been near. She said a last prayer, to Wesley more than God—"Let this thing *go*." Then her own mind joined him in quick black sleep.

What stayed awake in the house was Rato. His door was shut and his curiosity surely did not extend to wondering what Rosa and Wesley were doing in their new privacy. He just couldn't sleep. He was racing back and forth through what this meant—Wesley's reappearance, Rosa taking him in. Knowing them both, long as they'd known each other, still it never crossed Rato's mind to doubt that Wesley was back for good. These two had grown together more than half their lives ago. They couldn't disentangle now if they wanted to—and both their sets of eyes denied any serious thought of separation. He'd known that years ago, before they did. He'd told Rosa once she knew she was pregnant and wanted to run.

But him now, Rato? Everybody would expect him to pack his little duds and head up to Mama for thirty more years of country boredom. He'd really enjoyed these weeks in a town. Not that Raleigh was Berlin or even London, but it had the main good any city can offer — *nobody knew who you were*, at least not once you stepped into the street. You could be a guy with fourteen rich fat ex-wives dissolving in sulfuric acid under your bathroom floorboards, and people would think you were just a smiling shoesalesman or a bachelor Baptist preacher.

So if Rato could strangle his conscience well enough, he might just either rent a room from Wesley or find him a little efficiency apartment in the neighborhood or closer in toward N.C. State and the bowling alley, the doughnut shop, and the movies. His Army retirement check would probably stretch just about that far.

Or this new friend he'd met — Wave Wilbanks — had hinted at the chance of them rooming together somewhere clean and cheap (Wave had just got a job at a textbook store).

Jobs were the main thing here that worried Rato. He could probably hunt down some weird thing in a bar or a pawnshop — sweeping up, washing up, being the fool that customers called "Sarge" or "Old Timer." Rato had a special fear of *Old Timer*. The way he heard the words on television, he understood it was the name of the new disease you heard so much about now, where people lost their memory and lived on their family's kindness like big dirty turnips in bedroom corners — Old Timer's disease.

Afton and his mother's house wasn't so awful. The place would leave him alone. And his mother was all right too, if she just wouldn't ask too many questions about Raleigh and his doings. He could tell her about all the new things at Rosa's — the microwave and the twenty-gallon aquarium that Wesley had bought for a hobby and then left to Rosa. But there had been several surprising ways that Raleigh was different from Afton, the Army, and all of damned Europe.

The main thing was women. Once he left home at eighteen, so long ago, he got his first real chance to watch women. He had talked to Wave his bowling friend and to Wesley about how many women he'd really been next to, and he never flat lied. But he also never truly admitted how lonesome that made him—the women in every other place but Raleigh. He could pay some whore in Rhine-Main, Germany to touch his body any way he dreamed. Hell, he had known one girl that—free, for no money at all—had tried to lick off the ugly tattoo he regretted on his left wrist. But even if she could speak clear good English, she wouldn't ever ask what he wanted to hear.

Rato needed women to ask him for advice. He knew he understood the whole broad world, especially men, and he wanted women to profit from his knowledge. He could let them know what men thought of them, what men truly wanted from women in their private minds, how scared all men but Rato were of the secret whirlpool buried in women that caught men early and held them down there spinning forever. Rato had it all thought out in terms of the strong pull of water. Boys are *made*, from day one, in what seem like peaceful ponds hid deep inside their mothers' bodies. Then one day after nearly a long restful year, the mother flushes you out like some piece of festered trash—scared and dry and yelling. Then when you're maybe twelve or thirteen, every other girl in the world starts hinting to you that she's got that same warm peaceful piece of water inside her body just waiting for you—and that this time, there won't be any trouble. Well, dive in and *peaceful?* That's when you find out the meaning of whirlpools. By then though you're hooked. Or all other men but a few queers and Rato.

Rato wasn't scared because he'd escaped. Or had never been caught. The way he escaped was, he left his mother. From early in the crib, he understood how much he needed freedom. So something had made him turn from his mother—his only food!—and make her feed him a whole nother way. He was way too young to think it out. God or his mind had just helped him know. And now his mission was to pass that knowledge on—to men if they'd listen (which they'd seldom do) but mainly to women. His secret of happiness for all mankind. And up till now almost nobody anywhere had ever asked— not even Rosa lately, sad as she'd been.

He couldn't decide tonight anyhow. He'd need to talk to more people than Rato ever liked to involve—Wesley and Rosa, his mother, Wave, maybe a bunch of realtors and landladies. He couldn't think about all them at night.

He had all day tomorrow with nothing else planned. Matter of fact, nothing was planned between here and his grave. He'd save it for tomorrow then. He asked himself one last clear question—why does a young fellow like Wave (maybe twenty-five or six) want to live with somebody old as me? Then Rato was out too.

That left no one conscious but Waverly Wilbanks, on foot five blocks away, hoping to walk off the pain in his heart. In all the world, he was the one great mystery to himself—why he made the choices he made and when he made them. Rosa was by no means the first woman he'd forced to know him. Or to let him know them.

The idea of knowing had come to him in early childhood from Bible reading—"Now Adam knew Eve his wife, and she conceived and bore Cain." By the time Wave was fourteen, living east of Raleigh halfway to the ocean, he had determined in his mind really to *know* at least one woman.

No one that he'd met or dreamed about made him think that a woman would offer herself to him freely. Everything he could find, in books and movies and other boys' talk, convinced him that the kind of knowledge he craved—the deep dark sweetness and power— would yield only to a sudden hot thrust from his private body. Then just beyond the thrust would come an end to need and then a return flow of thanks and kindness from the woman. And the first girl that Wave ever forced responded in just the way he planned.

She was a neighbor to him and his mother in the country, a distant cousin two years behind him in school. They rode the same school-bus every morning and evening. And one spring afternoon when he was fourteen and pressure in his groin had built to the hurting point, Wave let the girl—Christine—walk ahead of him up the track toward their houses.

The low clear sun was falling behind her; and the light struck through her light skirt, showing the strength of her legs and hips. Wave felt, for the first time plainly, that if he couldn't get there—right in the center of her true power—he'd die or fall down at least in some kind of seizure that would prove his complete failure to be a man. He speeded up and touched her between the shoulder blades.

When Christine stopped and turned to face him, she was smiling slightly. She even said "I was wondering—"

Wave never let her say what she wondered. He dropped his books by the path, took her gently by the elbow, and led her a quarter-mile off toward the tall pine woods. When they were there in the half-dark, he first had to stop her from undressing (she volunteered to strip right off). He just motioned her to lie down in the soft straw and to be entirely silent.

So she obeyed and in another twenty minutes, Wave had done everything he ever dreamed of doing—and all of it with his gentle fingers and lips. Christine had cooperated fully with his hands. It was only when he moved his mouth down on her that she shook her head no. Wave rightly guessed how ashamed she was of that part of herself as dirty and ugly (because both women and men said so).

Well, there again Wave had another chance to redeem her pride and pleasure. When he'd worked a good quarter-hour with his mouth, Christine cut loose a sigh—long and thin as stocking thread. At first Wave thought he'd hurt her. But when he looked upward, her shut eyes were happy; her damp lips were smiling.

Finally Christine met Wave's waiting eyes and said "Can I stand up now?"

Before he could say "Yes," he thought "Thank Jesus, *that's* over. I was right all the way. I won't ever worry about that again." And it did fill the big howling hole in his chest for maybe three weeks—his memories of it, the dreams he built on it, the lovely chances it gave him to serve his own clean body again and again. But by the end of school and the start of tobacco season, the goodness had worn out of the memory. And Christine herself was asking for more. She'd wait evenings for him, as he came back from the fields. And two or three times, he walked off with her. She'd lie back and watch in the cool while he fiddled with her, got her twitching and yipping like a wind-up toy.

The trouble for Wave was, he knew Christine all the way by then. He could foretell every move she'd make the instant before she made it. He could say to himself "Put your little finger there; she'll do exactly *that*." And ten times in ten, he'd be dead right. That was when he began to think of older women.

And before he got his high-school diploma, Wave had known two of them. One was his dramatics teacher. The other was a librarian (he'd discovered books by then, the best source yet of mysterious women— really frank magazines hadn't yet penetrated rural North Carolina).

Forced was hardly the right word for what he accomplished with them. He knew that, out of loneliness and hunger, they mostly cooperated. But the way they obeyed his orders for silence and stillness and just lay back and watched him proceed, the way they almost never yelled or struck him but cried gently at the end—all those signs told him to believe what he hoped: that Waverly Wilbanks had won precious knowledge through his own strong force. He might not be the only wise man on earth; he'd never heard of any local rival at least, not down in the country or once he got to Raleigh.

Wave had dropped out in his sophomore year at N.C. State before he genuinely raped anybody. And the first real rape was also his first knowledge of a total stranger. She lived in his neighborhood over behind the Raleigh Little Theater, and he knew about her in that first drop-out year because his paper route served her house—the early-morning paper.

Once that spring she had been on the steps in her blue housecoat watering houseplants when Wave passed on his bike to sling her paper. She'd said firmly but quietly "Please don't throw it" and walked on toward him with her right hand out. He stopped and waited and handed it over smiling, knowing that instant what he'd do when enough time had passed for safety. He knew because she'd met his eyes and held onto them just that split-second longer than was usual—hunting, hunting for some good answer she couldn't foretell.

She wasn't bad-looking. So he checked round enough to know she was single, that she lived alone, and was no more than six years older than he. He learned that she worked as a legal secretary. So he figured that it meant—if he played his cards right and didn't really hurt her—she almost certainly wouldn't go to the Law for help.

Three weeks later, after planning every instant till his brain was smoking with the hopes, Wave shaved meticulously. Then he walked light-footedly to her backyard and checked her kitchen door at three-thirty in the morning. The screen was hooked but any kitten can unlock a screen. In four more minutes he found her bedroom in the one-story house, knelt on the shag rug by her knees, and began to stroke her upper thigh. It took a surprisingly long time to wake her.

But finally she came to, lay still, and said "I really do pray this isn't what I think it is."

Wave smiled in the dark and said "It isn't, no."

She said "What you want me to do then?"

"Lie flat on your back and let me take over."

She waited awhile to obey but then did. The only other words she said were "Don't cut me please."

Wave laughed gently. "Honey, never—not a scratch." Then he spent maybe half an hour slowly baring parts of her body, stroking, kissing, honoring her skin. He even reached a moment when he thought he'd put her back to sleep—her breathing steadied and slowed that much.

But when he rocked back and paused to see, she said "Can I go wash please?"

Wave wouldn't let himself think she was dirty. He had to say "No" and work himself back to where he'd been before—the aim to gentle her back to the moment when all her gates and bars went down, and he could board her quickly and *know*—really know forever—the absolute secrets of a woman compelled to take his attention, his own last secret, and then thank him for it.

For all Wave knew, that first strange woman had never complained—surely not to him and apparently not to the law. *Nor anybody else.* In fact, as he left her room before light, she said one peculiar last thing to his back—"Do you know my name?" He said "Yes ma'm. It's Kathleen, right?" And she said "Thank you."

He even went on as her paperboy for another four months till he got a better job. In the two years that lay between the first rape and Rosa's, he'd forced three other women—all alone at home in the quiet dark—and not one word of a cry for help as he crouched there beside them nor in the next day's news anywhere.

Rosa was somebody he planned for delicately. He had noticed her ever since his freshman year at State, at the office and in the cafeteria. It wasn't so much that she was beautiful or even attractive. She was after all literally old enough to be his mother, though she'd worn well enough—no fat or dyed hair.

What caught Wave in her face and shape was the same first thing that had caught Wesley. Somewhere behind her wide blue eyes, she guarded closely what Wave suspected was a big grand secret. This time, it was a secret that she herself understood; it was the rest of the world she was hiding her answer from. This woman knew the last little thing that Wave had missed. Week by week as he watched her— crossed her paths on campus, saw her smile eight times—he convinced himself that the two of them had a world to give each other. He knew every volt he had for her. And her rare smile said "Waverly Wilbanks, I can give you rest."

Just by occasional questions at school and in her neighborhood, Wave gradually put together the sense of a friendly woman with a cheerful-enough husband that didn't seem to fit her looks and her nature. It was that which gave him the most hope. Wave had discovered early that he somehow gave girls and then women more than most other men even began to offer—he *attended* to them.

He listened in stillness, heard their private needs, and filled them. Or so he believed. And didn't his safety, his freedom from jail or the fear of capture, prove him right?

So more and more in the days before that New Year's, he came to the urgent conclusion that not only could he get at Rosa but, without maybe knowing it, she wanted him to. How he was going to meet her with her husband in residence—that was his only big problem. Would it have to be his first attempt in daylight? (he'd noticed that Wesley worked till nine on two or three nights, usually late in the week).

But the first night Wesley disappeared, Wave picked up his absence—his car was gone from the drive and stayed gone right through Christmas. So his guess was right. Rosa wanted his attention. So did the sky, maybe God Himself—*the way was cleared*. It had seemed that plain, that wanted and right.

Even now—months later with her friendly watchdog, her guard-dog brother that couldn't hurt a gnat and her husband back home—Wave couldn't much doubt he had been flagged on, *led* on to force her. What had ruined him ever since New Year's was, he hadn't really finished. Out of all the women he'd really been near, Rosa was the only one who cried out and stopped him. She'd somehow lied in all those smiles and misled him badly. His mind couldn't leave her.

So now Wave stood in the midst of the night on the street outside her house, her room, her simple brother, and now this husband who couldn't deserve her. He suspected, even now, that he might be crazy. He'd read enough books, seen enough television, to know his kind were pitied and feared and dreaded by all. He himself might better off be locked in a cell, or hanged or gassed, than left out here on the streets free to roam. Yet he knew one thing more urgent than all—he was not a member of any common *kind*. He was a man in possession of a talent.

Surely what he had—a kind sweet gift that women seldom got, for all their pain—more than earned him room and air, the right to roam in darkness and strike where his hands knew best to strike. Surely nothing, in heaven or earth, meant for Wave to be this unknown and lonesome—this dreaded. Now that Wesley was back, surely Rato and Wave were the only two live adult souls in this end of town who wanted companions but took their rest with no warm shape to touch in the night.

He sat there opposite Rosa and Wesley's on the now chilly curb and tried to make his eyes pierce brick, thick drapes, and plaster to see their sleep. He knew they had to be unconscious by now, not talking or touching.

Just when his mind had made out the trail of Rosa's hair sideways on her pillow (her back to Wesley), a car roared around the nearest corner. And Wave had to jump back and find the dark—his own narrow bed, hopeless and dry. He who had this gift to give, this permanent pleasure, the actual worship that all women dream of—the one man alive who knew that secret in pure perfection and longed to give it night after night to willing women, every woman on earth, and no trace of harm.

ROSA JEAN RATO
WAVE WESLEY BRONNY

The third Friday in April was as fine a day as any live soul in Raleigh remembered. In the past week the trees had advanced from that day when new leaves break as a pale green mist, almost a hallucination, on the highest limbs. Now there were actual yellowish leaves. The dry warm air fell gently down through them, bearing a light sweet odor that seemed an actual promise from the sky—that one more winter had truly ended, that life was given one more round (earned or not).

Americans, Asians, smoky combinations of all the large and small, pink and brown races—the tens of thousands of students at N.C. State University had begun their annual grateful response to the single visible wheel of nature that responds, on time, to human hopes. The vernal thanksgiving consists of many acts in many stanzas, but the first is a sudden and forthright strip-to-essentials. The limbs of a race of well-fed children burst from the grim winter padding into a nearly blinding glare of grace and rank eros—a forest of gorgeous parts. And the upward rush of desire in their bodies is all but visible in the lilac snaking of arteries as they circle one another in the slow dances of noontime splendor. And though final examinations are hardly more than a week ahead, physics and calculus, hydraulics and architecture have slid from their minds as thoroughly as the grays and mists of February torpor.

Rosa and her office mate Jean Gillam (who'd given the New Year's party) had brought their lunches outdoors near the English Department. They'd eaten and now they were savoring the last minutes of freedom on a brick bench in the direct light that—for all the eons of human abuse—was as unscreened, kind, and caring as ever. Jean was no more than six years younger than Rosa; but her eyes frankly consumed the passing male bodies in the welcome new fashion of short-shorts and converted the bountiful information into a line of comment that (for all her good humor) Rosa could never have issued, though she laughed right along.

But finally Jean burst out with "First prize, no question! You could tear the last few threads off that child yonder, spray him white, and stand him up in Athens, Greece right this minute with no objection from anybody, least of all me."

And Rosa had to say "Nobody but the vice squad, you dirty old woman. That child could be yours."

Jean nodded. "Thank Jesus he's not. It was hard enough not stroking my own baby boy before he left home—those little running shorts of his, those curly gold hairs on his big calves!"

Rosa could still smile but she had to say "Jean, you may need a good long day in church on your knees. I never had one trace of trouble with Horace."

"No offense intended, Rosa—Horace is a sweet boy—but he can't compete with the Pillsbury *Doughboy* for beauty."

Rosa said "He didn't inherit Wesley's looks, I'll grant you."

Jean chose to let that one lie dead behind them. "Remember you promised to show me your old photos of Wesley? You never did."

"I'm afraid I burned them early last winter."

"General Sherman, you didn't! Lord, Rose, it's a sin to burn up history."

Rosa waited a good while. "Not *burn* really. I did fish them all out, shut them up with hot sealing-wax in a brown envelope, and bury them in a box in the basement."

"Well, rescue them now from the silverfish and bring them to the office for me to enjoy."

Rosa said "I'm not sure it's absolutely safe, not yet awhile. They may need to be something Horace finds when he's shoveled me under forty years from now."

"Or tomorrow noon. You and Wesley seem fine." Jean and her husband Hal had grilled burgers on their patio for Rosa and Wesley the previous weekend.

Rosa said "Did we really?"

Jean nodded emphatically. "Hal and I discussed it later. He said 'You'd never guess Wesley had missed a beat at home, would you?' I don't offer Hal as one of the world's most sensitive observation-posts (he's been known to miss a few H-bomb blasts in our own backyard). But he has got a pretty good sense of other men, when they're happy or sad. And Hal said 'Wesley Beavers is a lucky damned sucker; he knows it now if not a day sooner.'"

Rosa laughed. "You're lying."

"Swear to God on high." Jean raised her right hand with a last crust of bread.

Rosa said "Anybody swearing on Wonder Bread can't ask to be believed."

Jean flung the bread toward a pair of horny pigeons and swore again.

"He hasn't told me."

"He's showing you, Rose."

"How please? Tell me."

Jean said "He's here beside you smiling, not in Nashville or east Madagascar or Akron. Not with some bleached-blond X-ray technician in a mobile home cheap as sardine cans, eating cheese puffs and marshmallow whip on crackers. Wesley's promised you his life."

Rosa said "You've heard words I haven't heard, not from Wesley *this* year. The last plain thing he told me was, he was dead."

"I'll bet he's not dead when the lights are out."

Rosa faced Jean squarely, thought through the truth, then decided to tell it. "We've no more touched than brothers and sisters these past three weeks."

Jean said "Some brothers and sisters touch a lot. Read the paper every day. Fathers and daughters—"

"I can joke fast as you when it's joking time, Jean. It's not that yet, not at our house yet."

"But it's your house together, Rose. Wesley came back home. He knew what was his."

Before she remembered fully, Rosa said "Because he found out about—" Jean had never heard a word about the rape. So Rosa stayed calm and continued. "Wesley found out in his own heart how big a wrong he'd done."

Jean said "Shoot, that wouldn't have fazed Wesley. Wesley's as modern as any stud dragging Main with a Playboy Bunny insignia on his mirror and a pair of fur dice. Wesley's wild, Rose. One look at those eyes the other night, and I knew deep down that Wesley was as different from my Hal Gillan as Hal is from Nancy Reagan. Wesley won't say one word he doesn't mean."

Rosa nodded. "—Which is why he left."

"*And* came back."

Rosa said "He never changed his mind that fast before. I still don't know what happened with Wilson."

"Who?"

"That mess in the mobile home."

Jean said "I was scared you meant a man there for a minute."

"No. In this case, Wilson is a girl. We're talking about Wesley, Jean."

"I told you he was wild. Wesley gets *me* riled—pardon the personal confession."

Rosa smiled. "Careful or I might begin to wonder who *doesn't* rile you."

"Don't be mean now." Jean laughed the low gutter chuckle that won her forgiveness in so many quarters. "No, believe me, Miss Rose. If Wesley wanted or needed to be with that blondeened bitch, he'd be with her now."

Rosa said "The bitch may have had a word to say about it. She may have thrown him out. He's twice her age."

Jean said "He could be four times my age, with those dark eyes.

God, Rosa, those eyes can see on through me and every wall between me and Peking, China."

Rosa said "Me too but that's because those eyes aren't looking for you or me."

Jean said "Not me, for damned sure. But who?"

Rosa said "I've wondered since the day I first saw him. And so does he. He no more knows than you or me what he's hungry for."

"Then why did it take him thirty years to see you weren't it?"

"It didn't. He knew it well before our wedding. I forced his hand."

Jean said "The two of you got pregnant. Wesley wasn't exactly standing on the other side of the room when Horace cranked up in your tender womb. And Wesley knows that. Stop beating yourself."

Rosa smiled. "You ought to been present a lot earlier in my life."

"You might not have been such a woebegone sheep dog."

Rosa said "We're due back at work."

"Cool your jets," Jean said. "That office ain't going a step without us. We've earned a tardy, today anyhow."

"So you're telling me to take him back—Wesley, here and now? You're saying he won't bolt on me again? Won't ever surprise me? I couldn't stand that."

"I'm saying that much. But I'm not Wesley. Sit him down, sweet Rose, and ask him outright."

Rosa took ten seconds to study Jean's face in the frank sun, still as lovely as before. With all the fine young bodies around them, there was nothing in sight more generous or plainly trustworthy than the hands and face Jean Gillam had constructed in her years. So Rosa grinned broadly.

Jean knew it was a compliment. She responded gravely. "I love you too. But are you really telling me you haven't sat Wesley down and asked him the facts?"

"I haven't told you that, no. But you're guessing it right."

Jean waited an instant, then pointed sharply back toward their office. "Get your dumb ass in to that word processor. You no more deserve another minute of God's sun than these pink worms gnawing our feet."

Rosa smiled, studied the soles of her own shoes and then rose. "My shoes are safe."

Jean laughed and joined her. "Nothing else is though. You count on that."

"You just said the opposite. You said I was fine."

"I was lying," Jean said. She trotted three steps before looking back, younger in spirit than any student near them. "I don't do nothing but lie, old Rose. I'm sick as a dog, but oh please love me. I need human care."

Rosa said "I'll try. It'll be damned hard."

Jean stopped and said "You've done nothing else all your natural life. You're a pluperfect martyr. You *know* you know it, and you love every minute." She stepped back slowly till she bumped into Rosa. Then she took her kind but innocent friend's pale bare arm and steered her, like a lost untrained blind child, back to work in the world.

Rosa felt like a new-washed window in the light.

Two hours later just across the road, Rato sat in the bowling alley drinking a Pepsi and talking to Waverly, his only non-family friend in Raleigh. Rato had always lived on the policy of asking as few questions as possible of anybody—first, because he had the world's minimum of curiosity about other people and, second, because he didn't want to concede anyone else the right to question him. But after nearly a month of quiet job-hunting in the N.C. State neighborhood, Rato had about shot his bolt.

Home, the deep country, and more long years with his mother were staring him hard in the face. And while it wasn't all that bad an outlook, he did want to make one last few days' push to stay in town and keep the gains that a big city gives—excitement to watch, good noise to hear, more stuff than squirrels and foxes to study. It had pretty well come down to asking for Wave's help, so Rato said "Is there any work down at your place?" (Wave had said, a few days ago, that now he was working an early shift at a computer typesetting outfit.)

Wave waited and then said "Don't get me wrong but can you read good?"

"Ain't had a complaint since the third damned grade. What you want me to read? Anything but books—I can't stand a book."

"Oh nothing right now. What I mean is, a typesetter spends his time copying sentences from one piece of paper to a word processor. Could you do that?"

Rato said "You telling me they still have to do it that old way? Where the hell's the progress in that?"

Wave laughed. "Son, it would take a month to tell you." He'd called Rato *son* since the first week he knew him. It just seemed right, though Rato was old enough to be his natural father. Wave hadn't known his own father long enough. He'd been killed in some fast shoot-out with a deputy sheriff when Wave was five, a kind wiry man with a head of tight curls and a sweet gift of harmless practical jokes.

Rato was in no way like Wave's father except in one respect, his stillness. They both had the capacity to sit and watch some part of the world (a little thing nobody else would pause to snapshoot) till it opened up its inmost secret, if it had one. And neither one of them felt the need to report their findings. So Wave had grown a fondness for short doses of Rato's company, nothing intense or worrisome though. Now he said "It's a real small place, full of dumb-ass PhDs that think they're Einstein frosted with Jesus. But they might have some janitorial work, something like that."

Rato stared him down. "I pushed enough broom in my country's service to last me on to the grave and beyond."

"No offense. You asked."

Rato nodded. "I did." Then he sat still to down the remainder of his drink. "See, all it is—I'm aiming to stay here in Raleigh. Get me a job and a little place, maybe room with some quiet guy. Not have to go back to the miserable country and watch leaves develop."

Wave said "I wish I could *see* a leaf, just one more clean leaf."

Rato pointed to the big plate glass behind them. "Step out to the damned campus yonder and look."

Wave sneered. "They're so damned filthy they ain't even green, just a sick yellow-gray."

Rato said "I love them. City leaves deserve extra credit. They got to work harder. Up home they're lazy, get everything free."

Wave said "I was wondering what effect it would have—your sister's husband coming back."

"It don't have to have any effect on me. I'm welcome to be anywhere Wesley is; he said so plainly. I just plan to give them air to breathe."

"They still having trouble?"

"Ask them," Rato said.

Wave said "Cool down. I was just well-wishing."

"They'd be glad to know it. Go tell them so."

Wave laughed. "Thank you, no. I'll give it to her though, your sister is a lovely lady."

"Glad you noticed. I didn't know you'd seen that much of my sister."

Wave said "I haven't. Just two or three minutes—it don't take long. She shines out fast."

"She's naturally kind. Like natural curly hair. All her life and mine, Rosacoke has been kind from the roots of her hair."

"Rosa*coke?*" Wave asked.

"That's her full official name."

"Where the hell did that come from?"

Rato said "From God to our mother—you know, inspiration. But she dropped the *coke* when she moved here to town. Too country, I guess."

Wave smiled and nodded. "People might have thought she was dealing drugs. Just yesterday out here on Hillsboro Street, I saw a black dude in a big limousine with guess-what license plate?—S-M-A-C-K."

Rato said "Like I said though, my sister is *kind*."

"And she's been well paid, far as I can see."

Rato flushed. "What the hell does that mean? She don't work for pay. She's had real pain—a baby born dead after one live boy."

Wave said "I'm sorry. And I didn't mean money. I mean she has won her a happy life. I thought she had; now you say otherwise. I bow to your wisdom."

Again Rato took one of his pauses, time enough for atoms to race back and forth from pole to pole a few dozen times, making unseen auroras in the gloom of Greenland. Then he leaned forward. "Listen, how does this sound? If I head home in a week or so, would you come by the house the last night for supper? A little kind of party, my way to thank Rosa for letting me stay?—I'll buy all the food. Course I'll probably stay on."

Wave thought it through, then smiled sincerely. He knew Rato would have to leave soon. "If your folks don't mind, I'd be real honored."

Rato said "Anything I want is fine by them."

Wave said "I thought your sister had been kind of sick."

"Nervous, not sick—just from Wesley being gone."

Wave said "I thought you moved up to join her once she got sick."

It didn't raise any suspicion in Rato. "I never said that. You must have dreamed it."

Wave waited, then laughed much longer than he planned. "I dream so much I sometimes wonder if I'm ever awake."

Rato met his eyes head-on, then leaned closer quick and pressed a long fingernail hard in Wave's wrist. "Feel that?" he said.

Wave drew back. *"Yes."*

"You're awake now at least."

Wave said "I hope."

The same afternoon awhile past five, the spring light was holding at the rim of the sky; and the younger boys at Wesley's garage were dropping their equipment and heading home. His old boss Bronny walked up to Wesley, who was tuning a Volvo, and asked if he'd join him for a beer across the road?

Wesley said "Sure. Just give me ten minutes."

Bronny said "No longer. That woman can wait."

"I promised her I'd have it ready today. She's leaving for a wedding tomorrow at nine."

Bronny said "Yeah, her own—her own third, ain't it? You'd be doing both her and the guy a favor if you quit here and now, with the damned thing broke."

Wesley laughed but Bronny left him. And in another half-hour he'd finished the job, washed up, and was sitting with Bronny in the cool dim back of the Top Hat Lounge. Bronny had ordered Michelob, his idea of the finest in European beers; Wesley was nursing a double Jack Daniel's on the rocks. After two long draws, Bronny said "It looks like you're deep back in the groove and happy—am I wrong?"

Wesley said "I'm grateful to you for the raise. There's some few things I'm glad to have back. But Bron, I left here feeling cold dead. I won't lie to you and say that's changed."

Bronny pressed a dark enormous finger against the back of Wesley's hand. Blood flushed out of place. The flesh shone livid. Then the accustomed red streamed back. Bronny said "That's a test for life. You pass, flying colors."

Wesley smiled and pressed both palms to his temples. "The dead's up here between my ears."

Bronny asked "Since when were you any big genius? You live in your hands like me, not your brain. You're younger than me but you're still, what?—fifty?—and the store's shutting down. Got to slow down your dreams."

Wesley nodded. "I've got dreams old as my eyes, older than any cell alive in my body. I need one thing fulfilled at least. Then I'll shut up and die like everybody else."

Bronny said "Will you tell me?—that last thing you need."

Wesley said "Then give me your flat Bible oath, deep secret or death."

Bronny nodded in silence.

Wesley said "I need a strong woman maybe twenty-three. She'd work at home, keeping everything straight—no kids, just stuff: nice clean useful stuff. Good wholesome plain American food, no same dish more than once a month except sweet potato pie. Fine sex every night with a low light burning in the bathroom maybe—a good hour's worth, both of us repaid. Then the lights go out, I say my prayers, she tells me—I think her name may be Sandy—every last lie I need to hear. She makes it sound sincere as scripture, I trust every word, I sleep like a three-year-old and rise strong and rested to live more days like my best boyhood. That strong, that certain Wesley knows his way, that proud he's satisfied God and his family and will still not fail."

"That who you left in Nashville?"

Wesley's face clouded over.

"—Sandy, the girl? Is that who you lived with all those weeks?"

Wesley had to wonder. But he answered truly. "Some parts of her, yes. Her real name was Wilson. Wilson had some things I never saw matched—the sex part at first was like sweet magic: night, dawn, noon (if we got a day off). Wilson knew ways to lie there, facing my eyes, or even better ways to get up and *work*—ways I pray I never forget but can't never hope to meet again, not in this world. But then she stopped on a damned cold dime. The first day of spring I reached over to her and, Bron, she had *quit*. She said she quit lying, the real girl Wilson."

Bronny said "How'd you know?"

"She told me so. Said she'd been giving in to help me 'recover,' said now I'd need to manage myself. 'Work out your own cure—you're too old a guy to be rooting in just my skin for salvation.' Lying there that instant, my hand in her hair, I knew she was right. And it hurt worse than stabbing. I tucked tail and came on back here fast."

"I wondered what brought you."

Wesley nodded. "That was it." He hadn't yet mentioned the rape to anybody.

"And you're meaning to stay?"

"I don't think of anywhere else right now."

Bronny frowned. "I was hoping home had got some better."

Wesley said "Don't lose a good minute on me. I can still tighten bolts good as I ever did. I just can't face up to being grown. See, nobody but me ever knew how high I aimed—for happiness, I mean. Not money or power, nothing like that. Just a steady perfectly happy ride for my body, right on through this life to Paradise."

Bronny laughed. "Anybody ever get it? Anybody you've watched?"

"Course not," Wesley said. "I told you I was crazy."

"Then why not give up, admit you're normal, set back here with that fine wife you've got, and count your blessings once a year at Thanksgiving?"

Wesley nodded but then faced Bronny gravely. "Because I hurt too goddamned much."

Bronny said "I'm not exactly gliding on morphine. But hell, my mother warned me in the cradle. She said 'Ernest James, your dad and his brothers have ruined every woman's life that ever brushed past them. When you get grown enough to notice girls, remember your mother and let women *be*. They are just human beings, not angels in pearls. They can't make up to you for your bad luck. You'll be damned fortunate if you find one, in all your years, that can softboil an egg right four times in five—much less mend your broke heart every night.' I remembered her too, every word all my life. It saved me a lot."

Wesley smiled "Ernest *James*? Who in God's name is that?"

"The first two-thirds of my whole name. I let it slip out. Tell a soul and I'll kill you."

Wesley said "What you pay me?"

Bronny grinned at first and reached for his wallet, then put it back, and leaned to Wesley's eyes. "I've already give you a priceless gift— my good mother's words. You step on home now and live her advice. You might yet have a nice day or two in the thirty more years you're liable to get above ground."

Wesley said "Is it that long? Please say no."

Bronny said "May be longer, if you don't shape up. Something else Mama said, 'Whom the Lord loves, He kills.'"

Wesley shook his head. "Hot-damn, old Ernest! Your mama shot *straight*."

Bronny stood up to pay. "And is still aiming right this evening at fools. She'll be ninety-six this fourth of July."

"Then God must love her sweet butt to death."

Bronny said "He does. She's been stone-blind for the past ten years. But you knew that."

Wesley shook his head. "I didn't, no sir. I doubt I could have stood it."

Bronny strode on forward to the bleached cashier. "Sure you could. You'll stand far worse and be glad."

They all got home well before dark that evening. Rosa came first and when she had parked in the drive, she took the small bag of groceries and headed for the house before she thought to look. In all the months that Wesley was gone, she'd forced herself not to study home-sights (the details of where they'd spent their life—for instance, the dimestore white azalea that Wesley had brought her the week they moved here; now it was almost a neck-high tree).

But Rosa's right foot caught on a rock. When she paused to gain her balance, she saw the sun in the upstairs back-hall window ablaze. For an instant she thought the house was burning out of control, and for one more instant she felt relief. A leveling fire would bless them all—flush Rato to Afton, force Wesley's hand (to turn loose once for all and leave or to seize hold finally and rebuild a life).

Rosa's eyes brimmed water and the big can of yams in her grocery bag tore through the paper and struck her foot. She hollered "Oh!" and realized then that the fire was mere sunset, a commonplace. Next she thought "Thank God, it's all here—a lifetime's surroundings ready and waiting to work. Now we'll each take hold." By *each* she meant herself and Wesley.

Five minutes later Wesley pulled in behind her, paused at the wheel to spray his mouth with a sweet disguise to hide the bourbon (knowing Rosa still hated even one strong drink, whatever she said; it had killed her father). He tested his breath on the back of a hand, winced at the whorehouse stench, then aimed for the kitchen door. By then the sun had sunk enough to cool the back windows. What showed upstairs were the lamps Rosa had lit just now as she climbed up to change into kitchen clothes.

Wesley suddenly thought of the years he would race home here from work, hoping young Horace would still be playing and that Wesley could stretch out with Rosa ten minutes and fly back in time to their good first days before they stood back up to be parents. Could he do that now? Would his mind give the order and his body obey? Granting all that, would Rosa consent and not just laugh?

He kept on walking in the clean gray gravel. And in three more steps, he was saying again and again to himself Bronny's mother's old words—"You let women be. They are just human people, not angels in pearls." Was a word of it true? And if so, did Wesley want such a world—with no better dream?

Wesley prayed he'd know a workable livable answer by the time he reached for the door. But no he didn't. Still he went on in, with his own old key, and called upstairs to let her hear his voice. "It's nobody else but your old bud."

From somewhere farther away than the moon, what seemed Rosa's young voice said "Dear bud."

Wesley's dry heart leaned toward the flame. But no cell took fire, no answer came—not there or then.

Rato said goodbye to Wave at the corner two blocks away and scuffed on to Rosa and Wesley's in something very much like a trance. He'd counted as a last resort on Wave having job ideas or, at the least, an offer to bunk in with him. But Wave had met him with blank refusal. He'd seemed a real friend, almost like a son. Now Rato had scared him and flushed him off.

That had been the story every time in his life when Rato tried to open up to somebody. Something someway scared them. His strength was too big, or so he suspected. What he hadn't allowed for was another plain fact—that his own big eyes were wide as holes in the ocean floor off the Philippines sucking in all life, all rocks, boats, and whales. People, men especially, scrambled for high ground when Rato got anywhere near serious.

He'd tried fifty-odd years to change the problem—laughing more often, when nothing seemed funny, and letting folks know the last thing Rato needed was human help. But they still ran from him. All right, he'd take that as God's own will.

His mother once asked him not to get married. He didn't ask why at the time and had never asked since. She was bound to have had her own good reason (she never asked anything big without reason, generally good). When he got back home this time however, he'd ask her at last—*just tell me why*. And unless she barked back or sang a long stanza of partridge calls, Rato knew he'd obey. He was not a real human, not yet in this world.

But a voice said his name. "Horatio Junior Mustian."

Rato stopped—Wesley combed, clean, and dressed on his front-door stoop with *The Raleigh Times*.

Wesley also said "You look kind of lost."

Rato said "I'm not. I know my place."

Wesley said "Tell me mine."

"That's your next problem," Rato said, "nobody else's."

Wesley walked on to meet him and hugged his thin chest with one long arm.

Over his shoulder, from Wesley's mouth, Rato thought he could hear Wesley's deep voice whisper something like "Guess though. Guess where I belong. Please guess hard now. Help any way you can. It's got that bad."

Rato was confident he understood the words—Wesley was howling an S.O.S., something he'd never done in Rato's hearing in all the past years. Rato couldn't guess why though or what would help. His own hands stayed flat down at his sides. And in his natural voice at normal volume, he said "Just tell me what you want and when."

Wesley said "Take over, Ace. You lead from here."

Rato said "Then Jesus, we're blind in the night."

Wesley stepped back, turned loose of Rato's arm, and stared. Then he burst onto one long high laughing note.

By then Rosa had opened the front door behind them on the porch. She asked "Anybody but me bad hungry?"

Both men turned to face her, and Rato said "I may have to fall down here till you feed me with some kind of tube."

Wesley said "We both need you to save us."

Rosa smiled in their faces and said "All right." Her lean chin nodded again and again, the same agreement they'd seen her give throughout their lives when people (sometimes the two of them) needed her skills as badly as now.

Rato stepped forward, drawing Wesley behind. By the time they reached the screen door and entered, the last weak light had soaked back into the sky, and night swept up around all their tired legs.

In his own room two hours later than that, Wave lay in the dark and stared at a large hole of black night beyond him—his one clear window. He somehow knew that Rosa and Wesley, and Rato beside them, were still at their dining table still talking. He went on to think they would soon join hands and sing one song, not a hymn but some sweet statement of their care. They'd never have done it—Rato couldn't sing "Jesus Loves Me," much less harder songs—but the thought alone was sufficient to ease Wave off into sleep.

Fully dressed on top of his light army blanket, he slept five hours without turning once. Two or three times he spoke strange sentences plainly to the ceiling and woke himself briefly, long enough to realize he'd either said nonsense or told his dark secret to the walls and the window—that no man but Wave in all this state could serve lone women as fine as he, with his nice brand of tender care.

Then at one in the morning, Wave woke fully rested but chilly. He sat straight up. Rosa's face swam up at once in his head. He wanted above all things on earth to see her now and make up to her for all she'd suffered, all the world had kept from her.

He couldn't imagine how to break through the circles of guards that kept her—Rato in his room, yards down the hall, and Wesley right by her (he couldn't cut or kill; Wave had never cut yet).

But his wish was so strong, it took him to the street and in sight again of Rosa and Wesley and Rato's house—medium size and in need of paint—before he pulled up and saw his error. *This woman is happy. She's chosen her life and is glad to have it. Or it's chose her and she's bowed to take it.*

Wave had not shed actual tears since childhood; he shed none yet though his eyes felt full. Was his whole life wrong, founded on some sad or ridiculous mistake? What if the whole world out there, including all women, was happier than Wave? What if Wave was just one lonesome ludicrous clown out by himself in the cooling dark night acting on a simple boyhood mistake that everyone but he had long since corrected?

He still hadn't wept, not actual tears. But he couldn't have bet you his head wouldn't burst—in a screaming utterly silent explosion—in the next few seconds leaving Waverly Wilbanks no longer alive and present as a friend and no one noticing the hole he'd left or caring at least.

ROSA WESLEY

Five nights later at half-past eleven, Rosa climbed to their room, scrubbed her face, and was in her gown and robe before Wesley joined her. She'd spent a good part of the past few days thinking through her campus talk with Jean. Jean had even tried to keep up the sales pitch for Wesley. But Rosa had asked her to pull back please—she needed quiet air to test her own feelings and choose her own path. Jean had gladly agreed, saying only one more thing— "Don't even dream of finding another man that sweet to be around, that tried and true. They threw away the mold in 1945."

And by now it had come down pretty much to just that. If Rosa hung onto Wesley, and he to her, time might well be expected to sweeten their bodies again for one another. But *tried and true?* They'd sure God tried each other all their lives and might well have thought there were no surprises. But there were. Oh Jesus, there were awful shocks. And in all the problems the world could throw you, a surprise—anything from telephone reminders that you've missed a PTA meeting to announcements of death—was what Rosa dreaded most. She was living proof that a woman can walk into the house one evening to find it dark and cold and vacant, your long-trusted mate speeding west for Nashville and (whether he knows it or not) a young radiologist with fresh gifts to give him.

How could that be counted as something *true?* How could any such human be trusted again, much less lain down beside every night—even if he was the veteran of all you'd felt and done since early childhood? Maybe trust wasn't something anybody ever had a right to feel. Maybe all you could hope for was strength and courage and a steady share of luck.

One thing seemed sure—the rape hadn't made Rosa dread him or anyone except the sick rapist. She hadn't felt powerful bodily need for any known man in maybe ten years. That need has just slid from her for no visible cause. If Wesley badly needed to rekindle that, Rosa truly guessed he was welcome to try; she'd cooperate to the limits of her mind and present body. If a better life—deeper truth and trust—flowed forward from that, then praise all the angels, praise God (day or dark)!

By the time Rosa worked her way that far, she was sitting in the little straight chair she'd brought to Raleigh from her childhood bedroom, her grandfather's dark oak corner-chair (all rounds and slats, no foolish springs or stuffing and padding). She picked up *Quiet Time* from a low table, the devotional magazine that Mama gave her every year for her birthday—a scripture passage and a half-page meditation for each day. Rosa seldom kept up. In fact she hadn't so much as opened this month's copy yet.

Today's Bible verse was "Jesus wept," the shortest verse in either testament. When she was a girl, kids used it in Sunday school for all grades of fun—comic rhymes for instance. Milo could spin them out for the best part of a Sunday.

> *Jesus wept,*
> *Peter crept,*
> *Moses came a-crawling.*
> *Adam slept,*
> *Eve leapt,*
> *Cain came caterwauling.*

That night's meditation acknowledged that the verse had been cause for fun through centuries past but that now it was time for every believer to pause a long while and think of the meaning.

"Jesus weeps at the grave of his friend Lazarus. He weeps though

He knows that, in a moment, He will raise His friend from the stench of death into radiant life. It is the only time in the gospels when Jesus is shown to sorrow. Elsewhere He shows anger or consternation that evil has gained access to human flesh; but only here does he pay the tribute of tears, the fruit of love.

"Later, in the cool dark of Gethsemane when He foresees tomorrow's hot dust with the crowd jeering and cold spikes pounded through His tender flesh, He does not weep. In full awareness that tomorrow He must suffer, as hard as any man or woman ever, what rolls down is not tears but sweat, sweat like drops of blood streaks His flesh. The mystery in that! Tears for a friend who suffered death but will rise again, sweat for Himself who will die and rise. The fruit of sorrow, the fruit of labor—our deepest glimpses of what He paid to save all souls."

Wesley stepped on past her to the bathroom and brushed his teeth, gargled, combed his hair. By the time he was ready, Rosa had set her book down. Wesley stepped again past her to finish undressing. And again he took no notice of her, neither looking nor speaking—neat as she was.

In fifteen seconds he was bare before her, and he held there a minute—not preening or even aware of her eyes but wholly absorbed in a spot on his forearm. He finally licked at it lightly with short strokes of what seemed the tip of a puppy's pink tongue. Then he reached into his drawer, got a clean white T-shirt that once had been Horace's, and pulled it on. On the back it had Rosa's favorite message of all—

> If you love good music,
> Follow me home—

and he stepped toward the left-hand side of the bed. Rosa had already stood to follow before he turned to speak. But when his eyes met her, Wesley said anyhow "You planning on getting tired any night soon?"

Rosa said "No sir, I was coming for the music."

He didn't catch her meaning at first.

She pointed, "I mean your T-shirt. I'm following you home."

By then Wesley had thrown all the cover back. You could plainly see he was thinking of *home*. Was this really home she'd followed him to, his home anyhow? But suddenly he faced her from the edge of the mattress, pulled the hem of his shirt down in front, and blinked at her shyly. "I'd have dressed up better for a real lady-guest if you'd warned me you were here."

"I hoped I wasn't that much of a lady."

He was honestly baffled. "Why would you say that?"

"I sometimes think I hurt us with that, all my sense of what's fitting and right. I never was sure I could do it sincerely, be that easy at night with you."

Wesley waited awhile. "Oh no ma'm, you were — sincere all right. Eleanor Roosevelt was white trash next to you."

What could Rosa do but grin or run?

Before she could bolt though, Wesley laughed and climbed in the sheets and covered his body right to the chin.

Wesley stayed shy in the face, looking down. Steadily he moved from joking to gravity. Rosa's upright pride and dignity were things he'd also admired and sought in her. What was she meaning here now — cut and run? Was she saying they ought to bail out this Friday and drive to that sex motel near High Point and rent a big room with closed-circuit television, video porn, and maybe some hot deals with other starved couples to right and left?

Even though they never planned to try for more children or go to church regularly, Wesley knew he would hate it now if Rosa tried to rip out the broad base of decency they'd stood on. He couldn't even dream of a Rosa in make-up and crotchless panties from Frederick's of Hollywood (with all-night Saigon ticklers for Wesley to use by hand while he lay here lonesome and sad and watched her writhe). He said "Rosa, hush up and step on to bed." But he didn't turn the cover back and wave with his palm.

Rosa studied him in place for what seemed upward of half a minute. The front of his T-shirt was blank but clean (no other known housewife ironed T-shirts). Still she knew the back — *Good music . . . follow me*. Wasn't that what he'd said always since the Sunday she saw him up the tree staring off? — and not with his own voice but in some silent message from the empty air around him. Wesley was a promise and had evermore been. A promise of what? Well, she still didn't know. She had never really figured in nearly forty years. And had never really asked. Rosa couldn't stand here now and ask outright.

That left two choices. She could dress again warmly and leave for good. There were probably as many jobs for good secretaries in Nashville, or Charleston, as for good mechanics—well-combed women of the sad damned school that would water the office plants and cook for the Christmas parties on top of every well-spelled word she typed. Or else she could strip off further still and join that mainly strange man beyond her, begging her presence for his own secret need.

So eventually she did take the first step toward him. She switched off all the lights, laid her robe on the chair, and made a slow chilly way forward into cold cotton sheets till the zone of Wesley's established warmth broadcast through space and found her skin—just the warmth, no touch.

Rosa had time alone to say her night prayers. They were mostly calm requests for her mother as the one lone person in her family tonight. In the silence that followed, she could hear Wesley's body beside her awake. She figured it was she that would now have to talk. He was trapped as usual in his own natural quiet. But their hall door was still wide open, and next she heard Rato's big footsteps outside. His television was finished.

He paused by their door and listened for life or the rhythms of sleep.

Wesley was finally the one who spoke. "Hey, bud."

Rato said "Y'all asleep?"

Wesley said "For hours."

Rato said "Sleep on" and moved toward his room.

But Rosa said "Come back, hon. We're wide awake." She wondered if she'd ever called him *hon* before. Would he take offense or notice?

He noticed. He waited awhile and then began buzzing loudly like a bee. "Bzzzz."

Finally Wesley asked "What the hell is that?"

Rato said "I'm just cooking Rosa more honey."

Wesley said "Good business. Then you won't need me." He began to snore.

Rosa said "You two please hush; it's *night*. Rato, you got something to tell me or what?"

Rato said "Both of you. I'm leaving here soon."

Wesley said "No you ain't" and snored again.

Rosa said "Rato, why?"

"I got to head home."

"Something calling you there?" Rosa's voice by then was genuinely urgent.

"Nearest thing to home *I've* got, I guess." Rato was the last man alive who could say such words with no trace of self-pity.

Wesley said "You can live here long as I'm here." He meant it entirely.

Rosa said "Me too." And to her surprise, she was serious also. The peculiar brother who had been her good watchdog was suddenly now her friend and companion, a sure thing to lean on.

Rato said "Look, I've thought about it long as you two. I'm a retired U.S. soldier-boy and Afton's my address. Afton, N.C. is where the Army sends my check. If they come looking, they plan to find me there."

Wesley said "They won't come, Ace. They've used you up—you and me both, believe it. They're looking for men a lot younger than us."

Rosa smiled in the dark at both of them using the service for excuses. She said "Mama's making out all right alone."

Rato said "I ain't even studying Mama. God help the rapist that stumbles on Mama."

All three of them were struck dumb by that.

But Wesley broke the silence. He burst out laughing and the other two joined him.

Rato said "Wonder where he is right now?"

Wesley said "Out yonder in the bushes, hearing us."

Rosa said "Poor boy."

Rato said "I always thought he was grown."

Rosa said "Maybe so. He's a man anyhow; he sure was no lady." She could even laugh again.

Rato said "I can't find a job down here."

Wesley said "You ain't looked."

"I have, a long time. Nothing's turned up but pin boy at the bowling alley. And pin boys don't really work anymore; machines set the pins. They're just guys policing the floor backstage, picking up all the shit people throw with the balls—excuse me, Rosacoke" (excuse the word *shit*).

"Excused," she said.

Wesley said "I might could help you downtown."

Rato waited again. "Thank you, hear? But look, I worked a good hard thirty years for my country. Look how good a shape the damned country's in. The last thing my pride needs now is the minimum wage for a job some teenager dying of acne needs lot worse than me."

It was the nearest anybody had ever come to hearing Rato admit publicly how his strangeness affected the world's opinion of him. Rosa was too puzzled to respond. But Wesley said "You are a fine ranger."

Rato said "Beg your pardon?"

"—Forest Ranger, old Smoky the Bear."

Rato said "That I am. Can't say that I love it."

Rosa asked "How much you think we love our work—typing letters, tuning cars?"

Rato said "You don't?"

Wesley said "You'll notice I ain't gone wild with excitement. If I never had to touch one more sick Porsche, I wouldn't miss a beat."

Rato asked "Where would you rather be?"

Wesley didn't speak so Rosa said "I could be happy in my mother's house, once she's gone to Heaven, raising most of our food and watching the sky slide through a year's changes."

Wesley still didn't speak so Rato said "Wesley, you ain't said."

Wesley laughed. "I take what the Lord sends down."

Rato said "You ran."

Again they all were struck dumb. This time they knew they'd heard real judgment from the only one present who was fit to judge, a true bystander who (far as they knew) had never hurt one human soul for one instant. At last Wesley said "—Ran like a shot dog, then turned and came back."

"Ran from what?" Rato said. He was asking out of pure curiosity now with no trace of malice. They all understood.

So Wesley said "Rato, I was scared to death. Maybe scared of death. I'm three-fourths there anyhow; we all are—fifty's three-fourths of seventy on anybody's scale."

Rato said "Just about." When they'd all paused again, he said "I'll get the bus late tomorrow morning."

"No you won't," Wesley said. "The least I can do is drive you home Sunday. Please let me do that."

"Me too," Rosa said. "The bus is too sad."

Rato said "I've met a lot of girls on buses."

Wesley said "Well, now we don't want to butt in if you've got a hot plan."

Rato said "I'm joking. A ride would be nice."

Rosa said "I'll pack us a picnic lunch so Mama won't go into a big cooking tizzy."

Rato said "You do and you'll ruin her week. You know that's all she's living for now."

Rosa said "That's one place I learned we were wrong. Notice how very much Mama's liked these months of not having to feed."

Rato said "O.K." but he didn't sound pensive. He said "Good night, hear? And thank you both."

Wesley said "For what? It's us that thank you."

Rato said "I'm thanking you for all this much time in town. I've learned some things."

Wesley said "Name two."

Rosa said "No don't. We'll all be a lot better off with sleep."

Rato said "Maybe so. Good night again, hear?"

Wesley said "We hear you. Go get yourself dark."

Rosa heard that it was the most times Wesley had ever said *we* in his life. And calm as they were, it came as a shock. By the time she'd recovered, Rato was gone; and nothing else seemed important to say.

In a minute Wesley rolled to his left side, facing her. But still he didn't reach out or touch her skin at any point. He listened for a hint of sound from her, then he asked "That suit you?—what we just said?"

"I think so, yes."

"You want him to leave?"

Rosa said "I wouldn't need to put it that way. But I see what he means about his chances for work. And he couldn't stand to have us support him now. Long as he was guarding me, he let me keep him."

"I could leave again."

Rosa was also facing him. Even dark, she could see the dim lines of his features. "I won't ask that, just to keep a brother."

Wesley said "I'm absolutely serious. Understand me."

Nothing in his flat tone gave her the handholds to grasp a complete meaning. Was he claiming he needed to leave again? Was it that easy for him—to take *Go* or *Stay*, whichever she demanded? Eventually she said "No I don't understand. Can you go that easy?"

He said "Rosacoke, I think this is home. When I came back last month, I couldn't say that. Tonight though I almost think I can. It don't make me all that happy to admit it. It's not the real best I've dreamed to have; and whether you believe it or not, I've *dreamed*. I know that can't make you glad to hear. The trouble's not you, not the main part at least. The trouble's just life, the way it's made and *me* made in it—the turns I took and can't correct. With my mind now though, the way you've trained me, I don't think I can strike out and find better. That may mean I love you and that this must be home."

She thought "That's the longest speech he's ever made near me." And at first it promised to be a good thing, a new brand of freedom. But then she realized she'd heard two things. One was fine, the verge of a firm commitment for the rest of their lives. The other was as bad as she'd dreaded since Christmas week, the honest confession that what they'd had was not just imperfect but less than sufficient. To face Wesley now and accept all he'd said was somehow to lay down everything she'd fought for in knowing him and struggling to keep him. She faced the blank ceiling and waited for words. Not a clear true word rose up through her mind.

Wesley waited, slid into wheezing sleep (which Rosa could hear), then woke again to hear that she was silent. His brain's own clock couldn't tell if he'd lain there a minute or thirty. So he said "You still haven't said *Go* or *Stay*."

She told herself "If you cry now I'll kill you dead." But she said to Wesley "Better stay on tonight. I need to pause here. Tomorrow, or some sane day soon now, we both may have to pack up and go into separate rooms. I simply never heard your feelings before, not as clear as you laid them out just now. I've got to be sure I understood you right. Then I've got to be sure I can live with the meaning."

Wesley said "You sure my meaning is all that different from yours?"

"I think so, yes. I think it's got to be. It *has* been all these years anyhow."

Wesley said "Mine too. That's the main thing I said. I think—and hope—I can trim my sails and live like a human, not an angel on fire gazing off toward God."

Rosa said "Is that it? Maybe so. Oh Lord. I know I've felt on fire a lot."

"And burned, third degree."

Rosa nodded. "You too?"

"No you. I've watched you close, don't forget."

Rosa said "You're bound to have hurt."

Wesley said "Oh sure. But slower."

"Maybe deeper."

"I won't swap scars," he said. "It won't make sense."

Rosa touched him then—not thinking and never again knowing why. She'd been on her back; and when she turned, her left hand was uppermost. It went to his right shoulder and stroked him gently there.

At first he was startled, but then he lay still and waited for her gesture to clarify. In a minute he'd calmed to the point where he dreamed he had a fine tattoo under her palm, a sizable tiger stretched on the ground of Wesley's still-taut white hide. For so many years it had felt alone and not realized the danger in that. Now it roused and met Rosa and welcomed her notice.

Then for the first time in all his years with women, Wesley lay on quiet and let Rosa work her own slow will—partly because he started so tired but also because he was gambling there might be something to learn.

Rosa didn't share the hope. She'd learned all this, every move and sound, in her bedtime thoughts and dreams long ago. These were the ways she'd always loved Wesley, in her mind at least. The main thing she made was slow circles, small circles with her hand and (though she could only see a little) the syllables of tranquil comment and assurance that are most men's favorite of the sounds on earth.

She didn't assume he would somehow ignite and take over from her. She just kept going and he kept lying there. They'd got to a place that amazed them both, of mutual trust and precise alignment— lovely harmony and perfect rhythm.

And somehow they both moved on into sleep. In both their cases, it was sleep so profound their minds heard nothing from the house or street. Neither one knew a single thought or dream.

And when, blocks away, Wave Wilbanks woke suddenly, he sat bolt upright in hot stale sheets and said their full names in one short prayer. It was prayer for their life together hereafter, and it served to deepen the rest they'd earned tonight and enjoyed.

ROSA WESLEY RATO
HORACE PRIS WILSON

The next weekend—the last in April—Horace called from Charlotte on Saturday morning while Rosa, Wesley, and Rato were finishing breakfast. Because Rosa was cooking a last round of pancakes, Wesley was forced to answer the ring (he'd rather have drunk rat bane than answer a telephone). He said "Hey, son" and several other pleasantries, then "Sure" several times, and finally "Plan to stay for supper. Drive careful, hear?" He sat down again without comment, and stubborn Rosa decided not to ask.

Rato broke down finally. "Who else is coming to supper? And is it today?"

Wesley ate a whole mouthful before he said "Horace and, I think he said, Pris. They're leaving now and said they'd be here in maybe three hours. That'd be one o'clock."

Since they hadn't let him buy the groceries, Rato knew he lacked the right to object. But he did think how they would complicate the evening, his last one in Raleigh. Rosa had planned him a farewell supper, and he'd invited Wave (Wave's first meal here). Well, Rosa could handle it all someway.

Rosa had not returned to the table. She was still at the stove, cleaning up there. But finally she couldn't restrain her anger. "I sure do

wish you'd asked my opinion. I've already got to shop and cook for
Rato's farewell supper tonight, and now two extra mouths to feed—
one of them, that Pris! I'd rather cook for the baboon-squad at the
N.C. Zoo than that mean-mouthed bitch."

Wesley shot a look to Rato. They both raised their eyebrows—having grown up in homes where, whatever you thought of your kin, you
never spoke quite that frankly about them. Wesley though was the
first one to laugh.

Rosa said "She is. You prove I'm wrong."

Wesley said "I'm not her lawyer, no ma'm. I'll grant you Pris is no
tender shrinking vine. But our only son married her. What choice
have we got?"

Rosa said "—The choice I've made all year, when Horace kindly
volunteered to come and help me. I told him I'd handle my trouble
in place. I didn't have to say 'Without your spouse.' Horace knows I
tried to like his pick. But who, in their right mind, could warm up to
Pris? Hell, a polar bear doesn't crave warmth that much."

Even Rato broke down then and laughed. "Don't worry. Pris
knows you're more than her match. If they do stay for supper, you'll
hold her down. Wave'll think she's just a clean dog in a muzzle."

And Rosa had got to the point of a smile. "Pris has always been
respectful to me. If they stay, I trust she'll act all right."

Wesley said "Remind me to lay in some booze."

Rato said "Since Wave is my guest, I'll contribute. He likes foreign
beer." That meant a real outlay, maybe Heinekens. Never mind.
Wave had thoroughly earned it.

Rosa said "I'll put my foot down now. That way, nobody gets mad
later on. You can bring in maybe a case of beer, nothing too expensive. But stronger than that, we better not go. I'm not slaving my
lovely bubbies all day over this hot stove for a table of drunks. Anybody not sober enough to taste my cooking, can get up and walk. I
serve notice now."

Wesley said "Understood" and winked at Rato.

Six hours later they were all back there together in the kitchen.
Horace had kept Pris downtown shopping from two till four. Rosa was

laying out supper supplies. The men were drinking beer at the table. Pris was serving the nachos she'd just learned to make from *Family Circle*, a big success.

Rato said "I learned to love spice in Spain. I can't see why it don't work in America."

Pris said "It does now, at my house anyhow."

Horace said "She's got me *massaged* in garlic. I can't see how I grew up without it."

Rosa said "Well, you did. Somehow against all odds you survived. And look at you now, strong and healthy to watch."

For an instant, pure misery swept through Horace's eyes. Not only had his whole childhood been darkened by the fact that a sister younger than he had been born dead; but once he'd quit college, gone to work, and found a classy wife, then his wife and mother hated each other. And *hated* was not too strong a word. Whenever they were apart (which he arranged to be more than a hundred percent of the time), they each survived by pretending that the other one didn't exist. But when he couldn't help bringing them to the same room, then he had to face truths about humanity that nearly stove him in.

Horace had his father's gentle heart. He couldn't imagine jealousy this harsh. What was in such short supply in his heart that two smart women had to fight like Siamese fish in a bowl to get their threatened portion? He knew he'd never find out. And anyhow he and Pris would be leaving shortly. So Horace took his old way out. He grinned and said "The women in my life have kept me hopping. I'm grateful to them both." He bowed to Pris and then to Rosa.

They each eyed each other—noticing the order of his recognition—then bowed back to Horace. And Pris said "Glad I made up the pallet."

Wesley said "Beg your pardon?"

"A pallet in the car, for Sabu to sleep on the back seat homeward." Sabu was Pris and Horace's dog, a King Charles spaniel that Roger hoped to eat. She'd left it in the car to help keep peace but found a way every hour or so to remind everybody of her sacrifice. She bent herself double to see out the window; it was almost dusk. She said "Who is this eating dinner with y'all?"

Rosa said "A very rich friend of my brother's."

Rato looked to his sister, unbelieving.

But Rosa shot him a smiling signal, *"Hush!"* She knew how Pris worshiped money in her life. Then Rosa thought "Oh Lord, now she might stay." So she added "Course he won't come into his trust fund till when, Rato?—ten years?"

Rato said "Twenty-odd. He's flat-broke still. That explains the bugs."

Pris went lilac-colored at the ears but Horace said "Bugs?"

Wesley said "Rato doesn't mean real bugs. His hair does look like it's got legs though."

Rato said "I'm not sure what I mean." But he left it at that.

Pris began to rise. She brushed herself off carefully in place, then headed briskly for an upstairs bathroom where she suspected no visitors went.

And Rato, for his own unexplained reasons, all but ran out the back.

By then Wesley, Rosa, and Horace were seated at the kitchen table. Horace said "We'll need to get on the road, got just tomorrow to rest up in, then work again Monday."

Wesley smiled "Like everybody else on earth. You all that tired?"

Horace said "No sir, I didn't mean that. I just meant I didn't want to drive past midnight."

Rosa said "We well understand that, son. You've got no need to feel guilty with us. You've been a good boy. You don't owe us one single thing more."

As if his mother had tripped a switch he'd dreaded all day, a gallon of blood flushed through Horace's face. A vigorous red, then a strangulated purple—it passed through the visible stages of health. Then he finally said "You both look safe. Am I right or wrong?"

Baffled thoroughly, Wesley looked to Rosa. "You feeling in danger?"

Rosa smiled "Not a lot." Horace was one more person who didn't know about the rape.

Wesley said "Me neither. What you talking about, son?"

Horace's blush had calmed a little but renewed itself now. "I meant are you two feeling good together? You've been back under the same roof now for—what?—four weeks. Is it going to take? Have I got my parents back together again, or are you two staking out separate tents?"

Rosa wanted to answer quickly "Parents, two of them, back together." But something kept her silent, waiting.

So in his own time, Wesley said "I think this tent'll be big enough. Don't you, Mom?"

Horace grinned. "Outstanding."

But Rosa was staring seriously at Wesley. "Please never call me *Mom* again. I've asked you before. I'm Horace's mother, nobody else's yet."

Wesley nodded. "*I'm* ready. We still got the crib." He wasn't being cruel. The dead little girl was so far behind them, and they'd talked so long about other solutions. "Call the orphanage Monday."

Even Rosa could smile. "Maybe this tent does need a big annex—a few concubines, years younger than me."

Pris was back in the door, hair sprayed again—a hard-sugar helmet—and a clean new white blouse stiff at her neckline (she always brought an overnight bag of changeables, in case of filth or perspiration or a big change of mood). "There haven't been concubines since the Old Testament."

"There may be again though," Wesley said. "Any day, here and now. Brace yourself and come on forward toward me. My first wife just now give her permission which is all it takes, in the Bible at least."

Pris looked to Horace with a taut sick grin.

But Horace was already rising to leave. He'd grown up here; and he liked his parents, especially his father (a kind burdened man). But the wife Horace chose and all but worshiped was made for a better world than this—different at least, according to her. All her dreams were of order, of cut-glass chandeliers, mint-green velvet rugs, and everybody dressed for the hour of the day. It was time to rescue Pris and drive her and Sabu home to Charlotte. He and she both were prepared to work hard years—ten, twenty, thirty till arthritis crushed them—to buy their tickets toward her brand of taste.

When they'd said goodbye to Horace and Pris and were still in the yard, Wesley turned to Rosa. "I'm going to run in and buy me some magazines. Anything you need to get for the supper?"

She said "Bring me something decent to read."

"Whoa, what would that be? Most reading's indecent these days— whole point about reading."

Rosa said "How about *Southern Living?*"

Wesley said "That's decent but tame as hell, recipes and how to restore your old johnny-house."

"Bring it anyhow. I'll stay out of trouble."

He asked Rato when the friend was due.

"Six o'clock. He'll be here early though."

Wesley checked his watch. "Then I'll beat him back. Wouldn't want him to feel like he didn't have a host."

Wesley wished they hadn't but Rosa and Rato stood there to watch him out of sight as if he might be going for good. The whole point of the errand was, he wasn't. He was making the last arrangement to stay. And only that certainty made him push on through this little last afternoon deceit.

He stopped quickly at a newsstand near N.C. State, picked up fifteen dollars worth of magazines, and rushed on into the middle of town (near Capitol Square) to a pay phone he'd checked out the previous Friday. You couldn't see it easily from the street, and Wesley had laid in a big lot of change. As the number rang the first time, he did what he'd hardly planned to do—for whatever reasons, he prayed she'd be there.

It seemed she wasn't or the number had been changed. A strange woman answered and repeated the number.

He said "Look, I'm trying to get up with Wilson."

She said "Who are you?"

"An old friend, Wesley in North Carolina."

She said "Hey there" and yes, it was Wilson.

"Boy, you sure don't sound like the Wilson I knew."

She laughed a dry cough; had she started back smoking? "Maybe that's because I'm not. Leave me alone and I go all strange. You're not the first guy to run across that."

"Nor the last," Wesley said.

That was her turn to say "Look, what's the problem? I don't want to sit here and ruin a nice memory. You got something kind to say, say it or let's quit."

"You got you some company?"

"I'm curling hair," she said. "But just for tonight. Me and Eunice Dean are supervising permanents on each other's heads."

"I bet you look grand."

"And you win!" Wilson said. "By dark I'll look like a million in cash."

Wesley said "It's pretty here, a long bright Saturday."

"That's nice to know."

Then he couldn't think further. He forgot the reason he'd gone to these lengths.

Wilson still remembered him well enough to know that, if she was ever going to get back to curling hair, she'd have to spring his trap. She said "You miss me?"

That did it. In his mind Wesley felt a strong click as his meaning cleared up. "Wilson, I missed you before I ever left. I'll miss you every day long as I live."

"It's fun to hear," she said. "And I'm grateful. But don't overdo it. Your brain's got to have other memories by now."

Wesley said "It does. What I mean is, there'll be whole sets of minutes every day when I think of you as one real blessing in my sad life."

"That's so sweet, Wesley—you could've called collect!"

He laughed edgily. "It's every word true. But beyond it I also got to be honest. I'll be staying on here at home in my old stable."

Wilson said "I understood that. It's no kind of shock."

"I just didn't want it to be. I felt like the decent thing was to tell you myself."

In her privacy in Nashville, Wilson smiled to herself (even Eunice Dean near her couldn't have seen it). But she said "You were decent right along. I won't forget that. And you gave me eight or ten pictures yourself that'll stay with me always."

"I hope I did. It's about all any old boy can hope."

In an unguarded attempt to quit, Wilson said "So if you're back up here anytime, give me a ring for auld lang syne."

Wesley said "I won't be. Not unless I wake up one dreadful day turned overnight to a country-music star."

Wilson laughed. "I'll sit here waiting for that!"

"You do," he said. And his errand was ended. As he headed on to Rosa, he felt lighter weight by twenty pounds. He even whistled every country song he knew, smiling one or more times in each block.

Yet when he had entered the kitchen, given Rosa her *Southern Living* and Rato his *Playboy* and *Hustler* and *Cheri* (provisions for country life), Rosa said "If I didn't think it would mean I'm crazy, I'd say you've been out crying like a dog."

Wesley glanced at the small mirror by the refrigerator. By God he had but he said "No ma'm, just the breeze in my eyes."

Rato said "It's as still outside as Hell on Monday."

"That's still," Wesley said.

But they all quit there and turned back to supper tasks.

ROSA WESLEY
RATO WAVE

At five minutes to six (early as Rato foretold), Wave knocked at the kitchen door. Rosa was upstairs dressing, Wesley was watching television in the living room, Rato was nervous waiting beside him. And at the sound of the knock, Rato shot up like somebody struck with lethal voltage—"Goddammit, I told him the *front* door."

Wesley said "Be nice to him now. It's no big deal. Maybe he just ain't a front-door man."

Rato said "But it's my damned party, the only one ever. If I don't make the rules for this one, I won't get another chance."

Wesley laughed. "And if you don't go on and let your company in, you ain't going to have *this* chance."

So Rato went and there Wave was in black corduroy pants a little too short (with red socks showing), a dark blue shirt, and a grass-green tie. It was more than any of the family men were wearing.

Rato said "You can take off half of that stuff."

Wave said "Is it that ugly?" Never having been a supper guest, he was genuinely unsure.

Rato stepped aside and waved him in. "Hell no, walk in. You look so expensive I barely recognized you."

Wave smiled and entered. "I was hoping for that."

With no other word, Rato walked off toward the living room; and Wave fell in behind him shaking.

Wesley stood up to meet him and thrust out a hand. "Rato's told me you've been a good friend."

Wave said "Nothing hard in that" and looked around quickly. This was one room he'd never had time to see on his other trips here, in light and dark.

Already zombied by the television eye, Rato dropped on the sofa to watch the ball game.

So Wesley had to say "Take a load off your feet. Can I get you a beer?"

Wave said "Oh no sir, help yourself. I don't touch beer."

Wesley laughed. "You wouldn't have to touch it. I could bring you a straw."

But Wave shook his head and sat next to Rato neatly. In another second he was watching hard as Rato, though he knew less about any ball sport than a well-bred lady. Something in his mind said "Grab this hard, this moving picture. It'll get you through till she appears."

All the way over, he had wracked his brain to see if Rato had said where his sister would be. Maybe this was some sort of bachelor event? If so a whole door in his life would shut. He might never get to do the big thing he needed to do, the thing that might yet keep him alive and in hope.

But Wesley stood up and repeated his offer. "Last chance at a beverage." He loved the word *beverage*. It came into wide use after he was grown, and it fit his mouth nicely—*bev-er-age*.

Wave said "All right, sir," quickly dug two quarters out of his pocket, and held them toward Wesley.

Wesley grinned. "Lord, son. Be my guest. I'm a well-paid professional. I can handle the outlay, one night at least."

Wave blushed so fiercely it seemed to warn a hemorrhage. But then he smiled and Wesley went out.

The game had near ended, and the beers were finished when Rosa walked in. She came so silently nobody heard her but Wave, and he stood like a galvanized child—bolt upright, shivering. He thought she looked younger than ever before. He had never seen her smile up close, and it almost shook him past his power to resist. The thought that he'd touched her closely in darkness not four months ago—and run when she yelled—seemed more unlikely than world peace or Jesus walking through the front door next with several blind children all reading the news.

Rosa didn't think she had seen Wave before. But of course since he was the one stranger present, she risked his name and offered her hand.

He seemed to inspect it before responding. But then, with his face still grave, he held it longer than either of them intended.

Rosa didn't pull back but when he'd released her, she took a long instant to search his eyes. There was something strong here, way stronger than she'd looked for in Rato's friend. But no, no clue of the source came to her. She said "I'm glad you were free to join us. We wanted to let Rato know how we'd miss him. He said you were his best Raleigh friend. So you seemed the right one to share our sadness but celebrate the chance he'll be back soon."

Rato said "Don't hold y'alls' breath too long."

That let Wave laugh. But he told Rosa how glad he was to share. Then he said the first truth he planned to reveal. "I've never been asked out to supper before."

Wesley said "Son, how old are you?"

Wave said "Twenty-six."

Wesley reached for his beer (a good heavy bottle—he hated to drink anything from a can). He toasted the air and said to Wave "Consider yourself asked, again and again. We're here most nights, clicking against each other like dice on a board—Rosa and me, old married folks. Drop in when you're lonesome."

Rosa smiled, understanding how loosely it was meant.

But Wave stayed earnest. He said "Whooee, if I came that often, I'd move on in."

Wesley said "We got a spare room from tomorrow noon onward."

Wave said "Oh well, my rent's paid up. I better stay there and leave you be."

Something told Rosa to change the tune, so she said "Anybody need a refill here? Otherwise I'll head on back to serve supper." She faced Wave again.

And again he was swept by her actual power. It no longer drew him onward to her skin but warmed him lightly all over—spring light, though by now outdoors full dark had fallen.

Wave said "No ma'm. I'm saving myself. Home cooking's a general mystery to me."

"Don't hope too hard," Rosa said. "I'm a typist. My mother's the last great cook in our line."

Rato said "You're better than all of t.v." (television chefs were among his favorite actors).

Wave said "I've counted on that now for days." He risked confronting her eyes again.

She was laughing and shaking her head, "Don't believe him." But every watt of her energy reached him and said "Your chance is still here waiting." Then she left for the stove.

Dessert was the last of Rato's choices, an Eagle Brand condensed-milk lemon pie of sufficient richness to sink most battleships, not to mention submarines. When everyone had surfaced and Rosa had stood to start cleaning plates, Wave spoke for the first time without being questioned. His face went urgent. "You going somewhere?"

Rosa laughed for the hundredth time. "No farther than the dishwasher. Why? What you need?"

Wave said "I just need to get on home and—"

"Home?" Wesley said. "The night's still young."

"Thank you, no sir. I got some homework to do—I'm taking a course in the night school at State in Creative Writing. Got a story to write."

Wesley said "No sweat. I'll just tell you mine. That'll hold you through three or four more semesters."

Rosa sat back down and said "Please spare him."

Wesley said "You got you a story already?"

Wave nodded. "These nine things land on Earth next year from the Fourth Dimension. They look so much like human that nobody thinks they're strange. But one or two smart people notice their eyes, which don't reflect light. The eyelashes are about an inch long and straight, and the pupils are so flat black you can all but fall in and drown. Anyhow the things spread to all the real continents."

Rato asked "Are they men or women?"

"Neither one. They can be whichever they want—plus others—as the need arises."

Wesley said "Hot damn, it's going to get dirty."

Wave said "No sir. My class is mixed; most of them are working women with kids. Anyhow my spacelings each know one skill that the whole Earth lacks. They can heal fatal cancer or negotiate peace or prevent divorce by helping grown people in their bedrooms at night. The only thing all nine can do together is stop child abuse, just stop it dead. So the whole story shows how they each try to train their whole assigned continent the main thing they know. Their idea is, if all nine succeed then the continents can turn around and train others once the spacelings have left. Well, as you can guess, some of them succeed, some fail, some are killed—they can all be killed as easy as us; you just have to aim at their hearts or heads. They don't really have much muscle or bone. They're mainly just gristle. So their mission is not that big a success. As they leave all of them but two are in tears."

Wesley said "Don't get me wrong now please. But what kind of story would end like that?"

Wave said "Beg your pardon?"

Rato said "I like it a lot. It'd make a good show."

Rosa said "Me too. Do they teach some progressive people how to cure cancer?"

Wave said "No ma'm. That's another place they fail."

Wesley said "See there. That's all I mean. If you're making up a story, why the hell say that? Why not let the whole thing come out right? If you're making the story, you're the God of it—right?"

Wave smiled. "I guess so."

"Then *be* God, son. Do your best by the Earth. If I'm going to shell out hard-earned dollars to buy your book, I sure God don't want the Earth to end up with cancer and men's poor peckers still falling off from syphilis and such."

Rosa said "We're at the table, Wesley."

He said "Oh damn, I thought it was the pool room" but went on genuinely facing Wave, for an honest answer.

Wave said "I hadn't thought of it that way. My teacher neither—or at least he hasn't said so. I guess it's because we're telling the truth or trying to. The Earth's got cancer and even worse problems—"

Rosa was stunned to hear her mouth say "Women get raped too night after night."

Everybody was stunned. Rato and Wesley knew they understood. They figured Wave at least would be mystified. Finally Rato asked "You saying that's bad as cancer?"

Rosa said "Can be, in some situations."

Then Wesley got scared she had broke some leash and would, any instant now, throw her last room open to this strange guest. He said "Sugar, we're just talking school talk. It's no big deal."

But Wave faced Rosa too and dared a short smile. He said "Mrs. Beavers, two-thirds of raped women don't even call the cops when their bodies get forced."

Rosa waited a long time, still mystified by her mind's direction. Nothing had told her who this boy was, no clue in his voice or the line of his face "No, Wave, they don't. I understand why. They don't want to share that awful a secret."

Wave said "You sure it's always awful?"

"I'd have to say yes. But I haven't finished polling the rest of my sex." By then she'd found the breath and will to manage a laugh. She knew something she hadn't known before supper, not even ten minutes ago at this table. She couldn't yet say what it was or why. She just suspected a broad black weight, like a dense canvas tarp, was lifting back off her—her face and neck, her legs and feet. With grace and luck, by bedtime tonight she'd be drawing freer air than for months, for long years maybe. Was she crazy or not?

The whole room wondered, all the three men around her. Her skin and eyes were brighter and younger. She had the low still radiance of girls with the first baby in them, nested deep down and growing steady. It looked to them all that, if they could just wait here—minutes, not months—she'd give birth before them to something worth watching and helping to live.

Wave suddenly broke his eyes off her face and turned to Rato. He said "Old buddy, you let me know. I'll hop on a bus any weekend you say. I ain't seen the country for several years now. But I'll come on up and you reacquaint me."

Rosa said "Wave don't let me ruin it. Stay on yet awhile. Rato's got a good movie picked out on t.v."

Wave said "I'm serious, Mrs. Beavers, truly. That story of mine's due tomorrow night at eight."

Wesley said "O.K. Just let them cure lockjaw or whip Ronald Reagan's dyed hair at the polls or something as good. Make my dollar worth spending."

Rato said "You're showing your ignorance, Wesley. No book's cost a dollar since you were a boy." Then he stood and offered his hand to Wave. "I'll write you that postcard real soon, hear? I've got sights up yonder, country or not, that you'll never guess till I've got you in hand and can give you the tour."

Everybody stood and watched Wave turn toward the back door slowly.

Rosa said "You go out the front way, Wave."

Wave smiled. "The back door won't shame me, Mrs. Beavers." He headed on as planned.

So Rato, Rosa, and Wesley followed—standing in a crescent to shake his hand once more and wish him well as if a spring night outside were threatful, a trial to be faced.

As his face got to Rosa's, Wave's own face paled. He thought "In this last second, she could hurt me." He prayed she wouldn't say more than "Goodbye," and it seemed for the moment his prayer had won.

Wesley said "Don't speak to no girls in the street."

Rato said "You taught me some things," the highest thanks he knew how to give. What he meant was the air of kindness from Wave, the way Wave showed his good intentions in every move of his hand or eye.

And at last Rosa said "Whatever you felt in other times here, Wave, you're welcome next time. We'll be here to greet you."

Wesley and Rato barely heard her strangeness. If they had, they well might not have understood.

Rosa wasn't sure she understood herself. Something that was still a deep secret in her own mind had formed her meaning and sent it on out in words.

But to Wave they sounded clear as great boulders heaved off a tall cliff into water way down in the night and deep. One by one he felt their weight and power and plea. He had hurt this woman, not helped or pleased her. How on the Earth had he failed to know that? Was he meant to go home now and cut his own throat? Whatever strange planet had sent him here, it had also clouded his mission for now. He'd done more harm than he ever intended.

No number of years of life on Earth would let Wave make up for all he'd ruined. The kindest act would be to leave now. Nobody left but his mother would mind. Or maybe this woman here three feet beyond him, his friend Rato's sister—the main one he'd harmed. He couldn't turn from her, the big blue eyes. He said "I'm sorry."

Rosa said "Thank you, sir."

Wave took a whole minute to squat down to Roger and tell him goodbye. Since the first day he came here as Rato's friend, Wave had noticed how Roger pulled back from him. No snarls or barks but a cold-eyed stare. Wave couldn't remember if Roger had seen him New Year's night (there were surely no barks). Still there'd always been this stand-off between them. So now he extended a bare right hand to Roger's big mouth—lick it or rip off two or three fingers.

With more dignity than came natural to him, Roger kept his seat and sniffed at the hand from a courteous distance. Then he touched the back of the palm with his nose, no slobbering kiss.

Wave said "Thank you, sir." Then he rose up quick, facing no one else, and trotted off.

Roger stood to escort him at least to the curb.

But by then full darkness had folded Wave in. He was almost down to the corner before they could hear his final "Thank you all. Rato, hold it in the road." Then from farther still, they plainly heard a last "I may love you." Who was that meant for?—the few stars already straining to shine?

Rosa wanted to run, touch Wave's shoulder lightly, stop him and say "Think it over. Love who?" But of course she waited, and then he was gone. She faced the room and moved on in toward the cluttered table.

Wesley was making strong coffee at the sink, and Rato was already testing the new Sony FM tape box that Wesley had bought him—their farewell gift for a child that had maybe saved her life.

Neither man in her family looked up to watch her. And certainly neither one asked what they'd meant—Rosa and Wave in those last few words. They were just that tired. But when, in a minute, the loneliness struck her and she asked for help, they both turned to help. The three together had all dishes cleared in under ten minutes.

ROSA WESLEY
RATO EMMA MILO
SISSIE MARY

The next day was Sunday. After another substantial early meal, they hit the road at eleven. For the first twenty minutes, they rode without talking since Rosa was tuned to a Presbyterian service on the radio. But finally Wesley's imitation of the minister's desperately maintained Scottish brogue (by an American citizen who hadn't seen heather for forty years) forced even her to laugh and give up the effort. They spent the next twenty minutes watching the countryside before Louisburg, as all the after-shocks of Raleigh calmed down and the woods deepened out on both sides of them. There were some few oaks and shag-bark hickories, looking old as alligators stuck upright in the sandy ground. But mostly there were what seemed endless pines, each lovely as individual trees in Chinese paintings meant to teach us stillness and constant strength in adversity.

Nobody in the car thought quite that way, but all three had spent their lives close to pines a lot like these. So the lesson and the lonesome moan of the limbs in any slight wind was as much a part of what they knew as their mother's names or the plans of the rooms they were each born in.

When they'd crossed the high bridge and cleared the long Main

Street of Louisburg (the only town), then Wesley could say "Everybody remember now—no dirty words, no speed or crack, no crotch-shot magazines flashed in public. And Rato, no mention of your friend Brenda Walters."

Rato laughed, grinned at the woods on his side, but kept his own counsel.

Rosa finally turned back and said "Did I meet her?"

Rato shook his head no.

Wesley said "Sorry, Ace. I'd have never brought her up. I just thought Rosa might have walked in on her the way I did."

Rosa said "Walked *in*? What's been going on?"

Rato didn't meet her eyes. "Nothing you need to rile your mind with now."

Rosa said "It's my house and will be tonight when we get back home. I need to know who to call Monday morning—the flea exterminator or the health department." She gave a nervous laugh but was plainly interested.

Wesley said "She looked right clean to me." He craned up to catch Rato's eyes in the mirror.

Rato just nodded.

Rosa turned back to face him. "Rato, I'm a grown woman. I know you spent your young years in service. So don't look to hear any sermons from me. I'm just surprised to hear of a lady visitor while you were there with me. I'd have been pleased to meet her and welcome her in."

Wesley said "Two of your words there need a little tuning—*lady* and *welcome*. Scratch those two at least. I thought she looked like she had an education till she said she loved our 'old antiques' and that she still hoped to have 'two twins' and quit."

Rato said "She's no big scholar, no. How about when she said 'I've worked extra hard to keep my virgin's license, but I just keep failing the hand-signal test.'" He meant it to be the purest nonsense and laughed like a moron.

Wesley joined in the laughter.

But Rosa said "Boys, hand jokes are out now we've passed Louisburg. That's big-city talk. I've told you before. Don't forget hereafter."

Wesley said "She did have petal-soft hands."

"You'd better say how you know," Rosa said.

"Strictly eye-inspection—ain't I right? Back me, Rato."

"Absolutely," Rato said. "I had em both busy the whole time you saw her."

Rosa said "Stop here and let me out. It's still not too far for me to walk."

Wesley knew she wasn't serious, but he pulled to the shoulder and faced her gravely. It was then that he saw they'd pushed her too far with a manufactured joke. Nearly forty years of identical jive hadn't immunized Rosa to the rank male strut of their favorite fun.

She somehow still held on to the hope of men's sweetness, a hope for single-eyed devotion to her and her own fierce brand of love for them that would sweep the air clean of rival girls and their filthy threats. Wesley put out his long-boned index finger, pressed her left thigh, and kissed her cheek. "We made this whole thing up to cheer you. Won't you ever learn that?"

Rosa searched Wesley's eyes till she knew he was earnest. Then she turned back to Rato. "You backing him up?"

Rato nodded. "If you force me to, yes ma'am. I wish to God I'd met Brenda Any-Damned-Body in Raleigh or Rome. I wouldn't have brought her to your house though. So don't burn any of your towels or sheets."

"Or strip up the rugs?" Rosa asked and laughed.

"You might want to buy new rugs," Rato said. "I walked through them barefooted day after day. All sorts of my germans are teeming in there."

It was the first time in forty years she'd thought of Rato's *germans*, the word he used for *germs* through the war. She reached back and stroked his long dry cheek. "New rugs then," she said, "and cheap at the price—all the free care you gave me."

Rato said "No I didn't."

She said "You're not the soul to know the truth of that. I'd almost surely be dead of the blues or choked in my sheets if you hadn't been there those weeks of dark winter."

Rato said "You mean it?"

"You know I do. Don't forget it was *you* called me New Year's Day. You knew I was bad-off and volunteered help."

"That so?" Wesley said, slowly joining the road.

Rato nodded to Wesley's eyes in the rear-view mirror.

Wesley drove a whole mile, then at last swallowed down a wad that blocked his words. "I owe you a lot more thanks than is easy."

Rato said "Why's it hard?"

Wesley said "Goddamn. I'm the cause of it all—me running, her pain."

Rato said "You're crazy."

"No he's not," Rosa said.

That silenced them all, right to Emma's front porch.

By the time they'd climbed the gulches of the long drive, Emma had seen them and was out on the front porch waiting by the steps. When Rosa caught sight, she took a sharp breath. She hadn't seen her mother in exactly four Sundays, and in that time it seemed Emma had shrunk several sizes inward. And near the five steps, there seemed a good chance that the slightest breeze would tip her balance and fling her down broken.

Again Rosa suddenly felt she should come here and spend the rest of her mother's few years giving constant care and learning everything her mother had kept in. There was no real way to manage it though and stay close to Wesley; she forced back tears.

Wesley hadn't seen Mrs. Mustian since Thanksgiving, so the change came even more clearly to him. "You two didn't tell me she'd been so sick."

"She hasn't," Rosa said, "—just fast old age."

Rato said "She knows how to outlast us."

Wesley said "Then I just beg her not to tell me."

"That's the reason I dread coming back," Rato said.

Rosa said "You told us you'd be happy here.'"

Rato said "The main thing you learn in the Army is lying. I could tell you the sky was raining port wine, and you'd say 'Pour me a big slug quick.'" But by then he was already out of the car and waving at his mother.

Rosa and Wesley got out, stood, and watched Rato give Emma his standard greeting. He brushed her cheek as dry as sandpaper, said "I got to stash all this mess," and pushed on past her with his suitcase and grocery bag of new things.

Then Emma looked to them. "Wesley, I been afraid I'd go to my Maker without seeing you. You look good as ever—course I'm going blind." But she held out two long thin arms to take him.

Wesley had always liked her (she laughed at his jokes, none of them too risky). So he loped up the steps and hugged her hard till Rosa suspected she'd hear joints crack.

When she got to her, Emma said "Ain't we all lucky?"

Wesley was standing there but Rosa said "Why?"

"To have him alive."

It still scraped Rosa's throat to say it but she nodded. "Big as he is, a coffin would break me."

Wesley gave an old-fashioned boy's bow from the waist. "Miss Emma, many thanks. Miss Rosa, kiss my heiny."

Emma reached out and straightened Wesley's brows (like most men his age, he'd begun sprouting grasshopper eyebrows like tentacles tuned to the farthest planets). She said "I've cooked everything on the place, all but boiled the wood bowls."

Wesley said "Let's start" and they all moved in.

By one o'clock when dinner was ready, Milo and Sissie had rolled in from Henderson. So there were six around the table, all of Emma's live family and in-laws (the youngest child, Baby Sister, had died twenty years ago of Hodgkin's disease—divorced with no children). In Emma's generation when family gathered, a woman absolutely never said dinner-grace. But today when they'd all unfolded napkins big and white as old baby-diapers, they faced Emma silently.

At first she went cold—did she even know a grace? But then she accepted her duty and right. She even composed her speech as she went. "Good Lord, I'm proud to be here today. I thank You for the mind and hands to still work. Thank You for these strong children that have grown up doing good mostly. Let them outlast me and never be sorry they were mine and knew me." She looked straight up and said "Everybody eat till they fall out asleep."

Rato said "Amen."

Emma said "Beg your pardon?"

He said "You never ended the blessing. God's still on the phone."

Emma laughed. "Oh He's not. He invented the phone. He knows when to hang up, even when I don't."

Wesley reached for the biscuits.

But Rato wouldn't quit. He said "Alexander Graham Bell made the phone."

Milo said "But he credited God for the dialer."

Rato said "Say what?"

"Bell always said it was him made the mouthpiece, but God made the dialer—the really hard part."

Sissie said "It *is*. I still have trouble dialing numbers with zeroes; my finger gets stuck."

Milo reached out and squeezed Sissie's dialing finger. "Poor child, shut up now and eat till you drop like Mama said."

Sissie had heard such nonsense all her grown life, but she knew not to fight. So she quieted down and ate big helpings.

Everybody else did. In families like this only a few years past, hard and poorly rewarded labor in the fields was consoled by plentiful hot food. And in those who contributed their share of the outdoor work, a great deal of personal oddness or nonsense had always been allowed to pass in amused silence, if not laughter. Only genuinely frightening symptoms like filthy clothes and stinking skin or a failing appetite would be mentioned at once and warned of.

Emma continued watching. Silently but with eyes that still needed no glasses, she patrolled the various recipients of her food. Who was falling behind on this or that? And if so, was the trouble her own (too much salt, too little vinegar)? Or were Milo or Rosa dieting (a development of her own lifetime that Emma thought as foolish as it was unneeded)?

The only person present that she'd hesitate to warn was Rato at her left, and that was only because words spent on Rato might as well have been puffed up the chimney for all their effect. Still she was glad to see him and to know he was back. Not that she'd worried about him or been scared for herself in his absence. But now that his long tan horse-face was back, Emma could check every few minutes on its peace and be reminded (as nowhere else) that she'd done a fair enough mothering job. To raise such a strange child, lose him for years to the faceless Army, and now have him back here—at this much ease, blaming no one for nothing—was some reward for all her own pain, even if she hadn't had Milo and Rosa (she barely ever let herself recall Baby Sister; that was too far to go, for too much heartache).

Milo carefully reloaded his plate, then turned on Rato. "And now, Big Ace, forget these ladies here, and tell all you can about big-city life."

"I knew it," Wesley said. "Now you've breeched the damned dam. We'll all be swamped."

For the first time in anybody's memory, Rato looked up grinning and began to speak at once as though in fraternal affection and obedience. "The first morning there I asked Rosacoke, and she checked the phone book—those yellow pages; I could read those all night—and by noon that same day, my lifetime heart's desire was filled. I was enrolled in the Ajax Bible College learning God's whole will for my sinful life. So every day since then, that's where I been—just sitting there with my poor face scrubbed soaking up all the wisdom and goodness I've missed for so long. To be sure, I wish there'd been a few girls in at least one class. But no, I guess they know what they're—"

Emma said "Rato, sundown's not but four hours off. Don't spend all our daylight on one big lie." She was plainly not mad.

Milo said "You always wanted a preacher."

Emma gave a high sharp laugh. "Not here, not under my roof. Once a week, at Delight Church, is fine by me—no more, thank you please, here lately anyhow."

"Hell," Milo said, "we'd have had a lot more fun if you'd lost your religion back when we were kids, in time for us to enjoy the world."

Emma said "If you'd enjoyed it any more, your heart would've stopped. You well know what I mean. I hold onto all I ever believed. I just don't see the need to harp on it so."

Milo began to harp with both hands and to sing a tenor chorus of his personal favorite hymn from childhood, "Shall we gather at the river?"

It had all rubbed hard on Sissie's nerves, and her determination to stay shut-mouthed had worn thin. So to change the subject, she smiled at Wesley. "Is the new Opry Land good as everybody says?"

The fact that he had never set foot there didn't slow Wesley. He said "Yes m'am, every word's more than true. If Milo won't take you, then save your own allowance and hop a fast bus. Whatever you do, don't miss the Jacuzzi part."

Milo was already grinning in hope.

But Sissie was earnest with expectation. "You better explain."

Wesley said "You give them your name as you enter before the main show. Just say 'Ms. Milo Mustian, a widow.'"

Sissie said "But I'm not."

Milo touched her wrist. "Just do what he says. Wes knows how it's done in those big hillbilly towns out west."

Rosa caught Wesley's eye. "Have a heart now, hear?"

But Rato said "Sissie, you'll love this fine."

So Wesley lit out. "Once they have your name, they take you to your seat in the plush-lined box. You listen and eat on your complimentary cheese and crackers, and you drink your Cold Duck if so inclined. Once the last song's over at midnight—Kenny Rogers, Loretta Lynn, Mother Maybelle Carter—"

Sissie said "Mother Carter's been dead long years."

"Well, whoever else—it's all big stars. Once the music's done, your private attendant comes to lead you back. You change in your own spacious private lounge, then walk out into your own dimmed cubicle—deep blue mirrors on all sides and ceiling. Your private masseur, a young Christian gentleman in modest tights (they have to have bare chests, the work is so strenuous), he steps on in and commences his craft. Child, they are *well*-trained. The girl I got on my first visit had studied at Bob Jones University in South Carolina, and I still feel relaxed—that stiff neck of mine just laid down and died for good and *all*."

Milo said "I'll bet a dollar it did. But now just for curiosity's sake, could Sissie get a lady masseur herself?"

Sissie said "They have their rules set, hon, by the state boards and all. Anyhow I'm no kind of missionary."

"There have been times," Milo said, "when I wondered. But steam ahead, Wes."

"You got it," Wesley said, "—the steam comes next."

Emma said "No it don't. Sounds like a trip I might need to take, with my bad knees. But you and Sissie finish this plan in the yard, the details especially. What comes next at my dinner table is cake."

After dinner Rato took his new radio and went to the woods. Sissie napped (one of her punishing headaches). Rosa and Emma headed for the kitchen, and Milo asked Wesley to take a good look at his new Pontiac in the yard. The day had opened out on a seamless bright sky and shirtsleeve temperatures. Both men, for all their middle age and stopped hopes, felt fine with each other. They'd known and liked each other since the days when Rosa first fell for Wesley, and they'd played baseball together at John Graham High School. So now they could crouch down over an engine, study it like abstract iron sculpture, and barely need to speak.

Milo said "Tell me I didn't get a bargain."

Wesley said "Wait now. I'm a pro at this. You don't really want to hear a real pro's truth."

"What you think I'm standing out here with ugly you for, when I could be canoodling upstairs with my lovely wife?"

"If you touched her," Wesley said, "she'd *run* to damned Nashville, with your credit cards."

Milo said "Let's don't get mean and personal both. If I opened up on you, you'd be so full of buckshot you'd die of lead poison."

Wesley laughed. "You win. No, Milo, look—you love your new car. It's exactly what you wanted, and it matches Sissie's hair. Just roll back, cross both hands on your belly (it's swelling nicely, by the way), and try to forget that day by day Wesley works on Mercedes, BMWs, Bentley's, and moviestar-customized Alfa-Romeos. Every now and then I lower my standards, double my prices, and tune up a Jag. But it's been six years since my soft hands even touched a piece of Detroit tinfoil dogshit. I done you a favor by looking at this." When he faced Milo, Wesley saw that wide jaw clamping down hard. He'd been too cruel, one more time. So gently he rocked all the sparkplugs for tightness and checked the dipsticks. Then he could say "It's a clean neat baby and, sure, it's a bargain. I'll accept it right now, as an Easter present—you forgot me last Easter—and drive it straight home."

Milo smiled and nodded. "See, I'm real sorry about your Easter. But I didn't get any word from you, so I just assumed your ass would be as invisible then as it was at Christmas."

Wesley grinned. "No it wasn't. Me and Easter Bunny sat home all day waiting on your basket of eggs to show."

Milo said "Hold your breath. Anyhow if I'd sent so much as a biddy, Miss Sissie would've shot me in cold blood in bed."

"Might have been a welcome change," Wesley said, "—little noise and violence in you all's bed."

Not a note of that was meanly intended, and both of them knew it. It was their original mode of conversation. It meant how long they'd liked each other, how long they'd known each other's secrets and destruction buttons. The fact that in nearly forty years of such scuffling they'd never cut a serious wound in each other meant simply that they hoped to grow old together—old and even more knowing, more nearly each other's mirror-self like the best male friends who stop short of touch. (Wesley understood that one of the mysteries about himself was, though he'd had good times close to several queer men, it never crossed his mind to touch Milo or any other friend on his own initiative.)

Finished, Wesley stepped back and wiped his hands on a clean white handkerchief. Then he stepped aside to let Milo take the owner's prerogative, closing the hood. It gave the satisfying crunch of a new metal catch, and Milo said "You glad to be back?"

Wesley looked to the house, the dining-room window—no sign of Rosa or Sissie or Miss Emma. He said "You know what your own answer would be?"

Milo said "Sure I do."

"Then mine's the same."

"I'm sorry," Milo said. "I figured as much. She *is* a fine girl. It still shows in her. I noticed just now—how she sat there letting us play the tired fool. She laughed and winced but never tried to stop us. Looks damned good too for—what?—the change of life."

Wesley nodded. "The last lady left."

"Her and our mothers," Milo said.

Wesley took a step toward the house.

Milo said "What's wrong?"

Wesley kept his head turned and still watched the front door. But then he thought again and came back to Milo, within breathing distance. When he felt his breath echo off his friend, he said "What's wrong? You're bound to know. We're the same kind of man. We're near the same age."

Milo shook his head hard. "You're way past me. Wesley, your whole luck went way past me. Don't ever forget you had the big sense to leave here long enough to serve your country. You saw a whole lot, touched a lot of young women, and got back here with your hide in one piece. And your mind still hot with all that good memory, all that clean good hair you tasted."

Wesley smiled. "And some that went a long way past clean."

Milo waved a careless palm in the air. "All the diseases back then, they could cure. Just a juice glass of warm penicillin, and you were right back on the streets set to nail one more señorita by sundown."

Wesley said "So you had your share. Don't go get bitter."

"The hell you say."

"What?"

Milo's face was as pale as a veal cutlet, drained and tan. "I never told this to nobody but you. So if it ever gets back to me, I'll know where it come from. And I'll shoot you straight down the minute I find you." He clamped both eyes shut. "In all my whole life—boy and man—I touched one woman."

Wesley said "You mean Sissie?"

"I don't mean Rosa."

It shocked and hurt Wesley more than he'd have guessed, even that much of a hint about Rosa (who had always been Milo's choice kin). He said "I'm sorry. I thought you'd enjoyed yourself much as me."

"No boy of all that we grew up with was as lucky as you, Wesley. Look at Lonnie Williams—he went to Campbell College for two years. Got him right much of that sweet Baptist pussy, or so he claims right up to this day. And I for one believe him. Lonnie's too dumb to make it all up. Right today he can tell you what every gal said when he touched her left nipple for the first time. He said most of them—even then, that young—had hair on their nipples. Like to made me lose my dinner on the spot. You believe that?"

"I don't just believe it. I know it's true."

Milo shook his head, kicked in the dirt, and then laughed. By the time he met Wesley's eyes again, he could say "Makes me almost proud to be a virgin."

Wesley laughed in relief.

"Almost but not quite."

In the kitchen Emma and Rosa had finished washing dishes, and Rosa was storing everything away for the twelve millionth time. It was just in other people's houses—helping other people, especially her kin—that Rosa felt the real deep awfulness of housework. How it consisted almost entirely of wrecking something you'd built, clean and neat, just hours before. A drawer of knives and forks or shelves of dry plates, each one waiting to be fouled again. How had Mama stood it a whole life long?

She suddenly felt full of a question she'd never dared to ask her mother till now, "Are you ever sorry this is how you've lived?" But Emma's back was broadside to her, narrow as a dusty sparrow in the ditch; and her whole frame was half a head shorter than when Rosa was a girl. Pounded mercilessly down toward the earth by decades of walking from that sink to this green table here, on these pine floorboards that had someway not been worn to air by the traffic. Rosa opened her lips and what she said was "Go lie down a minute. I'm tired myself."

Emma said "You know I can't rest in daylight. You go yourself."

Rosa smiled. "That old room of mine is too full of sad ghosts."

"I always thought this house was good to you. It tried to be."

"Oh it was," Rosa said. "I didn't mean that."

Emma said "Then it's got to mean you're sad now."

Not really being sure, Rosa waited on that. Then she said "No ma'm, but I've been pushed back."

"Where to?"

"Years ago, the Sunday I first saw Wesley."

"Up a tree."

Rosa said "You remember?"

Emma grinned and gently slapped her own thigh. "You told me times enough. Lord knows, I can near about recite every move."

"I'll bet that's more than Wesley can do."

Emma said "He'd surprise you. Wesley's got a sweet heart."

"So sweet it could start home a few days before Christmas, take a little detour that lasted four months and saw me raped, saw a new woman on him, and the whole world ended."

"The *world* kept going up here," Emma said. "Least I thought it did. Check round and see."

Rosa actually looked around slowly. "It did, same as ever. Thank you again."

"Not me," Emma said. "I had no more to do with it lasting than this ant did." She'd seen a black ant pause on the counter. She crushed it slowly with the palm of her hand and then wiped the hand on her damp apron.

Rosa tried to conceal a wince.

But Emma laughed. "Get on back to town. You've lost your country nerves."

"Wish I had," Rosa said.

Emma asked "How so?"

Rosa smiled all through the answer. "Because if I had, me and Wesley wouldn't be here together today. I'd have told him to get his tail back to some place as common as Nashville, Tennessee—and that girl he found with the steaming butt and the big mobile home."

Emma said, "Rosacoke, I didn't raise children to talk mule manure."

"Mama, I'm talking the plain truth now."

"Very little that's plain true is worth bringing up."

Rosa said "That was my whole problem from the start. You taught me to be so Christian polite, I never told Wesley what the ground rules were."

"Rosa, that's a black lie. You been giving rules, to Wesley and me and the dogs on the porch, since you could stand on your own legs and say 'Shut up.'"

"If Wesley had truly known what I could and would stand for, he would never have put him and me through this pain." Big tears ran for the first time in months, surprising Rosa far more than her mother.

Emma said "Sit down at the table a minute"—the first real order she'd given in years. She herself sat first and Rosa slowly joined her. Then Emma said "I trust you've got some memory left, way beyond you and Wesley. If so you'll recall that suffering didn't start when you two met. You loved your daddy. Remember him? He had parents as kind as any child ever had. Him and me were good in our iron bedstead as any three whores on the modern t.v."

Emma blushed ferociously but still had to say it. It was a part of her truth, confirmed every hour now in every newspaper. "But Horatio Senior was ruined from the cradle somehow, just ruined. A terrible seed was born down in him. He needed liquor like the ground needs rain. And fine as he was to look at and touch, the seed bloomed gradually when he was fifteen. I already knew him and I saw when it started. The church picnic that year was nearby. Nobody had cars then to truck up the road to nice lakes or cabins. We went to the deep woods back of Mr. Isaac's house and pitched down there, spread our quilts in the shade, and ate a feast fit for the kings of the world and ample for the full five thousand plus orphans."

"You were how old?" Rosa asked.

"Thirteen, just turned—and already watching him like quail watch foxes. He didn't seem to know I was live on the ground, though no other girl seemed to have his eye either. What happened in the shank of the afternoon was, an older fellow—Dim Waters, a lawyer that practiced in Warrenton—came up and tapped your daddy on the shoulder. The two of them and one other boy, that died in the war, loped off farther in the woods. With my two parents, I'd barely heard liquor mentioned (much less seen it drunk). But right that instant in my heart I could say the two things I suddenly knew. I said 'Dim Waters will fry in Hell, and Horatio's going to be a drunkard for life.' I was as sure as I've ever been about any fact. But it seemed like my love was a train that, whoever was driving, it wasn't me. It just plunged hot right on down the line till I married him six years later, to the month, and had all of you and watched him kill himself way too slow."

Rosa waited, watching Emma closely so the words would register in a way that lasted—stamped onto one long moving-picture of faces, her mother and father's (with Milo, Rato, herself, and poor Baby Sister pale behind them, sucking strength). Then she thanked her mother simply.

Emma stood up and said "Wesley's right lucky. But so are you, Rosa. You forget that and you know you do."

"You want to tell me where the lucky part is? Just the fact that Wesley's not a falling-down drunk or hasn't ever beat me?"

Emma said "Thank you, no. I tell you what I see, from way out here in my seventies. You ought to be glad. And so ought he. Course I may be blind or crazy or soft-brained. You got to recognize your own damned luck."

Rosa had only heard her mother say *damn* maybe five times through the years, times that mattered. In Emma Mustian's mouth it had the force of the wildest outbursts in others less restrained. So then and there she decided to honor it at least, to search her own life hard for luck. She said "Please teach me."

Emma said "What you think I been teaching all your life?" But then she laughed and stepped toward the door, time for others now.

But by the time Emma combed her hair in her bedroom, her poor ears heard the others beyond her. Rosa had joined Milo and Wesley on the porch. No word from Sissie—she would still be asleep. And Rato would still be gone in the woods. Emma Mustian was all alone again, the way she'd been these past four months—the way she'd stay in the grave forever. She'd promised herself not to tell another soul. But while she was here alone in this house, she'd finally come to the hard conclusion that had tempted her since Horatio died.

There is no Hell or Heaven. There is no afterlife. We are here, one by one, with the pigs and chickens, the beetles and snakes. We work like miserable coal-black slaves, with the hope of some final gold-watch reward. Well, Jesus looks nice in the Sunday-school pictures (and can put you to sleep fast in the one-page devotions like the ones she sent Rosa every birthday that came). No doubt Jesus, the man on earth, was kind and polite. But the secret that Emma thought she'd learned these past lonely months was, Jesus himself wouldn't be her reward. Now she knew it was bound to be better than that. It was pure black sleep, perpetual *rest*.

How had Emma known, after all the wrong years? She couldn't quite have told you. Maybe by a kind of reverse revelation. Some saints in the night get gleaming pictures of God's throne with angels in endless harmony. Ten days or so after Rato left her, she settled back into new deeper silence. Life in the country—with no children home—had been quiet enough. But now, with even her last son gone, day and night passed in a quiet so deep that even a bird call got to be offensive, a raucous scrape down a perfect sky.

Then well before dawn at the end of two weeks, Emma woke in the dark surrounded by silence. Something had called her, she well knew that—no voice, some *absence* with a plain truth to tell. She lay in her warm sheets and waited, not scared. Maybe three blank minutes, then a long high scream. Beginning loud, then shrinking in size—some squirrel or rabbit seized by an owl and borne through the night farther off to be torn and swallowed. So she knew.

That was it. The final shock that was really such relief. It was all she'd waited for. All bets were off. The last easy truth was plain before her. There was nothing else to come. The world, the sky, the core of the ground was nothing but two things—eaters and food.

In the nights alone also she'd sat up late, doing additions with the little hand-calculator Rosa gave her last year. She figured up how many times in her life she'd done so and so—changed baby diapers, made love to Horatio, cooked hot meals (and for seven mouths generally), washed all their dishes, emptied slop jars till they got indoor plumbing. Could any old mule in the country say more, assuming you could still find one live mule?

The meals for instance. Emma started at age fifteen for her daddy, when her own mother died. And not one time had any black woman ever lent her a hand. So till now, she punched the plain facts on her keyboard—well there, it came to more than thirty-five thousand cooked hot meals. Every one of them laid out with at least good conscience. Could anybody, even her most loving child, recall one single dish and taste it in memory? She'd said it to the empty house when she finished, *Don't everybody fall down laughing at once.*

So *rest.* Lord Jesus, you lie back now and calm yourself—and thanks for your time—but bring on my *rest.*

The sound of Milo's laugh from the porch caught Emma where she spun far out on the string of her new lonely knowledge. She checked her face again in the mirror. All things considered, for its age, the mirror was in worse shape than she. Again she touched the wings of her hair, still bunned in the back and tight on her ears. Since she had never smoked so much as one cigarette, it was snow white and soft—a glory at last after long years of looking like packing straw.

She would step out now and join those children as if she was who they'd known all their lives. They'd be almost right. Very little had changed except that now she had this surety—rest like the finest hospital anesthesia, black silent sleep. No eternal glare on her tired eyes, no big reunion of all her old kin, grinning and singing and ready to eat.

By the time the children reached her age—if they ever did—they might well share her joy in the news of rest, pure rest. They would have to learn it without her help though. She'd given them the slim faith in God that sustained them this far. She wouldn't feel right now to walk out toward them on a nice spring Sunday and strip that off their ignorant faces. Let time teach them in the night like their mother. It would come with age, if they earned it at all. And by then, thank the stars, Emma Mustian would long since be underground. Or nowhere. *Nowhere.*

She went toward them smiling.

Whoever died, however many left, it still took an hour to withdraw from Emma's. First there were all the gifts to pack—the home-canned goods, the caramel cake she'd made for Wesley and kept hid till the last minute, the pan of her rolls laid out and ready to bake for Sunday supper as soon as they were home (the possibility of rolling in and defrosting a pizza would have horror-struck Emma), Rosa's tenth-grade autograph book she'd found preserved in a trunk.

Then the farewells—tying Rato down long enough to say goodbye and to hear Rosa's serious repeated thanks, extricating from Sissie without further insults, assuring Milo he'd be welcome to visit anytime he could come (he always asked, ever since the one good time, but still never came), facing up to what might be the last sight of Emma.

Then the lingering small talk through both car windows, then at last the slow drive downhill through gulches back out into whatever dream of freedom they could manage once they'd struck hard pavement and begun to thread the last country roads before they could aim unblocked for Raleigh.

In a while they passed Mr. Isaac Alston's, the biggest old house in Afton. When Mr. Isaac died it had run down badly till the long, front porch had fallen in. But now they'd heard of a rich Warrenton lady who fixed it up and moved in lately. Wesley figured they had daylight enough to see it, so he took a sharp right and rode on past.

And yes, she'd fixed it—brand-new gingerbread brackets in corners, fern baskets all along the porch ceiling, and every board painted a jaundiced yellow with barn-red trim. In the yard—instead of bird dogs, chickens, and sand—was thick lawn-grass in an unreal chemical blue dotted with painted concrete figures of colored boys wearing red sombreros and adorable matching yellow burros hauling carts of watermelons. The porch was hung with a new rope hammock. None of it looked like a human hand had participated. Rosa said "Sometimes I hope the dead *die*."

Wesley said "Why so?"

"At least Mr. Isaac wouldn't have to see this."

"He's in Heaven. To him it's all one more joke."

Rosa said "In my very humble opinion, it would take more than Heaven to make this a joke."

By then the insulted house and dirt were gone behind them in the dusk, but Wesley missed the first two chances to turn. At the third, Rosa started to ask were they lost. But "No," she thought, "I'll sit this out. Wherever we go, and I bet it's not Nashville, I guess I could find my way back home if Wesley fades on me."

The days now were longer; and every rock in the road was clear, every cone on the trees. The road had been paved twenty years ago, and the car picked up speed to pass Delight Church. Fine as it looked in its new white paint, its tall storm windows, Rosa didn't let herself think back to the night when there, in a Virgin Mary costume, she had watched her mind find its slow pained way to accept Wesley's offer and take his name for the bastard child they'd started growing in her secret womb. She made the only sane guess she could manage, "We stopping by to see your mother?"

"I called Mother three or four nights ago, remember?"

"You know she'll be home."

Wesley said "She'll be home, Rosa, when you and I have *flown*."

"I'd be glad to see her. Don't think I wouldn't."

"Rosa, don't go tell a king-size lie. We've had a nice day."

"Your mother has never been less than kind to me."

Not glancing toward her, Wesley's right hand reached out with perfect aim, found her mouth, and shut it gently. "I'm looking for something you long since forgot."

Rosa said "I remember how Mama's ribs looked from inside, with the sunlight slatting in through her skin when she pulled off her nightgown each dawn at the window. I can still recall my daddy's voice through Mama's belly when it reached me treading in her warm dark lake every night when he'd find his drunk way home and bunch up beside her and beg her hot pardon, worn out as it was. So don't tell Rosa she's forgot a damned thing, not anything old enough to matter tonight up here in the woods."

Wesley nodded. "Yes ma'am."

"What?"

"We're looking for woods."

Rosa still hadn't followed his line of thought. "You've found them, Columbus—hearty applause." Pines and cedars stretched on both sides, so deep beyond them that they might almost reach Canada unseen if they set out to walk.

Wesley pulled to the edge of the ditch and slowly stopped. He was looking past Rosa into the trees. Then he faced her at last. "You game to walk a ways?"

She had on new panty-hose. But this was so strange, she wouldn't have said no if her new hose were spun-gold thread. And even with all the past year's history, it never dawned on her that Wesley meant to harm her—the Afton Strangler. She set her purse in the glove compartment and said "Better lock this please—credit cards, a little cash."

So he turned the lock, came around, and politely helped Rosa out.

Then he took a slight lead and walked on to where the trees began to thicken and strain out light. The sun that reached them was a pale blue, but it gave their features a clarity that seemed to stream from within.

Wesley noticed it first. He turned on Rosa, studied her face, and said "You don't know where you are." Even he could hear that his voice was strange, more than the usual space between words. But his smile was normal.

Rosa had already checked the surroundings, a small circle in the tallest trees they'd seen all day. She said "You win this time. I'm lost."

Wesley's smile deepened. "But you brought me here, lord, thirty years ago. Remember?—the night we saw those deer out on the road and walked back in here, hoping to find them, and then laid down on the ground and did it. First time of all."

Rosa looked around once more, then checked his face for laughter. "It can't be so. The trees are too tall."

"You don't think they've stood still anymore than us?"

Rosa said "I've never been back here since."

"I have," Wesley said, "every five years or so."

"What for?" To Rosa it was all but incredible.

"I had a good time that night," Wesley said. "I hoped you did."

Rosa looked to her feet. The ground was clean, just dry leaves and sticks. "Can we sit down a minute?"

"You want to risk chiggers?"

"Too early for chiggers." She sat down slowly and pressed both hands in the compost beneath her, down to where the ground was still cold and damp.

Wesley sat clear of Rosa but in reaching distance.

"You're sure?" she asked.

"I'm sure you're you." He reached toward her face, then stopped his hand short in the darkening air. "Yes ma'am, I'm sure as I am that you're Rosa. This is where we were."

So they'd seen the buck out there on the road, in deep fall dark. It had been at a time when Rosa thought she was truly losing Wesley and must move fast and furious to stop and hold him. She'd asked him if they couldn't follow the deer and his two does on back in these woods, meaning—God, whatever million things had she meant? *Let's live forever, let's die right here, don't ever let's tear apart again, there'll never be any place better than this (any better night) to join together and make one thing.*

It had been her idea, she understood that, but Wesley had agreed in mind and body. And if he was right now—surely he was—this was where they'd done it (as he said), *made a thing.* She dug with her short nails deeper in the earth. Well, let it be true. Let this be the place. They'd made a real thing. And only part of it was Horace, a baby. The big part was them. Why cancel them here or anywhere else in this world or life? She met Wesley's eyes. "It's bound to be." She meant the place. He'd apparently found it, something she could not have done.

Wesley waited a long time to nod his thanks for what he thought was her final agreement. By then the sun had dropped another three notches toward night. If Rosa had just now seen him clearly, he could barely find her when he stepped on forward and leaned to give her his right hand again.

She found it though and rose to its strength. Far stronger and more certainly than all those years ago, she followed him out to the car and toward what might yet be home—no longer the old Mustian place (her mother's, with room for Milo and Sissie, Rato and Sister) but Raleigh, the house she and Wesley had bought with their earnings to shelter their own heads and the one child they'd started with young lovely bodies on the hard ground they'd just now touched in the woods.

They turned full-circle and drove toward the highway. Then in a half-mile the lights struck a tall shape coming against them with what seemed to Rosa no visible head. Then she saw it had to be a black woman.

Wesley recognized her first and began to pull over.

Rosa said "Who?" Then she saw it was old Mary Sutton alone in a heavy green sweater. When Wesley had stopped, Rosa cranked down her window. "Can we drive you home, Mary?"

Mary didn't know the car or the voice, but she said "Not unless this car's a damned *tank*." Mary's house was far too deep in the woods for a car, and the *damn* had to mean that she'd had a big drink.

Wesley laughed and leaned over. "It's Wesley and Rosacoke, heading to Raleigh. How you doing, Mary?"

So Mary relaxed her guard, walked over, set strong arms on the window ledge, and craned in to see them. "Right," she said. "I'd a knowed both of you if I had good sense." The odor of cheap fruit-brandy was clear but not rank.

Wesley asked "You got me a drink of pain-killer?"

Mary took two steps backward, then laughed loud. "What's hurting you, boy?"

"My whole life till now. I'm an *old* man."

"You a baby next to me. And I'm still grinning." Then she came near again. "Miss Rosa, don't tell me you hurting too."

Rosa said "I'm younger than either one of you. No, I'm proud to say Rosa's in fairly good health."

Mary said "Glad to hear it. You the only one left. Everybody else up in the sticks here's miserable." She looked past Rosa to Wesley. "You back I see."

"You knew I was gone?"

Mary said "Me and every sick sparrow in the trees. You was big bad news—in the paper, on the radio."

"I told her," Rosa said.

But Mary ignored her and went on to Wesley. "Where'd you go?"

"Nashville, Tennessee."

"Learn anything new?"

"Not new."

"But good?"

Wesley's eyes knicked the side of Rosa's taut face. "Neither one," he said. "Mary, I'm a plain boy. Can't handle rich good, these fast rich towns."

Mary said "Lord Jesus, then give me a chance. Give me a bus ticket out of here and I'll fly. Won't see me back." She'd never been farther than Baltimore, for more than a week during World War II.

Wesley said "I doubt you know what you're saying."

Mary held out her palm, again past Rosa. "You try me and watch."

Rosa knew Mary Sutton had always been hard. She'd gone to Mary several times years ago, when everybody else lied, for clear rough truth. But now was worse. Time had walled Mary off. Now was mean and useless. Rosa wanted to say a fast good night and leave.

Mary felt it someway. She laid a hand on Rosa's lean shoulder. "You proud of him, ain't you?"

"I'm used to him, Mary."

Mary drew back her hand and faced Wesley again. "That good enough for you?"

Wesley smiled. "May be the best offer I get."

Mary said "Think it over then. You a fine man. Still young enough to pick."

So Rosa firmed up. "You get home, Mary. It's not safe out here alone in the road."

Mary said "You used to ask *me* for advice."

Rosa smiled. "Yes well, I'm a grown woman now."

Mary stepped back again, took a good long look, and laughed.

"Ain't it so. Ain't it so!" Mary slapped her own firm thigh over and over.

Wesley said "Mary, come round here to my window."

She put a long hushing finger to her lip and tiptoed with obvious caution toward his side. Then she leaned in his window and gave him a pecking kiss on his ear.

He laughed but said "I'm spoke for now. Don't go tempting me." He dug in his wallet and handed her a bill.

Mary walked due left till the edge of the headlights shined on her hand. "This'll ease more grief than most folks I know." Then her voice broke up into chunks like concrete dumped from a loader. "Wesley, you too good. I'm praying for you."

Wesley said "I'm a saint in glory—believe it! But don't stop praying for us both anyhow. God loves you. You're so big a sinner, he's bound to."

Mary waited awhile to understand that. Then she said "I'm going to laugh at that once I get home, and the sting in it don't hurt nearly this much."

Wesley said "You do that." He blew her a second kiss, released the brake, and rolled ahead.

* * *

Miles up the road when they sighted the highway's chain of lights, Rosa said "Who is *both?*"

"Ma'm?"

"*Both*—you asked her to pray 'for us both.' "

"You and me," Wesley said. "You object to that?"

"Not really. She was drunk."

His voice wasn't angry but patient as a father's. "I knew that, Rosa. I also know Mary Sutton's prayers work. They've worked for me since I was a boy. I need them again and I thought you did."

"Thank you then," Rosa said.

In the dark they repeated the morning's trip—silence between them till they threaded Louisburg (all but deserted, a few young black men propping up buildings with their tall fine bodies). Then in full dark beyond it, with Raleigh ahead, Wesley said "Please tell me what you believe."

Rosa asked "About what?"

"Everything—God, Heaven and Hell, the fleas on dogs. You recall that radio show of Edward R. Murrow's, 'This I Believe'? He'd ask— you know—Einstein, Mrs. Roosevelt, General George C. Marshall. They'd answer too and fast."

Rosa said "I believe the Apostles' Creed and Jesus' Lord's Prayer."

"Don't be a damned missionary all your grown life." Wesley knocked her knee.

"It's true though, Wesley. What do you doubt?"

He said "Most of it. Oh, I guess there's a God. But it sure as hell looks like He's so far gone, He can't see us and barely hears even our loudest begging—when we beg help for children that are twisting in pain."

Rosa said "We had good luck with Horace, nothing worse than that one long bout of strep throat the winter he was two."

"—And being a pitiful jackass now."

"Wesley, that boy's the one thing we made together. Give him some little credit."

"For what—marrying a beehive hairdo with legs?" Wesley hoped he could hear Rosa strangle a laugh. He paused to see if she'd show her true colors, but she was watching the right side intently. So he went on and said "I'm ashamed now to think Horace was what forced me to marry you, a piss-poor shotgun."

She finally laughed and slid a few inches toward him but not quite touching. "He's got a sweet heart. We're not old yet. He'll be there ready when you're feeble and gray."

Wesley said "For you. You'll outlast me."

Rosa shook her head. "I don't take wear. I'm wrinkled, creased, threadbare in the seat."

"You're the thing I watched all those years ago. You're still broadcasting the signal that caught me."

Rosa smiled. "Thank you." But then she remembered. "You died though, Wesley—signal or no. You said you died toward the end of last year, and Rosa didn't save you."

"I did die truly. But I never blamed Rosa."

"She was right there beside you, the same girl as now. Nothing in me has changed."

Wesley said "*Me* then. I'm a different piece of work." He stared on at the road.

So Rosa looked carefully. And yes, he had changed again. All their time together, it was what had held her closest—the slow unpredictable speed at which each day he was turning like a tall plant into something, more or less or different anyhow. Times without number, she prayed he would stop, stand still, and *be*.

She'd tell herself she needed a fixed human star to plot by, a tall lone tree on a hill to watch as she cut her own path toward him or away. But he'd never been that. He'd always brought home peculiar faces (some scary, some grand) that she had to watch or at least learn to bear—faces that would vanish next day with no warning.

Could she—hell, *should* she—spend the next thirty years shifting the grounds of her care every few days to match Wesley's shifts? Well, first, he couldn't help it; he was built to change. And finally surely, it was what she loved deep down in her dark heart. It was what she had learned maybe from her father and two older brothers. She herself really needed that restless ground—a light that *burned* but wavered and sank and nearly dimmed out but always somehow, in her own eyes, demanded care. She'd watched Wesley's profile all through her thought.

Now he glanced over toward her, from as far off as that first day she'd seen him—grave as a watchman on the highest lighthouse. Then he faced the road.

Rosa said "All right"—meaning *All right*, change. *I can try to watch.*

In another quarter-hour of silent driving, they could see the gleam of Raleigh on the sky. It was still twenty minutes ahead at this rate. But either one of them, or both, could stop here. Turn back, choose another destination together or part company finally and go different ways. Wesley said "We could streak off right now for elsewhere. Just send Horace the keys and a letter saying where the deed's kept."

"And then go where?"

Wesley said "You choose."

"Together or apart?"

He smiled but ahead at the road and the dark. "You choose."

Rosa let a whole extra mile roll behind them. The gentle pad of the tires seemed the sound of their lives, eating whatever slim time was left. Then she said "Well, Raleigh. The same warm house. Us same two old dogs, the same old basket."

Wesley thought a whole minute, then gave a nod, pressed his foot down slightly, and the car took speed.

WAVE ROSA WESLEY

The whole day Sunday, Wave had stayed in his room. He'd slept a lot—long naps with dreams that changed faces so fast he never got to know who his actors were, much less what they needed from him or had volunteered to give in return for the use of his brain and time. Then he would wake up and read awhile in the short stack of books he always kept by his bed. His favorites were mysteries and science fiction. The mysteries were not detective stories but real human bafflements—the Bermuda Triangle or the Holy Shroud.

Wave had first run into the Shroud in *Time* magazine years ago, and ever since he'd pursued its truth. Since he left his mother, he'd never darkened a single church door and had no plans to. But that didn't mean he was an atheist or that he came anywhere near spitting on what others believed. If the Shroud was the actual cloth around Jesus in the thirty-odd black hours in the tomb, then all those yelling Baptists had one thing right anyhow—man had conquered death and would do so again.

Wave Wilbanks's body (this ramshackled five-foot-eleven-inch house thrown together of meat, bone, and hair) would stand up one day out of the grave into God's own actual truth-seeing eyesight and hear those blessed final words, "Well done, My good and faithful servant. You have honored My Loved ones. Accept My thanks."

Then Wave would climb out of worms and cold clay, his big skull

bored by tunnels of rot, and stride into hot clean light that streamed
no longer from the sun but from God's own eyes. As his legs gained
strength with each forward step, Wave would see on all sides the other
human eyes—eyes that, in his life, had hated and jeered: other children, his uncles, some women he'd tried to touch and help.

But now every eye would be weeping with thanks, begging somehow to stay near the risen Wave (stronger than ever) and finally share
what he'd offered again and again in the past—his harmless gifts that
could bring such joy, all permanent now in the land without death.
Even his father, that had died so long ago (God knew how), would
step up now with identification and show true pride in this great
son—pleading for just a seat at his side, to share the new glory. And
Wave would let him.

He got through the whole day till sundown like that, a good restful
time in sweet-smelling sheets. And unlike most healthy young men at
ease, he felt no need to seize on himself and masturbate. After a few
times in early adolescence, he'd come to see how sad that was—that
lonely showing-off. He preferred to wait for a warm other body.

Then in late afternoon—just before he would need any light—he
climbed out, showered, shaved, dressed in his only suit and prettiest
tie, and started his plan. The plan had not formed till the night
before, as he walked home alone from supper with the Beaverses and
Rato Mustian. They would all be out of the house Sunday from
morning till bedtime.

Wave would wait till dark, go over unseen, let himself in, and finish the business that Rosa had balked on New Year's night. There
would be some risk. Neither Wesley nor Rosa had said when they
expected to be home. Wave was guessing on the basis of what he'd
watched in other people's family visits—eat a little supper with them,
take your leave slowly, mosey on back in time for bed. But risk had been
the main excitement of his grown life, and it didn't slow him now.

So it was past seven when he jimmied the door-handle lock in the
Beavers' kitchen. They'd left on at least one light in every room, and
one quiet radio to fool the burglars. He had good company then and
a nice steady glow for the thorough inspection he needed to make—

every corner, every drawer. Wave had learned years ago how to do it invisibly.

Housebreakers in general leave a hateful mess behind, not Waverly Wilbanks. He could open every envelope, read every letter in a filing cabinet, and leave behind nothing but clean fingerprints (he'd never feared those and had never been caught, not even suspected). Methodically then he fingered, read, and memorized the souvenirs and hoarded junk of two lives no longer young as they'd been.

But Wave loved the chance. The thought that he, more than any old friend (even Rato himself), knew the hidden trail of two married lives and all they'd thought worth saving back—it drew him on through the downstairs and up like a bright warm light.

And then in the bedroom he found Wesley's secrets (a dozen new rubbers, three oldtime books with pictures of sailors with cocks like underground prize-winning State Fair tubers in their white blocked hats and short black socks screwing star-spangled whores, and a red rubber-dildo painted with a motto—"Forget your hairdo! Hang onto your heart!"). That was good, almost good enough.

But before Wave could carry out all his plan, he had to find something just right that was Rosa's. Some unmistakable clue, after Sunday night's kindness, that she wanted Wave to finish up here.

Her own drawer was nothing but a clothes drawer though, just neatly-folded underwear and blouses, stockings and scarves. Wave sifted those quickly with no sick interest in their feel or smell. Her bedside cabinet held nothing like the modern-day working girl's shelves (a diaphragm, modernistic battery-powered massager, or copies of *Playgirl*) but straight-trimmed recipes from family magazines and one moldly scrapbook with clippings about Horatio Beavers as a high-school student (the Audio-Visual Club, that sort of thing).

Wave's heart sank a notch. He might have to leave and not accomplish his one main hope. That would sadden him far more even than leaving here fast on New Year's night without the chance of showing Rosa his inmost meaning, his hope to ease her.

As he turned from the cabinet, he saw an old Bible. A thin *New Testament and Psalms*, dusty with the yellowed edges of clippings and photos kept there for safety. He sat on the edge of the mattress and opened the book, hoping to find any verses she'd marked for special memory or for help in trouble. Find that, in anybody's house, and you've got a key to their deepest back room. Nothing here though, not even real signs of wear and tear. None of the darkness of long needy use. Could she be the sort of person for whom a Bible was just a filing cabinet, a place to keep birth certificates or insurance receipts? It didn't seem likely but here were the facts.

Then Wave turned to his own favorite passage of scripture, St. Paul's Epistle to the Romans, chapter 8: verse 18 (*I consider that the sufferings of this present time are not worth comparing with the glory that is about to be revealed to us*). And laid in beside it was an old tan photograph, no writing on the back. So Wave had no idea of the subject.

It was Rosa's father, with two other boys, as a very young boy at Ocean View—long before liquor found his mouth and burned out the core of his body and soul, long before Rosa herself ever saw him, before he dreamed that this body of his would ever bloom in its own grinning babies. Yet it was still her favorite picture of him, of his innocence in the days when he had live dreams of a useful life—when his own four children were patiently waiting in the dry-seed fork of his strong bare legs.

Somehow the force of it tore through to Wave. Somehow he felt like that same boy, in his own life now. He also stood up smiling like that, in a strong counter-wind, with his mouth wide open trying to say something helpful and kind to a world that could see him but would not take his meaning. He even had the boy's dark eyes and hair. There seemed to be a bruise on the boy's right knee. Now, this day, on Wave's own knee was a brown mark big as a baby's palm—some permanent sign of who he was and had always been.

Could it someway be him, here in Rosa's Bible? Had he lived back there a whole life ago? Maybe without her knowing it at all? Was it why he'd felt so drawn to her life? Maybe that was why he'd known he could help her.

And had Rosa treasured him all this time? Whoever she thought the old picture was—a kin person?—she knew by now that it looked like him. Surely she'd plan to follow that up? Had he ruined his chance at knowing her again by forcing himself too soon or too late? He needed to know. Maybe someday he could ask her.

Or maybe he had to swear off here. Leave it to patience, time, and fate. And hope that at last Rosa would know that—whoever he was now, had always been—he'd stood at the edge of her whole recent life and wished her well. Surely she knew she could call for him and get all the help he'd saved for her?

How could he vow to leave her now though and make himself obey? What would convince his mind in the nights, when it brought up Rosa's face again and begged him onward, that she'd already known him?—that she had a version of him pictured by her pillow and would surely think of him whenever she opened the book in reach?

He could hide a penciled note here now on the back of the picture—*This old friend came back in once more but has left for good thinking you are happy. If that ever changes and you want him again, just say so quick. He will be nearby.*

Then a better way dawned. Wave stood up, borrowed a comb from the cabinet, and smoothed his hair in the glass of a picture near the bed. Neatly he checked his fly and all buttons, then straightened his necktie.

He sat back down on Rosa's edge of the mattress. He shut his eyes and said "Dear Lord and God, I was here once before in the hopes of doing Your will by one of your saints. I made some mistake and hurt her badly. You've let her give me a real second chance. And also I've found out she's known me before and values my face. Let me bless her now, once for all in her life, by resting in the place where I tried to touch her and begging Your strength to leave her for good unless she needs me."

A voice clear as anything on FM broadcasts said in a deep tone "Thank you, son. Now do the right thing." Next it gave him the right thing to do.

He lay back on Rosa's side of the mattress, slid himself to the center on top of the spread, touched both their pillows, shut his eyes again, and said "I'll never be back here again, not of my own will. I'll wait for her." He waved both long arms beside him like wings, the angel wings he saw so often in the night in dreams or awake above him in the dark overhead.

The clear voice said "Get up now and go. You've got three minutes. You were right. Amen."

Wave stayed another instant, sweet as any in his whole past life. Then he sprang to the floor, leaned back, and neatly composed the spread and pillows to where even Wesley and Rosa herself could never guess he and God the Judge had been present there and done great deeds. He went to the door, looked back once quickly. Then helpless to resist, he turned and bent and pressed a long dry kiss deep in the spread. In under a minute he was downstairs, out the back door, and gone—no trace behind.

And in one more minute, when Wesley drove in and Rosa faced the house, she could say what she said at the end of most trips but with real truth now "Home. Safe again. Thank heavens."

Wesley said "So right" and was also true.

Whatever the sky was—at least the cause of birth and death (all hardness and ease)—it had secretly honored the unlikely choice of two normal creatures to work again at a careful life. They could not know they were safe till their endings, which would be hard and slow a long way off. This modest house would be home till then. It had room enough for the small calm pleasures that would not be rare. They would live here till death. Death would find them with ease.

REYNOLDS PRICE

Reynolds Price was born in Macon, North Carolina in 1933. Educated in the public schools of his native state, he earned an A.B. *summa cum laude* from Duke University; and in 1955 he traveled as a Rhodes Scholar to Merton College, Oxford University to study English literature. After three years and the B.Litt. degree, he returned to Duke where he continues in his fifth decade of teaching. He is James B. Duke Professor of English.

In 1962 his novel A *Long and Happy Life* received the William Faulkner Award for a notable first novel and has never been out of print. Since, he has published more than thirty books. Among them, his novel *Kate Vaiden* received the National Book Critics Circle Award in 1986. His *Collected Stories* appeared in 1993, his *Collected Poems* in 1997; in 1995 he completed his trilogy A *Great Circle*, which consists of the novels *The Surface of Earth, The Source of Light,* and *The Promise of Rest.* He has also published volumes of plays, essays, and two volumes of memoir *Clear Pictures* and A *Whole New Life.* The latter is his account of a long survival of spinal cancer and ensuing paraplegia. He is a member of the American Academy of Arts and Letters, and his books have appeared in sixteen languages.